AGATHA CHRISTIE OMNIBUS

1920s

VOLUME TWO

The ABC Murders
The Adventure of the
   Christmas Pudding
After the Funeral
And Then There Were None
Appointment with Death
At Bertram's Hotel
The Big Four
The Body in the Library
By the Pricking of My Thumbs
Cards on the Table
A Caribbean Mystery
Cat Among the Pigeons
The Clocks
Crooked House
Curtain: Poirot's Last Case
Dead Man's Folly
Death Comes as the End
Death in the Clouds
Death on the Nile
Destination Unknown
Dumb Witness
Elephants Can Remember
Endless Night
Evil Under the Sun
Five Little Pigs
4.50 from Paddington
Hallowe'en Party
Hercule Poirot's Christmas
Hickory Dickory Dock
The Hollow
The Hound of Death
The Labours of Hercules
The Listerdale Mystery
Lord Edgware Dies
The Man in the Brown Suit
The Mirror Crack'd from Side
   to Side
Miss Marple's Final Cases
The Moving Finger
Mrs McGinty's Dead
The Murder at the Vicarage
Murder in Mesopotamia
Murder in the Mews
A Murder is Announced
Murder is Easy
The Murder of Roger Ackroyd
Murder on the Links
Murder on the Orient Express

The Mysterious Affair at Styles
The Mysterious Mr Quin
The Mystery of the Blue Train
Nemesis
N or M?
One, Two, Buckle My Shoe
Ordeal by Innocence
The Pale Horse
Parker Pyne Investigates
Partners in Crime
Passenger to Frankfurt
Peril at End House
A Pocket Full of Rye
Poirot Investigates
Poirot's Early Cases
Postern of Fate
Problem at Pollensa Bay
Sad Cypress
The Secret Adversary
The Secret of Chimneys
The Seven Dials Mystery
The Sittaford Mystery
Sleeping Murder
Sparkling Cyanide
Taken at the Flood
They Came to Baghdad
They Do It With Mirrors
Third Girl
The Thirteen Problems
Three-Act Tragedy
Towards Zero
Why Didn't They Ask Evans

*Novels under the Nom de Plume of
'Mary Westmacott'*
Absent in the Spring
The Burden
A Daughter's A Daughter
Giant's Bread
The Rose and the Yew Tree
Unfinished Portrait

*Books under the name of
Agatha Christie Mallowan*
Come Tell me How You Live
Star Over Bethlehem

Autobiography
Agatha Christie: An Autobiography

AGATHA CHRISTIE
OMNIBUS
1920S

— ⬦ —

VOLUME TWO

The Man in the Brown Suit
Poirot Investigates
The Secret of Chimneys

Background Notes by Jacques Baudou

HarperCollinsPublishers

HarperCollins*Publishers*
77-85 Fulham Palace Road
Hammersmith, London W6 8JB

This paperback edition 1995
3 5 7 9 8 6 4 2

The Man in the Brown Suit copyright Agatha Christie 1924
Poirot Investigates copyright Agatha Christie 1924
The Secret of Chimneys copyright Agatha Christie 1925

ISBN 0 00 649656 3

Set in Linotron Baskerville by
Rowland Phototypesetting Ltd
Bury St Edmunds, Suffolk

Printed and bound in Great Britain by
Caledonian International Book Manufacturing Ltd, Glasgow

Contents

THE MAN IN THE
BROWN SUIT

Prologue

Nadina, the Russian dancer who had taken Paris by storm, swayed to the sound of the applause, bowed and bowed again. Her narrow black eyes narrowed themselves still more, the long line of her scarlet mouth curved faintly upwards. Enthusiastic Frenchmen continued to beat the ground appreciatively as the curtain fell with a swish, hiding the reds and blues and magentas of the bizarre *décor*. In a swirl of blue and orange draperies the dancer left the stage. A bearded gentleman received her enthusiastically in his arms. It was the Manager.

'Magnificent, *petite*, magnificent,' he cried. 'Tonight you have surpassed yourself.' He kissed her gallantly on both cheeks in a somewhat matter-of-fact manner.

Madame Nadina accepted the tribute with the ease of long habit and passed on to her dressing-room, where bouquets were heaped carelessly everywhere, marvellous garments of futuristic design hung on pegs, and the air was hot and sweet with the scent of the massed blossoms and with the more sophisticated perfumes and essences. Jeanne, the dresser, ministered to her mistress, talking incessantly and pouring out a stream of fulsome compliments.

A knock at the door interrupted the flow, Jeanne went to answer it, and returned with a card in her hand.

'Madame will receive?'

'Let me see.'

The dancer stretched out a languid hand, but at the sight of the name on the card, 'Count Sergius Paulovitch', a sudden flicker of interest came into her eyes.

'I will see him. The maize *peignoir*, Jeanne, and quickly. And when the Count comes you may go.'

'*Bien, Madame.*'

Jeanne brought the *peignoir*, an exquisite wisp of corn-coloured chiffon and ermine. Nadina slipped into it, and sat smiling to herself, whilst one long white hand beat a slow tattoo on the glass of the dressing table.

The Count was prompt to avail himself of the privilege accorded to him – a man of medium height, very slim, very elegant, very pale, extraordinarily weary. In feature, little to take hold of, a man difficult to recognize again if one left his mannerisms out of account. He bowed over the dancer's hand with exaggerated courtliness.

'Madame, this is a pleasure indeed.'

So much Jeanne heard before she went out, closing the door behind her. Alone with her visitor, a subtle change came over Nadina's smile.

'Compatriots though we are, we will not speak Russian, I think,' she observed.

'Since we neither of us know a word of the language, it might be as well,' agreed her guest.

By common consent, they dropped into English, and nobody, now that the Count's mannerisms had dropped from him, could doubt that it was his native language. He had, indeed, started life as a quick-change music-hall artiste in London.

'You had great success tonight,' he remarked. 'I congratu-late you.'

'All the same,' said the woman, 'I am disturbed. My pos-ition is not what it was. The suspicions aroused during the War have never died down. I am continually watched and spied upon.'

'But no charge of espionage was ever brought against you?'

'Our chief lays his plans too carefully for that.'

'Long life to the "Colonel",' said the Count, smiling. 'Amaz-ing news, is it not, that he means to retire? To retire! Just like a doctor, or a butcher, or a plumber –'

'Or any other business man,' finished Nadina. 'It should not surprise us. That is what the "Colonel" has always been – an excellent man of business. He has organized crime as another man might organize a boot factory. Without committing himself, he has planned and directed a series of stupendous *coups*, embracing every branch of what we might call his "profession". Jewel robberies, forgery, espionage (the latter very profitable in war-time), sabotage, discreet assassination, there is hardly anything he has not touched. Wisest of all, he knows when to stop. The game begins to be dangerous? – he retires gracefully – with an enormous fortune!'

'H'm!' said the Count doubtfully. 'It is rather – upsetting for all of us. We are at a loose end, as it were.'

'But we are being paid off – on a most generous scale!'

Something, some undercurrent of mockery in her tone, made the man look at her sharply. She was smiling to herself, and the quality of her smile aroused his curiosity. But he proceeded diplomatically:

'Yes, the "Colonel" has always been a great paymaster. I attribute much of his success to that – and to his invariable plan of providing a suitable scapegoat. A great brain, undoubtedly a great brain! And an apostle of the maxim, "If you want a thing done safely, do not do it yourself!" Here are we, every one of us incriminated up to the hilt and absolutely in his power, and not one of us has anything on him.'

He paused, almost as though he were expecting her to disagree with him, but she remained silent, smiling to herself as before.

'Not one of us,' he mused. 'Still, you know, he is superstitious, the old man. Years ago, I believe, he went to one of these fortune-telling people. She prophesied a lifetime of success, but declared that his downfall would be brought about through a woman.'

He had interested her now. She looked up eagerly.

'That is strange, very strange! Through a woman you say?'

He smiled and shrugged his shoulders.

'Doubtless, now that he has – retired, he will marry. Some young society beauty, who will disperse his millions faster than he acquired them.'

Nadina shook her head.

'No, no, that is not the way of it. Listen, my friend, tomorrow I go to London.'

'But your contract here?'

'I shall be away only one night. And I go incognito, like Royalty. No one will ever know that I have left France. And why do you think that I go?'

'Hardly for pleasure at this time of the year. January, a detestable foggy month! It must be for profit, eh?'

'Exactly.' She rose and stood in front of him, every graceful line of her arrogant with pride. 'You said just now that none of us had anything on the chief. You were wrong. I have. I, a woman, have had the wit and, yes, the courage – for it needs courage – to double-cross him. You remember the De Beer diamonds?'

'Yes, I remember. At Kimberley, just before the war broke out? I had nothing to do with it, and I never heard the details, the case was hushed up for some reason, was it not? A fine haul too.'

'A hundred thousand pounds' worth of stones. Two of us worked it – under the "Colonel's" orders, of course. And it was then that I saw my chance. You see, the plan was to substitute some of the De Beer diamonds for some sample diamonds brought from South America by two young prospectors who happened to be in Kimberley at the time. Suspicion was then bound to fall on them.'

'Very clever,' interpolated the Count approvingly.

'The "Colonel" is always clever. Well, I did my part – but I also did one thing which the "Colonel" had not foreseen. I kept back some of the South American stones – one or two are unique and could easily be proved never to have passed through De Beers' hands. With these diamonds in my possession, I have the whip-hand of my esteemed chief. Once the two young men are cleared, his part in the matter is bound to be suspected. I have said nothing all these years, I have been content to know that I had this weapon in reserve, but now matters are different. I want my price – and it will be big, I might almost say a staggering price.'

'Extraordinary,' said the Count. 'And doubtless you carry these diamonds about with you everywhere?'

His eyes roamed gently around the disordered room.

Nadina laughed softly.

'You need suppose nothing of the sort. I am not a fool. The diamonds are in a safe place where no one will dream of looking for them.'

'I never thought you a fool, my dear lady, but may I venture to suggest that you are somewhat foolhardy? The "Colonel" is not the type of man to take kindly to being blackmailed, you know.'

'I am not afraid of him,' she laughed. 'There is only one man I have ever feared – and he is dead.'

The man looked at her curiously.

'Let us hope that he will not come to life again, then,' he remarked lightly.

'What do you mean?' cried the dancer sharply.

The Count looked slightly surprised.

'I only meant that resurrection would be awkward for you,' he explained. 'A foolish joke.'

She gave a sigh of relief.

'Oh, no, he is dead all right. Killed in the war. He was a man who once – loved me.'

'In South Africa?' asked the Count negligently.

'Yes, since you ask it, in South Africa.'

'That is your native country, is it not?'

She nodded. Her visitor rose and reached for his hat.

'Well,' he remarked, 'you know your own business best, but, if I were you, I should fear the "Colonel" far more than any disillusioned lover. He is a man whom it is particularly easy to – underestimate.'

She laughed scornfully.

'As if I did not know him after all these years!'

'I wonder if you do?' he said softly. 'I very much wonder if you do.'

'Oh, I am not a fool! And I am not alone in this. The South African mail-boat docks at Southampton tomorrow, and on board her is a man who has come specially from Africa at my request and who has carried out certain orders of mine. The "Colonel" will have not one of us to deal with, but two.'

'Is that wise?'

'It is necessary.'

'You are sure of this man?'

A rather peculiar smile played over the dancer's face.

'I am quite sure of him. He is inefficient, but perfectly trustworthy.' She paused, and then added in an indifferent tone of voice: 'As a matter of fact, he happens to be my husband.'

CHAPTER I

Everybody has been at me, right and left, to write this story, from the great (represented by Lord Nasby) to the small (represented by our late maid-of-all-work, Emily, whom I saw when I was last in England. 'Lor, miss, what a be-yewtiful book you might make out of it all – just like the pictures!')

I'll admit that I've certain qualifications for the task. I was mixed up in the affair from the very beginning, I was in the thick of it all through, and I was triumphantly 'in at the death'. Very fortunately, too, the gaps that I cannot supply from my own knowledge are amply covered by Sir Eustace Pedler's diary, of which he has kindly begged me to make use.

So here goes. Anne Beddingfeld starts to narrate her adventures.

I'd always longed for adventures. You see, my life had such a dreadful sameness. My father, Professor Beddingfeld, was one of England's greatest living authorities on Primitive Man. He really was a genius – everyone admits that. His mind dwelt in Palæolithic times, and the inconvenience of life for him was that his body inhabited the modern world. Papa did not care for modern man – even Neolithic Man he despised as a mere herder of cattle, and he did not rise to enthusiasm until he reached the Mousterian period.

Unfortunately one cannot entirely dispense with modern men. One is forced to have some kind of truck with butchers and bakers and milkmen and greengrocers. Therefore, Papa being immersed in the past, Mamma having died when I was a baby, it fell to me to undertake the practical side of living. Frankly, I hate Palæolithic Man, be he Aurignacian, Mouster-ian, Chellian, or anything else, and though I typed and revised most of Papa's *Neanderthal Man and his Ancestors*, Neanderthal men themselves fill me with loathing, and I always reflect what a fortunate circumstance it was that they became extinct in remote ages.

I do not know whether Papa guessed my feelings on the subject, probably not, and in any case he would not have been interested. The opinion of other people never interested him in the slightest degree. I think it was really a sign of his greatness. In the same way, he lived quite detached from the necessities of daily life. He ate what was put before him in an exemplary fashion, but seemed mildly pained when the question of paying for it arose. We never seemed to have any money. His celebrity was not of the kind that brought in a cash return. Although he was a fellow of almost every important society and had rows of letters after his name, the general public scarcely knew of his existence, and his long learned books, though adding signally to the sum-total of human knowledge, had no attraction for the masses. Only on one occasion did he leap into the public gaze. He had read a paper before some society on the subject of the young of the chimpanzee. The young of the human race show some anthropoid features, whereas the young of the chimpanzee approach more nearly to the human than the adult chimpanzee does. That seems to show that whereas our ancestors were more Simian than we are, the chimpanzee's were of a higher type than the present species – in other words, the chimpanzee is a degenerate. That enterprising newspaper, the *Daily Budget*, being hard up for something spicy, immediately brought itself out with large headlines. '*We* are not descended from monkeys, but are monkeys descended from *us*? Eminent Professor says chimpanzees are decadent humans.' Shortly afterwards, a reporter called to see Papa, and endeavoured to induce him to write a series of popular articles on the theory. I have seldom seen Papa so angry. He turned the reporter out of the house with scant ceremony, much to my secret sorrow, as we were particularly short of money at the moment. In fact, for a moment I meditated running after the young man and informing him that my father had changed his mind and would send the articles in question. I could easily have written them myself, and the probabilities were that Papa would never have learnt of the transaction, not being a reader of the *Daily Budget*. However, I rejected this course as being too risky, so I merely put on my best hat and went sadly down the village to interview our justly irate grocer.

The reporter from the *Daily Budget* was the only young man who ever came to our house. There were times when I envied Emily, our little servant, who 'walked out' whenever occasion offered with a large sailor to whom she was affianced. In between times, to 'keep her hand in', as she expressed it, she walked out with the greengrocer's young man, and the chemist's assistant. I reflected sadly that I had no one to 'keep my hand in' with. All Papa's friends were aged Professors – usually with long beards. It is true that Professor Peterson once clasped me affectionately and said I had a 'neat little waist' and then tried to kiss me. The phrase alone dated him hopelessly. No self-respecting female has had a 'neat little waist' since I was in my cradle.

I yearned for adventure, for love, for romance, and I seemed condemned to an existence of drab utility. The village possessed a lending library, full of tattered works of fiction, and I enjoyed perils and love-making at second hand, and went to sleep dreaming of stern silent Rhodesians, and of strong men who always 'felled their opponent with a single blow'. There was no one in the village who even looked as though they could 'fell' an opponent, with a single blow or several.

There was the cinema too, with a weekly episode of 'The Perils of Pamela'. Pamela was a magnificent young woman. Nothing daunted her. She fell out of aeroplanes, adventured in submarines, climbed skyscrapers and crept about in the Underworld without turning a hair. She was not really clever, The Master Criminal of the Underworld caught her each time, but as he seemed loath to knock her on the head in a simple way, and always doomed her to death in a sewer-gas-chamber or by some new and marvellous means, the hero was always able to rescue her at the beginning of the following week's episode. I used to come out with my head in a delirious whirl

– and then I would get home and find a notice from the Gas Company threatening to cut us off if the outstanding account was not paid!

And yet, though I did not suspect it, every moment was bringing adventure nearer to me.

It is possible that there are many people in the world who have never heard of the finding of an antique skull at the Broken Hill Mine in Northern Rhodesia. I came down one morning to find Papa excited to the point of apoplexy. He poured out the whole story to me.

'You understand, Anne? There are undoubtedly certain resemblances to the Java skull, but superficial – superficial only. No, here we have what I have always maintained – the ancestral form of the Neanderthal race. You grant that the Gibraltar skull is the most primitive of the Neanderthal skulls found? Why? The cradle of the race was in Africa. They passed to Europe –'

'Not marmalade on kippers, Papa,' I said hastily, arresting my parent's absent-minded hand. 'Yes, you were saying?'

'They passed to Europe on –'

Here he broke down with a bad fit of choking, the result of an immoderate mouthful of kipper bones.

'But we must start at once,' he declared, as he rose to his feet at the conclusion of the meal. 'There is no time to be lost. We must be on the spot – there are doubtless incalculable finds to be found in the neighbourhood. I shall be interested to note whether the implements are typical of the Mousterian period – there will be the remains of the primitive ox, I should say, but not those of the woolly rhinoceros. Yes, a little army will be starting soon. We must get ahead of them. You will write to Cook's today, Anne?'

'What about money, Papa?' I hinted delicately.

He turned a reproachful eye upon me.

'Your point of view always depresses me, my child. We must not be sordid. No, no, in the cause of science one must not be sordid.'

'I feel Cook's might be sordid, Papa.'

Papa looked pained.

'My dear Anne, you will pay them in ready money.'

'I haven't got any ready money.'

Papa looked thoroughly exasperated.

'My child, I really cannot be bothered with these vulgar money details. The bank – I had something from the Manager yesterday, saying I had twenty-seven pounds.'

'That's your overdraft, I fancy.'

'Ah, I have it! Write to my publishers.'

I acquiesced doubtfully, Papa's books bringing in more glory than money. I liked the idea of going to Rhodesia immensely. 'Stern silent men,' I murmured to myself in an ecstasy. Then something in my parent's appearance struck me as unusual.

'You have odd boots on, Papa,' I said. 'Take off the brown one and put on the other black one. And don't forget your muffler. It's a very cold day.'

In a few minutes Papa stalked off, correctly booted and well mufflered.

He returned late that evening, and, to my dismay, I saw his muffler and overcoat were missing.

'Dear me, Anne, you are quite right. I took them off to go into the cavern. One gets so dirty there.'

I nodded feelingly, remembering an occasion when Papa had returned literally plastered from head to foot with rich Pleistocene clay.

Our principal reason for settling in Little Hampsley had been the neighbourhood of Hampsley Cavern, a buried cave rich in deposits of the Aurignacian culture. We had a tiny museum in the village, and the curator and Papa spent most of their days messing about underground and bringing to light portions of woolly rhinoceros and cave bear.

Papa coughed badly all the evening, and the following morning I saw he had a temperature and sent for the doctor.

Poor Papa, he never had a chance. It was double pneumonia. He died four days later.

CHAPTER II

Everyone was very kind to me. Dazed as I was, I appreciated that. I felt no overwhelming grief. Papa had never loved me. I knew that well enough. If he had, I might have loved him in return. No, there had not been love between us, but we had belonged together, and I had looked after him, and had secretly admired his learning and his uncompromising devotion to science. And it hurt me that Papa should have died just when the interest of life was at its height for him. I should have felt happier if I could have buried him in a cave, with paintings of reindeer and flint implements, but the force of public opinion constrained a neat tomb (with marble slab) in our hideous local churchyard. The vicar's consolations, though well meant, did not console me in the least.

It took some time to dawn upon me that the thing I had always longed for – freedom – was at last mine. I was an orphan, and practically penniless, but free. At the same time I realized the extraordinary kindness of all these good people. The vicar did his best to persuade me that his wife was in urgent need of a companion help. Our tiny local library suddenly made up its mind to have an assistant librarian. Finally, the doctor called upon me, and after making various ridiculous excuses for failing to send a proper bill, he hummed and hawed a good deal and suddenly suggested I should marry him.

I was very much astonished. The doctor was nearer forty than thirty and a round, tubby little man. He was not at all like the hero of 'The Perils of Pamela', and even less like the stern and silent Rhodesian. I reflected a minute and then asked why he wanted to marry me. That seemed to fluster him a good deal, and he murmured that a wife was a great help to a general practitioner. The position seemed even more unromantic than before, and yet something in me urged towards its acceptance. Safety, that was what I was being offered.

Safety – and a Comfortable Home. Thinking it over now, I believe I did the little man an injustice. He was honestly in love with me, but a mistaken delicacy prevented him from pressing his suit on those lines. Anyway, my love of romance rebelled.

'It's extremely kind of you,' I said. 'But it's impossible. I could never marry a man unless I loved him madly.'

'You don't think –?'

'No, I don't,' I said firmly.

He sighed.

'But, my dear child, what do you propose to do?'

'Have adventures and see the world,' I replied, without the least hesitation.

'Miss Anne, you are very much a child still. You don't understand –'

'The practical difficulties? Yes, I do, doctor. I'm not a sentimental schoolgirl – I'm a hard-headed mercenary shrew! You'd know it if you married me!'

'I wish you would reconsider –'

'I can't.'

He sighed again.

'I have another proposal to make. An aunt of mine who lives in Wales is in want of a young lady to help her. How would that suit you?'

'No, doctor, I'm going to London. If things happen anywhere, they happen in London. I shall keep my eyes open and, you'll see, something will turn up! You'll hear of me next in China or Timbuctoo.'

My next visitor was Mr Flemming, Papa's London solicitor. He came down specially from town to see me. An ardent anthropologist himself, he was a great admirer of Papa's work. He was a tall, spare man with a thin face and grey hair. He rose to meet me as I entered the room and taking both my hands in his, patted them affectionately.

'My poor child,' he said. 'My poor, poor child.'

Without conscious hypocrisy, I found myself assuming the demeanour of a bereaved orphan. He hypnotized me into it.

He was benignant, kind and fatherly – and without the least doubt he regarded me as a perfect fool of a girl left adrift to face an unkind world. From the first I felt that it was quite useless to try to convince him of the contrary. As things turned out, perhaps it was just as well I didn't.

'My dear child, do you think you can listen to me whilst I try to make a few things clear to you?'

'Oh, yes.'

'Your father, as you know, was a very great man. Posterity will appreciate him. But he was not a good man of business.'

I knew that quite as well, if not better than Mr Flemming, but I restrained myself from saying so. He continued: 'I do not suppose you understand much of these matters. I will try to explain as clearly as I can.'

He explained at unnecessary length. The upshot seemed to be that I was left to face life with the sum of £87 17s. 4d. It seemed a strangely unsatisfying amount. I waited in some trepidation for what was coming next. I feared that Mr Flemming would be sure to have an aunt in Scotland who was in want of a bright young companion. Apparently, however, he hadn't.

'The question is,' he went on, 'the future. I understand you have no living relatives?'

'I'm alone in the world,' I said, and was struck anew by my likeness to a film heroine.

'You have friends?'

'Everyone has been very kind to me,' I said gratefully.

'Who would not be kind to one so young and charming?' said Mr Flemming gallantly. 'Well, well, my dear, we must see what can be done.' He hesitated a minute, and then said: 'Supposing – how would it be if you came to us for a time?'

I jumped at the chance. London! The place for things to happen.

'It's awfully kind of you,' I said. 'Might I really? Just while I'm looking around. I must start out to earn my living, you know?'

'Yes, yes, my dear child. I quite understand. We will look round for something – suitable.'

I felt instinctively that Mr Flemming's ideas of 'something suitable' and mine were likely to be widely divergent, but it was certainly not the moment to air my views.

'That is settled then. Why not return with me today?'

'Oh, thank you, but will Mrs Flemming –'

'My wife will be delighted to welcome you.'

I wonder if husbands know as much about their wives as they think they do. If I had a husband, I should hate him to bring home orphans without consulting me first.

'We will send her a wire from the station,' continued the lawyer.

My few personal belongings were soon packed. I contemplated my hat sadly before putting it on. It had originally been what I call a 'Mary' hat, meaning by that the kind of hat a housemaid ought to wear on her day out – but doesn't! A limp thing of black straw with a suitably depressed brim. With the inspiration of genius, I had kicked it once, punched it twice, dented in the crown and affixed to it a thing like a cubist's dream of a jazz carrot. The result had been distinctly chic. The carrot I had already removed, of course, and now I proceeded to undo the rest of my handiwork. The 'Mary' hat resumed its former status with an additional battered appearance which made it even more depressing than formerly. I might as well look as much like the popular conception of an orphan as possible. I was just a shade nervous of Mrs Flemming's reception, but hoped my appearance might have a sufficiently disarming effect.

Mr Flemming was nervous too. I realized that as we went up the stairs of the tall house in a quiet Kensington square. Mrs Flemming greeted me pleasantly enough. She was a stout, placid woman of the 'good wife and mother' type. She took me up to a spotless chintz-hung bedroom, hoped I had everything I wanted, informed me that tea would be ready in about a quarter of an hour, and left me to my own devices.

I heard her voice slightly raised, as she entered the drawing-room below on the first floor.

'Well, Henry, why on earth –' I lost the rest, but the acerbity of the tone was evident. And a few minutes later another phrase floated up to me, in an even more acid voice: 'I agree with you! She is certainly *very* good-looking.'

It is really a very hard life. Men will not be nice to you if you are not good-looking, and women will not be nice to you if you are.

With a deep sigh I proceeded to do things with my hair. I have nice hair. It is black – a real black, not dark brown – and it grows well back from my forehead and down over the ears. With a ruthless hand I dragged it upwards. As ears, my ears are quite all right, but there is no doubt about it, ears are *démodé* nowadays. They are quite like the 'Queen of Spain's legs' in Professor Peterson's young day. When I had finished I looked almost unbelievably like the kind of orphan that walks out in a queue with a little bonnet and red cloak.

I noticed when I went down that Mrs Flemming's eyes rested on my exposed ears with quite a kindly glance. Mr Flemming seemed puzzled. I had no doubt that he was saying to himself, 'What *has* the child done to herself?'

On the whole the rest of the day passed off well. It was settled that I was to start at once to look for something to do.

When I went to bed, I stared earnestly at my face in the glass. Was I really good-looking? Honestly I couldn't say I thought so! I hadn't got a straight Grecian nose, or a rosebud mouth, or any of the things you ought to have. It is true that a curate once told me that my eyes were like 'imprisoned sunshine in a dark, dark wood' – but curates always know so many quotations, and fire them off at random. I'd much prefer to have Irish blue eyes than dark green ones with yellow flecks! Still, green is a good colour for adventuresses.

I wound a black garment tightly round me, leaving my arms and shoulders bare. Then I brushed back my hair and pulled it well down over my ears again. I put a lot of powder on my face, so that the skin seemed even whiter than usual. I fished about until I found some lip-salve, and I put oceans of it on my lips. Then I did under my eyes with burnt cork. Finally I draped a red ribbon over my bare shoulder, stuck a scarlet feather in my hair, and placed a cigarette in one corner of my mouth. The whole effect pleased me very much.

'Anna the Adventuress,' I said aloud, nodding at my reflection. 'Anna the Adventuress. Episode I, "The House in Kensington"!'

Girls are foolish things.

CHAPTER III

In the succeeding weeks I was a good deal bored. Mrs Flemming and her friends seemed to me to be supremely uninteresting. They talked for hours of themselves and their children and of the difficulties of getting good milk for the children and of what they said to the dairy when the milk wasn't good. Then they would go on to the servants, and the difficulties of getting good servants and of what they had said to the woman at the registry office and of what the woman at the registry office had said to them. They never seemed to read the papers or to care about what went on in the world. They disliked travelling – everything was so different to England. The Riviera was all right, of course, because one met all one's friends there.

I listened and contained myself with difficulty. Most of these women were rich. The whole wide beautiful world was theirs to wander in and they deliberately stayed in dirty dull London and talked about milkmen and servants! I think now, looking back, that I was perhaps a shade intolerant. But they *were* stupid – stupid even at their chosen job: most of them kept the most extraordinarily inadequate and muddled housekeeping accounts.

My affairs did not progress very fast. The house and furniture had been sold, and the amount realized had just covered our debts. As yet, I had not been successful in finding a post. Not that I really wanted one! I had the firm conviction that, if I went about looking for adventure, adventure would meet me half-way. It is a theory of mine that one always gets what one wants.

My theory was about to be proved in practice.

It was early in January – the 8th, to be exact. I was returning from an unsuccessful interview with a lady who said she wanted a secretary-companion, but really seemed to require a strong charwoman who would work twelve hours a day for £25 a year. Having parted with mutual veiled impolitenesses, I walked down Edgware Road (the interview had taken place in a house in St John's Wood), and across Hyde Park to St George's Hospital. There I entered Hyde Park Corner Tube Station and took a ticket to Gloucester Road.

Once on the platform I walked to the extreme end of it. My inquiring mind wished to satisfy itself as to whether there really *were* points and an opening between the two tunnels just beyond the station in the direction of Down Street. I was foolishly pleased to find I was right. There were not many people on the platform, and at the extreme end there was only myself and one man. As I passed him, I sniffed dubiously. If there is one smell I cannot bear it is that of moth-balls! This man's heavy overcoat simply reeked of them. And yet most men begin to wear their winter overcoats before January, and consequently by this time the smell ought to have worn off. The man was beyond me, standing close to the edge of the tunnel. He seemed lost in thought, and I was able to stare at him without rudeness. He was a small thin man, very brown of face, with blue light eyes and a small dark beard.

'Just come from abroad,' I deduced. 'That's why his overcoat smells so. He's come from India. Not an officer, or he wouldn't have a beard. Perhaps a tea-planter.'

At this moment the man turned as though to retrace his steps along the platform. He glanced at me and then his eyes went on to something behind me, and his face changed. It was distorted by fear – almost panic. He took a step backwards as though involuntarily recoiling from some danger, forgetting that he was standing on the extreme edge of the platform, and went down and over. There was a vivid flash from the rails and a crackling sound. I shrieked. People came running up. Two station officials seemed to materialize from nowhere and took command.

I remained where I was, rooted to the spot by a sort of horrible fascination. Part of me was appalled at the sudden disaster, and another part of me was coolly and dispassionately

interested in the methods employed for lifting the man off the
live rail and back on to the platform.

'Let me pass, please. I am a medical man.'

A tall man with a brown beard pressed past me and bent
over the motionless body.

As he examined it, a curious sense of unreality seemed to
possess me. The thing wasn't real – couldn't be. Finally, the
doctor stood upright and shook his head.

'Dead as a door-nail. Nothing to be done.'

We had all crowded nearer, and an aggrieved porter raised
his voice. 'Now then, stand back there, will you? What's the
sense in crowding round?'

A sudden nausea seized me, and I turned blindly and ran up
the stairs again towards the lift. I felt that it was too horrible. I
must get out into the open air. The doctor who had examined
the body was just ahead of me. The lift was just about to go
up, another having descended, and he broke into a run. As
he did so, he dropped a piece of paper.

I stopped, picked it up, and ran after him. But the lift gates
clanged in my face, and I was left holding the paper in my
hand. By the time the second lift reached street level, there
was no sign of my quarry. I hoped it was nothing important
that he had lost, and for the first time I examined it. It was
a plain half-sheet of notepaper with some figures and words
scrawled upon it in pencil. This is a facsimile of it:

1 7·1 2 2   Kilmorden Castle

On the face of it, it certainly did not appear to be of any
importance. Still, I hesitated to throw it away. As I stood there
holding it, I involuntarily wrinkled my nose in displeasure.
Moth-balls again! I held the paper gingerly to my nose. Yes,
it smelt strongly of them. But, then –

I folded up the paper carefully and put it in my bag. I
walked home slowly and did a good deal of thinking.

I explained to Mrs Flemming that I had witnessed a nasty
accident in the Tube and that I was rather upset and would

go to my room and lie down. The kind woman insisted on my having a cup of tea. After that I was left to my own devices, and I proceeded to carry out a plan I had formed coming home. I wanted to know what it was that had produced that curious feeling of unreality whilst I was watching the doctor examine the body. First I lay down on the floor in the attitude of the corpse, then I laid a bolster down in my stead, and proceeded to duplicate, so far as I could remember, every motion and gesture of the doctor. When I had finished I had got what I wanted. I sat back on my heels and frowned at the opposite walls.

There was a brief notice in the evening papers that a man had been killed in the Tube, and a doubt was expressed whether it was suicide or accident. That seemed to me to make my duty clear, and when Mr Flemming heard my story he quite agreed with me.

'Undoubtedly you will be wanted at the inquest. You say no one else was near enough to see what happened?'

'I had the feeling someone was coming up behind me, but I can't be sure – and, anyway, they wouldn't be as near as I was.'

The inquest was held. Mr Flemming made all the arrangements and took me there with him. He seemed to fear that it would be a great ordeal for me, and I had to conceal from him my complete composure.

The deceased had been identified as L. B. Carton. Nothing had been found in his pockets except a house-agent's order to view a house on the river near Marlow. It was in the name of L. B. Carton, Russell Hotel. The bureau clerk from the hotel identified the man as having arrived the day before and booked a room under that name. He had registered as L. B. Carton, Kimberley, S. Africa. He had evidently come straight off the steamer.

I was the only person who had seen anything of the affair.

'You think it was an accident?' the coroner asked me.

'I am positive of it. Something alarmed him, and he stepped backwards blindly without thinking what he was doing.'

'But what could have alarmed him?'

'That I don't know. But there was something. He looked panic-stricken.'

A stolid juryman suggested that some men were terrified of cats. The man might have seen a cat. I didn't think his suggestion a very brilliant one, but it seemed to pass muster with the jury, who were obviously impatient to get home and only too pleased at being able to give a verdict of accident as opposed to suicide.

'It is extraordinary to me,' said the coroner, 'that the doctor who first examined the body has not come forward. His name and address should have been taken at the time. It was most irregular not to do so.'

I smiled to myself. I had my own theory in regard to the doctor. In pursuance of it, I determined to make a call upon Scotland Yard at an early date.

But the next morning brought a surprise. The Flemmings took in the *Daily Budget*, and the *Daily Budget* was having a day after its own heart.

EXTRAORDINARY SEQUEL TO TUBE ACCIDENT

WOMAN FOUND STRANGLED IN LONELY HOUSE

I read eagerly.

'A sensational discovery was made yesterday at the Mill House, Marlow. The Mill House, which is the property of Sir Eustace Pedler, MP, is to be let unfurnished, and an order to view this property was found in the pocket of the man who was at first thought to have commited suicide by throwing himself on the live rail at Hyde Park Corner Tube Station. In an upper room of the Mill House the body of a beautiful young woman was discovered yesterday, strangled. She is thought to be a foreigner, but so far has not been identified. The police are reported to have a clue. Sir Eustace Pedler, the owner of the Mill House, is wintering on the Riviera.'

CHAPTER IV

Nobody came forward to identify the dead woman. The inquest elicited the following facts.

Shortly after one o'clock on January 8th, a well-dressed woman with a slight foreign accent had entered the offices of Messrs Butler and Park, house-agents, in Knightsbridge. She explained that she wanted to rent or purchase a house on the Thames within easy reach of London. The particulars of several were given to her, including those of the Mill House. She gave the name of Mrs de Castina and her address at the Ritz, but there proved to be no one of that name staying there, and the hotel people failed to identify the body.

Mrs James, the wife of Sir Eustace Pedler's gardener, who acted as caretaker to the Mill House and inhabited the small lodge opening on the main road, gave evidence. About three o'clock that afternoon, a lady came to see over the house. She produced an order from the house-agents, and, as was the usual custom, Mrs James gave her the keys to the house. It was situated at some distance from the lodge, and she was not in the habit of accompanying prospective tenants. A few minutes later a young man arrived. Mrs James described him as tall and broad-shouldered, with a bronzed face and light grey eyes. He was clean-shaven and was wearing a brown suit. He explained to Mrs James that he was a friend of the lady who had come to look over the house, but had stopped at the post office to send a telegram. She directed him to the house, and thought no more about the matter.

Five minutes later he reappeared, handed back the keys and explained that he feared the house would not suit them. Mrs James did not see the lady, but thought that she had gone on ahead. What she did notice was that the young man seemed very much upset about something. 'He looked like a man who'd seen a ghost. I thought he was taken ill.'

On the following day another lady and gentleman came to see the property and discovered the body lying on the floor in one of the upstairs rooms. Mrs James identified it as that of the lady who had come the day before. The house-agents also recognized it as that of 'Mrs de Castina'. The police surgeon gave it as his opinion that the woman had been dead about twenty-four hours. The *Daily Budget* had jumped to the conclusion that the man in the Tube had murdered the woman and afterwards committed suicide. However, as the Tube victim was dead at two o'clock and the woman was alive and well at three o'clock, the only logical conclusion to come to was that the two occurrences had nothing to do with each other, and that the order to view the house at Marlow found in the dead man's pocket was merely one of those coincidences which so often occur in this life.

A verdict of 'Wilful Murder against some person or persons unknown' was returned, and the police (and the *Daily Budget*) were left to look for 'the man in the brown suit'. Since Mrs James was positive that there was no one in the house when the lady entered it, and that nobody except the young man in question entered it until the following afternoon, it seemed only logical to conclude that he was the murderer of the unfortunate Mrs de Castina. She had been strangled with a piece of stout black cord, and had evidently been caught unawares with no time to cry out. The black silk handbag which she carried contained a well-filled notecase and some loose change, a fine lace handkerchief, unmarked, and the return half of a first-class ticket to London. Nothing much there to go upon.

Such were the details published broadcast by the *Daily Budget*, and 'Find the Man in the Brown Suit' was their daily war-cry. On an average about five hundred people wrote daily to announce their success in the quest, and tall young men with well-tanned faces cursed the day when their tailors had persuaded them to a brown suit. The accident in the Tube, dismissed as a coincidence, faded out of the public mind.

Was it a coincidence? I was not so sure. No doubt I was prejudiced – the Tube incident was my own pet mystery – but

there certainly seemed to me to be a connexion of some kind
between the two fatalities. In each there was a man with a
tanned face – evidently an Englishman living abroad – and
there were other things. It was the consideration of these other
things that finally impelled me to what I considered a dashing
step. I presented myself at Scotland Yard and demanded to
see whoever was in charge of the Mill House case.

My request took some time to understand, as I had inadver-
tently selected the department for lost umbrellas, but eventually I was ushered into a small room and presented to
Detective Inspector Meadows.

Inspector Meadows was a small man with a ginger head
and what I considered a peculiarly irritating manner. A satel-
lite, also in plain clothes, sat unobtrusively in a corner.

'Good morning,' I said nervously.

'Good morning. Will you take a seat? I understand you've
something to tell me that you think may be of use to us.'

His tone seemed to indicate that such a thing was unlikely
in the extreme. I felt my temper stirred.

'Of course you know about the man who was killed in the
Tube? The man who had an order to view this same house at
Marlow in his pocket.'

'Ah!' said the inspector. 'You are the Miss Beddingfeld who
gave evidence at the inquest. Certainly the man had an order
in his pocket. A lot of other people may have had too – only
they didn't happen to be killed.'

I rallied my forces.

'You didn't think it odd that this man had no ticket in his
pocket?'

'Easiest thing in the world to drop your ticket. Done it
myself.'

'And no money.'

'He had some loose change in his trousers pocket.'

'But no notecase.'

'Some men don't carry a pocket-book or notecase of any
kind.'

I tried another tack.

'You don't think it's odd that the doctor never came forward afterwards?'

'A busy medical man very often doesn't read the papers. He probably forgot all about the accident.'

'In fact, inspector, you are determined to find nothing odd,' I said sweetly.

'Well, I'm inclined to think you're a little too fond of the word, Miss Beddingfeld. Young ladies are romantic, I know – fond of mysteries and such-like. But as I'm a busy man –'

I took the hint and rose.

The man in the corner raised a meek voice.

'Perhaps if the young lady would tell us briefly what her ideas really are on the subject, inspector?'

The inspector fell in with the suggestion readily enough.

'Yes, come now, Miss Beddingfeld, don't be offended. You've asked questions and hinted things. Just straight out what it is you've got in your head.'

I wavered between injured dignity and the overwhelming desire to express my theories. Injured dignity went to the wall.

'You said at the inquest you were positive it wasn't suicide?'

'Yes, I'm quite certain of that. The man was frightened. What frightened him? It wasn't me. But someone might have been walking up the platform towards us – someone he recognized.'

'You didn't see anyone?'

'No,' I admitted. 'I didn't turn my head. Then, as soon as the body was recovered from the line, a man pushed forward to examine it, saying he was a doctor.'

'Nothing unusual in that,' said the inspector dryly.

'But he wasn't a doctor.'

'What?'

'He wasn't a doctor,' I repeated.

'How do you know that, Miss Beddingfeld?'

'It's difficult to say, exactly. I've worked in hospitals during the war, and I've seen doctors handle bodies. There's a sort of deft professional callousness that this man hadn't got.

Besides, a doctor doesn't usually feel for the heart on the right side of the body.'

'He did that?'

'Yes. I didn't notice it specially at the time – except that I felt there was something wrong. But I worked it out when I got home, and then I saw why the whole thing had looked so unhandy to me at the time.'

'H'm,' said the inspector. He was reaching slowly for pen and paper.

'In running his hands over the upper part of the man's body he would have ample opportunity to take anything he wanted from the pockets.'

'Doesn't sound likely to me,' said the inspector. 'But – well, can you describe him at all?'

'He was tall and broad-shouldered, wore a dark overcoat and black boots, a bowler hat. He had a dark pointed beard and gold-rimmed eyeglasses.'

'Take away the overcoat, the beard and the eyeglasses, and there wouldn't be much to know him by,' grumbled the inspector. 'He could alter his appearance easily enough in five minutes if he wanted to – which he would do if he's the swell pickpocket you suggest.'

I had not intended to suggest anything of the kind. But from this moment I gave the inspector up as hopeless.

'Nothing more you can tell us about him?' he demanded, as I rose to depart.

'Yes,' I said. I seized my opportunity to fire a parting shot. 'His head was markedly brachycephalic. He will not find it so easy to alter that.'

I observed with pleasure that Inspector Meadows's pen wavered. It was clear that he did not know how to spell brachycephalic.

CHAPTER V

In the first heat of indignation, I found my next step unexpectedly easy to tackle. I had had a half-formed plan in my head when I went to Scotland Yard. One to be carried out if my interview there was unsatisfactory (it had been profoundly unsatisfactory). That is, if I had the nerve to go through with it.

Things that one would shrink from attempting normally are easily tackled in a flush of anger. Without giving myself time to reflect, I walked straight to the house of Lord Nasby.

Lord Nasby was the millionaire owner of the *Daily Budget*. He owned other papers – several of them, but the *Daily Budget* was his special child. It was as the owner of the *Daily Budget* that he was known to every householder in the United Kingdom. Owing to the fact that an itinerary of the great man's daily proceedings had just been published, I knew exactly where to find him at this moment. It was his hour for dictating to his secretary in his own house.

I did not, of course, suppose that any young woman who chose to come and ask for him would be at once admitted to the august presence. But I had attended to that side of the matter. In the card-tray in the hall of the Flemmings' house, I had observed the card of the Marquis of Loamsley, England's most famous sporting peer. I had removed the card, cleaned it carefully with bread-crumbs, and pencilled upon it the words: 'Please give Miss Beddingfeld a few moments of your time.' Adventuresses must not be too scrupulous in their methods.

The thing worked. A powdered footman received the card and bore it away. Presently a pale secretary appeared. I fenced with him successfully. He retired in defeat. He again reappeared and begged me to follow him. I did so. I entered a large room, a frightened-looking shorthand-typist fled past me like a visitant from the spirit-world. Then the door shut and I was face to face with Lord Nasby.

A big man. Big head. Big face. Big moustache. Big stomach. I pulled myself together. I had not come here to comment on Lord Nasby's stomach. He was already roaring at me.

'Well, what is it? What does Loamsley want? You are his secretary? What's it all about?'

'To begin with,' I said with as great an appearance of coolness as I could manage, 'I don't know Lord Loamsley, and he certainly knows nothing about me. I took his card from the tray in the house of the people I'm staying with, and I wrote those words on it myself. It was important that I should see you.'

For a moment it appeared to be a toss up as to whether Lord Nasby had apoplexy or not. In the end he swallowed twice and got over it.

'I admire your coolness, young woman. Well, you see me! If you interest me, you will continue to see me for exactly two minutes longer.'

'That will be ample,' I replied. 'And I shall interest you. It's the Mill House Mystery.'

'If you've found "The Man in the Brown Suit", write to the editor,' he interrupted hastily.

'If you will interrupt, I shall be more than two minutes,' I said sternly. 'I haven't found "The Man in the Brown Suit", but I'm quite likely to do so.'

In as few words as possible I put the facts of the Tube accident and the conclusions I had drawn from them before him. When I had finished he said unexpectedly, 'What do you know of brachycephalic heads?'

I mentioned Papa.

'The Monkey man? Eh? Well, you seem to have a head of some kind upon your shoulders, young woman. But it's all pretty thin, you know. Not much to go upon. And no use to us – as it stands.'

'I'm perfectly aware of that.'

'What d'you want, then?'

'I want a job on your paper to investigate this matter.'

'Can't do that. We've got our own special man on it.'

'And I've got my own special knowledge.'

'What you've just told me, eh?'

'Oh, no, Lord Nasby. I've still got something up my sleeve.'

'Oh, you have, have you? You seem a bright sort of girl. Well, what is it?'

'When this so-called doctor got into the lift, he dropped a piece of paper. I picked it up. It smelt of moth balls. So did the dead man. The doctor didn't. So I saw at once that the doctor must have taken it off the body. It had two words written on it and some figures.'

'Let's see it.'

Lord Nasby stretched out a careless hand.

'I think not,' I said, smiling. 'It's my find you see.'

'I'm right. You *are* a bright girl. Quite right to hang on to it. No scruples about not handing it over to the police?'

'I went there to do so this morning. They persisted in regarding the whole thing as having nothing to do with the Marlow affair, so I thought that in the circumstances I was justified in retaining the paper. Besides, the inspector put my back up.'

'Short-sighted man. Well, my dear girl, here's all I can do for you. Go on working on this line of yours. If you get any-thing – anything that's publishable – send it along and you shall have your chance. There's always room for real talent on the *Daily Budget*. But you've got to make good first. See?'

I thanked him and apologized for my methods.

'Don't mention it. I rather like cheek – from a pretty girl. By the way, you said two minutes and you've been three, allowing for interruptions. For a woman, that's quite remark-able! Must be your scientific training.'

I was in the street again, breathing hard as though I had been running. I found Lord Nasby rather wearing as a new acquaintance.

CHAPTER VI

I went home with a feeling of exultation. My scheme had succeeded far better than I could possibly have hoped. Lord Nasby had been positively genial. It only now remained for me to 'make good', as he expressed it. Once locked in my own room, I took out my precious piece of paper and studied it attentively. Here was the clue to the mystery.

To begin with, what did the figures represent? There were five of them, and a dot after the first two. 'Seventeen – one hundred and twenty two,' I murmured.

That did not seem to lead to anything.

Next I added them up. That is often done in works of fiction and leads to surprising deductions.

'One and seven make eight and one is nine and two are eleven and two are thirteen!'

Thirteen! Fateful number! Was this a warning to me to leave the whole thing alone? Very possibly. Anyway, except as a warning, it seemed to be singularly useless. I declined to believe that any conspirator would take that way of writing thirteen in real life. If he meant thirteen, he would write thirteen. '13' – like that.

There was a space between the one and the two. I accordingly subtracted twenty-two from a hundred and seventy-one. The result was a hundred and fifty-nine. I did it again and made it a hundred and forty-nine. These arithmetical exercises were doubtless excellent practice, but as regarded the solution of the mystery, they seemed totally ineffectual. I left arithmetic alone, not attempting fancy division or multiplication, and went on to the words.

Kilmorden Castle. That was something definite. A place. Probably the cradle of an aristocratic family. (Missing heir? Claimant to title?) Or possibly a picturesque ruin. (Buried treasure?)

Yes, on the whole I inclined to the theory of buried treasure. Figures always go with buried treasure. One pace to the right, seven paces to the left, dig one foot, descend twenty-two steps. That sort of idea. I could work out that later. The thing was to get to Kilmorden Castle as quickly as possible.

I made a strategic sally from my room, and returned laden with books of reference. *Who's Who*, Whitaker, a Gazetteer, a History of Scotch Ancestral Homes, and Somebody or other's British Isles.

Time passed. I searched diligently, but with growing annoyance. Finally, I shut the last book with a bang. There appeared to be no such place as Kilmorden Castle.

Here was an unexpected check. There *must* be such a place. Why should anyone invent a name like that and write it down on a piece of paper? Absurd!

Another idea occurred to me. Possibly it was a castellated abomination in the suburbs with a high-sounding name invented by its owner. But if so, it was going to be extraordinarily hard to find. I sat back gloomily on my heels (I always sit on the floor to do anything really important) and wondered how on earth I was to set about it.

Was there any other line I could follow? I reflected earnestly and then sprang to my feet delightedly. Of course! I must visit the 'scene of the crime'. Always done by the best sleuths! And no matter how long afterwards it may be they always find something that the police have overlooked. My course was clear. I must go to Marlow.

But how was I to get into the house? I discarded several adventurous methods, and plumped for stern simplicity. The house had been to let – presumably was still to let. I would be a prospective tenant.

I also decided on attacking the local house-agents, as having fewer houses on their books.

Here, however, I reckoned without my host. A pleasant clerk produced particulars of about half a dozen desirable properties. It took me all my ingenuity to find objections to them. In the end I feared I had drawn a blank.

'And you've really nothing else?' I asked, gazing pathetically into the clerk's eyes. 'Something right on the river, and with a fair amount of garden and a small lodge.' I added, summing up the main points of the Mill House, as I had gathered them from the papers.

'Well, of course, there's Sir Eustace Pedler's place,' said the man doubtfully. 'The Mill House, you know.'

'Not – not where –' I faltered. (Really, faltering is getting to be my strong point.)

'That's it! Where the murder took place. But perhaps you wouldn't like –'

'Oh, I don't think I should mind,' I said with an appearance of rallying. I felt my *bona fides* was now quite established. 'And perhaps I might get it cheap – in the circumstances.'

A master touch that, I thought.

'Well, it's possible. There's no pretending that it will be easy to let now – servants and all that, you know. If you like the place after you've seen it, I should advise you to make an offer. Shall I write you out an order?'

'If you please.'

A quarter of an hour later I was at the lodge of the Mill House. In answer to my knock, the door flew open and a tall middle-aged woman literally bounced out.

'Nobody can go into the house, do you hear that? Fairly sick of you reporters, I am. Sir Eustace's orders are –'

'I understood the house was to let,' I said freezingly, holding out my order. 'Of course, if it's already taken –'

'Oh, I'm sure I beg your pardon, miss. I've been fairly pestered with these newspaper people. Not a minute's peace. No, the house isn't let – nor likely to be now.'

'Are the drains wrong?' I asked in an anxious whisper.

'Oh, Lord, miss, the *drains* is all right! But surely you've heard about that foreign lady as was done to death here?'

'I believe I did read something about it in the papers,' I said carelessly.

My indifference piqued the good woman. If I had betrayed

any interest, she would probably have closed up like an oyster. As it was she positively bridled.

'I should say you did, miss! It's been in all the newspapers. The *Daily Budget's* out still to catch the man who did it. It seems, according to them, as our police are no good at all. Well I hope they'll get him – although a nice looking fellow he was and no mistake. A kind of soldierly look about him – ah, well, I dare say he'd been wounded in the war, and sometimes they go a bit queer afterwards; my sister's boy did. Perhaps she'd used him bad – they're a bad lot, those foreigners. Though she was a fine-looking woman. Stood there where you're standing now.'

'Was she dark or fair?' I ventured. 'You can't tell from these newspaper portraits.'

'Dark hair, and a very white face – too white for nature, I thought – had her lips reddened something cruel. I don't like to see it – a little powder now and then is quite another thing.'

We were conversing like old friends now. I put another question.

'Did she seem nervous or upset at all?'

'Not a bit. She was smiling to herself, quiet like, as though she was amused at something. That's why you could have knocked me down with a feather when, the next afternoon, those people came running out calling for the police and saying there'd been murder done. I shall never get over it, and as for setting foot in that house after dark I wouldn't do it, not if it was ever so. Why, I wouldn't even stay here at the lodge, if Sir Eustace hadn't been down on his bended knees to me.'

'I thought Sir Eustace Pedler was at Cannes?'

'So he was, miss. He came back to England when he heard the news, and, as to the bended knees, that was a figure of speech, his secretary, Mr Pagett, having offered us double pay to stay on, and, as my John says, money is money nowadays.'

I concurred heartily with John's by no means original remarks.

'The young man now,' said Mrs James, reverting suddenly to a former point in the conversation. 'He *was* upset. His eyes, light eyes, they were, I noticed them particular, was all shining. Excited, *I* thought. But I never dreamt of anything being wrong. Not even when he came out again looking all queer.'

'How long was he in the house?'

'Oh, not long, a matter of five minutes maybe.'

'How tall was he, do you think? About six foot?'

'I should say so maybe.'

'He was clean-shaven, you say?'

'Yes, miss – not even one of these toothbrush moustaches.'

'Was his chin at all shiny?' I asked on a sudden impulse.

Mrs James stared at me with awe.

'Well, now you come to mention it, miss, it *was*. However did you know?'

'It's a curious thing, but murderers often have shiny chins,' I explained wildly.

Mrs James accepted the statement in all good faith.

'Really, now, miss. I never heard that before.'

'You didn't notice what kind of head he had, I suppose?'

'Just the ordinary kind, miss. I'll fetch you the keys, shall I?'

I accepted them, and went on my way to the Mill House. My reconstructions so far I considered good. All along I had realized that the differences between the man Mrs James had described and my Tube 'doctor' were those of non-essentials. An overcoat, a beard, gold-rimmed eye-glasses. The 'doctor' had appeared middle-aged, but I remembered that he had stooped over the body like a comparatively young man. There had been a suppleness which told of young joints.

The victim of the accident (the Moth Ball man, as I called him to myself) and the foreign woman, Mrs de Castina, or whatever her real name was, had had an assignation to meet at the Mill House. That was how I pieced the thing together. Either because they feared they were being watched or for some other reason, they chose the rather ingenious method of both getting an order to view the same house. Thus their meeting there might have the appearance of pure chance.

That the Moth Ball man had suddenly caught sight of the

'doctor', and that the meeting was totally unexpected and alarming to him, was another fact of which I was fairly sure. What had happened next? The 'doctor' had removed his disguise and followed the woman to Marlow. But it was possible that had he removed it rather hastily traces of spirit-gum might still linger on his chin. Hence my question to Mrs James.

Whilst occupied with my thoughts I had arrived at the low old-fashioned door of the Mill House. Unlocking it with the key, I passed inside. The hall was low and dark, the place smelt forlorn and mildewy. In spite of myself, I shivered. Did the woman who had come here 'smiling to herself' a few days ago feel no chill of premonition as she entered this house? I wondered. Did the smile fade from her lips, and did a nameless dread close round her heart? Or had she gone upstairs, smiling still, unconscious of the doom that was so soon to overtake her? My heart beat a little faster. Was the house really empty? Was doom waiting for me in it also? For the first time, I understood the meaning of the much-used word, 'atmosphere'. There was an atmosphere in this house, an atmosphere of cruelty, of menace, of evil.

CHAPTER VII

Shaking off the feelings that oppressed me, I went quickly upstairs. I had no difficulty in finding the room of the tragedy. On the day the body was discovered it had rained heavily, and large muddy boots had trampled the uncarpeted floor in every direction. I wondered if the murderer had left any footmarks the previous day. It was likely that the police would be reticent on the subject if he had, but on consideration I decided it was unlikely. The weather had been fine and dry.

There was nothing of interest about the room. It was almost square with two big bay windows, plain white walls and a bare floor, the boards being stained round the edges where the carpet had ceased. I searched it carefully, but there was not so much as a pin lying about. The gifted young detective did not seem likely to discover a neglected clue.

I had brought with me a pencil and notebook. There did not seem much to note, but I duly dotted down a brief sketch of the room to cover my disappointment at the failing of my quest. As I was in the act of returning the pencil to my bag, it slipped from my fingers and rolled along the floor.

The Mill House was really old, and the floors were very uneven. The pencil rolled steadily, with increasing momentum, until it came to rest under one of the windows. In the recess of each window there was a broad window-seat, underneath which there was a cupboard. My pencil was lying right against the cupboard door. The cupboard was shut, but it suddenly occurred to me that if it had been open my pencil would have rolled inside. I opened the door, and my pencil immediately rolled in and sheltered modestly in the farthest corner. I retrieved it, noting as I did so that owing to lack of light and the peculiar formation of the cupboard one could not see it, but had to feel for it. Apart from my pencil the cupboard was empty, but being thorough by nature I tried the one under the opposite window.

At first sight, it looked as though that also was empty, but I grubbed about perseveringly, and was rewarded by feeling my hand close on a hard paper cylinder which lay in a sort of trough, or depression, in the far corner of the cupboard. As soon as I had it in my hand, I knew what it was. A roll of Kodak films. Here was a find!

I realized, of course, that these films might very well be an old roll belonging to Sir Eustace Pedler which had rolled in here and had not been found when the cupboard was emptied. But I did not think so. The red paper was far too fresh-looking. It was just as dusty as it would have been had it lain there for two or three days – that is to say, since the murder. Had it been there for any length of time, it would have been thickly coated.

Who had dropped it? The woman or the man? I remembered that the contents of her handbag had appeared to be intact. If it had been jerked open in the struggle and the roll of films had fallen out, surely some of the loose money would have been scattered about also? No, it was not the woman who had dropped the films.

I sniffed suddenly and suspiciously. Was the smell of moth-balls becoming an obsession with me? I could swear that the roll of films smelt of it also. I held them under my nose. They had, as usual, a strong smell of their own, but apart from that I could clearly detect the odour I disliked so much. I soon found the cause. A minute thread of cloth had caught on a rough edge of the centre wood, and that shred was strongly impregnated with moth-balls. At some time or another the films had been carried in the overcoat pocket of the man who was killed in the Tube. Was it he who had dropped them here? Hardly. His movements were all accounted for.

No, it was the other man, the 'doctor'. He had taken the films when he had taken the paper. It was he who had dropped them here during his struggle with the woman.

I had got my clue! I would have the roll developed, and

then I would have further developments to work upon.

Very elated, I left the house, returned the keys to Mrs James and made my way as quickly as possible to the station. On the way back to town, I took out my paper and studied it afresh. Suddenly the figures took on a new significance. Suppose they were a date? 17 1 22. The 17th of January, 1922. Surely that must be it! Idiot that I was not to have thought of it before. But in that case I *must* find out the whereabouts of Kilmorden Castle, for today was actually the 14th. Three days. Little enough – almost hopeless when one had no idea of where to look!

It was too late to hand in my roll today. I had to hurry home to Kensington so as not to be late for dinner. It occurred to me that there was an easy way of verifying whether some of my conclusions were correct. I asked Mr Flemming whether there had been a camera amongst the dead man's belongings. I knew that he had taken an interest in the case and was conversant with all the details.

To my surprise and annoyance he replied that there had been no camera. All Carton's effects had been gone over very carefully in the hopes of finding something that might throw light upon his state of mind. He was positive that there had been no photographic apparatus of any kind.

That was rather a set-back to my theory. If he had no camera, why should he be carrying a roll of films?

I set out early next morning to take my precious roll to be developed. I was so fussy that I went all the way to Regent Street to the big Kodak place. I handed it in and asked for a print of each film. The man finished stacking together a heap of films packed in yellow tin cylinders for the tropics, and picked up my roll.

He looked at me.

'You've made a mistake, I think,' he said, smiling.

'Oh, no,' I said. 'I'm sure I haven't.'

'You've given me the wrong roll. This is an *unexposed* one.'

I walked out with what dignity I could muster. I dare say

it is good for one now and again to realize what an idiot one can be! But nobody relishes the process.

And then, just as I was passing one of the big shipping offices, I came to a sudden halt. In the window was a beautiful model of one of the company's boats, and it was labelled 'Kenilworth Castle'. A wild idea shot through my brain. I pushed the door open and went in. I went up to the counter and in a faltering voice (genuine this time!) I murmured:

'Kilmorden Castle?'

'On the 17th from Southampton. Cape Town? First or second class?'

'How much is it?'

'First class, eighty-seven pounds –'

I interrupted him. The coincidence was too much for me. Exactly the amount of my legacy! I would put all my eggs in one basket.

'First class,' I said.

I was now definitely committed to the adventure.

CHAPTER VIII

(Extracts from the diary of Sir Eustace Pedler, MP)

It is an extraordinary thing that I never seem to get any peace. I am a man who likes a quiet life. I like my Club, my rubber of Bridge, a well-cooked meal, a sound wine. I like England in the summer, and the Riviera in the winter. I have no desire to participate in sensational happenings. Sometimes, in front of a good fire, I do not object to reading about them in the newspaper. But that is as far as I am willing to go. My object in life is to be thoroughly comfortable. I have devoted a certain amount of thought, and a considerable amount of money, to further that end. But I cannot say that I always succeed. If things do not actually happen to me, they happen round me, and frequently, in spite of myself, I become involved. I hate being involved.

All this because Guy Pagett came into my bedroom this morning with a telegram in his hand and a face as long as a mute at a funeral.

Guy Pagett is my secretary, a zealous, painstaking, hard-working fellow, admirable in every respect. I know no one who annoys me more. For a long time I have been racking my brains as to how to get rid of him. But you cannot very well dismiss a secretary because he prefers work to play, likes getting up early in the morning, and has positively no vices. The only amusing thing about the fellow is his face. He has the face of a fourteenth-century poisoner – the sort of man the Borgias got to do their odd jobs for them.

I wouldn't mind so much if Pagett didn't make me work too. My idea of work is something that should be undertaken lightly and airily – trifled with, in fact! I doubt if Guy Pagett has ever trifled with anything in his life. He takes everything seriously. That is what makes him so difficult to live with.

Last week I had the brilliant idea of sending him off to Florence. He talked about Florence and how much he wanted to go there.

'My dear fellow,' I cried, 'you shall go tomorrow. I will pay all your expenses.'

January isn't the usual time for going to Florence, but it would be all one to Pagett. I could imagine him going about, guidebook in hand, religiously doing all the picture galleries. And a week's freedom was cheap to me at the price.

It has been a delightful week. I have done everything I wanted to, and nothing that I did not want to do. But when I blinked my eyes open, and perceived Pagett standing between me and the light at the unearthly hour of 9 A.M. this morning, I realized that freedom was over.

'My dear fellow,' I said, 'has the funeral already taken place, or is it for later in the morning?'

Pagett does not appreciate dry humour. He merely stared.

'So you know, Sir Eustace?'

'Know what?' I said crossly. 'From the expression on your face I inferred that one of your near and dear relatives was to be interred this morning.'

Pagett ignored the sally as far as possible.

'I thought you couldn't know about this.' He tapped the telegram. 'I know you dislike being aroused early – but it *is* nine o'clock' – Pagett insists on regarding 9 A.M. as practically the middle of the day – 'and I thought that under the circumstances –' He tapped the telegram again.

'What is that thing?' I asked.

'It's a telegram from the police at Marlow. A woman has been murdered in your house.'

That aroused me in earnest.

'What colossal cheek,' I exclaimed. 'Why in *my* house? Who murdered her?'

'They don't say. I suppose we shall go back to England at once, Sir Eustace?'

'You need suppose nothing of the kind. Why should we go back?'

'The police –'

'What on earth have I to do with the police?'

'Well, it is your house.'

'That,' I said, 'appears to be more my misfortune than my fault.'

Guy Pagett shook his head gloomily.

'It will have a very unfortunate effect upon the constituency,' he remarked lugubriously.

I don't see why it should have – and yet I have a feeling that in such matters Pagett's instincts are always right. On the face of it, a Member of Parliament will be none the less efficient because a stray young woman comes and gets herself murdered in an empty house that belongs to him – but there is no accounting for the view the respectable British public takes of a matter.

'She's a foreigner too, and that makes it worse,' continued Pagett gloomily.

Again I believe he is right. If it is disreputable to have a woman murdered in your house, it becomes more disreputable if the woman is a foreigner. Another idea struck me.

'Good heavens,' I exclaimed, 'I hope this won't upset Caroline.'

Caroline is the lady who cooks for me. Incidentally she is the wife of my gardener. What kind of a wife she makes I do not know, but she is an excellent cook. James, on the other hand, is not a good gardener – but I support him in idleness and give him the lodge to live in solely on account of Caroline's cooking.

'I don't suppose she'll stay after this,' said Pagett.

'You always were a cheerful fellow,' I said.

I expect I shall have to go back to England. Pagett clearly intends that I shall. And there is Caroline to pacify.

Three days later.

It is incredible to me that anyone who can get away from

England in winter does not do so! It is an abominable climate. All this trouble is very annoying. The house-agents say it will be next to impossible to let the Mill House after all the publicity. Caroline has been pacified – with double pay. We could have sent her a cable to that effect from Cannes. In fact, as I have said all along, there was no earthly purpose to serve by our coming over. I shall go back tomorrow.

One day later.

Several very surprising things have occurred. To begin with, I met Augustus Milray, the most perfect example of an old ass the present Government has produced. His manner oozed diplomatic secrecy as he drew me aside in the Club into a quiet corner. He talked a good deal. About South Africa and the industrial situation there. About the growing rumours of a strike on the Rand. Of the secret causes actuating that strike. I listened as patiently as I could. Finally, he dropped his voice to a whisper and explained that certain documents had come to light which ought to be placed in the hands of General Smuts.

'I've no doubt you're quite right,' I said, stifling a yawn.

'But how are we to get them to him? Our position in the matter is delicate – very delicate.'

'What's wrong with the post?' I said cheerfully. 'Put a twopenny stamp on and drop 'em in the nearest letterbox.'

He seemed quite shocked at the suggestion.

'My dear Pedler! The common post!'

It has always been a mystery to me why Governments employ Kings' Messengers and draw such attention to their confidential documents.

'If you don't like the post, send one of your own young fellows. He'll enjoy the trip.'

'Impossible,' said Milray, wagging his head in a senile fashion. 'There are reasons, my dear Pedler – I assure you there are reasons.'

'Well,' I said rising, 'all this is very interesting, but I must be off –'

'One minute, my dear Pedler, one minute, I beg of you. Now tell me, in confidence, is it not true that you intend visiting South Africa shortly yourself? You have large interests in Rhodesia, I know, and the question of Rhodesia joining in the Union is one in which you have a vital interest.'

'Well, I had thought of going out in about a month's time.'

'You couldn't possibly make it sooner? This month? This week, in fact?'

'I could,' I said, eyeing him with some interest. 'But I don't know that I particularly want to.'

'You would be doing the Government a great service – a very great service. You would not find them – er – ungrateful.'

'Meaning, you want me to be the postman?'

'Exactly. Your position is an unofficial one, your journey is *bona fide*. Everything would be eminently satisfactory.'

'Well,' I said slowly, 'I don't mind if I do. The one thing I am anxious to do is to get out of England again as soon as possible.'

'You will find the climate of South Africa delightful – quite delightful.'

'My dear fellow, I know all about the climate. I was out there shortly before the war.'

'I am really much obliged to you, Pedler. I will send you round the package by messenger. To be placed in General Smuts's own hands, you understand? The *Kilmorden Castle* sails on Saturday – quite a good boat.'

I accompanied him a short way along Pall Mall, before we parted. He shook me warmly by the hand, and thanked me again effusively. I walked home reflecting on the curious by-ways of Governmental policy.

It was the following evening that Jarvis, my butler, informed me that a gentleman wished to see me on private business, but declined to give his name. I have always a lively apprehension of insurance touts, so told Jarvis to say I could not see him. Guy Pagett, unfortunately, when he might for once have been of real use, was laid up with a bilious attack. These earnest, hard-working young men with weak stomachs are always liable to bilious attacks.

Jarvis returned.

'The gentleman asked me to tell you, Sir Eustace, that he comes to you from Mr Milray.'

That altered the complexion of things. A few minutes later I was confronting my visitor in the library. He was a well-built young fellow with a deeply tanned face. A scar ran diagonally from the corner of his eye to the jaw, disfiguring what would otherwise have been a handsome though somewhat reckless countenance.

'Well,' I said, 'what's the matter?'

'Mr Milray sent me to you, Sir Eustace. I am to accompany you to South Africa as your secretary.'

'My dear fellow,' I said, 'I've got a secretary already. I don't want another.'

'I think you do, Sir Eustace. Where is your secretary now?'

'He's down with a bilious attack,' I explained.

'You are sure it's only a bilious attack?'

'Of course it is. He's subject to them.'

My visitor smiled.

'It may or may not be a bilious attack. Time will show. But I can tell you this, Sir Eustace, Mr Milray would not be surprised if an attempt were made to get your secretary out of the way. Oh, you need have no fear for yourself' – I suppose a momentary alarm had flickered across my face – 'you are not threatened. Your secretary out of the way, access to you would be easier. In any case, Mr Milray wishes me to accompany you. The passage-money will be our affair, of course, but you will take the necessary steps about the passport, as though you had decided that you needed the services of a second secretary.'

He seemed a determined young man. We stared at each other and he stared me down.

'Very well,' I said feebly.

'You will say nothing to anyone as to my accompanying you.'

'Very well,' I said again.

After all, perhaps it was better to have this fellow with me, but I had a premonition that I was getting into deep waters. Just when I thought I had attained peace!

I stopped my visitor as he was turning to depart.

'It might be just as well if I knew my new secretary's name,' I observed sarcastically.

He considered for a minute.

'Harry Rayburn seems quite a suitable name,' he observed.

It was a curious way of putting it.

'Very well,' I said for the third time.

CHAPTER IX

(Anne's Narrative Resumed)

It is most undignified for a heroine to be sea-sick. In books the more it rolls and tosses, the better she likes it. When everybody else is ill, she alone staggers along the deck, braving the elements and positively rejoicing in the storm. I regret to say that at the first roll the *Kilmorden* gave, I turned pale and hastened below. A sympathetic stewardess received me. She suggested dry toast and ginger ale.

I remained groaning in my cabin for three days. Forgotten was my quest. I had no longer any interest in solving mysteries. I was a totally different Anne to the one who had rushed back to the South Kensington square so jubilantly from the shipping office.

I smiled now as I remembered my abrupt entry into the drawing-room. Mrs Flemming was alone there. She turned her head as I entered.

'Is that you, Anne, my dear? There is something I want to talk over with you.'

'Yes?' I said, curbing my impatience.

'Miss Emery is leaving me.' Miss Emery was the governess. 'As you have not yet succeeded in finding anything, I wondered if you would care – it would be so nice if you remained with us altogether?'

I was touched. She didn't want me, I knew. It was sheer Christian charity that prompted the offer. I felt remorseful for my secret criticism of her. Getting up, I ran impulsively across the room and flung my arms round her neck.

'You're a dear,' I said. 'A dear, a dear, a dear! And thank you ever so much. But it's all right, I'm off to South Africa on Saturday.'

My abrupt onslaught had startled the good lady. She was

not used to sudden demonstrations of affection. My words startled her still more.

'To South Africa? My dear Anne. We would have to look into anything of that kind very carefully.'

That was the last thing I wanted. I explained that I had already taken my passage, and that upon arrival I proposed to take up duties as a parlourmaid. It was the only thing I could think of on the spur of the moment. There was, I said, a great demand for parlourmaids in South Africa. I assured her that I was equal to taking care of myself, and in the end, with a sigh of relief at getting me off her hands, she accepted the project without further query. At parting, she slipped an envelope into my hand. Inside it I found five new crisp five-pound notes and the words: 'I hope you will not be offended and will accept this with my love.' She was a very good, kind woman. I could not have continued to live in the same house with her, but I did recognize her intrinsic worth.

So here I was, with twenty-five pounds in my pocket, facing the world and pursuing my adventure.

It was on the fourth day that the stewardess finally urged me up on deck. Under the impression that I should die quicker below, I had steadfastly refused to leave my bunk. She now tempted me with the advent of Madeira. Hope rose in my breast. I could leave the boat and go ashore and be a parlourmaid there. Anything for dry land.

Muffled in coats and rugs, and weak as a kitten on my legs, I was hauled up and deposited, an inert mass, on a deck-chair. I lay there with my eyes closed, hating life. The purser, a fair-haired young man, with a round boyish face, came and sat down beside me.

'Hullo! Feeling rather sorry for yourself, eh?'

'Yes,' I replied, hating him.

'Ah, you won't know yourself in another day or two. We've had a rather nasty dusting in the Bay, but there's smooth weather ahead. I'll be taking you on at quoits tomorrow.'

I did not reply.

'Think you'll never recover, eh? But I've seen people much

worse than you, and two days later they were the life and soul of the ship. You'll be the same.'

I did not feel sufficiently pugnacious to tell him outright that he was a liar. I endeavoured to convey it by a glance. He chatted pleasantly for a few minutes more, then he mercifully departed. People passed and repassed, brisk couples 'exercising', curveting children, laughing young people. A few other pallid sufferers lay, like myself, in deck-chairs.

The air was pleasant, crisp, not too cold, and the sun was shining brightly. Insensibly, I felt a little cheered. I began to watch the people. One woman in particular attracted me. She was about thirty, of medium height and very fair with a round dimpled face and very blue eyes. Her clothes, though perfectly plain, had that indefinable air of 'cut' about them which spoke of Paris. Also, in a pleasant but self-possessed way, she seemed to own the ship!

Deck stewards ran to and fro obeying her commands. She had a special deck-chair, and an apparently inexhaustible supply of cushions. She changed her mind three times as to where she would like it placed. Throughout everything she remained attractive and charming. She appeared to be one of those rare people in the world who know what they want, see that they get it, and manage to do so without being offensive. I decided that if ever I recovered – but of course I shouldn't – it would amuse me to talk to her.

We reached Madeira about midday. I was still too inert to move, but I enjoyed the picturesque-looking merchants who came on board and spread their merchandise about the decks. There were flowers too. I buried my nose in an enormous bunch of sweet wet violets and felt distinctly better. In fact, I thought I might just possibly last out the end of the voyage. When my stewardess spoke of the attractions of a little chicken broth, I only protested feebly. When it came I enjoyed it.

My attractive woman had been ashore. She came back escorted by a tall, soldierly-looking man with dark hair and a bronzed face whom I had noticed striding up and down the deck earlier in the day. I put him down at once as one of the strong silent men of Rhodesia. He was about forty, with a touch of greying hair at either temple, and was easily the best-looking man on board.

When the stewardess brought me up an extra rug, I asked her if she knew who my attractive woman was.

'That's a well-known society lady, the Hon. Mrs Clarence Blair. You must have read about her in the papers.'

I nodded, looking at her with renewed interest. Mrs Blair was very well known indeed as one of the smartest women of the day. I observed, with some amusement, that she was the centre of a good deal of attention. Several people essayed to scrape acquaintance with the pleasant informality that a boat allows. I admired the polite way that Mrs Blair snubbed them. She appeared to have adopted the strong, silent man as her special cavalier, and he seemed duly sensible of the privilege accorded him.

The following morning, to my surprise, after taking a few turns round the deck with her attentive companion, Mrs Blair came to a halt by my chair.

'Feeling better this morning?'

I thanked her, and said I felt slightly more like a human being.

'You did look ill yesterday. Colonel Race and I decided that we should have the excitement of a funeral at sea – but you've disappointed us.'

I laughed.

'Being up in the air has done me good.'

'Nothing like fresh air,' said Colonel Race, smiling.

'Being shut up in those stuffy cabins would kill anyone,' declared Mrs Blair, dropping into a seat by my side and dismissing her companion with a little nod. 'You've got an outside one, I hope?'

I shook my head.

'My dear girl! Why don't you change? There's plenty of room. A lot of people got off at Madeira, and the boat's very empty. Talk to the purser about it. He's a nice little boy – he changed me into a beautiful cabin because I didn't care for the one I'd got. You talk to him at lunch-time when you go down.'

I shuddered.

'I couldn't move.'

'Don't be silly. Come and take a walk now with me.'

She dimpled at me encouragingly. I felt very weak on my legs at first, but as we walked briskly up and down I began to feel a brighter and better being.

After a turn or two, Colonel Race joined us again.

'You can see the Grand Peak of Tenerife from the other side.'

'Can we? Can I get a photograph of it, do you think?'

'No – but that won't deter you from snapping off at it.'

Mrs Blair laughed.

'You are unkind. Some of my photographs are very good.'

'About three per cent effective, I should say.'

We all went round to the other side of the deck. There, glimmering white and snowy, enveloped in a delicate rose-coloured mist, rose the glistening pinnacle. I uttered an exclamation of delight. Mrs Blair ran for her camera.

Undeterred by Colonel Race's sardonic comments, she snapped vigorously:

'There, that's the end of the roll. Oh,' her tone changed to one of chagrin, 'I've had the thing at "bulb" all the time.'

'I always like to see a child with a new toy,' murmured the Colonel.

'How horrid you are – but I've got another roll.'

She produced it in triumph from the pocket of her sweater. A sudden roll of the boat upset her balance, and as she caught at the rail to steady herself the roll of films flashed over the side.

'Oh!' cried Mrs Blair, comically dismayed. She leaned over. 'Do you think they have gone overboard?'

'No, you may have been fortunate enough to brain an unlucky steward in the deck below.'

A small boy who had arrived unobserved a few paces to our rear blew a deafening blast on a bugle.

'Lunch,' declared Mrs Blair ecstatically. 'I've had nothing to eat since breakfast, except two cups of beef-tea. Lunch, Miss Beddingfeld?'

'Well,' I said waveringly. 'Yes, I *do* feel rather hungry.'

'Splendid. You're sitting at the purser's table, I know. Tackle him about the cabin.'

I found my way down to the saloon, began to eat gingerly, and finished by consuming an enormous meal. My friend of yesterday congratulated me on my recovery. Everyone was changing cabins today, he told me, and he promised that my things should be moved to an outside one without delay.

There were only four at our table. Myself, a couple of elderly ladies, and a missionary who talked a lot about 'our poor black brothers'.

I looked round at the other tables. Mrs Blair was sitting at the Captain's table. Colonel Race next to her. On the other side of the Captain was a distinguished-looking, grey-haired man. A good many people I had already noticed on deck, but there was one man who had not previously appeared. Had he done so, he could hardly have escaped my notice. He was tall and dark, and had such a peculiarly sinister type of countenance that I was quite startled. I asked the purser, with some curiosity, who he was.

'That man? Oh, that's Sir Eustace Pedler's secretary. Been very sea-sick, poor chap, and not appeared before. Sir Eustace has got two secretaries with him, and the sea's been too much for both of them. The other fellow hasn't turned up yet. This man's name is Pagett.'

So Sir Eustace Pedler, the owner of the Mill House, was on board. Probably only a coincidence, and yet –

'That's Sir Eustace,' my informant continued, 'sitting next to the Captain. Pompous old ass.'

The more I studied the secretary's face, the less I liked it. Its even pallor, the secretive, heavy-lidded eyes, the curiously flattened head – it all gave a feeling of distaste, of apprehension.

Leaving the saloon at the same time as he did, I was close

behind him as he went up on deck. He was speaking to Sir Eustace, and I overheard a fragment or two.

'I'll see about the cabin at once then, shall I? It's impossible to work in yours, with all your trunks.'

'My dear fellow,' Sir Eustace replied. 'My cabin is intended (*a*) for me to sleep in, and (*b*) to attempt to dress in. I never had any intentions of allowing you to sprawl about the place making an infernal clicking with that typewriter of yours.'

'That's just what I say, Sir Eustace, we must have somewhere to work –'

Here I parted company from them, and went below to see if my removal was in progress. I found my steward busy at the task.

'Very nice cabin, miss. On D deck. No. 13.'

'Oh, no!' I cried. '*Not* 13.'

13 is the one thing I am superstitious about. It was a nice cabin too. I inspected it, wavered, but a foolish superstition prevailed. I appealed almost tearfully to the steward.

'Isn't there any other cabin I can have?'

The steward reflected.

'Well, there's 17, just along the starboard side. That was empty this morning, but I rather fancy it's been allotted to someone. Still, as the gentleman's things aren't in yet, and as gentlemen aren't anything like so superstitious as ladies, I dare say he wouldn't mind changing.'

I hailed the proposition gratefully, and the steward departed to obtain permission from the purser. He returned grinning.

'That's all right, miss. We can go along.'

He led the way to 17. It was not quite as large as No. 13, but I found it eminently satisfactory.

'I'll fetch your things right away, miss,' said the steward.

But at that moment the man with the sinister face (as I had nicknamed him) appeared in the doorway.

'Excuse me,' he said, 'but this cabin is reserved for the use of Sir Eustace Pedler.'

'That's all right, sir,' explained the steward. 'We're fitting up No. 13 instead.'

'No, it was No. 17 I was to have.'

'No. 13 is a better cabin, sir – larger.'

'I specially selected No. 17, and the purser said I could have it.'

'I'm sorry,' I said coldly. 'But No. 17 has been allotted to me.'

'I can't agree to that.'

The steward put in his oar.

'The other cabin's just the same, only better.'

'I want No. 17.'

'What's all this?' demanded a new voice. 'Steward, put my things in here. This is my cabin.'

It was my neighbour at lunch, the Rev. Edward Chichester.

'I beg your pardon,' I said. 'It's my cabin.'

'It is allotted to Sir Eustace Pedler,' said Mr Pagett.

We were all getting rather heated.

'I'm sorry to have to dispute the matter,' said Chichester with a meek smile which failed to mask his determination to get his own way. Meek men are always obstinate, I have noticed.

He edged himself sideways into the doorway.

'You're to have No. 28 on the port side,' said the steward. 'A very good cabin, sir.'

'I am afraid that I must insist. No. 17 was the cabin promised to me.'

We had come to an impasse. Each one of us was determined not to give way. Strictly speaking, I, at any rate, might have retired from the contest and eased matters by offering to accept Cabin 28. So long as I did not have 13 it was immaterial to me what other cabin I had. But my blood was up. I had not the least intention of being the first to give way. And I disliked Chichester. He had false teeth that clicked when he ate. Many men have been hated for less.

We all said the same things over again. The steward assured us, even more strongly, that both the other cabins were better cabins. None of us paid any attention to him.

Pagett began to lose his temper. Chichester kept his

serenely. With an effort I also kept mine. And still none of us would give way an inch.

A wink and a whispered word from the steward gave me my cue. I faded unobtrusively from the scene. I was lucky enough to encounter the purser almost immediately.

'Oh, please,' I said, 'you did say I could have cabin 17? And the others won't go away. Mr Chichester and Mr Pagett. You *will* let me have it, won't you?'

I always say that there are no people like sailors for being nice to women. My little purser came to scratch splendidly. He strode to the scene, informed the disputants that No. 17 was my cabin, they could have Nos 13 and 28 respectively or stay where they were – whichever they chose.

I permitted my eyes to tell him what a hero he was and then installed myself in my new domain. The encounter had done me worlds of good. The sea was smooth, the weather growing daily warmer. Sea-sickness was a thing of the past!

I went up on deck and was initiated into the mysteries of deck-quoits. I entered my name for various sports. Tea was served on deck, and I ate heartily. After tea, I played shovel-board with some pleasant young men. They were extraordinarily nice to me. I felt that life was satisfactory and delightful.

The dressing bugle came as a surprise and I hurried to my new cabin. The stewardess was awaiting me with a troubled face.

'There's a terrible smell in your cabin, miss. What it is, I'm sure I can't think, but I doubt if you'll be able to sleep here. There's a deck cabin up on C deck. You might move into that – just for the night, anyway.'

The smell really was pretty bad – quite nauseating. I told the stewardess I would think over the question of moving whilst I dressed. I hurried over my toilet, sniffing distastefully as I did so.

What *was* the smell? Dead rat? No, worse than that – and quite different. Yet I knew it! It was something I had smelt before. Something – Ah! I had got it. Asafoetida! I had worked in a hospital dispensary during the war for a short time and had become acquainted with various nauseous drugs.

Asafoetida, that was it. But how –

I sank down on the sofa, suddenly realizing the thing. Somebody had put a pinch of asafoetida in my cabin. Why? So that I should vacate it? Why were they so anxious to get me out? I thought of the scene this afternoon from a rather different point of view. What was it about Cabin 17 that made so many people anxious to get hold of it? The other two cabins were better cabins; why had both men insisted on sticking to 17?

17. How the number persisted! It was on the 17th I had sailed from Southampton. It was a 17 – I stopped with a sudden gasp. Quickly I unlocked my suit-case, and took my precious paper from its place of concealment in some rolled stockings.

17 1 22 – I had taken that for a date, the date of departure of the *Kilmorden Castle*. Supposing I was wrong. When I came to think of it, would anyone, writing down a date, think it necessary to put the year as well as the month? Supposing 17 meant *Cabin* 17? and 1? The time – one o'clock. Then 22 must be the date. I looked up at my little almanac.

Tomorrow was the 22nd!

CHAPTER X

I was violently excited. I was sure that I had hit on the right trail at last. One thing was clear, I must not move out of the cabin. The asafoetida had got to be borne. I examined my facts again.

Tomorrow was the 22nd, and at 1 A.M. or 1 P.M. something would happen. I plumped for 1 A.M. It was now seven o'clock. In six hours I should know.

I don't know how I got through the evening. I retired to my cabin fairly early. I had told the stewardess that I had a cold in the head and didn't mind smells. She still seemed distressed, but I was firm.

The evening seemed interminable. I duly retired to bed, but in view of emergencies I swathed myself in a thick flannel dressing-gown, and encased my feet in slippers. Thus attired I felt that I could spring up and take an active part in anything that happened.

What did I expect to happen? I hardly knew. Vague fancies, most of them wildly improbable, flitted through my brain. But one thing I was firmly convinced of, at one o'clock *something* would happen.

At various times I heard fellow-passengers coming to bed. Fragments of conversation, laughing good-nights, floated in through the open transom. Then, silence. Most of the lights went out. There was still one in the passage outside, and there was therefore a certain amount of light in my cabin. I heard eight bells go. The hour that followed seemed the longest I had ever known. I consulted my watch surreptitiously to be sure I had not overshot the time.

If my deductions were wrong, if nothing happened at one o'clock, I should have made a fool of myself, and spent all the money I had in the world on a mare's nest. My heart beat painfully.

Two bells went overhead. One o'clock! And nothing. Wait – what was that? I heard the quick light patter of feet running – running along the passage.

Then with the suddenness of a bombshell my cabin door burst open and a man almost fell inside.

'Save me,' he said hoarsely. 'They're after me.'

It was not a moment for argument or explanation. I could hear footsteps outside. I had about forty seconds in which to act. I had sprung to my feet and was standing facing the stranger in the middle of the cabin.

A cabin does not abound in hiding-places for a six-foot man. With one arm I pulled out my cabin trunk. He slipped down behind it under the bunk. I raised the lid. At the same time, with the other hand I pulled down the wash-basin. A deft movement and my hair was screwed into a tiny knot on the top of my head. From the point of view of appearance it was inartistic, from another standpoint it was supremely artistic. A lady, with her hair screwed into an unbecoming knob and in the act of removing a piece of soap from her trunk with which, apparently, to wash her neck, could hardly be suspected of harbouring a fugitive.

There was a knock at the door, and without waiting for me to say 'Come in' it was pushed open.

I don't know what I expected to see. I think I had vague ideas of Mr Pagett brandishing a revolver. Or my missionary friend with a sandbag, or some other lethal weapon. But I certainly did not expect to see a night stewardess, with an inquiring face and looking the essence of respectability.

'I beg your pardon, miss, I thought you called out.'

'No,' I said, 'I didn't.'

'I'm sorry for interrupting you.'

'That's all right,' I said. 'I couldn't sleep. I thought a wash would do me good.' It sounded rather as though it were a thing I never had as a general rule.

'I'm so sorry, miss,' said the stewardess again. 'But there's a gentleman about who's rather drunk and we are afraid he might get into one of the ladies' cabins and frighten them.'

'How dreadful!' I said, looking alarmed. 'He won't come in here, will he?'

'Oh, I don't think so, miss. Ring the bell if he does. Good night.'

'Good night.'

I opened the door and peeped down the corridor. Except for the retreating form of the stewardess, there was nobody in sight.

Drunk! So that was the explanation of it. My histrionic talents had been wasted. I pulled the cabin trunk out a little farther and said: 'Come out at once, please,' in an acid voice.

There was no answer. I peered under the bunk. My visitor lay immoveable. He seemed to be asleep. I tugged at his shoulder. He did not move.

'Dead drunk,' I thought vexedly. 'What *am* I to do?'

Then I saw something that made me catch my breath, a small scarlet spot on the floor.

Using all my strength, I succeeded in dragging the man out into the middle of the cabin. The dead whiteness of his face showed that he had fainted. I found the cause of his fainting easily enough. He had been stabbed under the left shoulder-blade – a nasty deep wound. I got his coat off and set to work to attend to it.

At the sting of the cold water he stirred, then sat up.

'Keep still, please,' I said.

He was the kind of young man who recovers his faculties very quickly. He pulled himself to his feet and stood there swaying a little.

'Thank you; I don't need anything done for me.'

His manner was defiant, almost aggressive. Not a word of thanks – of even common gratitude!

'That is a nasty wound. You must let me dress it.'

'You will do nothing of the kind.'

He flung the words in my face as though I had been begging a favour of him. My temper, never placid, rose.

'I cannot congratulate you on your manners,' I said coldly.

'I can at least relieve you of my presence.' He started for

the door, but reeled as he did so. With an abrupt movement
I pushed him down upon the sofa.

'Don't be a fool,' I said unceremoniously. 'You don't want
to go bleeding all over the ship, do you?'

He seemed to see the sense of that, for he sat quietly whilst
I bandaged up the wound as best I could.

'There,' I said, bestowing a pat on my handiwork, 'that will
have to do for the present. Are you better-tempered now and
do you feel inclined to tell me what it's all about?'

'I'm sorry that I can't satisfy your very natural curiosity.'

'Why not?' I said, chagrined.

He smiled nastily.

'If you want a thing broadcast, tell a woman. Otherwise
keep your mouth shut.'

'Don't you think I could keep a secret?'

'I don't think – I know.'

He rose to his feet.

'At any rate,' I said spitefully, 'I shall be able to do a little
broadcasting about the events of this evening.'

'I've no doubt you will too,' he said indifferently.

'How dare you!' I cried angrily.

We were facing each other, glaring at each other with the
ferocity of bitter enemies. For the first time, I took in the
details of his appearance, the close-cropped dark head,
the lean jaw, the scar on the brown cheek, the curious light
grey eyes that looked into mine with a sort of reckless mockery hard to describe. There was something dangerous about
him.

'You haven't thanked me yet for saving your life!' I said
with false sweetness.

I hit him there. I saw him flinch distinctly. Intuitively I
knew that he hated above all to be reminded that he owed his
life to me. I didn't care. I wanted to hurt him. I had never
wanted to hurt anyone so much.

'I wish to God you hadn't!' he said explosively. 'I'd be
better dead and out of it.'

'I'm glad you acknowledge the debt. You can't get out of

it. I saved your life and I'm waiting for you to say "Thank you."'

If looks could have killed, I think he would have liked to kill me then. He pushed roughly past me. At the door he turned back, and spoke over his shoulder.

'I shall not thank you – now or at any other time. But I acknowledge the debt. Some day I will pay it.'

He was gone, leaving me with clenched hands, and my heart beating like a mill race.

CHAPTER XI

There were no further excitements that night. I had breakfast in bed and got up late the next morning. Mrs Blair hailed me as I came on deck.

'Good morning, gipsy girl. Sit down here by me. You look as though you hadn't slept well.'

'Why do you call me that?' I asked, as I sat down obediently.

'Do you mind? It suits you somehow. I've called you that in my own mind from the beginning. It's the gipsy element in you that makes you so different from anyone else. I decided in my own mind that you and Colonel Race were the only two people on board who wouldn't bore me to death to talk to.'

'That's funny,' I said. 'I thought the same about you – only it's more understandable in your case. You're – you're such an exquisitely finished product.'

'Not badly put,' said Mrs Blair, nodding her head. 'Tell me about yourself, gipsy girl. Why are you going to South Africa?'

I told her something about Papa's life work.

'So you're Charles Beddingfeld's daughter? I thought you weren't a mere provincial miss! Are you going to Broken Hill to grub up more skulls?'

'I may,' I said cautiously. 'I've got other plans as well.'

'What a mysterious minx you are. But you do look tired this morning. Didn't you sleep well? I can't keep awake on board a boat. Ten hours' sleep for a fool, they say! I could do with twenty!'

She yawned, looking like a sleepy kitten. 'An idiot of a steward woke me up in the middle of the night to return me that roll of films I dropped yesterday. He did it in the most melodramatic manner, stuck his arm through the ventilator and dropped them neatly in the middle of my tummy. I thought it was a bomb for a moment!'

'Here's your Colonel,' I said, as the tall soldierly figure of Colonel Race appeared on the deck.

'He's not my Colonel particularly. In fact he admires *you* very much, gipsy girl. So don't run away.'

'I want to tie something round my head. It will be more comfortable than a hat.'

I slipped quickly away. For some reason or other I was uncomfortable with Colonel Race. He was one of the few people who were capable of making me feel shy.

I went down to my cabin and began looking for something with which I could restrain my rebellious locks. Now I am a tidy person, I like my things always arranged in a certain way and I keep them so. I had no sooner opened my drawer than I realized that somebody had been disarranging my things. Everything had been turned over and scattered. I looked in the other drawers and the small hanging cupboard. They told the same tale. It was as though someone had been making a hurried and ineffectual search for something.

I sat down on the edge of the bunk with a grave face. Who had been searching my cabin and what had they been looking for? Was it the half-sheet of paper with scribbled figures and words? I shook my head, dissatisfied. Surely that was past history now. But what else could there be?

I wanted to think. The events of last night, though exciting, had not really done anything to elucidate matters. Who was the young man who had burst into my cabin so abruptly? I had not seen him on board previously, either on deck or in the saloon. Was he one of the ship's company or was he a passenger? Who had stabbed him? Why had they stabbed him? And why, in the name of goodness, should Cabin No 17 figure so prominently? It was all a mystery, but there was no doubt that some very peculiar occurrences were taking place on the *Kilmorden Castle*.

I counted off on my fingers the people on whom it behoved me to keep watch.

Setting aside my visitor of the night before, but promising myself that I would discover him on board before another day had passed, I selected the following persons as worthy of my notice:

(1) Sir Eustace Pedler. He was the owner of the Mill House, and his presence on the *Kilmorden Castle* seemed something of a coincidence.

(2) Mr Pagett, the sinister-looking secretary, whose eagerness to obtain Cabin 17 had been so very marked. N. B. – Find out whether he had accompanied Sir Eustace to Cannes.

(3) The Rev. Edward Chichester. All I had against him was his obstinacy over Cabin 17, and that might be entirely due to his own peculiar temperament. Obstinacy can be an amazing thing.

But a little conversation with Mr Chichester would not come amiss, I decided. Hastily tying a handkerchief round my hair, I went up on deck again, full of purpose. I was in luck. My quarry was leaning against the rail, drinking beef tea. I went up to him.

'I hope you've forgiven me over Cabin 17,' I said, with my best smile.

'I consider it unchristian to bear a grudge,' said Mr Chichester coldly. 'But the purser had distinctly promised me that cabin.'

'Pursers are such busy men, aren't they?' I said vaguely. 'I suppose they're bound to forget sometimes.'

Mr Chichester did not reply.

'Is this your first visit to South Africa?' I inquired conversationally.

'To South Africa, yes. But I have worked for the last two years amongst the cannibal tribes in the interior of East Africa.'

'How thrilling! Have you had many narrow escapes?'

'Escapes?'

'Of being eaten, I mean?'

'You should not treat sacred subjects with levity, Miss Beddingfeld.'

'I didn't know that cannibalism was a sacred subject,' I retorted, stung.

As the words left my lips, another idea struck me. If Mr Chichester had indeed spent the last two years in the interior of Africa, how was it that he was not more sunburnt? His skin was as pink and white as a baby's. Surely there was something fishy there? Yet his manner and voice were so absolutely *it*. Too much so, perhaps. Was he – or was he not – just a little like a *stage* clergyman?

I cast my mind back to the curates I had known at Little Hampsley. Some of them I had liked, some of them I had not, but certainly none of them had been quite like Mr Chichester. They had been human – he was a glorified type.

I was debating all this when Sir Eustace Pedler passed down the deck. Just as he was abreast of Mr Chichester, he stooped and picked up a piece of paper which he handed to him, remarking, 'You've dropped something.'

He passed on without stopping, and so probably did not notice Mr Chichester's agitation. I did. Whatever it was he had dropped, its recovery agitated him considerably. He turned a sickly green, and crumpled up the sheet of paper into a ball. My suspicions were accentuated a hundredfold.

He caught my eye, and hurried into explanations.

'A – a – fragment of a sermon I was composing,' he said with a sickly smile.

'Indeed?' I rejoined politely.

A fragment of a sermon, indeed! No, Mr Chichester – too weak for words!

He soon left me with a muttered excuse. I wished, oh, how I wished, that I had been the one to pick up that paper and not Sir Eustace Pedler! One thing was clear, Mr Chichester could not be exempted from my list of suspects. I was inclined to put him top of the three.

After lunch, when I came up to the lounge for coffee, I noticed Sir Eustace and Pagett sitting with Mrs Blair and Colonel Race. Mrs Blair welcomed me with a smile, so I went over and joined them. They were talking about Italy.

'But it *is* misleading,' Mrs Blair insisted. '*Aqua calda* certainly *ought* to be cold water – not hot.'

'You're not a Latin scholar,' said Sir Eustace, smiling.

'Men are so superior about their Latin,' said Mrs Blair. 'But all the same I notice that when you ask them to translate inscriptions in old churches they can never do it! They hem and haw, and get out of it somehow.'

'Quite right,' said Colonel Race. 'I always do.'

'But I love the Italians,' continued Mrs Blair. 'They're so obliging – though even that has its embarrassing side. You ask them the way somewhere, and instead of saying "first to the right, second to the left" or something that one could follow, they pour out a flood of well-meaning directions, and when you look bewildered they take you kindly by the arm and walk all the way there with you.'

'Is that your experience in Florence, Pagett?' asked Sir Eustace, turning with a smile to his secretary.

For some reason the question seemed to disconcert Mr Pagett. He stammered and flushed.

'Oh, quite so, yes – er quite so.'

Then with a murmured excuse, he rose and left the table.

'I am beginning to suspect Guy Pagett of having committed some dark deed in Florence,' remarked Sir Eustace, gazing after his secretary's retreating figure. 'Whenever Florence or Italy is mentioned, he changes the subject or bolts precipitately.'

'Perhaps he murdered someone there,' said Mrs Blair hopefully. 'He looks – I hope I'm not hurting your feelings, Sir Eustace – but he does look as though he might murder someone.'

'Yes, pure Cinquecento! It amuses me sometimes – especially when one knows as well as I do how essentially law-abiding and respectable the poor fellow really is.'

'He's been with you some time, hasn't he, Sir Eustace?' asked Colonel Race.

'Six years,' said Sir Eustace with a deep sigh.

'He must be quite invaluable to you,' said Mrs Blair.

'Oh, invaluable! Yes, quite invaluable.' The poor man sounded even more depressed, as though the invaluableness of Mr Pagett was a secret grief to him. Then he added more briskly: 'But his face should really inspire you with confidence, my dear lady. No self-respecting murderer would ever consent to look like one. Crippen, now, I believe, was one of the pleasantest fellows imaginable.'

'He was caught on a liner, wasn't he?' murmured Mrs Blair.

There was a slight rattle behind us. I turned quickly. Mr Chichester had dropped his coffee-cup.

Our party soon broke up; Mrs Blair went below to sleep and I went out on deck. Colonel Race followed me.

'You're very elusive, Miss Beddingfeld. I looked for you everywhere last night at the dance.'

'I went to bed early,' I explained.

'Are you going to run away tonight too? Or are you going to dance with me?'

'I shall be very pleased to dance with you,' I murmured shyly. 'But Mrs Blair –'

'Our friend, Mrs Blair, doesn't care for dancing.'

'And do you?'

'I care for dancing with you.'

'Oh!' I said nervously.

I was a little afraid of Colonel Race. Nevertheless I was enjoying myself. This was better than discussing fossilized skulls with stuffy old professors! Colonel Race was really just my ideal of a stern silent Rhodesian. Possibly I might marry him! I hadn't been asked, it is true, but, as the Boy Scouts say, Be Prepared! And all women, without in the least meaning it, consider every man they meet as a possible husband for themselves or their best friend.

I danced several times with him that evening. He danced well. When the dancing was over, and I was thinking of going to bed, he suggested a turn round the deck. We walked round three times and finally subsided into two deck-chairs. There was nobody else in sight. We made desultory conversation for some time.

'Do you know, Miss Beddingfeld, I think I once met your father? A very interesting man – on his own subject, and it's a subject that has a special fascination for me. In my humble way, I've done a bit in that line myself. Why, when I was in the Dordogne region –'

Our talk became technical. Colonel Race's boast was not an idle one. He knew a great deal. At the same time, he made one or two curious mistakes – slips of the tongue, I might almost have thought them. But he was quick to take his cue from me and to cover them up. Once he spoke of the Mousterian period as succeeding the Aurignacian – an absurd mistake for one who knew anything of the subject.

It was twelve o'clock when I went to my cabin. I was still puzzling over those queer discrepancies. Was it possible that he had 'got the whole subject up' for the occasion – that really he knew nothing of archaeology? I shook my head, vaguely dissatisfied with that solution.

Just as I was dropping off to sleep, I sat up with a sudden start as another idea flashed into my head. Had *he* been pumping *me*? Were those slight inaccuracies just tests – to see whether I really knew what I was talking about? In other words, he suspected me of not being genuinely Anne Beddingfeld.

Why?

CHAPTER XII

(Extract from the diary of Sir Eustace Pedler)

There is something to be said for life on board ship. It is peaceful. My grey hairs fortunately exempt me from the indignities of bobbing for apples, running up and down deck with potatoes and eggs, and the more painful sports of 'Brother Bill' and Bolster Bar. What amusement people can find in these painful proceedings has always been a mystery to me. But there are many fools in the world. One praises God for their existence and keeps out of their way.

Fortunately I am an excellent sailor. Pagett, poor fellow, is not. He began turning green as soon as we were out of the Solent. I presume my other so-called secretary is also sea-sick. At any rate he has not yet made an appearance. But perhaps it is not sea-sickness, but high diplomacy. The great thing is that *I* have not been worried by him.

On the whole, the people on board are a mangy lot. Only two decent Bridge players and one decent-looking woman – Mrs Clarence Blair. I've met her in town, of course. She is one of the only women I know who can lay claim to a sense of humour. I enjoy talking to her, and should enjoy it more if it were not for a long-legged taciturn ass who attached himself to her like a limpet. I cannot think that this Colonel Race really amuses her. He's good-looking in his way, but dull as ditch water. One of these strong silent men that lady novelists and young girls always rave over.

Guy Pagett struggled up on deck after we left Madeira and began babbling in a hollow voice about work. What the devil does anyone want to work for on board ship? It is true that I promised my publishers my 'Reminiscences' early in the summer, but what of it? Who really reads reminiscences? Old ladies in the suburbs. And what do my reminiscences amount to? I've knocked against a certain number of so-called famous people in my lifetime. With the assistance of Pagett, I invented insipid anecdotes about them. And, the truth of the matter is, Pagett is too honest for the job. He won't let me invent anecdotes about the people I might have met but haven't.

I tried kindness with him.

'You look a perfect wreck still, my dear chap,' I said easily. 'What you need is a deck-chair in the sun. No – not another word. The work must wait.'

The next thing I knew he was worrying about an extra cabin. 'There's no room to work in your cabin, Sir Eustace. It's full of trunks.'

From his tone, you might have thought the trunks were black beetles, something that had no business to be there.

I explained to him that, though he might not be aware of the fact, it was usual to take a change of clothing with one when travelling. He gave the wan smile with which he always greets my attempts at humour, and then reverted to the business in hand.

'And we could hardly work in my little hole.'

I know Pagett's 'little holes' – he usually has the best cabin on the ship.

'I'm sorry the Captain didn't turn out for you this time,' I said sarcastically. 'Perhaps you'd like to dump some of your extra luggage in my cabin?'

Sarcasm is dangerous with a man like Pagett. He brightened up at once.

'Well, if I could get rid of the typewriter and the stationery trunk –'

The stationery trunk weighs several solid tons. It causes endless unpleasantness with the porters, and it is the aim of Pagett's life to foist it on me. It is a perpetual struggle between us. He seems to regard it as my special personal property. I, on the other hand, regard the charge of it as the only thing where a secretary is really useful.

'We'll get an extra cabin,' I said hastily.

The thing seemed simple enough, but Pagett is a person who loves to make mysteries. He came to me the next day with a face like a Renaissance conspirator.

'You know you told me to get Cabin 17 for an office?'

'Well, what of it? Has the stationery trunk jammed in the doorway?'

'The doorways are the same size in all the cabins,' replied Pagett seriously. 'But I tell you, Sir Eustace, there's something very queer about that cabin.'

Memories of reading *The Upper Berth* floated through my mind.

'If you mean that it's haunted,' I said, 'we're not going to sleep there, so I don't see that it matters. Ghosts don't affect typewriters.'

Pagett said that it wasn't a ghost and that, after all, he hadn't got Cabin 17. He told me a long, garbled story. Apparently, he and a Mr Chichester, and a girl called Beddingfeld, had almost come to blows over the cabin. Needless to say, the girl had won, and Pagett was apparently feeling sore over the matter.

'Both 13 and 28 are better cabins,' he reiterated. 'But they wouldn't look at them.'

'Well,' I said, stifling a yawn, 'for that matter, no more would you, my dear Pagett.'

He gave me a reproachful look.

'You *told* me to get Cabin 17.'

There is a touch of the 'boy upon the burning deck' about Pagett.

'My dear fellow,' I said testily, 'I mentioned No. 17 because I happened to observe that it was vacant. But I didn't mean you to make a stand to the death about it – 13 or 28 would have done us equally well.'

He looked hurt.

'There's something more, though,' he insisted. 'Miss Beddingfeld got the cabin, but this morning I saw Chichester coming out of it in a furtive sort of way.'

I looked at him severely.

'If you're trying to get up a nasty scandal about Chichester, who is a missionary – though a perfectly poisonous person – and that attractive child, Anne Beddingfeld, I don't believe a word of it,' I said coldly. 'Anne Beddingfeld is an extremely nice girl – with particularly good legs. I should say she had far and away the best legs on board.'

Pagett did not like my reference to Anne Beddingfeld's legs. He is the sort of man who never notices legs himself – or, if he does, would die sooner than say so. Also he thinks my appreciation of such things frivolous. I like annoying Pagett, so I continued maliciously:

'As you've made her acquaintance, you might ask her to dine at our table tomorrow night. It's the Fancy Dress dance. By the way, you'd better go down to the barber and select a fancy costume for me.'

'Surely you will not go in fancy dress?' said Pagett, in tones of horror.

I could see that it was quite incompatible with his idea of my dignity. He looked shocked and pained. I had really had no intention of donning fancy dress, but the complete discomfiture of Pagett was too tempting to be forborne.

'What do you mean?' I said. 'Of course I shall wear fancy dress. So will you.'

Pagett shuddered.

'So go down to the barber's and see about it,' I finished.

'I don't think he'll have any outsizes,' murmured Pagett, measuring my figure with his eye.

Without meaning it, Pagett can occasionally be extremely offensive.

'And order a table for six in the saloon,' I said. 'We'll have the Captain, the girl with the nice legs, Mrs Blair –'

'You won't get Mrs Blair, without Colonel Race,' Pagett interposed. 'He's asked her to dine with him, I know.'

Pagett always knows everything. I was justifiably annoyed.

'Who *is* Race?' I demanded, exasperated.

As I said before, Pagett always knows everything – or thinks he does. He looked mysterious again.

'They say he's a Secret Service chap, Sir Eustace. Rather a great gun too. But of course I don't know for certain.'

'Isn't that like the Government?' I exclaimed. 'Here's a man on board whose business it is to carry about secret documents, and they go giving them to a peaceful outsider, who only asks to be let alone.'

Pagett looked even more mysterious. He came a pace nearer and dropped his voice.

'If you ask me, the whole thing is very queer, Sir Eustace. Look at the illness of mine before we started –'

'My dear fellow,' I interrupted brutally, 'that was a bilious attack. You're always having bilious attacks.'

Pagett winced slightly.

'It wasn't the usual sort of bilious attack. This time –'

'For God's sake, don't go into details of your condition, Pagett. I don't want to hear them.'

'Very well, Sir Eustace. But my belief is that I was deliberately *poisoned*!'

'Ah!' I said. 'You've been talking to Rayburn.'

He did not deny it.

'At any rate, Sir Eustace, *he* thinks so – and he should be in a position to know.'

'By the way, where is the chap?' I asked. 'I've not set eyes on him since we came on board.'

'He gives out that he's ill, and stays in his cabin, Sir Eustace.' Pagett's voice dropped again. 'But that's *camouflage*, I'm sure. So that he can watch better.'

'Watch?'

'Over your safety, Sir Eustace. In case an attack should be made upon you.'

'You're such a cheerful fellow, Pagett,' I said. 'I trust that your imagination runs away with you. If I were you I should go to the dance as a death's head or an executioner. It will suit your mournful style of beauty.'

That shut him up for the time being. I went on deck. The Beddingfeld girl was deep in conversation with the missionary parson, Chichester. Women always flutter round parsons.

A man of my figure hates stooping, but I had the courtesy to pick up a bit of paper that was fluttering round the parson's feet.

I got no word of thanks for my pains. As a matter of fact I couldn't help seeing what was written on the sheet of paper. There was just one sentence.

'Don't try to play a lone hand or it will be the worse for you.'

That's a nice thing for a parson to have. Who is this fellow Chichester, I wonder? He *looks* mild as milk. But looks are deceptive. I shall ask Pagett about him. Pagett always knows everything.

I sank gracefully into my deck-chair by the side of Mrs Blair, thereby interrupting her *tête-à-tête* with Race, and remarked that I didn't know what the clergy were coming to nowadays.

Then I asked her to dine with me on the night of the Fancy Dress dance. Somehow or other Race managed to get included in the invitation.

After lunch the Beddingfeld girl came and sat with us for coffee. I was right about her legs. They *are* the best on the ship. I shall certainly ask her to dinner as well.

I would very much like to know what mischief Pagett was up to in Florence. Whenever Italy is mentioned, he goes to pieces. If I did not know how intensely respectable he is – I should suspect him of some disreputable *amour* . . .

I wonder now! Even the most respectable men – It would cheer me up enormously if it was so.

Pagett – with a guilty secret! Splendid!

CHAPTER XIII

It has been a curious evening.

The only costume that fitted me in the barber's emporium was that of a Teddy Bear. I don't mind playing bears with some nice young girls on a winter's evening in England – but it's hardly an ideal costume for the equator. However, I created a good deal of merriment, and won first prize for 'brought on board' – an absurd term for a costume hired for the evening. Still, as nobody seemed to have the least idea whether they were made or brought, it didn't matter.

Mrs Blair refused to dress up. Apparently she is at one with Pagett on the matter. Colonel Race followed her example. Anne Beddingfeld had concocted a gipsy costume for herself, and looked extraordinarily well. Pagett said he had a headache and didn't appear. To replace him I asked a quaint little fellow called Reeves. He's a prominent member of the South African Labour party. Horrible little man, but I want to keep in with him, as he gives me information that I need. I want to understand this Rand business from both sides.

Dancing was a hot affair. I danced twice with Anne Beddingfeld and she had to pretend she liked it. I danced once with Mrs Blair, who didn't trouble to pretend, and I victimized various other damsels whose appearance struck me favourably.

Then we went down to supper. I had ordered champagne; the steward suggested Clicquot 1911 as being the best they had on the boat and I fell in with his suggestion. I seemed to have hit on the one thing that would loosen Colonel Race's tongue. Far from being taciturn, the man became actually talkative. For a while this amused me, then it occurred to me that Colonel Race, and not myself, was becoming the life and soul of the party. He chaffed me at length about keeping a diary.

'It will reveal all your indiscretions one of these days, Pedler.'

'My dear Race,' I said, 'I venture to suggest that I am not quite the fool you think me. I may commit indiscretions, but I don't write them down in black and white. After my death, my executors will know my opinion of a great many people, but I doubt if they will find anything to add or detract from their opinion of *me*. A diary is useful for recording the idiosyncrasies of other people – but not one's own.'

'There is such a thing as unconscious self-revelation, though.'

'In the eyes of the psycho-analyst, all things are vile,' I replied sententiously.

'You must have had a very interesting life, Colonel Race?' said Miss Beddingfeld, gazing at him with wide, starry eyes.

That's how they do it, these girls! Othello charmed Desdemona by telling her stories, but, oh, didn't Desdemona charm Othello by the way she listened?

Anyway, the girl set Race off all right. He began to tell lion stories. A man who has shot lions in large quantities has an unfair advantage over other men. It seemed to me that it was time I, too, told a lion story. One of a more sprightly character.

'By the way,' I remarked, 'that reminds me of a rather exciting tale I heard. A friend of mine was out on a shooting trip somewhere in East Africa. One night he came out of his tent for some reason, and was startled by a low growl. He turned sharply and saw a lion crouching to spring. He had left his rifle in the tent. Quick as thought, he ducked, and the lion sprang right over his head. Annoyed at having missed him, the animal growled and prepared to spring again. Again he ducked, and again the lion sprang right over him. This happened a third time, but by now he was close to the entrance of his tent, and he darted in and seized his rifle. When he emerged, rifle in hand, the lion had disappeared. That puzzled him greatly. He crept round the back of the tent, where there was a little clearing. There, sure enough, was the lion, busily practising low jumps.'

This was received by a roar of applause. I drank some champagne.

'On another occasion,' I remarked, 'this friend of mine had a second curious experience. He was trekking across country, and being anxious to arrive at his destination before the heat of the day he ordered his boys to inspan whilst it was still dark. They had some trouble in doing so, as the mules were very restive, but at last they managed it, and a start was made. The mules raced along like the wind, and when daylight came they saw why. In the darkness, the boys had inspanned a lion as the near wheeler.'

This, too, was well received, a ripple of merriment going round the table, but I am not sure that the greatest tribute did not come from my friend the Labour Member, who remained pale and serious.

'My God!' he said anxiously. 'Who un'arnessed them?'

'I must go to Rhodesia,' said Mrs Blair. 'After what you have told us, Colonel Race, I simply must. It's a horrible journey though, five days in the train.'

'You must join me in my private car,' I said gallantly.

'Oh, Sir Eustace, how sweet of you! Do you really mean it?'

'Do I mean it!' I exclaimed reproachfully, and drank another glass of champagne.

'Just about another week, and we shall be in South Africa,' sighed Mrs Blair.

'Ah, South Africa,' I said sentimentally, and began to quote from a recent speech of mine at the Colonial Institute. 'What has South Africa to show the world? What indeed? Her fruit and her farms, her wool and her wattles, her herds and her hides, her gold mines and her diamonds –'

I was hurrying on, because I knew that as soon as I paused Reeves would butt in and inform me that the hides were worthless because the animals hung themselves up on barbed wire or something of that sort, would crab everything else, and end up with the hardships of the miners on the Rand. And I was not in the mood to be abused as a Capitalist. However, the interruption came from another source at the magic word diamonds.

'Diamonds!' said Mrs Blair ecstatically.

'Diamonds!' breathed Miss Beddingfeld.

They both addressed Colonel Race.

'I suppose you've been to Kimberley?'

I had been to Kimberley too, but I didn't manage to say so in time. Race was being inundated with questions. What were mines like? Was it true that the natives were kept shut up in compounds? And so on.

Race answered their questions and showed a good knowledge of his subject. He described the methods of housing the natives, the searches instituted, and the various precautions that De Beers took.

'Then it's practically impossible to steal any diamonds?' asked Mrs Blair with as keen an air of disappointment as though she had been journeying there for the express purpose.

'Nothing's impossible, Mrs Blair. Thefts do occur – like the case I told you of where the Kafir hid the stone in his wound.'

'Yes, but on a large scale?'

'Once, in recent years. Just before the War, in fact. You must remember the case, Pedler. You were in South Africa at the time?'

I nodded.

'Tell us,' cried Miss Beddingfeld. 'Oh, do tell us!'

Race smiled.

'Very well, you shall have the story. I suppose most of you have heard of Sir Laurence Eardsley, the great South African mining magnate? His mines were gold mines, but he comes into the story through his son. You may remember that just before the War rumours were afield of a new potential Kimberley hidden somewhere in the rocky floor of the British Guiana jungles. Two young explorers, so it was reported, had returned from that part of South America bringing with them a remarkable collection of rough diamonds, some of them of considerable size. Diamonds of small size had been found before in the neighbourhood of the Essequibo and Mazaruni rivers, but these two young men, John Eardsley and his friend Lucas, claimed to have discovered beds of great carbon deposits at the common head of two streams. The diamonds were of every colour, pink, blue, yellow, green, black, and the purest white. Eardsley and Lucas came to Kimberley, where they were to submit their gems to inspection. At the same time a sensational robbery was found to have taken place at De Beers. When sending diamonds to England they are made up into a packet. This remains in the big safe, of which the two keys are held by two different men whilst a third man knows the combination. They are handed to the Bank, and the Bank send them to England. Each package is worth, roughly, about £100,000.

'On this occasion the Bank were struck by something a little unusual about the sealing of the packet. It was opened, and found to contain knobs of sugar!

'Exactly how suspicion came to fasten on John Eardsley I do not know. It was remembered that he had been very wild at Cambridge and that his father had paid his debts more than once. Anyhow, it soon got about that this story of South American diamond fields was all a fantasy. John Eardsley was arrested. In his possesion was found a portion of the De Beers diamonds.

'But the case never came to court. Sir Laurence Eardsley paid over a sum equal to the missing diamonds, and De Beers did not prosecute. Exactly how the robbery was committed has never been known. But the knowledge that his son was a thief broke the old man's heart. He had a stroke shortly afterwards. As for John, his Fate was in a way merciful. He enlisted, went to the War, fought there bravely, and was killed, thus wiping out the stain on his name. Sir Laurence himself had a third stroke and died about a month ago. He died intestate and his vast fortune passed to his next of kin, a man whom he hardly knew.'

The Colonel paused. A babel of ejaculations and questions broke out. Something seemed to attract Miss Beddingfeld's attention, and she turned in her chair. At the little gasp she gave, I, too, turned.

My new secretary, Rayburn, was standing in the doorway. Under his tan, his face had the pallor of one who has seen a ghost. Evidently Race's story had moved him profoundly.

Suddenly conscious of our scrutiny, he turned abruptly and disappeared.

'Do you know who that is?' asked Anne Beddingfeld abruptly.

'That's my other secretary,' I explained. 'Mr Rayburn. He's been seedy up to now.'

She toyed with the bread by her plate.

'Has he been your secretary long?'

'Not very long,' I said cautiously.

But caution is useless with a woman, the more you hold back, the more she presses forward. Anne Beddingfeld made no bones about it.

'How long?' she asked bluntly.

'Well – er – I engaged him just before I sailed. Old friend of mine recommended him.'

She said nothing more, but relapsed into a thoughtful silence. I turned to Race with the feeling that it was my turn to display an interest in his story.

'Who is Sir Laurence's next of kin, Race? Do you know?'

'I should do so,' he replied, with a smile. 'I am!'

CHAPTER XIV

(Anne's Narrative Resumed)

It was on the night of the Fancy Dress dance that I decided that the time had come for me to confide in someone. So far I had played a lone hand and rather enjoyed it. Now suddenly everything was changed. I distrusted my own judgement and for the first time a feeling of loneliness and desolation crept over me.

I sat on the edge of my bunk, still in my gipsy dress, and considered the situation. I thought first of Colonel Race. He had seemed to like me. He would be kind, I was sure. And he was no fool. Yet, as I thought it over, I wavered. He was a man of commanding personality. He would take the whole matter out of my hands. And it was *my* mystery! There were other reasons, too, which I would hardly acknowledge to myself, but which made it inadvisable to confide in Colonel Race.

Then I thought of Mrs Blair. She, too, had been kind to me. I did not delude myself into the belief that that really meant anything. It was probably a mere whim of the moment. All the same, I had it in my power to interest her. She was a woman who had experienced most of the ordinary sensations in life. I proposed to supply her with an extraordinary one! And I liked her; liked her ease of manner, her lack of sentimentality, her freedom from any form of affectation.

My mind was made up. I decided to seek her out then and there. She would hardly be in bed yet.

Then I remembered that I did not know the number of her cabin. My friend, the night stewardess, would probably know.

I rang the bell. After some delay it was answered by a man. He gave me the information I wanted. Mrs Blair's cabin was

No. 71. He apologized for the delay in answering the bell, but explained that he had all the cabins to attend to.

'Where is the stewardess, then?' I asked.

'They all go off duty at ten o'clock.'

'No – I mean the night stewardess.'

'No stewardess on at night, miss.'

'But – but a stewardess came the other night – about one o'clock.'

'You must have been dreaming, miss. There's no stewardess on duty after ten.'

He withdrew and I was left to digest this morsel of information. Who was the woman who had come to my cabin on the night of the 22nd? My face grew graver as I realized the cunning and audacity of my unknown antagonists. Then, pulling myself together, I left my own cabin and sought that of Mrs Blair. I knocked at the door.

'Who's that?' called her voice from within.

'It's me – Anne Beddingfeld.'

'Oh, come in, gipsy girl.'

I entered. A good deal of scattered clothing lay about, and Mrs Blair herself was draped in one of the loveliest kimonos I had ever seen. It was all orange and gold and black and made my mouth water to look at it.

'Mrs Blair,' I said abruptly, 'I want to tell you the story of my life – that is, if it isn't too late, and you won't be bored.'

'Not a bit. I always hate going to bed,' said Mrs Blair, her face crinkling into smiles in the delightful way it had. 'And I should love to hear the story of your life. You're a most unusual creature, gipsy girl. Nobody else would think of bursting in on me at 1 A.M. to tell me the story of their life. Especially after snubbing my natural curiosity for weeks as you have done! I'm not accustomed to being snubbed. It's been quite a pleasing novelty. Sit down on the sofa and unburden your soul.'

I told her the whole story. It took some time as I was conscientious over all the details. She gave a deep sigh when I had finished, but she did not say at all what I had expected her to say. Instead she looked at me, laughed a little and said:

'Do you know, Anne, you're a very unusual girl? Haven't you ever had qualms?'

'Qualms?' I asked, puzzled.

'Yes, qualms, qualms, qualms! Starting off alone with practically no money. What will you do when you find yourself in a strange country with all your money gone?'

'It's no good bothering about that until it comes. I've got plenty of money still. The twenty-five pounds that Mrs Flemming gave me is practically intact, and then I won the sweep yesterday. That's another fifteen pounds. Why, I've got *lots* of money. Forty pounds!'

'Lots of money! My God!' murmured Mrs Blair. 'I couldn't do it, Anne, and I've plenty of pluck in my own way. I couldn't start off gaily with a few pounds in my pocket and no idea as to what I was doing and where I was going.'

'But that's the fun of it,' I cried, thoroughly roused. 'It gives one such a splendid feeling of adventure.'

She looked at me, nodded once or twice, and then smiled.

'Lucky Anne! There aren't many people in the world who feel as you do.'

'Well,' I said impatiently, 'what do you think of it all, Mrs Blair?'

'I think it's the most thrilling thing I ever heard! Now, to begin with, you will stop calling me Mrs Blair. Suzanne will be ever so much better. Is that agreed?'

'I should love it, Suzanne.'

'Good girl. Now let's get down to business. You say that in Sir Eustace's secretary – not that long-faced Pagett, the other one – you recognized the man who was stabbed and came into your cabin for shelter?'

I nodded.

'That gives us two links connecting Sir Eustace with the tangle. The woman was murdered in *his* house, and it's *his* secretary who gets stabbed at the mystic hour of one o'clock. I don't suspect Sir Eustace himself, but it can't be all coincidence. There's a connexion somewhere even if he himself is unaware of it.

'Then there's the queer business of the stewardess,' she continued thoughtfully. 'What was she like?'

'I hardly noticed her. I was so excited and strung up – and a stewardess seemed such an anticlimax. But – yes – I did think her face was familiar. Of course it would be if I'd seen her about the ship.'

'Her face seemed familiar to you,' said Suzanne. 'Sure she wasn't a man?'

'She was very tall,' I admitted.

'Hum. Hardly Sir Eustace, I should think, nor Mr Pagett – Wait!'

She caught up a scrap of paper and began drawing feverishly. She inspected the result with her head poised on one side.

'A very good likeness of the Rev. Edward Chichester. Now for the etceteras.' She passed the paper over to me. 'Is that your stewardess?'

'Why, yes,' I cried. 'Suzanne, how clever of you!'

She disdained the compliment with a light gesture.

'I've always had suspicions about that Chichester creature. Do you remember how he dropped his coffee-cup and turned a sickly green when we were discussing Crippen the other day?'

'And he tried to get Cabin 17!'

'Yes, it all fits in so far. But what does it all *mean*? What was really meant to happen at one o'clock in Cabin 17? It can't be the stabbing of the secretary. There would be no point in timing that for a special hour on a special day in a special place. No, it must have been some kind of appointment and he was on his way to keep it when they knifed him. But who was the appointment with? Certainly not with you. It might have been with Chichester. Or it might have been with Pagett.'

'That seems unlikely,' I objected; 'they can see each other any time.'

We both sat silent for a minute or two, then Suzanne started off on another tack.

'Could there have been anything hidden in the cabin?'

'That seems more probable,' I agreed. 'It would explain my things being ransacked the next morning. But there was nothing hidden there, I'm sure of it.'

'The young man couldn't have slipped something into a drawer the night before?'

I shook my head.

'I should have seen him.'

'Could it have been your precious bit of paper they were looking for?'

'It might have been, but it seems rather senseless. It was only a time and a date – and they were both past by then.'

Suzanne nodded.

'That's so, of course. No, it wasn't the paper. By the way, have you got it with you? I'd rather like to see it.'

I had brought the paper with me as Exhibit A, and I handed it over to her. She scrutinized it, frowning.

'There's a dot after the 17. Why isn't there a dot after the 1 too?'

'There's a space,' I pointed out.

'Yes, there's a space, but –'

Suddenly she rose and peered at the paper, holding it as close under the light as possible. There was a repressed excitement in her manner.

'Anne, that isn't a dot! That's a flaw in the paper! A flaw in the paper, you see? So you've got to ignore it, and just go by the spaces – the spaces!'

I had risen and was standing by her. I read out the figures as I now saw them.

'1 71 22.'

'You see,' said Suzanne. 'It's the same, but not quite. It's one o'clock still, and the 22nd – but it's Cabin 71! *My* cabin, Anne!'

We stood staring at each other, so pleased with our new discovery and so rapt with excitement that you might have thought we had solved the whole mystery. Then I fell to earth with a bump.

'But, Suzanne, nothing happened here at one o'clock on the 22nd?'

Her face fell also.

'No – it didn't.'

Another idea struck me.

'This isn't your own cabin, is it, Suzanne? I mean not the one you originally booked?'

'No, the purser changed me into it.'

'I wonder if it was booked before sailing for someone – someone who didn't turn up. I suppose we could find out.'

'We don't need to find out, gipsy girl,' cried Suzanne. 'I know! The purser was telling me about it. The cabin was booked in the name of Mrs Grey – but it seems that Mrs Grey was merely a pseudonym for the famous Madame Nadina. She's a celebrated Russian dancer, you know. She's never appeared in London, but Paris has been quite mad about her. She had a terrific success there all through the War. A thoroughly bad lot, I believe, but most attractive. The purser expressed his regrets that she wasn't on board in a most heart-felt fashion when he gave me her cabin, and then Colonel Race told me a lot about her. It seems there were very queer stories afloat in Paris. She was suspected of espionage, but they couldn't prove anything. I rather fancy Colonel Race was over there simply on that account. He's told me some very interesting things. There was a regular organized gang, not German in origin at all. In fact the head of it, a man always referred to as 'the Colonel', was thought to be an Englishman, but they never got any clue to his identity. But there is no doubt that he controlled a considerable organization of inter-national crooks. Robberies, espionage, assaults, he undertook them all – and usually provided an innocent scapegoat to pay the penalty. Diabolically clever, he must have been! This woman was supposed to be one of his agents, but they couldn't get hold of anything to go upon. Yes, Anne, we're on the right tack. Nadina is just the woman to be mixed up in this business. The appointment on the morning of the 22nd was with her in this cabin. But where is she? Why didn't she sail?'

A light flashed upon me.

'She meant to sail,' I said slowly.

'Then why didn't she?'

'*Because she was dead*. Suzanne, Nadina was the woman murdered at Marlow!'

My mind went back to the bare room in the empty house and there swept over me again the indefinable sensation of menace and evil. With it came the memory of the falling pencil and the discovery of the roll of films. A roll of films – that struck a more recent note. Where had I heard of a roll of films? And why did I connect that thought with Mrs Blair?

Suddenly I flew at her and almost shook her in my excitement.

'Your films! The ones that were passed to you through the ventilator? Wasn't that on the 22nd?'

'The ones I lost?'

'How do you know they were the same? Why would anyone return them to you that way – in the middle of the night? It's a mad idea. No – they were a message, the films had been taken out of the yellow tin case, and something else put inside. Have you still got it?'

'I may have used it. No, here it is. I remember I tossed it into the rack at the side of the bunk.'

She held it out to me.

It was an ordinary round tin cylinder, such as films are packed in for the tropics. I took it with trembling hand, but even as I did so my heart leapt. It was noticeably heavier than it should have been.

With shaking fingers I peeled off the strip of adhesive plaster that kept it air-tight. I pulled off the lid, and a stream of dull glassy pebbles rolled on to the bed.

'Pebbles,' I said, keenly disappointed.

'Pebbles?' cried Suzanne.

The ring in her voice excited me.

'Pebbles? No, Anne, not pebbles! *Diamonds!*'

CHAPTER XV

Diamonds!

I stared, fascinated, at the glassy heap on the bunk. I picked up one which, but for the weight, might have been a fragment of broken bottle.

'Are you sure, Suzanne?'

'Oh, yes, my dear. I've seen rough diamonds too often to have any doubts. They're beauties too, Anne – and some of them are unique, I should say. There's a history behind these.'

'The history we heard tonight,' I cried.

'You mean –'

'Colonel Race's story. It can't be a coincidence. He told it for a purpose.'

'To see its effect, you mean?'

I nodded.

'Its effect on Sir Eustace?'

'Yes.'

But, even as I said it, a doubt assailed me. *Was it* Sir Eustace who had been subjected to a test, or had the story been told for *my* benefit? I remembered the impression I had received on that former night of having been deliberately 'pumped'. For some reason or other, Colonel Race was suspicious. But where did he come in? What possible connexion could he have with the affair?

'Who *is* Colonel Race?' I asked.

'That's rather a question,' said Suzanne. 'He's pretty well known as a big-game hunter, and, as you heard him say tonight, he was a distant cousin of Sir Laurence Eardsley. I've never actually met him until this trip. He journeys to and from Africa a good deal. There's a general idea that he does Secret Service work. I don't know whether it's true or not. He's certainly rather a mysterious creature.'

'I suppose he came into a lot of money as Sir Laurence Eardsley's heir?'

'My dear Anne, he must be *rolling*. You know, he'd be a splendid match for you.'

'I can't have a good go at him with you aboard the ship,' I said, laughing. 'Oh, these married women!'

'We do have a pull,' murmured Suzanne complacently. 'And everybody knows that I am absolutely devoted to Clarence – my husband, you know. It's so safe and pleasant to make love to a devoted wife.'

'It must be very nice for Clarence to be married to someone like you.'

'Well, I'm wearing to live with! Still, he can always escape to the Foreign Office, where he fixes his eyeglass in his eye, and goes to sleep in a big arm-chair. We might cable him to tell us all he knows about Race. I love sending cables. And they annoy Clarence so. He always says a letter would have done as well. I don't suppose he'd tell us anything though. He is so frightfully discreet. That's what makes him so hard to live with for long on end. But let us go on with our match-making. I'm sure Colonel Race is very attracted to you, Anne. Give him a couple of glances from those wicked eyes of yours, and the deed is done. Everyone gets engaged on board ship. There's nothing else to do.'

'I don't want to get married.'

'Don't you?' said Suzanne. 'Why not? I love being married – even to Clarence!'

I disdained her flippancy.

'What I want to know is,' I said with determination, 'what has Colonel Race got to do with this? He's in it somewhere.'

'You don't think it was mere chance, his telling that story?'

'No, I don't,' I said decidedly. 'He was watching us all narrowly. You remember, *some* of the diamonds were recovered, not all. Perhaps these are the missing ones – or perhaps –'

'Perhaps what?'

I did not answer directly.

'I should like to know,' I said, 'what became of the other young man. Not Eardsley but – what was his name? – Lucas!'

'We're getting some light on the thing, anyway. It's the diamonds all these people are after. It must have been to obtain possession of the diamonds that "The Man in the Brown Suit" killed Nadina.'

'He didn't kill her,' I said sharply.

'Of course he killed her. Who else could have done so?'

'I don't know. But I'm sure he didn't kill her.'

'He went into the house three minutes after her and came out as white as a sheet.'

'Because he found her dead.'

'But nobody else went in.'

'Then the murderer was in the house already, or else he got in some other way. There's no need for him to pass the lodge, he could have climbed over the wall.'

Suzanne glanced at me sharply.

'"The Man in the Brown Suit,"' she mused. 'Who was he, I wonder? Anyway, he was identical with the "doctor" in the Tube. He would have had time to remove his make-up and follow the woman to Marlow. She and Carton were to have met there, they both had an order to view the same house, and if they took such elaborate precautions to make their meeting appear accidental they must have suspected they were being followed. All the same, Carton did *not* know that his shadower was the "Man in the Brown Suit". When he recognized him, the shock was so great that he lost his head completely and stepped back on to the line. That all seems pretty clear, don't you think so, Anne!'

I did not reply.

'Yes, that's how it was. He took the paper from the dead man, and in his hurry to get away he dropped it. Then he followed the woman to Marlow. What did he do when he left there, when he had killed her – or, according to you, found her dead? Where did he go?'

Still I said nothing.

'I wonder, now,' said Suzanne musingly. 'Is it posssible that he induced Sir Eustace Pedler to bring him on board as his secretary? It would be a unique chance of getting safely out of England, and dodging the hue and cry. But how did he square Sir Eustace? It looks as though he had some hold over him.'

'Or over Pagett,' I suggested in spite of myself.

'You don't seem to like Pagett, Anne. Sir Eustace says he's a most capable and hard-working young man. And, really, he may be for all we know against him. Well, to continue my surmises, Rayburn is "The Man in the Brown Suit". He had read the paper he dropped. Therefore, misled by the dot as you were, he attempts to reach Cabin 17 at one o'clock on the 22nd, having previously tried to get possession of the cabin through Pagett. On the way there somebody knifes him –'

'Who?' I interpolated.

'Chichester. Yes, it all fits in. Cable to Lord Nasby that you have found "The Man in the Brown Suit", and your fortune's made, Anne!'

'There are several things you've overlooked.'

'What things? Rayburn's got a scar, I know – but a scar can be faked easily enough. He's the right height and build. What's the description of a head with which you pulverized them at Scotland Yard?'

I trembled. Suzanne was a well-educated, well-read woman, but I prayed that she might not be conversant with technical terms of anthropology.

'Dolichocephalic,' I said lightly.

Susanne looked doubtful.

'Was that it?'

'Yes. Long-headed, you know. A head whose width is less than 75 per cent of its length,' I explained fluently.

There was a pause. I was just beginning to breathe freely when Suzanne said suddenly:

'What's the opposite?'

'What do you mean – the opposite?'

'Well, there must be an opposite. What do you call heads whose breadth is more than 75 per cent of their length?'

'Brachycephalic,' I murmured unwillingly.

'That's it. I thought that was what you said.'

'Did I? It was a slip of the tongue. I meant dolichocephalic,' I said with all the assurance I could muster.

Suzanne looked at me searchingly. Then she laughed.

'You lie very well, gipsy girl. But it will save time and trouble now if you tell me all about it.'

'There is nothing to tell,' I said unwillingly.

'Isn't there?' said Suzanne gently.

'I suppose I shall have to tell you,' I said slowly. 'I'm not ashamed of it. You can't be ashamed of something that just – happens to you. That's what he did. He was detestable – rude and ungrateful – but that I think I understand. It's like a dog that's been chained up – or badly treated – it'll bite anybody. That's what he was like – bitter and snarling. I don't know why I care – but I do. I care horribly. Just seeing him has turned my whole life upside-down. I love him. I want him. I'll walk all over Africa barefoot till I find him, and I'll make him care for me. I'd die for him. I'd work for him, slave for him, steal for him, even beg or borrow for him! There – now you know!'

Suzanne looked at me for a long time.

'You're very un-English, gipsy girl,' she said at last. 'There's not a scrap of the sentimental about you. I've never met anyone who was at once so practical and so passionate. I shall never care for anyone like that – mercifully for me – and yet – and yet I envy you, gipsy girl. It's something to be able to care. Most people can't. But what a mercy for your little doctor man that you didn't marry him. He doesn't sound at all the sort of individual who would enjoy keeping high explosive in the house! So there's to be no cabling to Lord Nasby?'

I shook my head.

'And yet you believe him to be innocent?'

'I also believe that innocent people can be hanged.'

'H'm! yes. But, Anne dear, you can face facts, face them now. In spite of all you say, he may have murdered this woman.'

'No,' I said. 'He didn't.'

'That's sentiment.'

'No, it isn't. He might have killed her. He may even have followed her there with that idea in mind. But he wouldn't take a bit of black cord and strangle her with it. If he'd done it, he would have strangled her with his bare hands.'

Suzanne gave a little shiver. Her eyes narrowed appreciatively.

'H'm! Anne, I am beginning to see why you find this young man of yours so attractive!'

CHAPTER XVI

I got an opportunity of tackling Colonel Race on the following morning. The auction of the sweep had just been concluded, and we walked up and down the deck together.

'How's the gipsy this morning? Longing for land and her caravan?'

I shook my head.

'Now that the sea is behaving so nicely, I feel I should like to stay on it for ever and ever.'

'What enthusiasm!'

'Well, isn't it lovely this morning?'

We leant together over the rail. It was a glassy calm. The sea looked as though it had been oiled. There were great patches of colour on it, blue, pale green, emerald, purple and deep orange, like a cubist picture. There was an occasional flash of silver that showed the flying fish. The air was moist and warm, almost sticky. Its breath was like a perfumed caress.

'That was a very interesting story you told us last night,' I said, breaking the silence.

'Which one?'

'The one about the diamonds.'

'I believe women are always interested in diamonds.'

'Of course we are. By the way, what became of the other young man? You said there were two of them.'

'Young Lucas? Well, of course, they couldn't prosecute one without the other, so he went scot-free too.'

'And what happened to him? – eventually, I mean. Does anyone know?'

Colonel Race was looking straight ahead of him out to sea. His face was as devoid of expression as a mask, but I had an idea that he did not like my questions. Nevertheless, he replied readily enough.

'He went to the War and acquitted himself bravely. He was reported missing and wounded – believed killed.'

That told me what I wanted to know. I asked no more. But more than ever I wondered how much Colonel Race knew. The part he was playing in all this puzzled me.

One other thing I did. That was to interview the night steward. With a little financial encouragement, I soon got him to talk.

'The lady wasn't frightened, was she miss? It seemed a harmless sort of joke. A bet, or so I understood.'

I got it all out of him, little by little. On the voyage from Cape Town to England one of the passengers had handed him a roll of film with instructions that they were to be dropped on to the bunk in Cabin 71 at 1 A.M. on January 22nd on the outward journey. A lady would be occupying the cabin, and the affair was described as a bet. I gathered the steward had been liberally paid for his part in the transaction. The lady's name had not been mentioned. Of course, as Mrs Blair went straight into Cabin 71, interviewing the purser as soon as she got on board, it never occurred to the steward that she was not the lady in question. The name of the passenger who had arranged the transaction was Carton, and his description tallied exactly with that of the man killed on the Tube.

So one mystery, at all events, was cleared up, and the diamonds were obviously the key to the whole situation.

Those last days on the *Kilmorden* seemed to pass very quickly. As we drew nearer and nearer to Cape Town, I was forced to consider carefully my future plans. There were so many people I wanted to keep an eye on. Mr Chichester, Sir Eustace and his secretary, and – yes, Colonel Race! What was I to do about it? Naturally it was Chichester who had first claim on my attention. Indeed, I was on the point of reluctantly dismissing Sir Eustace and Mr Pagett from their position of suspicious characters when a chance conversation awakened fresh doubts in my mind.

I had forgotten Mr Pagett's incomprehensible emotion at the mention of Florence. On the last evening on board we

were all sitting on deck and Sir Eustace addressed a perfectly
innocent question to his secretary. I forget exactly what it was,
something to do with railway delays in Italy, but at once I
noticed that Mr Pagett was displaying the same uneasiness
which had caught my attention before. When Sir Eustace
claimed Mrs Blair for a dance, I quickly moved into the chair
next to the secretary. I was determined to get to the bottom
of the matter.

'I have always longed to go to Italy,' I said. 'And especially
to Florence. Didn't you enjoy it very much there?'

'Indeed I did, Miss Beddingfeld. If you will excuse me,
there is some correspondence of Sir Eustace's that –'

I took hold of him firmly by his coat sleeve.

'Oh, you mustn't run away!' I cried with the skittish accent
of an elderly dowager. 'I'm sure Sir Eustace wouldn't like you
to leave me alone with no one to talk to. You never seem to
want to talk about Florence. Oh, Mr Pagett, I believe you
have a guilty secret!'

I still had my hand on his arm, and I could feel the sudden
start he gave.

'Not at all, Miss Beddingfeld, not at all,' he said earnestly.
'I should be only too delighted to tell you all about it, but
there really are some cables –'

'Oh, Mr Pagett, what a thin pretence! I shall tell Sir
Eustace –'

I got no further. He gave another jump. The man's nerves
seemed in a shocking state.

'What is it you want to know?'

The resigned martyrdom of his tone made me smile
inwardly.

'Oh, everything! The pictures, the olive trees –'

I paused, rather at a loss myself.

'I suppose you speak Italian?' I resumed.

'Not a word, unfortunately. But of course, with hall porters
and – er – guides.'

'Exactly,' I hastened to reply. 'And which was your favourite picture?'

'Oh, er – the Madonna – er, Raphael, you know.'

'Dear old Florence,' I murmured sentimentally. 'So picturesque on the banks of the Arno. A beautiful river. And the
Duomo, you remember the Duomo?'

'Of course, of course.'

'Another beautiful river, is it not?' I hazarded. 'Almost more
beautiful than the Arno?'

'Decidedly so, I should say.'

Emboldened by the success of my little trap, I proceeded
further. But there was little room for doubt. Mr Pagett
delivered himself into my hands with every word he uttered.
The man had never been in Florence in his life.

But if not in Florence, where had he been? In England?
Actually in England at the time of the Mill House Mystery?
I decided on a bold step.

'The curious thing is,' I said, 'that I fancied I had seen you
before somewhere. But I must be mistaken – since you were
in Florence at the time. And yet –'

I studied him frankly. There was a hunted look in his eyes.
He passed his tongue over dry lips.

'Where – er – where –'

'Did I think I had seen you?' I finished for him. 'At Marlow.
You know Marlow? Why, of course, how stupid of me, Sir
Eustace has a house there!'

But with an incoherent muttered excuse, my victim rose
and fled.

That night I invaded Suzanne's cabin, alight with
excitement.

'You see, Suzanne,' I urged, as I finished my tale, 'he was
in England, in Marlow, at the time of the murder. Are you so
sure now that "The Man in the Brown Suit" is guilty?'

'I'm sure of one thing,' Suzanne said, twinkling, unexpectedly.

'What's that?'

'That "The Man in the Brown Suit" is better looking than
poor Mr Pagett. No, Anne, don't get cross. I was only teasing.
Sit down here. Joking apart, I think you've made a very impor-

tant discovery. Up till now, we've considered Pagett as having an alibi. Now we know he hasn't.'

'Exactly,' I said. 'We must keep an eye on him.'

'As well as everybody else,' she said ruefully. 'Well, that's one of the things I wanted to talk to you about. That – and finance. No, don't stick your nose in the air. I know you are absurdly proud and independent, but you've got to listen to horse sense over this. We're partners – I wouldn't offer you a penny because I liked you, or because you're a friendless girl – what I want is a thrill, and I'm prepared to pay for it. We're going into this together regardless of expense. To begin with you'll come with me to the Mount Nelson Hotel at my expense, and we'll plan out our campaign.'

We argued the point. In the end I gave in. But I didn't like it. I wanted to do the thing on my own.

'That's settled,' said Suzanne at last, getting up and stretching herself with a big yawn. 'I'm exhausted with my own eloquence. Now then, let us discuss our victims. Mr Chichester is going on to Durban. Sir Eustace is going to the Mount Nelson Hotel in Cape Town and then up to Rhodesia. He's going to have a private car on the railway, and in a moment of expansion, after his fourth glass of champagne the other night, he offered me a place in it. I dare say he didn't really mean it, but, all the same, he can't very well back out if I hold him to it.'

'Good,' I approved. 'You keep an eye on Sir Eustace and Mr Pagett, and I take on Chichester. But what about Colonel Race?'

Suzanne looked at me queerly.

'Anne, you can't possibly suspect –'

'I do. I suspect everybody. I'm in the mood when one looks round for the most unlikely person.'

'Colonel Race is going to Rhodesia too,' said Suzanne thoughtfully. 'If we could arrange for Sir Eustace to invite him also –'

'You can manage it. You can manage anything.'

'I love butter,' purred Suzanne.

We parted on the understanding that Suzanne should employ her talents to her best advantage.

I felt too excited to go to bed immediately. It was my last night on board. Early tomorrow morning we should be in Table Bay.

I slipped up on deck. The breeze was fresh and cool. The boat was rolling a little in the choppy sea. The decks were dark and deserted. It was after midnight.

I leaned over the rail, watching the phosphorescent trail of foam. Ahead of us lay Africa, we were rushing towards it through the dark water. I felt alone in a wonderful world. Wrapped in a strange peace, I stood there, taking no heed of time, lost in a dream.

And suddenly I had a curious intimate premonition of danger. I had heard nothing, but I swung round instinctively. A shadowy form had crept up behind me. As I turned, it sprang. One hand gripped my throat, stifling any cry I might have uttered. I fought desperately, but I had no chance. I was half choking from the grip on my throat, but I bit and clung and scratched in the most approved feminine fashion. The man was handicapped by having to keep me from crying out. If he had succeeded in reaching me unawares it would have been easy enough for him to sling me overboard with a sudden heave. The sharks would have taken care of the rest.

Struggle as I would, I felt myself weakening. My assailant felt it too. He put out all his strength. And then, running on swift noiseless feet, another shadow joined in. With one blow of his fist, he sent my opponent crashing headlong to the deck. Released, I fell back against the rail, sick and trembling.

My rescuer turned to me with a quick movement.

'You're hurt!'

There was something savage in his tone – a menace against the person who had dared to hurt me. Even before he spoke I had recognized him. It was my man – the man with the scar.

But that one moment in which his attention had been diverted to me had been enough for the fallen enemy. Quick as a flash he had risen to his feet and taken to his heels down the deck. With an oath Rayburn sprang after him.

I always hate being out of things. I joined the chase – a bad third. Round the deck we went to the starboard side of the ship. There by the saloon door lay the man in a crumpled heap. Rayburn was bending over him.

'Did you hit him again?' I called breathlessly.

'There was no need,' he replied grimly. 'I found him collapsed by the door. Or else he couldn't get it open and is shamming. We'll soon see about that. And we'll see who he is too.'

With a beating heart I drew nearer. I had realized at once that my assailant was a bigger man than Chichester. Anyway, Chichester was a flabby creature who might use a knife at a pinch, but who would have little strength in his bare hands.

Rayburn struck a match. We both uttered an ejaculation. The man was Guy Pagett.

Rayburn appeared absolutely stupefied by the discovery.

'Pagett,' he muttered. 'My God, Pagett.'

I felt a slight sense of superiority.

'You seem surprised.'

'I am,' he said heavily. 'I never suspected –' He wheeled suddenly round on me. 'And you? You're not? You recognized him, I suppose, when he attacked you?'

'No, I didn't. All the same, I'm not so very surprised.'

He stared at me suspiciously.

'Where do you come in, I wonder? And how much do you know?'

I smiled.

'A good deal, Mr – er – Lucas!'

He caught my arm, the unconscious strength of his grip made me wince.

'Where did you get that name?' he asked hoarsely.

'Isn't it yours?' I demanded sweetly. 'Or do you prefer to be called "The Man in the Brown Suit"?'

That did stagger him. He released my arm and fell back a pace or two.

'Are you a girl, or a witch?' he breathed.

'I'm a friend,' I advanced a step towards him. 'I offered you my help once – I offer it again. Will you have it?'

The fierceness of his answer took me aback.

'No. I'll have no truck with you or with any woman. Do your damnedest.'

As before, my own temper began to rise.

'Perhaps,' I said, 'you don't realize how much in my power you are? A word from me to the Captain –'

'Say it,' he sneered. Then advancing with a quick step: 'And whilst we're realizing things, my dear girl, do you realize you're in *my* power this minute? I could take you by the throat like this.' With a swift gesture he suited the action to the word. I felt his two hands clasp my throat and press – ever so little. 'Like this – and squeeze the life out of you! And then – like our unconscious friend here, but with more success – fling your dead body to the sharks. What do you say to that?'

I said nothing. I laughed. And yet I knew that the danger was real. Just at that moment he hated me. But I knew that I loved the danger, loved the feeling of his hands on my throat. That I would not have exchanged that moment for any moment in my life.

With a short laugh he released me.

'What's your name?' he asked abruptly.

'Anne Beddingfeld.'

'Does nothing frighten you, Anne Beddingfeld?'

'Oh, yes,' I said, with an assumption of coolness I was far from feeling. 'Wasps, sarcastic women, very young men, cockroaches, and superior shop assistants.'

He gave the same short laugh as before. Then he stirred the unconscious form of Pagett with his feet.

'What shall we do with this junk? Throw it overboard?' he asked carelessly.

'If you like,' I answered with equal calm.

'I admire your whole-hearted, bloodthirsty instincts, Miss Beddingfeld. But we will leave him to recover at his leisure. He is not seriously hurt.'

'You shrink from a second murder, I see,' I said sweetly.

'A second murder?'

He looked genuinely puzzled.

'The woman at Marlow,' I reminded him, watching the effect of my words closely.

An ugly brooding expression settled down on his face. He seemed to have forgotten my presence.

'I might have killed her,' he said. 'Sometimes I believe that I meant to kill her . . .'

A wild rush of feeling, hatred of the dead woman, surged through me. *I* could have killed her that moment, had she stood before me . . . For he must have loved her once – he must – he must – to have felt like that!

I regained control of myself and spoke in my normal voice:

'We seem to have said all there is to be said – except good night.'

'Good night and goodbye, Miss Beddingfeld.'

'Au revoir, Mr Lucas.'

Again he flinched at the name. He came nearer.

'Why do you say that – au revoir, I mean?'

'Because I have a fancy that we shall meet again.'

'Not if I can help it!'

Emphatic as his tone was, it did not offend me. On the contrary, I hugged myself with secret satisfaction. I am not quite a fool.

'All the same,' I said gravely, 'I think we shall.'

'Why?'

I shook my head, unable to explain the feeling that had actuated my words.

'I never wish to see you again,' he said suddenly, and violently.

It was really a very rude thing to say, but I only laughed softly and slipped away into the darkness.

I heard him start after me, and then pause, and a word floated down the deck. I think it was 'witch'!

CHAPTER XVII

(Extract from the diary of Sir Eustace Pedler)

MOUNT NELSON HOTEL, CAPE TOWN.

It is really the greatest relief to get off the *Kilmorden*. The whole time that I was on board I was conscious of being surrounded by a network of intrigue. To put the lid on everything, Guy Pagett must needs engage in a drunken brawl the last night. It is all very well to explain it away, but that is what it actually amounts to. What else would you think if a man comes to you with a lump the size of an egg on the side of his head and an eye coloured all the tints of the rainbow?

Of course Pagett would insist on trying to be mysterious about the whole thing. According to him, you would think his black eye was the direct result of his devotion to my interests. His story was extraordinarily vague and rambling and it was a long time before I could make head or tail of it.

To begin with, it appears he caught sight of a man behaving suspiciously. Those are Pagett's words. He has taken them straight from the pages of a German spy story. What he means by a man behaving suspiciously he doesn't know himself. I said so to him.

'He was slinking along in a very furtive manner, and it was the middle of the night, Sir Eustace.'

'Well, what were you doing yourself? Why weren't you in bed and asleep like a good Christian?' I demanded irritably.

'I had been coding those cables of yours, Sir Eustace, and typing the diary up to date.'

Trust Pagett to be always in the right and a martyr over it!

'Well?'

'I just thought I would have a look round before turning in, Sir Eustace. The man was coming down the passage from your cabin. I thought at once there was something wrong by the way he looked about him. He slunk up the stairs by the saloon. I followed him.

'My dear Pagett,' I said, 'why shouldn't the poor chap go on deck without having his footsteps dogged? Lots of people even sleep on deck – very uncomfortable, I've always thought. The sailors wash you down with the rest of the deck at five in the morning.' I shuddered at the idea.

'Anyway,' I continued, 'if you went worrying some poor devil who was suffering from insomnia, I don't wonder he landed you one.'

Pagett looked patient.

'If you would hear me out, Sir Eustace. I was convinced the man had been prowling about near your cabin where he had no business to be. The only two cabins down that passage are yours and Colonel Race's.'

'Race,' I said, lighting a cigar carefully, 'can look after himself without your assistance, Pagett.' I added as an afterthought: 'So can I.'

Pagett came nearer and breathed heavily as he always does before imparting a secret.

'You see, Sir Eustace, I fancied – and now indeed I am sure – it was Rayburn.'

'Rayburn?'

'Yes, Sir Eustace.'

I shook my head.

'Rayburn has far too much sense to attempt to wake me up in the middle of the night.'

'Quite so, Sir Eustace. I think it was Colonel Race he went to see. A secret meeting – for orders!'

'Don't hiss at me, Pagett,' I said, drawing back a little, 'and do control your breathing. Your idea is absurd. Why should they want to have a secret meeting in the middle of the night? If they'd anything to say to each other, they could hobnob over beef-tea in a perfectly casual and natural manner.'

I could see that Pagett was not in the least convinced.

'*Something* was going on last night, Sir Eustace,' he urged, 'or why should Rayburn assault me so brutally?'

'You're quite sure it was Rayburn?'

Pagett appeared to be perfectly convinced of that. It was the only part of the story that he wasn't vague about.

'There's something very queer about all this,' he said. 'To begin with, where *is* Rayburn?'

It's perfectly true that we haven't seen the fellow since we came on shore. He did not come up to the hotel with us. I decline to believe that he is afraid of Pagett, however.

Altogether the whole thing is very annoying. One of my secretaries has vanished into the blue, and the other looks like a disreputable prize-fighter. I can't take him about with me in his present condition. I shall be the laughing-stock of Cape Town. I have an appointment later in the day to deliver old Milray's *billet-doux*, but I shall not take Pagett with me. Confound the fellow and his prowling ways.

Altogether I am decidedly out of temper. I had a poisonous breakfast with poisonous people. Dutch waitresses with thick ankles who took half an hour to bring me a bad bit of fish. And this farce of getting up at 5 AM on arrival at the port to see a blinking doctor and hold your hands above your head simply makes me tired.

Later.

A very serious thing has occurred. I went to my appointment with the Prime Minister, taking Milray's sealed letter. It didn't look as though it had been tampered with, but inside was a blank sheet of paper!

Now, I suppose, I'm in the devil of a mess. Why I ever let that bleating old fool Milray embroil me in the matter I can't think.

Pagett is a famous Job's comforter. He displays a certain gloomy satisfaction that maddens me. Also, he had taken advantage of my perturbation to saddle me with the stationery trunk. Unless he is careful, the next funeral he attends will be his own.

However in the end I had to listen to him.

'Supposing, Sir Eustace, that Rayburn had overheard a word or two of your conversation with Mr Milray in the street? Remember, you had no written authority from Mr Milray. You accepted Rayburn on his own valuation.'

'You think Rayburn is a crook, then?' I said slowly.

Pagett did. How far his views were influenced by resentment over his black eye I don't know. He made out a pretty fair case against Rayburn. And the appearance of the latter told against him. My idea was to do nothing in the matter. A man who has permitted himself to be made a thorough fool of is not anxious to broadcast the fact.

But Pagett, his energy unimpaired by his recent misfortunes, was all for vigorous measures. He had his way, of course. He bustled out to the police station, sent innumerable cables, and brought a herd of English and Dutch officials to drink whiskies and sodas at my expense.

We got Milray's answer that evening. He knew nothing of my late secretary! There was only one spot of comfort to be extracted from the situation.

'At any rate,' I said to Pagett, 'you weren't poisoned. You had one of your ordinary bilious attacks.'

I saw him wince. It was my only score.

Later.

Pagett is in his element. His brain positively scintillates with bright ideas. He will have it now that Rayburn is none other than the famous 'Man in the Brown Suit'. I dare say he is right. He usually is. But all this is getting unpleasant. The sooner I get off to Rhodesia the better. I have explained to Pagett that he is not to accompany me.

'You see, my dear fellow,' I said, 'you must remain here on the spot. You might be required to identify Rayburn any minute. And, besides, I have my dignity as an English Member of Parliament to think of. I can't go about with a secretary who has apparently recently been indulging in a vulgar street-brawl.'

Pagett winced. He is such a respectable fellow that his appearance is pain and tribulation to him.

'But what will you do about your correspondence, and the notes for your speeches, Sir Eustace?'

'I shall manage,' I said airily.

'Your private car is to be attached to the eleven-o'clock train tomorrow, Wednesday, morning,' Pagett continued. 'I have made all arrangements. Is Mrs Blair taking a maid with her?'

'Mrs Blair?' I gasped.

'She tells me you offered her a place.'

So I did, now I come to think of it. On the night of the Fancy Dress ball. I even urged her to come. But I never thought she would. Delightful as she is, I do not know that I want Mrs Blair's society all the way to Rhodesia and back. Women require such a lot of attention. And they are confoundedly in the way sometimes.

'Have I asked anyone else?' I said nervously. One does these things in moments of expansion.

'Mrs Blair seemed to think you had asked Colonel Race as well.'

I groaned.

'I must have been very drunk if I asked Race. Very drunk indeed. Take my advice, Pagett, and let your black eye be a warning to you, don't go on the bust again.'

'As you know, I am a teetotaller, Sir Eustace.'

'Much wiser to take the pledge if you have a weakness that way. I haven't asked anyone else, have I, Pagett?'

'Not that I know of, Sir Eustace.'

I heaved a sigh of relief.

'There's Miss Beddingfeld,' I said thoughtfully. 'She wants to get to Rhodesia to dig up bones, I believe. I've a good mind to offer her a temporary job as a secretary. She can typewrite, I know, for she told me so.'

To my surprise, Pagett opposed the idea vehemently. He

does not like Anne Beddingfeld. Ever since the night of the black eye, he has displayed uncontrollable emotion whenever she is mentioned. Pagett is full of mysteries nowadays.

Just to annoy him, I shall ask the girl. As I said before, she has extremely nice legs.

CHAPTER XVIII

(Anne's Narrative Resumed)

I don't suppose that as long as I live I shall forget my first sight of Table Mountain. I got up frightfully early and went out on deck. I went right up to the boat deck, which I believe is a heinous offence, but I decided to dare something in the cause of solitude. We were just steaming into Table Bay. There were fleecy white clouds hovering above Table Mountain, and nestling on the slopes below, right down to the sea, was the sleeping town, gilded and bewitched by the morning sunlight.

It made me catch my breath and have that curious hungry pain inside that seizes one sometimes when one comes across something that's extra beautiful. I'm not very good at expressing these things, but I knew well enough that I had found, if only for a fleeting moment, the thing that I had been looking for ever since I left Little Hampsley. Something new, something hitherto undreamed of, something that satisfied my aching hunger for romance.

Perfectly silently, or so it seemed to me, the *Kilmorden* glided nearer and nearer. It was still very like a dream. Like all dreamers, however, I could not let my dream alone. We poor humans are so anxious not to miss anything.

'This is South Africa,' I kept saying to myself industriously. 'South Africa, South Africa. You are seeing the world. This is the world. You are seeing it. Think of it, Anne Beddingfeld, you pudding-head. You're seeing the world.'

I had thought that I had the boat deck to myself, but now I observed another figure leaning over the rail, absorbed as I had been in the rapidly approaching city. Even before he turned his head I knew who it was. The scene of last night seemed unreal and melodramatic in the peaceful morning sunshine. What must he have thought of me? It made me hot to

realize the things that I had said. And I hadn't meant them
– or had I?

I turned my head resolutely away, and stared hard at Table
Mountain. If Rayburn had come up here to be alone, I, at
least, need not disturb him by advertising my presence.

But to my intense surprise I heard a light footfall on the
deck behind me, and then his voice, pleasant and normal:

'Miss Beddingfeld.'

'Yes?'

I turned.

'I want to apologize to you. I behaved like a perfect boor
last night.'

'It – it was a peculiar night,' I said hastily.

It was not a very lucid remark, but it was absolutely the
only thing I could think of.

'Will you forgive me?'

I held out my hand without a word. He took it.

'There's something else I want to say.' His gravity deep-
ened. 'Miss Beddingfeld, you may not know it, but you are
mixed up in a rather dangerous business.'

'I gather as much,' I said.

'No, you don't. You can't possibly know. I want to warn
you. Leave the whole thing alone. It can't concern you really.
Don't let your curiosity lead you to tamper with other people's
business. No, please don't get angry again. I'm not speaking
of myself. You've no idea of what you might come up against
– these men will stop at nothing. They are absolutely ruthless.
Already you're in danger – look at last night. They fancy you
know something. Your only chance is to persuade them that
they're mistaken. But be careful, always be on the lookout for
danger, and, look here, if at any time you should fall into their
hands, don't try and be clever – tell the whole truth; it will
be your only chance.'

'You make my flesh creep, Mr Rayburn,' I said, with some
truth. 'Why do you take the trouble to warn me?'

He did not answer for some minutes, then he said in a low
voice:

'It may be the last thing I can do for you. Once on shore I shall be all right – but I may not get on shore.'

'What?' I cried.

'You see, I'm afraid you're not the only person on board who knows that I am "The Man in the Brown Suit".'

'If you think that I told –' I said hotly.

He reassured me with a smile.

'I don't doubt you, Miss Beddingfeld. If I ever said I did, I lied. No, but there's one person on board who's known all along. He's only to speak – and my number's up. All the same, I'm taking a sporting chance that he won't speak.'

'Why?'

'Because he's a man who likes playing a lone hand. And when the police have got me I should be of no further use to him. Free, I might be! Well, an hour will show.'

He laughed rather mockingly, but I saw his face harden. If he had gambled with Fate, he was a good gambler. He could lose and smile.

'In any case,' he said lightly, 'I don't suppose we shall meet again.'

'No,' I said slowly. 'I suppose not.'

'So – goodbye.'

'Goodbye.'

He gripped my hand hard, just for a minute his curious light eyes seemed to burn into mine, then he turned abruptly and left me. I heard his footsteps ringing along the deck. They echoed and re-echoed. I felt that I should hear them always. Footsteps – going out of my life.

I can admit frankly that I did not enjoy the next two hours. Not till I stood on the wharf, having finished with most of the ridiculous formalities that bureaucracies require, did I breathe freely once more. No arrest had been made, and I realized that it was a heavenly day, and that I was extremely hungry. I joined Suzanne. In any case, I was staying the night with her at the hotel. The boat did not go on to Port Elizabeth and Durban until the following morning. We got into a taxi and drove to the Mount Nelson.

It was all heavenly. The sun, the air, the flowers! When I thought of Little Hampsley in January, the mud knee-deep, and the sure-to-be-falling rain, I hugged myself with delight. Suzanne was not nearly so enthusiastic. She has travelled a great deal of course. Besides, she is not the type that gets excited before breakfast. She snubbed me severely when I let out an enthusiastic yelp at the sight of a giant blue convolvulus.

By the way, I should like to make clear here and now that this story will not be a story of South Africa. I guarantee no genuine local colour – you know the sort of thing – half a dozen words in italics on every page. I admire it very much, but I can't do it. In South Sea Islands, of course, you make an immediate reference to *bêche-de-mer*. I don't know what *bêche-de-mer* is, I have never known, I probably never shall know. I've guessed once or twice and guessed wrong. In South Africa I know you at once begin to talk about a *stoep* – I do know what a *stoep* is – it's the thing round a house and you sit on it. In various other parts of the world you call it a veranda, a piazza, and a ha-ha. Then again, there are pawpaws. I had often read of pawpaws. I discovered at once what they were, because I had one plumped down in front of me for breakfast. I thought at first that it was a melon gone bad. The Dutch waitress enlightened me, and persuaded me to use lemon juice and sugar and try again. I was very pleased to meet a pawpaw. I had always vaguely associated it with a *hulahula*, which, I believe, though I may be wrong, is a kind of straw skirt that Hawaiian girls dance in. No, I think I am wrong – that is a *lava-lava*.

At any rate, all these things are very cheering after England. I can't help thinking that it would brighten our cold Island life if one could have a breakfast of *bacon-bacon*, and then go out clad in a *jumper-jumper* to pay the books.

Suzanne was a little tamer after breakfast. They had given me a room next to hers with a lovely view right out over Table Bay. I looked at the view whilst Suzanne hunted for some special facecream. When she had found it and started an immediate application, she became capable of listening to me.

'Did you see Sir Eustace?' I asked. 'He was marching out of the breakfast-room as we went in. He'd had some bad fish or something and was just telling the head waiter what he thought about it, and he bounced a peach on the floor to show how hard it was – only it wasn't quite as hard as he thought and it squashed.'

Suzanne smiled.

'Sir Eustace doesn't like getting up early any more than I do. But, Anne, did you see Mr Pagett? I ran against him in the passage. He's got a black eye. What can he have been doing?'

'Only trying to push me overboard,' I replied nonchalantly.

It was a distinct score for me. Suzanne left her face half anointed and pressed for details. I gave them to her.

'It all gets more and more mysterious,' she cried. 'I thought I was going to have the soft job sticking to Sir Eustace, and that you would have all the fun with the Rev. Edward Chichester, but now I'm not so sure. I hope Pagett won't push me off the train some dark night.'

'I think you're still above suspicion, Suzanne. But, if the worst happens I'll wire to Clarence.'

'That reminds me – give me a cable form. Let me see now, what shall I say? "Implicated in the most thrilling mystery please send me a thousand pounds at once Suzanne."'

I took the form from her, and pointed out that she could eliminate a 'the', an 'a', and possibly, if she didn't care about being polite, a 'please'. Suzanne, however, appears to be perfectly reckless in money matters. Instead of attending to my economical suggestions, she added three more words: 'enjoying myself hugely'.

Suzanne was engaged to lunch with friends of hers, who came to the hotel about eleven o'clock to fetch her. I was left to my own devices. I went down through the grounds of the hotel, crossed the tram-lines and followed a cool shady avenue right down till I came to the main street. I strolled about, seeing the sights, enjoying the sunlight and the black-faced sellers of flowers and fruits. I also discovered a place where they had the most delicious ice-cream sodas. Finally, I bought a sixpenny basket of peaches and retraced my steps to the hotel.

To my surprise and pleasure I found a note awaiting me. It was from the curator of the Museum. He had read of my arrival on the *Kilmorden*, in which I was described as the daughter of the late Professor Beddingfeld. He had known my father slightly and had had great admiration for him. He went on to say that his wife would be delighted if I would come out and have tea with them that afternoon at their Villa at Muizenberg. He gave me instructions for getting there.

It was pleasant to think that poor Papa was still remembered and highly thought of. I foresaw that I would have to be personally escorted round the Museum before I left Cape Town, but I risked that. To most people it would have been a treat – but one can have too much of a good thing if one is brought up on it, morning, noon, and night.

I put on my best hat (one of Suzanne's cast-offs) and my least crumpled white linen and started off after lunch. I caught a fast train to Muizenberg and got there in about half an hour. It was a nice trip. We wound slowly round the base of Table Mountain, and some of the flowers were lovely. My geography being weak, I had never fully realized that Cape Town is on a peninsula, consequently I was rather surprised on getting out of the train to find myself facing the sea once more. There was some perfectly entrancing bathing going on. The people had short curved boards and came floating in on the waves. It was far too early to go to tea. I made for the bathing pavilion, and when they said would I have a surf board, I said 'Yes, please.' Surfing looks perfectly easy. *It isn't.* I say no more. I got very angry and fairly hurled my plank from me. Nevertheless, I determined to return on the first possible opportunity and have another go. I would not be beaten. Quite by mistake I then got a good run on my board, and came out delirious with happiness. Surfing is like that. You are either

vigorously cursing or else you are idiotically pleased with
yourself.

I found the Villa Medgee after some difficulty. It was right
up on the side of the mountain, isolated from the other cottages
and villas. I rang the bell, and a smiling Kafir boy answered
it.

'Mrs Raffini?' I inquired.

He ushered me in, preceded me down the passage and flung
open a door. Just as I was about to pass in, I hesitated. I felt
a sudden misgiving. I stepped over the threshold and the door
swung sharply behind me.

A man rose from his seat behind a table and came forward
with outstretched hand.

'So glad we have persuaded you to visit us, Miss Beddingfeld,' he said.

He was a tall man, obviously a Dutchman, with a flaming
orange beard. He did not look in the least like the curator of
a museum. In fact, I realized in a flash that I had made a
fool of myself.

I was in the hands of the enemy.

CHAPTER XIX

It reminded me forcibly of Episode III in 'The Perils of Pamela'. How often had I not sat in the sixpenny seats, eating a twopenny bar of milk chocolate, and yearning for similar things to happen to me! Well, they had happened with a vengeance. And somehow it was not nearly so amusing as I had imagined. It's all very well on the screen – you have the comfortable knowledge that there's bound to be an Episode IV. But in real life there was absolutely no guarantee that Anna the Adventuress might not terminate abruptly at the end of any Episode.

Yes, I was in a tight place. All the things that Rayburn had said that morning came back to me with unpleasant distinctness. Tell the truth, he had said. Well, I could always do that, but was it going to help me? To begin with, would my story be believed? Would they consider it likely or possible that I had started off on this mad escapade simply on the strength of a scrap of paper smelling of mothballs? It sounded to me a wildly incredible tale. In that moment of cold sanity I cursed myself for a melodramatic idiot, and yearned for the peaceful boredom of Little Hampsley.

All this passed through my mind in less time than it takes to tell. My first instinctive movement was to step backwards and feel for the handle of the door. My captor merely grinned.

'Here you are and here you stay,' he remarked facetiously.

I did my best to put a bold face upon the matter.

'I was invited to come here by the curator of the Cape Town Museum. If I have made a mistake –'

'A mistake? Oh, yes, a big mistake!'

He laughed coarsely.

'What right have you to detain me? I shall inform the police –'

'Yap, yap, yap – like a little toy dog.' He laughed.

I sat down on a chair.

'I can only conclude that you are a dangerous lunatic,' I said coldly.

'Indeed?'

'I should like to point out to you that my friends are perfectly well aware where I have gone, and that if I have not returned by this evening, they will come in search of me. You understand?'

'So your friends know where you are, do they? Which of them?'

Thus challenged, I did a lightning calculation of chances. Should I mention Sir Eustace? He was a well-known man, and his name might carry weight. But if they were in touch with Pagett, they might know I was lying. Better not risk Sir Eustace.

'Mrs Blair, for one,' I said lightly. 'A friend of mine with whom I am staying.'

'I think not,' said my captor, slyly shaking his orange head. 'You have not seen her since eleven this morning. And you received our note, bidding you to come here, at lunchtime.'

His words showed me how closely my movements had been followed, but I was not going to give in without a fight.

'You are very clever,' I said. 'Perhaps you have heard of that useful invention, the telephone? Mrs Blair called me up on it when I was resting in my room after lunch. I told her then where I was going this afternoon.'

To my great satisfaction, I saw a shade of uneasiness pass over his face. Clearly he had overlooked the possibility that Suzanne might have telephoned me. I wished she really had done so!

'Enough of this,' he said harshly, rising.

'What are you going to do with me?' I asked, still endeavouring to appear composed.

'Put you where you can do no harm in case your friends come after you.'

For a moment my blood ran cold, but his next words reassured me.

'Tomorrow you'll have some questions to answer, and after you've answered them we shall know what to do with you. And I can tell you, young lady, we've more ways than one of making obstinate little fools talk.'

It was not cheering, but it was at least a respite. I had until tomorrow. This man was clearly an underling obeying the orders of a superior. Could that superior by any chance be Pagett?

He called and two Kafirs appeared. I was taken upstairs. Despite my struggles, I was gagged and then bound hand and foot. The room into which they had taken me was a kind of attic right under the roof. It was dusty and showed little signs of having been occupied. The Dutchman made a mock bow and withdrew, closing the door behind him.

I was quite helpless. Turn and twist as I would, I could not loosen my bonds in the slightest degree, and the gag prevented me from crying out. If, by any possible chance, anyone did come to the house, I could do nothing to attract their attention. Down below I heard the sound of a door shutting. Evidently the Dutchman was going out.

It was maddening not to be able to do anything. I strained again at my bonds, but the knots held. I desisted at last, and either fainted or fell asleep. When I awoke I was in pain all over. It was quite dark now, and I judged that the night must be well advanced, for the moon was high in the heavens and shining down through the dusty skylight. The gag was half choking me and the stiffness and pain were unendurable.

It was then that my eyes fell on a bit of broken glass lying in the corner. A moonbeam slanted right down on it, and its glistening had caught my attention. As I looked at it, an idea came into my head.

My arms and legs were helpless, but surely I could still *roll*. Slowly and awkwardly, I set myself in motion. It was not easy. Besides being extremely painful, since I could not guard my face with my arms, it was also exceedingly difficult to keep any particular direction.

I tended to roll in every direction except the one I wanted

to go. In the end, however, I came right up against my objective. It almost touched my bound hands.

Even then it was not easy. It took an infinity of time before I could wriggle the glass into such a position, wedged against the wall, that it would rub up and down on my bonds. It was a long heart-rending process, and I almost despaired, but in the end I succeeded in sawing through the cords that bound my wrists. The rest was a matter of time. Once I had restored the circulation to my hands by rubbing the wrists vigorously, I was able to undo the gag. One or two full breaths did a lot for me.

Very soon I had undone the last knot, though even then it was some time before I could stand on my feet, but at last I stood erect, swinging my arms to and fro to restore the circulation, and wishing above all things that I could get hold of something to eat.

I waited about a quarter of an hour, to be quite sure of my recovered strength. Then I tiptoed noiselessly to the door. As I had hoped, it was not locked, only latched. I unlatched it and peeped cautiously out.

Everything was still. The moonlight came in through a window and showed me the dusty uncarpeted staircase. Cautiously I crept down it. Still no sound – but as I stood on the landing below, a faint murmur of voices reached me. I stopped dead, and stood there for some time. A clock on the wall registered the fact that it was after midnight.

I was fully aware of the risks I might run if I descended lower, but my curiosity was too much for me. With infinite precautions I prepared to explore. I crept softly down the last flight of stairs and stood in the square hall. I looked round me – and then caught my breath with a gasp. A Kafir boy was sitting by the hall door. He had not seen me, indeed I soon realized by his breathing that he was fast asleep.

Should I retreat, or should I go on? The voices came from the room I had been shown into on arrival. One of them was that of my Dutch friend, the other I could not for the moment recognize, though it seemed vaguely familiar.

In the end I decided that it was clearly my duty to hear all I could. I must risk the Kafir boy waking up. I crossed the hall noiselessly and knelt by the study door. For a moment or two I could hear no better. The voices were louder, but I could not distinguish what they said.

I applied my eye to the keyhole instead of my ear. As I had guessed, one of the speakers was the big Dutchman. The other man was sitting outside my circumscribed range of vision.

Suddenly he rose to get himself a drink. His back, black-clad and decorous, came into view. Even before he turned round I knew who he was.

Mr Chichester!

Now I began to make out the words.

'All the same, it is dangerous. Suppose her friends come after her?'

It was the big man speaking. Chichester answered him. He had dropped his clerical voice entirely. No wonder I had not recognized it.

'All bluff. They haven't an idea where she is.'

'She spoke very positively.'

'I dare say. I've looked into the matter, and we've nothing to fear. Anyway, it's the "Colonel's" orders. You don't want to go against them, I suppose?'

The Dutchman ejaculated something in his own language. I judged it to be a hasty disclaimer.

'But why not knock her on the head?' he growled. 'It would be simple. The boat is all ready. She could be taken out to sea.'

'Yes,' said Chichester meditatively. 'That is what I should do. She knows too much, that is certain. But the "Colonel" is a man who likes to play a lone hand – though no one else must do so.' Something in his own words seemed to awaken a memory that annoyed him. 'He wants information of some kind from this girl.'

He had paused before the 'information', and the Dutchman was quick to catch him up.

'Information?'

'Something of the kind.'

'Diamonds,' I said to myself.

'And now,' continued Chichester, 'give me the lists.'

For a long time their conversation was quite incomprehensible to me. It seemed to deal with large quantities of vegetables. Dates were mentioned, prices, and various names of places which I did not know. It was quite half an hour before they had finished their checking and counting.

'Good,' said Chichester, and there was a sound as though he pushed back his chair. 'I will take these with me for the "Colonel" to see.'

'When do you leave?'

'Ten o'clock tomorrow morning will do.'

'Do you want to see the girl before you go?'

'No. There are strict orders that no one is to see her until the "Colonel" comes. Is she all right?'

'I looked in on her when I came in for dinner. She was asleep, I think. What about food?'

'A little starvation will do no harm. The "Colonel" will be here some time tomorrow. She will answer questions better if she is hungry. No one had better go near her till then. Is she securely tied up?'

The Dutchman laughed.

'What do you think?'

They both laughed. So did I, under my breath. Then, as the sounds seemed to betoken that they were about to come out of the room, I beat a hasty retreat. I was just in time. As I reached the head of the stairs, I heard the door of the room open, and at the same time the Kafir stirred and moved. My retreat by the way of the hall door was not to be thought of. I retired prudently to the attic, gathered my bonds round me and lay down again on the floor, in case they should take it into their heads to come and look at me.

They did not do so, however. After about an hour, I crept down the stairs, but the Kafir by the door was awake and humming softly to himself. I was anxious to get out of the house, but I did not quite see how to manage it.

In the end, I was forced to retreat to the attic again. The Kafir was clearly on guard for the night. I remained there patiently all through the sounds of early morning preparation. The men breakfasted in the hall, I could hear their voices distinctly floating up the stairs. I was getting thoroughly unnerved. How on earth was I to get out of the house?

I counselled myself to be patient. A rash move might spoil everything. After breakfast came the sounds of Chichester departing. To my intense relief, the Dutchman accompanied him.

I waited breathlessly. Breakfast was being cleared away, the work of the house was being done. At last, the various activities seemed to die down. I slipped out from my lair once more. Very carefully I crept down the stairs. The hall was empty. Like a flash I was across it, had unlatched the door, and was outside in the sunshine. I ran down the drive like one possessed.

Once outside, I resumed a normal walk. People stared at me curiously, and I do not wonder. My face and clothes must have been covered in dust from rolling about in the attic. At last I came to a garage. I went in.

'I have met with an accident,' I explained. 'I want a car to take me to Cape Town at once. I must catch the boat to Durban.'

I had not long to wait. Ten minutes later I was speeding along in the direction of Cape Town. I must know if Chichester was on the boat. Whether to sail on her myself or not, I could not determine, but in the end I decided to do so. Chichester would not know that I had seen him in the Villa at Muizenberg. He would doubtless lay further traps for me, but I was forewarned. And he was the man I was after, the man who was seeking the diamonds on behalf of the mysterious 'Colonel'.

Alas, for my plans! As I arrived at the docks, the *Kilmorden Castle* was steaming out to sea. And I had no means of knowing whether Chichester had sailed on her or not!

CHAPTER XX

I drove to the hotel. There was no one in the lounge that I knew. I ran upstairs and tapped on Suzanne's door. Her voice bade me 'come in'. When she saw who it was she literally fell on my neck.

'Anne, dear, where have you been? I've been worried to death about you. What have you been doing?'

'Having adventures,' I replied. 'Episode III of "The Perils of Pamela".'

I told her the whole story. She gave vent to a deep sigh when I finished.

'Why do these things always happen to you?' she demanded plaintively. 'Why does no one gag me and bind me hand and foot?'

'You wouldn't like it if they did,' I assured her. 'To tell you the truth, I'm not nearly so keen on having adventures myself as I was. A little of that sort of thing goes a long way.'

Suzanne seemed unconvinced. An hour or two of gagging and binding would have changed her view quickly enough. Suzanne likes thrills, but she hates being uncomfortable.

'And what are we all doing now?' she asked.

'I don't quite know,' I said thoughtfully. 'You still go to Rhodesia, of course, to keep an eye on Pagett –'

'And you?'

That was just my difficulty. Had Chichester gone on the *Kilmorden*, or had he not? Did he mean to carry out his original plan of going to Durban? The hour of his leaving Muizenberg seemed to point to an affirmative answer to both questions. In that case, I might go to Durban by train. I fancied that I should get there before the boat. On the other hand, if the news of my escape were wired to Chichester, and also the information that I had left Cape Town for Durban, nothing was simpler for him than to leave the boat at either Port

Elizabeth or East London and so give me the slip completely.

It was rather a knotty problem.

'We'll inquire about trains to Durban anyway,' I said.

'And it's not too late for morning tea,' said Suzanne. 'We'll have it in the lounge.'

The Durban train left at 8.15 that evening, so they told me at the office. For the moment I postponed decision, and joined Suzanne for somewhat belated 'eleven-o'clock tea'.

'Do you feel that you would really recognize Chichester again – in any other disguise, I mean?' asked Suzanne.

I shook my head ruefully.

'I certainly didn't recognize him as the stewardess, and never should have but for your drawing.'

'The man's a professional actor, I'm sure of it,' said Suzanne thoughtfully. 'His make-up is perfectly marvellous. He might come off the boat as a navvy or something, and you'd never spot him.'

'You're very cheering,' I said.

At that minute Colonel Race stepped in through the window and came and joined us.

'What is Sir Eustace doing?' asked Suzanne. 'I haven't seen him about today.'

Rather an odd expression passed over the Colonel's face.

'He's got a little trouble of his own to attend to which is keeping him busy.'

'Tell us about it.'

'I mustn't tell tales out of school.'

'Tell us something – even if you have to invent it for our special benefit.'

'Well, what would you say to the famous "Man in the Brown Suit" having made the voyage with us?'

'*What?*'

I felt the colour die out of my face and then surge back again. Fortunately Colonel Race was not looking at me.

'It's a fact, I believe. Every port watched for him and he bamboozled Pedler into bringing him out as his secretary!'

'Not Mr Pagett?'

'Oh, not Pagett – the other fellow. Rayburn, he called himself.'

'Have they arrested him?' asked Suzanne. Under the table she gave my hand a reassuring squeeze. I waited breathlessly for an answer.

'He seems to have disappeared into thin air.'

'How does Sir Eustace take it?'

'Regards it as a personal insult offered him by Fate.'

An opportunity of hearing Sir Eustace's views on the matter presented itself later in the day. We were awakened from a refreshing afternoon nap by a page-boy with a note. In touching terms it requested the pleasure of our company at tea in his sitting-room.

The poor man was indeed in a pitiable state. He poured out his troubles to us, encouraged by Suzanne's sympathetic murmurs. (She does that sort of thing very well.)

'First a perfectly strange woman has the impertinence to get herself murdered in my house – on purpose to annoy me, I do believe. Why my house? Why, of all the houses in Great Britain, choose the Mill House? What harm had I ever done the woman that she must needs get herself murdered there?'

Suzanne made one of her sympathetic noises again and Sir Eustace proceeded, in a still more aggrieved tone:

'And, if that's not enough, the fellow who murdered her has the impudence, the colossal impudence, to attach himself to me as my secretary. My secretary, if you please! I'm tired of secretaries, I won't have any more secretaries. Either they're concealed murderers or else they're drunken brawlers. Have you seen Pagett's black eye? But of course you have. How can I go about with a secretary like that? And his face is such a nasty shade of yellow too – just the colour that doesn't go with a black eye. I've done with secretaries – unless I have a girl. A nice girl, with liquid eyes, who'll hold my hand when I'm feeling cross. What about you, Miss Anne? Will you take on the job?'

'How often shall I have to hold your hand?' I asked, laughing.

'All day long,' replied Sir Eustace gallantly.

'I shan't get much typing done at that rate,' I reminded him.

'That doesn't matter. All this work is Pagett's idea. He works me to death. I'm looking forward to leaving him behind in Cape Town.'

'He is staying behind?'

'Yes, he'll enjoy himself thoroughly sleuthing about after Rayburn. That's the sort of thing that suits Pagett down to the ground. He adores intrigue. But I'm quite serious in my offer. Will you come? Mrs Blair here is a competent chaperone, and you can have a half-holiday every now and again to dig for bones.'

'Thank you very much, Sir Eustace,' I said cautiously, 'but I think I'm leaving for Durban tonight.'

'Now don't be an obstinate girl. Remember, there are lots of lions in Rhodesia. You'll like lions. All girls do.'

'Will they be practising low jumps?' I asked, laughing. 'No, thank you very much, but I must go to Durban.'

Sir Eustace looked at me, sighed deeply, then opened the door of the adjoining room, and called to Pagett.

'If you've quite finished your afternoon sleep, my dear fellow, perhaps you'd do a little work for a change.'

Guy Pagett appeared in the doorway. He bowed to us both, starting slightly at the sight of me, and replied in a melancholy voice:

'I have been typing that memorandum all this afternoon, Sir Eustace.'

'Well, stop typing it then. Go down to the Trade Commissioner's Office, or the Board of Agriculture, or the Chamber of Mines, or one of those places, and ask them to lend me some kind of a woman to take to Rhodesia. She must have liquid eyes and not object to my holding her hand.'

'Yes, Sir Eustace. I will ask for a competent shorthand-typist.'

'Pagett's a malicious fellow,' said Sir Eustace, after the secretary had departed. 'I'd be prepared to bet that he'll pick out some slab-faced creature on purpose to annoy me. She must have nice feet too – I forgot to mention that.'

I clutched Suzanne excitedly by the hand and almost dragged her along to her room.

'Now, Suzanne,' I said, 'we've got to make plans – and make them quickly. Pagett is staying behind here – you heard that?'

'Yes. I suppose that means that I shan't be allowed to go to Rhodesia – which is very annoying, because I *want* to go to Rhodesia. How tiresome.'

'Cheer up,' I said. 'You're going all right. I don't see how you could back out at the last moment without its appearing frightfully suspicious. And, besides, Pagett might suddenly be summoned by Sir Eustace, and it would be far harder for you to attach yourself to him for the journey up.'

'It would hardly be respectable,' said Suzanne, dimpling. 'I should have to pretend a fatal passion for him as an excuse.'

'On the other hand, if you were there when he arrived, it would all be perfectly simple and natural. Besides, I don't think we ought to lose sight of the other two entirely.'

'Oh, Anne, you surely can't suspect Colonel Race or Sir Eustace?'

'I suspect everybody,' I said darkly, 'and if you've read any detective stories, Suzanne, you must know that it's always the most unlikely person who's the villain. Lots of criminals have been cheerful fat men like Sir Eustace.'

'Colonel Race isn't particularly fat – or particularly cheerful either.'

'Sometimes they're lean and saturnine,' I retorted. 'I don't say I seriously suspect either of them, but, after all, the woman was murdered in Sir Eustace's house –'

'Yes, yes, we needn't go over all that again. I'll watch him for you, Anne, and if he gets any fatter and any more cheerful, I'll send you a telegram at once. "Sir E. swelling highly suspicious. Come at once."'

'Really, Suzanne,' I cried, 'you seem to think all this is a game!'

'I know I do,' said Suzanne, unabashed. 'It seems like that. It's your fault, Anne. I've got imbued with your "Let's have an adventure" spirit. It doesn't seem a bit real. Dear me, if Clarence knew that I was running about Africa tracking dangerous criminals, he'd have a fit.'

'Why don't you cable him about it?' I asked sarcastically.

Suzanne's sense of humour always fails her when it comes to sending cables. She considered my suggestion in perfectly good faith.

'I might. It would have to be a very long one.' Her eyes brightened at the thought. 'But I think it's better not. Husbands always want to interfere with perfectly harmless amusements.'

'Well,' I said, summing up the situation, 'you will keep an eye on Sir Eustace and Colonel Race –'

'I know why I've got to watch Sir Eustace,' interrupted Suzanne, 'because of his figure and his humorous conversation. But I think it's carrying it rather far to suspect Colonel Race; I do indeed. Why, he's something to do with the Secret Service. Do you know, Anne, I believe the best thing we could do would be to confide in him and tell him the whole story.'

I objected vigorously to this unsporting proposal. I recognized in it the disastrous effects of matrimony. How often have I not heard a perfectly intelligent female say, in the tone of one clinching an argument, '*Edgar* says –' And all the time you are perfectly aware that Edgar is a perfect fool. Suzanne, by reason of her married state, was yearning to lean upon some man or other.

However, she promised faithfully that she would not breathe a word to Colonel Race, and we went on with our plan-making.

'It's quite clear that I must stay here and watch Pagett, and this is the best way to do it. I must pretend to leave for Durban this evening, take my luggage down and so on, but really I shall go to some small hotel in the town. I can alter my appearance a little – wear a fair toupee and one of those thick white lace veils, and I shall have a much better chance of seeing what he's really at if he thinks I'm safely out of the way.'

Suzanne approved this plan heartily. We made due and ostentatious preparations, inquiring once more about the departure of the train at the office and packing my luggage.

We dined together in the restaurant. Colonel Race did not appear, but Sir Eustace and Pagett were at their table in the window. Pagett left the table half-way through the meal, which annoyed me, as I had planned to say goodbye to him. However, doubtless Sir Eustace would do as well. I went over to him when I had finished.

'Goodbye, Sir Eustace,' I said. 'I'm off tonight to Durban.'

Sir Eustace sighed heavily.

'So I heard. You wouldn't like me to come with you, would you?'

'I should love it.'

'Nice girl. Sure you won't change your mind and come and look for lions in Rhodesia?'

'Quite sure.'

'He must be a very handsome fellow,' said Sir Eustace plaintively. 'Some young whipper-snapper in Durban, I suppose, who puts my mature charms completely in the shade. By the way, Pagett's going down in the car in a minute or two. He could take you to the station.'

'Oh, no, thank you,' I said hastily. 'Mrs Blair and I have got our own taxi ordered.'

To go down with Guy Pagett was the last thing I wanted! Sir Eustace looked at me attentively.

'I don't believe you like Pagett. I don't blame you. Of all the officious, interfering asses – going about with the air of a martyr, and doing everything he can to annoy and upset me!'

'What has he done now?' I inquired with some curiosity.

'He's got hold of a secretary for me. You never saw such a woman! Forty, if she's a day, wears pince-nez and sensible boots and an air of brisk efficiency that will be the death of me. A regular slab-faced woman.'

'Won't she hold your hand?'

'I devoutly hope not!' exclaimed Sir Eustace. 'That would be the last straw. Well, goodbye, liquid eyes. If I shoot a lion I shan't give you the skin – after the base way you've deserted me.'

He squeezed my hand warmly and we parted. Suzanne was waiting for me in the hall. She was to come down to see me off.

'Let's start at once,' I said hastily, and motioned to the man to get a taxi.

Then a voice behind me made me start:

'Excuse me, Miss Beddingfeld, but I'm just going down in a car. I can drop you and Mrs Blair at the station.'

'Oh, thank you,' I said hastily. 'But there's no need to trouble you. I –'

'No trouble at all, I assure you. Put the luggage in, porter.'

I was helpless. I might have protested further, but a slight warning nudge from Suzanne urged me to be on my guard.

'Thank you, Mr Pagett,' I said coldly.

We all got into the car. As we raced down the road into the town, I racked my brains for something to say. In the end Pagett himself broke the silence.

'I have secured a very capable secretary for Sir Eustace,' he observed. 'Miss Pettigrew.'

'He wasn't exactly raving about her just now,' I remarked.

Pagett looked at me coldly.

'She is a proficient shorthand-typist,' he said repressively.

We pulled up in front of the station. Here surely he would leave us. I turned with outstretched hand – but no.

'I'll come and see you off. It's just eight o'clock, your train goes in a quarter of an hour.'

He gave efficient directions to porters. I stood helpless, not daring to look at Suzanne. The man suspected. He was determined to make sure that I did go by the train. And what could I do? Nothing. I saw myself, in a quarter of an hour's time, steaming out of the station with Pagett planted on the platform waving me adieu. He had turned the tables on me adroitly. His manner towards me had changed, moreover. It was full of an uneasy geniality which sat ill upon him, and which nauseated me. The man was an oily hypocrite. First he tried to murder me, and now he paid me compliments! Did he imagine for one minute that I hadn't recognized him that night on the boat? No, it was a pose, a pose which he forced me to acquiesce in, his tongue in his cheek all the while.

Helpless as a sheep, I moved along under his expert directions. My luggage was piled in my sleeping compartment – I had a two-berth one to myself. It was twelve minutes past eight. In three minutes the train would start.

But Pagett had reckoned without Suzanne.

'It will be a terribly hot journey, Anne,' she said suddenly. 'Especially going through the Karoo tomorrow. You've got some eau-de-Cologne or lavender water with you, haven't you?'

My cue was plain.

'Oh, dear,' I cried. 'I left my eau-de-Cologne on the dressing-table at the hotel.'

Suzanne's habit of command served her well. She turned imperiously to Pagett.

'Mr Pagett. Quick. You've just time. There's a chemist almost opposite the station. Anne must have some eau-de-Cologne.'

He hesitated, but Suzanne's imperative manner was too much for him. She is a born autocrat. He went. Suzanne followed him with her eyes till he disappeared.

'Quick, Anne, get out the other side – in case he hasn't really gone but is watching us from the end of the platform. Never mind your luggage. You can telegraph about that tomorrow. Oh, if only the train starts on time!'

I opened the gate on the opposite side to the platform and climbed down. Nobody was observing me. I could just see Suzanne standing where I had left her, looking up at the train and apparently chatting to me at the window. A whistle blew, the train began to draw out. Then I heard feet racing furiously up the platform. I withdrew to the shadow of a friendly bookstall and watched.

Suzanne turned from waving her handkerchief to the retreating train.

'Too late, Mr Pagett,' she said cheerfully. 'She's gone. Is that the eau-de-Cologne? What a pity we didn't think of it sooner!'

They passed not far from me on their way out of the station. Guy Pagett was extremely hot. He had evidently run all the way to the chemist and back.

'Shall I get you a taxi, Mrs Blair?'

Suzanne did not fail in her role.

'Yes, please. Can't I give you a lift back? Have you much to do for Sir Eustace? Dear me, I wish Anne Beddingfeld was coming with us tomorrow. I don't like the idea of a young girl like that travelling off to Durban all by herself. But she was set upon it. Some little attraction there, I fancy –'

They passed out of earshot. Clever Suzanne. She had saved me.

I allowed a minute or two to elapse and then I too made my way out of the station, almost colliding as I did so with a man – an unpleasant-looking man with a nose disproportionately big for his face.

CHAPTER XXI

I had no further difficulty in carrying out my plans. I found a small hotel in a back street, got a room there, paid a deposit as I had no luggage with me, and went placidly to bed.

On the following morning I was up early and went out into the town to purchase a modest wardrobe. My idea was to do nothing until after the departure of the eleven-o'clock train to Rhodesia with most of the party on board. Pagett was not likely to indulge in any nefarious activities until he had got rid of them. Accordingly I took a train out of the town and proceeded to enjoy a country walk. It was comparatively cool, and I was glad to stretch my legs after the long voyage and my close confinement at Muizenberg.

A lot hinges on small things. My shoe-lace came untied, and I stopped to do it up. The road had just turned a corner, and as I was bending over the offending shoe a man came right round and almost walked into me. He lifted his hat, murmuring an apology, and went on. It struck me at the time that his face was vaguely familiar, but at the moment I thought no more of it. I looked at my wrist-watch. The time was getting on. I turned my feet in the direction of Cape Town.

There was a tram on the point of going and I had to run for it. I heard other footsteps running behind me. I swung myself on and so did the other runner. I recognized him at once. It was the man who had passed me on the road when my shoe came untied, and in a flash I knew why his face was familiar. It was the small man with the big nose whom I had run into on leaving the station the night before.

The coincidence was rather startling. Could it be possible that the man was deliberately following me? I resolved to test that as promptly as possible. I rang the bell and got off at the next stop. The man did not get off. I withdrew into the shadow of a shop doorway and watched. He alighted at the next stop and walked back in my direction.

The case was clear enough. I was being followed. I had crowed too soon. My victory over Guy Pagett took on another aspect. I hailed the next tram and, as I expected, my shadower also got on. I gave myself up to some very serious thinking.

It was perfectly apparent that I had stumbled on a bigger thing than I knew. The murder in the house at Marlow was not an isolated incident committed by a solitary individual. I was up against a gang, and, thanks to Colonel Race's revelations to Suzanne, and what I had overheard at the house at Muizenberg, I was beginning to understand some of its manifold activities. Systematized crime, organized by the man known to his followers as the 'Colonel'! I remembered some of the talk I had heard on board ship, of the strike on the Rand and the causes underlying it – and the belief that some secret organization was at work fomenting the agitation. That was the 'Colonel's' work, his emissaries were acting according to plan. He took no part in these things himself, I had always heard, as he limited himself to directing and organizing. The brain-work – not the dangerous labour – for him. But still it well might be that he himself was on the spot, directing affairs from an apparently impeccable position.

That, then, was the meaning of Colonel Race's presence on the *Kilmorden Castle*. He was out after the arch-criminal. Everything fitted in with that assumption. He was someone high up in the Secret Service whose business it was to lay the 'Colonel' by the heels.

I nodded to myself – things were becoming very clear to me. What of my part in the affair? Where did I come in? Was it only diamonds they were after? I shook my head. Great as the value of the diamonds might be, they hardly accounted for the desperate attempts which had been made to get me out of the way. No, I stood for more than that. In some way, unknown to myself, I was a menace, a danger! Some knowledge that I had, or that they thought I had, made them anxious to remove me at all costs – and that knowledge was bound up somehow with the diamonds. There was one person, I felt sure, who could enlighten me – if he would! 'The Man in the Brown Suit' – Harry Rayburn. He knew the other half of the story. But he had vanished into the darkness, he was a hunted creature flying from pursuit. In all probability he and I would never meet again . . .

I brought myself back with a jerk to the actualities of the moment. It was no good thinking sentimentally of Harry Rayburn. He had displayed the greatest antipathy to me from the first. Or, at least – There I was again – dreaming! The real problem was what to do – *now!*

I, priding myself upon my role of watcher, had become the watched. And I was afraid! For the first time, I began to lose my nerve. I was the little bit of grit that was impeding the smooth working of the great machine – and I fancied that the machine would have a short way with little bits of grit. Once Harry Rayburn had saved me, once I had saved myself – but I felt suddenly that the odds were heavily against me. My enemies were all around me in every direction, and they were closing in. If I continued to play a lone hand I was doomed.

I rallied myself with an effort. After all, what could they do? I was in a civilized city – with policemen every few yards. I would be wary in future. They should not trap me again as they had done in Muizenberg.

As I reached this point in my meditations, the tram arrived at Adderley Street. I got out. Undecided what to do, I walked slowly up the left-hand side of the street. I did not trouble to look if my watcher was behind me. I knew he was. I walked into Cartwright's and ordered two coffee ice-cream sodas – to steady my nerves. A man, I suppose, would have had a stiff peg; but girls derive a lot of comfort from ice-cream sodas. I applied myself to the end of the straw with gusto. The cool liquid went trickling down my throat in the most agreeable manner. I pushed the first glass aside empty.

I was sitting on one of the little high stools in front of the counter. Out of the tail of my eye, I saw my tracker come in and sit down unostentatiously at a little table near the door.

I finished the second coffee soda and demanded a maple one. I can drink practically an unlimited amount of ice-cream sodas.

Suddenly the man by the door got up and went out. That surprised me. If he was going to wait ouside, why not wait outside from the beginning? I slipped down from my stool and went cautiously to the door. I drew back quickly into the shadow. The man was talking to Guy Pagett.

If I had ever had any doubts, that would have settled it. Pagett had his watch out and was looking at it. They exchanged a few brief words, and then the secretary swung on down the street towards the station. Evidently he had given his orders. But what were they?

Suddenly my heart leapt into my mouth. The man who had followed me crossed to the middle of the road and spoke to a policeman. He spoke at some length, gesticulating towards Cartwright's and evidently explaining something. I saw the plan at once. I was to be arrested on some charge or other – pocket-picking, perhaps. It would be easy enough for the gang to put through a simple little matter like that. Of what good to protest my innocence? They would have seen to every detail. Long ago they had brought a charge of robbing De Beers against Harry Rayburn, and he had not been able to disprove it, though I had little doubt but that he had been absolutely blameless. What chance had I against such a 'frame up' as the 'Colonel' could devise?

I glanced up at the clock almost mechanically, and immediately another aspect of the case struck me. I saw the point of Guy Pagett's looking at his watch. It was just on eleven, and at eleven the mail train left for Rhodesia bearing with it the influential friends who might otherwise come to my rescue. That was the reason of my immunity up to now. From last night till eleven this morning I had been safe, but now the net was closing in upon me.

I hurriedly opened my bag and paid for my drinks, and as I did so, my heart seemed to stand still, *for inside it was a man's wallet stuffed with notes!* It must have been deftly introduced into my handbag as I left the tram.

Promptly I lost my head. I hurried out of Cartwright's. The little man with the big nose and the policeman were just crossing the road. They saw me, and the little man designated me excitedly to the policeman. I took to my heels and ran. I judged him to be a slow policeman. I should get a start. But I had no plan, even then. I just ran for my life down Adderley Street. People began to stare. I felt that in another minute someone would stop me.

An idea flashed into my head.

'The station?' I asked, in a breathless gasp.

'Just down on the right.'

I sped on. It is permissible to run for a train. I turned into the station, but as I did so I heard footsteps close behind me. The little man with the big nose was a champion sprinter. I foresaw that I should be stopped before I got to the platform I was in search of. I looked up to the clock – one minute to eleven. I might just do it if my plan succeeded.

I had entered the station by the main entrance in Adderley Street. I now darted out again through the side exit. Directly opposite me was the side entrance to the post office, the main entrance to which is in Adderley Street.

As I expected, my pursuer, instead of following me in, ran down the street to cut me off when I emerged by the main entrance, or to warn the policeman to do so.

In an instant I slipped across the street again and back into the station. I ran like a lunatic. It was just eleven. The long train was moving as I appeared on the platform. A porter tried to stop me, but I wriggled myself out of his grasp and sprang upon the foot-board. I mounted the two steps and opened the gate. I was safe! The train was gathering way.

We passed a man standing by himself at the end of the platform. I waved to him.

'Goodbye Mr Pagett,' I shouted.

Never have I seen a man more taken aback. He looked as though he had seen a ghost.

In a minute or two I was having trouble with the conductor. But I took a lofty tone.

'I am Sir Eustace Pedler's secretary,' I said haughtily. 'Please take me to his private car.'

Suzanne and Colonel Race were standing on the rear observation platform. They both uttered an exclamation of utter surprise at seeing me.

'Hullo, Miss Anne,' cried Colonel Race, 'where have you turned up from? I thought you'd gone to Durban. What an unexpected person you are!'

Suzanne said nothing, but her eyes asked a hundred questions.

'I must report myself to my chief,' I said demurely. 'Where is he?'

'He's in the office – middle compartment – dictating at an incredible rate to the unfortunate Miss Pettigrew.'

'This enthusiasm for work is something new,' I commented.

'H'm!' said Colonel Race. 'His idea is, I think, to give her sufficient work to chain her to her typewriter in her own compartment for the rest of the day.'

I laughed. Then, followed by the other two, I sought out Sir Eustace. He was striding up and down the circumscribed space, hurling a flood of words at the unfortunate secretary whom I now saw for the first time. A tall, square woman in drab clothing, with pince-nez and an efficient air. I judged that she was finding it difficult to keep pace with Sir Eustace, for her pencil was flying along, and she was frowning horribly.

I stepped into the compartment.

'Come aboard, sir,' I said saucily.

Sir Eustace paused dead in the middle of a complicated sentence on the labour situation, and stared at me. Miss Pettigrew must be a nervous creature, in spite of her efficient air, for she jumped as though she had been shot.

'God bless my soul!' ejaculated Sir Eustace. 'What about the young man in Durban?'

'I prefer you,' I said softly.

'Darling,' said Sir Eustace. 'You can start holding my hand at once.'

Miss Pettigrew coughed, and Sir Eustace hastily withdrew his hand.

'Ah, yes,' he said. 'Let me see, where were we? Yes. Tylman Roos, in his speech at – What's the matter? Why aren't you taking it down?'

'I think,' said Colonel Race gently, 'that Miss Pettigrew has broken her pencil.'

He took it from her and sharpened it. Sir Eustace stared, and so did I. There was something in Colonel Race's tone that I did not quite understand.

CHAPTER XXII

(Extract from the diary of Sir Eustace Pedler)

I am inclined to abandon my Reminiscences. Instead, I shall write a short article entitled 'Secretaries I have had'. As regards secretaries, I seem to have fallen under a blight. At one minute I have no secretaries, at another I have too many. At the present minute I am journeying to Rhodesia with a pack of women. Race goes off with the two best looking, of course, and leaves me with the dud. That is what always happens to me – and, after all, this is *my* private car, not Race's.

Also Anne Beddingfield is accompanying me to Rhodesia on the pretext of being my temporary secretary. But all this afternoon she has been out on the observation platform with Race exclaiming at the beauty of the Hex River Pass. It is true that I told her her principal duty would be to hold my hand. But she isn't even doing that. Perhaps she is afraid of Miss Pettigrew. I don't blame her if so. There is nothing attractive about Miss Pettigrew – she is a repellent female with large feet, more like a man than a woman.

There is something very mysterious about Anne Beddingfield. She jumped on board the train at the last minute, puffing like a steam-engine, for all the world as though she'd been running a race – and yet Pagett told me that he'd seen her off to Durban last night! Either Pagett has been drinking again, or else the girl must have an astral body.

And she never explains. Nobody ever explains. Yes, 'Secretaries I have had'. No. 1, a murderer fleeing from justice. No. 2, a secret drinker who carries on disreputable intrigues in Italy. No. 3, a beautiful girl who possesses the useful faculty of being in two places at once. No. 4, Miss Pettigrew, who, I have no doubt, is really a particularly dangerous crook in disguise! Probably one of Pagett's Italian friends that he has palmed off on me. I shouldn't wonder if the world found some day that it had been grossly deceived by Pagett. On the whole, I think Rayburn was the best of the bunch. He never worried me or got in my way. Guy Pagett has had the impertinence to have the stationery trunk put in here. None of us can move without falling over it.

I went out on the observation platform just now, expecting my appearance to be greeted with hails of delight. Both the women were listening spellbound to one of Race's traveller's tales. I shall label this car – not 'Sir Eustace Pedler and Party', but 'Colonel Race and Harem'.

Then Mrs Blair must needs begin taking silly photographs. Every time we went round a particularly appalling curve, as we climbed higher and higher, she snapped at the engine.

'You see the point,' she cried delightedly. 'It must be some curve if you can photograph the front part of the train from the back, and with the mountain background it will look awfully dangerous.'

I pointed out to her that no one could possibly tell it had been taken from the back of the train. She looked at me pityingly.

'I shall write underneath it. "Taken from the train. Engine going round a curve."'

'You could write that under any snapshot of a train,' I said. Women never think of these simple things.

'I'm glad we've come up here in daylight,' cried Anne Beddingfeld. 'I shouldn't have seen this if I'd gone last night to Durban, should I?'

'No,' said Colonel Race, smiling. 'You'd have woken up tomorrow morning to find yourself in the Karoo, a hot, dusty desert of stones and rocks.'

'I'm glad I changed my mind,' said Anne, sighing contentedly, and looking round.

It was rather a wonderful sight. The great mountains all around, through which we turned and twisted and laboured ever steadily upwards.

'Is this the best train in the day to Rhodesia?' asked Anne Beddingfeld.

'In the day?' laughed Race. 'Why, my dear Miss Anne, there are only three trains a week. Mondays, Wednesdays, and Saturdays. Do you realize that you don't arrive at the Falls until Saturday next?'

'How well we shall know each other by that time!' said Mrs Blair maliciously. 'How long are you going to stay at the Falls, Sir Eustace?'

'That depends,' I said cautiously.

'On what?'

'On how things go at Johannesburg. My original idea was to stay a couple of days at the Falls – which I've never seen, though this is my third visit to Africa – and then go on to Jo'burg and study the conditions of things on the Rand. At home, you know, I pose as being an authority on South African politics. But from all I hear, Jo'burg will be a particularly unpleasant place to visit in about a week's time. I don't want to study conditions in the midst of a raging revolution.'

Race smiled in a rather superior manner.

'I think your fears are exaggerated, Sir Eustace. There will be no great danger in Jo'burg.'

The women immediately looked at him in the 'What a brave hero you are' manner. It annoyed me intensely. I am every bit as brave as Race – but I lack the figure. These long, lean, brown men have it all their own way.

'I suppose you'll be there,' I said coldly.

'Very possibly. We might travel together.'

'I'm not sure that I shan't stay on at the Falls a bit,' I answered non-committally. Why is Race so anxious that I should go to Jo'burg? He's got his eye on Anne, I believe. 'What are your plans, Miss Anne?'

'That depends,' she replied demurely, copying me.

'I thought you were my secretary,' I objected.

'Oh, but I've been cut out. You've been holding Miss Pettigrew's hand all the afternoon.'

'Whatever I've been doing, I can swear I've not been doing that,' I assured her.

Thursday night.

We have just left Kimberley. Race was made to tell the story of the diamond robbery all over again. Why are women so excited by anything to do with diamonds?

At last Anne Beddingfeld has shed her veil of mystery. It seems that she's a newspaper correspondent. She sent an immense cable from De Aar this morning. To judge by the jabbering that went on nearly all night in Mrs Blair's cabin she must have been reading aloud all her special articles for years to come.

It seems that all along she's been on the track of 'The Man in the Brown Suit'. Apparently she didn't spot him on the *Kilmorden* – in fact, she hardly had the chance, but she's now very busy cabling home: 'How I journeyed out with the Murderer', and inventing highly fictitious stories of 'What he said to me', etc. I know how these things are done. I do them myself, in my Reminiscences when Pagett will let me. And of course one of Nasby's efficient staff will brighten up the details still more, so that when it appears in the *Daily Budget* Rayburn won't recognize himself.

The girl's clever, though. All on her own, apparently, she's ferreted out the identity of the woman who was killed in my house. She was a Russian dancer called Nadina. I asked Anne Beddingfeld if she was sure of this. She replied that it was merely a deduction – quite in the Sherlock Holmes manner. However, I gather that she had cabled it home to Nasby as a proved fact. Women have these intuitions – I've no doubt that Anne Beddingfeld is perfectly right in her guess – but to call it a deduction is absurd.

How she ever got on the staff of the *Daily Budget* is more than I can imagine. But she is the kind of young woman who does these things. Impossible to withstand her. She is full of coaxing ways that mask an invincible determination. Look how she has got into my private car!

I am beginning to have an inkling why. Race said something about the police suspecting that Rayburn would make for Rhodesia. He might just have got off by Monday's train. They telegraphed all along the line, I presume, and no one of his description was found, but that says little. He's an astute young man and he knows Africa. He's probably exquisitely disguised as an old Kafir woman – and the simple police continue to look for a handsome young man with a scar, dressed in the height of European fashion. I never did quite swallow that scar.

Anyway, Anne Beddingfeld is on his track. She wants the glory of discovering him for herself and the *Daily Budget.* Young women are very cold-blooded nowadays. I hinted to her that it was an unwomanly action. She laughed at me. She assured me that did she run him to earth her fortune was made. Race doesn't like it, either, I can see. Perhaps Rayburn is on this train. If so, we may all be murdered in our beds. I said so to Mrs Blair – but she seemed quite to welcome the idea, and remarked that if I were murdered it would be really a terrific scoop for Anne! A scoop for Anne, indeed!

Tomorrow we shall be going through Bechuanaland. The dust will be atrocious. Also at every station little Kafir children come and sell you quaint wooden animals that they carve themselves. Also mealie bowls and baskets. I am rather afraid that Mrs Blair may run amok. There is a primitive charm about these toys that I feel will appeal to her.

Friday evening.

As I feared. Mrs Blair and Anne have bought forty-nine wooden animals!

CHAPTER XXIII

(Anne's Narrative Resumed)

I thoroughly enjoyed the journey up to Rhodesia. There was something new and exciting to see every day. First the wonderful scenery of the Hex River valley, then the desolate grandeur of the Karoo, and finally that wonderful straight stretch of line in Bechuanaland, and the perfectly adorable toys the natives brought to sell. Suzanne and I were nearly left behind at each station – if you could call them stations. It seemed to me that the train just stopped whenever it felt like it, and no sooner had it done so than a horde of natives materialized out of the empty landscape, holding up mealie bowls and sugar canes and fur karosses and adorable carved wooden animals. Suzanne began at once to make a collection of the latter. I imitated her example – most of them cost a 'tiki' (threepence) and each was different. There were giraffes and tigers and snakes and a melancholy-looking eland and absurd little black warriors. We enjoyed ourselves enormously.

Sir Eustace tried to restrain us – but in vain. I still think it was a miracle we were not left behind at some oasis of the line. South African trains don't hoot or get excited when they are going to start off again. They just glide quietly away, and you look up from your bargaining and run for your life.

Suzanne's amazement at seeing me climb upon the train at Cape Town can be imagined. We held an exhaustive survey of the situation on the first evening out. We talked half the night.

It had become clear to me that defensive tactics must be adopted as well as aggressive ones. Travelling with Sir Eustace Pedler and his party, I was fairly safe. Both he and Colonel Race were powerful protectors, and I judged that my enemies would not wish to stir up a hornet's nest about *my* ears. Also, as long as I was near Sir Eustace, I was more or less in touch with Guy Pagett – and Guy Pagett was the heart of the mystery. I asked Suzanne whether in her opinion it was possible that Pagett himself was the mysterious 'Colonel'. His subordinate position was, of course, against the assumption, but it had struck me once or twice that, for all his autocratic ways, Sir Eustace was really very much influenced by his secretary. He was an easy-going man, and one whom an adroit secretary might be able to twist round his little finger. The comparative obscurity of his position might in reality be useful to him, since he would be anxious to be well out of the limelight.

Suzanne, however, negatived these ideas very strongly. She refused to believe that Guy Pagett was the ruling spirit. The real head – the 'Colonel' – was somewhere in the background and had probably been already in Africa at the time of our arrival.

I agreed that there was much to be said for her view, but I was not entirely satisfied. For in each suspicious instance Pagett had been shown as the directing genius. It was true that his personality seemed to lack the assurance and decision that one would expect from a master criminal – but after all, according to Colonel Race, it was brain-work only that this mysterious leader supplied, and creative genius is often allied to a weak and timorous physical constitution.

'There speaks the Professor's daughter,' interrupted Suzanne, when I had got to this point in my argument.

'It's true, all the same. On the other hand, Pagett may be the Grand Vizier, so to speak, of the All Highest.' I was silent for a minute or two, and then went on musingly: 'I wish I knew how Sir Eustace made his money!'

'Suspecting him again?'

'Suzanne, I've got into that state that I can't help suspecting somebody! I don't really suspect him – but, after all, he *is* Pagett's employer, and he *did* own the Mill House.'

'I've always heard that he made his money in some way he isn't anxious to talk about,' said Suzanne thoughtfully. 'But that doesn't necessarily mean crime – it might be tintacks or hair restorer!'

I agreed ruefully.

'I suppose,' said Suzanne doubtfully, 'that we're not barking up the wrong tree? Being led completely astray, I mean, by assuming Pagett's complicity? Supposing that, after all, he is a perfectly honest man?'

I considered that for a minute or two, then I shook my head.

'I can't believe that.'

'After all, he has his explanations for everything.'

'Y – es, but they're not very convincing. For instance, the night he tried to throw me overboard on the *Kilmorden*, he says he followed Rayburn up on deck and Rayburn turned and knocked him down. Now we know that's not true.'

'No,' said Suzanne unwillingly. 'But we only heard the story at second-hand from Sir Eustace. If we'd heard it direct from Pagett himself, it might have been different. You know how people always get a story a little wrong when they repeat it.'

I turned the thing over in my mind.

'No,' I said at last, 'I don't see any way out. Pagett's guilty. You can't get away from the fact that he tried to throw me overboard, and everything else fits in. Why are you so persistent in this new idea of yours?'

'Because of his face.'

'His face? But –'

'Yes, I know what you're going to say. It's a sinister face. That's just it. No man with a face like that could be really sinister. It must be a colossal joke on the part of Nature.'

I did not believe much in Suzanne's argument. I know a lot about Nature in past ages. If she's got a sense of humour, she doesn't show it much. Suzanne is just the sort of person who would clothe Nature with all her own attributes.

We passed on to discuss our immediate plans. It was clear to me that I must have some kind of standing. I couldn't go on avoiding explanations for ever. The solution of all my difficulties lay ready to my hand, though I didn't think of it for some time. The *Daily Budget*! My silence or my speech could no longer affect Harry Rayburn. He was marked down as 'The Man in the Brown Suit' through no fault of mine. I could help him best by seeming to be against him. The 'Colonel' and his gang must have no suspicion that there existed any friendly feeling between me and the man they had elected to be the scapegoat of the murder at Marlow. As far as I knew, the woman killed was still unidentified. I would cable to Lord Nasby, suggesting that she was no other than the famous Russian dancer 'Nadina' who had been delighting Paris for so long. It seemed incredible to me that she had not been identified already – but when I learnt more of the case long afterwards I saw how natural it really was.

Nadina had never been to England, during her successful career in Paris. She was unknown to London audiences. The pictures in the papers of the Marlow victim were so blurred and unrecognizable that it is small wonder no one identified them. And, on the other hand, Nadina had kept her intention of visiting England a profound secret from everyone. The day after the murder, a letter had been received by her manager purporting to be from the dancer, in which she said that she was returning to Russia on urgent private affairs and that he must deal with her broken contract as best he could.

All this, of course, I only learned afterwards. With Suzanne's full approval, I sent a long cable from De Aar. It arrived at a psychological moment (this again, of course, I learnt afterwards). The *Daily Budget* was hard up for a sensation. My guess was verified and proved to be correct and the *Daily Budget* had the scoop of its lifetime. 'Victim of the Mill House Murder identified by our special reporter'. And so on. 'Our reporter makes voyage with the murderer. The Man in the Brown Suit. What he is really like.'

The main facts were, of course, cabled to the South African papers, but I only read my own lengthy articles at a much later date! I received approval and full instructions by cable at Bulawayo. I was on the staff of the *Daily Budget*, and I had a private word of congratulation from Lord Nasby himself. I was definitely accredited to hunt down the murderer, and I, and only I, knew that the murderer was not Harry Rayburn! But let the world think that it was he – best so for the present.

CHAPTER XXIV

We arrived at Bulawayo early on Saturday morning. I was disappointed in the place. It was very hot, and I hated the hotel. Also Sir Eustace was what I can only describe as thoroughly sulky. I think it was all our wooden animals that annoyed him – especially the big giraffe. It was a colossal giraffe with an impossible neck, a mild eye and a dejected tail. It had character. It had charm. A controversy was already arising as to whom it belonged to – me or Suzanne. We had each contributed a *tiki* to its purchase. Suzanne advanced the claims of seniority and the married state, I stuck to the position that I had been the first to behold its beauty.

In the meantime, I must admit, it occupied a good deal of this three-dimensional space of ours. To carry forty-nine wooden animals, all of awkward shape, and all of extremely brittle wood, is somewhat of a problem. Two porters were laden with a bunch of animals each – and one promptly dropped a ravishing group of ostriches and broke their heads off. Warned by this, Suzanne and I carried all we could, Colonel Race helped, and I pressed the big giraffe into Sir Eustace's arms. Even the correct Miss Pettigrew did not escape, a large hippopotamus and two black warriors fell to her share. I had a feeling Miss Pettigrew didn't like me. Perhaps she fancied I was a bold hussy. Anyway, she avoided me as much as she could. And the funny thing was, her face seemed vaguely familiar to me, though I couldn't quite place it.

We reposed ourselves most of the morning, and in the afternoon we drove out to the Matopos to see Rhodes's grave. That is to say, we were to have done so, but at the last moment Sir Eustace backed out. He was very nearly in as bad a temper as the morning we arrived at Cape Town when he bounced the peaches on the floor and they squashed! Evidently arriving early in the morning at places is bad for his temperament. He cursed the porters, he cursed the waiter at breakfast, he cursed the whole hotel management, he would doubtless have liked to curse Miss Pettigrew, who hovered around with her pencil and pad, but I don't think even Sir Eustace would have dared to curse Miss Pettigrew. She's just like the efficient secretary in a book. I only rescued our dear giraffe just in time. I feel Sir Eustace would have liked to dash him to the ground.

To return to our expedition, after Sir Eustace had backed out, Miss Pettigrew said she would remain at home in case he might want her. And at the very last minute Suzanne sent down a message to say she had a headache. So Colonel Race and I drove off alone.

He is a strange man. One doesn't notice it so much in a crowd. But when one is alone with him the sense of his personality seems really almost overpowering. He becomes more taciturn, and yet his silence seems to say more than speech might do.

It was so that day that we drove to the Matopos through the soft yellow-brown scrub. Everything seemed strangely silent – except our car, which I should think was the first Ford ever made by man! The upholstery of it was torn to ribbons and, though I know nothing about engines, even I could guess that all was not as it should be in its interior.

By and by the character of the country changed. Great boulders appeared, piled up into fantastic shapes. I felt suddenly that I had got into a primitive era. Just for a moment Neanderthal men seemed quite as real to me as they had to Papa. I turned to Colonel Race.

'There must have been giants once,' I said dreamily. 'And their children were just like children are today – they played with handfuls of pebbles, piling them up and knocking them down, and the more cleverly they balanced them, the better pleased they were. If I were to give a name to this place I should call it The Country of Giant Children.'

'Perhaps you're nearer the mark than you know,' said Colonel Race gravely. 'Simple, primitive, big – that is Africa.'

I nodded appreciatively.

'You love it, don't you?' I asked.

'Yes. But to live in it long – well, it makes one what you would call cruel. One comes to hold life and death very lightly.'

'Yes,' I said, thinking of Harry Rayburn. He had been like that too. 'But not cruel to weak things?'

'Opinions differ as to what are and are not "weak things", Miss Anne.'

There was a note of seriousness in his voice which almost startled me. I felt that I knew very little really of this man at my side.

'I meant children and dogs, I think.'

'I can truthfully say I've never been cruel to children or dogs. So you don't class women as "weak things"?'

I considered.

'No, I don't think I do – though they are, I suppose. That is, they are nowadays. But Papa always said that in the beginning men and women roamed the world together, equal in strength – like lions and tigers –'

'And giraffes?' interpolated Colonel Race slyly.

I laughed. Everyone makes fun of that giraffe.

'And giraffes. They were nomadic, you see. It wasn't till they settled down in communities, and women did one kind of thing and men another, that women got weak. And of course, underneath, one is still the same – one *feels* the same, I mean – and that is why women worship physical strength in men: it's what they once had and have lost.'

'Almost ancestor worship, in fact?'

'Something of the kind.'

'And you really think that's true? That women worship strength, I mean?'

'I think it's quite true – if one's honest. You think you admire moral qualities, but when you fall in love, you revert to the primitive where the physical is all that counts. But I don't think that's the end; if you lived in primitive conditions it would be all right, but you don't – and so, in the end, the other thing wins after all. It's the things that are apparently

conquered that always do win, isn't it? They win in the only
way that counts. Like what the Bible says about losing your
life and finding it.'

'In the end,' said Colonel Race thoughtfully, 'you fall in
love – and you fall out of it, is that what you mean?'

'Not exactly, but you can put it that way if you like.'

'But I don't think you've ever fallen out of love, Miss Anne?'

'No, I haven't,' I admitted frankly.

'Or fallen in love, either?'

I did not answer.

The car drew up at our destination and brought the conversation to a close. We got out and began the slow ascent to the
World's View. Not for the first time, I felt a slight discomfort
in Colonel Race's company. He veiled his thoughts so well
behind those impenetrable black eyes. He frightened me a
little. He had always frightened me. I never knew where I
stood with him.

We climbed in silence till we reached the spot where Rhodes
lies guarded by giant boulders. A strange eerie place, far from
the haunts of men, that sings a ceaseless paean of rugged
beauty.

We sat there for a time in silence. Then descended more,
but diverging slightly from the path. Sometimes it was a rough
scramble and once we came to a sharp slope or rock that was
almost sheer.

Colonel Race went first, then turned to help me.

'Better lift you,' he said suddenly, and swung me off my
feet with a quick gesture.

I felt the strength of him as he set me down and released
his clasp. A man of iron, with muscles like taut steel. And
again I felt afraid, especially as he did not move aside, but
stood directly in front of me, staring into my face.

'What are you really doing here, Anne Beddingfeld?' he said
abruptly.

'I'm a gipsy seeing the world.'

'Yes, that's true enough. The newspaper correspondent is
only a pretext. You've not the soul of a journalist. You're out

for your own hand – snatching at life. But that's not all.'

What was he going to make me tell him? I was afraid – afraid. I looked him full in the face. My eyes can't keep secrets like his, but they can carry the war into the enemy's country.

'What are *you* really doing here, Colonel Race?' I asked deliberately.

For a moment I thought he wasn't going to answer. He was clearly taken aback, though. At last he spoke, and his words seemed to afford him a grim amusement.

'Pursuing ambition,' he said. 'Just that – pursuing ambition. You will remember, Miss Beddingfeld, that "by that sin fell the angels," etc.'

'They say,' I said slowly, 'that you are really connected with the Government – that you are in the Secret Service. Is that true?'

Was it my fancy, or did he hesitate for a fraction of a second before he answered?

'I can assure you, Miss Beddingfeld, that I am out here strictly as a private individual travelling for my own pleasure.'

Thinking the answer over later, it struck me as slightly ambiguous. Perhaps he meant it to be so.

We rejoined the car in silence. Half-way back to Bulawayo we stopped for tea at a somewhat primitive structure at the side of the road. The proprietor was digging in the garden, and seemed annoyed at being disturbed. But he graciously promised to see what he could do. After an interminable wait, he brought us some stale cakes and some lukewarm tea. Then disappeared to his garden again.

No sooner had he departed than we were surrounded by cats, six of them all miaowing piteously at once. The racket was deafening. I offered them some pieces of cake. They devoured them ravenously. I poured all the milk there was into a saucer and they fought each other to get it.

'Oh,' I cried indignantly, 'they're starved! It's wicked. Please, please, order some more milk and another plate of cake.'

Colonel Race departed silently to do my bidding. The cats

had begun miaowing again. He returned with a big jug of milk and the cats finished it all.

I got up with determination on my face.

'I'm going to take those cats home with us – I shan't leave them here.'

'My dear child, don't be absurd. You can't carry six cats as well as fifty wooden animals round with you.'

'Never mind the wooden animals. These cats are alive. I shall take them back with me.'

'You will do nothing of the kind.' I looked at him resentfully but he went on: 'You think me cruel – but one can't go through life sentimentalizing over these things. It's no good standing out – I shan't allow you to take them. It's a primitive country, you know, and I'm stronger than you.'

I always know when I am beaten. I went down to the car with tears in my eyes.

'They're probably short of food just today,' he explained consolingly. 'That man's wife has gone into Bulawayo for stores. So it will be all right. And anyway, you know, the world's full of starving cats.'

'Don't – don't,' I said fiercely.

'I'm teaching you to realize life as it is. I'm teaching you to be hard and ruthless – like I am. That's the secret of strength – and the secret of success.'

'I'd sooner be dead than hard,' I said passionately.

We got into the car and started off. I pulled myself together again slowly. Suddenly, to my intense astonishment, he took my hand in his.

'Anne,' he said gently, 'I want you. Will you marry me?'

I was utterly taken aback.

'Oh, no,' I stammered. 'I can't.'

'Why not?'

'I don't care for you in that way. I've never thought of you like that.'

'I see. Is that the only reason?'

I had to be honest. I owed it him.

'No,' I said, 'it is not. You see – I – care for someone else.'

'I see,' he said again. 'And was that true at the beginning – when I first saw you – on the *Kilmorden*?'

'No,' I whispered. 'It was – since then.'

'I see,' he said for the third time, but this time there was a purposeful ring in his voice that made me turn and look at him. His face was grimmer than I had ever seen it.

'What – what do you mean?' I faltered.

He looked at me, inscrutable, dominating.

'Only – that I know now what I have to do.'

His words sent a shiver through me. There was a determination behind them that I did not understand – and it frightened me.

We neither of us said any more until we got back to the hotel. I went straight up to Suzanne. She was lying on her bed reading, and did not look in the least as though she had a headache.

'Here reposes the perfect gooseberry,' she remarked. '*Alias* the tactful chaperone. Why, Anne dear, what's the matter?'

For I had burst into a flood of tears.

I told her about the cats – I felt it wasn't fair to tell her about Colonel Race. But Suzanne is very sharp. I think she saw that there was something more behind.

'You haven't caught a chill, have you, Anne? Sounds absurd even to suggest such things in this heat, but you keep on shivering.'

'It's nothing,' I said. 'Nerves – or someone walking over my grave. I keep feeling something dreadful's going to happen.'

'Don't be silly,' said Suzanne, with decision. 'Let's talk of something interesting. Anne, about those diamonds –'

'What about them?'

'I'm not sure they're safe with me. It was all right before, no one could think they'd be amongst my things. But now that everyone knows we're such friends, you and I, I'll be under suspicion too.'

'Nobody knows they're in a roll of films, though,' I argued. 'It's a splendid hiding-place and I really don't think we could better it.'

She agreed doubtfully, but said we would discuss it again when we got to the Falls.

Our train went at nine o'clock. Sir Eustace's temper was still far from good, and Miss Pettigrew looked subdued. Colonel Race was completely himself. I felt that I had dreamed the whole conversation on the way back.

I slept heavily that night on my hard bunk, struggling with ill-defined, menacing dreams. I awoke with a headache and went out on the observation platform of the car. It was fresh and lovely, and everywhere, as far as one could see, were the undulating wooded hills. I loved it – loved it more than any place I had ever seen. I wished then that I could have a little hut somewhere in the heart of the scrub and live there always – always . . .

Just before half-past two, Colonel Race called me out from the 'office' and pointed to a bouquet-shaped white mist that hovered over one portion of the bush.

'The spray from the Falls,' he said. 'We are nearly there.'

I was still wrapped in that strange dream feeling of exaltation that had succeeded my troubled night. Very strongly implanted in me was the feeling that I had come home . . . Home! And yet I had never been here before – or had I in dreams?

We walked from the train to the hotel, a big white building closely wired against mosquitoes. There were no roads, no houses. We went out on the *stoep* and I uttered a gasp. There, half a mile away, facing us, were the Falls. I've never seen anything so grand and beautiful – I never shall.

'Anne, you're fey,' said Suzanne, as we sat down to lunch. 'I've never seen you like this before.'

She stared at me curiously.

'Am I?' I laughed, but I felt that my laugh was unnatural. 'It's just that I love it all.'

'It's more than that.'

A little frown crossed her brow – one of apprehension.

Yes, I was happy, but beyond that I had the curious feeling

that I was waiting for something – something that would happen soon. I was excited – restless.

After tea we strolled out, got on the trolley and were pushed by smiling blacks down the little tracks of rails to the bridge.

It was a marvellous sight, the great chasm and the rushing waters below, and the veil of mist and spray in front of us that parted every now and then for one brief minute to show the cataract of water and then closed up again in its impenetrable mystery. That, to my mind, has always been the fascination of the Falls – their elusive quality. You always think you're going to see – and you never do.

We crossed the bridge and walked slowly on by the path that was marked out with white stone on either side and led round the brink of the gorge. Finally we arrived in a big clearing where on the left a path led downwards towards the chasm.

'The palm gully,' explained Colonel Race. 'Shall we go down? Or shall we leave it until tomorrow? It will take some time, and it's a good climb up again.'

'We'll leave it until tomorrow,' said Sir Eustace with decision. He isn't at all fond of strenuous physical exercise, I have noticed.

He led the way back. As we went, we passed a fine native stalking along. Behind him came a woman who seemed to have the entire household belongings piled upon her head! The collection included a frying-pan.

'I never have my camera when I want it,' groaned Suzanne.

'That's an opportunity that will occur often enough, Mrs Blair,' said Colonel Race. 'So don't lament.'

We arrived back on the bridge.

'Shall we go into the rainbow forest?' he continued. 'Or are you afraid of getting wet?'

Suzanne and I accompanied him. Sir Eustace went back to the hotel. I was rather disappointed in the rainbow forest. There weren't nearly enough rainbows, and we got soaked to the skin, but every now and then we got a glimpse of the Falls opposite and realized how enormously wide they are. Oh, dear, dear Falls, how I love and worship you and always shall!

We got back to the hotel just in time to change for dinner. Sir Eustace seemed to have taken a positive antipathy to Colonel Race. Suzanne and I rallied him gently, but didn't get much satisfaction.

After dinner he retired to his sitting-room, dragging Miss Pettigrew with him. Suzanne and I talked for a while with Colonel Race, and then she declared, with an immense yawn, that she was going to bed. I didn't want to be left alone with him, so I got up too and went to my room.

But I was far too excited to go to sleep. I did not even undress. I lay back in a chair and gave myself up to dreaming. And all the time I was conscious of something coming nearer and nearer . . .

There was a knock at the door, and I started. I got up and went to it. A little black boy held out a note. It was addressed to me in a handwriting I did not know. I took it and came back into the room. I stood there holding it. At last I opened it. It was very short!

'I must see you. I dare not come to the hotel. Will you come to the clearing by the palm gully? In memory of Cabin 17 please come. The man you knew as Harry Rayburn.'

My heart beat to suffocation. He was here then! Oh, I had known it – I had known it all along! I had felt him near me. All unwittingly I had come to his place of retreat.

I wound a scarf round my head and stole to the door. I must be careful. He was hunted down. No one must see me meet him. I stole along to Suzanne's room. She was fast asleep. I could hear her breathing evenly.

Sir Eustace? I paused outside the door of his sitting-room. Yes, he was dictating to Miss Pettigrew, I could hear her monotonous voice repeating: 'I therefore venture to suggest, that in tackling this problem of coloured labour –' She paused for him to continue, and I heard him grunt something angrily.

I stole on again. Colonel Race's room was empty. I did not see him in the lounge. And he was the man I feared most!

Still, I could waste no more time. I slipped quickly out of the hotel, and took the path to the bridge.

I crossed it and stood there waiting in the shadow. If anyone had followed me, I should see them crossing the bridge. But the minutes passed, and no one came. I had not been followed. I turned and took the path to the clearing. I took six paces or so, and then stopped. Something had rustled behind me. It could not be anyone who had followed me from the hotel. It was someone who was already here, waiting.

And immediately, without rhyme or reason, but with the sureness of instinct, I knew that it was I myself who was threatened. It was the same feeling as I had had on the *Kilmorden* that night – a sure instinct warning me of danger.

I looked sharply over my shoulder. Silence. I moved on a pace or two. Again I heard that rustle. Still walking, I looked over my shoulder again. A man's figure came out of the shadow. He saw that I saw him, and jumped forward, hard on my track.

It was too dark to recognize anybody. All I could see was that he was tall, and a European, not a native. I took to my heels and ran. I heard him pounding behind. I ran quicker, keeping my eyes fixed on the white stones that showed me where to step, for there was no moon that night.

And suddenly my foot felt nothingness. I heard the man behind me laugh, an evil, sinister laugh. It rang in my ears, as I fell headlong – down – down – down to destruction far beneath.

CHAPTER XXV

I came to myself slowly and painfully. I was conscious of an aching head and a shooting pain down my left arm when I tried to move, and everything seemed dreamlike and unreal. Nightmare visions floated before me. I felt myself falling – falling again. Once Harry Rayburn's face seemed to come to me out of the mist. Almost I imagined it real. Then it floated away again, mocking me. Once, I remember, someone put a cup to my lips and I drank. A black face grinned into mine – a devil's face, I thought it, and screamed out. Then dreams again – long troubled dreams in which I vainly sought Harry Rayburn to warn him – warn him – what of? I did not know myself. But there was some danger – some great danger – and I alone could save him. Then darkness again, merciful darkness and real sleep.

I woke at last myself again. The long nightmare was over. I remembered perfectly everything that had happened: my hurried flight from the hotel to meet Harry, the man in the shadows and the last terrible moment of falling . . .

By some miracle or other I had not been killed. I was bruised and aching, and very weak, but I was alive. But where was I? Moving my head with difficulty I looked round me. I was in a small room with rough wooden walls. On them were huge skins of animals and various tusks of ivory. I was lying on a kind of rough couch, also covered with skins, and my left arm was bandaged up and felt stiff and uncomfortable. At first I thought I was alone, and then I saw a man's figure sitting between me and the light, his head turned towards the window. He was so still that he might have been carved out of wood. Something in the close-cropped black head was familiar to me, but I did not dare to let my imagination run astray. Suddenly he turned, and I caught my breath. It was Harry Rayburn. Harry Rayburn in the flesh.

He rose and came over to me.

'Feeling better?' he said a trifle awkwardly.

I could not answer. The tears were running down my face. I was weak still, but I held his hand in both of mine. If only I could die like this, whilst he stood there looking down on me with that new look in his eyes.

'Don't cry, Anne. Please don't cry. You're safe now. No one shall hurt you.'

He went and fetched a cup and brought it to me.

'Drink some of this milk.'

I drank obediently. He went on talking, in a low coaxing tone such as he might have used to a child.

'Don't ask any more questions now. Go to sleep again. You'll be stronger by and by. I'll go away if you like.'

'No,' I said urgently. 'No, no.'

'Then I'll stay.'

He brought a small stool over beside me and sat there. He laid his hand over mine, and, soothed and comforted, I dropped off to sleep once more.

It must have been evening then, but when I woke again the sun was high in the heavens. I was alone in the hut, but as I stirred an old native woman came running in. She was hideous as sin, but she grinned at me encouragingly. She brought me water in a basin and helped me wash my face and hands. Then she brought me a large bowl of soup, and I finished it every drop! I asked her several questions, but she only grinned and nodded and chattered away in a guttural language, so I gathered she knew no English.

Suddenly she stood up and drew back respectfully as Harry Rayburn entered. He gave her a nod of dismissal and she went out leaving us alone. He smiled at me.

'Really better today!'

'Yes, indeed, but very bewildered still. Where am I?'

'You're on a small island on the Zambesi about four miles up from the Falls.'

'Do – do my friends know I'm here?'

He shook his head.

'I must send word to them.'

'That is as you like, of course, but if I were you I should wait until you are a little stronger.'

'Why?'

He did not answer immediately, so I went on:

'How long have I been here?'

His answer amazed me.

'Nearly a month.'

'Oh!' I cried. 'I must send word to Suzanne. She'll be terribly anxious.'

'Who is Suzanne?'

'Mrs Blair. I was with her and Sir Eustace and Colonel Race at the hotel – but you knew that, surely?'

He shook his head.

'I know nothing, except that I found you, caught in the fork of a tree, unconscious and with a badly wrenched arm.'

'Where was the tree?'

'Overhanging the ravine. But for your clothes catching on the branches, you would certainly have been dashed to pieces.'

I shuddered. Then a thought struck me.

'You say you didn't know I was there. What about the note then?'

'What note?'

'The note you sent me, asking me to meet you in the clearing.'

He stared at me.

'I sent no note.'

I felt myself flushing up to the roots of my hair. Fortunately he did not seem to notice.

'How did you come to be on the spot in such a marvellous manner?' I asked, in as nonchalant a manner as I could assume. 'And what are you doing in this part of the world, anyway?'

'I live here,' he said simply.

'On this island?'

'Yes, I came here after the War. Sometimes I take parties

from the hotel out in my boat, but it costs me very little to live, and mostly I do as I please.'

'You live here all alone?'

'I am not pining for society, I assure you,' he replied coldly.

'I am sorry to have inflicted mine upon you,' I retorted, 'but I seem to have had very little to say in the matter.'

To my surprise, his eyes twinkled a little.

'None whatever. I slung you across my shoulders like a sack of coal and carried you to my boat. Quite like a primitive man of the Stone Age.'

'But for a different reason,' I put in.

He flushed this time, a deep burning blush. The tan of his face was suffused.

'But you haven't told me how you came to be wandering about so conveniently for me?' I said hastily, to cover his confusion.

'I couldn't sleep. I was restless – disturbed – had the feeling something was going to happen. In the end I took the boat and came ashore and tramped down towards the Falls. I was just at the head of the palm gully when I heard you scream.'

'Why didn't you get help from the hotel instead of carting me all the way here?' I asked.

He flushed again.

'I suppose it seems an unpardonable liberty to you – but I don't think that even now you realize your danger! You think I should have informed your friends? Pretty friends, who allowed you to be decoyed out to death. No, I swore to myself that I'd take better care of you than anyone else could. Not a soul comes to this island. I got old Batani, whom I cured of a fever once, to come and look after you. She's loyal. She'll never say a word. I could keep you here for months and no one would ever know.'

I could keep you here for months and no one would ever know! How some words please one!

'You did quite right,' I said quietly. 'And I shall not send word to anyone. A day or so more anxiety doesn't make much difference. It's not as though they were my own people.

They're only acquaintances really – even Suzanne. And whoever wrote that note must have known – a great deal! It was
not the work of an outsider.'

I managed to mention the note this time without blushing
at all.

'If you would be guided by me –' he said, hesitating.

'I don't expect I shall be,' I answered candidly. 'But there's
no harm in hearing.'

'Do you always do what you like, Miss Beddingfeld?'

'Usually,' I replied cautiously. To anyone else I would have
said 'Always.'

'I pity your husband,' he said unexpectedly.

'You needn't,' I retorted. 'I shouldn't dream of marrying
anyone unless I was madly in love with him. And of course
there is really nothing a woman enjoys so much as doing
all the things she doesn't like for the sake of someone she
does like. And the more self-willed she is, the more she likes
it.'

'I'm afraid I disagree with you. The boot is on the other
leg as a rule.' He spoke with a slight sneer.

'Exactly,' I cried eagerly. 'And that's why there are so many
unhappy marriages. It's all the fault of the men. Either they
give way to their women – and then the women despise them
– or else they are utterly selfish, insist on their own way and
never say "thank you". Successful husbands make their wives
do just what they want, and then make a frightful fuss of them
for doing it. Women like to be mastered, but they hate not to
have their sacrifices appreciated. On the other hand, men
don't really appreciate women who are nice to them all the
time. When I am married, I shall be a devil most of the time,
but every now and then, when my husband least expects it, I
shall show him what a perfect angel I can be.'

Harry laughed outright.

'What a cat-and-dog life you will lead!'

'Lovers always fight,' I assured him. 'Because they don't
understand each other. And by the time they do understand
each other they aren't in love any more.'

'Does the reverse hold true? Are people who fight each other always lovers?'

'I – I don't know,' I said, momentarily confused.

He turned away to the fireplace.

'Like some more soup?' he asked in a casual tone.

'Yes, please. I'm so hungry that I would eat a hippopotamus.'

'That's good.'

He busied himself with the fire. I watched.

'When I can get off the couch, I'll cook for you,' I promised.

'I don't suppose you know anything about cooking.'

'I can warm up things out of tins as well as you can,' I retorted, pointing to a row of tins on the mantelpiece.

'*Touché*,' he said and laughed.

His whole face changed when he laughed. It became boyish, happy – a different personality.

I enjoyed my soup. As I ate it I reminded him that he had not, after all, tendered me his advice.

'Ah, yes, what I was going to say was this. If I were you I would stay quietly *perdu* here until you are quite strong again. Your enemies will believe you dead. They will hardly be surprised at not finding the body. It would have been dashed to pieces on the rocks and carried down with the torrent.'

I shivered.

'Once you are completely restored to health, you can journey quietly on to Beira and get a boat to take you back to England.'

'That would be very tame,' I objected scornfully.

'There speaks a foolish schoolgirl.'

'I'm not a foolish schoolgirl,' I cried indignantly. 'I'm a woman.'

He looked at me with an expression I could not fathom, as I sat up flushed and excited.

'God help me, so you are,' he muttered and went abruptly out.

My recovery was rapid. The two injuries I had sustained were a knock on the head and a badly wrenched arm. The latter was the most serious and, to begin with, my rescuer had believed it to be actually broken. A careful examination, however, convinced him that it was not so, and although it was very painful I was recovering the use of it quite quickly.

It was a strange time. We were cut off from the world, alone together as Adam and Eve might have been – but with what a difference! Old Batani hovered about, counting no more than a dog might have done. I insisted on doing the cooking, or as much of it as I could manage with one arm. Harry was out a good part of the time, but we spent long hours together lying out in the shade of the palms, talking and quarrelling – discussing everything under high heaven, quarrelling and making it up again. We bickered a good deal, but there grew up between us a real and lasting comradeship such as I could never have believed possible. That – and something else.

The time was drawing near, I knew it, when I should be well enough to leave, and I realized it with a heavy heart. Was he going to let me go? Without a word? Without a sign? He had fits of silence, long moody intervals, moments when he would spring up and tramp off by himself. One evening the crisis came. We had finished our simple meal and were sitting in the doorway of the hut. The sun was sinking.

Hairpins were necessities of life with which Harry had not been able to provide me, and my hair, straight and black, hung to my knees. I sat, my chin on my hands, lost in meditation. I felt rather than saw Harry looking at me.

'You look like a witch, Anne,' he said at last, and there was something in his voice that had never been there before.

He reached out his hand and just touched my hair. I shivered. Suddenly he sprang up with an oath.

'You must leave here tomorrow, do you hear?' he cried. 'I – I can't bear any more. I'm only a man after all. You must go, Anne. You must. You're not a fool. You know yourself that this can't go on.'

'I suppose not,' I said slowly. 'But – it's been happy, hasn't it?'

'Happy? It's been hell!'

'As bad as that!'

'What do you torment me for? Why are you mocking at me? Why do you say that – laughing into your hair?'

'I wasn't laughing. And I'm not mocking. If you want me to go, I'll go. But if you want me to stay – I'll stay.'

'Not that!' he cried vehemently. 'Not that. Don't tempt me, Anne. Do you realize what I am? A criminal twice over. A man hunted down. They know me here as Harry Parker – they think I've been away on a trek up country, but any day they may put two and two together – and then the blow will fall. You're so young, Anne, and so beautiful – with the kind of beauty that sends men mad. All the world's before you – love, life, everything. Mine's behind me – scorched, spoiled, with a taste of bitter ashes.'

'If you don't want me –'

'You know I want you. You know that I'd give my soul to pick you up in my arms and keep you here, hidden away from the world, for ever and ever. And you're tempting me, Anne. You, with your long witch's hair, and your eyes that are golden and brown and green and never stop laughing even when your mouth is grave. But I'll save you from yourself and from me. You shall go tonight. You shall go to Beira –'

'I'm not going to Beira,' I interrupted.

'You are. You shall go to Beira if I have to take you there myself and throw you on to the boat. What do you think I'm made of? Do you think I'll wake up night after night, fearing they've got you? One can't go on counting on miracles happening. You must go back to England, Anne – and – and marry and be happy.'

'With a steady man who'll give me a good home!'

'Better that than – utter disaster.'

'And what of you?'

His face grew grim and set.

'I've got my work ready to hand. Don't ask what it is. You can guess, I dare say. But I'll tell you this – I'll clear my name, or die in the attempt, and I'll choke the life out of the damned scoundrel who did his best to murder you the other night.'

'We must be fair,' I said. 'He didn't actually push me over.'

'He'd no need to. His plan was cleverer than that. I went up to the path afterwards. Everything looked all right, but by the marks on the ground I saw that the stones which outline the path had been taken up and put down again in a slightly different place. There are tall bushes growing just over the edge. He'd balanced the outside stones on them, so that you'd think you were still on the path when in reality you were stepping into nothingness. God help him if I lay my hands upon him!'

He paused a minute and then said, in a totally different tone:

'We've never spoken of these things, Anne, have we? But the time's come. I want you to hear the whole story – from the beginning.'

'If it hurts you to go over the past, don't tell me,' I said in a low voice.

'But I want you to know. I never thought I should speak of that part of my life to anyone. Funny, isn't it, the tricks Fate plays?'

He was silent for a minute or two. The sun had set, and the velvety darkness of the African night was enveloping us like a mantle.

'Some of it I know,' I said gently.

'What do you know?'

'I know that your real name is Harry Lucas.'

Still he hesitated – not looking at me, but staring straight out in front of him. I had no clue as to what was passing in his mind, but at last he jerked his head forward as though acquiescing in some unspoken decision of his own, and began his story.

CHAPTER XXVI

'You are right. My real name is Harry Lucas. My father was a retired soldier who came out to farm in Rhodesia. He died when I was in my second year at Cambridge.'

'Were you fond of him?' I asked suddenly.

'I – don't know.'

Then he flushed and went on with sudden vehemence:

'Why do I say that? I *did* love my father. We said bitter things to each other the last time I saw him, and we had many rows over my wildness and my debts, but I cared for the old man. I know how much now – when it's too late,' he continued more quietly. 'It was at Cambridge that I met the other fellow –'

'Young Eardsley?'

'Yes – young Eardsley. His father, as you know, was one of South Africa's most prominent men. We drifted together at once, my friend and I. We had our love of South Africa in common and we both had a taste for the untrodden places of the world. After he left Cambridge, Eardsley had a final quarrel with his father. The old man had paid his debts twice, he refused to do so again. There was a bitter scene between them. Sir Laurence declared himself at the end of his patience – he would do no more for his son. He must stand on his own legs for a while. The result was, as you know, that those two young men went off to South America together, prospecting for diamonds. I'm not going into that now, but we had a wonderful time out there. Hardships in plenty, you understand, but it was a good life – a hand-to-mouth scramble for existence far from the beaten track – and, my God that's the place to know a friend. There was a bond forged between us two out there that only death could have broken. Well, as Colonel Race told you, our efforts were crowned with success. We found a second Kimberley in the heart of the British Guiana jungles. I can't tell you our elation. It wasn't so much the actual value in money of the find – you see, Eardsley was used to money, and he knew that when his father died he would be a millionaire, and Lucas had always been poor and was used to it. No, it was the sheer delight of discovery.'

He paused, and then added, almost apologetically,

'You don't mind my telling it this way, do you? As though I wasn't in it at all. It seems like that now when I look back and see those two boys. I almost forget that one of them was – Harry Rayburn.'

'Tell it any way you like,' I said, and he went on:

'We came to Kimberley – very cock-a-hoop over our find. We brought a magnificent selection of diamonds with us to submit to the experts. And then – in the hotel at Kimberley – we met her –'

I stiffened a little, and the hand that rested on the doorpost clenched itself involuntarily.

'Anita Grünberg – that was her name. She was an actress. Quite young and very beautiful. She was South African born, but her mother was a Hungarian, I believe. There was some sort of mystery about her, and that, of course, heightened her attraction for two boys home from the wilds. She must have had an easy task. We both fell for her right away, and we both took it hard. It was the first shadow that had ever come between us – but even then it didn't weaken our friendship. Each of us, I honestly believe, was willing to stand aside for the other to go in and win. But that wasn't her game. Sometimes, afterwards, I wondered why it hadn't been, for Sir Laurence Eardsley's only son was quite a *parti*. But the truth of it was that she was married – to a sorter in De Beers' – though nobody knew of it. She pretended enormous interest in our discovery, and we told her all about it and even showed her the diamonds. Delilah – that's what she should have been called – and she played her part well!

'The De Beers robbery was discovered, and like a thunderclap the police came down upon us. They seized our diamonds. We only laughed at first – the whole thing was so absurd. And then the diamonds were produced in court – and without question they were the stones stolen from De Beers'. Anita Grünberg had disappeared. She had effected the substitution neatly enough, and our story that these were not the stones originally in our possession was laughed to scorn.

'Sir Laurence Eardsley had enormous influence. He succeeded in getting the case dismissed – but it left two young men ruined and disgraced to face the world with the stigma of thief attached to their name, and it pretty well broke the old fellow's heart. He had one bitter interview with his son in which he heaped upon him every reproach imaginable. He had done what he could to save the family name, but from that day on his son was his son no longer.

He cast him off utterly. And the boy, like the proud young fool that he was, remained silent, disdaining to protest his innocence in the face of his father's disbelief. He came out furious from the interview – his friend was waiting for him. A week later, war was declared. The two friends enlisted together. You know what happened. The best pal a man ever had was killed, partly through his own mad recklessness in rushing into unnecessary danger. He died with his name tarnished . . .

'I swear to you, Anne, that it was mainly on his account that I was so bitter against that woman. It had gone deeper with him than with me. I had been madly in love with her for the moment – I even think that I frightened her sometimes – but with him it was a quieter and deeper feeling. She had been the very centre of his universe – and her betrayal of him tore up the very roots of life. The blow stunned him and left him paralysed.'

Harry paused. After a minute or two he went on:

'As you know, I was reported "Missing, presumed killed". I never troubled to correct the mistake. I took the name of Parker and came to this island, which I knew of old. At the beginning of the War I had had ambitious hopes of proving my innocence, but now all that spirit seemed dead. All I felt was, "What's the good?" My pal was dead, neither he nor I had any living relations who would care. I was supposed to be dead too; let it remain at that. I led a peaceful existence here, neither happy nor unhappy – numbed of all feeling. I see now, though I did not realize it at the time, that that was partly the effect of the War.

'And then one day something occurred to wake me right up again. I was taking a party of people in my boat on a trip up the river, and I was standing at the landing-stage, helping them in, when one of the men uttered a startled exclamation. It focused my attention on him. He was a small, thin man with a beard, and he was staring at me for all he was worth as though I was a ghost. So powerful was his emotion that it awakened my curiosity. I made inquiries about him at the hotel and learned that his name was Carton, that he came from Kimberley, and that he was a diamond-sorter employed by De Beers'. In a minute all the old sense of wrong surged over me again. I left the island and went to Kimberley.

'I could find out little more about him, however. In the end, I decided that I must force an interview. I took my revolver with me. In the brief glimpse I had had of him, I had realized that he was a physical coward. No sooner were we face to face than I recognized that he was afraid of me. I soon forced him to tell me all he knew. He had engineered part of the robbery and Anita Grünberg was his wife. He had once caught sight of both of us when we were dining with her at the hotel, and, having read that I was killed, my appearance in the flesh at the Falls had startled him badly. He and Anita had married quite young, but she had soon drifted away from him. She had got in with a bad lot, he told me – and it was then for the first time that I heard of the "Colonel". Carton himself had never been mixed up in anything except this one affair – so he solemnly assured me, and I was inclined to believe him. He was emphatically not of the stuff of which successful criminals are made.

'I still had the feeling that he was keeping back something. As a test, I threatened to shoot him there and then, declaring that I cared very little what became of me now. In a frenzy of terror he poured out a further story. It seems that Anita Grünberg did not quite trust the "Colonel". Whilst pretending to hand over to him the stones she had taken from the hotel, she kept back some in her own possession. Carton advised her, with his technical knowledge, which to keep. If, at any time, these stones were produced, they were of such colour and quality as to be readily identifiable, and the experts at De Beers' would admit at once that these stones had never passed through their hands. In this way, my story of a substitution would be supported, my name would be cleared, and suspicion would be diverted to the proper quarter. I gathered that, contrary to his usual practice, the "Colonel" himself had been concerned in this affair, therefore Anita felt satisfied that she had a real hold over him, should she need it. Carton now proposed that I should make a bargain with Anita Grünberg, or Nadina, as she now called herself. For a sufficient sum of money, he thought that she would be willing to give up the diamonds and betray her former employer. He would cable to her immediately.

'I was still suspicious of Carton. He was a man whom it was easy enough to frighten, but who, in his fright, would tell so many lies that to sift the truth out from them would be no easy job. I went back to the hotel and waited. By the following evening I judged that he would have received the reply to his cable. I called round to his house and was told that Mr Carton was away, but would be returning on the morrow. Instantly I became suspicious. In the nick of time I found out that he was in reality sailing for England on the *Kilmorden Castle*, which left Cape Town in two days' time. I had just time to journey down and catch the same boat.

'I had no intention of alarming Carton by revealing my presence on board. I had done a good deal of acting in my time at Cambridge, and it was comparatively easy for me to transform myself into a grave bearded gentleman of middle age. I avoided Carton carefully on board the boat, keeping to my own cabin as far as possible under the pretence of illness.

'I had no difficulty in trailing him when we got to London.

He went straight to an hotel and did not go out until the following day. He left the hotel shortly before one o'clock. I was behind him. He went straight to a house-agent in Knightsbridge. There he asked for particulars of houses to let on the river.

'I was at the next table also inquiring about houses. Then suddenly in walked Anita Grünberg, Nadina – whatever you like to call her. Superb, insolent, and almost as beautiful as ever. God! how I hated her. There she was, the woman who had ruined my life – and who had also ruined a better life than mine. At that minute I could have put my hands round her neck and squeezed the life out of her inch by inch! Just for a minute or two I saw red. I hardly took in what the agent was saying. It was her voice that I heard next, high and clear, with an exaggerated foreign accent: "The Mill House, Marlow. The property of Sir Eustace Pedler. That sounds as though it might suit me. At any rate, I will go and see it."

'The man wrote her an order, and she walked out again in her regal insolent manner. Not by word or a sign had she recognized Carton, yet I was sure that their meeting there was a preconceived plan. Then I started to jump to conclusions. Not knowing that Sir Eustace was at Cannes, I thought that this house-hunting business was a mere pretext for meeting him in the Mill House. I knew that he had been in South Africa at the time of the robbery, and never having seen him I immediately leaped to the conclusion that he himself was the mysterious "Colonel" of whom I had heard so much.

'I followed my two suspects along Knightsbridge. Nadina went into the Hyde Park Hotel. I quickened my pace and went in also. She walked straight into the restaurant, and I decided that I would not risk her recognizing me at the moment, but would continue to follow Carton. I was in great hopes that he was going to get the diamonds, and that by suddenly appearing and making myself known to him when he least expected it I might startle the truth out of him. I followed him down into the Tube station at Hyde Park Corner. He was standing by himself at the end of the platform. There was some girl standing near, but no one else. I decided that I would accost him then and there. You know what happened. In the sudden shock of seeing a man whom he imagined far away in South Africa, he lost his head and stepped back upon the line. He was always a coward. Under the pretext of being a doctor, I managed to search his pockets. There was a wallet with some notes in it and one or two unimportant letters, there was a roll of films – which I must have dropped somewhere later – and there was a piece of paper with an appointment made on it for the 22nd on the *Kilmorden Castle*. In my haste to get away before anyone detained me, I dropped that also, but fortunately I remembered the figures.

'I hurried to the nearest cloak-room and hastily removed my make-up. I did not want to be laid by the heels for picking a dead man's pocket. Then I retraced my steps to the Hyde Park Hotel. Nadina was still having lunch. I needn't describe in detail how I followed her down to Marlow. She went into the house, and I spoke to the woman at the lodge, pretending that I was with her. Then I, too, went in.'

He stopped. There was a tense silence.

'You will believe me, Anne, won't you? I swear before God that what I am going to say is true. I went into the house after her with something very like murder in my heart – and she was dead! I found her in that first-floor room – God! It was horrible. Dead – and I was not more than three minutes behind her. And there was no sign of anyone else in the house! Of course I realized at once the terrible position I was in. By one master-stroke the blackmailed had rid himself of the blackmailer, and at the same time had provided a victim to whom the crime would be ascribed. The hand of the "Colonel" was very plain. For the second time I was to be his victim. Fool that I had been to walk into the trap so easily!

'I hardly know what I did next. I managed to go out of the place looking fairly normal, but I knew that it could not be long before the crime was discovered and a description of my appearance telegraphed all over the country.

'I lay low for some days, not daring to make a move. In

the end, chance came to my aid. I overheard a conversation between two middle-aged gentlemen in the street, one of whom proved to be Sir Eustace Pedler. I at once conceived the idea of attaching myself to him as his secretary. The fragment of conversation I had overheard gave me my clue. I was now no longer so sure that Sir Eustace Pedler was the "Colonel". His house might have been appointed as a rendezvous by accident, or for some obscure motive that I had not fathomed.'

'Do you know,' I interrupted, 'that Guy Pagett was in Marlow at the date of the murder?'

'That settles it then. I thought he was at Cannes with Sir Eustace.'

'He was supposed to be in Florence – but he certainly never went *there*. I'm pretty certain he was really in Marlow, but of course I can't prove it.'

'And to think I never suspected Pagett for a minute until the night he tried to throw you overboard. The man's a marvellous actor.'

'Yes, isn't he?'

'That explains why the Mill House was chosen. Pagett could probably get in and out of it unobserved. Of course he made no objection to my accompanying Sir Eustace across in the boat. He didn't want me laid by the heels immediately. You see, evidently Nadina didn't bring the jewels with her to the rendezvous, as they had counted on her doing. I fancy that Carton really had them and concealed them somewhere on the *Kilmorden Castle* – that's where he came in. They hoped that I might have some clue as to where they were hidden. As long as the "Colonel" did not recover the diamonds, he was still in danger – hence his anxiety to get them at all costs. Where the devil Carton hid them – if he did hide them – I don't know.'

'That's another story,' I quoted. '*My story*. And I'm going to tell it to you now.'

CHAPTER XXVII

Harry listened attentively whilst I recounted all the events
that I have narrated in these pages. The thing that bewildered
and astonished him most was to find that all along the diamonds had been in my possession – or rather in Suzanne's.
That was a fact he had never suspected. Of course, after hearing his story, I realized the point of Carton's little arrangement
– or rather Nadina's, since I had no doubt that it was her
brain which had conceived the plan. No surprise tactics
executed against her or her husband could result in the seizure
of the diamonds. The secret was locked in her own brain,
and the 'Colonel' was not likely to guess that they had been
entrusted to the keeping of an ocean steward!

Harry's vindication from the old charge of theft seemed
assured. It was the other graver charge that paralysed all our
activities. For, as things stood, he could not come out in the
open to prove his case.

The one thing we came back to, again and again, was the
identity of the 'Colonel'. Was he, or was he not, Guy Pagett?

'I should say he was but for one thing,' said Harry. 'It
seems pretty much of a certainty that it was Pagett who murdered Anita Grünberg at Marlow – and that certainly lends
colour to the supposition that he is actually the 'Colonel', since
Anita's business was not of the nature to be discussed with a
subordinate. No – the only thing that militates against that
theory is the attempt to put you out of the way the night of
your arrival here. You saw Pagett left behind at Cape Town
– by no possible means could he have arrived here before the
following Wednesday. He is unlikely to have any emissaries
in this part of the world, and all his plans were laid to deal
with you in Cape Town. He might, of course, have cabled
instructions to some lieutenant of his in Johannesburg, who
could have joined the Rhodesian train at Mafeking, but his

instructions would have had to be particularly definite to allow of that note being written.'

We sat silent for a moment, then Harry went on slowly:

'You say that Mrs Blair was asleep when you left the hotel and that you heard Sir Eustace dictating to Miss Pettigrew? Where was Colonel Race?'

'I could not find him anywhere.'

'Had he any reason to believe that – you and I might be friendly with each other?'

'He might have had,' I answered thoughtfully, remembering our conversation on the way back from the Matopos. 'He's a very powerful personality,' I continued, 'but not at all my idea of the "Colonel". And, anyway, such an idea would be absurd. He's in the Secret Service.'

'How do we know that he is? It's the easiest thing in the world to throw out a hint of that kind. No one contradicts it, and the rumour spreads until everyone believes it as gospel truth. It provides an excuse for all sorts of doubtful doings. Anne, do you like Race?'

'I do – and I don't. He repels me and at the same time fascinates me; but I know one thing, I'm always a little afraid of him.'

'He was in South Africa, you know, at the time of the Kimberley robbery,' said Harry slowly.

'But it was he who told Suzanne all about the "Colonel" and how he had been in Paris trying to get on his track.'

'*Camouflage* – of a particularly clever kind.'

'But where does Pagett come in? Is he in Race's pay?'

'Perhaps,' said Harry slowly, 'he doesn't come in at all.'

'What?'

'Think back, Anne. Did you ever hear Pagett's own account of that night on the *Kilmorden*?'

'Yes – through Sir Eustace.'

I repeated it. Harry listened closely.

'He saw a man coming from the direction of Sir Eustace's cabin and followed him up on deck. Is that what he says? Now, who had the cabin opposite to Sir Eustace? Colonel

Race. Supposing Colonel Race crept up on deck, and, foiled in his attack on you, fled round the deck and met Pagett just coming through the saloon door. He knocks him down and springs inside, closing the door. We dash round and find Pagett lying there. How's that?'

'You forget that he declares positively it was you who knocked him down.'

'Well, suppose that just as he regains consciousness he sees me disappearing in the distance? Wouldn't he take it for granted that I was his assailant? Especially as he thought all along it was I he was following?'

'It's possible, yes,' I said slowly. 'But it alters all our ideas. And there are other things.'

'Most of them are open to explanation. The man who followed you in Cape Town spoke to Pagett, and Pagett looked at his watch. The man might have merely asked him the time.'

'It was just a coincidence, you mean?'

'Not exactly. There's a method in all this, connecting Pagett with the affair. Why was the Mill House chosen for the murder? Was it because Pagett had been in Kimberley when the diamonds were stolen? Would *he* have been made the scapegoat if I had not appeared so providentially upon the scene?'

'Then you think he may be entirely innocent?'

'It looks like it, but, if so, we've got to find out what he was doing in Marlow. If he's got a reasonable explanation of that, we're on the right tack.'

He got up.

'It's past midnight. Turn in, Anne, and get some sleep. Just before dawn I'll take you over in the boat. You must catch the train at Livingstone. I've got a friend there who will keep you hidden away until the train starts. You go to Bulawayo and catch the Beira train there. I can find out from my friend in Livingstone what's going on at the hotel and where your friends are now.'

'Beira,' I said meditatively.

'Yes, Anne, it's Beira for you. This is man's work. Leave it to me.'

We had had a momentary respite from emotion whilst we talked the situation out, but it was on us again now. We did not even look at each other.

'Very well,' I said, and passed into the hut.

I lay down on the skin-covered couch, but I didn't sleep, and outside I could hear Harry Rayburn pacing up and down, up and down through the long dark hours. At last he called me:

'Come, Anne, it's time to go.'

I got up and came out obediently. It was still quite dark, but I knew that dawn was not far off.

'We'll take the canoe, not the motor-boat –' Harry began, when suddenly he stopped dead and held up his hand.

'Hush! What's that?'

I listened, but could hear nothing. His ears were sharper than mine, however, the ears of a man who has lived long in the wilderness. Presently I heard it too – the faint splash of paddles in the water coming from the direction of the right bank of the river and rapidly approaching our little landing-stage.

We strained our eyes in the darkness, and could make out a dark blur on the surface of the water. It was a boat. Then there was a momentary spurt of flame. Someone had struck a match. By its light I recognized one figure, the red-bearded Dutchman of the villa at Muizenberg. The others were natives.

'Quick – back to the hut.'

Harry swept me back with him. He took down a couple of rifles and a revolver from the wall.

'Can you load a rifle?'

'I never have. Show me how.'

I grasped his instructions well enough. We closed the door and Harry stood by the window which overlooked the landing-stage. The boat was just about to run alongside it.

'Who's that?' called out Harry, in a ringing voice.

Any doubt we might have had as to our visitors' intentions was swiftly resolved. A hail of bullets splattered round us. Fortunately neither of us was hit. Harry raised the rifle. It spat murderously, and again and again. I heard two groans and a splash.

'That's given 'em something to think about,' he muttered grimly, as he reached for the second rifle. 'Stand well back, Anne, for God's sake. And load quickly.'

More bullets. One just grazed Harry's cheek. His answering fire was more deadly than theirs. I had the rifle reloaded when he turned for it. He caught me close with his left arm and kissed me once savagely before he turned to the window again. Suddenly he uttered a shout.

'They're going – had enough of it. They're a good mark out there on the water, and they can't see how many of us there are. They're routed for the moment – but they'll come back. We'll have to get ready for them.' He flung down the rifle and turned to me.

'Anne! You beauty! You wonder! You little queen! As brave as a lion. Black-haired witch!'

He caught me in his arms. He kissed my hair, my eyes, my mouth.

'And now to business,' he said, suddenly releasing me. 'Get out those tins of paraffin.'

I did as I was told. He was busy inside the hut. Presently I saw him on the roof of the hut, crawling along with something in his arms. He rejoined me in a minute or two.

'Go down to the boat. We'll have to carry it across the island to the other side.'

He picked up the paraffin as I disappeared.

'They're coming back,' I called softly. I had seen the blur moving out from the opposite shore.

He ran down to me.

'Just in time. Why – where the hell's the boat?'

Both had been cut adrift. Harry whistled softly.

'We're in a tight place, honey. Mind?'

'Not with you.'

'Ah, but dying together's not much fun. We'll do better than that. See – they've got two boat-loads this time. Going to land at two different points. Now for my little scenic effect.'

Almost as he spoke a long flame shot up from the hut. Its light illuminated two crouching figures huddled together on the roof.

'My old clothes – stuffed with rags – but they won't tumble to it for some time. Come, Anne, we've got to try desperate means.'

Hand in hand, we raced across the island. Only a narrow channel of water divided it from the shore on that side.

'We've got to swim for it. Can you swim at all, Anne? Not that it matters. I can get you across. It's the wrong side for a boat – too many rocks, but the right side for swimming, and the right side for Livingstone.'

'I can swim a little – further than that. What's the danger, Harry?' For I had seen the grim look on his face. 'Sharks?'

'No, you little goose. Sharks live in the sea. But you're sharp, Anne. Crocs, that's the trouble.'

'Crocodiles?'

'Yes, don't think of them – or say your prayers, whichever you feel inclined.'

We plunged in. My prayers must have been efficacious, for we reached the shore without adventure, and drew ourselves up wet and dripping on the bank.

'Now for Livingstone. It's rough going, I'm afraid, and wet clothes won't make it any better. But it's got to be done.'

That walk was a nightmare. My wet skirts flapped round my legs, and my stockings were soon torn off by the thorns. Finally, I stopped, utterly exhausted. Harry came back to me.

'Hold up, honey. I'll carry you for a bit.'

That was the way I came into Livingstone, slung across his shoulder like a sack of coals. How he did it for all that way, I don't know. The first faint light of dawn was just breaking. Harry's friend was a young man of twenty years old who kept a store of native curios. His name was Ned – perhaps he had another, but I never heard it. He didn't seem in the least surprised to see Harry walk in, dripping wet, holding an equally dripping female by the hand. Men are very wonderful.

He gave us food to eat, and hot coffee, and got our clothes dried for us whilst we rolled ourselves in Manchester blankets of gaudy hue. In the tiny back room of the hut we were safe from observation whilst he departed to make judicious inquiries as to what had become of Sir Eustace's party, and whether any of them were still at the hotel.

It was then that I informed Harry that nothing would induce me to go to Beira. I never meant to, anyway, but now all reason for such proceedings had vanished. The point of the plan had been that my enemies believed me dead. Now that they knew I wasn't dead, my going to Beira would do no good whatever. They could easily follow me there and murder me quietly. I should have no one to protect me. It was finally arranged that I should join Suzanne, wherever she was, and devote all my energies to taking care of myself. On no account was I to seek adventures or endeavour to checkmate the 'Colonel'.

I was to remain quietly with her and await instructions from Harry. The diamonds were to be deposited in the Bank at Kimberley under the name of Parker.

'There's one thing,' I said thoughtfully, 'we ought to have a code of some kind. We don't want to be hoodwinked again by messages purporting to come from one to the other.'

'That's easy enough. Any message that comes *genuinely* from me will have the word "and" crossed out in it.'

'Without trade-mark, none genuine,' I murmured. 'What about wires?'

'Any wires from me will be signed "Andy".'

'Train will be in before long, Harry,' said Ned, putting his head in, and withdrawing it immediately.

I stood up.

'And shall I marry a nice steady man if I find one?' I asked demurely.

Harry came close to me.

'My God! Anne, if you ever marry anyone else but me, I'll wring his neck. And as for you –'

'Yes,' I said, pleasurably excited.

'I shall carry you away and beat you black and blue!'

'What a delightful husband I have chosen!' I said satirically. 'And doesn't he change his mind overnight!'

CHAPTER XXVIII

(Extract from the diary of Sir Eustace Pedler)

As I remarked once before, I am essentially a man of peace. I yearn for a quiet life – and that's just the one thing I don't seem able to have. I am always in the middle of storms and alarms. The relief of getting away from Pagett with his incessant nosing out of intrigues was enormous, and Miss Pettigrew is certainly a useful creature. Although there is nothing of the houri about her, one or two of her accomplishments are invaluable. It is true that I had a touch of liver at Bulawayo and behaved like a bear in consequence, but I had had a disturbed night in the train. At 3 A.M. an exquisitely dressed young man looking like a musical-comedy hero of the Wild West entered my compartment and asked where I was going. Disregarding my first murmur of 'Tea – and for God's sake don't put sugar in it,' he repeated his question, laying stress on the fact that he was not a waiter but an Immigration officer. I finally succeeded in satisfying him that I was suffering from no infectious disease, that I was visiting Rhodesia from the purest of motives, and further gratified him with my full Christian names and my place of birth. I then endeavoured to snatch a little sleep, but some officious ass aroused me at 5.30 with a cup of liquid sugar which he called tea. I don't think I threw it at him, but I know that that was what I wanted to do. He brought me unsugared tea, stone cold, at 6, and I then fell asleep utterly exhausted, to awaken just outside Bulawayo and be landed with a beastly wooden giraffe, all legs and neck!

But for these small contretemps, all had been going smoothly. And then fresh calamity befell.

It was the night of our arrival at the Falls. I was dictating to Miss Pettigrew in my sitting-room, when suddenly Mrs

Blair burst in without a word of excuse and wearing most compromising attire.

'Where's Anne?' she cried.

A nice question to ask. As though I were responsible for the girl. What did she expect Miss Pettigrew to think? That I was in the habit of producing Anne Beddingfeld from my pocket at midnight or thereabouts? Very compromising for a man in my position.

'I presume,' I said coldly, 'that she is in her bed.'

I cleared my throat and glanced at Miss Pettigrew, to show that I was ready to resume dictating. I hoped Mrs Blair would take the hint. She did nothing of the kind. Instead she sank into a chair, and waved a slippered foot in an agitated manner.

'She's not in her room. I've been there. I had a dream – a terrible dream – that she was in some awful danger, and I got up and went to her room, just to reassure myself, you know. She wasn't there and her bed hadn't been slept in.'

She looked at me appealingly.

'What shall I do, Sir Eustace?'

Repressing the desire to reply, 'Go to bed, and don't worry over nothing. An able-bodied young woman like Anne Beddingfeld is perfectly well able to take care of herself,' I frowned judicially.

'What does Race say about it?'

Why should Race have it all his own way? Let him have some of the disadvantages as well as the advantages of female society.

'I can't find him anywhere.'

She was evidently making a night of it. I sighed, and sat down in a chair.

'I don't quite see the reason for your agitation,' I said patiently.

'My dream –'

'That curry we had for dinner!'

'Oh, Sir Eustace!'

The woman was quite indignant. And yet everybody knows that nightmares are a direct result of injudicious eating.

'After all,' I continued persuasively, 'why shouldn't Anne Beddingfeld and Race go out for a little stroll without having the whole hotel aroused about it?'

'You think they've just gone out for a stroll together? But it's after midnight?'

'One does these foolish things when one is young,' I murmured, 'though Race is certainly old enough to know better.'

'Do you really think so?'

'I dare say they've run away to make a match of it,' I continued soothingly, though fully aware that I was making an idiotic suggestion. For, after all, at a place like this, where is there to run away to?

I don't know how much longer I should have gone on making feeble remarks, but at that moment Race himself walked in upon us. At any rate, I had been partly right – *he* had been out for a stroll, but he hadn't taken Anne with him. However, I had been quite wrong in my way of dealing with the situation. I was soon shown that. Race had the whole hotel turned upside-down in three minutes. I've never seen a man more upset.

The thing is very extraordinary. Where did the girl go? She walked out of the hotel, full dressed, about ten minutes past eleven, and she was never seen again. The idea of suicide seems impossible. She was one of these energetic young women who are in love with life, and have not the faintest intention of quitting it. There was no train either way until midday on the morrow, so she can't have left the place. Then where the devil is she?

Race is almost beside himself, poor fellow. He has left no stone unturned. All the DC's, or whatever they call themselves, for hundreds of miles round have been pressed into the service. The native trackers have run about on all fours. Everything that can be done is being done – but no sign of Anne Beddingfeld. The accepted theory is that she walked in her sleep. There are signs on the path near the bridge which seem to show that the girl walked deliberately off the edge. If so, of course, she must have been dashed to pieces on the rocks below. Unfortunately, most of the footprints were obliterated by a party of tourists who chose to walk that way early on the Monday morning.

I don't know that it's a very satisfactory theory. In my young days, I was always told that sleep-walkers couldn't hurt themselves – that their own sixth sense took care of them. I don't think the theory satisfies Mrs Blair either.

I can't make that woman out. Her whole attitude towards Race has changed. She watches him now like a cat a mouse, and she makes obvious efforts to bring herself to be civil to him. And they used to be such friends. Altogether she is unlike herself, nervous, hysterical, starting and jumping at the least sound. I am beginning to think that it is high time I went to Jo'burg.

A rumour came along yesterday of a mysterious island somewhere up the river, with a man and a girl on it. Race got very excited. It turned out to be all a mare's nest however. The man had been there for years, and is well known to the manager of the hotel. He takes parties up and down the river in the season and points out crocodiles and a stray hippopotamus or so to them. I believe that he keeps a tame one which is trained to bite pieces out of the boat on occasions. Then he fends it off with a boathook, and the party feel they have really got to the back of beyond at last. How long the girl has been there is not definitely known, but it seems pretty clear that she can't be Anne, and there is a certain delicacy in interfering in other people's affairs. If I were this young fellow, I should certainly kick Race off the island if he came asking questions about my love affairs.

Later.

It is definitely settled that I go to Jo'burg tomorrow. Race urges me to do so. Things are getting unpleasant there, by all I hear, but I might as well go before they get worse. I dare say I shall be shot by a striker, anyway. Mrs Blair was to have accompanied me, but at the last minute she changed her mind and decided to stay on at the Falls. It seems as though she couldn't bear to take her eyes off Race. She came to me tonight, and said, with some hesitation, that she had a favour to ask. Would I take charge of her souvenirs for her?

'Not the animals?' I asked, in lively alarm. I always felt that I should get stuck with those beastly animals sooner or later.

In the end, we effected a compromise. I took charge of two small wooden boxes for her which contained fragile articles. The animals are to be packed by the local store in vast crates and sent to Cape Town by rail, where Pagett will see to their being stored.

The people who are packing them say that they are of a particularly awkward shape (!), and that special cases will have to be made. I pointed out to Mrs Blair that by the time she has got them home those animals will have cost her easily a pound apiece!

Pagett is straining at the leash to rejoin me in Jo'burg. I shall make an excuse of Mrs Blair's cases to keep him in Cape Town. I have written him that he must receive the cases and see to their safe disposal, as they contain rare curios of immense value.

So all is settled, and I and Miss Pettigrew go off into the blue together. And anyone who has seen Miss Pettigrew will admit that it is perfectly respectable.

CHAPTER XXIX

Johannesburg, *March 6th*.

There is something about the state of things here that is not at all healthy. To use the well-known phrase that I have so often read, we are all living on the edge of a volcano. Bands of strikers, or so-called strikers, patrol the streets and scowl at one in a murderous fashion. They are picking out the bloated capitalists ready for when the massacres begin, I suppose. You can't ride in a taxi – If you do, strikers pull you out again. And the hotels hint pleasantly that when the food gives out they will fling you out on the mat!

I met Reeves, my labour friend of the *Kilmorden*, last night. He has cold feet worse than any man I ever saw. He's like all the rest of these people; they make inflammatory speeches of enormous length, solely for political purposes, and then wish they hadn't. He's busy now going about and saying he didn't really do it. When I met him, he was just off to Cape Town, where he meditates making a three days' speech in Dutch, vindicating himself, and pointing out that the things he said really meant something entirely different. I am thankful that I do not have to sit in the Legislative Assembly of South Africa. The House of Commons is bad enough, but at least we have only one language, and some slight restriction as to length of speeches. When I went to the Assembly before leaving Cape Town, I listened to a grey-haired gentleman with a drooping moustache who looked exactly like the Mock Turtle in *Alice in Wonderland*. He dropped out his words one by one in a particularly melancholy fashion. Every now and then he galvanized himself to further efforts by ejaculating something that sounded like 'Platt Skeet', uttered *fortissimo* and in marked contrast to the rest of his delivery. When he did this, half his audience yelled 'whoof, whoof!' which is possibly Dutch for

'Hear, hear', and the other half woke up with a start from the pleasant nap they had been having. I was given to understand that the gentleman had been speaking for at least three days. They must have a lot of patience in South Africa.

I have invented endless jobs to keep Pagett in Cape Town, but at last the fertility of my imagination has given out, and he joins me tomorrow in the spirit of the faithful dog who comes to die by his master's side. And I was getting on so well with my Reminiscences too! I had invented some extraordinarily witty things that the strike leaders said to me and I said to the strike leaders.

This morning I was interviewed by a Government official. He was urbane, persuasive and mysterious in turn. To begin with, he alluded to my exalted position and importance, and suggested that I should remove myself, or be removed by him, to Pretoria.

'You expect trouble, then?' I asked.

His reply was so worded as to have no meaning whatsoever, so I gathered that they were expecting serious trouble. I suggested to him that his Government were letting things go rather too far.

'There is such a thing as giving a man enough rope, and letting him hang himself, Sir Eustace.'

'Oh, quite so, quite so.'

'It is not the strikers themselves who are causing the trouble. There is some organization at work behind them. Arms and explosives have been pouring in, and we have made a haul of certain documents which throw a good deal of light on the methods adopted to import them. There is a regular code. Potatoes mean "detonators", cauliflower, "rifles", other vegetables stand for various explosives.'

'That's very interesting,' I commented.

'More than that, Sir Eustace, we have every reason to believe that the man who runs the whole show, the directing genius of the affair, is at this minute in Johannesburg.'

He stared at me so hard that I began to fear that he suspected me of being the man. I broke out into a cold perspiration at the thought, and began to regret that I had ever conceived the idea of inspecting a miniature revolution at first hand.

'No trains are running from Jo'burg to Pretoria,' he continued. 'But I can arrange to send you over by private car. In case you should be stopped on the way, I can provide you with two separate passes, one issued by the Union Government, and the other stating that you are an English visitor who has nothing whatsoever to do with the Union.'

'One for your people, and one for the strikers, eh?'

'Exactly.'

The project did not appeal to me – I know what happens in a case of that kind. You get flustered and mix the things up. I should hand the wrong pass to the wrong person, and it would end in my being summarily shot by a bloodthirsty rebel, or one of the supporters of law and order whom I notice guarding the streets wearing bowler hats and smoking pipes, with rifles tucked carelessly under their arms. Besides, what should I do with myself in Pretoria? Admire the architecture of the Union buildings, and listen to the echoes of the shooting round Johannesburg? I should be penned up there God knows how long. They've blown up the railway line already, I hear. It isn't even as if one could get a drink there. They put the place under martial law two days ago.

'My dear fellow,' I said, 'you don't seem to realize that I'm studying conditions on the Rand. How the devil am I going to study them from Pretoria? I appreciate your care for my safety, but don't worry about me, I shall be all right.'

'I warn you, Sir Eustace, that the food question is already serious.'

'A little fasting will improve my figure,' I said, with a sigh.

We were interrupted by a telegram being handed to me. I read it with amazement.

'Anne is safe. Here with me at Kimberley. Suzanne Blair.'

I don't think I ever really believed in the annihilation of Anne. There is something peculiarly indestructible about that young woman – she is like the patent balls that one gives to terriers. She has an extraordinary knack of turning up smiling. I still don't see why it was necessary for her to walk out of the hotel in the middle of the night in order to get to Kimberley. There was no train, anyway. She must have put on a pair of angel's wings and flown there. And I don't suppose she will ever explain. Nobody does – to me. I always have to guess. It becomes monotonous after a while. The exigencies of journalism are at the bottom of it, I suppose. 'How I shot the rapids,' by our Special Correspondent.

I refolded the telegram and got rid of my Governmental friend. I don't like the prospect of being hungry, but I'm not alarmed for my personal safety. Smuts is perfectly capable of dealing with the revolution. But I would give a considerable sum of money for a drink! I wonder if Pagett will have the sense to bring a bottle of whisky with him when he arrives tomorrow?

I put on my hat and went out, intending to buy a few souvenirs. The curio-shops in Jo'burg are rather pleasant. I was just studying a window full of imposing karosses, when a man coming out of the shop cannoned into me. To my surprise it turned out to be Race.

I can't flatter myself that he looked pleased to see me. As a matter of fact, he looked distinctly annoyed, but I insisted on his accompanying me back to the hotel. I get tired of having no one but Miss Pettigrew to talk to.

'I had no idea you were in Jo'burg,' I said chattily. 'When did you arrive?'

'Last night.'

'Where are you staying?'

'With friends.'

He was disposed to be extraordinarily taciturn, and seemed to be embarrassed by my questions.

'I hope they keep poultry,' I remarked. 'A diet of newlaid eggs, and the occasional slaughtering of an old cock, will be decidedly agreeable soon, from all I hear.'

'By the way,' I said, when we were back in the hotel, 'have you heard that Miss Beddingfeld is alive and kicking?'

He nodded.

'She gave us quite a fright,' I said airily. 'Where the devil did she go to that night, that's what I'd like to know.'

'She was on the island all the time.'

'Which island? Not the one with the young man on it?'

'Yes.'

'How very improper,' I said. 'Pagett will be quite shocked. He always did disapprove of Anne Beddingfeld. I suppose that was the young man she originally intended to meet in Durban?'

'I don't think so.'

'Don't tell me anything if you don't want to,' I said, by way of encouraging him.

'I fancy that this is a young man we should all be very glad to lay our hands on.'

'Not –?' I cried, in rising excitement.

He nodded.

'Harry Rayburn, *alias* Harry Lucas – that's his real name, you know. He's given us all the slip once more, but we're bound to rope him in soon.'

'Dear me, dear me,' I murmured.

'We don't suspect the girl of complicity in any case. On her side it's – just a love-affair.'

I always did think Race was in love with Anne. The way he said those last words made me feel sure of it.

'She's gone to Beira,' he continued rather hastily.

'Indeed,' I said, staring. 'How do you know?'

'She wrote to me from Bulawayo, telling me she was going home that way. The best thing she can do, poor child.'

'Somehow, I don't fancy she is in Beira,' I said meditatively.

'She was just starting when she wrote.'

I was puzzled. Somebody was clearly lying. Without stopping to reflect that Anne might have excellent reasons for her misleading statements, I gave myself up to the pleasure of scoring off Race. He is always so cocksure. I took the telegram from my pocket and handed it to him.

'Then how do you explain this?' I asked nonchalantly.

He seemed dumbfounded. 'She said she was just starting for Beira,' he said, in a dazed voice.

I know that Race is supposed to be clever. He is, in my opinion, rather a stupid man. It never seemed to occur to him that girls do not always tell the truth.

'Kimberley too. What are they doing there?' he muttered.

'Yes, that surprised me. I should have thought Miss Anne would have been in the thick of it here, gathering copy for the *Daily Budget*.'

'Kimberley,' he said again. The place seemed to upset him. 'There's nothing to see there – the pits aren't being worked.'

'You know what women are,' I said vaguely.

He shook his head and went off. I have evidently given him something to think about.

No sooner had he departed than my Government official reappeared.

'I hope you will forgive me for troubling you again, Sir Eustace,' he apologized. 'But there are one or two questions I should like to ask you.'

'Certainly, my dear fellow,' I said cheerfully. 'Ask away.'

'It concerns your secretary –'

'I know nothing about him,' I said hastily. 'He foisted himself upon me in London, robbed me of valuable papers – for which I shall be hauled over the coals – and disappeared like a conjuring trick at Cape Town. It's true that I was at the Falls at the same time as he was, but I was at the hotel, and he was on an island. I can assure you that I never set eyes upon him the whole time that I was there.'

I paused for breath.

'You misunderstand me. It was of your other secretary that I spoke.'

'What? Pagett?' I cried, in lively astonishment. 'He's been with me eight years – a most trustworthy fellow.'

My interlocutor smiled.

'We are still at cross-purposes. I refer to the lady.'

'Miss Pettigrew?' I exclaimed.

'Yes. She has been seen coming out of Agrasato's Native Curio-shop.'

'God bless my soul!' I interrupted. 'I was going into that place myself this afternoon. You might have caught *me* coming out!'

There doesn't seem to be any innocent thing that one can do in Jo'burg without being suspected for it.

'Ah! but she has been seen there more than once – and in rather doubtful circumstances. I may as well tell you – in confidence, Sir Eustace – that the place is suspected of being a well-known rendezvous used by the secret organization behind this revolution. That is why I should be glad to hear all that you can tell me about this lady. Where and how did you come to engage her?'

'She was lent to me,' I replied coldly, 'by your own Government.'

He collapsed utterly.

CHAPTER XXX

(Anne's Narrative Resumed)

As soon as I got to Kimberley I wired to Suzanne. She joined me there with the utmost dispatch, heralding her arrival with telegrams sent off *en route*. I was awfully surprised to find that she really was fond of me – I thought I had been just a new sensation, but she positively fell on my neck and wept when we met.

When we had recovered from our emotion a little, I sat down on the bed and told her the whole story from A to Z.

'You always did suspect Colonel Race,' she said thoughtfully, when I had finished. 'I didn't until the night you disappeared. I liked him so much all along and thought he would make such a nice husband for you. Oh, Anne, dear, don't be cross, but how do you know that this young man of yours is telling the truth? You believe every word he says.'

'Of course I do,' I cried indignantly.

'But what is there in him that attracts you so? I don't see that there's anything in him at all except his rather reckless good looks and his modern Sheik-cum-Stone-Age lovemaking.'

I poured out the vials of my wrath upon Suzanne for some minutes.

'Just because you're comfortably married and getting fat, you've forgotten that there's any such thing as romance,' I ended.

'Oh, I'm not getting fat, Anne. All the worry I've had about you lately must have worn me to a shred.'

'You look particularly well nourished,' I said coldly. 'I should say you must have put on about half a stone.'

'And I don't know that I'm so comfortably married either,' continued Suzanne in a melancholy voice. 'I've been having the most dreadful cables from Clarence ordering me to come home at once. At last I didn't answer them, and now I haven't heard for over a fortnight.'

I'm afraid I didn't take Suzanne's matrimonial troubles very seriously. She will be able to get round Clarence all right when the time comes. I turned the conversation to the subject of the diamonds.

Suzanne looked at me with a dropped jaw.

'I must explain, Anne. You see, as soon as I began to suspect Colonel Race, I was terribly upset about the diamonds. I wanted to stay on at the Falls in case he might have kidnapped you somewhere close by, but didn't know what to do about the diamonds. I was afraid to keep them in my possession –'

Suzanne looked round her uneasily, as though she feared the walls might have ears, and then whispered vehemently in my ear.

'A distinctly good idea,' I approved. 'At the time, that is. It's a bit awkward now. What did Sir Eustace do with the cases?'

'The big ones were sent down to Cape Town. I heard from Pagett before I left the Falls, and he enclosed the receipt for their storage. He's leaving Cape Town today by the by, to join Sir Eustace in Johannesburg.'

'I see,' I said thoughtfully. 'And the small ones, where are they?'

'I suppose Sir Eustace has got them with him.'

I turned the matter over in my mind.

'Well,' I said at last, 'it's awkward – but it's safe enough. We'd better do nothing for the present.'

Suzanne looked at me with a little smile.

'You don't like doing nothing, do you, Anne?'

'Not very much,' I replied honestly.

The one thing I could do was to get hold of a time-table and see what time Guy Pagett's train would pass through Kimberley. I found that it would arrive at 5.40 on the following afternoon and depart again at 6. I wanted to see Pagett as soon as possible, and that seemed to me a good opportunity.

The situation on the Rand was getting very serious, and it might be a long time before I got another chance.

The only thing that livened up the day was a wire dispatched from Johannesburg. A most innocent-sounding telegram:

'Arrived safely. All going well. Eric here, also Eustace, but not Guy. Remain where you are for the present. Andy.'

Eric was our pseudonym for Race. I chose it because it is a name I dislike exceedingly. There was clearly nothing to be done until I could see Pagett. Suzanne employed herself in sending off a long soothing cable to the far-off Clarence. She became quite sentimental over him. In her way – which of course is quite different from me and Harry – she is really fond of Clarence.

'I do wish he was here, Anne,' she gulped. 'It's such a long time since I've seen him.'

'Have some face-cream,' I said soothingly.

Suzanne rubbed a little on the tip of her charming nose.

'I shall want some more face-cream soon too,' she remarked, 'and you can only get this kind in Paris.' She sighed. 'Paris!'

'Suzanne,' I said, 'very soon you'll have had enough of South Africa and adventure.'

'I should like a really nice hat,' admitted Suzanne wistfully. 'Shall I come with you to meet Guy Pagett tomorrow?'

'I prefer to go alone. He'd be shyer speaking before two of us.'

So it came about that I was standing in the doorway of the hotel on the following afternoon, struggling with a recalcitrant parasol that refused to go up, whilst Suzanne lay peacefully on her bed with a book and a basket of fruit.

According to the hotel porter, the train was on its good behaviour today and would be almost on time, though he was extremely doubtful whether it would ever get through to Johannesburg. The line had been blown up, so he solemnly assured me. It sounded cheerful!

The train drew in just ten minutes late. Everybody tumbled

out on the platform and began walking up and down feverishly. I had no difficulty in espying Pagett. I accosted him
eagerly. He gave his usual nervous start at seeing me – somewhat accentuated this time.

'Dear me, Miss Beddingfeld, I understood that you had
disappeared.'

'I have reappeared again,' I told him solemnly. 'And how
are you, Mr Pagett?'

'Very well, thank you – looking forward to taking up my
work again with Sir Eustace.'

'Mr Pagett,' I said, 'there is something I want to ask you.
I hope that you won't be offended, but a lot hangs on it, more
than you can possibly guess. I want to know what you were
doing at Marlow on the 8th of January last?'

He started violently.

'Really, Miss Beddingfeld – I – indeed –'

'You *were* there, weren't you?'

'I – for reasons of my own I was in the neighbourhood,
yes.'

'Won't you tell me what those reasons were?'

'Sir Eustace has not already told you?'

'Sir Eustace? Does he know?'

'I am almost sure that he does. I hoped he had not recognized me, but from the hints he has let drop, and his remarks,
I fear it is only too certain. In any case, I meant to make a
clean breast of the matter and offer my resignation. He is a
peculiar man, Miss Beddingfeld, with an abnormal sense of
humour. It seems to amuse him to keep me on tenterhooks.
All the time, I dare say, he was perfectly well aware of the
true facts. Possibly he has known them for years.'

I hoped that sooner or later I should be able to understand
what Pagett was talking about. He went on fluently:

'It is difficult for a man of Sir Eustace's standing to put
himself in my position. I know that I was in the wrong, but
it seemed a harmless deception. I would have thought it better
taste on his part to have tackled me outright – instead of
indulging in covert jokes at my expense.'

A whistle blew, and the people began to surge back into the train.

'Yes, Mr Pagett,' I broke in, 'I'm sure I quite agree with all you're saying about Sir Eustace. *But why did you go to Marlow?*'

'It was wrong of me, but natural under the circumstances – yes, I still feel natural under the circumstances.'

'What circumstances?' I cried desperately.

For the first time, Pagett seemed to recognize that I was asking him a question. His mind detached itself from the peculiarities of Sir Eustace, and his own justification, and came to rest on me.

'I beg your pardon, Miss Beddingfeld,' he said stiffly, 'but I fail to see your concern in the matter.'

He was back in the train now, leaning down to speak to me. I felt desperate. What could one do with a man like that?

'Of course, if it's so dreadful that you'd be ashamed to speak of it to me –' I began spitefully.

At last I had found the right stop. Pagett stiffened and flushed.

'Dreadful? Ashamed? I don't understand you.'

'Then tell me.'

In three short sentences he told me. At last I knew Pagett's secret! It was not in the least what I expected.

I walked slowly back to the hotel. There a wire was handed to me. I tore it open. It contained full and definite instructions for me to proceed forthwith to Johannesburg, or rather to a station this side of Johannesburg, where I should be met by a car. It was signed, not Andy, but Harry.

I sat down in a chair to do some very serious thinking.

CHAPTER XXXI

(From the diary of Sir Eustace Pedler)

Johannesburg, *March 7th.*
Pagett has arrived. He is in a blue funk, of course. Suggested at once that we should go off to Pretoria. Then, when I had told him kindly but firmly that we were going to remain here, he went to the other extreme, wished he had his rifle here, and began bucking about some bridge he guarded during the Great War. A railway bridge at Little Puddecombe junction, or something of that sort.

I soon cut that short by telling him to unpack the big typewriter. I thought that that would keep him employed for some time, because the typewriter was sure to have gone wrong – it always does – and he would have to take it somewhere to be mended. But I had forgotten Pagett's powers of being in the right.

'I've already unpacked all the cases, Sir Eustace. The typewriter is in perfect condition.'

'What do you mean – all the cases?'

'The two small cases as well.'

'I wish you wouldn't be so officious, Pagett. Those small cases were no business of yours. They belong to Mrs Blair.'

Pagett looked crestfallen. He hates to make a mistake.

'So you can just pack them up again neatly,' I continued. 'After that you can go out and look around you. Jo'burg will probably be a heap of smoking ruins by tomorrow, so it may be your last chance.'

I thought that that would get rid of him successfully for the morning, at any rate.

'There is something I want to say to you when you have the leisure, Sir Eustace.'

'I haven't got it now,' I said hastily. 'At this minute I have absolutely no leisure whatsoever.'

Pagett retired.

'By the way,' I called after him, 'what was there in those cases of Mrs Blair's?'

'Some fur rugs, and a couple of fur – hats, I think.'

'That's right,' I assented. 'She bought them on the train. They *are* hats – of a kind – though I hardly wonder at your not recognizing them. I dare say she's going to wear one of them at Ascot. What else was there?'

'Some rolls of films, and some baskets – a lot of baskets –'

'There would be,' I assured him. 'Mrs Blair is the kind of woman who never buys less than a dozen or so of anything.'

'I think that's all, Sir Eustace, except some miscellaneous odds and ends, a motor-veil and some odd gloves – that sort of thing.'

'If you hadn't been a born idiot, Pagett, you would have seen from the start that those couldn't possibly be my belongings.'

'I thought some of them might belong to Miss Pettigrew.'

'Ah, that reminds me – what do you mean by picking me out such a doubtful character as a secretary?'

And I told him about the searching cross-examination I had been put through. Immediately I was sorry, I saw a glint in his eye that I know only too well. I changed the conversation hurriedly. But it was too late. Pagett was on the war-path.

He next proceeded to bore me with a long pointless story about the *Kilmorden*. It was about a roll of films and a wager. The roll of films being thrown through a port-hole in the middle of the night by some steward who ought to have known better. I hate horse-play. I told Pagett so, and he began to tell me the story all over again. He tells a story extremely badly, anyway. It was a long time before I could make head or tail of this one.

I did not see him again until lunch-time. Then he came in brimming over with excitement, like a bloodhound on the scent. I never have cared for bloodhounds. The upshot of it all was that he had seen Rayburn.

'What?' I cried, startled.

Yes, he had caught sight of someone whom he was sure was Rayburn crossing the street. Pagett had followed him.

'And who do you think I saw him stop and speak to? Miss Pettigrew!'

'What?'

'Yes, Sir Eustace. And that's not all. I've been making inquiries about her –'

'Wait a bit. What happened to Rayburn?'

'He and Miss Pettigrew went into that corner curio-shop –'

I uttered an involuntary exclamation. Pagett stopped inquiringly.

'Nothing,' I said. 'Go on.'

'I waited outside for ages – but they didn't come out. At last I went in. Sir Eustace, there was no one in the shop! There must be another way out.'

I stared at him.

'As I was saying, I came back to the hotel and made some inquiries about Miss Pettigrew.' Pagett lowered his voice and breathed hard as he always does when he wants to be confidential. 'Sir Eustace, a man was seen coming out of her room last night.'

I raised my eyebrows.

'And I always regarded her as a lady of such eminent respectability,' I murmured.

Pagett went on without heeding.

'I went straight up and searched her room. What do you think I found?'

I shook my head.

'This!'

Pagett held up a safety razor and a stick of shaving soap.

'What should a woman want with these?'

I don't suppose Pagett ever reads the advertisements in the high-class ladies' papers. I do. Whilst not proposing to argue with him on the subject, I refused to accept the presence of the razor as proof positive of Miss Pettigrew's sex. Pagett is so hopelessly behind the times. I should not have been at all surprised if he had produced a cigarette-case to support his theory. However, even Pagett has his limits.

'You're not convinced, Sir Eustace. What do you say to *this*?'

I inspected the article which he dangled aloft triumphantly.

'It looks like hair,' I remarked distastefully.

'It is hair. I think it's what they call a toupee.'

'Indeed,' I commented.

'Now are you convinced that that Pettigrew woman is a man in disguise?'

'Really, my dear Pagett, I think I am. I might have known it by her feet.'

'Then that's that. And now, Sir Eustace, I want to speak to you about my private affairs. I cannot doubt, from your hints and your continual allusions to the time I was in Florence, that you have found me out.'

At last the mystery of what Pagett did in Florence is going to be revealed!

'Make a clean breast of it, my dear fellow,' I said kindly. 'Much the best way.'

'Thank you, Sir Eustace.'

'Is it her husband? Annoying fellows, husbands. Always turning up when they're least expected.'

'I fail to follow you, Sir Eustace. Whose husband?'

'The lady's husband.'

'What lady?'

'God bless my soul, Pagett, the lady you met in Florence. There must have been a lady. Don't tell me that you merely robbed a church or stabbed an Italian in the back because you didn't like his face.'

'I am quite at a loss to understand you, Sir Eustace. I suppose you are joking.'

'I am an amusing fellow sometimes, when I take the trouble, but I can assure you that I am not trying to be funny this minute.'

'I hoped that as I was a good way off you had not recognized me, Sir Eustace.'

'Recognized you where?'

'At Marlow, Sir Eustace?'

'At Marlow? What the devil were you doing at Marlow?'

'I thought you understood that –'

'I'm beginning to understand less and less. Go back to the beginning of the story and start again. You went to Florence –'

'Then you don't know after all – and you didn't recognize me!'

'As far as I can judge, you seem to have given yourself away needlessly – made a coward of by your conscience. But I shall be able to tell better when I've heard the whole story. Now, then, take a deep breath and start again. You went to Florence –'

'But I didn't go to Florence. That is just it.'

'Well, where did you go, then?'

'I went home – to Marlow.'

'What the devil did you want to go to Marlow for?'

'I wanted to see my wife. She was in delicate health and expecting –'

'Your wife? But I didn't know you were married!'

'No, Sir Eustace, that is just what I am telling you. I deceived you in this matter.'

'How long have you been married?'

'Just over eight years. I had been married just six months when I became your secretary. I did not want to lose the post. A resident secretary is not supposed to have a wife, so I suppressed the fact.'

'You take my breath away,' I remarked. 'Where has she been all these years?'

'We have had a small bungalow on the river at Marlow, quite close to the Mill House, for over five years.'

'God bless my soul,' I muttered. 'Any children?'

'Four children, Sir Eustace.'

I gazed at him in a kind of stupor. I might have known, all along, that a man like Pagett couldn't have a guilty secret. The respectability of Pagett has always been my bane. That's just the kind of secret he would have – a wife and four children.

'Have you told this to anyone else?' I demanded at last, when I had gazed at him in fascinated interest for quite a long while.

'Only Miss Beddingfeld. She came to the station at Kimberley.'

I continued to stare at him. He fidgeted under my glance.

'I hope, Sir Eustace, that you are not seriously annoyed?'

'My dear fellow,' I said, 'I don't mind telling you here and now that you've blinking well torn it!'

I went out seriously ruffled. As I passed the corner curio-shop, I was assailed by a sudden irresistible temptation and went in. The proprietor came forward obsequiously, rubbing his hands.

'Can I show you something? Furs, curios?'

'I want something quite out of the ordinary,' I said. 'It's for a special occasion. Will you show me what you've got?'

'Perhaps you will come into my back room? We have many specialities there.'

That is where I made a mistake. And I thought I was going to be so clever. I followed him through the swinging *portières*.

CHAPTER XXXII

(Anne's Narrative Resumed)

I had great trouble with Suzanne. She argued, she pleaded, she even wept before she would let me carry out my plan. But in the end I got my own way. She promised to carry out my instructions to the letter and came down to the station to bid me a tearful farewell.

I arrived at my destination the following morning early. I was met by a short black-bearded Dutchman whom I had never seen before. He had a car waiting and we drove off. There was a queer booming in the distance, and I asked him what it was. 'Guns,' he answered laconically. So there was fighting going on in Jo'burg!

I gathered that our objective was a spot somewhere in the suburbs of the city. We turned and twisted and made several detours to get there, and every minute the guns were nearer. It was an exciting time. At last we stopped before a somewhat ramshackle building. The door was opened by a Kafir boy. My guide signed to me to enter. I stood irresolute in the dingy square hall. The man passed me and threw open a door.

'The young lady to see Mr Harry Rayburn,' he said, and laughed.

Thus announced, I passed in. The room was sparsely furnished and smelt of cheap tobacco smoke. Behind a desk a man sat writing. He looked up and raised his eyebrows.

'Dear me,' he said, 'if it isn't Miss Beddingfeld!'

'I must be seeing double,' I apologized. 'Is it Mr Chichester, or is it Miss Pettigrew? There is an extraordinary resemblance to both of them.'

'Both characters are in abeyance for the moment. I have doffed my petticoats – and my cloth likewise. Won't you sit down?'

I accepted a seat composedly.

'It would seem,' I remarked, 'that I have come to the wrong address.'

'From your point of view, I am afraid you have. Really, Miss Beddingfeld, to fall into the trap a second time!'

'It was not very bright of me,' I admitted meekly.

Something about my manner seemed to puzzle him.

'You hardly seem upset by the occurrence,' he remarked dryly.

'Would my going into heroics have any effect upon you?' I asked.

'It certainly would not.'

'My Great-aunt Jane always used to say that a true lady was neither shocked nor surprised at anything that might happen,' I murmured dreamily. 'I endeavour to live up to her precepts.'

I read Mr Chichester-Pettigrew's opinion so plainly written on his face that I hastened into speech once more.

'You really are positively marvellous at make-up,' I said generously. 'All the time you were Miss Pettigrew I never recognized you – even when you broke your pencil in the shock of seeing me climb upon the train at Cape Town.'

He tapped upon the desk with the pencil he was holding in his hand at the minute.

'All this is very well in its way, but we must get to business. Perhaps, Miss Beddingfeld, you can guess why we required your presence here?'

'You will excuse me,' I said, 'but I never do business with anyone but principals.'

I had read the phrase or something like it in a moneylender's circular, and I was rather pleased with it. It certainly had a devastating effect upon Mr Chichester-Pettigrew. He opened his mouth and then shut it again. I beamed upon him.

'My Great-uncle George's maxim,' I added, as an afterthought. 'Great-aunt Jane's husband, you know. He made knobs for brass beds.'

I doubt if Chichester-Pettigrew had ever been ragged before. He didn't like it at all.

'I think you would be wise to alter your tone, young lady.'

I did not reply, but yawned – a delicate little yawn that hinted at intense boredom.

'What the devil –' he began forcibly.

I interrupted him.

'I can assure you it's no good shouting at me. We are only wasting time here. I have no intention of talking with underlings. You will save a lot of time and annoyance by taking me straight to Sir Eustace Pedler.'

'To –'

He looked dumbfounded.

'Yes,' I said. 'Sir Eustace Pedler.'

'I – I – excuse me –'

He bolted from the room like a rabbit. I took advantage of the respite to open my bag and powder my nose thoroughly. Also I settled my hat at a more becoming angle. Then I settled myself to wait with patience for my enemy's return.

He reappeared in a subtly chastened mood.

'Will you come this way, Miss Beddingfeld?'

I followed him up the stairs. He knocked at the door of a room, a brisk 'Come in' sounded from inside, and he opened the door and motioned to me to pass inside.

Sir Eustace Pedler sprang up to greet me, genial and smiling.

'Well, well, Miss Anne.' He shook me warmly by the hand. 'I'm delighted to see you. Come and sit down. Not tired after your journey? That's good.'

He sat down facing me, still beaming. It left me rather at a loss. His manner was so completely natural.

'Quite right to insist on being brought straight to me,' he went on. 'Minks is a fool. A clever actor – but a fool. That was Minks you saw downstairs.'

'Oh, really,' I said feebly.

'And now,' said Sir Eustace cheerfully, 'let's get down to facts. How long have you known that I was the "Colonel"?'

'Ever since Mr Pagett told me that he had seen you in Marlow when you were supposed to be in Cannes.'

Sir Eustace nodded ruefully.

'Yes, I told the fool he'd blinking well torn it. He didn't understand, of course. His whole mind was set on whether *I'd* recognized *him*. It never occurred to him to wonder what I was doing down there. A piece of sheer bad luck that was. I arranged it all so carefully too, sending him off to Florence, telling the hotel I was going over to Nice for one night or possibly two. Then, by the time the murder was discovered, I was back again in Cannes, with nobody dreaming that I'd ever left the Riviera.'

He still spoke quite naturally and unaffectedly. I had to pinch myself to understand that this was all real – that the man in front of me was really that deep-dyed criminal, the 'Colonel'. I followed things out in my mind.

'Then it was you who tried to throw me overboard on the *Kilmorden*,' I said slowly. 'It was you that Pagett followed up on deck that night?'

He shrugged his shoulders.

'I apologize, my dear child, I really do. I always liked you – but you were so confoundedly interfering. I couldn't have all my plans brought to naught by a chit of a girl.'

'I think your plan at the Falls was really the cleverest,' I said, endeavouring to look at the thing in a detached fashion. 'I would have been ready to swear anywhere that you were in the hotel when I went out. Seeing is believing in future.'

'Yes, Minks had one of his greatest successes, as Miss Pettigrew, and he can imitate my voice quite creditably.'

'There is one thing I should like to know.'

'Yes?'

'How did you induce Pagett to engage her?'

'Oh, that was quite simple. She met Pagett in the doorway of the Trade Commissioner's office or the Chamber of Mines, or wherever it was he went – told him I had 'phoned down in a hurry, and that she had been selected by the Government department in question. Pagett swallowed it like a lamb.'

'You're very frank,' I said, studying him.

'There's no earthly reason why I shouldn't be.'

I didn't like the sound of that. I hastened to put my own interpretation on it.

'You believe in the success of this Revolution? You've burnt your boats.'

'For an otherwise intelligent young woman, that's a singularly unintelligent remark. No, my dear child, I do not believe in this Revolution. I give it a couple of days longer and it will fizzle out ignominiously.'

'Not one of your successes, in fact?' I said nastily.

'Like all women, you've no idea of business. The job I took on was to supply certain explosives and arms – heavily paid for – to foment feeling generally, and to incriminate certain people up to the hilt. I've carried out my contract with complete success, and I was careful to be paid in advance. I took special care over the whole thing, as I intended it be my last contract before retiring from business. As for burning my boats, as you call it, I simply don't know what you mean. I'm not the rebel chief, or anything of that kind – I'm a distinguished English visitor, who had the misfortune to go nosing into a certain curio-shop – and saw a little more than he was meant to, and so the poor fellow was kidnapped. Tomorrow, or the day after, when circumstances permit, I shall be found tied up somewhere, in a pitiable state of terror and starvation.'

'Ah!' I said slowly. 'But what about me?'

'That's just it,' said Sir Eustace softly. 'What about you? I've got you here – I don't want to rub it in in any way – but I've got you here very neatly. The question is, what am I going to do with you? The simplest way of disposing of you – and, I may add, the pleasantest to myself – is the way of marriage. Wives can't accuse their husbands, you know, and I'd rather like a pretty young wife to hold my hand and glance at me out of liquid eyes – don't flash them at me so! You quite frighten me. I see that the plan does not commend itself to you?'

'It does not.'

Sir Eustace sighed.

'A pity! But I am no Adelphi villain. The usual trouble, I suppose. You love another, as the books say.'

'I love another.'

'I thought as much – first I thought it was that long-legged, pompous ass, Race, but I suppose it's the young hero who fished you out of the Falls that night. Women have no taste. Neither of those two have half the brains that I have. I'm such an easy person to underestimate.'

I think he was right about that. Although I knew well enough the kind of man he was and must be, I could not bring myself to realize it. He had tried to kill me on more than one occasion, he had actually killed another woman, and he was responsible for endless other deeds of which I knew nothing, and yet I was quite unable to bring myself into the frame of mind for appreciating his deeds as they deserved. I could not think of him as other than our amusing, genial travelling companion. I could not even feel frightened of him – and yet I knew he was capable of having me murdered in cold blood if it struck him as necessary. The only parallel I can think of is the case of Stevenson's Long John Silver. He must have been much the same kind of man.

'Well, well,' said this extraordinary person, leaning back in his chair. 'It's a pity that the idea of being Lady Pedler doesn't appeal to you. The other alternatives are rather crude.'

I felt a nasty feeling going up and down my spine. Of course I had known all along that I was taking a big risk, but the prize had seemed worth it. Would things turn out as I had calculated, or would they not?

'The fact of the matter is,' Sir Eustace was continuing, 'I've a weakness for you. I really don't want to proceed to extremes. Suppose you tell me the whole story, from the very beginning, and let's see what we can make of it. But no romancing, mind – I want the truth.'

I was not going to make any mistake over that. I had a great deal of respect for Sir Eustace's shrewdness. It was a moment for the truth, the whole truth, and nothing but the truth. I told him the whole story, omitting nothing, up to the moment of my rescue by Harry. When I had finished, he nodded his head in approval.

'Wise girl. You've made a clean breast of the thing. And let me tell you I should soon have caught you out if you hadn't. A lot of people wouldn't believe your story, anyway, expecially the beginning part, but I do. You're the kind of girl who would start off like that – at a moment's notice, on the slenderest of motives. You've had amazing luck, of course, but sooner or later the amateur runs up against the professional and then the result is a foregone conclusion. I am the professional. I started on this business when I was quite a youngster. All things considered, it seemed to me a good way of getting rich quickly. I always could think things out and devise ingenious schemes – and I never made the mistake of trying to carry out my schemes myself. Always employ the expert – that has been my motto. The one time I departed from it I came to grief – but I couldn't trust anyone to do that job for me. Nadina knew too much. I'm an easy-going man, kind-hearted and good-tempered so long as I'm not thwarted. Nadina both thwarted me and threatened me – just as I was at the apex of a successful career. Once she was dead and the diamonds were in my possession, I was safe. I've come to the conclusion now that I bungled the job. That idiot Pagett, with his wife and family! My fault – it tickled my sense of humour to employ the fellow, with his Cinquecento poisoner's face and his mid-Victorian soul. A maxim for you, my dear Anne. Don't let your sense of humour carry you away. For years I've had an instinct that it would be wise to get rid of Pagett, but the fellow was so hard-working and conscientious that I honestly couldn't find an excuse for sacking him. So I let things drift.

'But we're wandering from the point. The question is what to do with you. Your narrative was admirably clear, but there is one thing that still escapes me. Where are the diamonds now?'

'Harry Rayburn has them,' I said, watching him.

His face did not change, it retained its expression of sardonic good-humour.

'H'm. I want those diamonds.'

'I don't see much chance of your getting them,' I replied.

'Don't you? Now I do. I don't want to be unpleasant, but I should like you to reflect that a dead girl or so found in this quarter of the city will occasion no surprise. There's a man downstairs who does those sort of jobs very neatly. Now, you're a sensible young woman. What I propose is this: you will sit down and write to Harry Rayburn, telling him to join you here and bring the diamonds with him –'

'I won't do anything of the kind.'

'Don't interrupt your elders. I propose to make a bargain with you. The diamonds in exchange for your life. And don't make any mistake about it, your life is absolutely in my power.'

'And Harry?'

'I'm far too tender-hearted to part two young lovers. He shall go free too – on the understanding, of course, that neither of you interfere with me in the future.'

'And what guarantee have I that you will keep your side of the bargain?'

'None whatever, my dear girl. You'll have to trust me and hope for the best. Of course, if you're in an heroic mood and prefer annihilation, that's another matter.'

This was what I had been playing for. I was careful not to jump at the bait. Gradually I allowed myself to be bullied and cajoled into yielding. I wrote at Sir Eustace's dictation:

'Dear Harry,

I think I see a chance of establishing your innocence beyond any possible doubt. Please follow my instructions minutely. Go to Agrasato's curio-shop. Ask to see something "out of the ordinary", "for a special occasion". The man will then ask you to "come into the back room". Go with him. You will find a messenger who will bring you to me. Do exactly as he tells you. Be sure and bring the diamonds with you. Not a word to anyone.'

Sir Eustace stopped.

'I leave the fancy touches to your own imagination,' he remarked. 'But be careful to make no mistakes.'

'"Yours for ever and ever, Anne," will be sufficient,' I remarked.

I wrote in the words. Sir Eustace stretched out his hand for the letter and read it through.

'That seems all right. Now the address.'

I gave it him. It was that of a small shop which received letters and telegrams for a consideration.

He struck the bell upon the table with his hand. Chichester-Pettigrew, *alias* Minks, answered the summons.

'This letter is to go immediately – the usual route.'

'Very well, Colonel.'

He looked at the name on the envelope. Sir Eustace was watching him keenly.

'A friend of yours, I think?'

'Of mine?' The man seemed startled.

'You had a prolonged conversation with him in Johannesburg yesterday.'

'A man came up and questioned me about your movements and those of Colonel Race. I gave him misleading information.'

'Excellent, my dear fellow, excellent,' said Sir Eustace genially. 'My mistake.'

I chanced to look at Chichester-Pettigrew as he left the room. He was white to the lips, as though in deadly terror. No sooner was he outside, than Sir Eustace picked up a speaking-tube that rested by his elbow, and spoke down it. 'That you, Schwart? Watch Minks. He's not to leave the house without orders.'

He put the speaking-tube down again, and frowned, slightly tapping the table with his hand.

'May I ask you a few questions, Sir Eustace,' I said, after a minute or two of silence.

'Certainly. What excellent nerves you have, Anne! You are capable of taking an intelligent interest in things when most girls would be sniffling and wringing their hands.'

'Why did you take Harry as your secretary instead of giving him up to the police?'

'I wanted those cursed diamonds. Nadina, the little devil, was playing off your Harry against me. Unless I gave her the price she wanted, she threatened to sell them back to him. That was another mistake I made – I thought she'd have them with her that day. But she was too clever for that. Carton, her husband, was dead too – I'd no clue whatsoever as to where the diamonds were hidden. Then I managed to get a copy of a wireless message sent to Nadina by someone on board the *Kilmorden* – either Carton or Rayburn, I didn't know which. It was a duplicate of that piece of paper you picked up. "Seventeen one twenty two", it ran. I took it to be an appointment with Rayburn, and when he was so desperate to get aboard the *Kilmorden* I was convinced that I was right. So I pretended to swallow his statements, and let him come. I kept a pretty sharp watch upon him and hoped that I should learn more. Then I found Minks trying to play a lone hand, and interfering with me. I soon stopped that. He came to heel all right. It was annoying not getting Cabin 17, and it worried me not being able to place you. Were you the innocent young girl you seemed, or were you not? When Rayburn set out to keep the appointment that night, Minks was told off to intercept him. Minks muffed it, of course.'

'But why did the wireless message say "seventeen" instead of "seventy-one"?'

'I've thought that out. Carton must have given that wireless operator his own memorandum to copy off on to a form, and he never read the copy through. The operator made the same mistake we all did, and read it as 17.1.22 instead of 1.71.22. The thing I don't know is how Minks got on to Cabin 17. It must have been sheer instinct.'

'And the dispatch to General Smuts? Who tampered with that?'

'My dear Anne, you don't suppose I was going to have a lot of my plans given away, without making an effort to save them? With an escaped murderer as a secretary, I had no hesitation whatever in substituting blanks. Nobody would think of suspecting poor old Pedler.'

'What about Colonel Race?'

'Yes, that was a nasty jar. When Pagett told me he was a Secret Service fellow, I had an unpleasant feeling down the spine. I remembered that he'd been nosing around Nadina in Paris during the War – and I had a horrible suspicion that he was out after *me*! I don't like the way he's stuck to me ever since. He's one of those strong, silent men who have always got something up their sleeve.'

A whistle sounded. Sir Eustace picked up the tube, listened for a minute or two, then answered:

'Very well, I'll see him now.'

'Business,' he remarked. 'Miss Anne, let me show you your room.'

He ushered me into a small shabby apartment, a Kafir boy brought up my small suit-case, and Sir Eustace, urging me to ask for anything I wanted, withdrew, the picture of a courteous host. A can of hot water was on the washstand, and I proceeded to unpack a few necessaries. Something hard and unfamiliar in my sponge-bag puzzled me greatly. I untied the string and looked inside.

To my utter amazement I drew out a small pearl-handled revolver. It hadn't been there when I started from Kimberley. I examined the thing gingerly. It appeared to be loaded.

I handled it with a comfortable feeling. It was a useful thing to have in a house such as this. But modern clothes are quite unsuited to the carrying of fire-arms. In the end I pushed it gingerly into the top of my stocking. It made a terrible bulge, and I expected every minute that it would go off and shoot me in the leg, but it really seemed the only place.

CHAPTER XXXIII

I was not summoned to Sir Eustace's presence until late in the afternoon. Eleven-o'clock tea and a substantial lunch had been served to me in my own apartment, and I felt fortified for further conflict.

Sir Eustace was alone. He was walking up and down the room, there was a gleam in his eye and a restlessness in his manner which did not escape me. He was exultant about something. There was a subtle change in his manner towards me.

'I have news for you. Your young man is on his way. He will be here in a few minutes. Moderate your transports – I have something more to say. You attempted to deceive me this morning. I warned you that you would be wise to stick to the truth, and up to a certain point you obeyed me. Then you ran off the rails. You attempted to make me believe that the diamonds were in Harry Rayburn's possession. At the time I accepted your statement because it facilitated my task – the task of inducing you to decoy Harry Rayburn here. But, my dear Anne, the diamonds have been in my possession ever since I left the Falls – though I only discovered the fact yesterday.'

'You know!' I gasped.

'It may interest you to hear that it was Pagett who gave the show away. He insisted on boring me with a long pointless story about a wager and a tin of films. It didn't take me long to put two and two together – Mrs Blair's distrust of Colonel Race, her agitation, her entreaty that I would take care of her souvenirs for her. The excellent Pagett had already unfastened the cases through an excess of zeal. Before leaving the hotel, I simply transferred all the rolls of films to my own pocket. They are in the corner there. I admit that I haven't had time to examine them yet, but I notice that one is of a totally different weight to the others, rattles in a peculiar fashion, and has evidently been stuck down with seccotine, which will necessitate the use of a tin-opener. The case seems clear, does it not? And now, you see, I have you both nicely in the trap . . . It's a pity that you didn't take kindly to the idea of becoming Lady Pedler.'

I did not answer. I stood looking at him.

There was the sound of feet on the stairs, the door was flung open, and Harry Rayburn was hustled into the room between two men. Sir Eustace flung me a look of triumph.

'According to plan,' he said softly. 'You amateurs *will* pit yourselves against professionals.'

'What's the meaning of this?' cried Harry hoarsely.

'It means that you have walked into my parlour – said the spider to the fly,' remarked Sir Eustace facetiously. 'My dear Rayburn, you are extraordinarily unlucky.'

'You said I could come safely, Anne.'

'Do not reproach her, my dear fellow. That note was written at my dictation, and the lady could not help herself. She would have been wiser not to write it, but I did not tell her so at the time. You followed her instructions, went to the curio-shop, were taken through the secret passage from the back room – and found yourself in the hands of your enemies!'

Harry looked at me. I understood his glance and edged nearer to Sir Eustace.

'Yes,' murmured the latter, 'decidedly you are not lucky! This is – let me see, the third encounter.'

'You are right,' said Harry. 'This is the third encounter. Twice you have worsted me – have you never heard that the third time the luck changes? This is my round – cover him, Anne.'

I was all ready. In a flash I had whipped the pistol out of my stocking and was holding it to his head. The two men guarding Harry sprang forward, but his voice stopped them.

'Another step – and he dies! If they come any nearer, Anne, pull the trigger – don't hesitate.'

'I shan't,' I replied cheerfully. 'I'm rather afraid of pulling it, anyway.'

I think Sir Eustace shared my fears. He was certainly shaking like a jelly.

'Stay where you are,' he commanded, and the men stopped obediently.

'Tell them to leave the room,' said Harry.

Sir Eustace gave the order. The men filed out, and Harry shot the bolt across the door behind them.

'Now we can talk,' he observed grimly, and, coming across the room, he took the revolver out of my hand.

Sir Eustace uttered a sigh of relief and wiped his forehead with a handkerchief.

'I'm shockingly out of condition,' he observed. 'I think I must have a weak heart. I am glad that revolver is in competent hands. I didn't trust Miss Anne with it. Well, my young friend, as you say, now we can talk. I'm willing to admit that you stole a march upon me. Where the devil that revolver came from I don't know. I had the girl's luggage searched when she arrived. And where did you produce it from now? You hadn't got it on you a minute ago?'

'Yes, I had,' I replied. 'It was in my stocking.'

'I don't know enough about women. I ought to have studied them more,' said Sir Eustace sadly. 'I wonder if Pagett would have known that?'

Harry rapped sharply on the table.

'Don't play the fool. If it weren't for your grey hairs, I'd throw you out of the window. You damned scoundrel! Grey hairs, or no grey hairs, I – '

He advanced a step or two, and Sir Eustace skipped nimbly behind the table.

'The young are always so violent,' he said reproachfully. 'Unable to use their brains, they rely solely on their muscles. Let us talk sense. For the moment you have the upper hand. But that state of affairs cannot continue. The house is full of my men. You are hopelessly outnumbered. Your momentary ascendancy has been gained by an accident – '

'Has it?'

Something in Harry's voice, a grim raillery, seemed to attract Sir Eustace's attention. He stared at him.

'Has it?' said Harry again. 'Sit down, Sir Eustace, and listen to what I have to say.' Still covering him with the revolver, he went on: 'The cards are against you this time. To begin with, listen to *that!*'

That was a dull banging at the door below. There were shouts, oaths, and then a sound of firing. Sir Eustace paled.

'What's that?'

'Race – and his people. You didn't know, did you, Sir Eustace, that Anne had an arrangement with me by which we should know whether communications from one to the other were genuine? Telegrams were to be signed "Andy", letters were to have the word "and" crossed out somewhere in them. Anne knew that your telegram was a fake. She came here of her own free will, walked deliberately into the snare, in the hope that she might catch you in your own trap. Before leaving Kimberley she wired both to me and to Race. Mrs Blair has been in communication with us ever since. I received the letter written at your dictation, which was just what I expected. I had already discussed the probabilities of a secret passage leading out of the curio-shop with Race, and he had discovered the place where the exit was situated.'

There was a screaming, tearing sound, and a heavy explosion which shook the room.

'They're shelling this part of the town. I must get you out of here, Anne.'

A bright light flared up. The house opposite was on fire. Sir Eustace had risen and was pacing up and down. Harry kept him covered with the revolver.

'So you see, Sir Eustace, the game is up. It was you yourself who very kindly provided us with the clue of your whereabouts. Race's men were watching the exit of the secret passage. In spite of the precautions you took, they were successful in following me here.'

Sir Eustace turned suddenly.

'Very clever. Very creditable. But I've still a word to say. If I've lost the trick, so have you. You'll never be able to bring the murder of Nadina home to me. I was in Marlow on that day, that's all you've got against me. No one can prove that I even knew the woman. But you knew her, you had a motive for killing her – and your record's against you. You're a thief, remember, a thief. There's one thing you don't know, perhaps. *I've got the diamonds.* And here goes –'

With an incredibly swift movement, he stooped, swung up his arm and threw. There was a tinkle of breaking glass, as the object went through the window and disappeared into the blazing mass opposite.

'There goes your only hope of establishing your innocence over the Kimberley affair. And now we'll talk. I'll drive a bargain with you. You've got me cornered. Race will find all he needs in this house. There's a chance for me if I can get away. I'm done for if I stay, but so are you, young man! There's a skylight in the next room. A couple of minutes' start and I shall be all right. I've got one or two little arrangements all ready made. You let me out of the way, and give me a start – and I leave you a signed confession that I killed Nadina.'

'*Yes*, Harry,' I cried. 'Yes, yes, yes!'

He turned a stern face on me.

'No, Anne, a thousand times, no. You don't know what you're saying.'

'I do. It solves everything.'

'I'd never be able to look Race in the face again. I'll take my chance, but I'm damned if I'll let this slippery old fox get away. It's no good, Anne. I won't do it.'

Sir Eustace chuckled. He accepted defeat without the least emotion.

'Well, well,' he remarked. 'You seem to have met your master, Anne. But I can assure you both that moral rectitude does not always pay.'

There was a crash of rending wood, and footsteps surged up the stairs. Harry drew back the bolt. Colonel Race was the first to enter the room. His face lit at the sight of us.

'You're safe, Anne. I was afraid –' He turned to Sir Eustace. 'I've been after you for a long time, Pedler – and at last I've got you.'

'Everybody seems to have gone completely mad,' declared Sir Eustace airily. 'These young people have been threatening me with revolvers and accusing me of the most shocking things. I don't know what it's all about.'

'Don't you? It means that I've found the "Colonel". It means that on January 8th last you were not at Cannes, but at Marlow. It means that when your tool, Madame Nadina, turned against you, you planned to do away with her – and at last we shall be able to bring the crime home to you.'

'Indeed? And from whom did you get all this interesting information? From the man who is even now being looked for by the police? His evidence will be very valuable.'

'We have other evidence. There is someone else who knew that Nadina was going to meet you at the Mill House.'

Sir Eustace looked surprised. Colonel Race made a gesture with his hand. Arthur Minks *alias* the Rev. Edward Chichester *alias* Miss Pettigrew stepped forward. He was pale and nervous, but he spoke clearly enough:

'I saw Nadina in Paris the night before she went over to England. I was posing at the time as a Russian Count. She told me of her purpose. I warned her, knowing what kind of man she had to deal with, but she did not take my advice. There was a wireless message on the table. I read it. Afterwards I thought I would have a try for the diamonds myself. In Johannesburg Mr Rayburn accosted me. He persuaded me to come over to his side.'

Sir Eustace looked at him. He said nothing, but Minks seemed visibly to wilt.

'Rats always leave a sinking ship,' observed Sir Eustace. 'I don't care for rats. Sooner or later, I destroy vermin.'

'There's just one thing I'd like to tell you, Sir Eustace,' I remarked. 'That tin you threw out of the window didn't contain the diamonds. It had common pebbles in it. The diamonds are in a perfectly safe place. As a matter of fact they're in the big giraffe's stomach. Suzanne hollowed it out, put the diamonds in with cotton wool, so that they wouldn't rattle, and plugged it up again.'

Sir Eustace looked at me for some time. His reply was characteristic:

'I always did hate that blinking giraffe,' he said. 'It must have been instinct.'

CHAPTER XXXIV

We were not able to return to Johannesburg that night. The shells were coming over pretty fast, and I gathered that we were now more or less cut off, owing to the rebels having obtained possession of a new part of the suburbs.

Our place of refuge was a farm some twenty miles or so from Johannesburg – right out on the veld. I was dropping with fatigue. All the excitement and anxiety of the last two days had left me little better than a limp rag.

I kept repeating to myself, without being able to believe it, that our troubles were really over. Harry and I were together and we should never be separated again. Yet all through I was conscious of some barrier between us – a constraint on his part, the reason of which I could not fathom.

Sir Eustace had been driven off in an opposite direction accompanied by a strong guard. He waved his hand airily to us on departing.

I came out on to the *stoep* early on the following morning and looked across the veld in the direction of Johannesburg. I could see the great dumps glistening in the pale morning sunshine, and I could hear the low rumbling mutter of the guns. The Revolution was not over yet.

The farmer's wife came out and called me in to breakfast. She was a kind, motherly soul, and I was already very fond of her. Harry had gone out at dawn and had not yet returned, so she informed me. Again I felt a stir of uneasiness pass over me. What was this shadow of which I was so conscious between us?

After breakfast I sat out on the *stoep*, a book in my hand which I did not read. I was so lost in my own thoughts that I never saw Colonel Race ride up and dismount from his horse. It was not until he said 'Good morning, Anne,' that I became aware of his presence.

'Oh,' I said, with a flush, 'it's you.'

'Yes. May I sit down?'

He drew a chair up beside me. It was the first time we had been alone together since that day at the Matopos. As always, I felt that curious mixture of fascination and fear that he never failed to inspire in me.

'What is the news?' I asked.

'Smuts will be in Johannesburg tomorrow. I give this outbreak three days more before it collapses utterly. In the meantime the fighting goes on.'

'I wish,' I said, 'that one could be sure that the right people were the ones to get killed. I mean the ones who wanted to fight – not just all the poor people who happen to live in the parts where the fighting is going on.'

He nodded.

'I know what you mean, Anne. That's the unfairness of war. But I've other news for you.'

'Yes?'

'A confession of incompetency on my part. Pedler has managed to escape.'

'What?'

'Yes. No one knows how he managed it. He was securely locked up for the night – in an upper-storey room of one of the farms roundabouts which the Military have taken over, but this morning the room was empty and the bird had flown.'

Secretly, I was rather pleased. Never, to this day, have I been able to rid myself of a sneaking fondness for Sir Eustace. I dare say it's reprehensible, but there it is. I admired him. He was a thorough-going villain, I dare say – but he was a pleasant one. I've never met anyone half so amusing since.

I concealed my feelings, of course. Naturally Colonel Race would feel quite differently about it. He wanted Sir Eustace brought to justice. There was nothing very surprising in his escape when one came to think of it. All round Jo'burg he must have innumerable spies and agents. And, whatever Colonel Race might think, I was exceedingly doubtful that they would ever catch him. He probably had a well-planned line of retreat. Indeed, he had said as much to us.

I expressed myself suitably, though in a rather lukewarm manner, and the conversation languished. Then Colonel Race asked suddenly for Harry. I told him that he had gone off at dawn and that I hadn't seen him this morning.

'You understand, don't you, Anne, that apart from formalities, he is completely cleared? There are technicalities, of course, but Sir Eustace's guilt is well assured. There is nothing now to keep you apart.'

He said this without looking at me, in a slow, jerky voice.

'I understand,' I said gratefully.

'And there is no reason why he should not at once resume his real name.'

'No, of course not.'

'You know his real name?'

The question surprised me.

'Of course I do. Harry Lucas.'

He did not answer, and something in the quality of his silence struck me as peculiar.

'Anne, do you remember that, as we drove home from the Matopos that day, I told you that I knew what I had to do?'

'Of course I remember.'

'I think that I may fairly say I have done it. The man you love is cleared of suspicion.'

'Was that what you meant?'

'Of course.'

I hung my head, ashamed of the baseless suspicion I had entertained. He spoke again in a thoughtful voice:

'When I was a mere youngster, I was in love with a girl who jilted me. After that I thought only of my work. My career meant everything to me. Then I met you, Anne – and all that seemed worth nothing. But youth calls to youth . . . I've still got my work.'

I was silent. I suppose one can't really love two men at once – but you can feel like it. The magnetism of this man was very great. I looked up at him suddenly.

'I think that you'll go very far,' I said dreamily. 'I think that you've got a great career ahead of you. You'll be one of the world's big men.'

I felt as though I was uttering a prophecy.

'I shall be alone, though.'

'All the people who do really big things are.'

'You think so?'

'I'm sure of it.'

He took my hand, and said in a low voice:

'I'd rather have had – the other.'

Then Harry came striding round the corner of the house. Colonel Race rose.

'Good morning – Lucas,' he said.

For some reason Harry flushed up to the roots of his hair.

'Yes,' I said gaily, 'you must be known by your real name now.'

But Harry was still staring at Colonel Race.

'So you know, sir,' he said at last.

'I never forget a face. I saw you once as a boy.'

'What's all this about?' I asked, puzzled, looking from one to the other.

It seemed a conflict of wills between them. Race won. Harry turned slightly away.

'I suppose you're right, sir. Tell her my real name.'

'Anne, this isn't Harry Lucas. Harry Lucas was killed in the War. This is John Harold Eardsley.'

CHAPTER XXXV

With his last words, Colonel Race had swung away and left us. I stood staring after him. Harry's voice recalled me to myself.

'Anne, forgive me, say you forgive me.'

He took my hand in his and almost mechanically I drew it away.

'Why did you deceive me?'

'I don't know that I can make you understand. I was afraid of all that sort of thing - the power and fascination of wealth. I wanted you to care for me just for myself – for the man I was – without ornaments and trappings.'

'You mean you didn't trust me?'

'You can put it that way if you like, but it isn't quite true. I'd become embittered, suspicious – always prone to look for ulterior motives – and it was so wonderful to be cared for in the way you cared for me.'

'I see,' I said slowly. I was going over in my own mind the story he had told me. For the first time I noted discrepancies in it which I had disregarded – an assurance of money, the power to buy back the diamonds of Nadina, the way in which he had preferred to speak of both men from the point of view of an outsider. And when he had said 'my friend' he had meant not Eardsley, but Lucas. It was Lucas, the quiet fellow, who had loved Nadina so deeply.

'How did it come about?' I asked.

'We were both reckless – anxious to get killed. One night we exchanged identification discs – for luck! Lucas was killed the next day – blown to pieces.'

I shuddered.

'But why didn't you tell me now? This morning? You couldn't have doubted my caring for you by this time?'

'Anne, I didn't want to spoil it all. I wanted to take you

back to the island. What's the good of money? It can't buy happiness. We'd have been happy on the island. I tell you I'm afraid of that other life – it nearly rotted me through once.'

'Did Sir Eustace know who you really were?'

'Oh, yes.'

'And Carton?'

'No. He saw us both with Nadina at Kimberley one night, but he didn't know which was which. He accepted my statement that I was Lucas, and Nadina was deceived by his cable. She was never afraid of Lucas. He was a quiet chap – very deep. But I always had the devil's own temper. She'd have been scared out of her life if she'd known that I'd come to life again.'

'Harry, if Colonel Race hadn't told me, what did you mean to do?'

'Say nothing. Go on as Lucas.'

'And your father's millions?'

'Race was welcome to them. Anyway, he would make a better use of them than I ever shall. Anne, what are you thinking about? You're frowning so.'

'I'm thinking,' I said slowly, 'that I almost wish Colonel Race hadn't made you tell me.'

'No. He was right. I owed you the truth.'

He paused, then said suddenly:

'You know, Anne, I'm jealous of Race. He loves you too – and he's a bigger man than I am or ever shall be.'

I turned to him, laughing.

'Harry, you idiot. It's you I want – and that's all that matters.'

As soon as possible we started for Cape Town. There Suzanne was waiting to greet me, and we disembowelled the big giraffe together. When the Revolution was finally quelled, Colonel Race came down to Cape Town and at his suggestion the big villa at Muizenberg that had belonged to Sir Laurence Eardsley was reopened and we all took up our abode in it.

There we made our plans. I was to return to England with Suzanne and to be married from her house in London. And the trousseau was to be bought in Paris! Suzanne enjoyed planning all these details enormously. So did I. And yet the future seemed curiously unreal. And sometimes, without knowing why, I felt absolutely stifled – as though I couldn't breathe.

It was the night before we were to sail. I couldn't sleep. I was miserable, and I didn't know why. I hated leaving Africa. When I came back to it, would it be the same thing? Would it ever be the same thing again?

And then I was startled by an authoritative rap on the shutter. I sprang up. Harry was on the *stoep* outside.

'Put some clothes on, Anne, and come out. I want to speak to you.'

I huddled on a few garments, and stepped out into the cool night air – still and scented, with its velvety feel. Harry beckoned me out of earshot of the house. His face looked pale and determined and his eyes were blazing.

'Anne, do you remember saying to me once that women enjoyed doing things they disliked for the sake of someone they liked?'

'Yes,' I said, wondering what was coming.

He caught me in his arms.

'Anne, come away with me – now – tonight. Back to Rhodesia – back to the island. I can't stand all this tomfoolery. I can't wait for you any longer.'

I disengaged myself a minute.

'And what about my French frocks?' I lamented mockingly.

To this day, Harry never knows when I'm in earnest, and when I'm only teasing him.

'Damn your French frocks. Do you think I want to put frocks on you? I'm a damned sight more likely to want to tear them off you. I'm not going to let you go, do you hear? You're my woman. If I let you go away, I may lose you. I'm never sure of you. You're coming with me now – tonight – and damn everybody.'

He held me to him, kissing me until I could hardly breathe.

'I can't do without you any longer, Anne. I can't indeed. I

hate all this money. Let Race have it. Come on. Let's go.'

'My toothbrush?' I demurred.

'You can buy one. I know I'm a lunatic, but for God's sake, *come!*'

He stalked off at a furious pace. I followed him as meekly as the Barotsi woman I had observed at the Falls. Only I wasn't carrying a frying-pan on my head. He walked so fast that it was very difficult to keep up with him.

'Harry,' I said at last, in a meek voice, 'are we going to walk all the way to Rhodesia?'

He turned suddenly, and with a great shout of laughter gathered me up in his arms.

'I'm mad, sweetheart, I know it. But I do love you so.'

'We're a couple of lunatics. And, oh, Harry, you never asked me, but I'm not making a sacrifice at all! I *wanted* to come!'

CHAPTER XXXVI

That was two years ago. We still live on the island. Before me, on the rough wooden table, is the letter that Suzanne wrote me.

> Dear Babes in the Wood – Dear Lunatics in Love,
>   I'm not surprised – not at all. All the time we've been talking Paris and frocks I felt that it wasn't a bit real – that you'd vanish into the blue some day to be married over the tongs in the good old gipsy fashion. But you *are* a couple of lunatics! This idea of renouncing a vast fortune is absurd. Colonel Race wanted to argue the matter, but I have persuaded him to leave the argument to time. He can administer the estate for Harry – and none better. Because, after all, honeymoons don't last for ever – you're not here, Anne, so I can safely say that without having you fly out at me like a little wild-cat – Love in the wilderness will last a good while, but one day you will suddenly begin to dream of houses in Park Lane, sumptuous furs, Paris frocks, the largest thing in motors and the latest thing in perambulators, French maids and Norland nurses! Oh, yes, you will!
>   But have your honeymoon, dear lunatics, and let it be a long one. And think of me sometimes, comfortably putting on weight amidst the fleshpots!
> Your loving friend,
Suzanne Blair

> P.S. – I am sending you an assortment of frying-pans as a wedding present, and an enormous *terrine* of *pâté de foie gras* to remind you of me.

There is another letter that I sometimes read. It came a good while after the other and was accompanied by a bulky parcel. It appeared to be written from somewhere in Bolivia.

My dear Anne Beddingfeld,
I can't resist writing to you, not so much for the pleasure it gives me to write, as for the enormous pleasure I know it will give you to hear from me. Our friend Race wasn't quite as clever as he thought himself, was he?

I think I shall appoint you my literary executor. I'm sending you my diary. There's nothing in it that would interest Race and his crowd, but I fancy that there are passages in it which may amuse you. Make use of it in any way you like. I suggest an article for the *Daily Budget*, 'Criminals I have met.' I only stipulate that I shall be the central figure.

By this time I have no doubt that you are no longer Anne Beddingfeld, but Lady Eardsley, queening it in Park Lane. I should just like to say that I bear you no malice whatever. It is hard, of course, to have to begin all over again at my time of life, but, *entre nous*, I had a little reserve fund carefully put aside for such a contingency. It has come in very usefully and I am getting together a nice little connexion. By the way, if you ever come across that funny friend of yours, Arthur Minks, just tell him that I haven't forgotten him, will you? That will give him a nasty jar.

On the whole I think I have displayed a most Christian and forgiving spirit. Even to Pagett. I happened to hear that he – or rather Mrs Pagett – had brought a sixth child into the world the other day. England will be entirely populated by Pagetts soon. I sent the child a silver mug, and, on a post card, declared my willingness to act as godfather. I can see Pagett taking both mug and post card straight to Scotland Yard without a smile on his face!

Bless you, liquid eyes. Some day you will see what a mistake you have made in not marrying me.
> Yours ever
> Eustace Pedler

Harry was furious. It is the one point on which he and I do not see eye to eye. To him, Sir Eustace was the man who tried to murder me and whom he regards as responsible for the death of his friend. Sir Eustace's attempts on my life have always puzzled me. They are not in the picture, so to speak. For I am sure that he always had a genuinely kindly feeling towards me.

Then why did he twice attempt to take my life? Harry says 'because he's a damned scoundrel,' and seems to think that settles the matter. Suzanne was more discriminating. I talked it over with her, and she put it down to a 'fear complex'. Suzanne goes in rather for psycho-analysis. She pointed out to me that Sir Eustace's whole life was actuated by a desire to be safe and comfortable. He had an acute sense of self-preservation. And the murder of Nadina removed certain inhibitions. His actions did not represent the state of his feeling towards me, but were the result of his acute fears for his own safety. I think Suzanne is right. As for Nadina, she was the kind of woman who deserved to die. Men do all sorts of questionable things in order to get rich, but women shouldn't pretend to be in love when they aren't for ulterior motives.

I can forgive Sir Eustace easily enough, but I shall never forgive Nadina. Never, never, never!

The other day I was unpacking some tins that were wrapped in bits of an old *Daily Budget*, and I suddenly came upon the words, 'The Man in the Brown Suit'. How long ago it seemed! I had, of course, severed my connexion with the *Daily Budget* long ago – I had done with it sooner than it had done with me. MY ROMANTIC WEDDING was given a halo of publicity.

My son is lying in the sun, kicking his legs. There's a 'man in a brown suit' if you like. He's wearing as little as possible, which is the best costume for Africa, and is as brown as a berry. He's always burrowing in the earth. I think he takes after Papa. He'll have that same mania for Pleistocene clay.

Suzanne sent me a cable when he was born:

'Congratulations and love to the latest arrival on Lunatics' Island. Is his head dolichocephalic or brachycephalic?'

I wasn't going to stand that from Suzanne. I sent her a reply of one word, economical and to the point:

'Platycephalic!'

Postscript

In between the writing of Murder on the Links *and* The Man in
the Brown Suit, *Agatha Christie and her husband travelled round the
world. Many years later, in her* Autobiography, *Christie devoted an
entire chapter to their journey, which she remembered as 'one of the most
exciting things that ever happened to me'.*

The Man in the Brown Suit *owes much to this journey round the
world, not least its starting point.*

*Archie had a friend, Major Belcher, who had been a professor at
Clifton and who was, according to Agatha, 'a character – with terrific
powers of bluff'. He had, according to his own story, bluffed himself
into the position of Controller of Potatoes during the war, even though
he confessed he didn't know a thing about potatoes. Similarly, in 1922,
he was elected director for the British Empire Mission, with the responsibility of preparing the great 1924 British Empire Exhibition. Since the
Major valued Archie's knowledge of economics, Belcher hired him for
his mission as a financial consultant.*

*Shortly before their departure, during a dinner at the Major's house
in Dorney known as 'The Mill', he asked Agatha Christie to write a
detective story entitled* The Mystery of the Mill House *in which he
would be a character. Christie tried, in vain, to tell him that she couldn't
'do anything with real people' since 'she had to imagine them'. The
Major insisted that he had always wanted to be a hero in a detective
story. Eventually giving in to the Major's constant questions about his
place in her future novel, Agatha agreed that she would make him her
victim. But the Major insisted on being cast as the murderer since 'the
murderer is always the most interesting character in the book'.*

*Agatha Christie eventually made him a villain: Sir Eustace Pedler.
'He wasn't Belcher, of course, but he used several of Belcher's phrases,
and told some of his stories. He too was a master of the art of bluff, and
behind the bluff could easily be sensed an unscrupulous and interesting*

character. Soon I had forgotten Belcher and had Sir Eustace Pedler himself wielding the pen.'

The plot of The Man in the Brown Suit *was largely sketched out during the time the mission spent in South Africa. There, Agatha Christie decided it would be more in the nature of a thriller than a detective story. Partly taking place in South Africa, Christie pictured the heroine as a 'gay, adventurous, young woman, an orphan, who started out to seek adventure'.*

Several episodes in the novel were inspired by their journey: like Agatha Christie, who suffered greatly from seasickness on board the 'Kildonan Castle', the boat that took her to South Africa, so her heroine, Anne Beddingfeld, is seasick on the 'Kilmordan', which takes her to the Cape.

During her visit to South Africa Agatha Christie witnessed a certain amount of social upheaval; the events in The Man in a Brown Suit *were a direct reflection of these disturbances. Finally, another reason why Agatha Christie was keen to write the book was because Archie, who had left his job in the City in order to work for Belcher, had difficulty finding an interesting job on his return. Pursuing her writing certainly provided the possibility of earning some money.*

When The Mystery of the Mill House *was finished, Christie sent it to her Publisher who, though slightly reluctant, nevertheless decided to publish it.*

Disappointed by the way in which her editor John Lane had treated her and had taken advantage of her lack of experience by offering her an unfavourable contract that tied her to The Bodley Head Company for her next five books, Agatha Christie was determined to look for a new Publisher as well as a literary agent. When she met Edmund Cork, Hughes Massie's successor – the same Massie who had been recommended to her by Eden Philpotts – Agatha placed her career in his hands. When John Lane approached her with a new contract, she refused without giving any definite reason.

The Mystery of the Mill House *was finally published under the title* The Man in the Brown Suit, *as the original title sounded too similar to* Murder on the Links. The Evening News, *an important paper, bought the serialisation rights for £500 which, at the time, was a considerable sum. Although Agatha Christie did not approve of the*

title under which they wanted to publish it, Anna the Adventuress
*– 'as silly a title as I have ever heard' – she was nevertheless pleased
with the money she made from it and, on Archie's suggestion, bought
herself a car.*

*'I will confess here and now that of the two things that have excited
me most in my life, the first was my car: my grey bottle-nosed Morris
Cowley. The second was dining with the Queen at Buckingham Palace
about forty years later. Both of these happenings, you see, had something
of a fairy-tale quality about them.'*

POIROT INVESTIGATES

Contents

The Adventure of 'The Western Star'

I was standing at the window of Poirot's rooms looking out idly on the street below.

'That's queer,' I ejaculated suddenly beneath my breath.

'What is, *mon ami*?' asked Poirot placidly, from the depths of his comfortable chair.

'Deduce, Poirot, from the following facts! Here is a young lady, richly dressed – fashionable hat, magnificent furs. She is coming along slowly, looking up at the houses as she goes. Unknown to her, she is being shadowed by three men and a middle-aged woman. They have just been joined by an errand boy who points after the girl, gesticulating as he does so. What drama is this being played? Is the girl a crook, and are the shadows detectives preparing to arrest her? Or are *they* the scoundrels, and are they plotting to attack an innocent victim? What does the great detective say?'

'The great detective, *mon ami*, chooses, as ever, the simplest course. He rises to see for himself.' And my friend joined me at the window.

In a minute he gave vent to an amused chuckle.

'As usual, your facts are tinged with your incurable romanticism. This is Miss Mary Marvell, the film star. She is being followed by a bevy of admirers who have recognized her. And, *en passant*, my dear Hastings, she is quite aware of the fact!'

I laughed.

'So all is explained! But you get no marks for that, Poirot. It was a mere matter of recognition.'

'*En vérité!* And how many times have you seen Mary Marvell on the screen, *mon cher?*'

I thought.

'About a dozen times perhaps.'

'And I – once! Yet *I* recognize her, and *you* do not.'

'She looks so different,' I replied rather feebly.

'Ah! *Sacré!*' cried Poirot. 'Is it that you expect her to promenade herself in the streets of London in a cowboy hat, or with bare feet, and a bunch of curls, as an Irish colleen? Always with you it is the non-essentials! Remember the case of the dancer, Valerie Saintclair.'

I shrugged my shoulders, slightly annoyed.

'But console yourself, *mon ami*,' said Poirot, calming down. 'All cannot be as Hercule Poirot! I know it well.'

'You really have the best opinion of yourself of anyone I ever knew!' I cried, divided between amusement and annoyance.

'What will you? When one is unique, one knows it! And others share that opinion – even, if I mistake it not, Miss Mary Marvell.'

'What?'

'Without doubt. She is coming here.'

'How do you make that out?'

'Very simply. This street, it is not aristocratic, *mon ami*! In it there is no fashionable doctor, no fashionable dentist – still less is there a fashionable milliner! But there *is* a fashionable detective. *Oui*, my friend, it is true – I am become the mode, the *dernier cri*! One says to another: "*Comment?* You have lost your gold pencil-case? You must go to the little Belgian. He is too marvellous! Everyone goes! *Courez!* And they arrive! In flocks, *mon ami*! With problems of the most foolish!"' A bell rang below. 'What did I tell you? That is Miss Marvell.'

As usual, Poirot was right. After a short interval, the American film star was ushered in, and we rose to our feet.

Mary Marvell was undoubtedly one of the most popular actresses on the screen. She had only lately arrived in England in company with her husband, Gregory B. Rolf, also a film actor. Their marriage had taken place about a year ago in the

States and this was their first visit to England. They had been given a great reception. Everyone was prepared to go mad over Mary Marvell, her wonderful clothes, her furs, her jewels, above all one jewel, the great diamond which had been nick-named, to match its owner, 'The Western Star'. Much, true and untrue, had been written about this famous stone which was reported to be insured for the enormous sum of fifty thousand pounds.

All these details passed rapidly through my mind as I joined with Poirot in greeting our fair client.

Miss Marvell was small and slender, very fair and girlish looking, with the wide innocent blue eyes of a child.

Poirot drew forward a chair for her, and she commenced talking at once.

'You will probably think me very foolish, Monsieur Poirot, but Lord Cronshaw was telling me last night how wonderfully you cleared up the mystery of his nephew's death, and I felt that I just must have your advice. I dare say it's only a silly hoax – Gregory says so – but it's just worrying me to death.'

She paused for breath. Poirot beamed encouragement.

'Proceed, madame. You comprehend, I am still in the dark.'

'It's these letters.' Miss Marvell unclasped her handbag, and drew out three envelopes which she handed to Poirot.

The latter scrutinized them closely.

'Cheap paper – the name and address carefully printed. Let us see the inside.' He drew out the enclosure.

I had joined him, and was leaning over his shoulder.

The writing consisted of a single sentence, carefully printed like the envelope. It ran as follows:

'The great diamond which is the left eye of the god must return whence it came.'

The second letter was couched in precisely the same terms, but the third was more explicit:

'You have been warned. You have not obeyed. Now the diamond will be taken from you. At the full of the moon, the two diamonds which are the left and right eye of the god shall return. So it is written.'

'The first letter I treated as a joke,' explained Miss Marvell. 'When I got the second, I began to wonder. The third one came yesterday, and it seemed to me that, after all, the matter might be more serious than I had imagined.'

'I see they did not come by post, these letters.'

'No; they were left by hand – by a *Chinaman*. That is what frightens me.'

'Why?'

'Because it was from a Chink in San Francisco that Gregory bought the stone three years ago.'

'I see, madame, that you believe the diamond referred to to be –'

'"The Western Star,"' finished Miss Marvell. 'That's so. At the time, Gregory remembers that there was some story attached to the stone, but the Chink wasn't handing out any information. Gregory says he seemed just scared to death, and in a mortal hurry to get rid of the thing. He only asked about a tenth of its value. It was Greg's wedding present to me.'

Poirot nodded thoughtfully.

'The story seems of an almost unbelievable romanticism. And yet – who knows? I pray of you, Hastings, hand me my little almanac.'

I complied.

'*Voyons!*' said Poirot, turning the leaves. 'When is the date of the full moon? Ah, Friday next. That is in three days' time. *Eh bien*, madame, you seek my advice – I give it to you. This *belle histoire* may be a hoax – but it may not! Therefore I counsel you to place the diamond in my keeping until after Friday next. Then we can take what steps we please.'

A slight cloud passed over the actress's face, and she replied constrainedly:

'I'm afraid that's impossible.'

'You have it with you – *hein?*' Poirot was watching her narrowly.

The girl hesitated a moment, then slipped her hand into the bosom of her gown, drawing out a long thin chain. She leaned forward, unclosing her hand. In the palm, a stone of white fire, exquisitely set in platinum, lay and winked at us solemnly.

Poirot drew in his breath with a long hiss.

'*Épatant!*' he murmured. 'You permit, madame?' He took the jewel in his own hand and scrutinized it keenly, then restored it to her with a little bow. 'A magnificent stone – without a flaw. Ah, *cent tonnerres!* and you carry it about with you, *comme ça!*'

'No, no, I'm very careful really, Monsieur Poirot. As a rule it's locked up in my jewel-case, and left in the hotel safe deposit. We're staying at the *Magnificent*, you know. I just brought it along today for you to see.'

'And you will leave it with me, *n'est-ce pas?* You will be advised by Papa Poirot?'

'Well, you see, it's this way, Monsieur Poirot. On Friday we're going down to Yardly Chase to spend a few days with Lord and Lady Yardly.'

Her words awoke a vague echo of remembrance in my mind. Some gossip – what was it now? A few years ago Lord and Lady Yardly had paid a visit to the States, rumour had it that his lordship had rather gone the pace out there with the assistance of some lady friends – but surely there was something more, more gossip which coupled Lady Yardly's name with that of a 'movie' star in California – why! it came to me in a flash – of course it was none other than Gregory B. Rolf.

'I'll let you into a little secret, Monsieur Poirot,' Miss Marvell was continuing. 'We've got a deal on with Lord Yardly. There's some chance of our arranging to film a play down there in his ancestral pile.'

'At Yardly Chase?' I cried, interested. 'Why, it's one of the showplaces of England.'

Miss Marvell nodded.

'I guess it's the real old feudal stuff all right. But he wants a pretty stiff price, and of course I don't know yet whether the deal will go through, but Greg and I always like to combine business with pleasure.'

'But – I demand pardon if I am dense, madame – surely it is possible to visit Yardly Chase without taking the diamond with you?'

A shrewd, hard look came into Miss Marvell's eyes which belied their childlike appearance. She looked suddenly a good deal older.

'I want to wear it down there.'

'Surely,' I said suddenly, 'there are some very famous jewels in the Yardly collection, a large diamond amongst them?'

'That's so,' said Miss Marvell briefly.

I heard Poirot murmur beneath his breath: 'Ah, *c'est comme ça!*' Then he said aloud, with his usual uncanny luck in hitting the bull's-eye (he dignifies it by the name of psychology): 'Then you are without doubt already acquainted with Lady Yardly, or perhaps your husband is?'

'Gregory knew her when she was out West three years ago,' said Miss Marvell. She hesitated a moment, and then added abruptly: 'Do either of you ever see *Society Gossip*?'

We both pleaded guilty rather shamefacedly.

'I ask because in this week's number there is an article on famous jewels, and it's really very curious –' She broke off.

I rose, went to the table at the other side of the room and returned with the paper in question in my hand. She took it from me, found the article, and began to read aloud:

'. . . Amongst other famous stones may be included The Star of the East, a diamond in the possession of the Yardly family. An ancestor of the present Lord Yardly brought it back with him from China, and a romantic story is said to attach to it. According to this, the stone was once the right eye of a temple god. Another diamond, exactly similar in form and size, formed the left eye, and the story goes that this jewel, too, would in course of time be stolen. "One eye shall go West, the other East, till they shall meet once more. Then, in triumph shall they return to the god." It is a curious coincidence that there is at the present time a stone corresponding closely in description with this one, and known as "The Star of the West", or "The Western Star". It is the property of the celebrated film star, Miss Mary Marvell. A comparison of the two stones would be interesting.'

She stopped.

'*Épatant!*' murmured Poirot. 'Without doubt a romance of the first water.' He turned to Mary Marvell. 'And you are not afraid, madame? You have no superstitious terrors? You do not fear to introduce these two Siamese twins to each other lest a Chinaman should appear and, hey presto! whisk them both back to China?'

His tone was mocking, but I fancied that an undercurrent of seriousness lay beneath it.

'I don't believe that Lady Yardly's diamond is anything like as good as mine,' said Miss Marvell. 'Anyway, I'm going to see.'

What more Poirot would have said I do not know, for at that moment the door flew open, and a splendid-looking man strode into the room. From his crisply curling black head, to the tips of his patent-leather boots, he was a hero fit for romance.

'I said I'd call round for you, Mary,' said Gregory Rolf, 'and here I am. Well, what does Monsieur Poirot say to our little problem? Just one big hoax, same as I do?'

Poirot smiled up at the big actor. They made a ridiculous contrast.

'Hoax or no hoax, Mr Rolf,' he said dryly, 'I have advised Madame your wife not to take the jewel with her to Yardly Chase on Friday.'

'I'm with you there, sir. I've already said so to Mary. But there! She's a woman through and through, and I guess she can't bear to think of another woman outshining her in the jewel line.'

'What nonsense, Gregory!' said Mary Marvell sharply. But she flushed angrily.

Poirot shrugged his shoulders.

'Madame, I have advised. I can do no more. *C'est fini.*'

He bowed them both to the door.

'Ah! *la la,*' he observed, returning. '*Histoire des femmes!* The good husband, he hit the nail – *tout de même*, but he was not tactful! Assuredly not.'

I imparted to him my vague remembrances, and he nodded vigorously.

'So I thought. All the same, there is something curious underneath all this. With your permission, *mon ami*, I will take the air. Await my return, I beg of you, I shall not be long.'

I was half asleep in my chair when the landlady tapped on the door, and put her head in.

'It's another lady to see Mr Poirot, sir. I've told her he was out, but she says as how she'll wait, seeing as she's come up from the country.'

'Oh, show her in here, Mrs Murchinson. Perhaps I can do something for her.'

In another moment the lady had been ushered in. My heart gave a leap as I recognized her. Lady Yardly's portrait had figured too often in the Society papers to allow her to remain unknown.

'Do sit down, Lady Yardly,' I said, drawing forward a chair. 'My friend, Poirot, is out, but I know for a fact that he'll be back very shortly.'

She thanked me and sat down. A very different type, this, from Miss Mary Marvell. Tall, dark, with flashing eyes, and a pale proud face – yet something wistful in the curves of the mouth.

I felt a desire to rise to the occasion. Why not? In Poirot's presence I have frequently felt a difficulty – I do not appear at my best. And yet there is no doubt that I, too, possess the deductive sense in a marked degree. I leant forward on a sudden impulse.

'Lady Yardly,' I said, 'I know why you have come here.

You have received blackmailing letters about the diamond.'

There was no doubt as to my bolt having shot home. She stared at me open-mouthed, all colour banished from her cheeks.

'You know?' she gasped. 'How?'

I smiled.

'By a perfectly logical process. If Miss Marvell has had warning letters –'

'Miss Marvell? She has been here?'

'She has just left. As I was saying, if she, as the holder of one of the twin diamonds, has received a mysterious series of warnings, you, as the holder of the other stone, must necessarily have done the same. You see how simple it is? I am right, then, you have received these strange communications also?'

For a moment she hesitated, as though in doubt whether to trust me or not, then she bowed her head in assent with a little smile.

'That is so,' she acknowledged.

'Were yours, too, left by hand – by a Chinaman?'

'No, they came by post; but tell me, has Miss Marvell undergone the same experience, then?'

I recounted to her the events of the morning. She listened attentively.

'It all fits in. My letters are the duplicate of hers. It is true that they came by post, but there is a curious perfume impregnating them – something in the nature of joss-stick – that at once suggested the East to me. What does it all mean?'

I shook my head.

'That is what we must find out. You have the letters with you? We might learn something from the postmarks.'

'Unfortunately I destroyed them. You understand, at the time I regarded it as some foolish joke. Can it be true that some Chinese gang are really trying to recover the diamonds? It seems too incredible.'

We went over the facts again and again, but could get no

further towards the elucidation of the mystery. At last Lady Yardly rose.

'I really don't think I need wait for Monsieur Poirot. You can tell him all this, can't you? Thank you so much Mr –'

She hesitated, her hand outstretched.

'Captain Hastings.'

'Of course! How stupid of me. You're a friend of the Cavendishes, aren't you? It was Mary Cavendish who sent me to Monsieur Poirot.'

When my friend returned, I enjoyed telling him the tale of what had occurred during his absence. He cross-questioned me rather sharply over the details of our conversation and I could read between the lines that he was not best pleased to have been absent. I also fancied that the dear old fellow was just the least inclined to be jealous. It had become rather a pose with him to consistently belittle my abilities, and I think he was chagrined at finding no loophole for criticism. I was secretly rather pleased with myself, though I tried to conceal the fact for fear of irritating him. In spite of his idiosyncrasies, I was deeply attached to my quaint little friend.

'*Bien!*' he said at length, with a curious look on his face. 'The plot develops. Pass me, I pray you, that *Peerage* on the top shelf there.' He turned the leaves. 'Ah, here we are! "Yardly . . . 10th viscount, served South African War" . . . *tout ça n'a pas d'importance*. . . "mar. 1907 Hon Maude Stopperton, fourth daughter of 3rd Baron Cotteril" . . . um, um, um . . . "has iss. two daughters, born 1908, 1910 . . . Clubs, residences" . . . *Voilà*, that does not tell us much. But tomorrow morning we see this *milord*!'

'What?'

'Yes. I telephoned to him.'

'I thought you had washed your hands of the case?'

'I am not acting for Miss Marvell since she refuses to be guided by my advice. What I do now is for my own satisfaction – the satisfaction of Hercule Poirot! Decidedly, I must have a finger in this pie.'

'And you calmly wire Lord Yardly to dash up to town just to suit your convenience. He won't be pleased.'

'*Au contraire*, if I preserve for him his family diamond, he ought to be very grateful.'

'Then you really think there is any chance of it being stolen?' I asked eagerly.

'Almost a certainty,' replied Poirot placidly. 'Everything points that way.'

'But how –'

Poirot stopped my eager questions with an airy gesture of the hand.

'Not now, I pray you. Let us not confuse the mind. And observe that *Peerage* – how you have replaced him! See you not that the tallest books go in the top shelf, the next tallest in the row beneath, and so on. Thus we have order, *method*, which, as I have often told you, Hastings –'

'Exactly,' I said hastily, and put the offending volume in its proper place.

Lord Yardly turned out to be a cheery, loud-voiced sportsman with a rather red face, but with a good-humoured bonhomie about him that was distinctly attractive and made up for any lack of mentality.

'Extraordinary business this, Monsieur Poirot. Can't make head or tail of it. Seems my wife's been getting odd kind of letters, and that Miss Marvell's had 'em too. What does it all mean?'

Poirot handed him the copy of *Society Gossip*.

'First, *milord*, I would ask you if these facts are substantially correct?'

The peer took it. His face darkened with anger as he read.

'Damned nonsense!' he spluttered. 'There's never been any romantic story attaching to the diamond. It came from India originally, I believe. I never heard of all this Chinese god stuff.'

'Still, the stone is known as "The Star of the East".'

'Well, what if it is?' he demanded wrathfully.

Poirot smiled a little, but made no direct reply.

'What I would ask you to do, *milord*, is to place yourself in my hands. If you do so unreservedly, I have great hopes of averting the catastrophe.'

'Then you think there's actually something in these wildcat tales?'

'Will you do as I ask you?'

'Of course I will, but –'

'*Bien!* Then permit that I ask you a few questions. This affair of Yardly Chase, is it, as you say, all fixed up between you and Mr Rolf?'

'Oh, he told you about it, did he? No, there's nothing settled.' He hesitated, the brick-red colour of his face deepening. 'Might as well get the thing straight. I've made rather an ass of myself in many ways, Monsieur Poirot – and I'm head over ears in debt – but I want to pull up. I'm fond of the kids, and I want to straighten things up, and be able to live on at the old place. Gregory Rolf is offering me big money – enough to set me on my feet again. I don't want to do it – I hate the thought of all that crowd play-acting round the Chase – but I may have to, unless –' He broke off.

Poirot eyed him keenly. 'You have, then, another string to your bow? Permit that I make a guess? It is to sell The Star of the East?'

Lord Yardly nodded. 'That's it. It's been in the family for some generations, but it's not essential. Still, it's not the easiest thing in the world to find a purchaser. Hoffberg, the Hatton Garden man, is on the lookout for a likely customer, but he'll have to find one soon, or it's a washout.'

'One more question, *permettez* – Lady Yardly, which plan does she approve?'

'Oh, she's bitterly opposed to my selling the jewel. You know what women are. She's all for this film stunt.'

'I comprehend,' said Poirot. He remained a moment or so in thought, then rose briskly to his feet. 'You return to Yardly Chase at once? *Bien!* Say no word to anyone – to *anyone*, mind

– but expect us there this evening. We will arrive shortly after five.'

'All right, but I don't see –'

'*Ça n'a pas d'importance*,' said Poirot kindly. 'You will that I preserve for you your diamond, *n'est-ce pas?*'

'Yes, but –'

'Then do as I say.'

A sadly bewildered nobleman left the room.

It was half-past five when we arrived at Yardly Chase, and followed the dignified butler to the old panelled hall with its fire of blazing logs. A pretty picture met our eyes: Lady Yardly and her two children, the mother's proud dark head bent down over the two fair ones. Lord Yardly stood near, smiling down on them.

'Monsieur Poirot and Captain Hastings,' announced the butler.

Lady Yardly looked up with a start, for her husband came forward uncertainly, his eyes seeking instruction from Poirot. The little man was equal to the occasion.

'All my excuses! It is that I investigate still this affair of Miss Marvell's. She comes to you on Friday, does she not? I make a little tour first to make sure that all is secure. Also I wanted to ask Lady Yardly if she recollected at all the postmarks on the letters she received?'

Lady Yardly shook her head regretfully. 'I'm afraid I don't. It's stupid of me. But, you see, I never dreamt of taking them seriously.'

'You'll stay the night?' said Lord Yardly.

'Oh, *milord*, I fear to incommode you. We have left our bags at the inn.'

'That's all right.' Lord Yardly had his cue. 'We'll send down for them. No, no – no trouble, I assure you.'

Poirot permitted himself to be persuaded, and sitting down by Lady Yardly, began to make friends with the children. In a short time they were all romping together, and had dragged me into the game.

'*Vous êtes bonne mère,*' said Poirot, with a gallant little bow, as the children were removed reluctantly by a stern nurse.

Lady Yardly smoothed her ruffled hair.

'I adore them,' she said with a little catch in her voice.

'And they you – with reason!' Poirot bowed again.

A dressing-gong sounded, and we rose to go up to our rooms. At that moment the butler emerged with a telegram on a salver which he handed to Lord Yardly. The latter tore it open with a brief word of apology. As he read it he stiffened visibly.

With an ejaculation he handed it to his wife. Then he glanced at my friend.

'Just a minute, Monsieur Poirot, I feel you ought to know about this. It's from Hoffberg. He thinks he's found a customer for the diamond – an American, sailing for the States tomorrow. They're sending down a chap tonight to vet the stone. By Jove, though, if this goes through –' Words failed him.

Lady Yardly had turned away. She still held the telegram in her hand.

'I wish you wouldn't sell it, George,' she said, in a low voice. 'It's been in the family so long.' She waited, as though for a reply, but when none came her face hardened. She shrugged her shoulders. 'I must go and dress. I suppose I had better display "the goods".' She turned to Poirot with a slight grimace. 'It's one of the most hideous necklaces that was ever designed! George has always promised to have the stones reset for me, but it's never been done.' She left the room.

Half an hour later, we three were assembled in the great drawing-room awaiting the lady. It was already a few minutes past the dinner hour.

Suddenly there was a low rustle, and Lady Yardly appeared framed in the doorway, a radiant figure in a long white shimmering dress. Round the column of her neck was a rivulet of fire. She stood there with one hand just touching the necklace.

'Behold the sacrifice,' she said gaily. Her ill-humour seemed to have vanished. 'Wait while I turn the big light on and you shall feast your eyes on the ugliest necklace in England.'

The switches were just outside the door. As she stretched out her hand to them, the incredible thing happened. Suddenly, without any warning, every light was extinguished, the door banged, and from the other side of it came a long-drawn piercing woman's scream.

'My God!' cried Lord Yardly. 'That was Maude's voice! What has happened?'

We rushed blindly for the door, cannoning into each other in the darkness. It was some minutes before we could find it. What a sight met our eyes! Lady Yardly lay senseless on the marble floor, a crimson mark on her white throat where the necklace had been wrenched from her neck.

As we bent over her, uncertain for the moment whether she was dead or alive, her eyelids opened.

'The Chinaman,' she whispered painfully. 'The Chinaman – the side door.'

Lord Yardly sprang up with an oath. I accompanied him, my heart beating wildly. The Chinaman again! The side door in question was a small one in the angle of the wall, not more than a dozen yards from the scene of the tragedy. As we reached it, I gave a cry. There, just short of the threshold, lay the glittering necklace, evidently dropped by the thief in the panic of his flight. I swooped joyously down on it. Then I uttered another cry which Lord Yardly echoed. For in the middle of the necklace was a great gap. The Star of the East was missing!

'That settles it,' I breathed. 'These were no ordinary thieves. This one stone was all they wanted.'

'But how did the fellow get in?'

'Through this door.'

'But it's always locked.'

I shook my head. 'It's not locked now. See.' I pulled it open as I spoke.

As I did so something fluttered to the ground. I picked it up. It was a piece of silk, and the embroidery was unmistakable. It had been torn from a Chinaman's robe.

'In his haste it caught in the door,' I explained. 'Come, hurry. He cannot have gone far as yet.'

But in vain we hunted and searched. In the pitch darkness of the night, the thief had found it easy to make his getaway. We returned reluctantly, and Lord Yardly sent off one of the footmen post-haste to fetch the police.

Lady Yardly, aptly ministered to by Poirot, who is as good as a woman in these matters, was sufficiently recovered to be able to tell her story.

'I was just going to turn on the other light,' she said, 'when a man sprang on me from behind. He tore my necklace from my neck with such force that I fell headlong to the floor. As I fell I saw him disappearing through the side door. Then I realized by the pigtail and the embroidered robe that he was a Chinaman.' She stopped with a shudder.

The butler reappeared. He spoke in a low voice to Lord Yardly.

'A gentleman from Mr Hoffberg's, m'lord. He says you expect him.'

'Good heavens!' cried the distracted nobleman. 'I must see him, I suppose. No, not here, Mullings, in the library.'

I drew Poirot aside.

'Look here, my dear fellow, hadn't we better get back to London?'

'You think so, Hastings? Why?'

'Well' – I coughed delicately – 'things haven't gone very well, have they? I mean, you tell Lord Yardly to place himself in your hands and all will be well – and then the diamond vanishes from under your very nose!'

'True,' said Poirot, rather crestfallen. 'It was not one of my most striking triumphs.'

This way of describing events almost caused me to smile, but I stuck to my guns.

'So, having – pardon the expression – rather made a mess of things, don't you think it would be more graceful to leave immediately?'

'And the dinner, the without doubt excellent dinner, that the *chef* of Lord Yardly has prepared?'

'Oh, what's dinner!' I said impatiently.

Poirot held up his hands in horror.

'*Mon Dieu!* It is that in this country you treat the affairs gastronomic with a criminal indifference.'

'There's another reason why we should get back to London as soon as possible,' I continued.

'What is that, my friend?'

'The other diamond,' I said, lowering my voice. 'Miss Marvell's.'

'*Eh bien*, what of it?'

'Don't you see?' His unusual obtuseness annoyed me. What had happened to his usually keen wits? 'They've got one, now they'll go for the other.'

'*Tiens!*' cried Poirot, stepping back a pace and regarding me with admiration. 'But your brain marches to a marvel, my friend! Figure to yourself that for the moment I had not thought of that! But there is plenty of time. The full of the moon, it is not until Friday.'

I shook my head dubiously. The full of the moon theory left me entirely cold. I had my way with Poirot, however, and we departed immediately, leaving behind us a note of explanation and apology for Lord Yardly.

My idea was to go at once to the *Magnificent*, and relate to Miss Marvell what had occurred, but Poirot vetoed the plan, and insisted that the morning would be time enough. I gave in rather grudgingly.

In the morning Poirot seemed strangely disinclined to stir out. I began to suspect that, having made a mistake to start with, he was singularly loath to proceed with the case. In answer to my persuasions, he pointed out, with admirable common sense, that as the details of the affair at Yardly Chase were already in the morning papers the Rolfs would know quite as much as we could tell them. I gave way unwillingly.

Events proved my forebodings to be justified. About two o'clock, the telephone rang. Poirot answered it. He listened for some moments, then with a brief '*Bien, j'y serai*' he rang off, and turned to me.

'What do you think, *mon ami*?' He looked half ashamed, half excited. 'The diamond of Miss Marvell, it has been stolen.'

'What?' I cried, springing up. 'And what about the "full of the moon" now?' Poirot hung his head. 'When did this happen?'

'This morning, I understand.'

I shook my head sadly. 'If only you had listened to me. You see I was right.'

'It appears so, *mon ami*,' said Poirot cautiously. 'Appearances are deceptive, they say, but it certainly appears so.'

As we hurried in a taxi to the *Magnificent*, I puzzled out the true inwardness of the scheme.

'That "full of the moon" idea was clever. The whole point of it was to get us to concentrate on the Friday, and so be off our guard beforehand. It is a pity you did not realize that.'

'*Ma foi!*' said Poirot airily, his nonchalance quite restored after its brief eclipse. 'One cannot think of everything!'

I felt sorry for him. He did so hate failure of any kind.

'Cheer up,' I said consolingly. 'Better luck next time.'

At the *Magnificent*, we were ushered at once into the manager's office. Gregory Rolf was there with two men from Scotland Yard. A pale-faced clerk sat opposite them.

Rolf nodded to us as we entered.

'We're getting to the bottom of it,' he said. 'But it's almost unbelievable. How the guy had the nerve I can't think.'

A very few minutes sufficed to give us the facts. Mr Rolf had gone out of the hotel at 11.15. At 11.30, a gentleman, so like him in appearance as to pass muster, entered the hotel and demanded the jewel-case from the safe deposit. He duly signed the receipt, remarking carelessly as he did so: 'Looks a bit different from my ordinary one, but I hurt my hand getting out of the taxi.' The clerk merely smiled and remarked that he saw very little difference. Rolf laughed and said: 'Well, don't run me in as a crook this time, anyway. I've been getting threatening letters from a Chinaman, and the worst of it is I look rather like a Chink myself – it's something about the eyes.'

'I looked at him,' said the clerk who was telling us this,

'and I saw at once what he meant. The eyes slanted up at the corners like an Oriental's. I'd never noticed it before.'

'Darn it all, man,' roared Gregory Rolf, leaning forward, 'do you notice it now?'

The man looked up at him and started.

'No, sir,' he said. 'I can't say I do.' And indeed there was nothing even remotely Oriental about the frank brown eyes that looked into ours.

The Scotland Yard man grunted. 'Bold customer. Thought the eyes might be noticed, and took the bull by the horns to disarm suspicion. He must have watched you out of the hotel, sir, and nipped in as soon as you were well away.'

'What about the jewel-case?' I asked.

'It was found in the corridor of the hotel. Only one thing had been taken – "The Western Star".'

We stared at each other – the whole thing was so bizarre, so unreal.

Poirot hopped briskly to his feet. 'I have not been of much use, I fear,' he said regretfully. 'Is it permitted to see Madame?'

'I guess she's prostrated with the shock,' exclaimed Rolf.

'Then perhaps I might have a few words alone with you, monsieur?'

'Certainly.'

In about five minutes Poirot reappeared.

'Now, my friend,' he said gaily. 'To a post office. I have to send a telegram.'

'Who to?'

'Lord Yardly.' He discounted further inquiries by slipping his arm through mine. 'Come, come, *mon ami*. I know all that you feel about this terrible business. I have not distinguished myself! You, in my place, might have distinguished yourself. *Bien!* All is admitted. Let us forget it and have lunch.'

It was about four o'clock when we entered Poirot's rooms. A figure rose from a chair by the window. It was Lord Yardly. He looked haggard and distraught.

'I got your wire and came up at once. Look here, I've been

round to Hoffberg, and they know nothing about that man of theirs last night, or the wire either. Do you think that –'

Poirot held up his hand.

'My excuses! I sent that wire, and hired the gentleman in question.'

'*You* – but why? What?' The nobleman spluttered impotently.

'My little idea was to bring things to a head,' explained Poirot placidly.

'Bring things to a head! Oh, my God!' cried Lord Yardly.

'And the ruse succeeded,' said Poirot cheerfully. 'Therefore, *milord*, I have much pleasure in returning you – this!' With a dramatic gesture he produced a glittering object. It was a great diamond.

'The Star of the East,' gasped Lord Yardly. 'But I don't understand –'

'No?' said Poirot. 'It makes no matter. Believe me, it was necessary for the diamond to be stolen. I promised you that it would be preserved to you, and I have kept my word. You must permit me to keep my little secret. Convey, I beg of you, the assurance of my deepest respect to Lady Yardly, and tell her how pleased I am to be able to restore her jewel to her. What *beau temps*, is it not? Good day, *milord*.'

And smiling and talking, the amazing little man conducted the bewildered nobleman to the door. He returned gently rubbing his hands.

'Poirot,' I said. 'Am I quite demented?'

'No, *mon ami*, but you are, as always, in a mental fog.'

'How did you get the diamond?'

'From Mr Rolf.'

'Rolf?'

'*Mais oui!* The warning letters, the Chinaman, the article in *Society Gossip*, all sprang from the ingenious brain of Mr Rolf! The two diamonds, supposed to be so miraculously alike – bah! they did not exist. There was only *one* diamond, my friend! Originally in the Yardly collection, for three years it has been in the possession of Mr Rolf. He stole it this morning with the assistance of a touch of grease paint at the corner of each eye! Ah, I must see him on the film, he is indeed an artist, *celui-là*!'

'But why should he steal his own diamond?' I asked, puzzled.

'For many reasons. To begin with, Lady Yardly was getting restive.'

'Lady Yardly?'

'You comprehend she was left much alone in California. Her husband was amusing himself elsewhere. Mr Rolf was handsome, he had an air about him of romance. But *au fond*, he is very businesslike, *ce monsieur*! He made love to Lady Yardly, and then he blackmailed her. I taxed the lady with the truth the other night, and she admitted it. She swore that she had only been indiscreet, and I believe her. But, undoubtedly, Rolf had letters of hers that could be twisted to bear a different interpretation. Terrified by the threat of a divorce, and the prospect of being separated from her children, she agreed to all he wished. She had no money of her own, and she was forced to permit him to substitute a paste replica for the real stone. The coincidence of the date of the appearance of "The Western Star" struck me at once. All goes well. Lord Yardly prepares to range himself – to settle down. And then comes the menace of the possible sale of the diamond. The substitution will be discovered. Without doubt she writes off frantically to Gregory Rolf who has just arrived in England. He soothes her by promising to arrange all – and prepares for a double robbery. In this way he will quiet the lady, who might conceivably tell all to her husband, an affair which would not suit our blackmailer at all, he will have £50,000 insurance money (aha, you had forgotten that!), and he will still have the diamond! At this point I put my fingers in the pie. The arrival of a diamond expert is announced. Lady Yardly, as I felt sure she would, immediately arranges a robbery – and does it very well too! But Hercule Poirot, he sees nothing but facts. What happens in actuality? The lady switches off the light, bangs the door, throws the necklace down the passage, and screams. She has already wrenched out the diamond with pliers upstairs –'

'But we saw the necklace round her neck!' I objected.

'I demand pardon, my friend. Her hand concealed the part of it where the gap would have shown. To place a piece of silk in the door beforehand is child's play! Of course, as soon as Rolf read of the robbery, he arranged his own little comedy. And very well he played it!'

'What did you say to him?' I asked with lively curiosity.

'I said to him that Lady Yardly had told her husband all, that I was empowered to recover the jewel, and that if it were not immediately handed over proceedings would be taken. Also a few more little lies which occurred to me. He was as wax in my hands!'

I pondered the matter.

'It seems a little unfair on Mary Marvell. She has lost her diamond through no fault of her own.'

'Bah!' said Poirot brutally. 'She has a magnificent advertisement. That is all she cares for, that one! Now the other, she is different. *Bonne mère, très femme!*'

'Yes,' I said doubtfully, hardly sharing Poirot's views on femininity. 'I suppose it was Rolf who sent her the duplicate letters.'

'*Pas du tout,*' said Poirot briskly. 'She came by the advice of Mary Cavendish to seek my aid in her dilemma. Then she heard that Mary Marvell, whom she knew to be her enemy, had been here, and she changed her mind jumping at a pretext that *you*, my friend, offered her. A very few questions sufficed to show me that *you* told her of the letters, not she you! She jumped at the chance your words offered.'

'I don't believe it,' I cried, stung.

'*Si, si, mon ami,* it is a pity that you study not the psychology. She told you that the letters were destroyed? Oh, *la la, never* does a woman destroy a letter if she can avoid it! Not even if it would be more prudent to do so!'

'It's all very well,' I said, my anger rising, 'but you've made a perfect fool of me! From beginning to end! No, it's all very well to try and explain it away afterwards. There really is a limit!'

'But you were so enjoying yourself, my friend, I had not the heart to shatter your illusions.'

'It's no good. You've gone a bit too far this time.'

'*Mon Dieu!* but how you enrage yourself for nothing, *mon ami!*'

'I'm fed up!' I went out, banging the door. Poirot had made an absolute laughing-stock of me. I decided that he needed a sharp lesson. I would let some time elapse before I forgave him. He had encouraged me to make a perfect fool of myself.

The Tragedy at Marsdon Manor

I had been called away from town for a few days, and on my return found Poirot in the act of strapping up his small valise.

'*A la bonne heure*, Hastings, I feared you would not have returned in time to accompany me.'

'You are called away on a case, then?'

'Yes, though I am bound to admit that, on the face of it, the affair does not seem promising. The Northern Union Insurance Company have asked me to investigate the death of a Mr Maltravers who a few weeks ago insured his life with them for the large sum of fifty thousand pounds.'

'Yes?' I said, much interested.

'There was, of course, the usual suicide clause in the policy. In the event of his committing suicide within a year the premiums would be forfeited. Mr Maltravers was duly examined by the Company's own doctor, and although he was a man slightly past the prime of life was passed as being in quite sound health. However, on Wednesday last – the day before yesterday – the body of Mr Maltravers was found in the grounds of his house in Essex, Marsdon Manor, and the cause of his death is described as some kind of internal haemorrhage. That in itself would be nothing remarkable, but sinister rumours as to Mr Maltravers' financial position have been in the air of late, and the Northern Union have ascertained beyond any possible doubt that the deceased gentleman stood upon the verge of bankruptcy. Now that alters matters considerably. Maltravers had a beautiful young wife, and it is suggested that he got together all the ready money he could for the purpose of paying the premiums on a life insurance for his wife's benefit, and then committed suicide. Such a thing is not uncommon. In any case, my friend Alfred Wright, who is a director of the Northern Union, has asked me to investigate the facts of the case, but, as I told him, I am not very hopeful of success. If the cause of the death had been heart failure, I should have been more sanguine. Heart failure may always be translated as the inability of the local GP to discover what his patient really did die of, but a haemorrhage seems fairly definite. Still, we can but make some necessary inquiries. Five minutes to pack your bag, Hastings, and we will take a taxi to Liverpool Street.'

About an hour later, we alighted from a Great Eastern train at the little station of Marsdon Leigh. Inquiries at the station yielded the information that Marsdon Manor was about a mile distant. Poirot decided to walk, and we betook ourselves along the main street.

'What is our plan of campaign?' I asked.

'First I will call upon the doctor. I have ascertained that there is only one doctor in Marsdon Leigh, Dr Ralph Bernard. Ah, here we are at his house.'

The house in question was a kind of superior cottage, standing back a little from the road. A brass plate on the gate bore the doctor's name. We passed up the path and rang the bell.

We proved to be fortunate in our call. It was the doctor's consulting hour, and for the moment there were no patients waiting for him. Dr Bernard was an elderly man, high-shouldered and stooping, with a pleasant vagueness of manner.

Poirot introduced himself and explained the purpose of our visit, adding that Insurance Companies were bound to investigate fully in a case of this kind.

'Of course, of course,' said Dr Bernard vaguely. 'I suppose, as he was such a rich man, his life was insured for a big sum?'

'You consider him a rich man, doctor?'

The doctor looked rather surprised.

'Was he not? He kept two cars, you know, and Marsdon Manor is a pretty big place to keep up, although I believe he bought it very cheap.'

'I understand that he had had considerable losses of late,' said Poirot, watching the doctor narrowly.

The latter, however, merely shook his head sadly.

'Is that so? Indeed. It is fortunate for his wife, then, that there is this life insurance. A very beautiful and charming young creature, but terribly unstrung by this sad catastrophe. A mass of nerves, poor thing. I have tried to spare her all I can, but of course the shock was bound to be considerable.'

'You had been attending Mr Maltravers recently?'

'My dear sir, I never attended him.'

'What?'

'I understand Mr Maltravers was a Christian Scientist – or something of that kind.'

'But you examined the body?'

'Certainly. I was fetched by one of the under-gardeners.'

'And the cause of death was clear?'

'Absolutely. There was blood on the lips, but most of the bleeding must have been internal.'

'Was he still lying where he had been found?'

'Yes, the body had not been touched. He was lying at the edge of a small plantation. He had evidently been out shooting rooks, a small rook rifle lay beside him. The haemorrhage must have occurred quite suddenly. Gastric ulcer, without a doubt.'

'No question of his having been shot, eh?'

'My dear sir!'

'I demand pardon,' said Poirot humbly. 'But, if my memory is not at fault, in the case of a recent murder, the doctor first gave a verdict of heart failure – altering it when the local constable pointed out that there was a bullet wound through the head!'

'You will not find any bullet wounds on the body of Mr Maltravers,' said Dr Bernard dryly. 'Now gentlemen, if there is nothing further –'

We took the hint.

'Good morning, and many thanks to you, doctor, for so

kindly answering our questions. By the way, you saw no need for an autopsy?'

'Certainly not.' The doctor became quite apoplectic. 'The cause of death was clear, and in my profession we see no need to distress unduly the relatives of a dead patient.'

And, turning, the doctor slammed the door sharply in our faces.

'And what do you think of Dr Bernard, Hastings?' inquired Poirot, as we proceeded on our way to the Manor.

'Rather an old ass.'

'Exactly. Your judgements of character are always profound, my friend.'

I glanced at him uneasily, but he seemed perfectly serious. A twinkle, however, came into his eye, and he added slyly:

'That is to say, where there is no question of a beautiful woman!'

I looked at him coldly.

On our arrival at the manor house, the door was opened to us by a middle-aged parlourmaid. Poirot handed her his card, and a letter from the Insurance Company for Mrs Maltravers. She showed us into a small morning room, and retired to tell her mistress. About ten minutes elapsed, and then the door opened, and a slender figure in widow's weeds stood upon the threshold.

'Monsieur Poirot?' she faltered.

'Madame!' Poirot sprang gallantly to his feet and hastened towards her. 'I cannot tell you how I regret to derange you in this way. But what will you? *Les affaires* – they know no mercy.'

Mrs Maltravers permitted him to lead her to a chair. Her eyes were red with weeping, but the temporary disfigurement could not conceal her extraordinary beauty. She was about twenty-seven or -eight, and very fair, with large blue eyes and a pretty pouting mouth.

'It is something about my husband's insurance, is it? But must I be bothered *now* – so soon?'

'Courage, my dear madame. Courage! You see, your late

husband insured his life for rather a large sum, and in such a case the Company always has to satisfy itself as to a few details. They have empowered me to act for them. You can rest assured that I will do all in my power to render the matter not too unpleasant for you. Will you recount to me briefly the sad events of Wednesday?'

'I was changing for tea when my maid came up – one of the gardeners had just run to the house. He had found –'

Her voice trailed away. Poirot pressed her hand sympathetically.

'I comprehend. Enough! You had seen your husband earlier in the afternoon?'

'Not since lunch. I had walked down to the village for some stamps, and I believe he was out pottering round the grounds.'

'Shooting rooks, eh?'

'Yes, he usually took his little rook rifle with him, and I heard one or two shots in the distance.'

'Where is this little rook rifle now?'

'In the hall, I think.'

She led the way out of the room and found and handed the little weapon to Poirot, who examined it cursorily.

'Two shots fired, I see,' he observed, as he handed it back. 'And now, madame, if I might see –'

He paused delicately.

'The servant shall take you,' she murmured, averting her head.

The parlourmaid, summoned, led Poirot upstairs. I remained with the lovely and unfortunate woman. It was hard to know whether to speak or remain silent. I essayed one or two general reflections to which she responded absently, and in a very few minutes Poirot rejoined us.

'I thank you for all your courtesy, madame. I do not think you need be troubled any further with this matter. By the way, do you know anything of your husband's financial position?'

She shook her head.

'Nothing whatever. I am very stupid over business things.'

'I see. Then you can give us no clue as to why he suddenly

decided to insure his life? He had not done so previously, I understand.'

'Well, we had only been married a little over a year. But, as to why he insured his life, it was because he had absolutely made up his mind that he would not live long. He had a strong premonition of his own death. I gather that he had had one haemorrhage already, and that he knew that another one would prove fatal. I tried to dispel these gloomy fears of his, but without avail. Alas, he was only too right!'

Tears in her eyes, she bade us a dignified farewell. Poirot made a characteristic gesture as we walked down the drive together.

'*Eh bien*, that is that! Back to London, my friend, there appears to be no mouse in this mouse-hole. And yet –'

'Yet what?'

'A slight discrepancy, that is all! You noticed it? You did not? Still, life is full of discrepancies, and assuredly the man cannot have taken his life – there is no poison that would fill his mouth with blood. No, no, I must resign myself to the fact that all here is clear and above board – but who is this?'

A tall young man was striding up the drive towards us. He passed us without making any sign, but I noted that he was not ill-looking, with a lean, deeply-bronzed face that spoke of life in a tropic clime. A gardener who was sweeping up leaves had paused for a minute in his task, and Poirot ran quickly up to him.

'Tell me, I pray you, who is that gentleman? Do you know him?'

'I don't remember his name, sir, though I did hear it. He was staying down here last week for a night. Tuesday, it was.'

'Quick, *mon ami*, let us follow him.'

We hastened up the drive after the retreating figure. A glimpse of a black-robed figure on the terrace at the side of the house, and our quarry swerved and we after him, so that we were witnesses of the meeting.

Mrs Maltravers almost staggered where she stood, and her face blanched noticeably.

'You,' she gasped. 'I thought you were on the sea – on your way to East Africa?'

'I got some news from my lawyers that detained me,' explained the young man. 'My old uncle in Scotland died unexpectedly and left me some money. Under the circumstances I thought it better to cancel my passage. Then I saw this bad news in the paper and I came down to see if there was anything I could do. You'll want someone to look after things for you a bit perhaps.'

At that moment they became aware of our presence. Poirot stepped forward, and with many apologies explained that he had left his stick in the hall. Rather reluctantly, it seemed to me, Mrs Maltravers made the necessary introduction.

'Monsieur Poirot, Captain Black.'

A few minutes' chat ensued, in the course of which Poirot elicited the fact that Captain Black was putting up at the Anchor Inn. The missing stick not having been discovered (which was not surprising), Poirot uttered more apologies and we withdrew.

We returned to the village at a great pace, and Poirot made a beeline for the Anchor Inn.

'Here we establish ourselves until our friend the Captain returns,' he explained. 'You noticed that I emphasized the point that we were returning to London by the first train? Possibly you thought I meant it. But no – you observed Mrs Maltravers' face when she caught sight of this young Black? She was clearly taken aback, and he – *eh bien*, he was very devoted, did you not think so? And he was here on Tuesday night – the day before Mr Maltravers died. We must investigate the doings of Captain Black, Hastings.'

In about half an hour we espied our quarry approaching the inn. Poirot went out and accosted him and presently brought him up to the room we had engaged.

'I have been telling Captain Black of the mission which brings us here,' he explained. 'You can understand, *monsieur le capitaine*, that I am anxious to arrive at Mr Maltravers' state of mind immediately before his death, and that at the same time I do not wish to distress Mrs Maltravers unduly by asking her painful questions. Now, you were here just before the occurrence, and can give us equally valuable information.'

'I'll do anything I can to help you, I'm sure,' replied the young soldier; 'but I'm afraid I didn't notice anything out of the ordinary. You see, although Maltravers was an old friend of my people's, I didn't know him very well myself.'

'You came down – when?'

'Tuesday afternoon. I went up to town early Wednesday morning, as my boat sailed from Tilbury about twelve o'clock. But some news I got made me alter my plans, as I dare say you heard me explain to Mrs Maltravers.'

'You were returning to East Africa, I understand?'

'Yes. I've been out there ever since the War – a great country.'

'Exactly. Now what was the talk about at dinner on Tuesday night?'

'Oh, I don't know. The usual odd topics. Maltravers asked after my people, and then we discussed the question of German reparations, and then Mr Maltravers asked a lot of questions about East Africa, and I told them one or two yarns, that's about all, I think.'

'Thank you.'

Poirot was silent for a moment, then he said gently: 'With your permission, I should like to try a little experiment. You have told us all that your conscious self knows, I want now to question your subconscious self.'

'Psychoanalysis, what?' said Black, with visible alarm.

'Oh, no,' said Poirot reassuringly. 'You see, it is like this, I give you a word, you answer with another, and so on. Any word, the first you think of. Shall we begin?'

'All right,' said Black slowly, but he looked uneasy.

'Note down the words, please, Hastings,' said Poirot. Then he took from his pocket his big turnip-faced watch and laid it on the table beside him. 'We will commence. Day.'

There was a moment's pause, and then Black replied:
'*Night.*'

As Poirot proceeded, his answers came quicker.
'Name,' said Poirot.
'*Place.*'
'Bernard.'
'*Shaw.*'
'Tuesday.'
'*Dinner.*'
'Journey.'
'*Ship.*'
'Country.'
'*Uganda.*'
'Story.'
'*Lions.*'
'Rook Rifle.'
'*Farm.*'
'Shot.'
'*Suicide.*'
'Elephant.'
'*Tusks.*'
'Money.'
'*Lawyers.*'
'Thank you, Captain Black. Perhaps you could spare me a few minutes in about half an hour's time?'

'Certainly.' The young soldier looked at him curiously and wiped his brow as he got up.

'And now, Hastings,' said Poirot, smiling at me as the door closed behind him. 'You see it all, do you not?'

'I don't know what you mean.'

'Does that list of words tell you nothing?'

I scrutinized it, but was forced to shake my head.

'I will assist you. To begin with, Black answered well within the normal time limit, with no pauses, so we can take it that he himself has no guilty knowledge to conceal. "Day" to "Night" and "Place" to "Name" are normal associations. I began work with "Bernard," which might have suggested the local doctor had he come across him at all. Evidently he had not. After our recent conversation, he gave "Dinner" to my

"Tuesday", but "Journey" and "Country" were answered by "Ship" and "Uganda", showing clearly that it was his journey abroad that was important to him and not the one which brought him down here. "Story" recalls to him one of the "Lion" stories he told at dinner. I proceeded to "Rook Rifle" and he answered with the totally unexpected word "Farm". When I say "Shot", he answers at once "Suicide". The association seems clear. A man he knows committed suicide with a rook rifle on a farm somewhere. Remember, too, that his mind is still on the stories he told at dinner, and I think you will agree that I shall not be far from the truth if I recall Captain Black and ask him to repeat the particular suicide story which he told at the dinner-table on Tuesday evening.'

Black was straightforward enough over the matter.

'Yes, I did tell them that story now that I come to think of it. Chap shot himself on a farm out there. Did it with a rook rifle through the roof of the mouth, bullet lodged in the brain. Doctors were no end puzzled over it – there was nothing to show except a little blood on the lips. But what –?'

'What has it got to do with Mr Maltravers? You did not know, I see, that he was found with a rook rifle by his side.'

'You mean my story suggested to him – oh, but that is awful!'

'Do not distress yourself – it would have been one way or another. Well, I must get on the telephone to London.'

Poirot had a lengthy conversation over the wire, and came back thoughtful. He went off by himself in the afternoon, and it was not till seven o'clock that he announced that he could put it off no longer, but must break the news to the young widow. My sympathy had already gone out to her unreservedly. To be left penniless, and with the knowledge that her husband had killed himself to assure her future, was a hard burden for any woman to bear. I cherished a secret hope, however, that young Black might prove capable of consoling her after her first grief had passed. He evidently admired her enormously.

Our interview with the lady was painful. She refused vehemently to believe the facts that Poirot advanced, and when she was at last convinced broke down into bitter weeping. An examination of the body turned our suspicions into certainty. Poirot was very sorry for the poor lady, but, after all, he was employed by the Insurance Company, and what could he do? As he was preparing to leave he said gently to Mrs Maltravers:

'Madame, you of all people should know that there are no dead!'

'What do you mean?' she faltered, her eyes growing wide.

'Have you never taken part in any spiritualistic séances? You are mediumistic, you know.'

'I have been told so. But you do not believe in Spiritualism, surely?'

'Madame, I have seen some strange things. You know that they say in the village that this house is haunted?'

She nodded, and at that moment the parlourmaid announced that dinner was ready.

'Won't you just stay and have something to eat?'

We accepted gracefully, and I felt that our presence could not but help distract her a little from her own griefs.

We had just finished our soup, when there was a scream outside the door, and the sound of breaking crockery. We jumped up. The parlourmaid appeared, her hand to her heart.

'It was a man – standing in the passage.'

Poirot rushed out, returning quickly.

'There is no one there.'

'Isn't there, sir?' said the parlourmaid weakly. 'Oh it did give me a start!'

'But why?'

She dropped her voice to a whisper.

'I thought – I thought it was the master – it looked like 'im.'

I saw Mrs Maltravers give a terrified start, and my mind flew to the old superstition that a suicide cannot rest. She thought of it too, I am sure, for a minute later, she caught Poirot's arm with a scream.

'Didn't you hear that? Those three taps on the window?

That's how *he* always used to tap when he passed round the house.'

'The ivy,' I cried. 'It was the ivy against the pane.'

But a sort of terror was gaining on us all. The parlourmaid was obviously unstrung, and when the meal was over Mrs Maltravers besought Poirot not to go at once. She was clearly terrified to be left alone. We sat in the little morning room. The wind was getting up, and moaning round the house in an eerie fashion. Twice the door of the room came unlatched and the door slowly opened, and each time she clung to me with a terrified gasp.

'Ah, but this door, it is bewitched!' cried Poirot angrily at last. He got up and shut it once more, then turned the key in the lock. 'I shall lock it, so!'

'Don't do that,' she gasped. 'If it should come open now –'

And even as she spoke the impossible happened. The locked door slowly swung open. I could not see into the passage from where I sat, but she and Poirot were facing it. She gave one long shriek as she turned to him.

'You saw him – there in the passage?' she cried.

He was staring down at her with a puzzled face, then shook his head.

'I saw him – my husband – you must have seen him too?'

'Madame, I saw nothing. You are not well – unstrung –'

'I am perfectly well, I – Oh, God!'

Suddenly, without warning, the lights quivered and went out. Out of the darkness came three loud raps. I could hear Mrs Maltravers moaning.

And then – I saw!

The man I had seen on the bed upstairs stood there facing us, gleaming with a faint ghostly light. There was blood on his lips, and he held his right hand out, pointing. Suddenly a brilliant light seemed to proceed from it. It passed over Poirot and me, and fell on Mrs Maltravers. I saw her white terrified face, and something else!

'My God, Poirot!' I cried. 'Look at her hand, her right hand. It's all red!'

Her own eyes fell on it, and she collapsed in a heap on the floor.

'Blood,' she cried hysterically. 'Yes, it's blood. I killed him. I did it. He was showing me, and then I put my hand on the trigger and pressed. Save me from him – save me! He's come back!'

Her voice died away in a gurgle.

'Lights,' said Poirot briskly.

The lights went on as if by magic.

'That's it,' he continued. 'You heard, Hastings? And you, Everett? Oh, by the way, this is Mr Everett, rather a fine member of the theatrical profession. I phoned to him this afternoon. His make-up is good, isn't it? Quite like the dead man, and with a pocket torch and the necessary phosphorescence he made the proper impression. I shouldn't touch her right hand if I were you, Hastings. Red paint marks so. When the lights went out I clasped her hand, you see. By the way, we mustn't miss our train. Inspector Japp is outside the window. A bad night – but he has been able to while away the time by tapping on the window every now and then.'

'You see,' continued Poirot, as we walked briskly through the wind and rain, 'there was a little discrepancy. The doctor seemed to think the deceased was a Christian Scientist, and who could have given him that impression but Mrs Maltravers? But to us she represented him as being in a great state of apprehension about his own health. Again, why was she so taken aback by the reappearance of young Black? And lastly although I know that convention decrees that a woman must make a decent pretence of mourning for her husband, I do not care for such heavily-rouged eyelids! You did not observe them, Hastings? No? As I always tell you, you see nothing!

'Well, there it was. There were the two possibilities. Did Black's story suggest an ingenious method of committing suicide to Mr Maltravers, or did his other listener, the wife, see an equally ingenious method of committing murder? I inclined to the latter view. To shoot himself in the way indicated, he would probably have had to pull the trigger with his toe – or at least so I imagine. Now if Maltravers had been found with one boot off, we should almost certainly have heard of it from someone. An odd detail like that would have been remembered.

'No, as I say, I inclined to the view that it was the case of murder, not suicide, but I realized that I had not a shadow of proof in support of my theory. Hence the elaborate little comedy you saw played tonight.'

'Even now I don't quite see all the details of the crime,' I said.

'Let us start from the beginning. Here is a shrewd and scheming woman who, knowing of her husband's financial *débâcle* and tired of the elderly mate she had only married for his money, induces him to insure his life for a large sum, and then seeks for the means to accomplish her purpose. An accident gives her that – the young soldier's strange story. The next afternoon when *monsieur le capitaine*, as she thinks, is on the high seas, she and her husband are strolling round the grounds. "What a curious story that was last night!" she observes. "Could a man shoot himself in such a way? Do show me if it is possible!" The poor fool – he shows her. He places the end of his rifle in his mouth. She stoops down, and puts her finger on the trigger, laughing up at him. "And now, sir," she says saucily, "supposing I pull the trigger?"

'And then – and then, Hastings – she pulls it!'

The Adventure of the Cheap Flat

So far, in the cases which I have recorded, Poirot's investigations have started from the central fact, whether murder or robbery, and have proceeded from thence by a process of logical deduction to the final triumphant unravelling. In the events I am now about to chronicle a remarkable chain of circumstances led from the apparently trivial incidents which first attracted Poirot's attention to the sinister happenings which completed a most unusual case.

I had been spending the evening with an old friend of mine, Gerald Parker. There had been, perhaps, about half a dozen people there besides my host and myself, and the talk fell, as it was bound to do sooner or later wherever Parker found himself, on the subject of house-hunting in London. Houses and flats were Parker's special hobby. Since the end of the War, he had occupied at least half a dozen different flats and maisonettes. No sooner was he settled anywhere than he would light unexpectedly upon a new find, and would forthwith depart bag and baggage. His moves were nearly always accomplished at a slight pecuniary gain, for he had a shrewd business head, but it was sheer love of the sport that actuated him, and not a desire to make money at it. We listened to Parker for some time with the respect of the novice for the expert. Then it was our turn, and a perfect babel of tongues was let loose. Finally the floor was left to Mrs Robinson, a charming little bride who was there with her husband. I had never met them before, as Robinson was only a recent acquaintance of Parker's.

'Talking of flats,' she said, 'have you heard of our piece of luck, Mr Parker? We've got a flat – at last! In Montagu Mansions.'

'Well,' said Parker, 'I've always said there are plenty of flats – at a price!'

'Yes, but this isn't at a price. It's dirt cheap. Eighty pounds a year!'

'But – but Montagu Mansions is just off Knightsbridge, isn't it? Big handsome building. Or are you talking of a poor relation of the same name stuck in the slums somewhere?'

'No, it's the Knightsbridge one. That's what makes it so wonderful.'

'Wonderful is the word! It's a blinking miracle. But there must be a catch somewhere. Big premium, I suppose?'

'No premium!'

'No prem – oh, hold my head, somebody!' groaned Parker.

'But we've got to buy the furniture,' continued Mrs Robinson.

'Ah!' Parker bristled up. 'I knew there was a catch!'

'For fifty pounds. And it's beautifully furnished!'

'I give it up,' said Parker. 'The present occupants must be lunatics with a taste for philanthropy.'

Mrs Robinson was looking a little troubled. A little pucker appeared between her dainty brows.

'It *is* queer, isn't it? You don't think that – that – the place is *haunted*?'

'Never heard of a haunted flat,' declared Parker decisively.

'No-o.' Mrs Robinson appeared far from convinced. 'But there were several things about it all that struck me as – well, queer.'

'For instance –' I suggested.

'Ah,' said Parker, 'our criminal expert's attention is aroused! Unburden yourself to him, Mrs Robinson. Hastings is a great unraveller of mysteries.'

I laughed, embarrassed, but not wholly displeased with the rôle thrust upon me.

'Oh, not really queer, Captain Hastings, but when we went

to the agents, Stosser and Paul – we hadn't tried them before because they only have the expensive Mayfair flats, but we thought at any rate it would do no harm – everything they offered us was four and five hundred a year, or else huge premiums, and then, just as we were going, they mentioned that they had a flat at eighty, but that they doubted if it would be any good our going there, because it had been on their books some time and they had sent so many people to see it that it was almost sure to be taken – "snapped up" as the clerk put it – only people were so tiresome in not letting them know, and then they went on sending, and people get annoyed at being sent to a place that had, perhaps, been let some time.'

Mrs Robinson paused for some much needed breath, and then continued:

'We thanked him, and said that we quite understood it would probably be no good, but that we should like an order all the same – just in case. And we went there straight away in a taxi, for, after all, you never know. No 4 was on the second floor, and just as we were waiting for the lift, Elsie Ferguson – she's a friend of mine, Captain Hastings, and they are looking for a flat too – came hurrying down the stairs. "Ahead of you for once, my dear," she said. "But it's no good. It's already let." That seemed to finish it, but – well, as John said, the place was very cheap, we could afford to give more, and perhaps if we offered a premium. A horrid thing to do, of course, and I feel quite ashamed of telling you, but you know what flat-hunting is.'

I assured her that I was well aware that in the struggle for house-room the baser side of human nature frequently triumphed over the higher, and that the well-known rule of dog eat dog always applied.

'So we went up and, would you believe it, the flat wasn't let at all. We were shown over it by the maid, and then we saw the mistress, and the thing was settled then and there. Immediate possession and fifty pounds for the furniture. We signed the agreement next day, and we are to move in tomorrow!' Mrs Robinson paused triumphantly.

'And what about Mrs Ferguson?' asked Parker. 'Let's have your deductions, Hastings.'

'"Obvious, my dear Watson,"' I quoted lightly. 'She went to the wrong flat.'

'Oh, Captain Hastings, how clever of you!' cried Mrs Robinson admiringly.

I rather wished Poirot had been there. Sometimes I have the feeling that he rather underestimates my capabilities.

The whole thing was rather amusing, and I propounded the thing as a mock problem to Poirot on the following morning. He seemed interested, and questioned me rather narrowly as to the rents of flats in various localities.

'A curious story,' he said thoughtfully. 'Excuse me, Hastings, I must take a short stroll.'

When he returned, about an hour later, his eyes were gleaming with a peculiar excitement. He laid his stick on the table, and brushed the nap of his hat with his usual tender care before he spoke.

'It is as well, *mon ami*, that we have no affairs of moment on hand. We can devote ourselves wholly to the present investigation.'

'What investigation are you talking about?'

'The remarkable cheapness of your friend, Mrs Robinson's, new flat.'

'Poirot, you are not serious!'

'I am most serious. Figure to yourself, my friend, that the real rent of those flats is £350. I have just ascertained that from the landlord's agents. And yet this particular flat is being sublet at eighty pounds! Why?'

'There must be something wrong with it. Perhaps it is haunted, as Mrs Robinson suggested.'

Poirot shook his head in a dissatisfied manner.

'Then again how curious it is that her friend tells her the flat is let, and, when she goes up, behold, it is not so at all!'

'But surely you agree with me that the other woman must have gone to the wrong flat. That is the only possible solution.'

'You may or may not be right on that point, Hastings. The fact still remains that numerous other applicants were sent to see it, and yet, in spite of its remarkable cheapness, it was still in the market when Mrs Robinson arrived.'

'That shows that there *must* be something wrong about it.'

'Mrs Robinson did not seem to notice anything amiss. Very curious, is it not? Did she impress you as being a truthful woman, Hastings?'

'She was a delightful creature!'

'*Evidemment!* since she renders you incapable of replying to my question. Describe her to me, then.'

'Well, she's tall and fair; her hair's really a beautiful shade of auburn –'

'Always you have had a penchant for auburn hair!' murmured Poirot. 'But continue.'

'Blue eyes and a very nice complexion and – well, that's all, I think,' I concluded lamely.

'And her husband?'

'Oh, he's quite a nice fellow – nothing startling.'

'Dark or fair?'

'I don't know – betwixt and between, and just an ordinary sort of face.'

Poirot nodded.

'Yes, there are hundreds of these average men – and anyway, you bring more sympathy and appreciation to your description of women. Do you know anything about these people? Does Parker know them well?'

'They are just recent acquaintances, I believe. But surely, Poirot, you don't think for an instant –'

Poirot raised his hand.

'*Tout doucement, mon ami.* Have I said that I think anything? All I say is – it is a curious story. And there is nothing to throw light upon it; except perhaps the lady's name, eh, Hastings?'

'Her name is Stella,' I said stiffly, 'but I don't see –'

Poirot interrupted me with a tremendous chuckle. Something seemed to be amusing him vastly.

'And Stella means a star, does it not? Famous!'

'What on earth –?'

'And stars give light! *Voilà!* Calm yourself, Hastings. Do not put on that air of injured dignity. Come, we will go to Montagu Mansions and make a few inquiries.'

I accompanied him, nothing loath. The Mansions were a handsome block of buildings in excellent repair. A uniformed porter was sunning himself on the threshold, and it was to him that Poirot addressed himself.

'Pardon, but would you tell me if a Mr and Mrs Robinson reside here?'

The porter was a man of few words and apparently of a sour or suspicious disposition. He hardly looked at us and grunted out:

'No 4. Second floor.'

'I thank you. Can you tell me how long they have been here?'

'Six months.'

I started forward in amazement, conscious as I did so of Poirot's malicious grin.

'Impossible,' I cried. 'You must be making a mistake.'

'Six months.'

'Are you sure? The lady I mean is tall and fair with reddish gold hair and –'

'That's 'er,' said the porter. 'Come in the Michaelmas quarter, they did. Just six months ago.'

He appeared to lose interest in us and retreated slowly up the hall. I followed Poirot outside.

'*Eh bien*, Hastings?' my friend demanded slyly. 'Are you so sure now that delightful women always speak the truth?'

I did not reply.

Poirot had steered his way into Brompton Road before I asked him what he was going to do and where we were going.

'To the house agents, Hastings. I have a great desire to have a flat in Montagu Mansions. If I am not mistaken, several interesting things will take place there before long.'

We were fortunate in our quest. No 8, on the fourth floor, was to be let furnished at ten guineas a week, Poirot promptly took it for a month. Outside in the street again, he silenced my protests:

'But I make money nowadays! Why should I not indulge a whim? By the way, Hastings, have you a revolver?'

'Yes – somewhere,' I answered, slightly thrilled. 'Do you think –'

'That you will need it? It is quite possible. The idea pleases you, I see. Always the spectacular and romantic appeals to you.'

The following day saw us installed in our temporary home. The flat was pleasantly furnished. It occupied the same position in the building as that of the Robinsons, but was two floors higher.

The day after our installation was a Sunday. In the afternoon, Poirot left the front door ajar, and summoned me hastily as a bang reverberated from somewhere below.

'Look over the banisters. Are those your friends? Do not let them see you.'

I craned my neck over the staircase.

'That's them,' I declared in an ungrammatical whisper.

'Good. Wait awhile.'

About half an hour later, a young woman emerged in brilliant and varied clothing. With a sigh of satisfaction, Poirot tiptoed back into the flat.

'*C'est ça.* After the master and mistress, the maid. The flat should now be empty.'

'What are we going to do?' I asked uneasily.

Poirot had trotted briskly into the scullery and was hauling at the rope of the coal-lift.

'We are about to descend after the method of the dustbins,' he explained cheerfully. 'No one will observe us. The Sunday concert, the Sunday "afternoon out", and finally the Sunday nap after the Sunday dinner of England – *le rosbif* – all these will distract attention from the doings of Hercule Poirot. Come, my friend.'

He stepped into the rough wooden contrivance and I followed him gingerly.

'Are we going to break into the flat?' I asked dubiously.

Poirot's answer was not too reassuring:

'Not precisely today,' he replied.

Pulling on the rope, we descended slowly till we reached the second floor. Poirot uttered an exclamation of satisfaction as he perceived that the wooden door into the scullery was open.

'You observe? Never do they bolt these doors in the daytime. And yet anyone could mount or descend as we have done. At night, yes – though not always then – and it is against that that we are going to make provision.'

He had drawn some tools from his pocket as he spoke, and at once set deftly to work, his object being to arrange the bolt so that it could be pulled back from the lift. The operation only occupied about three minutes. Then Poirot returned the tools to his pocket, and we reascended once more to our own domain.

On Monday Poirot was out all day, but when he returned in the evening he flung himself into his chair with a sigh of satisfaction.

'Hastings, shall I recount to you a little history? A story after your own heart and which will remind you of your favourite cinema?'

'Go ahead,' I laughed. 'I presume that it is a true story, not one of your efforts of fancy.'

'It is true enough. Inspector Japp of Scotland Yard will vouch for its accuracy, since it was through his kind offices that it came to my ears. Listen, Hastings. A little over six months ago some important Naval plans were stolen from an American Government department. They showed the position of some of the most important Harbour defences, and would be worth a considerable sum to any foreign Government – that of Japan, for example. Suspicion fell upon a young man named Luigi Valdarno, an Italian by birth, who was employed in a minor capacity in the Department and who was missing at the same time as the papers. Whether Luigi Valdarno was the thief or not, he was found two days later on the East Side in New York, shot dead. The papers were not on him. Now for some time past Luigi Valdarno had been going about with a Miss Elsa Hardt, a young concert singer who had recently appeared and who lived with a brother in an apartment in Washington. Nothing was known of the antecedents of Miss Elsa Hardt, and she disappeared suddenly about the time of Valdarno's death. There are reasons for believing that she was in reality an accomplished international spy who has done much nefarious work under various aliases. The American Secret Service, while doing their best to trace her, also kept an eye upon certain insignificant Japanese gentlemen living in Washington. They felt pretty certain that, when Elsa Hardt had covered her tracks sufficiently, she would approach the gentlemen in question. One of them left suddenly for England a fortnight ago. On the face of it, therefore, it would seem that Elsa Hardt is in England.' Poirot paused, and then added softly: 'The official description of Elsa Hardt is: Height 5 ft 7, eyes blue, hair auburn, fair complexion, nose straight, no special distinguishing marks.'

'Mrs Robinson!' I gasped.

'Well, there is a chance of it, anyhow,' amended Poirot. 'Also I learn that a swarthy man, a foreigner of some kind, was inquiring about the occupants of No 4 only this morning. Therefore, *mon ami*, I fear that you must forswear your beauty sleep tonight, and join me in my all-night vigil in that flat below – armed with that excellent revolver of yours, *bien entendu!*'

'Rather,' I cried with enthusiasm. 'When shall we start?'

'The hour of midnight is both solemn and suitable, I fancy. Nothing is likely to occur before then.'

At twelve o'clock precisely, we crept cautiously into the coal-lift and lowered ourselves to the second floor. Under Poirot's manipulation, the wooden door quickly swung inwards, and we climbed into the flat. From the scullery we passed into the kitchen where we established ourselves comfortably in two chairs with the door into the hall ajar.

'Now we have but to wait,' said Poirot contentedly, closing his eyes.

To me, the waiting appeared endless. I was terrified of going to sleep. Just when it seemed to me that I had been there about eight hours – and had, as I found out afterwards, in reality been exactly one hour and twenty minutes – a faint scratching sound came to my ears. Poirot's hand touched mine. I rose, and together we moved carefully in the direction of the hall. The noise came from there. Poirot placed his lips to my ear.

'Outside the front door. They are cutting out the lock. When I give the word, not before, fall upon him from behind and hold him fast. Be careful, he will have a knife.'

Presently there was a rending sound, and a little circle of light appeared through the door. It was extinguished immediately and then the door was slowly opened. Poirot and I flattened ourselves against the wall. I heard a man's breathing as he passed us. Then he flashed on his torch, and as he did so, Poirot hissed in my ear:

'*Allez.*'

We sprang together, Poirot with a quick movement enveloped the intruder's head with a light woollen scarf whilst I pinioned his arms. The whole affair was quick and noiseless. I twisted a dagger from his hand, and as Poirot brought down the scarf from his eyes, whilst keeping it wound tightly round his mouth, I jerked up my revolver where he could see it and understand that resistance was useless. As he ceased to struggle Poirot put his mouth close to his ear and began to whisper rapidly. After a minute the man nodded. Then enjoining silence with a movement of the hand, Poirot led the way out of the flat and down the stairs. Our captive followed, and I brought up the rear with the revolver. When we were out in the street, Poirot turned to me.

'There is a taxi waiting just round the corner. Give me the revolver. We shall not need it now.'

'But if this fellow tries to escape?'

Poirot smiled.

'He will not.'

I returned in a minute with the waiting taxi. The scarf had been unwound from the stranger's face, and I gave a start of surprise.

'He's not a Jap,' I ejaculated in a whisper to Poirot.

'Observation was always your strong point, Hastings! Nothing escapes you. No, the man is not a Jap. He is an Italian.'

We got into the taxi, and Poirot gave the driver an address in St John's Wood. I was by now completely fogged. I did not like to ask Poirot where we were going in front of our captive, and strove in vain to obtain some light upon the proceedings.

We alighted at the door of a small house standing back from the road. A returning wayfarer, slightly drunk, was lurching along the pavement and almost collided with Poirot, who said something sharply to him which I did not catch. All three of us went up the steps of the house. Poirot rang the bell and motioned us to stand a little aside. There was no answer and he rang again and then seized the knocker which he plied for some minutes vigorously.

A light appeared suddenly above the fanlight, and the door opened cautiously a little way.

'What the devil do you want?' a man's voice demanded harshly.

'I want the doctor. My wife is taken ill.'

'There's no doctor here.'

The man prepared to shut the door, but Poirot thrust his foot in adroitly. He became suddenly a perfect caricature of an infuriated Frenchman.

'What you say, there is no doctor? I will have the law of you. You must come! I will stay here and ring and knock all night.'

'My dear sir –' The door was opened again, the man, clad in a dressing-gown and slippers, stepped forward to pacify Poirot with an uneasy glance round.

'I will call the police.'

Poirot prepared to descend the steps.

'No, don't do that for Heaven's sake!' The man dashed after him.

With a neat push Poirot sent him staggering down the steps. In another minute all three of us were inside the door and it was pushed to and bolted.

'Quick – in here.' Poirot led the way into the nearest room, switching on the light as he did so. 'And you – behind the curtain.'

'Si, Signor,' said the Italian and slid rapidly behind the full folds of rose-coloured velvet which draped the embrasure of the window.

Not a minute too soon. Just as he disappeared from view a woman rushed into the room. She was tall with reddish hair and held a scarlet kimono round her slender form.

'Where is my husband?' she cried, with a quick frightened glance. 'Who are you?'

Poirot stepped forward with a bow.

'It is to be hoped your husband will not suffer from a chill. I observed that he had slippers on his feet, and that his dressing-gown was a warm one.'

'Who are you? What are you doing in my house?'

'It is true that none of us have the pleasure of your acquaintance, madame. It is especially to be regretted as one of our number has come specially from New York in order to meet you.'

The curtains parted and the Italian stepped out. To my horror I observed that he was brandishing my revolver, which Poirot must doubtless have put down through inadvertence in the cab.

The woman gave a piercing scream and turned to fly, but Poirot was standing in front of the closed door.

'Let me by,' she shrieked. 'He will murder me.'

'Who was it dat croaked Luigi Valdarno?' asked the Italian hoarsely, brandishing the weapon, and sweeping each one of us with it. We dared not move.

'My God, Poirot, this is awful. What shall we do?' I cried.

'You will oblige me by refraining from talking so much,

Hastings. I can assure you that our friend will not shoot until I give the word.'

'Youse sure o' dat, eh?' said the Italian, leering unpleasantly.

It was more than I was, but the woman turned to Poirot like a flash.

'What is it you want?'

Poirot bowed.

'I do not think it is necessary to insult Miss Elsa Hardt's intelligence by telling her.'

With a swift movement, the woman snatched up a big black velvet cat which served as a cover for the telephone.

'They are stitched in the lining of that.'

'Clever,' murmured Poirot appreciatively. He stood aside from the door. 'Good evening, madame. I will detain your friend from New York whilst you make your getaway.'

'Whatta fool!' roared the big Italian, and raising the revolver he fired point-blank at the woman's retreating figure just as I flung myself upon him.

But the weapon merely clicked harmlessly and Poirot's voice rose in mild reproof.

'Never will you trust your old friend, Hastings. I do not care for my friends to carry loaded pistols about with them and never would I permit a mere acquaintance to do so. No, no, *mon ami*.' This to the Italian who was swearing hoarsely. Poirot continued to address him in a tone of mild reproof: 'See now, what I have done for you. I have saved you from being hanged. And do not think that our beautiful lady will escape. No, no, the house is watched, back and front. Straight into the arms of the police they will go. Is not that a beautiful and consoling thought? Yes, you may leave the room now. But be careful – be very careful. I – Ah, he is gone! And my friend Hastings looks at me with eyes of reproach. But it's all so simple! It was clear, from the first, that out of several hundred, probably, applicants for No 4 Montagu Mansions, only the Robinsons were considered suitable. Why? What was there that singled them out from the rest – at practically a glance.

Their appearance? Possibly, but it was not so unusual. Their name, then!'

'But there's nothing unusual about the name of Robinson,' I cried. 'It's quite a common name.'

'Ah! *Sapristi*, but exactly! That was the point. Elsa Hardt and her husband, or brother or whatever he really is, come from New York, and take a flat in the name of Mr and Mrs Robinson. Suddenly they learn that one of these secret societies, the Mafia, or the Camorra, to which doubtless Luigi Valdarno belonged, is on their track. What do they do? They hit on a scheme of transparent simplicity. Evidently they knew that their pursuers were not personally acquainted with either of them. What, then, can be simpler? They offer the flat at an absurdly low rental. Of the thousands of young couples in London looking for flats, there cannot fail to be several Robinsons. It is only a matter of waiting. If you will look at the name of Robinson in the telephone directory, you will realize that a fair-haired Mrs Robinson was pretty sure to come along sooner or later. Then what will happen? The avenger arrives. He knows the name, he knows the address. He strikes! All is over, vengeance is satisfied, and Miss Elsa Hardt has escaped by the skin of her teeth once more. By the way, Hastings, you must present me to the real Mrs Robinson – that delightful and truthful creature! What will they think when they find their flat has been broken into! We must hurry back. Ah, that sounds like Japp and his friends arriving.'

A mighty tattoo sounded on the knocker.

'How do you know this address?' I asked as I followed Poirot out into the hall. 'Oh, of course, you had the first Mrs Robinson followed when she left the other flat.'

'*A la bonne heure*, Hastings. You use your grey cells at last. Now for a little surprise for Japp.'

Softly unbolting the door, he stuck the cat's head round the edge and ejaculated a piercing 'Miaow'.

The Scotland Yard inspector, who was standing outside with another man, jumped in spite of himself.

'Oh, it's only Monsieur Poirot at one of his little jokes!' he exclaimed, as Poirot's head followed that of the cat. 'Let us in, moosior.'

'You have our friends safe and sound?'

'Yes, we've got the birds all right. But they hadn't got the goods with them.'

'I see. So you come to search. Well, I am about to depart with Hastings, but I should like to give you a little lecture upon the history and habits of the domestic cat.'

'For the Lord's sake, have you gone completely barmy?'

'The cat,' declaimed Poirot, 'was worshipped by the ancient Egyptians. It is still regarded as a symbol of good luck if a black cat crosses your path. This cat crossed your path tonight, Japp. To speak of the interior of any animal or any person is not, I know, considered polite in England. But the interior of this cat is perfectly delicate. I refer to the lining.'

With a sudden grunt, the second man seized the cat from Poirot's hand.

'Oh, I forgot to introduce you,' said Japp. 'Mr Poirot, this is Mr Burt of the United States Secret Service.'

The American's trained fingers had felt what he was looking for. He held out his hand, and for a moment speech failed him. Then he rose to the occasion.

'Pleased to meet you,' said Mr Burt.

The Mystery of Hunter's Lodge

'After all,' murmured Poirot, 'it is possible that I shall not die this time.'

Coming from a convalescent influenza patient, I hailed the remark as showing a beneficial optimism. I myself had been the first sufferer from the disease. Poirot in his turn had gone down. He was now sitting up in bed, propped up with pillows, his head muffled in a woollen shawl, and was slowly sipping a particularly noxious *tisane* which I had prepared according to his directions. His eye rested with pleasure upon a neatly graduated row of medicine bottles which adorned the mantelpiece.

'Yes, yes,' my little friend continued. 'Once more shall I be myself again, the great Hercule Poirot, the terror of evildoers! Figure to yourself, *mon ami*, that I have a little paragraph to myself in *Society Gossip*. But yes! Here it is: "Go it – criminals – all out! Hercule Poirot – and believe me, girls, he's some Hercules! – our own pet society detective can't get a grip on you. 'Cause why? 'Cause he's got *la grippe* himself"!'

I laughed.

'Good for you, Poirot. You are becoming quite a public character. And fortunately you haven't missed anything of particular interest during this time.'

'That is true. The few cases I have had to decline did not fill me with any regret.'

Our landlady stuck her head in at the door.

'There's a gentleman downstairs. Says he must see Monsieur Poirot or you, Captain. Seeing as he was in a great to-do – and with all that quite the gentleman – I brought up 'is card.'

She handed me a bit of pasteboard. 'Mr Roger Havering,' I read.

Poirot motioned with his head towards the bookcase, and I obediently pulled forth *Who's Who*. Poirot took it from me and scanned the pages rapidly.

'Second son of fifth Baron Windsor. Married 1913 Zoe, fourth daughter of William Crabb.'

'H'm!' I said. 'I rather fancy that's the girl who used to act at the Frivolity – only she called herself Zoe Carrisbrook. I remember she married some young man about town just before the War.'

'Would it interest you, Hastings, to go down and hear what our visitor's particular little trouble is? Make him all my excuses.'

Roger Havering was a man of about forty, well set up and of smart appearance. His face, however, was haggard, and he was evidently labouring under great agitation.

'Captain Hastings? You are Monsieur Poirot's partner, I understand. It is imperative that he should come with me to Derbyshire today.'

'I'm afraid that's impossible,' I replied. 'Poirot is ill in bed – influenza.'

His face fell.

'Dear me, that is a great blow to me.'

'The matter on which you want to consult him is serious?'

'My God, yes! My uncle, the best friend I have in the world, was foully murdered last night.'

'Here in London?'

'No, in Derbyshire. I was in town and received a telegram from my wife this morning. Immediately upon its receipt I determined to come round and beg Monsieur Poirot to undertake the case.'

'If you will excuse me a minute,' I said, struck by a sudden idea.

I rushed upstairs, and in a few brief words acquainted Poirot with the situation. He took any further words out of my mouth.

'I see. I see. You want to go yourself, is it not so? Well, why not? You should know my methods by now. All I ask is that you should report to me fully every day, and follow implicitly any instructions I may wire you.'

To this I willingly agreed.

An hour later I was sitting opposite Mr Havering in a first-class carriage on the Midland Railway, speeding rapidly away from London.

'To begin with, Captain Hastings, you must understand that Hunter's Lodge, where we are going, and where the tragedy took place, is only a small shooting-box in the heart of the Derbyshire moors. Our real home is near Newmarket, and we usually rent a flat in town for the season. Hunter's Lodge is looked after by a housekeeper who is quite capable of doing all we need when we run down for an occasional weekend. Of course, during the shooting season, we take down some of our own servants from Newmarket. My uncle, Mr Harrington Pace (as you may know, my mother was a Miss Pace of New York), has, for the last three years, made his home with us. He never got on well with my father, or my elder brother, and I suspect that my being somewhat of a prodigal son myself rather increased than diminished his affection towards me. Of course I am a poor man, and my uncle was a rich one – in other words, he paid the piper! But, though exacting in many ways, he was not really hard to get on with, and we all three lived very harmoniously together. Two days ago, my uncle, rather wearied with some recent gaieties of ours in town, suggested that we should run down to Derbyshire for a day or two. My wife telegraphed to Mrs Middleton, the housekeeper, and we went down that same afternoon. Yesterday evening I was forced to return to town, but my wife and my uncle remained on. This morning I received this telegram.' He handed it over to me:

'Come at once uncle Harrington murdered last night bring good detective if you can but do come – Zoe.'

'Then, as yet you know no details?'

'No, I suppose it will be in the evening papers. Without doubt the police are in charge.'

It was about three o'clock when we arrived at the little station of Elmer's Dale. From there a five-mile drive brought us to a small grey stone building in the midst of the rugged moors.

'A lonely place,' I observed with a shiver.

Havering nodded.

'I shall try and get rid of it. I could never live here again.'

We unlatched the gate and were walking up the narrow path to the oak door when a familiar figure emerged and came to meet us.

'Japp!' I ejaculated.

The Scotland Yard inspector grinned at me in a friendly fashion before addressing my companion.

'Mr Havering, I think? I've been sent down from London to take charge of this case, and I'd like a word with you, if I may, sir.'

'My wife –'

'I've seen your good lady, sir – and the housekeeper. I won't keep you a moment, but I am anxious to get back to the village now that I've seen all there is to see here.'

'I know nothing as yet as to what –'

'Ex-actly,' said Japp soothingly. 'But there are just one or two little points I'd like your opinion about all the same. Captain Hastings here, he knows me, and he'll go on up to the house and tell them you're coming. What have you done with the little man, by the way, Captain Hastings?'

'He's ill in bed with influenza.'

'Is he now? I'm sorry to hear that. Rather the case of the cart without the horse, you being here without him, isn't it?'

And on his rather ill-timed jest I went on to the house. I rang the bell, as Japp had closed the door behind him. After some moments it was opened to me by a middle-aged woman in black.

'Mr Havering will be here in a moment,' I explained. 'He

has been detained by the inspector. I have come down with him from London to look into the case. Perhaps you can tell me briefly what occurred last night.'

'Come inside, sir.' She closed the door behind me, and we stood in the dimly-lighted hall. 'It was after dinner last night, sir, that the man came. He asked to see Mr Pace, sir, and, seeing that he spoke the same way, I thought it was an American gentleman friend of Mr Pace's and I showed him into the gun-room, and then went to tell Mr Pace. He wouldn't give any name, which, of course, was a bit odd, now I come to think of it. I told Mr Pace, and he seemed puzzled like, but he said to the mistress: "Excuse me, Zoe, while I see what this fellow wants." He went off to the gun-room, and I went back to the kitchen, but after a while I heard loud voices, as if they were quarrelling, and I came out into the hall. At the same time, the mistress she comes out too, and just then there was a shot and then a dreadful silence. We both ran to the gun-room door, but it was locked and we had to go round to the window. It was open, and there inside was Mr Pace, all shot and bleeding.'

'What became of the man?'

'He must have got away through the window, sir, before we got to it.'

'And then?'

'Mrs Havering sent me to fetch the police. Five miles to walk it was. They came back with me, and the constable he stayed all night, and this morning the police gentleman from London arrived.'

'What was this man like who called to see Mr Pace?'

The housekeeper reflected.

'He had a black beard, sir, and was about middle-aged, and had on a light overcoat. Beyond the fact that he spoke like an American I didn't notice much about him.'

'I see. Now I wonder if I can see Mrs Havering?'

'She's upstairs, sir. Shall I tell her?'

'If you please. Tell her that Mr Havering is outside with Inspector Japp, and that the gentleman he has brought back with him from London is anxious to speak to her as soon as possible.'

'Very good, sir.'

I was in a fever of impatience to get all the facts. Japp had two or three hours' start on me, and his anxiety to be gone made me keen to be close at his heels.

Mrs Havering did not keep me waiting long. In a few minutes I heard a light step descending the stairs, and looked up to see a very handsome young woman coming towards me. She wore a flame-coloured jumper, that set off the slender boyishness of her figure. On her dark head was a little hat of flame-coloured leather. Even the present tragedy could not dim the vitality of her personality.

I introduced myself, and she nodded in quick comprehension.

'Of course I have often heard of you and your colleague, Monsieur Poirot. You have done some wonderful things together, haven't you? It was very clever of my husband to get you so promptly. Now will you ask me questions? That is the easiest way, isn't it, of getting to know all you want to about this dreadful affair?'

'Thank you, Mrs Havering. Now what time was it that this man arrived?'

'It must have been just before nine o'clock. We had finished dinner, and were sitting over our coffee and cigarettes.'

'Your husband had already left for London?'

'Yes, he went up by the 6.15.'

'Did he go by car to the station, or did he walk?'

'Our own car isn't down here. One came out from the garage in Elmer's Dale to fetch him in time for the train.'

'Was Mr Pace quite his usual self?'

'Absolutely. Most normal in every way.'

'Now, can you describe this visitor at all?'

'I'm afraid not. I didn't see him. Mrs Middleton showed him straight into the gun-room and then came to tell my uncle.'

'What did your uncle say?'

'He seemed rather annoyed, but went off at once. It was about five minutes later that I heard the sound of raised voices. I ran out into the hall and almost collided with Mrs Middleton. Then we heard the shot. The gun-room door was locked on the inside, and we had to go right round the house to the window. Of course that took some time, and the murderer had been able to get well away. My poor uncle' – her voice faltered – 'had been shot through the head. I saw at once that he was dead. I sent Mrs Middleton for the police, I was careful to touch nothing in the room but to leave it exactly as I found it.'

I nodded approval.

'Now, as to the weapon?'

'Well, I can make a guess at it, Captain Hastings. A pair of revolvers of my husband's were mounted upon the wall. One of them is missing. I pointed this out to the police, and they took the other one away with them. When they have extracted the bullet, I suppose they will know for certain.'

'May I go to the gun-room?'

'Certainly. The police have finished with it. But the body has been removed.'

She accompanied me to the scene of the crime. At that moment Havering entered the hall, and with a quick apology his wife ran to him. I was left to undertake my investigations alone.

I may as well confess at once that they were rather disappointing. In detective novels clues abound, but here I could find nothing that struck me as out of the ordinary except a large blood-stain on the carpet where I judged the dead man had fallen. I examined everything with painstaking care and took a couple of pictures of the room with my little camera which I had brought with me. I also examined the ground outside the window, but it appeared to have been so heavily trampled underfoot that I judged it was useless to waste time over it. No, I had seen all that Hunter's Lodge had to show me. I must go back to Elmer's Dale and get into touch with Japp. Accordingly I took leave of the Haverings, and was driven off in the car that had brought us from the station.

I found Japp at the Matlock Arms and he took me forthwith to see the body. Harrington Pace was a small, spare, clean-shaven man, typically American in appearance. He had been shot through the back of the head, and the revolver had been discharged at close quarters.

'Turned away for a moment,' remarked Japp, 'and the other fellow snatched up a revolver and shot him. The one Mrs Havering handed over to us was fully loaded and I suppose the other one was also. Curious what darn fool things people do. Fancy keeping two loaded revolvers hanging up on your wall.'

'What do you think of the case?' I asked, as we left the gruesome chamber behind us.

'Well, I'd got my eye on Havering to begin with. Oh, yes!' – noting my exclamation of astonishment. 'Havering has one or two shady incidents in his past. When he was a boy at Oxford there was some funny business about the signature on one of his father's cheques. All hushed up of course. Then, he's pretty heavily in debt now, and they're the kind of debts he wouldn't like to go to his uncle about, whereas you may be sure the uncle's will would be in his favour. Yes, I'd got my eye on him, and that's why I wanted to speak to him before he saw his wife, but their statements dovetail all right, and I've been to the station and there's no doubt whatever that he left by the 6.15. That gets up to London about 10.30. He went straight to his club, he says, and if that's confirmed all right – why, he couldn't have been shooting his uncle here at nine o'clock in a black beard!'

'Ah, yes, I was going to ask you what you thought about that beard?'

Japp winked.

'I think it grew pretty fast – grew in the five miles from Elmer's Dale to Hunter's Lodge. Americans that I've met are mostly clean-shaven. Yes, it's amongst Mr Pace's American associates that we'll have to look for the murderer. I questioned the housekeeper first, and then her mistress, and their stories agree all right, but I'm sorry Mrs Havering didn't get a look at the fellow. She's a smart woman, and she might have noticed something that would set us on the track.'

I sat down and wrote a minute and lengthy account to Poirot. I was able to add various further items of information before I posted the letter.

The bullet had been extracted and was proved to have been fired from a revolver identical with the one held by the police. Furthermore, Mr Havering's movements on the night in question had been checked and verified, and it was proved beyond doubt that he had actually arrived in London by the train in question. And, thirdly, a sensational development had occurred. A city gentleman, living at Ealing, on crossing Haven Green to get to the District Railway Station that morning, had observed a brown-paper parcel stuck between the railings. Opening it, he found that it contained a revolver. He handed the parcel over to the local police station, and before night it was proved to be the one we were in search of, the fellow to that given us by Mrs Havering. One bullet had been fired from it.

All this I added to my report. A wire from Poirot arrived whilst I was at breakfast the following morning:

'Of course black-bearded man was not Havering only you or Japp would have such an idea wire me description of housekeeper and what clothes she wore this morning same of Mrs Havering do not waste time taking photographs of interiors they are underexposed and not in the least artistic.'

It seemed to me that Poirot's style was unnecessarily facetious. I also fancied he was a shade jealous of my position on the spot with full facilities for handling the case. His request for a description of the clothes worn by the two women appeared to me to be simply ridiculous, but I complied as well as I, a mere man, was able to.

At eleven a reply wire came from Poirot:

'Advise Japp arrest housekeeper before it is too late.'

Dumbfounded, I took the wire to Japp. He swore softly under his breath.

'He's the goods, Monsieur Poirot: if he says so, there's something in it. And I hardly noticed the woman. I don't know that I can go so far as arresting her, but I'll have her watched. We'll go up right away, and take another look at her.'

But it was too late. Mrs Middleton, that quiet middle-aged woman, who had appeared so normal and respectable, had vanished into thin air. Her box had been left behind. It contained only ordinary wearing apparel. There was no clue to her identity, or as to her whereabouts.

From Mrs Havering we elicited all the facts we could:

'I engaged her about three weeks ago when Mrs Emery, our former housekeeper, left. She came to me from Mrs Selbourne's Agency in Mount Street – a very well-known place. I get all my servants from there. They sent several women to see me, but this Mrs Middleton seemed much the nicest, and had splendid references. I engaged her on the spot, and notified the Agency of the fact. I can't believe that there was anything wrong with her. She was such a nice quiet woman.'

The thing was certainly a mystery. Whilst it was clear that the woman herself could not have committed the crime, since at the moment the shot was fired Mrs Havering was with her in the hall, nevertheless she must have some connection with the murder, or why should she suddenly take to her heels and bolt?

I wired the latest development to Poirot and suggested returning to London and making inquiries at Selbourne's Agency.

Poirot's reply was prompt:

'Useless to inquire at agency they will never have heard of her find out what vehicle took her up to hunters lodge when she first arrived there.'

Though mystified, I was obedient. The means of transport in Elmer's Dale were limited. The local garage had two battered

Ford cars, and there were two station flies. None of these had been requisitioned on the date in question. Questioned, Mrs Havering explained that she had given the woman the money for her fare down to Derbyshire and sufficient to hire a car or fly to take her up to Hunter's Lodge. There was usually one of the Fords at the station on the chance of its being required. Taking into consideration the further fact that nobody at the station had noticed the arrival of a stranger, black-bearded or otherwise, on the fatal evening, everything seemed to point to the conclusion that the murderer had come to the spot in a car, which had been waiting near at hand to aid his escape, and that the same car had brought the mysterious housekeeper to her new post. I may mention that inquiries at the Agency in London bore out Poirot's prognostication. No such woman as 'Mrs Middleton' had ever been on their books. They had received the Hon. Mrs Havering's application for a housekeeper, and had sent her various applicants for the post. When she sent them the engagement fee, she omitted to mention which woman she had selected.

Somewhat crestfallen, I returned to London. I found Poirot established in an armchair by the fire in a garish silk dressing-gown. He greeted me with much affection.

'*Mon ami* Hastings! But how glad I am to see you. Veritably I have for you a great affection! And you have enjoyed yourself? You have run to and fro with the good Japp? You have interrogated and investigated to your heart's content?'

'Poirot,' I cried, 'the thing's a dark mystery! It will never be solved.'

'It is true that we are not likely to cover ourselves with glory over it.'

'No, indeed. It's a hard nut to crack.'

'Oh, as far as that goes, I am very good at cracking the nuts! A veritable squirrel! It is not that which embarrasses me. I know well enough who killed Mr Harrington Pace.'

'You know? How did you find out?'

'Your illuminating answers to my wires supplied me with the truth. See here, Hastings, let us examine the facts methodically and in order. Mr Harrington Pace is a man with a considerable fortune which at his death will doubtless pass to his nephew. Point No 1. His nephew is known to be desperately hard up. Point No 2. His nephew is also known to be – shall we say a man of rather loose moral fibre? Point No 3.'

'But Roger Havering is proved to have journeyed straight up to London.'

'*Précisément* – and therefore, as Mr Havering left Elmer's Dale at 6.15, and since Mr Pace cannot have been killed before he left, or the doctor would have spotted the time of the crime as being given wrongly when he examined the body, we conclude quite rightly, that Mr Havering did *not* shoot his uncle. But there is a Mrs Havering, Hastings.'

'Impossible! The housekeeper was with her when the shot was fired.'

'Ah, yes, the housekeeper. But she has disappeared.'

'She will be found.'

'I think not. There is something peculiarly elusive about that housekeeper, don't you think so, Hastings? It struck me at once.'

'She played her part, I suppose, and then got out in the nick of time.'

'And what was her part?'

'Well, presumably to admit her confederate, the black-bearded man.'

'Oh, no, that was not her part! Her part was what you have just mentioned, to provide an alibi for Mrs Havering at the moment the shot was fired. And no one will ever find her, *mon ami*, because she does not exist! "There's no such person," as your so great Shakespeare says.'

'It was Dickens,' I murmured, unable to suppress a smile. 'But what do you mean, Poirot?'

'I mean that Zoe Havering was an actress before her marriage, that you and Japp only saw the housekeeper in a dark hall, a dim middle-aged figure in black with a faint subdued voice, and finally that neither you nor Japp, nor the local police whom the housekeeper fetched, ever saw Mrs Middleton and her mistress at one and the same time. It was child's play for that clever and daring woman. On the pretext of summoning her mistress, she runs upstairs, slips on a bright jumper and a hat with black curls attached which she jams down over the grey transformation. A few deft touches, and the make-up is removed, a slight dusting of rouge, and the brilliant Zoe Havering comes down with her clear ringing voice. Nobody looks particularly at the housekeeper. Why should they? There is nothing to connect her with the crime. She, too, has an alibi.'

'But the revolver that was found at Ealing? Mrs Havering could not have placed it there?'

'No, that was Roger Havering's job – but it was a mistake on their part. It put me on the right track. A man who has committed murder with a revolver which he found on the spot would fling it away at once, he would not carry it up to London with him. No, the motive was clear, the criminals wished to focus the interest of the police on a spot far removed from Derbyshire, they were anxious to get the police away as soon as possible from the vicinity of Hunter's Lodge. Of course the revolver found at Ealing was not the one with which Mr Pace was shot. Roger Havering discharged one shot from it, brought it up to London, went straight to his club to establish his alibi, then went quickly out to Ealing by the District, a matter of about twenty minutes only, placed the parcel where it was found and so back to town. That charming creature, his wife, quietly shoots Mr Pace after dinner – you remember he was shot from behind? Another significant point, that! – reloads the revolver and puts it back in its place, and then starts off with her desperate little comedy.'

'It's incredible,' I muttered, fascinated, 'and yet –'

'And yet it is true. *Bien sur*, my friend, it is true. But to bring that precious pair to justice, that is another matter. Well, Japp must do what he can – I have written him fully – but I very much fear, Hastings, that we shall be obliged to leave them to Fate, or *le bon Dieu*, whichever you prefer.'

'The wicked flourish like a green bay tree,' I reminded him.

'But at a price, Hastings, always at a price, *croyez-moi*!'

Poirot's forebodings were confirmed, Japp, though convinced of the truth of his theory, was unable to get together the necessary evidence to ensure a conviction.

Mr Pace's huge fortune passed into the hands of his murderers. Nevertheless, Nemesis did overtake them, and when I read in the paper that the Hon. Roger and Mrs Havering were amongst those killed in the crashing of the Air Mail to Paris I knew that Justice was satisfied.

The Million Dollar Bond Robbery

'What a number of bond robberies there have been lately!' I observed one morning, laying aside the newspaper. 'Poirot, let us forsake the science of detection, and take to crime instead!'

'You are on the – how do you say it? – get-rich-quick tack, eh, *mon ami*?'

'Well, look at this last *coup*, the million dollars' worth of Liberty Bonds which the London and Scottish Bank were sending to New York, and which disappeared in such a remarkable manner on board the *Olympia*.'

'If it were not for *mal de mer*, and the difficulty of practising the so excellent method of Laverguier for a longer time than the few hours of crossing the Channel, I should delight to voyage myself on one of these big liners,' murmured Poirot dreamily.

'Yes, indeed,' I said enthusiastically. 'Some of them must be perfect palaces; the swimming-baths, the lounges, the restaurant, the palm courts – really, it must be hard to believe that one is on the sea.'

'Me, I always know when I am on the sea,' said Poirot sadly. 'And all those bagatelles that you enumerate, they say nothing to me; but, my friend, consider for a moment the geniuses that travel as it were incognito! On board these floating palaces, as you so justly call them, one would meet the élite, the *haute noblesse* of the criminal world!'

I laughed.

'So that's the way your enthusiasm runs! You would have liked to cross swords with the man who sneaked the Liberty Bonds?'

The landlady interrupted us.

'A young lady as wants to see you, Mr Poirot. Here's her card.'

The card bore the inscription: Miss Esmée Farquhar, and Poirot, after diving under the table to retrieve a stray crumb, and putting it carefully in the waste-paper basket, nodded to the landlady to admit her.

In another minute one of the most charming girls I have ever seen was ushered into the room. She was perhaps about five-and-twenty, with big brown eyes and a perfect figure. She was well-dressed and perfectly composed in manner.

'Sit down, I beg of you, mademoiselle. This is my friend, Captain Hastings, who aids me in my little problems.'

'I am afraid it is a big problem I have brought you today, Monsieur Poirot,' said the girl, giving me a pleasant bow as she seated herself. 'I dare say you have read about it in the papers. I am referring to the theft of Liberty Bonds on the *Olympia*.' Some astonishment must have shown itself on Poirot's face, for she continued quickly: 'You are doubtless asking yourself what have I to do with a grave institution like the London and Scottish Bank. In one sense nothing, in another sense everything. You see, Monsieur Poirot, I am engaged to Mr Philip Ridgeway.'

'Aha! and Mr Philip Ridgeway –'

'Was in charge of the bonds when they were stolen. Of course no actual blame can attach to him, it was not his fault in any way. Nevertheless, he is half distraught over the matter, and his uncle, I know, insists that he must carelessly have mentioned having them in his possession. It is a terrible set-back to his career.'

'Who is his uncle?'

'Mr Vavasour, joint general manager of the London and Scottish Bank.'

'Suppose, Miss Farquhar, that you recount to me the whole story?'

'Very well. As you know, the Bank wished to extend their credits in America, and for this purpose decided to send over

a million dollars in Liberty Bonds. Mr Vavasour selected his
nephew, who had occupied a position of trust in the Bank for
many years and who was conversant with all the details of the
Bank's dealings in New York, to make the trip. The *Olympia*
sailed from Liverpool on the 23rd, and the bonds were handed
over to Philip on the morning of that day by Mr Vavasour
and Mr Shaw, the two joint general managers of the London
and Scottish Bank. They were counted, enclosed in a package, and sealed in his presence, and he then locked the package
at once in his portmanteau.'

'A portmanteau with an ordinary lock?'

'No, Mr Shaw insisted on a special lock being fitted to it
by Hubbs. Philip, as I say, placed the package at the bottom
of the trunk. It was stolen just a few hours before reaching
New York. A rigorous search of the whole ship was made, but
without result. The bonds seemed literally to have vanished
into thin air.'

Poirot made a grimace.

'But they did not vanish absolutely, since I gather that they
were sold in small parcels within half an hour of the docking
of the *Olympia*! Well, undoubtedly the next thing is for me to
see Mr Ridgeway.'

'I was about to suggest that you should lunch with me at
the "Cheshire Cheese". Philip will be there. He is meeting
me, but does not yet know that I have been consulting you
on his behalf.'

We agreed to this suggestion readily enough, and drove
there in a taxi.

Mr Philip Ridgeway was there before us, and looked somewhat surprised to see his fiancée arriving with two complete
strangers. He was a nice-looking young fellow, tall and spruce,
with a touch of greying hair at the temples, though he could
not have been much over thirty.

Miss Farquhar went up to him and laid her hand on his
arm.

'You must forgive me acting without consulting you, Philip,'
she said. 'Let me introduce you to Monsieur Hercule Poirot,

of whom you must often have heard, and his friend, Captain Hastings.'

Ridgeway looked very astonished.

'Of course I have heard of you, Monsieur Poirot,' he said, as he shook hands. 'But I had no idea that Esmée was thinking of consulting you about my – our trouble.'

'I was afraid you would not let me do it, Philip,' said Miss Farquhar meekly.

'So you took care to be on the safe side,' he observed, with a smile. 'I hope Monsieur Poirot will be able to throw some light on this extraordinary puzzle, for I confess frankly that I am nearly out of my mind with worry and anxiety about it.'

Indeed, his face looked drawn and haggard and showed only too clearly the strain under which he was labouring.

'Well, well,' said Poirot. 'Let us lunch, and over lunch we will put our heads together and see what can be done. I want to hear Mr Ridgeway's story from his own lips.'

Whilst we discussed the excellent steak and kidney pudding of the establishment, Philip Ridgeway narrated the circumstances leading to the disappearance of the bonds. His story agreed with that of Miss Farquhar in every particular. When he had finished, Poirot took up the thread with a question.

'What exactly led you to discover that the bonds had been stolen, Mr Ridgeway?'

He laughed rather bitterly.

'The thing stared me in the face, Monsieur Poirot. I couldn't have missed it. My cabin trunk was half out from under the bunk and all scratched and cut about where they'd tried to force the lock.'

'But I understood that it had been opened with a key?'

'That's so. They tried to force it, but couldn't. And in the end, they must have got it unlocked somehow or other.'

'Curious,' said Poirot, his eyes beginning to flicker with the green light I knew so well. 'Very curious! They waste much, much time trying to prise it open, and then – *sapristi!* they find they have the key all the time – for each of Hubbs's locks are unique.'

'That's just why they couldn't have had the key. It never left me day or night.'

'You are sure of that?'

'I can swear to it, and besides, if they had had the key or a duplicate, why should they waste time trying to force an obviously unforceable lock?'

'Ah! there is exactly the question we are asking ourselves! I venture to prophesy that the solution, if we ever find it, will hinge on that curious fact. I beg of you not to assault me if I ask you one more question: *Are you perfectly certain that you did not leave the trunk unlocked?*'

Philip Ridgeway merely looked at him, and Poirot gesticulated apologetically.

'Ah, but these things can happen, I assure you! Very well, the bonds were stolen from the trunk. What did the thief do with them? How did he manage to get ashore with them?'

'Ah!' cried Ridgeway. 'That's just it. How? Word was passed to the Customs authorities, and every soul that left the ship was gone over with a toothcomb!'

'And the bonds, I gather, made a bulky package?'

'Certainly they did. They could hardly have been hidden on board – and anyway we know they weren't, because they were offered for sale within half an hour of the *Olympia's* arrival, long before I got the cables going and the numbers sent out. One broker swears he bought some of them even before the *Olympia* got in. But you can't send bonds by wireless.'

'Not by wireless, but did any tug come alongside?'

'Only the official ones, and that was after the alarm was given when everyone was on the look-out. I was watching out myself for their being passed over to someone that way. My God, Monsieur Poirot, this thing will drive me mad! People are beginning to say I stole them myself.'

'But you also were searched on landing, weren't you?' asked Poirot gently.

'Yes.'

The young man stared at him in a puzzled manner.

'You do not catch my meaning, I see,' said Poirot, smiling enigmatically. 'Now I should like to make a few inquiries at the Bank.'

Ridgeway produced a card and scribbled a few words on it.

'Send this in and my uncle will see you at once.'

Poirot thanked him, bade farewell to Miss Farquhar, and together we started out for Threadneedle Street and the head office of the London and Scottish Bank. On production of Ridgeway's card, we were led through the labyrinth of counters and desks, skirting paying-in clerks and paying-out clerks and up to a small office on the first floor where the joint general managers received us. They were two grave gentlemen, who had grown grey in the service of the Bank. Mr Vavasour had a short white beard, Mr Shaw was clean shaven.

'I understand you are strictly a private inquiry agent?' said Mr Vavasour. 'Quite so, quite so. We have, of course, placed ourselves in the hands of Scotland Yard. Inspector McNeil has charge of the case. A very able officer, I believe.'

'I am sure of it,' said Poirot politely. 'You will permit a few questions, on your nephew's behalf? About this lock, who ordered it from Hubbs's?'

'I ordered it myself,' said Mr Shaw. 'I would not trust to any clerk in the matter. As to the keys, Mr Ridgeway had one, and the other two are held by my colleague and myself.'

'And no clerk has had access to them?'

Mr Shaw turned inquiringly to Mr Vavasour.

'I think I am correct in saying that they have remained in the safe where we placed them on the 23rd,' said Mr Vavasour. 'My colleague was unfortunately taken ill a fortnight ago – in fact on the very day that Philip left us. He has only just recovered.'

'Severe bronchitis is no joke to a man of my age,' said Mr Shaw ruefully. 'But I'm afraid Mr Vavasour has suffered from the hard work entailed by my absence, especially with this unexpected worry coming on top of everything.'

Poirot asked a few more questions. I judged that he was

endeavouring to gauge the exact amount of intimacy between uncle and nephew. Mr Vavasour's answers were brief and punctilious. His nephew was a trusted official of the Bank, and had no debts or money difficulties that he knew of. He had been entrusted with similar missions in the past. Finally we were politely bowed out.

'I am disappointed,' said Poirot, as we emerged into the street.

'You hoped to discover more? They are such stodgy old men.'

'It is not their stodginess which disappoints me, *mon ami*. I do not expect to find in a Bank manager, a "keen financier with an eagle glance", as your favourite works of fiction put it. No, I am disappointed in the case – it is too easy!'

'*Easy?*'

'Yes, do you not find it almost childishly simple?'

'You know who stole the bonds?'

'I do.'

'But then – we must – why –'

'Do not confuse and fluster yourself, Hastings. We are not going to do anything at present.'

'But why? What are you waiting for?'

'For the *Olympia*. She is due on her return trip from New York on Tuesday.'

'But if you know who stole the bonds, why wait? He may escape.'

'To a South Sea island where there is no extradition? No, *mon ami*, he would find life very uncongenial there. As to why I wait – *eh bien*, to the intelligence of Hercule Poirot the case is perfectly clear, but for the benefit of others, not so greatly gifted by the good God – the Inspector, McNeil, for instance – it would be as well to make a few inquiries to establish the facts. One must have consideration for those less gifted than oneself.'

'Good Lord, Poirot! Do you know, I'd give a considerable sum of money to see you make a thorough ass of yourself – just for once. You're so confoundedly conceited!'

'Do not enrage yourself, Hastings. In verity, I observe that there are times when you almost detest me! Alas, I suffer the penalties of greatness!'

The little man puffed out his chest, and sighed so comically that I was forced to laugh.

Tuesday saw us speeding to Liverpool in a first-class carriage of the L and NWR. Poirot had obstinately refused to enlighten me as to his suspicions – or certainties. He contented himself with expressing surprise that I, too, was not equally *au fait* with the situation. I disdained to argue, and entrenched my curiosity behind a rampart of pretended indifference.

Once arrived at the quay alongside which lay the big transatlantic liner, Poirot became brisk and alert. Our proceedings consisted in interviewing four successive stewards and inquiring after a friend of Poirot's who had crossed to New York on the 23rd.

'An elderly gentleman, wearing glasses. A great invalid, hardly moved out of his cabin.'

The description appeared to tally with one Mr Ventnor who had occupied the cabin C24 which was next to that of Philip Ridgeway. Although unable to see how Poirot had deduced Mr Ventnor's existence and personal appearance, I was keenly excited.

'Tell me,' I cried, 'was this gentleman one of the first to land when you got to New York?'

The steward shook his head.

'No, indeed, sir, he was one of the last off the boat.'

I retired crestfallen, and observed Poirot grinning at me. He thanked the steward, a note changed hands, and we took our departure.

'It's all very well,' I remarked heatedly, 'but that last answer must have damned your precious theory, grin as you please!'

'As usual, you see nothing, Hastings. That last answer is, on the contrary, the coping-stone of my theory.'

I flung up my hands in despair.

'I give it up.'

*   *   *

When we were in the train, speeding towards London, Poirot wrote busily for a few minutes, sealing up the result in an envelope.

'This is for the good Inspector McNeil. We will leave it at Scotland Yard in passing, and then to the Rendezvous Restaurant, where I have asked Miss Esmée Farquhar to do us the honour of dining with us.'

'What about Ridgeway?'

'What about him?' asked Poirot with a twinkle.

'Why, you surely don't think – you can't –'

'The habit of incoherence is growing upon you, Hastings. As a matter of fact I *did* think. If Ridgeway had been the thief – which was perfectly possible – the case would have been charming; a piece of neat methodical work.'

'But not so charming for Miss Farquhar.'

'Possibly you are right. Therefore all is for the best. Now, Hastings, let us review the case. I can see that you are dying to do so. The sealed package is removed from the trunk and vanishes, as Miss Farquhar puts it, into thin air. We will dismiss the thin air theory, which is not practicable at the present stage of science, and consider what is likely to have become of it. Everyone asserts the incredulity of its being smuggled ashore –'

'Yes, but we know –'

'*You* may know, Hastings, I do not. I take the view that, since it seemed incredible, it *was* incredible. Two possibilities remain: it was hidden on board – also rather difficult – or it was thrown overboard.'

'With a cork on it, do you mean?'

'Without a cork.'

I stared.

'But if the bonds were thrown overboard, they couldn't have been sold in New York.'

'I admire your logical mind, Hastings. The bonds were sold in New York, therefore they were not thrown overboard. You see where that leads us?'

'Where we were when we started.'

'*Jamais de la vie!* If the package was thrown overboard and the bonds were sold in New York, the package could not have contained the bonds. Is there any evidence that the package *did* contain the bonds? Remember, Mr Ridgeway never opened it from the time it was placed in his hands in London.'

'Yes, but then –'

Poirot waved an impatient hand.

'Permit me to continue. The last moment that the bonds are seen as bonds is in the office of the London and Scottish Bank on the morning of the 23rd. They reappear in New York half an hour after the *Olympia* gets in, and according to one man, whom nobody listens to, actually *before* she gets in. Supposing then, that they have never been on the Olympia at all? Is there any other way they could get to New York? Yes. The *Gigantic* leaves Southampton on the same day as the *Olympia*, and she holds the record for the Atlantic. Mailed by the *Gigantic*, the bonds would be in New York the day before the *Olympia* arrived. All is clear, the case begins to explain itself. The sealed packet is only a dummy, and the moment of its substitution must be in the office in the bank. It would be an easy matter for any of the three men present to have prepared a duplicate package which could be substituted for the genuine one. *Trés bien*, the bonds are mailed to a confederate in New York, with instructions to sell as soon as the *Olympia* is in, but someone must travel on the *Olympia* to engineer the supposed moment of robbery.'

'But why?'

'Because if Ridgeway merely opens the packet and finds it a dummy, suspicion flies at once to London. No, the man on board in the cabin next door does his work, pretends to force the lock in an obvious manner so as to draw immediate attention to the theft, really unlocks the trunk with a duplicate key, throws the package overboard and waits until the last to leave the boat. Naturally he wears glasses to conceal his eyes, and is an invalid since he does not want to run the risk of meeting Ridgeway. He steps ashore in New York and returns by the first boat available.'

'But who – which was he?'

'The man who had a duplicate key, the man who ordered the lock, the man who has *not* been severely ill with bronchitis at his home in the country – *enfin*, the "stodgy" old man, Mr Shaw! There are criminals in high places sometimes, my friend. Ah, here we are, Mademoiselle, I have succeeded! You permit?'

And, beaming, Poirot kissed the astonished girl lightly on either cheek!

The Adventure of the Egyptian Tomb

I have always considered that one of the most thrilling and dramatic of the many adventures I have shared with Poirot was that of our investigation into the strange series of deaths which followed upon the discovery and opening of the Tomb of King Men-her-Ra.

Hard upon the discovery of the Tomb of Tutankh-Amen by Lord Carnarvon, Sir John Willard and Mr Bleibner of New York, pursuing their excavations not far from Cairo, in the vicinity of the Pyramids of Gizeh, came unexpectedly on a series of funeral chambers. The greatest interest was aroused by their discovery. The Tomb appeared to be that of King Men-her-Ra, one of those shadowy kings of the Eighth Dynasty, when the Old Kingdom was falling to decay. Little was known about this period, and the discoveries were fully reported in the newspapers.

An event soon occurred which took a profound hold on the public mind. Sir John Willard died quite suddenly of heart failure.

The more sensational newspapers immediately took the opportunity of reviving all the old superstitious stories connected with the ill luck of certain Egyptian treasures. The unlucky Mummy at the British Museum, that hoary old chestnut, was dragged out with fresh zest, was quietly denied by the Museum, but nevertheless enjoyed all its usual vogue.

A fortnight later Mr Bleibner died of acute blood poisoning, and a few days afterwards a nephew of his shot himself in New York. The 'Curse of Men-her-Ra' was the talk of the day, and the magic power of dead-and-gone Egypt was exalted to a fetish point.

It was then that Poirot received a brief note from Lady Willard, widow of the dead archaeologist, asking him to go and see her at her house in Kensington Square. I accompanied him.

Lady Willard was a tall, thin woman, dressed in deep mourning. Her haggard face bore eloquent testimony to her recent grief.

'It is kind of you to have come so promptly, Monsieur Poirot.'

'I am at your service, Lady Willard. You wished to consult me?'

'You are, I am aware, a detective, but it is not only as a detective that I wish to consult you. You are a man of original views, I know, you have imagination, experience of the world; tell me, Monsieur Poirot, what are your views on the supernatural?'

Poirot hesitated for a moment before he replied. He seemed to be considering. Finally he said:

'Let us not misunderstand each other, Lady Willard. It is not a general question that you are asking me there. It has a personal application, has it not? You are referring obliquely to the death of your late husband?'

'That is so,' she admitted.

'You want me to investigate the circumstances of his death?'

'I want you to ascertain for me exactly how much is newspaper chatter, and how much may be said to be founded on fact? Three deaths, Monsieur Poirot – each one explicable taken by itself, but taken together surely an almost unbelievable coincidence, and all within a month of the opening of the tomb! It may be mere superstition, it may be some potent curse from the past that operates in ways undreamed of by modern science. The fact remains – three deaths! And I am afraid, Monsieur Poirot, horribly afraid. It may not yet be the end.'

'For whom do you fear?'

'For my son. When the news of my husband's death came I was ill. My son, who has just come down from Oxford, went out there. He brought the – the body home, but now he has gone out again, in spite of my prayers and entreaties. He is so fascinated by the work that he intends to take his father's place and carry on the system of excavations. You may think me a foolish, credulous woman, but, Monsieur Poirot, I am afraid. Supposing that the spirit of the dead King is not yet appeased? Perhaps to you I seem to be talking nonsense –'

'No, indeed, Lady Willard,' said Poirot quickly. 'I, too, believe in the force of superstition, one of the greatest forces the world has ever known.'

I looked at him in surprise. I should never have credited Poirot with being superstitious. But the little man was obviously in earnest.

'What you really demand is that I shall protect your son? I will do my utmost to keep him from harm.'

'Yes, in the ordinary way, but against an occult influence?'

'In volumes of the Middle Ages, Lady Willard, you will find many ways of counteracting black magic. Perhaps they knew more than we moderns with all our boasted science. Now let us come to facts, that I may have guidance. Your husband had always been a devoted Egyptologist, hadn't he?'

'Yes, from his youth upwards. He was one of the greatest living authorities upon the subject.'

'But Mr Bleibner, I understand, was more or less of an amateur?'

'Oh, quite. He was a very wealthy man who dabbled freely in any subject that happened to take his fancy. My husband managed to interest him in Egyptology, and it was his money that was so useful in financing the expedition.'

'And the nephew? What do you know of his tastes? Was he with the party at all?'

'I do not think so. In fact I never knew of his existence till I read of his death in the paper. I do not think he and Mr Bleibner can have been at all intimate. He never spoke of having any relations.'

'Who are the other members of the party?'

'Well, there's Dr Tosswill, a minor official connected with the British Museum; Mr Schneider of the Metropolitan Museum in New York; a young American secretary; Dr Ames, who accompanies the expedition in his professional capacity; and Hassan, my husband's devoted native servant.'

'Do you remember the name of the American secretary?'

'Harper, I think, but I cannot be sure. He had not been with Mr Bleibner very long, I know. He was a very pleasant young fellow.'

'Thank you, Lady Willard.'

'If there is anything else –'

'For the moment, nothing. Leave it now in my hands, and be assured that I will do all that is humanly possible to protect your son.'

They were not exactly reassuring words, and I observed Lady Willard wince as he uttered them. Yet, at the same time, the fact that he had not pooh-poohed her fears seemed in itself to be a relief to her.

For my part I had never before suspected that Poirot had so deep a vein of superstition in his nature. I tackled him on the subject as we went homewards. His manner was grave and earnest.

'But yes, Hastings. I believe in these things. You must not underrate the force of superstition.'

'What are we going to do about it?'

'*Toujours pratique*, the good Hastings! *Eh bien*, to begin with we are going to cable to New York for fuller details of young Mr Bleibner's death.'

He duly sent off his cable. The reply was full and precise. Young Rupert Bleibner had been in low water for several years. He had been a beachcomber and a remittance man in several South Sea islands, but had returned to New York two years ago, where he had rapidly sunk lower and lower. The most significant thing, to my mind, was that he had recently managed to borrow enough money to take him to Egypt. 'I've a good friend there I can borrow from,' he had declared. Here, however, his plans had gone awry. He had returned to New York cursing his skinflint of an uncle who cared more for the bones of dead and gone kings than his own flesh and blood. It was during his sojourn in Egypt that the death of Sir John Willard had occurred. Rupert had plunged once more into his life of dissipation in New York, and then, without warning, he had committed suicide, leaving behind him a letter which contained some curious phrases. It seemed written in a sudden fit of remorse. He referred to himself as a leper and an outcast, and the letter ended by declaring that such as he were better dead.

A shadowy theory leapt into my brain. I had never really believed in the vengeance of a long dead Egyptian king. I saw here a more modern crime. Supposing this young man had decided to do away with his uncle – preferably by poison. By mistake, Sir John Willard receives the fatal dose. The young man returns to New York, haunted by his crime. The news of his uncle's death reaches him. He realizes how unnecessary his crime has been, and stricken with remorse takes his own life.

I outlined my solution to Poirot. He was interested.

'It is ingenious what you have thought of there – decidedly it is ingenious. It may even be true. But you leave out of count the fatal influence of the Tomb.'

I shrugged my shoulders.

'You still think that has something to do with it?'

'So much so, *mon ami*, that we start for Egypt tomorrow.'

'What?' I cried, astonished.

'I have said it.' An expression of conscious heroism spread over Poirot's face. Then he groaned. 'But oh,' he lamented, 'the sea! The hateful sea!'

It was a week later. Beneath our feet was the golden sand of the desert. The hot sun poured down overhead. Poirot, the picture of misery, wilted by my side. The little man was not a good traveller. Our four days' voyage from Marseilles had been one long agony to him. He had landed at Alexandria the wraith of his former self, even his usual neatness had deserted him. We had arrived in Cairo and had driven out at once to the Mena House Hotel, right in the shadow of the Pyramids.

The charm of Egypt had laid hold of me. Not so Poirot. Dressed precisely the same as in London, he carried a small clothes-brush in his pocket and waged an unceasing war on the dust which accumulated on his dark apparel.

'And my boots,' he wailed. 'Regard them, Hastings. My boots, of the neat patent leather, usually so smart and shining. See, the sand is inside them, which is painful, and outside them, which outrages the eyesight. Also the heat, it causes my moustaches to become limp – but limp!'

'Look at the Sphinx,' I urged. 'Even I can feel the mystery and the charm it exhales.'

Poirot looked at it discontentedly.

'It has not the air happy,' he declared. 'How could it, half-buried in sand in that untidy fashion. Ah, this cursed sand!'

'Come, now, there's a lot of sand in Belgium,' I reminded him, mindful of a holiday spent at Knocke-sur-mer in the midst of *Les dunes impeccables*' as the guide-book had phrased it.

'Not in Brussels,' declared Poirot. He gazed at the Pyramids thoughtfully. 'It is true that they, at least, are of a shape solid and geometrical, but their surface is of an unevenness most unpleasing. And the palm-trees I like them not. Not even do they plant them in rows!'

I cut short his lamentations, by suggesting that we should start for the camp. We were to ride there on camels, and the beasts were patiently kneeling, waiting for us to mount, in charge of several picturesque boys headed by a voluble dragoman.

I pass over the spectacle of Poirot on a camel. He started by groans and lamentations and ended by shrieks, gesticulations and invocations to the Virgin Mary and every Saint in the calendar. In the end, he descended ignominiously and finished the journey on a diminutive donkey. I must admit that a trotting camel is no joke for the amateur. I was stiff for several days.

At last we neared the scene of the excavations. A sunburnt

man with a grey beard, in white clothes and wearing a helmet, came to meet us.

'Monsieur Poirot and Captain Hastings? We received your cable. I'm sorry that there was no one to meet you in Cairo. An unforeseen event occurred which completely disorganized our plans.'

Poirot paled. His hand, which had stolen to his clothes-brush, stayed its course.

'Not another death?' he breathed.

'Yes.'

'Sir Guy Willard?' I cried.

'No, Captain Hastings. My American colleague, Mr Schneider.'

'And the cause?' demanded Poirot.

'Tetanus.'

I blanched. All around me I seemed to feel an atmosphere of evil, subtle and menacing. A horrible thought flashed across me. Supposing I were next?

'*Mon Dieu*,' said Poirot, in a very low voice, 'I do not understand this. It is horrible. Tell me, monsieur, there is no doubt that it was tetanus?'

'I believe not. But Dr Ames will tell you more than I can do.'

'Ah, of course, you are not the doctor.'

'My name is Tosswill.'

This, then, was the British expert described by Lady Willard as being a minor official at the British Museum. There was something at once grave and steadfast about him that took my fancy.

'If you will come with me,' continued Dr Tosswill. 'I will take you to Sir Guy Willard. He was most anxious to be informed as soon as you should arrive.'

We were taken across the camp to a large tent. Dr Tosswill lifted up the flap and we entered. Three men were sitting inside.

'Monsieur Poirot and Captain Hastings have arrived, Sir Guy,' said Tosswill.

The youngest of the three men jumped up and came forward to greet us. There was a certain impulsiveness in his manner which reminded me of his mother. He was not nearly so sun-burnt as the others, and that fact, coupled with a certain haggardness round the eyes, made him look older than his twenty-two years. He was clearly endeavouring to bear up under a severe mental strain.

He introduced his two companions, Dr Ames, a capable-looking man of thirty-odd, with a touch of greying hair at the temples, and Mr Harper, the secretary, a pleasant lean young man wearing the national insignia of horn-rimmed spectacles.

After a few minutes' desultory conversation the latter went out, and Dr Tosswill followed him. We were left alone with Sir Guy and Dr Ames.

'Please ask any questions you want to ask, Monsieur Poirot,' said Willard. 'We are utterly dumbfounded at this strange series of disasters, but it isn't – it can't be, anything but coincidence.'

There was a nervousness about his manner which rather belied the words. I saw that Poirot was studying him keenly.

'Your heart is really in this work, Sir Guy?'

'Rather. No matter what happens, or what comes of it, the work is going on. Make up your mind to that.'

Poirot wheeled round on the other.

'What have you to say to that, *monsieur le docteur?*'

'Well,' drawled the doctor, 'I'm not for quitting myself.'

Poirot made one of those expressive grimaces of his.

'Then, *évidemment*, we must find out just how we stand. When did Mr Schneider's death take place?'

'Three days ago.'

'You are sure it was tetanus?'

'Dead sure.'

'It couldn't have been a case of strychnine poisoning, for instance?'

'No, Monsieur Poirot, I see what you are getting at. But it was a clear case of tetanus.'

'Did you not inject anti-serum?'

'Certainly we did,' said the doctor dryly. 'Every conceivable thing that could be done was tried.'

'Had you the anti-serum with you?'

'No. We procured it from Cairo.'

'Have there been any other cases of tetanus in the camp?'

'No, not one.'

'Are you certain that the death of Mr Bleibner was not due to tetanus?'

'Absolutely plumb certain. He had a scratch upon his thumb which became poisoned, and septicaemia set in. It sounds pretty much the same to a layman, I dare say, but the two things are entirely different.'

'Then we have four deaths – all totally dissimilar, one heart failure, one blood poisoning, one suicide and one tetanus.'

'Exactly, Monsieur Poirot.'

'Are you certain that there is nothing which might link the four together?'

'I don't quite understand you?'

'I will put it plainly. Was any act committed by those four men which might seem to denote disrespect to the spirit of Men-her-Ra?'

The doctor gazed at Poirot in astonishment.

'You're talking through your hat, Monsieur Poirot. Surely you've not been guyed into believing all that fool talk?'

'Absolute nonsense,' muttered Willard angrily.

Poirot remained placidly immovable, blinking a little out of his green cat's eyes.

'So you do not believe it, *monsieur le docteur*?'

'No, sir, I do not,' declared the doctor emphatically. 'I am a scientific man, and I believe only what science teaches.'

'Was there no science then in Ancient Egypt?' asked Poirot softly. He did not wait for a reply, and indeed Dr Ames seemed rather at a loss for the moment. 'No, no, do not answer me, but tell me this. What do the native workmen think?'

'I guess,' said Dr Ames, 'that, where white folk lose their

heads, natives aren't going to be far behind. I'll admit that they're getting what you might call scared – but they've no cause to be.'

'I wonder,' said Poirot non-committally.

Sir Guy leant forward.

'Surely,' he cried incredulously, 'you cannot believe in – oh, but the thing's absurd! You can know nothing of Ancient Egypt if you think that.'

For answer Poirot produced a little book from his pocket – an ancient tattered volume. As he held it out I saw its title, *The Magic of the Egyptians and Chaldeans.* Then, wheeling round, he strode out of the tent. The doctor stared at me.

'What is his little idea?'

The phrase, so familiar on Poirot's lips, made me smile as it came from another.

'I don't know exactly,' I confessed. 'He's got some plan of exorcizing the evil spirits, I believe.'

I went in search of Poirot, and found him talking to the lean-faced young man who had been the late Mr Bleibner's secretary.

'No,' Mr Harper was saying, 'I've only been six months with the expedition. Yes, I knew Mr Bleibner's affairs pretty well.'

'Can you recount to me anything concerning his nephew?'

'He turned up here one day, not a bad-looking fellow. I'd never met him before, but some of the others had – Ames, I think, and Schneider. The old man wasn't at all pleased to see him. They were at it in no time, hammer and tongs. "Not a cent," the old man shouted. "Not one cent now or when I'm dead. I intend to leave my money to the furtherance of my life's work. I've been talking it over with Mr Schneider today." And a bit more of the same. Young Bleibner lit out for Cairo right away.'

'Was he in perfectly good health at the time?'

'The old man?'

'No, the young one.'

'I believe he did mention there was something wrong with

him. But it couldn't have been anything serious, or I should have remembered.'

'One thing more, has Mr Bleibner left a will?'

'So far as we know, he has not.'

'Are you remaining with the expedition, Mr Harper?'

'No, sir, I am not. I'm for New York as soon as I can square up things here. You may laugh if you like, but I'm not going to be this blasted Men-her-Ra's next victim. He'll get me if I stop here.'

The young man wiped the perspiration from his brow.

Poirot turned away. Over his shoulder he said with a peculiar smile:

'Remember, he got one of his victims in New York.'

'Oh, hell!' said Mr Harper forcibly.

'That young man is nervous,' said Poirot thoughtfully. 'He is on the edge, but absolutely on the edge.'

I glanced at Poirot curiously, but his enigmatical smile told me nothing. In company with Sir Guy Willard and Dr Tosswill we were taken round the excavations. The principal finds had been removed to Cairo, but some of the tomb furniture was extremely interesting. The enthusiasm of the young baronet was obvious, but I fancied that I detected a shade of nervousness in his manner as though he could not quite escape from the feeling of menace in the air. As we entered the tent which had been assigned to us, for a wash before joining the evening meal, a tall dark figure in white robes stood aside to let us pass with a graceful gesture and a murmured greeting in Arabic. Poirot stopped.

'You are Hassan, the late Sir John Willard's servant?'

'I served my Lord Sir John, now I serve his son.' He took a step nearer to us and lowered his voice. 'You are a wise one, they say, learned in dealing with evil spirits. Let the young master depart from here. There is evil in the air around us.'

And with an abrupt gesture, not waiting for a reply, he strode away.

'Evil in the air,' muttered Poirot. 'Yes, I feel it.'

Our meal was hardly a cheerful one. The floor was left to

Dr Tosswill, who discoursed at length upon Egyptian antiquities. Just as we were preparing to retire to rest, Sir Guy caught Poirot by the arm and pointed. A shadowy figure was moving amidst the tents. It was no human one: I recognized distinctly the dog-headed figure I had seen carved on the walls of the tomb.

'My blood froze at the sight.

'*Mon Dieu!*' murmured Poirot, crossing himself vigorously. 'Anubis, the jackal-headed, the god of departing souls.'

'Someone is hoaxing us,' cried Dr Tosswill, rising indignantly to his feet.

'It went into your tent, Harper,' muttered Sir Guy, his face dreadfully pale.

'No,' said Poirot, shaking his head, 'into that of the Dr Ames.'

The doctor stared at him incredulously; then, repeating Dr Tosswill's words, he cried:

'Someone is hoaxing us. Come, we'll soon catch the fellow.'

He dashed energetically in pursuit of the shadowy apparition. I followed him, but, search as we would, we could find no trace of any living soul having passed that way. We returned, somewhat disturbed in mind, to find Poirot taking energetic measures, in his own way, to ensure his personal safety. He was busily surrounding our tent with various diagrams and inscriptions which he was drawing in the sand. I recognized the five-pointed star or Pentagon many times repeated. As was his wont, Poirot was at the same time delivering an impromptu lecture on witchcraft and magic in general, White magic as opposed to Black, with various references to the Ka and the Book of the Dead thrown in.

It appeared to excite the liveliest contempt in Dr Tosswill, who drew me aside, literally snorting with rage.

'Balderdash, sir,' he exclaimed angrily. 'Pure balderdash. The man's an imposter. He doesn't know the difference between the superstitions of the Middle Ages and the beliefs of Ancient Egypt. Never have I heard such a hotch-potch of ignorance and credulity.'

I calmed the excited expert, and joined Poirot in the tent. My little friend was beaming cheerfully.

'We can now sleep in peace,' he declared happily. 'And I can do with some sleep. My head, it aches abominably. Ah, for a good *tisane!*'

As though in answer to prayer, the flap of the tent was lifted and Hassan appeared, bearing a steaming cup which he offered to Poirot. It proved to be camomile tea, a beverage of which he is inordinately fond. Having thanked Hassan and refused his offer of another cup for myself, we were left alone once more. I stood at the door of the tent some time after undressing, looking out over the desert.

'A wonderful place,' I said aloud, 'and a wonderful work. I can feel the fascination. This desert life, this probing into the heart of a vanished civilization. Surely, Poirot, you, too, must feel the charm?'

I got no answer, and I turned, a little annoyed. My annoyance was quickly changed to concern. Poirot was lying back across the rude couch, his face horribly convulsed. Beside him was the empty cup. I rushed to his side, then dashed out and across the camp to Dr Ames's tent.

'Dr Ames!' I cried. 'Come at once.'

'What's the matter?' said the doctor, appearing in pyjamas.

'My friend. He's ill. Dying. The camomile tea. Don't let Hassan leave the camp.'

Like a flash the doctor ran to our tent. Poirot was lying as I left him.

'Extraordinary,' cried Ames. 'Looks like a seizure – or – what did you say about something he drank?' He picked up the empty cup.

'Only I did not drink it!' said a placid voice.

We turned in amazement. Poirot was sitting up on the bed. He was smiling.

'No,' he said gently. 'I did not drink it. While my good friend Hastings was apostrophizing the night, I took the opportunity of pouring it, not down my throat, but into a little bottle. That little bottle will go to the analytical chemist. No'

– as the doctor made a sudden movement – 'as a sensible
man, you will understand that violence will be of no avail.
During Hastings' absence to fetch you, I have had time to put
the bottle in safe keeping. Ah, quick, Hastings, hold him!'

I misunderstood Poirot's anxiety. Eager to save my friend,
I flung myself in front of him. But the doctor's swift movement
had another meaning. His hand went to his mouth, a smell
of bitter almonds filled the air, and he swayed forward and
fell.

'Another victim,' said Poirot gravely, 'but the last. Perhaps
it is the best way. He has three deaths on his head.'

'Dr Ames?' I cried, stupefied. 'But I thought you believed
in some occult influence?'

'You misunderstood me, Hastings. What I meant was that
I believe in the terrific force of superstition. Once get it firmly
established that a series of deaths are supernatural, and you
might almost stab a man in broad daylight, and it would still
be put down to the curse, so strongly is the instinct of the
supernatural implanted in the human race. I suspected from
the first that a man was taking advantage of that instinct. The
idea came to him, I imagine, with the death of Sir John Willard. A fury of superstition arose at once. As far as I could
see, nobody could derive any particular profit from Sir John's
death. Mr Bleibner was a different case. He was a man of great
wealth. The information I received from New York contained
several suggestive points. To begin with, young Bleibner was
reported to have said he had a good friend in Egypt from
whom he could borrow. It was tacitly understood that he
meant his uncle, but it seemed to me that in that case he
would have said so outright. The words suggest some boon
companion of his own. Another thing, he scraped up enough
money to take him to Egypt, his uncle refused outright to
advance him a penny, yet he was able to pay the return passage to New York. Someone must have lent him the money.'

'All that was very thin,' I objected.

'But there was more. Hastings, there occur often enough
words spoken metaphorically which are taken literally. The

opposite can happen too. In this case, words which were meant literally were taken metaphorically. Young Bleibner wrote plainly enough: "I am a leper," but nobody realized that he shot himself because he believed that he contracted the dread disease of leprosy.'

'What?' I ejaculated.

'It was the clever invention of a diabolical mind. Young Bleibner was suffering from some minor skin trouble; he had lived in the South Sea Islands, where the disease is common enough. Ames was a former friend of his, and a well-known medical man, he would never dream of doubting his word. When I arrived here, my suspicions were divided between Harper and Dr Ames, but I soon realized that only the doctor could have perpetrated and concealed the crimes, and I learn from Harper that he was previously acquainted with young Bleibner. Doubtless the latter at some time or another had made a will or had insured his life in favour of the doctor. The latter saw his chance of acquiring wealth. It was easy for him to inoculate Mr Bleibner with the deadly germs. Then the nephew, overcome with despair at the dread news his friend had conveyed to him, shot himself. Mr Bleibner, whatever his intentions, had made no will. His fortune would pass to his nephew and from him to the doctor.'

'And Mr Schneider?'

'We cannot be sure. He knew young Bleibner too, remember, and may have suspected something, or, again, the doctor may have thought that a further death motiveless and purposeless would strengthen the coils of superstition. Furthermore, I will tell you an interesting psychological fact, Hastings. A murderer has always a strong desire to repeat his successful crime, the performance of it grows upon him. Hence my fears for young Willard. The figure of Anubis you saw tonight was Hassan dressed up by my orders. I wanted to see if I could frighten the doctor. But it would take more than the supernatural to frighten him. I could see that he was not entirely taken in by my pretences of belief in the occult. The little comedy I played for him did not deceive him. I suspected that he would endeavour to make me the next victim. Ah, but in spite of *la mer maudite*, the heat abominable, and the annoyances of the sand, the little grey cells still functioned!'

Poirot proved to be perfectly right in his premises. Young Bleibner, some years ago, in a fit of drunken merriment, had made a jocular will, leaving 'my cigarette-case you admire so much and everything else of which I die possessed which will be principally debts to my good friend Robert Ames who once saved my life from drowning.'

The case was hushed up as far as possible, and, to this day, people talk of the remarkable series of deaths in connection with the Tomb of Men-her-Ra as a triumphal proof of the vengeance of a bygone king upon the desecrators of his tomb – a belief which, as Poirot pointed out to me, is contrary to all Egyptian belief and thought.

The Jewel Robbery at the Grand Metropolitan

'Poirot,' I said, 'a change of air would do you good.'

'You think so, *mon ami?*'

'I am sure of it.'

'Eh – eh?' said my friend, smiling. 'It is all arranged, then?'

'You will come?'

'Where do you propose to take me?'

'Brighton. As a matter of fact, a friend of mine in the City put me on to a very good thing, and – well, I have money to burn, as the saying goes. I think a weekend at the Grand Metropolitan would do us all the good in the world.'

'Thank you, I accept most gratefully. You have the good heart to think of an old man. And the good heart, it is in the end worth all the little grey cells. Yes, yes, I who speak to you am in danger of forgetting that sometimes.'

I did not relish the implication. I fancy that Poirot is sometimes a little inclined to underestimate my mental capacities. But his pleasure was so evident that I put my slight annoyance aside.

'Then, that's all right,' I said hastily.

Saturday evening saw us dining at the Grand Metropolitan in the midst of a gay throng. All the world and his wife seemed to be at Brighton. The dresses were marvellous, and the jewels – worn sometimes with more love of display than good taste – were something magnificent.

'*Hein*, it is a good sight, this!' murmured Poirot. 'This is the home of the Profiteer, is it not so, Hastings?'

'Supposed to be,' I replied. 'But we'll hope they aren't all tarred with the Profiteering brush.'

Poirot gazed round him placidly.

'The sight of so many jewels makes me wish I had turned my brains to crime, instead of to its detection. What a magnificent opportunity for some thief of distinction! Regard, Hastings, that stout woman by the pillar. She is, as you would say, plastered with gems.'

I followed his eyes.

'Why,' I exclaimed, 'it's Mrs Opalsen.'

'You know her?'

'Slightly. Her husband is a rich stockbroker who made a fortune in the recent oil boom.'

After dinner we ran across the Opalsens in the lounge, and I introduced Poirot to them. We chatted for a few minutes, and ended by having our coffee together.

Poirot said a few words in praise of some of the costlier gems displayed on the lady's ample bosom, and she brightened up at once.

'It's a perfect hobby of mine, Mr Poirot. I just *love* jewellery. Ed knows my weakness, and every time things go well he brings me something new. You are interested in precious stones?'

'I have had a good deal to do with them one time and another, madame. My profession has brought me into contact with some of the most famous jewels in the world.'

He went on to narrate, with discreet pseudonyms, the story of the historic jewels of a reigning house, and Mrs Opalsen listened with bated breath.

'There now,' she exclaimed, as he ended. 'If it isn't just like a play! You know, I've got some pearls of my own that have a history attached to them. I believe it's supposed to be one of the finest necklaces in the world – the pearls are so beautifully matched and so perfect in colour. I declare I really must run up and get it!'

'Oh, madame,' protested Poirot, 'you are too amiable. Pray do not derange yourself!'

'Oh, but I'd like to show it to you.'

The buxom dame waddled across to the lift briskly enough. Her husband, who had been talking to me, looked at Poirot inquiringly.

'Madame your wife is so amiable as to insist on showing me her pearl necklace,' explained the latter.

'Oh, the pearls!' Opalsen smiled in a satisfied fashion. 'Well, they *are* worth seeing. Cost a pretty penny too! Still, the money's there all right; I could get what I paid for them any day – perhaps more. May have to, too, if things go on as they are now. Money's confoundedly tight in the City. All this infernal EPD.' He rambled on, launching into technicalities where I could not follow him.

He was interrupted by a small page-boy who approached him and murmured something in his ear.

'Eh – what? I'll come at once. Not taken ill, is she? Excuse me, gentlemen.'

He left us abruptly. Poirot leaned back and lit one of his tiny Russian cigarettes. Then, carefully and meticulously, he arranged the empty coffee-cups in a neat row, and beamed happily on the result.

The minutes passed. The Opalsens did not return.

'Curious,' I remarked, at length. 'I wonder when they will come back.'

Poirot watched the ascending spirals of smoke, and then said thoughtfully:

'They will not come back.'

'Why?'

'Because, my friend, something has happened.'

'What sort of thing? How do you know?' I asked curiously.

Poirot smiled.

'A few minutes ago the manager came hurriedly out of his office and ran upstairs. He was much agitated. The liftboy is deep in talk with one of the pages. The lift-bell has rung three times, but he heeds it not. Thirdly, even the waiters are *distrait*; and to make a waiter *distrait* –' Poirot shook his head with an air of finality. 'The affair must indeed be of the first magnitude. Ah, it is as I thought! Here come the police.'

Two men had just entered the hotel – one in uniform, the other in plain clothes. They spoke to a page, and were immediately ushered upstairs. A few minutes later, the same boy descended and came up to where we were sitting.

'Mr Opalsen's compliments, and would you step upstairs?'

Poirot sprang nimbly to his feet. One would have said that he awaited the summons. I followed with no less alacrity.

The Opalsens' apartments were situated on the first floor. After knocking on the door, the page-boy retired, and we answered the summons. 'Come in!' A strange scene met our eyes. The room was Mrs Opalsen's bedroom, and in the centre of it, lying back in an armchair, was the lady herself, weeping violently. She presented an extraordinary spectacle, with the tears making great furrows in the powder with which her complexion was liberally coated. Mr Opalsen was striding up and down angrily. The two police officials stood in the middle of the room, one with a notebook in hand. An hotel chambermaid, looking frightened to death, stood by the fireplace; and on the other side of the room a Frenchwoman, obviously Mrs Opalsen's maid, was weeping and wringing her hands, with an intensity of grief that rivalled that of her mistress.

Into this pandemonium stepped Poirot, neat and smiling. Immediately, with an energy surprising in one of her bulk Mrs Opalsen sprang from her chair towards him.

'There now; Ed may say what he likes, but I believe in luck, I do. It was fated I should meet you the way I did this evening, and I've a feeling that if you can't get my pearls back for me nobody can.'

'Calm yourself, I pray of you, madame.' Poirot patted her hand soothingly. 'Reassure yourself. All will be well. Hercule Poirot will aid you!'

Mr Opalsen turned to the police inspector.

'There will be no objection to my – er – calling in this gentleman, I suppose?'

'None at all, sir,' replied the man civilly, but with complete indifference. 'Perhaps now your lady's feeling better she'll just let us have the facts?'

Mrs Opalsen looked helplessly at Poirot. He led her back to her chair.

'Seat yourself, madame, and recount to us the whole history without agitating yourself.'

Thus abjured, Mrs Opalsen dried her eyes gingerly, and began.

'I came upstairs after dinner to fetch my pearls for Mr Poirot here to see. The chambermaid and Célestine were both in the room as usual –'

'Excuse me, madame, but what do you mean by "as usual"?' Mr Opalsen explained.

'I make it a rule that no one is to come into this room unless Célestine, the maid, is there also. The chambermaid does the room in the morning while Célestine is present, and comes in after dinner to turn down the beds under the same conditions; otherwise she never enters the room.'

'Well, as I was saying,' continued Mrs Opalsen, 'I came up. I went to the drawer here' – she indicated the bottom right-hand drawer of the knee-hole dressing-table – 'took out my jewel-case and unlocked it. It seemed quite as usual – but the pearls were not there!'

The inspector had been busy with his notebook. 'When had you last seen them?' he asked.

'They were there when I went down to dinner.'

'You are sure?'

'Quite sure. I was uncertain whether to wear them or not, but in the end I decided on the emeralds, and put them back in the jewel-case.'

'Who locked up the jewel-case?'

'I did. I wear the key on a chain round my neck.' She held it up as she spoke.

The inspector examined it, and shrugged his shoulders.

'The thief must have had a duplicate key. No difficult matter. The lock is quite a simple one. What did you do after you'd locked the jewel-case?'

'I put it back in the bottom drawer where I always keep it.'

'You didn't lock the drawer?'

'No, I never do. My maid remains in the room till I come up, so there's no need.'

The inspector's face grew greyer.

'Am I to understand that the jewels were there when you went down to dinner, and that since then *the maid has not left the room?*'

Suddenly, as though the horror of her own situation for the first time burst upon her, Célestine uttered a piercing shriek, and, flinging herself upon Poirot, poured out a torrent of incoherent French.

The suggestion was infamous! That she should be suspected of robbing Madame! The police were well known to be of a stupidity incredible! But Monsieur, who was a Frenchman –

'A Belgian,' interjected Poirot, but Célestine paid no attention to the correction.

Monsieur would not stand by and see her falsely accused, while that infamous chambermaid was allowed to go scot-free. She had never liked her – a bold, red-faced thing – a born thief. She had said from the first that she was not honest. And had kept a sharp watch over her too, when she was doing Madame's room! Let those idiots of policemen search her, and if they did not find Madame's pearls on her it would be very surprising!

Although this harangue was uttered in rapid and virulent French, Célestine had interlarded it with a wealth of gesture, and the chambermaid realized at least a part of her meaning. She reddened angrily.

'If that foreign woman's saying I took the pearls, it's a lie!' she declared heatedly. 'I never so much as saw them.'

'Search her!' screamed the other. 'You will find it is as I say.'

'You're a lair – do you hear?' said the chambermaid, advancing upon her. 'Stole 'em yourself, and want to put it on me. Why, I was only in the room about three minutes before the lady came up, and then you were sitting here the whole time, as you always do, like a cat watching a mouse.'

The inspector looked across inquiringly at Célestine. 'Is that true? Didn't you leave the room at all?'

'I did not actually leave her alone,' admitted Célestine reluctantly, 'but I went into my own room through the door here twice – once to fetch a reel of cotton, and once for my scissors. She must have done it then.'

'You wasn't gone a minute,' retorted the chambermaid angrily. 'Just popped out and in again. I'd be glad if the police *would* search me. *I've* nothing to be afraid of.'

At this moment there was a tap at the door. The inspector went to it. His face brightened when he saw who it was.

'Ah!' he said. 'That's rather fortunate. I sent for one of our female searchers, and she's just arrived. Perhaps if you wouldn't mind going into the room next door.'

He looked at the chambermaid, who stepped across the threshold with a toss of her head, the searcher following her closely.

The French girl had sunk sobbing into a chair. Poirot was looking round the room, the main features of which I have made clear by a sketch.

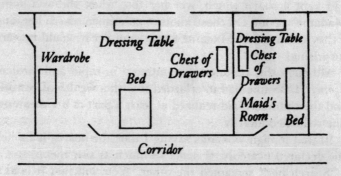

'Where does that door lead?' he inquired, nodding his head towards the one by the window.

'Into the next apartment, I believe,' said the inspector. 'It's bolted, anyway, on this side.'

Poirot walked across to it, tried it, then drew back the bolt and tried it again.

'And on the other side as well,' he remarked. 'Well, that seems to rule out that.'

He walked over to the windows, examining each of them in turn.

'And again – nothing. Not even a balcony outside.'

'Even if there were,' said the inspector impatiently, 'I don't see how that would help us, if the maid never left the room.'

'*Évidemment*,' said Poirot, not disconcerted. 'As Mademoiselle is positive she did not leave the room –'

He was interrupted by the reappearance of the chambermaid and the police searcher.

'Nothing,' said the latter laconically.

'I should hope not, indeed,' said the chambermaid virtuously. 'And that French hussy ought to be ashamed of herself taking away an honest girl's character.'

'There, there, my girl; that's all right,' said the inspector, opening the door. 'Nobody suspects you. You go along and get on with your work.'

The chambermaid went unwillingly.

'Going to search *her*?' she demanded, pointing at Célestine.

'Yes, yes!' He shut the door on her and turned the key.

Célestine accompanied the searcher into the small room in her turn. A few minutes later she also returned. Nothing had been found on her.

The inspector's face grew graver.

'I'm afraid I'll have to ask you to come along with me all the same, miss.' He turned to Mrs Opalsen. 'I'm sorry, madam, but all the evidence points that way. If she's not got them on her, they're hidden somewhere about the room.'

Célestine uttered a piercing shriek, and clung to Poirot's arm. The latter bent and whispered something in the girl's ear. She looked up at him doubtfully.

'*Si, si, mon enfant* – I assure you it is better not to resist.' Then he turned to the inspector. 'You permit, monsieur? A little experiment – purely for my own satisfaction.'

'Depends on what it is,' replied the police officer noncommittally.

Poirot addressed Célestine once more.

'You have told us that you went into your room to fetch a reel of cotton. Whereabouts was it?'

'On top of the chest of drawers, monsieur.'

'And the scissors?'

'They also.'

'Would it be troubling you too much, mademoiselle, to ask you to repeat those two actions? You were sitting here with your work, you say?'

Célestine sat down, and then, at a sign from Poirot, rose, passed into the adjoining room, took up an object from the chest of drawers, and returned.

Poirot divided his attention between her movements and a large turnip of a watch which he held in the palm of his hand.

'Again, if you please, mademoiselle.'

At the conclusion of the second performance, he made a note in his pocket-book, and returned the watch to his pocket.

'Thank you, mademoiselle. And you, monsieur' – he bowed to the inspector – 'for your courtesy.'

The inspector seemed somewhat entertained by this excessive politeness. Célestine departed in a flood of tears, accompanied by the woman and the plain-clothes official.

Then, with a brief apology to Mrs Opalsen, the inspector set to work to ransack the room. He pulled out drawers, opened cupboards, completely unmade the bed, and tapped the floor. Mr Opalsen looked on sceptically.

'You really think you will find them?'

'Yes, sir. It stands to reason. She hadn't time to take them out of the room. The lady's discovering the robbery so soon upset her plans. No, they're here right enough. One of the two must have hidden them – and it's very unlikely for the chambermaid to have done so.'

'More than unlikely – impossible!' said Poirot quietly.

'Eh?' The inspector stared.

Poirot smiled modestly.

'I will demonstrate. Hastings, my good friend, take my watch in your hand – with care. It is a family heirloom! Just now I timed Mademoiselle's movements – her first absence from the room was of twelve seconds, her second of fifteen. Now observe my actions. Madame will have the kindness to give me the key of the jewel-case. I thank you. My friend Hastings will have the kindness to say "Go!"'

'Go!' I said.

With almost incredible swiftness, Poirot wrenched open the drawer of the dressing-table, extracted the jewel-case, fitted the key in the lock, opened the case, selected a piece of jewellery, shut and locked the case, and returned it to the drawer, which he pushed to again. His movements were like lightning.

'Well, *mon ami?*' he demanded of me breathlessly.

'Forty-six seconds,' I replied.

'You see?' He looked round. 'There would have not been time for the chambermaid even to take the necklace out, far less hide it.'

'Then that settles it on the maid,' said the inspector with satisfaction, and returned to his search. He passed into the maid's bedroom next door.

Poirot was frowning thoughtfully. Suddenly he shot a question at Mr Opalsen.

'This necklace – it was, without doubt, insured?'

Mr Opalsen looked a trifle surprised at the question.

'Yes,' he said hesitatingly, 'that is so.'

'But what does that matter?' broke in Mrs Opalsen tearfully. 'It's my necklace I want. It was unique. No money could be the same.'

'I comprehend, madame,' said Poirot soothingly. 'I comprehend perfectly. To *la femme* sentiment is everything – is it not so? But, monsieur, who has not the so fine susceptibility, will doubtless find some slight consolation in the fact.'

'Of course, of course,' said Mr Opalsen rather uncertainly. 'Still –'

He was interrupted by a shout of triumph from the inspector. He came in dangling something from his fingers.

With a cry, Mrs Opalsen heaved herself up from her chair. She was a changed woman.

'Oh, oh, my necklace!'

She clasped it to her breast with both hands. We crowded round.

'Where was it?' demanded Opalsen.

'Maid's bed. In among the springs of the wire mattress. She must have stolen it and hidden it there before the chambermaid arrived on the scene.'

'You permit, madame?' said Poirot gently. He took the necklace from her and examined it closely; then handed it back with a bow.

'I'm afraid, madame, you'll have to hand it over to us for the time being,' said the inspector. 'We shall want it for the charge. But it shall be returned to you as soon as possible.'

Mr Opalsen frowned.

'Is that necessary?'

'I'm afraid so, sir. Just a formality.'

'Oh, let him take it, Ed!' cried his wife. 'I'd feel safer if he did. I shouldn't sleep a wink thinking someone else might try to get hold of it. That wretched girl! And I would never have believed it of her.'

'There, there, my dear, don't take on so.'

I felt a gentle pressure on my arm. It was Poirot.

'Shall we slip away, my friend? I think our services are no longer needed.'

Once outside, however, he hesitated, and then, much to my surprise, he remarked:

'I should rather like to see the room next door.'

The door was not locked, and we entered. The room, which was a large double one, was unoccupied. Dust lay about rather noticeably, and my sensitive friend gave a characteristic grimace as he ran his finger round a rectangular mark on a table near the window.

'The *service* leaves to be desired,' he observed dryly.

He was staring thoughtfully out of the window, and seemed to have fallen into a brown study.

'Well?' I demanded impatiently. 'What did we come in here for?'

He started.

'*Je vous demande pardon, mon ami*. I wished to see if the door was really bolted on this side also.'

'Well,' I said, glancing at the door which communicated with the room we had just left, 'it *is* bolted.'

Poirot nodded. He still seemed to be thinking.

'And anyway,' I continued, 'what does it matter? The case is over. I wish you'd had more chance of distinguishing yourself. But it was the kind of case that even a stiff-backed idiot like that inspector couldn't go wrong over.'

Poirot shook his head.

'The case is not over, my friend. It will not be over until we find out who stole the pearls.'

'But the maid did!'

'Why do you say that?'

'Why,' I stammered, 'they were found – actually in her mattress.'

'Ta, ta, ta!' said Poirot impatiently. 'Those were not the pearls.'

'What?'

'Imitation, *mon ami*.'

The statement took my breath away. Poirot was smiling placidly.

'The good inspector obviously knows nothing of jewels. But presently there will be a fine hullabaloo!'

'Come!' I cried, dragging at his arm.

'Where?'

'We must tell the Opalsens at once.'

'I think not.'

'But that poor woman –'

'*Eh bien*; that poor woman, as you call her, will have a much better night believing the jewels to be safe.'

'But the thief may escape with them!'

'As usual, my friend, you speak without reflection. How do you know that the pearls Mrs Opalsen locked up so carefully tonight were not the false ones, and that the real robbery did not take place at a much earlier date?'

'Oh!' I said, bewildered.

'Exactly,' said Poirot, beaming. 'We start again.'

He led the way out of the room, paused a moment as though considering, and then walked down to the end of the corridor, stopping outside the small den where the chambermaids and valets of the respective floors congregated. Our particular chambermaid appeared to be holding a small court there, and to be retailing her late experiences to an appreciative audience. She stopped in the middle of a sentence. Poirot bowed with his usual politeness.

'Excuse that I derange you, but I shall be obliged if you will unlock for me the door of Mr Opalsen's room.'

The woman rose willingly, and we accompanied her down the passage again. Mr Opalsen's room was on the other side of the corridor, its door facing that of his wife's room. The chambermaid unlocked it with her pass-key, and we entered.

As she was about to depart Poirot detained her.

'One moment; have you ever seen among the effects of Mr Opalsen a card like this?'

He held out a plain white card, rather highly glazed and uncommon in appearance. The maid took it and scrutinized it carefully.

'No, sir, I can't say I have. But, anyway, the valet has most to do with the gentlemen's rooms.'

'I see. Thank you.'

Poirot took back the card. The woman departed. Poirot appeared to reflect a little. Then he gave a short, sharp nod of the head.

'Ring the bell, I pray you, Hastings. Three times for the valet.'

I obeyed, devoured with curiosity. Meanwhile Poirot had emptied the waste-paper basket on the floor, and was swiftly going through its contents.

In a few moments the valet answered the bell. To him Poirot put the same question, and handed him the card to examine. But the response was the same. The valet had never seen a card of that particular quality among Mr Opalsen's belong-

ings. Poirot thanked him, and he withdrew, somewhat unwillingly, with an inquisitive glance at the overturned waste-paper
basket and the litter on the floor. He could hardly have helped
overhearing Poirot's thoughtful remark as he bundled the torn
papers back again:

'And the necklace was heavily insured . . .'

'Poirot,' I cried, 'I see –'

'You see nothing, my friend,' he replied quickly. 'As usual,
nothing at all! It is incredible – but there it is. Let us return
to our own apartments.'

We did so in silence. Once there, to my intense surprise,
Poirot effected a rapid change of clothing.

'I go to London tonight,' he explained. 'It is imperative.'

'What?'

'Absolutely. The real work, that of the brain (ah, those
brave little grey cells), it is done. I go to seek the confirmation.
I shall find it! Impossible to deceive Hercule Poirot!'

'You'll come a cropper one of these days,' I observed, rather
disgusted by his vanity.

'Do not be enraged, I beg of you, *mon ami*. I count on you
to do me a service – of your friendship.'

'Of course,' I said eagerly, rather ashamed of my morose-
ness. 'What is it?'

'The sleeve of my coat that I have taken off – will you brush
it? See you, a little white powder has clung to it. You without
doubt observed me run my finger round the drawer of the
dressing-table?'

'No, I didn't.'

'You should observe my actions, my friend. Thus I obtained
the powder on my finger, and, being a little overexcited, I
rubbed it on my sleeve; an action without method which I
deplore – false to all my principles.'

'But what was the powder?' I asked, not particularly interested in Poirot's principles.

'Not the poison of the Borgias,' replied Poirot with a twinkle.
'I see your imagination mounting. I should say it was French
chalk.'

'French chalk?'

'Yes, cabinet-makers use it to make drawers run smoothly.'

I laughed.

'You old sinner! I thought you were working up to something exciting.'

'Au revoir, my friend. I save myself. I fly!'

The door shut behind him. With a smile, half of derision, half of affection, I picked up the coat and stretched out my hand for the clothes brush.

The next morning, hearing nothing from Poirot, I went out for a stroll, met some old friends, and lunched with them at their hotel. In the afternoon we went for a spin. A punctured tyre delayed us, and it was past eight when I got back to the Grand Metropolitan.

The first sight that met my eyes was Poirot, looking even more diminutive than usual, sandwiched between the Opalsens, beaming in a state of placid satisfaction.

'*Mon ami* Hastings!' he cried, and sprang to meet me. 'Embrace me, my friend; all has marched to a marvel!'

Luckily, the embrace was merely figurative – not a thing one is always sure of with Poirot.

'Do you mean –' I began.

'Just wonderful, I call it!' said Mrs Opalsen, smiling all over her fat face. 'Didn't I tell you, Ed, that if he couldn't get back my pearls nobody would?'

'You did, my dear, you did. And you were right.'

I looked helplessly at Poirot, and he answered the glance.

'My friend Hastings is, as you say in England, all at the seaside. Seat yourself, and I will recount to you all the affair that has so happily ended.'

'Ended?'

'But yes. They are arrested.'

'Who are arrested?'

'The chambermaid and the valet, *parbleu*! You did not suspect? Not with my parting hint about the French chalk?'

'You said cabinet-makers used it.'

'Certainly they do – to make drawers slide easily. Somebody wanted the drawer to slide in and out without any noise. Who could that be? Obviously, only the chambermaid. The plan was so ingenious that it did not at once leap to the eye – not even to the eye of Hercule Poirot.

'Listen, this was how it was done. The valet was in the empty room next door, waiting. The French maid leaves the room. Quick as a flash the chambermaid whips open the drawer, takes out the jewel-case and, slipping back the bolt, passes it through the door. The valet opens it at his leisure with the duplicate key with which he has provided himself, extracts the necklace, and waits his time. Célestine leaves the room again, and – pst! – in a flash the case is passed back again and replaced in the drawer.

'Madame arrives, the theft is discovered. The chambermaid demands to be searched, with a good deal of righteous indignation, and leaves the room without a stain on her character. The imitation necklace with which they have provided themselves has been concealed in the French girl's bed that morning by the chambermaid – a master stroke, *ça!*'

'But what did you go to London for?'

'You remember the card?'

'Certainly. It puzzled me – and puzzles me still. I thought –'

I hesitated delicately, glancing at Mr Opalsen.

Poirot laughed heartily.

'*Une blague!* For the benefit of the valet. The card was one with a specially prepared surface – for fingerprints. I went straight to Scotland Yard, asked for our old friend Inspector Japp, and laid the facts before him. As I had suspected, the fingerprints proved to be those of two well-known jewel thieves who have been "wanted" for some time. Japp came down with me, the thieves were arrested, and the necklace was discovered in the valet's possession. A clever pair, but they failed in *method*. Have I not told you, Hastings, at least thirty-six times, that without method –'

'At least thirty-six thousand times!' I interrupted. 'But where did their "method" break down?'

'*Mon ami*, it is a good plan to take a place as chambermaid or valet – but you must not shirk your work. They left an empty room undusted; and therefore, when the man put down the jewel-case on the little table near the communicating door, it left a square mark –'

'I remember,' I cried.

'Before, I was undecided. Then – I *knew*!'

There was a moment's silence.

'And I've got my pearls,' said Mrs Opalsen as a sort of Greek chorus.

'Well,' I said, 'I'd better have some dinner.'

Poirot accompanied me.

'This ought to mean kudos for you,' I observed.

'*Pas du tout*,' replied Poirot tranquilly. 'Japp and the local inspector will divide the credit between them. But' – he tapped his pocket – 'I have a cheque here, from Mr Opalsen, and, how you say, my friend? This weekend has not gone according to plan. Shall we return here next weekend – at my expense this time?'

VIII

The Kidnapped Prime Minister

Now that war and the problems of war are things of the past, I think I may safely venture to reveal to the world the part which my friend Poirot played in a moment of national crisis. The secret has been well guarded. Not a whisper of it reached the Press. But, now that the need for secrecy has gone by, I feel it is only just that England should know the debt it owes to my quaint little friend, whose marvellous brain so ably averted a great catastrophe.

One evening after dinner – I will not particularize the date; it suffices to say that it was at the time when 'Peace by negotiation' was the parrot-cry of England's enemies – my friend and I were sitting in his rooms. After being invalided out of the Army I had been given a recruiting job, and it had become my custom to drop in on Poirot in the evenings after dinner and talk with him of any cases of interest that he might have had on hand.

I was attempting to discuss with him the sensational news of the day – no less than an attempted assassination of Mr David MacAdam, England's Prime Minister. The account in the papers had evidently been carefully censored. No details were given, save that the Prime Minister had had a marvellous escape, the bullet just grazing his cheek.

I considered that our police must have been shamefully careless for such an outrage to be possible. I could well understand that the German agents in England would be willing to risk much for such an achievement. 'Fighting Mac', as his own party had nicknamed him, had strenuously and unequivocally combated the Pacifist influence which was becoming so prevalent.

He was more than England's Prime Minister – he *was* England; and to have removed him from his sphere of influence would have been a crushing and paralysing blow to Britain.

Poirot was busy mopping a grey suit with a minute sponge. Never was there a dandy such as Hercule Poirot. Neatness and order were his passion. Now, with the odour of benzene filling the air, he was quite unable to give me his full attention.

'In a little minute I am with you, my friend. I have all but finished. The spot of grease – he is not good – I remove him – so!' He waved his sponge.

I smiled as I lit another cigarette.

'Anything interesting on?' I inquired, after a minute or two.

'I assist a – how do you call it? – "charlady" to find her husband. A difficult affair, needing the tact. For I have a little idea that when he is found he will not be pleased. What would you? For my part, I sympathize with him. He was a man of discrimination to lose himself.'

I laughed.

'At last! The spot of grease, he is gone! I am at your disposal.'

'I was asking you what you thought of this attempt to assassinate MacAdam?'

'*Enfantillage!*' replied Poirot promptly. 'One can hardly take it seriously. To fire with the rifle – never does it succeed. It is a device of the past.'

'It was very near succeeding this time,' I reminded him.

Poirot shook his head impatiently. He was about to reply when the landlady thrust her head round the door and informed him that there were two gentlemen below who wanted to see him.

'They won't give their names, sir, but they says as it's very important.'

'Let them mount,' said Poirot, carefully folding his grey trousers.

In a few minutes the two visitors were ushered in, and my heart gave a leap as in the foremost I recognized no less a personage than Lord Estair, Leader of the House of Commons; whilst his companion, Mr Bernard Dodge, was also a member of the War Cabinet, and, as I knew, a close personal friend of the Prime Minister.

'Monsieur Poirot?' said Lord Estair interrogatively. My friend bowed. The great man looked at me and hesitated. 'My business is private.'

'You may speak freely before Captain Hastings,' said my friend, nodding to me to remain. 'He has not all the gifts, no! But I answer for his discretion.'

Lord Estair still hesitated, but Mr Dodge broke in abruptly:

'Oh, come on – don't let's beat about the bush! As far as I can see, the whole of England will know the hole we're in soon enough. Time's everything.'

'Pray be seated, messieurs,' said Poirot politely. 'Will you take the big chair, *milord*?'

Lord Estair started slightly. 'You know me?'

Poirot smiled. 'Certainly. I read the little papers with the pictures. How should I not know you?'

'Monsieur Poirot, I have come to consult you upon a matter of the most vital urgency. I must ask for absolute secrecy.'

'You have the word of Hercule Poirot – I can say no more!' said my friend grandiloquently.

'It concerns the Prime Minister. We are in grave trouble.'

'We're up a tree!' interposed Mr Dodge.

'The injury is serious then?' I asked.

'What injury?'

'The bullet wound.'

'Oh, that!' cried Mr Dodge contemptuously. 'That's old history.'

'As my colleague says,' continued Lord Estair, 'that affair is over and done with. Luckily, it failed. I wish I could say as much for the second attempt.'

'There has been a second attempt, then?'

'Yes, though not of the same nature. Monsieur Poirot, the Prime Minister has disappeared.'

'What?'

'He has been kidnapped!'

'Impossible!' I cried, stupefied.

Poirot threw a withering glance at me, which I knew enjoined me to keep my mouth shut.

'Unfortunately, impossible as it seems, it is only too true,' continued his lordship.

Poirot looked at Mr Dodge. 'You said just now, monsieur, that time was everything. What did you mean by that?'

The two men exchanged glances, and then Lord Estair said:

'You have heard, Monsieur Poirot, of the approaching Allied Conference?'

My friend nodded.

'For obvious reasons, no details have been given of when and where it is to take place. But, although it has been kept out of the newspapers, the date is, of course, widely known in diplomatic circles. The Conference is to be held tomorrow – Thursday – evening at Versailles. Now you perceive the terrible gravity of the situation. I will not conceal from you that the Prime Minister's presence at the Conference is a vital necessity. The Pacifist propaganda, started and maintained by the German agents in our midst, has been very active. It is the universal opinion that the turning-point of the Conference will be the strong personality of the Prime Minister. His absence may have the most serious results – possibly a premature and disastrous peace. And we have no one who can be sent in his place. He alone can represent England.'

Poirot's face had grown very grave. 'Then you regard the kidnapping of the Prime Minister as a direct attempt to prevent his being present at the Conference?'

'Most certainly I do. He was actually on his way to France at the time.'

'And the Conference is to be held?'

'At nine o'clock tomorrow night.'

Poirot drew an enormous watch from his pocket.

'It is now a quarter to nine.'

'Twenty-four hours,' said Mr Dodge thoughtfully.

'And a quarter,' amended Poirot. 'Do not forget the quarter, monsieur – it may come in useful. Now for the details – the abduction, did it take place in England or in France?'

'In France. Mr MacAdam crossed to France this morning. He was to stay tonight as the guest of the Commander-in-Chief, proceeding tomorrow to Paris. He was conveyed across the Channel by destroyer. At Boulogne he was met by a car from General Headquarters and one of the Commander-in-Chief's ADCs.'

'*Eh bien?*'

'Well, they started from Boulogne – but they never arrived.'

'What?'

'Monsieur Poirot, it was a bogus car and a bogus ADC. The real car was found in a side road, with the chauffeur and the ADC neatly gagged and bound.'

'And the bogus car?'

'Is still at large.'

Poirot made a gesture of impatience. 'Incredible! Surely it cannot escape attention for long?'

'So we thought. It seemed merely a question of searching thoroughly. That part of France is under Military Law. We were convinced that the car could not go long unnoticed. The French police and our own Scotland Yard men and the military are straining every nerve. It is, as you say, incredible – but nothing has been discovered!'

At that moment a tap came at the door, and a young officer entered with a heavily sealed envelope which he handed to Lord Estair.

'Just through from France, sir. I brought it on here, as you directed.'

The Minister tore it open eagerly, and uttered an exclamation. The officer withdrew.

'Here is news at last! This telegram has just been decoded. They have found the second car, also the secretary, Daniels, chloroformed, gagged, and bound, in an abandoned farm near C–. He remembers nothing, except something being pressed against his mouth and nose from behind, and struggling to

free himself. The police are satisfied as to the genuineness of
his statement.'

'And they have found nothing else?'

'No.'

'Not the Prime Minister's dead body? Then, there is hope.
But it is strange. Why, after trying to shoot him this morning,
are they now taking so much trouble to keep him alive?'

Dodge shook his head. 'One thing's quite certain. They're
determined at all costs to prevent his attending the Conference.'

'If it is humanly possible, the Prime Minister shall be there.
God grant it is not too late. Now, messieurs, recount to me
everything – from the beginning. I must know about this
shooting affair as well.'

'Last night, the Prime Minister, accompanied by one of his
secretaries, Captain Daniels –'

'The same who accompanied him to France?'

'Yes. As I was saying, they motored down to Windsor,
where the Prime Minister was granted an Audience. Early
this morning he returned to town, and it was on the way that
the attempted assassination took place.'

'One moment, if you please. Who is this Captain Daniels?
You have his dossier?'

Lord Estair smiled. 'I thought you would ask me that. We
do not know very much of him. He is of no particular family.
He has served in the English Army, and is an extremely able
secretary, being an exceptionally fine linguist. I believe he
speaks seven languages. It is for that reason that the Prime
Minister chose him to accompany him to France.'

'Has he any relatives in England?'

'Two aunts. A Mrs Everard, who lives at Hampstead, and
a Miss Daniels, who lives near Ascot.'

'Ascot? That is near to Windsor, is it not?'

'That point has not been overlooked. But it has led to
nothing.'

'You regard the Capitaine Daniels, then, as above suspicion?'

A shade of bitterness crept into Lord Estair's voice, as he replied:

'No, Monsieur Poirot. In these days, I should hesitate before I pronounced *anyone* above suspicion.'

'*Très bien*. Now I understand, *milord*, that the Prime Minister would, as a matter of course, be under vigilant police protection, which ought to render any assault upon him an impossibility?'

Lord Estair bowed his head. 'That is so. The Prime Minister's car was closely followed by another car containing detectives in plain clothes. Mr MacAdam knew nothing of these precautions. He is personally a most fearless man, and would be inclined to sweep them away arbitrarily. But, naturally, the police make their own arrangements. In fact, the Premier's chauffeur, O'Murphy, is a CID man.'

'O'Murphy? That is a name of Ireland, is it not so?'

'Yes, he is an Irishman.'

'From what part of Ireland?'

'County Clare, I believe.'

'*Tiens!* But proceed, *milord*.'

'The Premier started for London. The car was a closed one. He and Captain Daniels sat inside. The second car followed as usual. But, unluckily, for some unknown reason, the Prime Minister's car deviated from the main road –'

'At a point where the road curves?' interrupted Poirot.

'Yes – but how did you know?'

'Oh, *c'est évident*! Continue!'

'For some unknown reason,' continued Lord Estair, 'the Premier's car left the main road. The police car, unaware of the deviation, continued to keep to the high road. At a short distance down the unfrequented lane, the Prime Minister's car was suddenly held up by a band of masked men. The chauffeur –'

'That brave O'Murphy!' murmured Poirot thoughtfully.

'The chauffeur, momentarily taken aback, jammed on the brakes. The Prime Minister put his head out of the window. Instantly a shot rang out – then another. The first one grazed his cheek, the second, fortunately, went wide. The chauffeur, now realizing the danger, instantly forged straight ahead, scattering the band of men.'

'A near escape,' I ejaculated, with a shiver.

'Mr MacAdam refused to make any fuss over the slight wound he had received. He declared it was only a scratch. He stopped at a local cottage hospital, where it was dressed and bound up – he did not, of course, reveal his identity. He then drove, as per schedule, straight to Charing Cross, where a special train for Dover was awaiting him, and, after a brief account of what had happened had been given to the anxious police by Captain Daniels, he duly departed for France. At Dover, he went on board the waiting destroyer. At Boulogne, as you know, the bogus car was waiting for him, carrying the Union Jack, and correct in every detail.'

'That is all you have to tell me?'

'Yes.'

'There is no other circumstance that you have omitted, *milord*?'

'Well, there is one rather peculiar thing.'

'Yes?'

'The Prime Minister's car did not return home after leaving the Prime Minister at Charing Cross. The police were anxious to interview O'Murphy, so a search was instituted at once. The car was discovered standing outside a certain unsavoury little restaurant in Soho, which is well known as a meeting-place of German agents.'

'And the chauffeur?'

'The chauffeur was nowhere to be found. He, too, had disappeared.'

'So,' said Poirot thoughtfully, 'there are two disappearances: the Prime Minister in France, and O'Murphy in London.'

He looked keenly at Lord Estair, who made a gesture of despair.

'I can only tell you, Monsieur Poirot, that, if anyone had suggested to me yesterday that O'Murphy was a traitor, I should have laughed in his face.'

'And today?'

'Today I do not know what to think.'

Poirot nodded gravely. He looked at his turnip of a watch again.

'I understand that I have *carte blanche*, messieurs – in every way, I mean? I must be able to go where I choose, and how I choose.'

'Perfectly. There is a special train leaving for Dover in an hour's time, with a further contingent from Scotland Yard. You shall be accompanied by a Military officer and a CID man, who will hold themselves at your disposal in every way. Is that satisfactory?'

'Quite. One more question before you leave, messieurs. What made you come to me? I am unknown, obscure in this great London of yours.'

'We sought you out on the express recommendation and wish of a very great man of your own country.'

'*Comment?* My old friend the *Préfet –*?'

Lord Estair shook his head.

'One higher than the *Préfet*. One whose word was once law in Belgium – and shall be again! That England has sworn!'

Poirot's hand flew swiftly to a dramatic salute. 'Amen to that! Ah, but my Master does not forget ... Messieurs, I, Hercule Poirot, will serve you faithfully. Heaven only send that it will be in time. But this is dark – dark ... I cannot see.'

'Well, Poirot,' I cried impatiently, as the door closed behind the Ministers, 'what do you think?'

My friend was busy packing a minute suitcase, with quick, deft movements. He shook his head thoughtfully.

'I don't know what to think. My brains desert me.'

'Why, as you said, kidnap him, when a knock on the head would do as well?' I mused.

'Pardon me, *mon ami*, but I did not quite say that. It is undoubtedly far more their affair to kidnap him.'

'But why?'

'Because uncertainty creates panic. That is one reason.

Were the Prime Minister dead, it would be a terrible calamity, but the situation would have to be faced. But now you have paralysis. Will the Prime Minister reappear, or will he not? Is he dead or alive? Nobody knows, and until they know nothing definite can be done. And, as I tell you, uncertainty breeds panic, which is what *les Boches* are playing for. Then, again, if the kidnappers are holding him secretly somewhere, they have the advantage of being able to make terms with both sides. The German Government is not a liberal paymaster, as a rule, but no doubt they can be made to disgorge substantial remittances in such a case as this. Thirdly, they run no risk of the hangman's rope. Oh, decidedly, kidnapping is their affair.'

'Then, if that is so, why should they first try to shoot him?'

Poirot made a gesture of anger. 'Ah, that is just what I do not understand! It is inexplicable – stupid! They have all their arrangements made (and very good arrangements too!) for the abduction, and yet they imperil the whole affair by a melodramatic attack, worthy of a cinema, and quite as unreal. It is almost impossible to believe in it, with its band of masked men, not twenty miles from London!'

'Perhaps they were two quite separate attempts which happened irrespective of each other,' I suggested.

'Ah, no, that would be too much of a coincidence! Then, further – who is the traitor? There must have been a traitor – in the first affair, anyway. But who was it – Daniels or O'Murphy? It must have been one of the two, or why did the car leave the main road? We cannot suppose that the Prime Minister connived at his own assassination! Did O'Murphy take that turning of his own accord, or was it Daniels who told him to do so?'

'Surely it must have been O'Murphy's doing.'

'Yes, because if it was Daniels' the Prime Minister would have heard the order, and would have asked the reason. But there are altogether too many "whys" in this affair, and they contradict each other. If O'Murphy is an honest man, *why* did he leave the main road? But if he was a dishonest man, *why* did he start the car again when only two shots had been fired – thereby, in all probability, saving the Prime Minister's life? And, again, if he was honest, why did he, immediately on leaving Charing Cross, drive to a well-known rendezvous of German spies?'

'It looks bad,' I said.

'Let us look at the case with method. What have we for and against these two men? Take O'Murphy first. Against: that his conduct in leaving the main road was suspicious; that he is an Irishman from County Clare; that he has disappeared in a highly suggestive manner. For: that his promptness in restarting the car saved the Premier's life; that he is a Scotland Yard man, and, obviously, from the post allotted to him, a trusted detective. Now for Daniels. There is not much against him, except the fact that nothing is known of his antecedents, and that he speaks too many languages for a good Englishman! (Pardon me, *mon ami*, but, as linguists, you are deplorable!) Now *for* him, we have the fact that he was found gagged, bound, and chloroformed – which does not look as though he had anything to do with the matter.'

'He might have gagged and bound himself, to divert suspicion.'

Poirot shook his head. 'The French police would make no mistake of that kind. Besides, once he had attained his object, and the Prime Minister was safely abducted, there would not be much point in his remaining behind. His accomplices *could* have gagged and chloroformed him, of course, but I fail to see what object they hoped to accomplish by it. He can be of little use to them now, for, until the circumstances concerning the Prime Minister have been cleared up, he is bound to be closely watched.'

'Perhaps he hoped to start the police on a false scent?'

'Then why did he not do so? He merely says that something was pressed over his nose and mouth, and that he remembers nothing more. There is no false scent there. It sounds remarkably like the truth.'

'Well,' I said, glancing at the clock, 'I suppose we'd better start for the station. You may find more clues in France.'

'Possibly, *mon ami*, but I doubt it. It is still incredible to me that the Prime Minister has not been discovered in that limited area, where the difficulty of concealing him must be tremendous. If the military and the police of two countries have not found him, how shall I?'

At Charing Cross we were met by Mr Dodge.

'This is Detective Barnes, of Scotland Yard, and Major Norman. They will hold themselves entirely at your disposal. Good luck to you. It's a bad business, but I've not given up hope. Must be off now.' And the Minister strode rapidly away.

We chatted in a desultory fashion with Major Norman. In the centre of the little group of men on the platform I recognized a little ferret-faced fellow talking to a tall, fair man. He was an old acquaintance of Poirot's – Detective-Inspector Japp, supposed to be one of the smartest of Scotland Yard's officers. He came over and greeted my friend cheerfully.

'I heard you were on this job too. Smart bit of work. So far they've got away with the goods all right. But I can't believe they can keep him hidden long. Our people are going through France with a toothcomb. So are the French. I can't help feeling it's only a matter of hours now.'

'That is, if he's still alive,' remarked the tall detective gloomily.

Japp's face fell. 'Yes . . . but somehow I've got the feeling he's still alive all right.'

Poirot nodded. 'Yes, yes; he's alive. But can he be found in time? I, like you, did not believe he could be hidden so long.'

The whistle blew, and we all trooped up into the Pullman car. Then, with a slow, unwilling jerk, the train drew out of the station.

It was a curious journey. The Scotland Yard men crowded together. Maps of Northern France were spread out, and eager forefingers traced the lines of roads and villages. Each man had his own pet theory. Poirot showed none of his usual loquacity, but sat staring in front of him, with an expression on his face that reminded me of a puzzled child. I talked to

Norman, whom I found quite an amusing fellow. On arriving at Dover Poirot's behaviour moved me to intense amusement. The little man, as he went on board the boat, clutched desperately at my arm. The wind was blowing lustily.

'*Mon Dieu!*' he murmured. 'This is terrible!'

'Have courage, Poirot,' I cried. 'You will succeed. You will find him. I am sure of it.'

'Ah, *mon ami*, you mistake my emotion. It is this villainous sea that troubles me! The *mal de mer* – it is horrible suffering!'

'Oh!' I said, rather taken aback.

The first throb of the engines was felt, and Poirot groaned and closed his eyes.

'Major Norman has a map of Northern France if you would like to study it?'

Poirot shook his head impatiently.

'But no, but no! Leave me, my friend. See you, to think, the stomach and the brain must be in harmony. Laverguier has a method most excellent for averting the *mal de mer*. You breathe in – and out – slowly, so – turning the head from left to right and counting six between each breath.'

I left him to his gymnastic endeavours, and went on deck.

As we came slowly into Boulogne Harbour Poirot appeared, neat and smiling, and announced to me in a whisper that Laverguier's system had succeeded 'to a marvel!'

Japp's forefinger was still tracing imaginary routes on his map. 'Nonsense! The car started from Boulogne – here they branched off. Now, my idea is that they transferred the Prime Minister to another car. See?'

'Well,' said the tall detective, 'I shall make for the seaports. Ten to one, they've smuggled him on board a ship.'

Japp shook his head. 'Too obvious. The order went out at once to close all the ports.'

The day was just breaking as we landed. Major Norman touched Poirot on the arm. 'There's a military car here waiting for you, sir.'

'Thank you, monsieur. But, for the moment, I do not propose to leave Boulogne.'

'What?'

'No, we will enter this hotel here, by the quay.'

He suited the action to the word, demanded and was accorded a private room. We three followed him, puzzled and uncomprehending.

He shot a quick glance at us. 'It is not so that the good detective should act, eh? I perceive your thought. He must be full of energy. He must rush to and fro. He should prostrate himself on the dusty road and seek the marks of tyres through a little glass. He must gather up the cigarette-end, the fallen match? That is your idea, is it not?'

His eyes challenged us. 'But I – Hercule Poirot – tell you that it is not so! The true clues are within – *here!*' He tapped his forehead. 'See you, I need not have left London. It would have been sufficient for me to sit quietly in my rooms there. All that matters is the little grey cells within. Secretly and silently they do their part, until suddenly I call for a map, and I lay my finger on a spot – so – and I say: the Prime Minister is *there!* And it is so! With method and logic one can accomplish anything! This frantic rushing to France was a mistake – it is playing a child's game of hide-and-seek. But now, though it may be too late, I will set to work the right way, from within. Silence, my friends, I beg of you.'

And for five long hours the little man sat motionless, blinking his eyelids like a cat, his green eyes flickering and becoming steadily greener and greener. The Scotland Yard man was obviously contemptuous, Major Norman was bored and impatient, and I myself found the time pass with wearisome slowness.

Finally, I got up, and strolled as noiselessly as I could to the window. The matter was becoming a farce. I was secretly concerned for my friend. If he failed, I would have preferred him to fail in a less ridiculous manner. Out of the window I idly watched the daily leave boat, belching forth columns of smoke, as she lay alongside the quay.

Suddenly I was aroused by Poirot's voice close to my elbow.

'*Mes amis*, let us start!'

I turned. An extraordinary transformation had come over my friend. His eyes were flickering with excitement, his chest was swelled to the uttermost.

'I have been an imbecile, my friends! But I see daylight at last.'

Major Norman moved hastily to the door. 'I'll order the car.'

'There is no need. I shall not use it. Thank Heaven the wind has fallen.'

'Do you mean you are going to walk, sir?'

'No, my young friend. I am no St Peter. I prefer to cross the sea by boat.'

'To cross the *sea*?'

'Yes. To work with method, one must begin from the beginning. And the beginning of this affair was in England. Therefore, we return to England.'

At three o'clock, we stood once more upon Charing Cross platform. To all our expostulations, Poirot turned a deaf ear, and reiterated again and again that to start at the beginning was not a waste of time, but the only way. On the way over, he had conferred with Norman in a low voice, and the latter had despatched a sheaf of telegrams from Dover.

Owing to the special passes held by Norman, we got through everywhere in record time. In London, a large police car was waiting for us, with some plain-clothes men, one of whom handed a typewritten sheet of paper to my friend. He answered my inquiring glance.

'A list of the cottage hospitals within a certain radius west of London. I wired for it from Dover.'

We were whirled rapidly through the London streets. We were on the Bath Road. On we went, through Hammersmith, Chiswick and Brentford. I began to see our objective. Through Windsor and so on to Ascot. My heart gave a leap. Ascot was where Daniels had an aunt living. We were after *him*, then, not O'Murphy.

We duly stopped at the gate of a trim villa. Poirot jumped

out and rang the bell. I saw a perplexed frown dimming the radiance of his face. Plainly, he was not satisfied. The bell was answered. He was ushered inside. In a few moments he reappeared, and climbed into the car with a short, sharp shake of his head. My hopes began to die down. It was past four now. Even if he found certain evidence incriminating Daniels, what would be the good of it, unless he could wring from someone the exact spot in France where they were holding the Prime Minister?

Our return progress towards London was an interrupted one. We deviated from the main road more than once, and occasionally stopped at a small building, which I had no difficulty in recognizing as a cottage hospital. Poirot only spent a few minutes at each, but at every halt his radiant assurance was more and more restored.

He whispered something to Norman, to which the latter replied:

'Yes, if you turn off to the left, you will find them waiting by the bridge.'

We turned up a side road, and in the failing light I discerned a second car, waiting by the side of the road. It contained two men in plain clothes. Poirot got down and spoke to them, and then we started off in a northerly direction, the other car following close behind.

We drove for some time, our objective being obviously one of the northern suburbs of London. Finally, we drove up to the front door of a tall house, standing a little back from the road in its own grounds.

Norman and I were left in the car. Poirot and one of the detectives went up to the door and rang. A neat parlourmaid opened it. The detective spoke.

'I am a police officer, and I have a warrant to search this house.'

The girl gave a little scream, and a tall, handsome woman of middle age appeared behind her in the hall.

'Shut the door, Edith. They are burglars, I expect.'

But Poirot swiftly inserted his foot in the door, and at the same moment blew a whistle. Instantly the other detectives ran up, and poured into the house, shutting the door behind them.

Norman and I spent about five minutes cursing our forced inactivity. Finally the door reopened, and the men emerged, escorting three prisoners – a woman and two men. The woman, and one of the men, were taken to the second car. The other man was placed in our car by Poirot himself.

'I must go with the others, my friend. But have great care of this gentleman. You do not know him, no? *Eh bien*, let me present to you, Monsieur O'Murphy!'

O'Murphy! I *gaped* at him open-mouthed as we started again. He was not handcuffed, but I did not fancy he would try to escape. He sat there staring in front of him as though dazed. Anyway, Norman and I would be more than a match for him.

To my surprise, we still kept a northerly route. We were not returning to London, then! I was much puzzled. Suddenly, as the car slowed down, I recognized that we were close to Hendon Aerodrome. Immediately I grasped Poirot's idea. He proposed to reach France by aeroplane.

It was a sporting idea, but, on the face of it, impracticable. A telegram would be far quicker. Time was everything. He must leave the personal glory of rescuing the Prime Minister to others.

As we drew up, Major Norman jumped out, and a plain-clothes man took his place. He conferred with Poirot for a few minutes, and then went off briskly.

I, too, jumped out, and caught Poirot by the arm.

'I congratulate you, old fellow! They have told you the hiding-place? But, look here, you must wire to France at once. You'll be too late if you go yourself.'

Poirot looked at me curiously for a minute or two.

'Unfortunately, my friend, there are some things that cannot be sent by telegram.'

* * *

At that moment Major Norman returned, accompanied by a young officer in the uniform of the Flying Corps.

'This is Captain Lyall, who will fly you over to France. He can start at once.'

'Wrap up warmly, sir,' said the young pilot. 'I can lend you a coat, if you like.'

Poirot was consulting his enormous watch. He murmured to himself: 'Yes, there is time – just time.' Then he looked up and bowed politely to the young officer. 'I thank you, monsieur. But it is not I who am your passenger. It is this gentleman here.'

He moved a little aside as he spoke, and a figure came forward out of the darkness. It was the second male prisoner who had gone in the other car, and as the light fell on his face, I gave a start of surprise.

It was the Prime Minister!

'For Heaven's sake, tell me all about it,' I cried impatiently, as Poirot, Norman and I motored back to London. 'How in the world did they manage to smuggle him back to England?'

'There was no need to smuggle him back,' replied Poirot dryly. 'The Prime Minister has never left England. He was kidnapped on his way from Windsor to London.'

'*What?*'

'I will make all clear. The Prime Minister was in his car, his secretary beside him. Suddenly a pad of chloroform is clapped on his face –'

'But by whom?'

'By the clever linguistic Captain Daniels. As soon as the Prime Minister is unconscious, Daniels picks up the speaking-tube, and directs O'Murphy to turn to the right, which the chauffeur, quite unsuspicious, does. A few yards down that unfrequented road a large car is standing, apparently broken down. Its driver signals to O'Murphy to stop. O'Murphy slows up. The stranger approaches. Daniels leans out of the window, and, probably with the aid of an instantaneous anaesthetic, such as ethylchloride, the chloroform trick is repeated.

In a few seconds, the two helpless men are dragged out and transferred to the other car, and a pair of substitutes take their places.'

'Impossible!'

'*Pas du tout!* Have you not seen music-hall turns imitating celebrities with marvellous accuracy? Nothing is easier than to personate a public character. The Prime Minister of England is far easier to understudy than Mr John Smith of Clapham, say. As for O'Murphy's "double", no one was going to take much notice of him until after the departure of the Prime Minister, and by then he would have made himself scarce. He drives straight from Charing Cross to the meeting-place of his friends. He goes in as O'Murphy, he emerges as someone quite different. O'Murphy has disappeared, leaving a conveniently suspicious trail behind him.'

'But the man who personated the Prime Minister was seen by everyone!'

'He was not seen by anyone who knew him privately or intimately. And Daniels shielded him from contact with anyone as much as possible. Moreover, his face was bandaged up, and anything unusual in his manner would be put down to the fact that he was suffering from shock as a result of the attempt upon his life. Mr MacAdam has a weak throat, and always spares his voice as much as possible before any great speech. The deception was perfectly easy to keep up as far as France. There it would be impracticable and impossible – so the Prime Minister disappears. The police of this country hurry across the Channel, and no one bothers to go into the details of the first attack. To sustain the illusion that the abduction has taken place in France, Daniels is gagged and chloroformed in a convincing manner.'

'And the man who has enacted the part of the Prime Minister?'

'Rids himself of his disguise. He and the bogus chauffeur may be arrested as suspicious characters, but no one will dream of suspecting their real part in the drama, and they will eventually be released for lack of evidence.'

'And the real Prime Minister?'

'He and O'Murphy were driven straight to the house of "Mrs Everard," at Hampstead, Daniels' so-called "aunt". In reality, she is Frau Bertha Ebenthal, and the police have been looking for her for some time. It is a valuable little present that I have made them – to say nothing of Daniels! Ah, it was a clever plan, but he did not reckon on the cleverness of Hercule Poirot!'

I think my friend might well be excused his moment of vanity.

'When did you first begin to suspect the truth of the matter?'

'When I began to work the right way – from *within*! I could not make that shooting affair fit in – but when I saw that the net result of it was that *the Prime Minister went to France with his face bound up* I began to comprehend! And when I visited all the cottage hospitals between Windsor and London, and found that no one answering to my description had had his face bound up and dressed that morning, I was sure! After that, it was child's play for a mind like mine!'

The following morning, Poirot showed me a telegram he had just received. It had no place of origin, and was unsigned. It ran:

'In time.'

Later in the day the evening papers published an account of the Allied Conference. They laid particular stress on the magnificent ovation accorded to Mr David MacAdam, whose inspiring speech had produced a deep and lasting impression.

The Disappearance of Mr Davenheim

Poirot and I were expecting our old friend Inspector Japp of Scotland Yard to tea. We were sitting round the tea-table awaiting his arrival. Poirot had just finished carefully straightening the cups and saucers which our landlady was in the habit of throwing, rather than placing, on the table. He had also breathed heavily on the metal teapot, and polished it with a silk handkerchief. The kettle was on the boil, and a small enamel saucepan beside it contained some thick, sweet chocolate which was more to Poirot's palate than what he described as 'your English poison'.

A sharp 'rat-tat' sounded below, and a few minutes afterwards Japp entered briskly.

'Hope I'm not late,' he said as he greeted us. 'To tell the truth, I was yarning with Miller, the man who's in charge of the Davenheim case.'

I pricked up my ears. For the last three days the papers had been full of the strange disappearance of Mr Davenheim, senior partner of Davenheim and Salmon, the well-known bankers and financiers. On Saturday last he had walked out of his house, and had never been seen since. I looked forward to extracting some interesting details from Japp.

'I should have thought,' I remarked, 'that it would be almost impossible for anyone to "disappear" nowadays.'

Poirot moved a plate of bread and butter the eighth of an inch, and said sharply:

'Be exact, my friend. What do you mean by "disappear"? To which class of disappearance are you referring?'

'Are disappearances classified and labelled, then?' I laughed.

Japp smiled also. Poirot frowned at both of us.

'But certainly they are! They fall into three categories: First, and most common, the voluntary disappearance. Second, the much abused "loss of memory" case – rare, but occasionally genuine. Third, murder, and a more or less successful disposal of the body. Do you refer to all three as impossible of execution?'

'Very nearly so, I should think. You might lose your own memory, but someone would be sure to recognize you – especially in the case of a well-known man like Davenheim. Then "bodies" can't be made to vanish into thin air. Sooner or later they turn up, concealed in lonely places, or in trunks. Murder will out. In the same way, the absconding clerk, or the domestic defaulter, is bound to be run down in these days of wireless telegraphy. He can be headed off from foreign countries; ports and railway stations are watched; and as for concealment in this country, his features and appearance will be known to everyone who reads a daily newspaper. He's up against civilization.'

'*Mon ami,*' said Poirot, 'you make one error. You do not allow for the fact that a man who had decided to make away with another man – or with himself in a figurative sense – might be that rare machine, a man of method. He might bring intelligence, talent, a careful calculation of detail to the task; and then I do not see why he should not be successful in baffling the police force.'

'But not *you*, I suppose?' said Japp good-humouredly, winking at me. 'He couldn't baffle you, eh, Monsieur Poirot?'

Poirot endeavoured, with a marked lack of success, to look modest. 'Me also! Why not? It is true that I approach such problems with an exact science, a mathematical precision, which seems, alas, only too rare in the new generation of detectives!'

Japp grinned more widely.

'I don't know,' he said. 'Miller, the man who's on this case, is a smart chap. You may be very sure he won't overlook a footprint, or a cigar-ash, or a crumb even. He's got eyes that see everything.'

'So, *mon ami*,' said Poirot, 'has the London sparrow. But all the same, I should not ask the little brown bird to solve the problem of Mr Davenheim.'

'Come now, monsieur, you're not going to run down the value of details as clues?'

'By no means. These things are all good in their way. The danger is they may assume undue importance. Most details are insignificant; one or two are vital. It is the brain, the little grey cells' – he tapped his forehead – 'on which one must rely. The senses mislead. One must seek the truth within – not without.'

'You don't mean to say, Monsieur Poirot, that you would undertake to solve a case without moving from your chair, do you?'

'That is exactly what I do mean – granted the facts were placed before me. I regard myself as a consulting specialist.'

Japp slapped his knee. 'Hanged if I don't take you at your word. Bet you a fiver that you can't lay your hand – or rather tell me where to lay my hand – on Mr Davenheim, dead or alive, before a week is out.'

Poirot considered. '*Eh bien, mon ami*, I accept. *Le sport*, it is the passion of you English. Now – the facts.'

'On Saturday last, as is his usual custom, Mr Davenheim took the 12.40 train from Victoria to Chingside, where his palatial country seat, The Cedars, is situated. After lunch, he strolled round the grounds, and gave various directions to the gardeners. Everybody agrees that his manner was absolutely normal and as usual. After tea he put his head into his wife's boudoir, saying that he was going to stroll down to the village and post some letters. He added that he was expecting a Mr Lowen, on business. If he should come before he himself returned, he was to be shown into the study and asked to wait. Mr Davenheim then left the house by the front door, passed leisurely down the drive, and out at the gate, and – was never seen again. From that hour, he vanished completely.'

'Pretty – very pretty – altogether a charming little problem,' murmured Poirot. 'Proceed, my good friend.'

'About a quarter of an hour later a tall, dark man with a thick black moustache rang the front door-bell, and explained that he had an appointment with Mr Davenheim. He gave the name of Lowen, and in accordance with the banker's instructions was shown into the study. Nearly an hour passed. Mr Davenheim did not return. Finally Mr Lowen rang the bell, and explained that he was unable to wait any longer, as he must catch his train back to town.

'Mrs Davenheim apologized for her husband's absence, which seemed unaccountable, as she knew him to have been expecting the visitor. Mr Lowen reiterated his regrets and took his departure.

'Well, as everyone knows, Mr Davenheim did *not* return. Early on Sunday morning the police were communicated with, but could make neither head nor tail of the matter. Mr Davenheim seemed literally to have vanished into thin air. He had not been to the post office; nor had he been seen passing through the village. At the station they were positive he had not departed by any train. His own motor had not left the garage. If he had hired a car to meet him in some lonely spot, it seems almost certain that by this time, in view of the large reward offered for information, the driver of it would have come forward to tell what he knew. True, there was a small race-meeting at Entfield, five miles away, and if he had walked to that station he might have passed unnoticed in the crowd. But since then his photograph and a full description of him have been circulated in every newspaper, and nobody has been able to give any news of him. We have, of course, received many letters from all over England, but each clue, so far, has ended in disappointment.

'On Monday morning a further sensational discovery came to light. Behind a *portière* in Mr Davenheim's study stands a safe, and that safe had been broken into and rifled. The windows were fastened securely on the inside, which seems to put an ordinary burglary out of court, unless, of course, an accomplice within the house fastened them again afterwards. On the other hand, Sunday having intervened, and the household being in a state of chaos, it is likely that the burglary was committed on the Saturday, and remained undetected until Monday.'

'*Précisément*,' said Poirot dryly. 'Well, is he arrested, *ce pauvre M Lowen?*'

Japp grinned. 'Not yet. But he's under pretty close supervision.'

Poirot nodded. 'What was taken from the safe? Have you any idea?'

'We've been going into that with the junior partner of the firm and Mrs Davenheim. Apparently there was a considerable amount in bearer bonds, and a very large sum in notes, owing to some large transaction having been just carried through. There was also a small fortune in jewellery. All Mrs Davenheim's jewels were kept in the safe. The purchasing of them had become a passion with her husband of late years, and hardly a month passed that he did not make her a present of some rare and costly gem.'

'Altogether a good haul,' said Poirot thoughtfully. 'Now, what about Lowen? Is it known what his business was with Davenheim that evening?'

'Well, the two men were apparently not on very good terms. Lowen is a speculator in quite a small way. Nevertheless, he has been able once or twice to score a coup off Davenheim in the market, though it seems they seldom or never actually met. It was a matter concerning some South American shares which led the banker to make his appointment.'

'Had Davenheim interests in South America, then?'

'I believe so. Mrs Davenheim happened to mention that he spent all last autumn in Buenos Aires.'

'Any trouble in his home life? Were the husband and wife on good terms?'

'I should say his domestic life was quite peaceful and

uneventful. Mrs Davenheim is a pleasant, rather unintelligent woman. Quite a nonentity, I think.'

'Then we must not look for the solution of the mystery there. Had he any enemies?'

'He had plenty of financial rivals, and no doubt there are many people whom he has got the better of who bear him no particular goodwill. But there was no one likely to make away with him – and, if they had, where is the body?'

'Exactly. As Hastings says, bodies have a habit of coming to light with fatal persistency.'

'By the way, one of the gardeners says he saw a figure going round to the side of the house towards the rose-garden. The long french window of the study opens on to the rose-garden, and Mr Davenheim frequently entered and left the house that way. But the man was a good way off, at work on some cucumber frames, and cannot even say whether it was the figure of his master or not. Also, he cannot fix the time with any accuracy. It must have been before six, as the gardeners cease work at that time.'

'And Mr Davenheim left the house?'

'About half-past five or thereabouts.'

'What lies beyond the rose-garden?'

'A lake.'

'With a boathouse?'

'Yes, a couple of punts are kept there. I suppose you're thinking of suicide, Monsieur Poirot? Well, I don't mind telling you that Miller's going down tomorrow expressly to see that piece of water dragged. That's the kind of man he is!'

Poirot smiled faintly, and turned to me. 'Hastings, I pray you, hand me that copy of *Daily Megaphone*. If I remember rightly, there is an unusually clear photograph there of the missing man.'

I rose, and found the sheet required. Poirot studied the features attentively.

'H'm!' he murmured. 'Wears his hair rather long and wavy, full moustache and pointed beard, bushy eyebrows. Eyes dark?'

'Yes.'

'Hair and beard turning grey?'

The detective nodded. 'Well, Monsieur Poirot, what have you got to say to it all? Clear as daylight, eh?'

'On the contrary, most obscure.'

The Scotland Yard man looked pleased.

'Which gives me great hopes of solving it,' finished Poirot placidly.

'Eh?'

'I find it a good sign when a case is obscure. If a thing is clear as daylight – *eh bien*, mistrust it! Someone has made it so.'

Japp shook his head almost pityingly. 'Well, each to their fancy. But it's not a bad thing to see your way clear ahead.'

'I do not see,' murmured Poirot. 'I shut my eyes – and think.'

Japp sighed. 'Well, you've got a clear week to think in.'

'And you will bring me any fresh developments that arise – the result of the labours of the hard-working and lynx-eyed Inspector Miller, for instance?'

'Certainly. That's in the bargain.'

'Seems a shame, doesn't it?' said Japp to me as I accompanied him to the door. 'Like robbing a child!'

I could not help agreeing with a smile. I was still smiling as I re-entered the room.

'*Eh bien!*' said Poirot immediately. 'You make fun of Papa Poirot, is it not so?' He shook his finger at me. 'You do not trust his grey cells? Ah, do not be confused! Let us discuss this little problem – incomplete as yet, I admit, but already showing one or two points of interest.'

'The lake!' I said significantly.

'And even more than the lake, the boathouse!'

I looked sidewise at Poirot. He was smiling in his most inscrutable fashion. I felt that, for the moment, it would be quite useless to question him further.

We heard nothing of Japp until the following evening, when he walked in about nine o'clock. I saw at once by his expression that he was bursting with news of some kind.

'*Eh bien*, my friend,' remarked Poirot. 'All goes well? But do not tell me that you have discovered the body of Mr Davenheim in your lake, because I shall not believe you.'

'We haven't found the body, but we did find his *clothes* – the identical clothes he was wearing that day. What do you say to that?'

'Any other clothes missing from the house?'

'No, his valet was quite positive on that point. The rest of his wardrobe is intact. There's more. We've arrested Lowen. One of the maids, whose business it is to fasten the bedroom windows, declares that she saw Lowen coming *towards* the study through the rose-garden about a quarter past six. That would be about ten minutes before he left the house.'

'What does he himself say to that?'

'Denied first of all that he had ever left the study. But the maid was positive, and he pretended afterwards that he had forgotten just stepping out of the window to examine an unusual species of rose. Rather a weak story! And there's fresh evidence against him come to light. Mr Davenheim always wore a thick gold ring set with a solitaire diamond on the little finger of his right hand. Well, that ring was pawned in London on Saturday night by a man called Billy Kellett! He's already known to the police – did three months last autumn for lifting an old gentleman's watch. It seems he tried to pawn the ring at no less than five different places, succeeded at the last one, got gloriously drunk on the proceeds, assaulted a policeman, and was run in in consequence. I went to Bow Street with Miller and saw him. He's sober enough now, and I don't mind admitting we pretty well frightened the life out of him, hinting he might be charged with murder. This is his yarn, and a very queer one it is.

'He was at Entfield races on Saturday, though I dare say scarfpins was his line of business, rather than betting. Anyway, he had a bad day, and was down on his luck. He was tramping along the road to Chingside, and sat down in a ditch to rest just before he got into the village. A few minutes later he noticed a man coming along the road to the village, "dark-complexioned gent, with a big moustache, one of them city toffs," is his description of the man.

'Kellett was half concealed from the road by a heap of stones. Just before he got abreast of him, the man looked quickly up and down the road, and seeing it apparently deserted he took a small object from his pocket and threw it over the hedge. Then he went on towards the station. Now, the object he had thrown over the hedge had fallen with a slight "chink" which aroused the curiosity of the human derelict in the ditch. He investigated and, after a short search, discovered the ring! That is Kellett's story. It's only fair to say that Lowen denies it utterly, and of course the word of a man like Kellett can't be relied upon in the slightest. It's within the bounds of possibility that he met Davenheim in the lane and robbed and murdered him.'

Poirot shook his head.

'Very improbable, *mon ami*. He had no means of disposing of the body. It would have been found by now. Secondly, the open way in which he pawned the ring makes it unlikely that he did murder to get it. Thirdly, your sneak-thief is rarely a murderer. Fourthly, as he has been in prison since Saturday, it would be too much of a coincidence that he is able to give so accurate a description of Lowen.'

Japp nodded. 'I don't say you're not right. But all the same, you won't get a jury to take much note of a jailbird's evidence. What seems odd to me is that Lowen couldn't find a cleverer way of disposing of the ring.'

Poirot shrugged his shoulders. 'Well, after all, if it were found in the neighbourhood, it might be argued that Davenheim himself had dropped it.'

'But why remove it from the body at all?' I cried.

'There might be a reason for that,' said Japp. 'Do you know that just beyond the lake, a little gate leads out on to the hill, and not three minutes' walk brings you to – what do you think? – a *lime kiln*.'

'Good heavens!' I cried. 'You mean that the lime which

destroyed the body would be powerless to affect the metal of the ring?'

'Exactly.'

'It seems to me,' I said, 'that that explains everything. What a horrible crime!'

By common consent we both turned and looked at Poirot. He seemed lost in reflection, his brow knitted, as though with some supreme mental effort. I felt at last his keen intellect was asserting itself. What would his first words be? We were not long left in doubt. With a sigh, the tension of his attitude relaxed and turning to Japp, he asked:

'Have you any idea, my friend, whether Mr and Mrs Davenheim occupied the same bedroom?'

The question seemed so ludicrously inappropriate that for a moment we both stared in silence. Then Japp burst into a laugh. 'Good Lord, Monsieur Poirot, I thought you were coming out with something startling. As to your question, I'm sure I don't know.'

'You could find out?' asked Poirot with curious persistence.

'Oh, certainly – if you *really* want to know.'

'*Merci, mon ami.* I should be obliged if you would make a point of it.'

Japp stared at him a few minutes longer, but Poirot seemed to have forgotten us both. The detective shook his head sadly at me, and murmuring, 'Poor old fellow! War's been too much for him!' gently withdrew from the room.

As Poirot seemed sunk in a daydream, I took a sheet of paper, and amused myself by scribbling notes upon it. My friend's voice aroused me. He had come out of his reverie, and was looking brisk and alert.

'*Que faites-vous là, mon ami?*'

'I was jotting down what occurred to me as the main points of interest in this affair.'

'You become methodical – at last!' said Poirot approvingly.

I concealed my pleasure. 'Shall I read them to you?'

'By all means.'

I cleared my throat.

' "One: All the evidence points to Lowen having been the man who forced the safe.

' "Two: He had a grudge against Davenheim.

' "Three: He lied in his first statement that he had never left the study.

' "Four: If you accept Billy Kellett's story as true, Lowen is unmistakably implicated." '

I paused. 'Well?' I asked, for I felt that I had put my finger on all the vital facts.

Poirot looked at me pityingly, shaking his head very gently. '*Mon pauvre ami!* But it is that you have not the gift! The important detail, you appreciate him never! Also, your reasoning is false.'

'How?'

'Let me take your four points.'

'One: Mr Lowen could not possibly know that he would have the chance to open the safe. He came for a business interview. He could not know beforehand that Mr Davenheim would be absent posting a letter, and that he would consequently be alone in the study!'

'He might have seized the opportunity,' I suggested.

'And the tools? City gentlemen do not carry round housebreaker's tools on the off chance! And one could not cut into that safe with penknife, *bien entendu!* '

'Well, what about Number Two?'

'You say Lowen had a grudge against Mr Davenheim. What you mean is that he had once or twice got the better of him. And presumably those transactions were entered into with the view of benefiting himself. In any case you do not as a rule bear a grudge against a man you have got the better of – it is more likely to be the other way about. Whatever grudge there might have been would have been on Mr Davenheim's side.'

'Well, you can't deny that he lied about never having left the study?'

'No. But he may have been frightened. Remember, the missing man's clothes had just been discovered in the lake. Of course, as usual, he would have done better to speak the truth.'

'And the fourth point?'

'I grant you that. If Kellett's story is true, Lowen is undeniably implicated. That is what makes the affair so very interesting.'

'Then I *did* appreciate one vital fact?'

'Perhaps – but you have entirely overlooked the two most important points, the ones which undoubtedly hold the clue to the whole matter.'

'And pray, what are they?'

'One, the passion which has grown upon Mr Davenheim in the last few years for buying jewellery. Two, his trip to Buenos Aires last autumn.'

'Poirot, you are joking?'

'I am serious. Ah, sacred thunder, but I hope Japp will not forget my little commission.'

But the detective, entering into the spirit of the joke, had remembered it so well that a telegram was handed to Poirot about eleven o'clock the next day. At his request I opened it and read it out:

'"Husband and wife have occupied separate rooms since last winter."'

'Aha!' cried Poirot. 'And now we are in mid June! All is solved!'

I stared at him.

'You have no moneys in the bank of Davenheim and Salmon, *mon ami?*'

'No,' I said wondering. 'Why?'

'Because I should advise you to withdraw it – before it is too late.'

'Why, what do you expect?'

'I expect a big smash in a few days – perhaps sooner. Which reminds me, we will return the compliment of a *dépêche* to Japp. A pencil, I pray you, and a form. *Voilà!* "Advise you to withdraw any money deposited with firm in question." That will intrigue him, the good Japp! His eyes will open wide –

wide! He will not comprehend in the slightest – until tomorrow, or the next day!'

I remained sceptical, but the morrow forced me to render tribute to my friend's remarkable powers. In every paper was a huge headline telling of the sensational failure of the Davenheim bank. The disappearance of the famous financier took on a totally different aspect in the light of the revelation of the financial affairs of the bank.

Before we were half-way through breakfast, the door flew open and Japp rushed in. In his left hand was a paper; in his right was Poirot's telegram, which he banged down on the table in front of my friend.

'How did you know, Monsieur Poirot? How the blazes could you know?'

Poirot smiled placidly at him. 'Ah, *mon ami*, after your wire, it was a certainty! From the commencement, see you, it struck me that the safe burglary was somewhat remarkable. Jewels, ready money, bearer bonds – all so conveniently arranged for – whom? Well, the good Monsieur Davenheim was of those who "look after Number One" as your saying goes! It seemed almost certain that it was arranged for – himself! Then his passion of late years for buying jewellery! How simple! The funds he embezzled, he converted into jewels, very likely replacing them in turn with paste duplicates, and so he put away in a safe place, under another name, a considerable fortune to be enjoyed all in good time when everyone has been thrown off the track. His arrangements completed, he makes an appointment with Mr Lowen (who has been imprudent enough in the past to cross the great man once or twice), drills a hole in the safe, leaves orders that the guest is to be shown into the study, and walks out of the house – where?' Poirot stopped, and stretched out his hand for another boiled egg. He frowned. 'It is really insupportable,' he murmured, 'that every hen lays an egg of a different size! What symmetry can there be on the breakfast table? At least they should sort them in dozens at the shop!'

'Never mind the eggs,' said Japp impatiently. 'Let 'em lay

'em square if they like. Tell us where our customer went to when he left The Cedars – that is, if you know!'

'*Eh bien*, he went to his hiding place. Ah, this Monsieur Davenheim, there may be some malformation in his grey cells, but they are of the first quality!'

'Do you know where he is hiding?'

'Certainly! It is most ingenious.'

'For the Lord's sake, tell us, then!'

Poirot gently collected every fragment of shell from his plate, placed them in the egg-cup, and reversed the empty egg-shell on top of them. This little operation concluded, he smiled on the neat effect, and then beamed affectionately on us both.

'Come, my friends, you are men of intelligence. Ask yourself the question I asked myself. "If I were this man, where should *I* hide?" Hastings, what do you say?'

'Well,' I said, 'I'm rather inclined to think I'd not do a bolt at all. I'd stay in London – in the heart of things, travel by tubes and buses; ten to one I'd never be recognized. There's safety in a crowd.'

Poirot turned inquiringly to Japp.

'I don't agree. Get clear away at once – that's the only chance. I would have had plenty of time to prepare things beforehand. I'd have a yacht waiting, with steam up, and I'd be off to one of the most out-of-the-way corners of the world before the hue and cry began!'

We both looked at Poirot. 'What do *you* say, monsieur?'

For a moment he remained silent. Then a very curious smile flitted across his face.

'My friends, if *I* were hiding from the police, do you know *where* I should hide? *In a prison!*'

'*What?*'

'You are seeking Monsieur Davenheim in order to put him in prison, so you never dream of looking to see if he may not be already there!'

'What do you mean?'

'You tell me Madame Davenheim is not a very intelligent

woman. Nevertheless I think if you took her up to Bow Street and confronted her with the man Billy Kellett she would recognize him! In spite of the fact that he has shaved his beard and moustache and those bushy eyebrows, and has cropped his hair close. A woman nearly always knows her husband, though the rest of the world may be deceived.'

'Billy Kellett? But he's known to the police!'

'Did I not tell you Davenheim was a clever man? He prepared his alibi long beforehand. He was not in Buenos Aires last autumn – he was creating the character of Billy Kellett, "doing three months", so that the police should have no suspicions when the time came. He was playing, remember, for a large fortune, as well as liberty. It was worth while doing the thing thoroughly. Only –'

'Yes?'

'*Eh bien*, afterwards he had to wear a false beard and wig, had to *make up as himself again*, and to sleep with a false beard is not easy – it invites detection! He cannot risk continuing to share the chamber of madame his wife. You found out for me that for the last six months, or ever since his supposed return from Buenos Aires, he and Mrs Davenheim occupied separate rooms. Then I was sure! Everything fitted in. The gardener who fancied he saw his master going round to the side of the house was quite right. He went to the boathouse, donned his "tramp" clothes, which you may be sure had been safely hidden from the eyes of his valet, dropped the others in the lake, and proceeded to carry out his plan by pawning the ring in an obvious manner, and then assaulting a policeman, getting himself safely into the haven of Bow Street, where nobody would ever dream of looking for him!'

'It's impossible,' murmured Japp.

'Ask Madame,' said my friend, smiling.

The next day a registered letter lay beside Poirot's plate. He opened it and a five-pound note fluttered out. My friend's brow puckered.

'*Ah, sacré!* But what shall I do with it? I have much remorse! *Ce pauvre Japp?* Ah, an idea! We will have a little dinner, we

three! That consoles me. It was really too easy. I am ashamed.
I, who would not rob a child – *mille tonnerres! Mon ami*, what
have you, that you laugh so heartily?'

X

The Adventure of the Italian Nobleman

Poirot and I had many friends and acquaintances of an informal nature. Amongst these was to be numbered Dr Hawker, a near neighbour of ours, and a member of the medical profession. It was the genial doctor's habit to drop in sometimes of an evening and have a chat with Poirot, of whose genius he was an ardent admirer. The doctor himself, frank and unsuspicious to the last degree, admired the talents so far removed from his own.

On one particular evening in early June, he arrived about half past eight and settled down to a comfortable discussion on the cheery topic of the prevalence of arsenical poisoning in crimes. It must have been about a quarter of an hour later when the door of our sitting room flew open, and a distracted female precipitated herself into the room.

'Oh, doctor, you're wanted! Such a terrible voice. It gave me a turn, it did indeed.'

I recognized in our new visitor Dr Hawker's housekeeper, Miss Rider. The doctor was a bachelor, and lived in a gloomy old house a few streets away. The usually placid Miss Rider was now in a state bordering on incoherence.

'What terrible voice? Who is it, and what's the trouble?'

'It was the telephone, doctor. I answered it – and a voice spoke. "Help," it said. "Doctor – help. They've killed me!" Then it sort of tailed away. "Who's speaking?" I said. "Who's speaking?" Then I got a reply, just a whisper, it seemed, "Foscatine" – something like that – "Regent's Court."'

The doctor uttered an exclamation.

'Count Foscatini. He has a flat in Regent's Court. I must go at once. What can have happened?'

'A patient of yours?' asked Poirot.

'I attended him for some slight ailment a few weeks ago. An Italian, but he speaks English perfectly. Well, I must wish you good night, Monsieur Poirot, unless –' He hesitated.

'I perceive the thought in your mind,' said Poirot, smiling. 'I shall be delighted to accompany you. Hastings, run down and get hold of a taxi.'

Taxis always make themselves sought for when one is particularly pressed for time, but I captured one at last, and we were soon bowling along in the direction of Regent's Park. Regent's Court was a new block of flats, situated just off St John's Wood Road. They had only recently been built, and contained the latest service devices.

There was no one in the hall. The doctor pressed the lift-bell impatiently, and when the lift arrived questioned the uniformed attendant sharply.

'Flat 11. Count Foscatini. There's been an accident there, I understand.'

The man stared at him.

'First I've heard of it. Mr Graves – that's Count Foscatini's man – went out about half an hour ago, and he said nothing.'

'Is the Count alone in the flat?'

'No, sir, he's got two gentlemen dining with him.'

'What are they like?' I asked eagerly.

We were in the lift now, ascending rapidly to the second floor, on which Flat 11 was situated.

'I didn't see them myself, sir, but I understand that they were foreign gentlemen.'

He pulled back the iron door, and we stepped out on the landing. No 11 was opposite to us. The doctor rang the bell. There was no reply, and we could hear no sound from within. The doctor rang again and again; we could hear the bell trilling within, but no sign of life rewarded us.

'This is getting serious,' muttered the doctor. He turned to the lift attendant.

'Is there any pass-key to this door?'

'There is one in the porter's office downstairs.'

'Get it, then, and, look here, I think you'd better send for the police.'

Poirot approved with a nod of the head.

The man returned shortly; with him came the manager.

'Will you tell me, gentlemen, what is the meaning of all this?'

'Certainly. I received a telephone message from Count Foscatini stating that he had been attacked and was dying. You can understand that we must lose no time – if we are not already too late.'

The manager produced the key without more ado, and we all entered the flat.

We passed first into the small square lounge hall. A door on the right of it was half open. The manager indicated it with a nod.

'The dining room.'

Dr Hawker led the way. We followed close on his heels. As we entered the room I gave a gasp. The round table in the centre bore the remains of a meal; three chairs were pushed back, as though their occupants had just risen. In the corner, to the right of the fireplace, was a big writing-table, and sitting at it was a man – or what had been a man. His right hand still grasped the base of the telephone, but he had fallen forward, struck down by a terrific blow on the head from behind. The weapon was not far to seek. A marble statue stood where it had been hurriedly put down, the base of it stained with blood.

The doctor's examination did not take a minute. 'Stone dead. Must have been almost instantaneous. I wonder he even managed to telephone. It will be better not to move him until the police arrive.'

On the manager's suggestion we searched the flat, but the result was a foregone conclusion. It was not likely that the murderers would be concealed there when all they had to do was to walk out.

We came back to the dining room. Poirot had not accompanied us in our tour. I found him studying the centre table with close attention. I joined him. It was a well-polished round mahogany table. A bowl of roses decorated the centre, and white lace mats reposed on the gleaming surface. There was a dish of fruit, but the three dessert plates were untouched. There were three coffee-cups with remains of coffee in them – two black, one with milk. All three men had taken port, and the decanter, half-full, stood before the centre plate. One of the men had smoked a cigar, the other two cigarettes. A tortoiseshell-and-silver box, holding cigars and cigarettes, stood open upon the table.

I enumerated all these facts to myself, but I was forced to admit that they did not shed any brilliant light on the situation. I wondered what Poirot saw in them to make him so intent. I asked him.

'*Mon ami*,' he replied, 'you miss the point. I am looking for something that I do *not* see.'

'What is that?'

'A mistake – even a little mistake – on the part of the murderer.'

He stepped swiftly to the small adjoining kitchen, looked in, and shook his head.

'Monsieur,' he said to the manager, 'explain to me, I pray, your system of serving meals here.'

The manager stepped to a small hatch in the wall.

'This is the service lift,' he explained. 'It runs to the kitchens at the top of the building. You order through this telephone, and the dishes are sent down in the lift, one course at a time. The dirty plates and dishes are sent up in the same manner. No domestic worries, you understand, and at the same time you avoid the wearying publicity of always dining in a restaurant.'

Poirot nodded.

'Then the plates and dishes that were used tonight are on high in the kitchen. You permit that I mount there?'

'Oh, certainly, if you like! Roberts, the lift man, will take you up and introduce you; but I'm afraid you won't find anything that's of any use. They're handling hundreds of plates and dishes, and they'll be all lumped together.'

Poirot remained firm, however, and together we visited the kitchens and questioned the man who had taken the order from Flat 11.

'The order was given from the à la carte menu – for three,' he explained. 'Soup julienne, filet de sole normande, tournedos of beef, and a rice soufflé. What time? Just about eight o'clock, I should say. No, I'm afraid the plates and dishes have been all washed up by now. Unfortunate. You were thinking of fingerprints, I suppose?'

'Not exactly,' said Poirot, with an enigmatical smile. 'I am more interested in Count Foscatini's appetite. Did he partake of every dish?'

'Yes; but of course I can't say how much of each he ate. The plates were all soiled, and the dishes empty – that is to say, with the exception of the rice soufflé. There was a fair amount of that left.'

'Ah!' said Poirot, and seemed satisfied with the fact.

As we descended to the flat again he remarked in a low tone:

'We have decidedly to do with a man of method.'

'Do you mean the murderer, or Count Foscatini?'

'The latter was undoubtedly an orderly gentleman. After imploring help and announcing his approaching demise, he carefully hung up the telephone receiver.'

I stared at Poirot. His words now and his recent inquiries gave me the glimmering of an idea.

'You suspect poison?' I breathed. 'The blow on the head was a blind.'

Poirot merely smiled.

We re-entered the flat to find the local inspector of police had arrived with two constables. He was inclined to resent our appearance, but Poirot calmed him with the mention of our Scotland Yard friend, Inspector Japp, and we were accorded a grudging permission to remain. It was a lucky thing we were, for we had not been back five minutes before an agitated middle-aged man came rushing into the room with every appearance of grief and agitation.

This was Graves, valet-butler to the late Count Foscatini. The story he had to tell was a sensational one.

On the previous morning, two gentlemen had called to see his master. They were Italians, and the elder of the two, a man of about forty, gave his name as Signor Ascanio. The younger was a well-dressed lad of about twenty-four.

Count Foscatini was evidently prepared for their visit and immediately sent Graves out upon some trivial errand. Here the man paused and hesitated in his story. In the end, however, he admitted that, curious as to the purport of the interview, he had not obeyed immediately, but had lingered about endeavouring to hear something of what was going on.

The conversation was carried on in so low a tone that he was not as successful as he had hoped; but he gathered enough to make it clear that some kind of monetary proposition was being discussed, and that the basis of it was a threat. The discussion was anything but amicable. In the end, Count Foscatini raised his voice slightly, and the listener heard these words clearly:

> 'I have no time to argue further now, gentlemen. If you will dine with me tomorrow night at eight o'clock, we will resume the discussion.'

Afraid of being discovered listening, Graves had then hurried out to do his master's errand. This evening the two men had arrived punctually at eight. During dinner they had talked of indifferent matters – politics, the weather, and the theatrical world. When Graves had placed the port upon the table and brought in the coffee his master told him that he might have the evening off.

'Was that a usual proceeding of his when he had guests?' asked the inspector.

'No, sir; it wasn't. That's what made me think it must be

some business of a very unusual kind that he was going to discuss with these gentlemen.'

That finished Graves's story. He had gone out about 8.30, and meeting a friend, had accompanied him to the Metropolitan Music Hall in Edgware Road.

Nobody had seen the two men leave, but the time of the murder was fixed clearly enough at 8.47. A small clock on the writing-table had been swept off by Foscatini's arm, and had stopped at that hour, which agreed with Miss Rider's telephone summons.

The police surgeon had made his examination of the body, and it was now lying on the couch. I saw the face for the first time – the olive complexion, the long nose, the luxuriant black moustache, and the full red lips drawn back from the dazzlingly white teeth. Not altogether a pleasant face.

'Well,' said the inspector, refastening his notebook. 'The case seems clear enough. The only difficulty will be to lay our hands on this Signor Ascanio. I suppose his address is not in the dead man's pocket-book by any chance?'

As Poirot had said, the late Foscatini was an orderly man. Neatly written in small, precise handwriting was the inscription, 'Signor Paolo Ascanio, Grosvenor Hotel.'

The inspector busied himself with the telephone, then turned to us with a grin.

'Just in time. Our fine gentleman was off to catch the boat train to the Continent. Well, gentlemen, that's about all we can do here. It's a bad business, but straightforward enough. One of these Italian vendetta things, as likely as not.'

Thus airily dismissed, we found our way downstairs. Dr Hawker was full of excitement.

'Like the beginning of a novel, eh? Real exciting stuff. Wouldn't believe it if you read about it.'

Poirot did not speak. He was very thoughtful. All the evening he had hardly opened his lips.

'What says the master detective, eh?' asked Hawker, clapping him on the back. 'Nothing to work your grey cells over this time.'

'You think not?'

'What could there be?'

'Well, for example, there is the window.'

'The window? But it was fastened. Nobody could have got out or in that way. I noticed it specially.'

'And why were you able to notice it?'

The doctor looked puzzled. Poirot hastened to explain.

'It is to the curtains that I refer. They were not drawn. A little odd, that. And then there was the coffee. It was very black coffee.'

'Well, what of it?'

'Very black,' repeated Poirot. 'In conjunction with that let us remember that very little of the rice soufflé was eaten, and we get – what?'

'Moonshine,' laughed the doctor. 'You're pulling my leg.'

'Never do I pull the leg. Hastings here knows that I am perfectly serious.'

'I don't know what you are getting at, all the same,' I confessed. 'You don't suspect the manservant, do you? He might have been in with the gang, and put some dope in the coffee. I suppose they'll test his alibi?'

'Without doubt, my friend; but it is the alibi of Signor Ascanio that interests me.'

'You think he has an alibi?'

'That is just what worries me. I have no doubt that we shall soon be enlightened on that point.'

The *Daily Newsmonger* enabled us to become conversant with succeeding events.

Signor Ascanio was arrested and charged with the murder of Count Foscatini. When arrested, he denied knowing the Count, and declared he had never been near Regent's Court either on the evening of the crime or on the previous morning. The younger man had disappeared entirely. Signor Ascanio had arrived alone at the Grosvenor Hotel from the Continent two days before the murder. All efforts to trace the second man failed.

Ascanio, however, was not sent for trial. No less a personage than the Italian Ambassador himself came forward and testified at the police-court proceedings that Ascanio had been with him at the Embassy from eight till nine that evening. The prisoner was discharged. Naturally, a lot of people thought that the crime was a political one, and was being deliberately hushed up.

Poirot had taken a keen interest in all these points. Nevertheless, I was somewhat surprised when he suddenly informed me one morning that he was expecting a visitor at eleven o'clock, and that the visitor was none other than Ascanio himself.

'He wishes to consult you?'

'*Du tout*, Hastings, I wish to consult him.'

'What about?'

'The Regent's Court murder.'

'You are going to prove that he did it?'

'A man cannot be tried twice for murder, Hastings. Endeavour to have the common sense. Ah, that is our friend's ring.'

A few minutes later Signor Ascanio was ushered in – a small, thin man with a secretive and furtive glance in his eyes. He remained standing, darting suspicious glances from one to the other of us.

'Monsieur Poirot?'

My little friend tapped himself gently on the chest.

'Be seated, signor. You received my note. I am determined to get to the bottom of this mystery. In some small measure you can aid me. Let us commence. You – in company with a friend – visited the late Count Foscatini on the morning of Tuesday the 9th –'

The Italian made an angry gesture.

'I did nothing of the sort. I have sworn in court –'

'*Précisément* – and I have a little idea that you have sworn falsely.'

'You threaten me? Bah! I have nothing to fear from you. I have been acquitted.'

'Exactly; and as I am not an imbecile, it is not with the gallows I threaten you – but with publicity. Publicity! I see

that you do not like the word. I had an idea that you would
not. My little ideas, you know, they are very valuable to me.
Come, signor, your only chance is to be frank with me. I do
not ask to know whose indiscretions brought you to England.
I know this much, you came for the special purpose of seeing
Count Foscatini.'

'He was not a count,' growled the Italian.

'I have already noted the fact that his name does not appear
in the *Almanach de Gotha*. Never mind, the title of count is often
useful in the profession of blackmailing.'

'I suppose I might as well be frank. You seem to know a
good deal.'

'I have employed my grey cells to some advantage. Come,
Signor Ascanio, you visited the dead man on the Tuesday
morning – that is so, is it not?'

'Yes; but I never went there on the following evening. There
was no need. I will tell you all. Certain information concerning
a man of great position in Italy had come into this scoundrel's
possession. He demanded a big sum of money in return for
the papers. I came over to England to arrange the matter. I
called upon him by appointment that morning. One of the
young secretaries of the Embassy was with me. The Count
was more reasonable than I had hoped, although even then
the sum of money I paid him was a huge one.'

'Pardon, how was it paid?'

'In Italian notes of comparatively small denomination. I
paid over the money then and there. He handed me the incriminating papers. I never saw him again.'

'Why did you not say all this when you were arrested?'

'In my delicate position I was forced to deny any association
with the man.'

'And how do you account for the events of the evening then?'

'I can only think that someone must have deliberately
impersonated me. I understand that no money was found in
the flat.'

Poirot looked at him and shook his head.

'Strange,' he murmured. 'We all have the little grey cells.

And so few of us know how to use them. Good morning, Signor Ascanio. I believe your story. It is very much as I had imagined. But I had to make sure.'

After bowing his guest out, Poirot returned to his armchair and smiled at me.

'Let us hear M le Capitaine Hastings on the case.'

'Well, I suppose Ascanio is right – somebody impersonated him.'

'Never, never will you use the brains the good God has given you. Recall to yourself some words I uttered after leaving the flat that night. I referred to the window-curtains not being drawn. We are in the month of June. It is still light at eight o'clock. The light is failing by half-past. *Ça vous dit quelque chose?* I perceive a struggling impression that you will arrive some day. Now let us continue. The coffee was, as I said, very black. Count Foscatini's teeth were magnificently white. Coffee stains the teeth. We reason from that that Count Foscatini did not drink any coffee. Yet there was coffee in all three cups. Why should anyone pretend Count Foscatini had drunk coffee when he had not done so?'

I shook my head, utterly bewildered.

'Come, I will help you. What evidence have we that Ascanio and his friend, or two men posing as them, ever came to the flat that night? Nobody saw them go in; nobody saw them go out. We have the evidence of one man and of a host of inanimate objects.'

'You mean?'

'I mean knives and forks and plates and empty dishes. Ah, but it was a clever idea! Graves is a thief and a scoundrel, but what a man of method! He overhears a portion of the conversation in the morning, enough to realize that Ascanio will be in an awkward position to defend himself. The following evening, about eight o'clock, he tells his master he is wanted at the telephone. Foscatini sits down, stretches out his hand to the telephone, and from behind Graves strikes him down with the marble figure. Then quickly to the service telephone – dinner for three! It comes, he lays the table, dirties the plates, knives, and forks, etc. But he has to get rid of the food too. Not only is he a man of brain; he has a resolute and capacious stomach! But after eating three tournedos, the rice soufflé is too much for him! He even smokes a cigar and two cigarettes to carry out the illusion. Ah, but it was magnificently thorough! Then, having moved on the hands of the clock to 8.47, he smashes it and stops it. The one thing he does not do is to draw the curtains. But if there had been a real dinner party the curtains would have been drawn as soon as the light began to fail. Then he hurries out, mentioning the guests to the lift man in passing. He hurries to a telephone box, and as near as possible to 8.47 rings up the doctor with his master's dying cry. So successful is his idea that no one ever inquires if a call was put through from Flat 11 at that time.'

'Except Hercule Poirot, I suppose?' I said sarcastically.

'Not even Hercule Poirot,' said my friend, with a smile. 'I am about to inquire now. I had to prove my point to you first. But you will see, I shall be right; and then Japp, to whom I have already given a hint, will be able to arrest the respectable Graves. I wonder how much of the money he has spent.'

Poirot *was* right. He always is, confound him!

The Case of the Missing Will

The problem presented to us by Miss Violet Marsh made rather a pleasant change from our usual routine work. Poirot had received a brisk and businesslike note from the lady asking for an appointment, and had replied asking her to call upon him at eleven o'clock the following day.

She arrived punctually – a tall, handsome young woman, plainly but neatly dressed, with an assured and businesslike manner. Clearly a young woman who meant to get on in the world. I am not a great admirer of the so-called New Woman myself, and, in spite of her good looks, I was not particularly prepossessed in her favour.

'My business is of a somewhat unusual nature, Monsieur Poirot,' she began, after she had accepted a chair. 'I had better begin at the beginning and tell you the whole story.'

'If you please, mademoiselle.'

'I am an orphan. My father was one of two brothers, sons of a small yeoman farmer in Devonshire. The farm was a poor one, and the elder brother, Andrew, emigrated to Australia, where he did very well indeed, and by means of successful speculation in land became a very rich man. The younger brother, Roger (my father), had no leanings towards the agricultural life. He managed to educate himself a little, and obtained a post as clerk with a small firm. He married slightly above him; my mother was the daughter of a poor artist. My father died when I was six years old. When I was fourteen, my mother followed him to the grave. My only living relation then was my uncle Andrew, who had recently returned from Australia and bought a small place, Crabtree Manor, in his native county. He was exceedingly kind to his brother's orphan

child, took me to live with him, and treated me in every way
as though I was his own daughter.

'Crabtree Manor, in spite of its name, is really only an old
farmhouse. Farming was in my uncle's blood, and he was
intensely interested in various modern farming experiments.
Although kindness itself to me, he had certain peculiar and
deeply-rooted ideas as to the upbringing of women. Himself
a man of little or no education, though possessing remarkable
shrewdness, he placed little value on what he called "book
knowledge". He was especially opposed to the education of
women. In his opinion, girls should learn practical housework
and dairy-work, be useful about the home, and have as little
to do with book learning as possible. He proposed to bring
me up on these lines, to my bitter disappointment and annoyance. I rebelled frankly. I knew that I possessed a good brain,
and had absolutely no talent for domestic duties. My uncle
and I had many bitter arguments on the subject, for, though
much attached to each other, we were both self-willed. I was
lucky enough to win a scholarship, and up to a certain point
was successful in getting my own way. The crisis arose when
I resolved to go to Girton. I had a little money of my own,
left me by my mother, and I was quite determined to make
the best use of the gifts God had given me. I had one long,
final argument with my uncle. He put the facts plainly before
me. He had no other relations, and he had intended me to be
his sole heiress. As I have told you, he was a very rich man.
If I persisted in these "new-fangled notions" of mine, however,
I need look for nothing from him. I remained polite, but firm.
I should always be deeply attached to him, I told him, but I
must lead my own life. We parted on that note. "You fancy
your brains, my girl," were his last words. "I've no book
learning, but, for all that, I'll pit mine against yours any day.
We'll see what we shall see."'

'That was nine years ago. I have stayed with him for a
weekend occasionally, and our relations were perfectly amicable, though his views remained unaltered. He never referred
to my having matriculated, nor to my BSc. For the last three

years his health had been failing, and a month ago he died.

'I am now coming to the point of my visit. My uncle left a most extraordinary will. By its terms, Crabtree Manor and its contents are to be at my disposal for a year from his death – "during which time my clever niece may prove her wits", the actual words run. At the end of that period, "my wits having been proved better than hers", the house and all my uncle's large fortune pass to various charitable institutions.'

'That is a little hard on you, mademoiselle, seeing that you were Mr Marsh's only blood relation.'

'I do not look on it in that way. Uncle Andrew warned me fairly, and I chose my own path. Since I would not fall in with his wishes, he was at perfect liberty to leave his money to whom he pleased.'

'Was the will drawn up by a lawyer?'

'No; it was written on a printed will-form and witnessed by the man and his wife who live at the house and do for my uncle.'

'There might be a possibility of upsetting such a will?'

'I would not even attempt to do such a thing.'

'You regard it then as a sporting challenge on the part of your uncle?'

'That is exactly how I look upon it.'

'It bears that interpretation, certainly,' said Poirot thoughtfully. 'Somewhere in this rambling old manor-house your uncle has concealed either a sum of money in notes or possibly a second will, and has given you a year in which to exercise your ingenuity to find it.'

'Exactly, Monsieur Poirot; and I am paying you the compliment of assuming that your ingenuity will be greater than mine.'

'Eh, eh! but that is very charming of you. My grey cells are at your disposal. You have made no search yourself?'

'Only a cursory one; but I have too much respect for my uncle's undoubted abilities to fancy that the task will be an easy one.'

'Have you the will or a copy of it with you?'

Miss Marsh handed a document across the table. Poirot ran through it, nodding to himself.

'Made three years ago. Dated March 25; and the time is given also – 11 AM – that is very suggestive. It narrows the field of search. Assuredly it is another will we have to seek for. A will made even half an hour later would upset this. *Eh bien*, mademoiselle, it is a problem charming and ingenious that you have presented to me here. I shall have all the pleasure in the world in solving it for you. Granted that your uncle was a man of ability, his grey cells cannot have been of the quality of Hercule Poirot's!'

(Really, Poirot's vanity is blatant!)

'Fortunately, I have nothing of moment on hand at the minute. Hastings and I will go down to Crabtree Manor tonight. The man and wife who attended on your uncle are still there, I presume?'

'Yes, their name is Baker.'

The following morning saw us started on the hunt proper. We had arrived late the night before. Mr and Mrs Baker, having received a telegram from Miss Marsh, were expecting us. They were a pleasant couple, the man gnarled and pink-cheeked, like a shrivelled pippin, and his wife a woman of vast proportion and true Devonshire calm.

Tired with our journey and the eight-mile drive from the station, we had retired at once to bed after a supper of roast chicken, apple pie, and Devonshire cream. We had now disposed of an excellent breakfast, and were sitting in a small panelled room which had been the late Mr Marsh's study and living room. A roll-top desk stuffed with papers, all neatly docketed, stood against the wall, and a big leather armchair showed plainly that it had been its owner's constant resting-place. A big chintz-covered settee ran along the opposite wall, and the deep low window seats were covered with the same faded chintz of an old-fashioned pattern.

'*Eh bien, mon ami*,' said Poirot, lighting one of his tiny cigarettes, 'we must map out our plan of campaign. Already I have made a rough survey of the house, but I am of the opinion that any clue will be found in this room. We shall have to go through the documents in the desk with meticulous care. Naturally, I do not expect to find the will amongst them, but it is likely that some apparently innocent paper may conceal the clue to its hiding-place. But first we must have a little information. Ring the bell, I pray of you.'

I did so. While we were waiting for it to be answered, Poirot walked up and down, looking about him approvingly.

'A man of method, this Mr Marsh. See how neatly the packets of papers are docketed; then the key to each drawer has its ivory label – so has the key of the china cabinet on the wall; and see with what precision the china within is arranged. It rejoices the heart. Nothing here offends the eye –'

He came to an abrupt pause, as his eye was caught by the key of the desk itself, to which a dirty envelope was affixed. Poirot frowned at it and withdrew it from the lock. On it were scrawled the words: 'Key of Roll Top Desk,' in a crabbed handwriting, quite unlike the neat superscriptions on the other keys.

'An alien note,' said Poirot, frowning. 'I could swear that here we have no longer the personality of Mr Marsh. But who else has been in the house? Only Miss Marsh, and she, if I mistake not, is also a young lady of method and order.'

Baker came in answer to the bell.

'Will you fetch madame your wife, and answer a few questions?'

Baker departed, and in a few moments returned with Mrs Baker, wiping her hands on her apron and beaming all over her face.

In a few clear words Poirot set forth the object of his mission. The Bakers were immediately sympathetic.

'Us don't want to see Miss Violet done out of what's hers,' declared the woman. 'Cruel hard 'twould be for hospitals to get it all.'

Poirot proceeded with his questions. Yes, Mr and Mrs Baker remembered perfectly witnessing the will. Baker had previously been sent into the neighbouring town to get two printed will-forms.

'Two?' said Poirot sharply.

'Yes, sir, for safety like, I suppose, in case he should spoil one – and sure enough, so he did do. Us had signed one –'

'What time of day was that?'

Baker scratched his head, but his wife was quicker.

'Why, to be sure, I'd just put the milk on for the cocoa at eleven. Don't ee remember? It had all boiled over on the stove when us got back to kitchen.'

'And afterwards?'

"Twould be about an hour later. Us had to go in again. "I've made a mistake," said old master, "had to tear the whole thing up. I'll trouble you to sign again," and us did. And afterwards master gave us a tidy sum of money each. "I've left you nothing in my will," says he, "but each year I live you'll have this to be a nest-egg when I'm gone": and sure enough, so he did.'

Poirot reflected.

'After you had signed the second time, what did Mr Marsh do? Do you know?'

'Went out to the village to pay tradesmen's books.'

That did not seem very promising. Poirot tried another tack. He held out the key of the desk.

'Is that your master's writing?'

I may have imagined it, but I fancied that a moment or two elapsed before Baker replied: 'Yes, sir, it is.'

'He's lying,' I thought. 'But why?'

'Has your master let the house? – have there been any strangers in it during the last three years?'

'No, sir.'

'No visitors?'

'Only Miss Violet.'

'No strangers of any kind been inside this room?'

'No, sir.'

'You forget the workmen, Jim,' his wife reminded him.

'Workmen?' Poirot wheeled round on her. 'What workmen?'

The woman explained that about two years and a half ago workmen had been in the house to do certain repairs. She was quite vague as to what the repairs were. Her view seemed to be that the whole thing was a fad of her master's quite unnecessary. Part of the time the workmen had been in the study; but what they had done there she could not say, as her master had not let either of them into the room whilst the work was in progress. Unfortunately, they could not remember the name of the firm employed, beyond the fact that it was a Plymouth one.

'We progress, Hastings,' said Poirot, rubbing his hands as the Bakers left the room. 'Clearly he made a second will and then had workmen from Plymouth in to make a suitable hiding-place. Instead of wasting time taking up the floor and tapping the walls, we will go to Plymouth.'

With a little trouble, we were able to get the information we wanted. After one or two essays we found the firm employed by Mr Marsh.

Their employees had all been with them many years, and it was easy to find the two men who had worked under Mr Marsh's orders. They remembered the job perfectly. Amongst various other minor jobs, they had taken up one of the bricks of the old-fashioned fireplace, made a cavity beneath, and so cut the brick that it was impossible to see the join. By pressing on the second brick from the end, the whole thing was raised. It had been quite a complicated piece of work, and the old gentleman had been very fussy about it. Our informant was a man called Coghan, a big, gaunt man with a grizzled moustache. He seemed an intelligent fellow.

We returned to Crabtree Manor in high spirits, and, locking the study door, proceeded to put our newly acquired knowledge into effect. It was impossible to see any sign on the bricks, but when we pressed in the manner indicated, a deep cavity was at once disclosed.

Eagerly Poirot plunged in his hand. Suddenly his face fell from complacent elation to consternation. All he held was a charred fragment of stiff paper. But for it, the cavity was empty.

'*Sacre!*' cried Poirot angrily. 'Someone has been before us.'

We examined the scrap of paper anxiously. Clearly it was a fragment of what we sought. A portion of Baker's signature remained, but no indication of what the terms of the will had been.

Poirot sat back on his heels. His expression would have been comical if we had not been so overcome. 'I understand it not,' he growled. 'Who destroyed this? And what was their object?'

'The Bakers?' I suggested.

'*Pourquoi?* Neither will makes any provision for them, and they are more likely to be kept on with Miss Marsh than if the place became the property of a hospital. How could it be to anyone's advantage to destroy the will? The hospitals benefit – yes; but one cannot suspect institutions.'

'Perhaps the old man changed his mind and destroyed it himself,' I suggested.

Poirot rose to his feet, dusting his knees with his usual care.

'That may be,' he admitted. 'One of your more sensible observations, Hastings. Well, we can do no more here. We have done all that mortal man can do. We have successfully pitted our wits against the late Andrew Marsh's; but, unfortunately, his niece is not better off for our success.'

By driving to the station at once, we were just able to catch a train to London, though not the principal express. Poirot was sad and dissatisfied. For my part, I was tired and dozed in a corner. Suddenly, as we were just moving out of Taunton, Poirot uttered a piercing squeal.

'*Vite*, Hastings! Awake and jump! But jump I say!'

Before I knew where I was we were standing on the platform, bareheaded and minus our valises, whilst the train disappeared into the night. I was furious. But Poirot paid no attention.

'Imbecile that I have been!' he cried. 'Triple imbecile! Not again will I vaunt my little grey cells!'

'That's a good job at any rate,' I said grumpily. 'But what is this all about?'

As usual, when following out his own ideas, Poirot paid absolutely no attention to me.

'The tradesmen's books – I have left them entirely out of account? Yes, but where? Where? Never mind, I cannot be mistaken. We must return at once.'

Easier said than done. We managed to get a slow train to Exeter, and there Poirot hired a car. We arrived back at Crabtree Manor in the small hours of the morning. I pass over the bewilderment of the Bakers when we had at last aroused them. Paying no attention to anybody, Poirot strode at once to the study.

'I have been, not a triple imbecile, but thirty-six times one, my friend,' he deigned to remark. 'Now, behold!'

Going straight to the desk he drew out the key, and detached the envelope from it. I stared at him stupidly. How could he possibly hope to find a big will-form in that tiny envelope? With great care he cut open the envelope, laying it out flat. Then he lighted the fire and held the plain inside surface of the envelope to the flame. In a few minutes faint characters began to appear.

'Look, *mon ami!*' cried Poirot in triumph.

I looked. There were just a few lines of faint writing stating briefly that he left everything to his niece, Violet Marsh. It was dated March 25 12.30 P.M., and witnessed by Albert Pike, confectioner, and Jessie Pike, married woman.

'But is it legal?' I gasped.

'As far as I know, there is no law against writing your will in a blend of disappearing and sympathetic ink. The intention of the testator is clear, and the beneficiary is his only living relation. But the cleverness of him! He foresaw every step that a searcher would take – that I, miserable imbecile, took. He gets two will-forms, makes the servants sign twice, then sallies out with his will written on the inside of a dirty envelope and a fountain-pen containing his little ink mixture. On some excuse he gets the confectioner and his wife to sign their names under his own signature, then he ties it to the key of his desk and chuckles to himself. If his niece sees through his little ruse, she will have justified her choice of life and elaborate education and be thoroughly welcome to his money.'

'She didn't see through it, did she?' I said slowly. 'It seems rather unfair. The old man really won.'

'But no, Hastings. It is *your* wits that go astray. Miss Marsh proved the astuteness of her wits and the value of the higher education for women by at once putting the matter in *my* hands. Always employ the expert. She has amply proved her right to the money.'

I wonder – I very much wonder – what old Andrew Marsh would have thought!

Postscript

Of those who had read The Mysterious Affair at Styles, *one reader was particularly impressed by the character of Hercule Poirot, Bruce Ingram, who was then editor of* The Sketch *magazine. Ingram liked Poirot so much that he got in touch with Agatha Christie and suggested she should write a series of Poirot stories for* The Sketch. *Christie thought this a wonderful idea, particularly since the Sketch was such a prestigious and well-known magazine: 'At last I was becoming a success. To be in* The Sketch – *wonderful!'*

Bruce Ingram commissioned Agatha Christie to write a series of Poirot stories for his paper. She wrote eight of them fairly swiftly which, at first, seemed to be enough. But four others were commissioned quite soon afterwards and she had to write them rather more hastily than she wanted.

The first of the Poirot stories appeared in The Sketch *on March 7th 1923. Ingram was so keen on the project that he commissioned the illustrator W. Smithson to draw a special portrait of Hercule Poirot. Agatha Christie wrote: 'He was not unlike my idea of him, though he was depicted as a little smarter and more aristocratic than I had envisaged him.' When John Lane published the twelve novellas in one volume, Agatha Christie insisted on using Poirot's portrait from* The Sketch *as a cover.*

Several titles were envisaged for this volume. The first was the title of the story The Curious Disappearance of the Opalsen Pearls, *eventually published as* The Jewel Robbery at the Grand Metropolitan. *Since Christie wanted a better title, her editor asked her to choose between* The Grey Cells of Monsieur Poirot *and* Poirot Investigates. *Christie chose the latter.*

It was through writing the stories in Poirot Investigates *that Agatha Christie became aware of the extent to which she was now tied to her characters: 'I quite enjoyed Captain Hastings. He was a stereotyped creation, but he and Poirot represented my idea of a detective team. I was still writing in the Sherlock Holmes tradition – eccentric detective, stooge assistant, with a Lestrade-type Scotland Yard detective, Inspector Japp.' Undoubtedly the genre and form of the short story, which Conan Doyle had used so successfully, reinforced the influence of the Sherlock Holmes tradition.*

In any case, Poirot Investigates *marks Agatha Christie's first steps as a short story writer. Throughout her career she wrote more than a hundred and they represent an important part of her oeuvre.*

THE SECRET
OF CHIMNEYS

To my nephew
In memory of an inscription
At Compton Castle and a day at the Zoo

CHAPTER I

Anthony Cade Signs On

'Gentleman Joe!'

'Why, if it isn't old Jimmy McGrath,'

Castle's Select Tour, represented by seven depressed-looking females and three perspiring males, looked on with considerable interest. Evidently their Mr Cade had met an old friend. They all admired Mr Cade so much, his tall lean figure, his sun-tanned face, the light-hearted manner with which he settled disputes and cajoled them all into good temper. This friend of his now – surely rather a peculiar-looking man. About the same height as Mr Cade, but thickset and not nearly so good-looking. The sort of man one read about in books, who probably kept a saloon. Interesting though. After all, that was what one came abroad for – to see all these peculiar things one read about in books. Up to now they had been rather bored with Bulawayo. The sun was unbearably hot, the hotel was uncomfortable, there seemed to be nowhere particular to go until the moment should arrive to motor to the Matoppos. Very fortunately, Mr Cade had suggested picture postcards. There was an excellent supply of picture postcards.

Anthony Cade and his friend had stepped a little apart.

'What the hell are you doing with this pack of females?' demanded McGrath. 'Starting a harem?'

'Not with this little lot,' grinned Anthony. 'Have you taken a good look at them?'

'I have that. Thought maybe you were losing your eyesight.'

'My eyesight's as good as ever it was. No, this is a Castle's Select Tour. I'm Castle – the local Castle, I mean.'

'What the hell made you take on a job like that?'

'A regrettable necessity for cash. I can assure you it doesn't suit my temperament.'

Jimmy grinned.

'Never a hog for regular work, were you?'

Anthony ignored this aspersion.

'However, something will turn up soon, I expect,' he remarked hopefully. 'It usually does.'

Jimmy chuckled.

'If there's any trouble brewing, Anthony Cade is sure to be in it sooner or later, I know that,' he said. 'You've an absolute instinct for rows – *and* the nine lives of a cat. When can we have a yarn together?'

Anthony sighed.

'I've got to take these cackling hens to see Rhodes' grave.'

'That's the stuff,' said Jimmy approvingly. 'They'll come back bumped black and blue with the ruts in the road, and clamouring for bed to rest the bruises on. Then you and I will have a spot or two and exchange the news.'

'Right. So long, Jimmy.'

Anthony rejoined his flock of sheep. Miss Taylor, the youngest and most skittish of the party, instantly attacked him.

'Oh, Mr Cade, was that an old friend of yours?'

'It was, Miss Taylor. One of the friends of my blameless youth.'

Miss Taylor giggled.

'I thought he was such an interesting-looking man.'

'I'll tell him you said so.'

'Oh, Mr Cade, how can you be so naughty! The very idea! What was that name he called you?'

'Gentleman Joe?'

'Yes. Is your name Joe?'

'I thought you knew it was Anthony, Miss Taylor.'

'Oh, go on with you!' cried Miss Taylor coquettishly.

Anthony had by now well mastered his duties. In addition to making the necessary arrangements of travel, they included soothing down irritable old gentlemen when their dignity was ruffled, seeing that elderly matrons had ample opportunities to buy picture postcards, and flirting with everything under a catholic forty years of age. The last task was rendered easier for him by the extreme readiness of the ladies in question to read a tender meaning into his most innocent remarks.

Miss Taylor returned to the attack.

'Why does he call you Joe, then?'

'Oh, just because it isn't my name.'

'And why Gentleman Joe?'

'The same kind of reason.'

'Oh, Mr Cade,' protested Miss Taylor, much distressed, 'I'm sure you shouldn't say that. Papa was only saying last night what gentlemanly manners you had.'

'Very kind of your father, I'm sure, Miss Taylor.'

'And we are all agreed that you are quite the gentleman.'

'I'm overwhelmed.'

'No, really, I mean it.'

'Kind hearts are more than coronets,' said Anthony vaguely, without a notion of what he meant by the remark, and wishing fervently it was lunchtime.

'That's such a beautiful poem, I always think. Do you know much poetry, Mr Cade?'

'I might recite "The boy stood on the burning deck" at a pinch. "The boy stood on the burning deck, whence all but he had fled." That's all I know, but I can do that bit with action if you like. "The boy stood on the burning deck" – whoosh – whoosh – whoosh – (the flames, you see) "Whence all but he had fled" – for that bit I run to and fro like a dog.'

Miss Taylor screamed with laughter.

'Oh, do look at Mr Cade! Isn't he funny?'

'Time for morning tea,' said Anthony briskly. 'Come this way. There is an excellent café in the next street.'

'I presume,' said Mrs Caldicott in her deep voice, 'that the expense is included in the Tour?'

'Morning tea, Mrs Caldicott,' said Anthony, assuming his professional manner, 'is an extra.'

'Disgraceful.'

'Life is full of trials, isn't it?' said Anthony cheerfully.

Mrs Caldicott's eyes gleamed, and she remarked with the air of one springing a mine:

'I suspected as much, and in anticipation I poured off some tea into a jug at breakfast this morning! I can heat that up on the spirit-lamp. Come, Father.'

Mr and Mrs Caldicott sailed off triumphantly to the hotel, the lady's back complacent with successful forethought.

'Oh, Lord,' muttered Anthony, 'what a lot of funny people it does take to make a world.'

He marshalled the rest of the party in the direction of the café. Miss Taylor kept by his side, and resumed her catechism.

'Is it a long time since you saw your friend?'

'Just over seven years.'

'Was it in Africa you knew him?'

'Yes, not this part, though. The first time I ever saw Jimmy McGrath he was all trussed up ready for the cooking pot. Some of the tribes in the interior are cannibals, you know. We got there just in time.'

'What happened?'

'Very nice little shindy. We potted some of the beggars, and the rest took to their heels.'

'Oh, Mr Cade, what an adventurous life you must have led.'

'Very peaceful, I assure you.'

But it was clear that the lady did not believe him.

It was about ten o'clock that night when Anthony Cade walked into the small room where Jimmy McGrath was busy manipulating various bottles.

'Make it strong, James,' he implored. 'I can tell you, I need it.'

'I should think you did, my boy. I wouldn't take on that job of yours for anything.'

'Show me another, and I'll jump out of it fast enough.'

McGrath poured out his own drink, tossed it off with a practised hand and mixed a second one. Then he said slowly:

'Are you in earnest about that, old son?'

'About what?'

'Chucking this job of yours if you could get another?'

'Why? You don't mean to say that you've got a job going begging? Why don't you grab it yourself?'

'I have grabbed it – but I don't much fancy it, that's why I'm trying to pass it on to you.'

Anthony became suspicious.

'What's wrong with it? They haven't engaged you to teach in a Sunday school, have they?'

'Do you think anyone would choose me to teach in a Sunday school?'

'Not if they knew you well, certainly.'

'It's a perfectly good job – nothing wrong with it whatsoever.'

'Not in South America by any lucky chance? I've rather got my eye on South America. There's a very tidy little revolution coming off in one of those little republics soon.'

McGrath grinned.

'You always were keen on revolutions – anything to be mixed up in a really good row.'

'I feel my talents might be appreciated out there. I tell you, Jimmy, I can be jolly useful in a revolution – to one side or the other. It's better than making an honest living any day.'

'I think I've heard that sentiment from you before, my son. No, the job isn't in South America – it's in England.'

'England? Return of hero to his native land after many long years. They can't dun you for bills after seven years, can they, Jimmy?'

'I don't think so. Well, are you on for hearing more about it?'

'I'm on all right. The thing that worries me is why you're not taking it on yourself.'

'I'll tell you. I'm after gold, Anthony – far up in the interior.'

Anthony whistled and looked at him.

'You've always been after gold, Jimmy, ever since I knew you. It's your weak spot – your own particular little hobby. You've followed up more wild-cat trails than anyone I know.'

'And in the end I'll strike it. You'll see.'

'Well, everyone his own hobby. Mine's rows, yours is gold.'

'I'll tell you the whole story. I suppose you know all about Herzoslovakia?'

Anthony looked up sharply.

'Herzoslovakia?' he said, with a curious ring in his voice.

'Yes. Know anything about it?'

There was quite an appreciable pause before Anthony answered. Then he said slowly:

'Only what everyone knows. It's one of the Balkan States, isn't it? Principal rivers, unknown. Principal mountains, also unknown, but fairly numerous. Capital, Ekarest. Population, chiefly brigands. Hobby, assassinating kings and having revolutions. Last king, Nicholas IV, assassinated about seven years ago. Since then it's been a republic. Altogether a very likely spot. You might have mentioned before that Herzoslovakia came into it.'

'It doesn't except indirectly.'

Anthony gazed at him more in sorrow than in anger.

'You ought to do something about this, James,' he said. 'Take a correspondence course, or something. If you'd told a story like this in the good old Eastern days, you'd have been hung up by the heels and bastinadoed or something equally unpleasant.'

Jimmy pursued his course quite unmoved by these strictures.

'Ever heard of Count Stylptitch?'

'Now you're talking,' said Anthony. 'Many people who have never heard of Herzoslovakia would brighten at the mention of Count Stylptitch. The Grand Old Man of the Balkans. The Greatest Statesman of Modern Times. The biggest villain unhung. The point of view all depends on which newspaper you take in. But be sure of this, Count Stylptitch will be remembered long after you and I are dust and ashes, James. Every move and counter-move in the Near East for the last twenty years has had Count Stylptitch at the bottom of it.

He's been a dictator and a patriot and a statesman – and nobody knows exactly what he has been, except that he's been a perfect king of intrigue. Well, what about him?'

'He was Prime Minister of Herzoslovakia – that's why I mentioned it first.'

'You've no sense of proportion, Jimmy. Herzoslovakia is of no importance at all compared to Stylptitch. It just provided him with a birthplace and a post in public affairs. But I thought he was dead?'

'So he is. He died in Paris about two months ago. What I'm telling you about happened some years ago.'

'The question is,' said Anthony, 'what *are* you telling me about?'

Jimmy accepted the rebuke and hastened on.

'It was like this. I was in Paris – just four years ago, to be exact. I was walking along one night in rather a lonely part, when I saw half a dozen French toughs beating up a respectable-looking old gentleman. I hate a one-sided show, so I promptly butted in and proceeded to beat up the toughs. I guess they'd never been hit really hard before. They melted like snow!'

'Good for you, James,' said Anthony softly. 'I'd like to have seen that scrap.'

'Oh, it was nothing much,' said Jimmy modestly. 'But the old boy was no end grateful. He'd had a couple, no doubt about that, but he was sober enough to get my name and address out of me, and he came along and thanked me next day. Did the thing in style, too. It was then that I found out it was Count Stylptitch I'd rescued. He'd got a house up by the Bois.'

Anthony nodded.

'Yes, Stylptitch went to live in Paris after the assassination of King Nicholas. They wanted him to come back and be president later, but he wasn't taking any. He remained sound to his monarchical principles, though he was reported to have his finger in all the backstairs pies that went on in the Balkans. Very deep, the late Count Stylptitch.'

'Nicholas IV was the man who had a funny taste in wives, wasn't he?' said Jimmy suddenly.

'Yes,' said Anthony. 'And it did for him, too, poor beggar. She was some little guttersnipe of a music-hall artiste in Paris – not even suitable for a morganatic alliance. But Nicholas had a frightful crush on her, and she was all out for being a queen. Sounds fantastic, but they managed it somehow. Called her the Countess Popoffsky, or something, and pretended she had Romanoff blood in her veins. Nicholas married her in the cathedral at Ekarest with a couple of unwilling archbishops to do the job, and she was crowned as Queen Varaga. Nicholas squared his ministers, and I suppose he thought that was all that mattered – but he forgot to reckon with the populace. They're very aristocratic and reactionary in Herzoslovakia. They like their kings and queens to be the genuine article. There were mutterings and discontent, and the usual ruthless suppressions, and the final uprising which stormed the palace, murdered the King and Queen, and proclaimed a republic. It's been a republic ever since – but things still manage to be pretty lively there, so I've heard. They've assassinated a president or two, just to keep their hand in. But *revenons à nos moutons*. You had got to where Count Stylptitch was hailing you as his preserver.'

'Yes. Well, that was the end of that business. I came back to Africa and never thought of it again until about two weeks ago I got a queer-looking parcel which had been following me all over the place for the Lord knows how long. I'd seen in a paper that Count Stylptitch had recently died in Paris. Well, this parcel contained his memoirs – or reminiscences, or whatever you call the things. There was a note enclosed to the effect that if I delivered the manuscript at a certain firm of publishers in London on or before October 13th, they were instructed to hand me a thousand pounds.'

'A thousand pounds? Did you say a thousand pounds, Jimmy?'

'I did, my son. I hope to God it's not a hoax. Put not your trust in princes or politicians, as the saying goes. Well, there it is. Owing to the way the manuscript had been following me around, I had no time to lose. It was a pity, all the same. I'd just fixed up this trip to the interior, and I'd set my heart on going. I shan't get such a good chance again.'

'You're incurable, Jimmy. A thousand pounds in the hand is worth a lot of mythical gold.'

'And supposing it's all a hoax? Anyway, here I am, passage booked and everything, on the way to Cape Town – and then you blow along!'

Anthony got up and lit a cigarette.

'I begin to perceive your drift, James. You go gold-hunting as planned, and I collect the thousand pounds for you. How much do I get out of it?'

'What do you say to a quarter?'

'Two hundred and fifty pounds free of income tax, as the saying goes?'

'That's it.'

'Done, and just to make you gnash your teeth I'll tell you that I would have gone for a hundred! Let me tell you, James McGrath, *you* won't die in your bed counting up your bank balance.'

'Anyway, it's a deal?'

'It's a deal all right. I'm on. And confusion to Castle's Select Tours.'

They drank the toast solemnly.

CHAPTER II

A Lady in Distress

'So that's that,' said Anthony, finishing off his glass and replacing it on the table. 'What boat were you going on?'

'*Granarth Castle.*'

'Passage booked in your name, I suppose, so I'd better travel as James McGrath. We've outgrown the passport business, haven't we.'

'No odds either way. You and I are totally unlike, but we'd probably have the same description on one of those blinking things. Height six feet, hair brown, eyes blue, nose ordinary, chin ordinary –'

'Not so much of this "ordinary" stunt. Let me tell you that Castle's selected me out of several applicants solely on account of my pleasing appearance and nice manners.'

Jimmy grinned.

'I noticed your manners this morning.'

'The devil you did.'

Anthony rose and paced up and down the room. His brow was slightly wrinkled, and it was some minutes before he spoke.

'Jimmy,' he said at last. 'Stylptitch died in Paris. What's the point of sending a manuscript from Paris to London via Africa?'

Jimmy shook his head helplessly.

'I don't know.'

'Why not do it up in a nice little parcel and send it by post?'

'Sounds a damn sight more sensible, I agree.'

'Of course,' continued Anthony, 'I know that kings and queens and government officials are prevented by etiquette from doing anything in a simple, straightforward fashion.

Hence King's Messengers and all that. In medieval days you gave a fellow a signet ring as a sort of open sesame. "The King's Ring! Pass, my lord!" And usually it was the other fellow who had stolen it. I always wonder why some bright lad never hit on the expedient of copying the ring – making a dozen or so, and selling them at a hundred ducats apiece. They seem to have had no initiative in the Middle Ages.'

Jimmy yawned.

'My remarks on the Middle Ages don't seem to amuse you. Let us get back to Count Stylptitch. From France to England via Africa seems a bit thick even for a diplomatic personage. If he merely wanted to ensure that you should get a thousand pounds he could have left it you in his will. Thank God neither you nor I are too proud to accept a legacy! Stylptitch must have been barmy.'

'You'd think so, wouldn't you?'

Anthony frowned and continued his pacing.

'Have you read the thing at all?' he asked suddenly.

'Read what?'

'The manuscript.'

'Good Lord, no. What do you think I want to read a thing of that kind for?'

Anthony smiled.

'I just wondered, that's all. You know a lot of trouble has been caused by memoirs. Indiscreet revelations, that sort of thing. People who have been close as an oyster all their lives seem positively to relish causing trouble when they themselves shall be comfortably dead. It gives them a kind of malicious glee. Jimmy, what sort of a man was Count Stylptitch? You met him and talked to him, and you're a pretty good judge of raw human nature. Could you imagine him being a vindictive old devil?'

Jimmy shook his head.

'It's difficult to tell. You see, that first night he was distinctly canned, and the next day he was just a high-toned old boy with the most beautiful manners overwhelming me with compliments till I didn't know where to look.'

'And he didn't say anything interesting when he was drunk?'

Jimmy cast his mind back, wrinkling his brows as he did so.

'He said he knew where the Koh-i-noor was,' he volunteered doubtfully.

'Oh, well,' said Anthony, 'we all know that. They keep it in the Tower, don't they? Behind thick plate-glass and iron bars, with a lot of gentlemen in fancy dress standing round to see you don't pinch anything.'

'That's right,' agreed Jimmy.

'Did Stylptitch say anything else of the same kind? That he knew which city the Wallace Collection was in, for instance?'

Jimmy shook his head.

'Hm!' said Anthony.

He lit another cigarette, and once more began pacing up and down the room.

'You never read the papers, I suppose, you heathen?' he threw out presently.

'Not very often,' said McGrath simply. 'They're not about anything that interests me as a rule.'

'Thank heaven I'm more civilized. There have been several mentions of Herzoslovakia lately. Hints at a royalist restoration.'

'Nicholas IV didn't leave a son,' said Jimmy. 'But I don't suppose for a minute that the Obolovitch dynasty is extinct. There are probably shoals of young 'uns knocking about, cousins and second cousins and third cousins once removed.'

'So that there wouldn't be any difficulty in finding a king?'

'Not in the least, I should say,' replied Jimmy. 'You know, I don't wonder at their getting tired of republican institutions. A full-blooded, virile people like that must find it awfully tame to pot at presidents after being used to kings. And talking of kings, that reminds me of something else old Stylptitch let out that night. He said he knew the gang that was after him. They were King Victor's people, he said.'

'What?' Anthony wheeled round suddenly.

A short grin widened on McGrath's face.

'Just a mite excited, aren't you, Gentleman Joe?' he drawled.

'Don't be an ass, Jimmy. You've just said something rather important.'

He went over to the window and stood there looking out.

'Who is this King Victor, anyway?' demanded Jimmy. 'Another Balkan monarch?'

'No,' said Anthony slowly. 'He isn't that kind of a king.'

'What is he, then?'

There was a pause, and then Anthony spoke.

'He's a crook, Jimmy. The most notorious jewel thief in the world. A fantastic, daring fellow, not to be daunted by anything. King Victor was the nickname he was known by in Paris. Paris was the headquarters of his gang. They caught him there and put him away for seven years on a minor charge. They couldn't prove the more important things against him. He'll be out soon – or he may be out already.'

'Do you think Count Stylptitch had anything to do with putting him away? Was that why the gang went for him? Out of revenge?'

'I don't know,' said Anthony. 'It doesn't seem likely on the face of it. King Victor never stole the crown jewels of Herzoslovakia as far as I've heard. But the whole thing seems rather suggestive, doesn't it? The death of Stylptitch, the memoirs, and the rumours in the papers – all vague but interesting. And there's a further rumour to the effect that they've found oil in Herzoslovakia. I've a feeling in my bones, James, that people are getting ready to be interested in that unimportant little country.'

'What sort of people?'

'Hebraic people. Yellow-faced financiers in city offices.'

'What are you driving at with all this?'

'Trying to make an easy job difficult, that's all.'

'You can't pretend there's going to be any difficulty in handing over a simple manuscript at a publisher's office?'

'No,' said Anthony regretfully. 'I don't suppose there'll be anything difficult about that. But shall I tell you, James, where

I propose to go with my two hundred and fifty pounds?'

'South America?'

'No, my lad, Herzoslovakia. I shall stand in with the republic, I think. Very probably I shall end up as president.'

'Why not announce yourself as the principal Obolovitch and be a king whilst you're about it?'

'No, Jimmy. Kings are for life. Presidents only take on the job for four years or so. It would quite amuse me to govern a kingdom like Herzoslovakia for four years.'

'The average for kings is even less, I should say,' interpolated Jimmy.

'It will probably be a serious temptation to me to embezzle your share of the thousand pounds. You won't want it, you know, when you get back weighed down with nuggets. I'll invest it for you in Herzoslovakian oil shares. You know, James, the more I think of it, the more pleased I am with this idea of yours. I should never have thought of Herzoslovakia if you hadn't mentioned it. I shall spend one day in London, collecting the booty, and then away by the Balkan Express!'

'You won't get off quite as fast as that. I didn't mention it before, but I've got another little commission for you.'

Anthony sank into a chair and eyed him severely.

'I knew all along that you were keeping something dark. This is where the catch comes in.'

'Not a bit. It's just something that's got to be done to help a lady.'

'Once and for all, James, I refuse to be mixed up in your beastly love affairs.'

'It's not a love affair. I've never seen the woman. I'll tell you the whole story.'

'If I've got to listen to more of your long, rambling stories, I shall have to have another drink.'

His host complied hospitably with this demand, then began the tale.

'It was when I was up in Uganda. There was a dago there whose life I had saved –'

'If I were you, Jimmy, I should write a short book entitled

"Lives I have Saved". This is the second I've heard of this evening.'

'Oh, well, I didn't really do anything this time. Just pulled the dago out of the river. Like all dagos, he couldn't swim.'

'Wait a minute, has this story anything to do with the other business?'

'Nothing whatever, though, oddly enough, now I remember it, the man was a Herzoslovakian. We always called him Dutch Pedro, though.'

Anthony nodded indifferently.

'Any name's good enough for a dago,' he remarked. 'Get on with the good work, James.'

'Well, the fellow was sort of grateful about it. Hung around like a dog. About six months later he died of fever. I was with him. Last thing, just as he was pegging out, he beckoned me and whispered some excited jargon about a secret – a gold mine, I thought he said. Shoved an oilskin packet into my hand which he'd always worn next his skin. Well, I didn't think much of it at the time. It wasn't until a week afterwards that I opened the packet. Then I was curious, I must confess. I shouldn't have thought that Dutch Pedro would have had the sense to know a gold mine when he saw it – but there's no accounting for luck –'

'And at the mere thought of gold, your heart beat pitterpat as always,' interrupted Anthony.

'I was never so disgusted in my life. Gold mine, indeed! I dare say it may have been a gold mine to him, the dirty dog. Do you know what it was? A woman's letters – yes, a woman's letters, and an Englishwoman at that. The skunk had been blackmailing her – and he had the impudence to pass on his dirty bag of tricks to me.'

'I like to see your righteous heat, James, but let me point out to you that dagos will be dagos. He meant well. You had saved his life, he bequeathed to you a profitable source of raising money – your high-minded British ideals did not enter his horizon.'

'Well, what the hell was I to do with the things? Burn 'em, that's what I thought at first. And then it occurred to me that there would be that poor dame, not knowing they'd been destroyed, and always living in a quake and a dread lest that dago should turn up again one day.'

'You've more imagination than I gave you credit for, Jimmy,' observed Anthony, lighting a cigarette. 'I admit that the case presented more difficulties than were at first apparent. What about just sending them to her by post?'

'Like all women, she'd put no date and no address on most of the letters. There was a kind of address on one – just one word. "Chimneys".'

Anthony paused in the act of blowing out his match, and he dropped it with a quick jerk of the wrist as it burned his finger.

'Chimneys?' he said. 'That's rather extraordinary.'

'Why, do you know it?'

'It's one of the stately homes of England, my dear James. A place where kings and queens go for weekends, and diplomatists forgather and diplome.'

'That's one of the reasons why I'm so glad that you're going to England instead of me. You know all these things,' said Jimmy simply. 'A josser like myself from the backwoods of Canada would be making all sorts of bloomers. But someone like you who's been to Eton and Harrow –'

'Only one of them,' said Anthony modestly.

'Will be able to carry it through. Why didn't I send them to her, you say? Well, it seemed to me dangerous. From what I could make out, she seemed to have a jealous husband. Suppose he opened the letter by mistake. Where would the poor dame be then? Or she might be dead – the letters looked as though they'd been written some time. As I figured it out, the only thing was for someone to take them to England and put them into her own hands.'

Anthony threw away his cigarette, and coming across to his friend, clapped him affectionately on the back.

'You're a real knight-errant, Jimmy,' he said. 'And the backwoods of Canada should be proud of you. I shan't do the job half as prettily as you would.'

'You'll take it on, then?'

'Of course.'

McGrath rose, and going across to a drawer, took out a bundle of letters and threw them on the table.

'Here you are. You'd better have a look at them.'

'Is it necessary? On the whole, I'd rather not.'

'Well, from what you say about this Chimneys place, she may have been staying there only. We'd better look through the letters and see if there's any clue as to where she really hangs out.'

'I suppose you're right.'

They went through the letters carefully, but without finding what they had hoped to find. Anthony gathered them up again thoughtfully.

'Poor little devil,' he remarked. 'She was scared stiff.'

Jimmy nodded.

'Do you think you'll be able to find her all right?' he asked anxiously.

'I won't leave England till I have. You're very concerned about this unknown lady, James?'

Jimmy ran his finger thoughtfully over the signature.

'It's a pretty name,' he said apologetically. '*Virginia Revel*.'

CHAPTER III

Anxiety in High Places

'Quite so, my dear fellow, quite so,' said Lord Caterham.

He had used the same words three times already, each time in the hope that they would end the interview and permit him to escape. He disliked very much being forced to stand on the steps of the exclusive London club to which he belonged and listen to the interminable eloquence of the Hon George Lomax.

Clement Edward Alistair Brent, ninth Marquis of Caterham, was a small gentleman, shabbily dressed, and entirely unlike the popular conception of a marquis. He had faded blue eyes, a thin melancholy nose, and a vague but courteous manner.

The principal misfortune of Lord Caterham's life was to have succeeded his brother, the eighth marquis, four years ago. For the previous Lord Caterham had been a man of mark, a household word all over England. At one time Secretary of State for Foreign Affairs, he had always bulked largely in the counsels of the Empire, and his country seat, Chimneys, was famous for its hospitality. Ably seconded by his wife, a daughter of the Duke of Perth, history had been made and unmade at informal weekend parties at Chimneys, and there was hardly anyone of note in England – or indeed in Europe – who had not, at one time or another, stayed there.

That was all very well. The ninth Marquis of Caterham had the utmost respect and esteem for the memory of his brother. Henry had done that kind of thing magnificently. What Lord Caterham objected to was the assumption that Chimneys was a national possession rather than a private country house. There was nothing that bored Lord Caterham more than politics – unless it was politicians. Hence his impatience under the continued eloquence of George Lomax. A robust man, George Lomax, inclined to *embonpoint*, with a red face and protuberant eyes, and an immense sense of his own importance.

'You see the point, Caterham? We can't – we simply can't afford a scandal of any kind just now. The position is one of the utmost delicacy.'

'It always is,' said Lord Caterham, with a flavour of irony.

'My dear fellow, I'm in a position to *know*!'

'Oh, quite so, quite so,' said Lord Caterham, falling back upon his previous line of defence.

'One slip over this Herzoslovakian business and we're done. It is most important that the oil concessions should be granted to a British company. You must see that?'

'Of course, of course.'

'Prince Michael Obolovitch arrives the end of the week, and the whole thing can be carried through at Chimneys under the guise of a shooting party.'

'I was thinking of going abroad this week,' said Lord Caterham.

'Nonsense, my dear Caterham, no one goes abroad in early October.'

'My doctor seems to think I'm in rather a bad way,' said Lord Caterham, longingly eyeing a taxi that was crawling past.

He was quite unable to make a dash for liberty, however, since Lomax had the unpleasant habit of retaining a hold upon a person with whom he was engaged in serious conversation – doubtless the result of long experience. In this case, he had a firm grip of the lapel of Lord Caterham's coat.

'My dear man, I put it to you imperially. In a moment of national crisis, such as is fast approaching –'

Lord Caterham wriggled uneasily. He felt suddenly that he would rather give any number of house parties than listen to George Lomax quoting from one of his own speeches. He knew by experience that Lomax was quite capable of going on for twenty minutes without a stop.

'All right,' he said hastily, 'I'll do it. You'll arrange the whole thing, I suppose.'

'My dear fellow, there's nothing to arrange. Chimneys, quite apart from its historic associations, is ideally situated. I shall be at the Abbey, less than seven miles away. It wouldn't do, of course, for me to be actually a member of the house party.'

'Of course not,' agreed Lord Caterham, who had no idea why it would not do, and was not interested to learn.

'Perhaps you wouldn't mind having Bill Eversleigh, though. He'd be useful to run messages.'

'Delighted,' said Lord Caterham, with a shade more animation. 'Bill's quite a decent shot, and Bundle likes him.'

'The shooting, of course, is not really important. It's only the pretext, as it were.'

Lord Caterham looked depressed again.

'That will be all, then. The Prince, his suite, Bill Eversleigh, Herman Isaacstein –'

'Who?'

'Herman Isaacstein. The representative of the syndicate I spoke to you about.'

'The all-British syndicate?'

'Yes. Why?'

'Nothing – nothing – I only wondered, that's all. Curious names these people have.'

'Then, of course, there ought to be one or two outsiders – just to give the thing a *bona fide* appearance. Lady Eileen could see to that – young people, uncritical, and with no idea of politics.'

'Bundle would attend to that all right, I'm sure.'

'I wonder now.' Lomax seemed struck by an idea. 'You remember the matter I was speaking about just now?'

'You've been speaking about so many things.'

'No, no, I mean this unfortunate contretemps' – he lowered his voice to a mysterious whisper – 'the memoirs – Count Stylptitch's memoirs.'

'I think you're wrong about that,' said Lord Caterham,

suppressing a yawn. 'People *like* scandal. Damn it all, I read reminiscences myself – and enjoy 'em too.'

'The point is not whether people will read them or not – they'll read them fast enough – but their publication at this juncture might ruin everything – everything. The people of Herzoslovakia wish to restore the monarchy, and are prepared to offer the crown to Prince Michael, who has the support and encouragement of His Majesty's Government –'

'And who is prepared to grant concessions to Mr Ikey Hermanstein and Co in return for the loan of a million or so to set him on the throne –'

'Caterham, Caterham,' implored Lomax in an agonized whisper. 'Discretion, I beg of you. Above all things, discretion.'

'And the point is,' continued Lord Caterham, with some relish, though he lowered his voice in obedience to the other's appeal, 'that some of Stylptitch's reminiscences may upset the apple-cart. Tyranny and misbehaviour of the Obolovitch family generally, eh? Questions asked in the House. Why replace the present broad-minded and democratic form of government by an obsolete tyranny? Policy dictated by the blood-sucking capitalists. Down with the Government. That kind of thing – eh?'

Lomax nodded.

'And there might be worse still,' he breathed. 'Suppose – only suppose that some reference should be made to – to that unfortunate disappearance – you know what I mean.'

Lord Caterham stared at him.

'No, I don't. What disappearance?'

'You must have heard of it? Why, it happened while they were at Chimneys. Henry was terribly upset about it. It almost ruined his career.'

'You interest me enormously,' said Lord Caterham. 'Who or what disappeared?'

Lomax leant forward and put his mouth to Lord Caterham's ear. The latter withdrew it hastily.

'For God's sake, don't hiss at me.'

'You heard what I said?'

'Yes, I did,' said Lord Caterham reluctantly. 'I remember now hearing something about it at the time. Very curious affair. I wonder who did it. It was never recovered?'

'Never. Of course we had to go about the matter with the utmost discretion. No hint of the loss could be allowed to leak out. But Stylptitch was there at the time. He knew something. Not all, but something. We were at loggerheads with him once or twice over the Turkish question. Suppose that in sheer malice he has set the whole thing down for the world to read. Think of the scandal – of the far-reaching results. Everyone would say – why was it hushed up?'

'Of course they would,' said Lord Caterham, with evident enjoyment.

Lomax, whose voice had risen to a high pitch, took a grip on himself.

'I must keep calm,' he murmured. 'I must keep calm. But I ask you this, my dear fellow. If he didn't mean mischief, why did he send the manuscript to London in this roundabout way?'

'It's odd, certainly. You are sure of your facts?'

'Absolutely. We – er – had our agents in Paris. The memoirs were conveyed away secretly some weeks before his death.'

'Yes, it looks as though there's something in it,' said Lord Caterham, with the same relish he had displayed before.

'We have found out that they were sent to a man called Jimmy, or James, McGrath, a Canadian at present in Africa.'

'Quite an Imperial affair, isn't it?' said Lord Caterham cheerily.

'James McGrath is due to arrive by the *Granarth Castle* tomorrow – Thursday.'

'What are you going to do about it?'

'We shall, of course, approach him at once, point out the possibly serious consequences, and beg him to defer publication of the memoirs for at least a month, and in any case to permit them to be judiciously – er – edited.'

'Supposing that he says "No, sir," or "I'll goddarned well

see you in hell first," or something bright and breezy like that?' suggested Lord Caterham.

'That's just what I'm afraid of,' said Lomax simply. 'That's why it suddenly occurred to me that it might be a good thing to ask him down to Chimneys as well. He'd be flattered, naturally, at being asked to meet Prince Michael, and it might be easier to handle him.'

'I'm not going to do it,' said Lord Caterham hastily. 'I don't get on with Canadians, never did – especially those that have lived much in Africa!'

'You'd probably find him a splendid fellow – a rough diamond, you know.'

'No, Lomax. I put my foot down there absolutely. Somebody else has got to tackle him.'

'It has occurred to me,' said Lomax, 'that a woman might be very useful here. Told enough and not too much, you understand. A woman could handle the whole thing delicately and with tact – put the position before him, as it were, without getting his back up. Not that I approve of women in politics – St Stephen's is ruined, absolutely ruined, nowadays. But woman in her own sphere can do wonders. Look at Henry's wife and what she did for him. Marcia was magnificent, unique, a perfect political hostess.'

'You don't want to ask Marcia down for this party, do you?' asked Lord Caterham faintly, turning a little pale at the mention of his redoubtable sister-in-law.

'No, no, you misunderstand me. I was speaking of the influence of women in general. No, I suggest a young woman, a woman of charm, beauty, intelligence?'

'Not Bundle? Bundle would be no use at all. She's a red-hot Socialist if she's anything at all, and she'd simply scream with laughter at the suggestion.'

'I was not thinking of Lady Eileen. Your daughter, Caterham, is charming, simply charming, but quite a child. We need some one with *savoir faire*, poise, knowledge of the world – Ah, of course, the very person. My cousin Virginia.'

'Mrs Revel?' Lord Caterham brightened up. He began to

feel that he might possibly enjoy the party after all. 'A very good suggestion of yours, Lomax. The most charming woman in London.'

'She is well up in Herzoslovakian affairs too. Her husband was at the Embassy there, you remember. And, as you say, a woman of great personal charm.'

'A delightful creature,' murmured Lord Caterham.

'That is settled, then.'

Mr Lomax relaxed his hold on Lord Caterham's lapel, and the latter was quick to avail himself of the chance.

'Bye-bye, Lomax, you'll make all the arrangements, won't you?'

He dived into a taxi. As far as it is possible for one upright Christian gentleman to dislike another upright Christian gentleman, Lord Caterham disliked the Hon George Lomax. He disliked his puffy red face, his heavy breathing, and his prominent earnest blue eyes. He thought of the coming week-end and sighed. A nuisance, an abominable nuisance. Then he thought of Virginia Revel and cheered up a little.

'A delightful creature,' he murmured to himself. 'A most delightful creature.'

CHAPTER IV

Introducing a Very Charming Lady

George Lomax returned straightway to Whitehall. As he entered the sumptuous apartment in which he transacted affairs of State, there was a scuffling sound.

Mr Bill Eversleigh was assiduously filing letters, but a large armchair near the window was still warm from contact with a human form.

A very likeable young man, Bill Eversleigh. Age at a guess, twenty-five, big and rather ungainly in his movements, a pleasantly ugly face, a splendid set of white teeth and a pair of honest brown eyes.

'Richardson sent up that report yet?'

'No, sir. Shall I get on to him about it?'

'It doesn't matter. Any telephone messages?'

'Miss Oscar is dealing with most of them. Mr Isaacstein wants to know if you can lunch with him at the Savoy tomorrow.'

'Tell Miss Oscar to look in my engagement book. If I'm not engaged, she can ring up and accept.'

'Yes, sir.'

'By the way, Eversleigh, you might ring up a number for me now. Look it up in the book. Mrs Revel, 487 Pont Street.'

'Yes, sir.'

Bill seized the telephone book, ran an unseeing eye down a column of M's, shut the book with a bang and moved to the instrument on the desk. With his hand upon it, he paused, as though in sudden recollection.

'Oh, I say, sir, I've just remembered. Her line's out of order. Mrs Revel's, I mean. I was trying to ring her up just now.'

George Lomax frowned.

'Annoying,' he said, 'distinctly annoying.' He tapped the table undecidedly.

'If it's anything important, sir, perhaps I might go round there now in a taxi. She is sure to be in at this time in the morning.'

George Lomax hesitated, pondering the matter. Bill waited expectantly, poised for instant flight, should the reply be favourable.

'Perhaps that would be the best plan,' said Lomax at last. 'Very well, then, take a taxi there, and ask Mrs Revel if she will be at home this afternoon at four o'clock as I am very anxious to see her about an important matter.'

'Right, sir.'

Bill seized his hat and departed.

Ten minutes later, a taxi deposited him at 487 Pont Street. He rang the bell and executed a loud rat-tat on the knocker. The door was opened by a grave functionary to whom Bill nodded with the ease of long acquaintance.

'Morning, Chilvers, Mrs Revel in?'

'I believe, sir, that she is just going out.'

'Is that you, Bill?' called a voice over the banisters. 'I thought I recognized that muscular knock. Come up and talk to me.'

Bill looked up at the face that was laughing down on him, and which was always inclined to reduce him – and not him alone – to a state of babbling incoherency. He took the stairs two at a time and clasped Virginia Revel's outstretched hands tightly in his.

'Hullo, Virginia!'

'Hullo, Bill!'

Charm is a very peculiar thing; hundreds of young women, some of them more beautiful than Virginia Revel, might have said 'Hullo, Bill,' with exactly the same intonation, and yet have produced no effect whatever. But those two simple words, uttered by Virginia, had the most intoxicating effect upon Bill.

Virginia Revel was just twenty-seven. She was tall and of an exquisite slimness – indeed, a poem might have been written to her slimness, it was so exquisitely proportioned. Her hair was of real bronze, with the greenish tint in its gold; she had a determined little chin, a lovely nose, slanting blue eyes that showed a gleam of deepest cornflower between the half-closed lids, and a delicious and quite indescribable mouth that tilted ever so slightly at one corner in what is known as 'the signature of Venus'. It was a wonderfully expressive face, and there was a sort of radiant vitality about her that always challenged attention. It would have been quite impossible ever to ignore Virginia Revel.

She drew Bill into the small drawing-room which was all pale mauve and green and yellow, like crocuses surprised in a meadow.

'Bill, darling,' said Virginia, 'isn't the Foreign Office missing you? I thought they couldn't get on without you.'

'I've brought a message for you from Codders.'

Thus irreverently did Bill allude to his chief.

'And by the way, Virginia, in case he asks, remember that your telephone was out of order this morning.'

'But it hasn't been.'

'I know that. But I said it was.'

'Why? Enlighten me as to this Foreign Office touch.' Bill threw her a reproachful glance.

'So that I could get here and see you, of course.'

'Oh, darling Bill, how dense of me! And how perfectly sweet of you!'

'Chilvers said you were going out.'

'So I was – to Sloane Street. There's a place there where they've got a perfectly wonderful new hip band.'

'A hip band?'

'Yes, Bill, H-I-P hip, B-A-N-D band. A band to confine the hips. You wear it next the skin.'

'I blush for you Virginia. You shouldn't describe your underwear to a young man to whom you are not related. It isn't delicate.'

'But, Bill dear, there's nothing indelicate about hips. We've all got hips – although we poor women are trying awfully hard to pretend we haven't. This hip band is made of red rubber and comes to just above the knees, and it's simply impossible to walk in it.'

'How awful!' said Bill. 'Why do you do it?'

'Oh, because it gives one such a noble feeling to suffer for one's silhouette. But don't let's talk about my hip band. Give me George's message.'

'He wants to know whether you'll be in at four o'clock this afternoon.'

'I shan't. I shall be at Ranelagh. Why this sort of formal call? Is he going to propose to me, do you think?'

'I shouldn't wonder.'

'Because, if so, you can tell him that I much prefer men who propose on impulse.'

'Like me?'

'It's not an impulse with you, Bill. It's habit.'

'Virginia, won't you ever –'

'No, no, no, Bill. I won't have it in the morning before lunch. Do try and think of me as a nice motherly person approaching middle age who has your interests thoroughly at heart.'

'Virginia, I do love you so.'

'I know, Bill, I know. And I simply love being loved. Isn't it wicked and dreadful of me? I should like every nice man in the world to be in love with me.'

'Most of them are, I expect,' said Bill gloomily.

'But I hope George isn't in love with me. I don't think he can be. He's so wedded to his career. What else did he say?'

'Just that it was very important.'

'Bill, I'm getting intrigued. The things that George thinks important are so awfully limited. I think I must chuck Ranelagh. After all, I can go to Ranelagh any day. Tell George that I shall be awaiting him meekly at four o'clock.'

Bill looked at his wristwatch.

'It seems hardly worthwhile to go back before lunch. Come out and chew something, Virginia.'

'I'm going out to lunch somewhere or other.'

'That doesn't matter. Make a day of it, and chuck everything all round.'

'It would be rather nice,' said Virginia, smiling at him.

'Virginia, you're a darling. Tell me, you do like me rather, don't you? Better than other people.'

'Bill, I adore you. If I had to marry someone – simply had to – I mean if it was in a book and a wicked mandarin said to me, "Marry someone or die by slow torture," I should choose you at once – I should indeed. I should say, "Give me little Bill".'

'Well, then –'

'Yes, but I haven't got to marry anyone. I love being a wicked widow.'

'You could do all the same things still. Go about, and all that. You'd hardly notice me about the house.'

'Bill, you don't understand. I'm the kind of person who marries enthusiastically if they marry at all.'

Bill gave a hollow groan.

'I shall shoot myself one of these days, I expect,' he murmured gloomily.

'No, you won't, Bill darling. You'll take a pretty girl out to supper – like you did the night before last.'

Mr Eversleigh was momentarily confused.

'If you mean Dorothy Kirkpatrick, the girl who's in *Hooks and Eyes*, I – well, dash it all, she's a thoroughly nice girl, straight as they make 'em. There was no harm in it.'

'Bill darling, of course there wasn't. I love you to enjoy yourself. But don't pretend to be dying of a broken heart, that's all.'

Mr Eversleigh recovered his dignity.

'You don't understand at all, Virginia,' he said severely. 'Men –'

'Are polygamous! I know they are. Sometimes I have a shrewd suspicion that I am polyandrous. If you really love me, Bill, take me out to lunch quickly.'

CHAPTER V

First Night in London

There is often a flaw in the best-laid plans. George Lomax had made one mistake – there was a weak spot in his preparations. The weak spot was Bill.

Bill Eversleigh was an extremely nice lad. He was a good cricketer and a scratch golfer, he had pleasant manners, and an amiable disposition, but his position in the Foreign Office had been gained, not by brains, but by good connexions. For the work he had to do he was quite suitable. He was more or less George's dog. He did no responsible or brainy work. His part was to be constantly at George's elbow, to interview unimportant people whom George didn't want to see, to run errands, and generally to make himself useful. All this Bill carried out faithfully enough. When George was absent, Bill stretched himself out in the biggest chair and read the sporting news, and in so doing he was merely carrying out a time-honoured tradition.

Being accustomed to send Bill on errands, George had dispatched him to the Union Castle offices to find out when the *Granarth Castle* was due in. Now, in common with most well-educated young Englishmen, Bill had a pleasant but quite inaudible voice. Any elocution master would have found fault with his pronunciation of the word Granarth. It might have been anything. The clerk took it to be Carnfrae.

The *Carnfrae Castle* was due in on the following Thursday. He said so. Bill thanked him and went out. George Lomax accepted the information and laid his plans accordingly. He knew nothing about Union Castle liners, and took it for granted that James McGrath would duly arrive on Thursday.

Therefore, at the moment he was buttonholing Lord Caterham on the steps of the club on Wednesday morning, he would have been greatly surprised to learn that the *Granarth Castle* had docked at Southampton the preceding afternoon. At two o'clock that afternoon Anthony Cade, travelling under the name of Jimmy McGrath, stepped out of the boat train at Waterloo, hailed a taxi, and after a moment's hesitation, ordered the driver to proceed to the Blitz Hotel.

'One might as well be comfortable,' said Anthony to himself as he looked with some interest out of the taxi windows.

It was exactly fourteen years since he had been in London.

He arrived at the hotel, booked a room, and then went for a short stroll along the Embankment. It was rather pleasant to be back in London again. Everything was changed of course. There had been a little restaurant there – just past Blackfriars Bridge – where he had dined fairly often, in company with other earnest lads. He had been a Socialist then, and worn a flowing red tie. Young – very young.

He retraced his steps back to the Blitz. Just as he was crossing the road, a man jostled against him, nearly making him lose his balance. They both recovered themselves, and the man muttered an apology, his eyes scanning Anthony's face narrowly. He was a short, thick-set man of the working classes, with something foreign in his appearance.

Anthony went on into the hotel, wondering, as he did so, what had inspired that searching glance. Nothing in it probably. The deep tan of his face was somewhat unusual looking amongst these pallid Londoners and it had attracted the fellow's attention. He went up to his room and, led by a sudden impulse, crossed to the looking-glass and stood studying his face in it. Of the few friends of the old days – just a chosen few – was it likely that any of them would recognize him now if they were to meet him face to face? He shook his head slowly.

When he had left London he had been just eighteen – a fair, slightly chubby boy, with a misleadingly seraphic expression. Small chance that that boy would be recognized in the lean, brown-faced man with the quizzical expression.

The telephone beside the bed rang, and Anthony crossed to the receiver.

'Hullo!'

The voice of the desk clerk answered him.

'Mr James McGrath?'

'Speaking.'

'A gentleman has called to see you.'

Anthony was rather astonished.

'To see *me*?'

'Yes, sir, a foreign gentleman.'

'What's his name?'

There was a slight pause, and then the clerk said:

'I will send up a page-boy with his card.'

Anthony replaced the receiver and waited. In a few minutes there was a knock on the door and a small page appeared bearing a card upon a salver.

Anthony took it. The following was the name engraved upon it.

Baron Lolopretjzyl

He now fully appreciated the desk clerk's pause.

For a moment or two he stood studying the card, and then made up his mind.

'Show the gentleman up.'

'Very good, sir.'

In a few minutes the Baron Lolopretjzyl was ushered into the room, a big man with an immense fan-like black beard and a high, bald forehead.

He brought his heels together with a click, and bowed.

'Mr McGrath,' he said.

Anthony imitated his movements as nearly as possible.

'Baron,' he said. Then, drawing forward a chair, 'Pray sit down. I have not, I think, had the pleasure of meeting you before?'

'That is so,' agreed the Baron, seating himself. 'It is my misfortune,' he added politely.

'And mine also,' responded Anthony, on the same note.

'Let us now to business come,' said the Baron. 'I represent in London the Loyalist party of Herzoslovakia.'

'And represent it admirably, I am sure,' murmured Anthony.

The Baron bowed in acknowledgement of the compliment.

'You are too kind,' he said stiffly. 'Mr McGrath, I will not from you conceal anything. The moment has come for the restoration of the monarchy, in abeyance since the martyrdom of His Most Gracious Majesty King Nicholas IV of blessed memory.'

'Amen,' murmured Anthony. 'I mean hear, hear.'

'On the throne will be placed His Highness Prince Michael, who the support of the British Government has.'

'Splendid,' said Anthony. 'It's very kind of you to tell me all this.'

'Everything arranged is – when you come here to trouble make.'

The Baron fixed him with a stern eye.

'My dear Baron,' protested Anthony.

'Yes, yes, I know what I am talking about. You have with you the memoirs of the late Count Stylptitch.'

He fixed Anthony with an accusing eye.

'And if I have? What have the memoirs of Count Stylptitch to do with Prince Michael?'

'They will cause scandals.'

'Most memoirs do that,' said Anthony soothingly.

'Of many secrets he the knowledge had. Should he reveal but the quarter of them, Europe into war plunged may be.'

'Come, come,' said Anthony. 'It can't be as bad as all that.'

'An unfavourable opinion of the Obolovitch will abroad be spread. So democratic is the English spirit.'

'I can quite believe,' said Anthony, 'that the Obolovitch may have been a trifle high-handed now and again. It runs in the blood. But people in England expect that sort of thing from the Balkans. I don't know why they should, but they do.'

'You do not understand,' said the Baron. 'You do not understand at all. And my lips sealed are.' He sighed.

'What exactly are you afraid of?' asked Anthony.

'Until I have read the memoirs I do not know,' explained the Baron simply. 'But there is sure to be something. These great diplomats are always indiscreet. The apple-cart upset will be, as the saying goes.'

'Look here,' said Anthony kindly. 'I'm sure you're taking altogether too pessimistic a view of the thing. I know all about publishers – they sit on manuscripts and hatch 'em like eggs. It will be at least a year before the thing is published.'

'Either a very deceitful or a very simple young man you are. All is arranged for the memoirs in a Sunday newspaper to come out immediately.'

'Oh!' Anthony was somewhat taken aback. 'But you can always deny everything,' he said hopefully.

The Baron shook his head sadly.

'No, no, through the hat you talk. Let us to business come. One thousand pounds you are to have, is it not so? You see, I have the good information got.'

'I certainly congratulate the Intelligence Department of the Loyalists.'

'Then I to you offer fifteen hundred.'

Anthony stared at him in amazement, then shook his head ruefully.

'I'm afraid it can't be done,' he said, with regret.

'Good. I to you offer two thousand.'

'You tempt me, Baron, you tempt me. But I still say it can't be done.'

'Your own price name, then.'

'I'm afraid you don't understand the position. I'm perfectly willing to believe that you are on the side of the angels, and that these memoirs may damage your cause. Nevertheless, I've undertaken the job, and I've got to carry it through. See? I can't allow myself to be bought off by the other side. That kind of thing isn't done.'

The Baron listened very attentively. At the end of Anthony's speech he nodded his head several times.

'I see. Your honour as an Englishman it is?'

'Well, we don't put it that way ourselves,' said Anthony. 'But I dare say, allowing for a difference in vocabulary, that we both mean much the same thing.'

The Baron rose to his feet.

'For the English honour I much respect have,' he announced. 'We must another way try. I wish you good morning.'

He drew his heels together, clicked, bowed and marched out of the room, holding himself stiffly erect.

'Now I wonder what he meant by that,' mused Anthony. 'Was it a threat? Not that I'm in the least afraid of old Lollipop. Rather a good name for him, that, by the way. I shall call him Baron Lollipop.'

He took a turn or two up and down the room, undecided on his next course of action. The date stipulated upon for delivering the manuscript was a little over a week ahead. Today was the 5th of October. Anthony had no intention of handing it over before the last moment. Truth to tell, he was by now feverishly anxious to read these memoirs. He had meant to do so on the boat coming over, but had been laid low with a touch of fever, and not at all in the mood for deciphering crabbed and illegible handwriting, for none of the manuscript was typed. He was now more than ever determined to see what all the fuss was about.

There was the other job too.

On an impulse, he picked up the telephone book and looked up the name of Revel. There were six Revels in the book: Edward Henry Revel, surgeon, of Harley Street; and James Revel and Co, saddlers; Lennox Revel of Abbotbury Mansions, Hampstead; Miss Mary Revel with an address in Ealing; Hon Mrs Timothy Revel of 487 Pont Street; and Mrs Willis Revel of 42 Cadogan Square. Eliminating the saddlers and Miss Mary Revel, that gave him four names to investigate – and there was no reason to suppose that the lady lived in

London at all! He shut up the book with a short shake of the head.

'For the moment I'll leave it to chance,' he said. 'Something usually turns up.'

The luck of the Anthony Cades of this world is perhaps in some measure due to their own belief in it. Anthony found what he was after not half an hour later, when he was turning over the pages of an illustrated paper. It was a representation of some tableaux organized by the Duchess of Perth. Below the central figure, a woman in Eastern dress, was the inscription:

The Hon Mrs Timothy Revel as Cleopatra. Before her marriage, Mrs Revel was the Hon Virginia Cawthron, a daughter of Lord Edgbaston.

Anthony looked at the picture some time, slowly pursing up his lips as though to whistle. Then he tore out the whole page, folded it up and put it in his pocket. He went upstairs again, unlocked his suitcase and took out the packet of letters. He took out the folded page from his pocket and slipped it under the string that held them together.

Then at a sudden sound behind him, he wheeled round sharply. A man was standing in the doorway, the kind of man whom Anthony had fondly imagined existed only in the chorus of a comic opera. A sinister-looking figure, with a squat brutal head and lips drawn back in an evil grin.

'What the devil are you doing here?' asked Anthony. 'And who let you come up?'

'I pass where I please,' said the stranger. His voice was guttural and foreign, though his English was idiomatic enough.

'Another dago,' thought Anthony.

'Well, get out, do you hear?' he went on aloud.

The man's eyes were fixed on the packet of letters which Anthony had caught up.

'I will get out when you have given me what I have come for.'

'And what's that, may I ask?'

The man took a step nearer.

'The memoirs of Count Stylptitch,' he hissed.

'It's impossible to take you seriously,' said Anthony. 'You're so completely the stage villain. I like your get-up very much. Who sent you here? Baron Lollipop?'

'Baron? – ' The man jerked out a string of harsh sounding consonants.

'So that's how you pronounce it, is it? A cross between gargling and barking like a dog. I don't think I could say it myself – my throat's not made that way. I shall have to go on calling him Lollipop. So he sent you, did he?'

But he received a vehement negative. His visitor went so far as to spit upon the suggestion in a very realistic manner. Then he drew from his pocket a sheet of paper which he threw upon the table.

'Look,' he said. 'Look and tremble, accursed Englishman.'

Anthony looked with some interest, not troubling to fulfil the latter part of the command. On the paper was traced the crude design of a human hand in red.

'It looks like a hand,' he remarked. 'But, if you say so, I'm quite prepared to admit that it's a Cubist picture of Sunset at the North Pole.'

'It is the sign of the Comrades of the Red Hand. I am a Comrade of the Red Hand.'

'You don't say so,' said Anthony, looking at him with much interest. 'Are the others all like you? I don't know what the Eugenic Society would have to say about it.'

The man snarled angrily.

'Dog,' he said. 'Worse than dog. Paid slave of an effete monarchy. Give me the memoirs, and you shall go unscathed. Such is the clemency of the Brotherhood.'

'It's very kind of them, I'm sure,' said Anthony, 'but I'm afraid that both they and you are labouring under a misapprehension. My instructions are to deliver the manuscript – not to your amiable society, but to a certain firm of publishers.'

'Pah!' laughed the other. 'Do you think you will ever be

permitted to reach that office alive? Enough of this fool's talk. Hand over the papers, or I shoot.'

He drew a revolver from his pocket and brandished it in the air.

But there he misjudged his Anthony Cade. He was not used to men who could act as quickly – or quicker than they could think. Anthony did not wait to be covered by the revolver. Almost as soon as the other got it out of his pocket, Anthony had sprung forward and knocked it out of his hand. The force of the blow sent the man swinging round, so that he presented his back to his assailant.

The chance was too good to be missed. With one mighty, well-directed kick, Anthony sent the man flying through the doorway into the corridor, where he collapsed in a heap.

Anthony stepped out after him, but the doughty Comrade of the Red Hand had had enough. He got nimbly to his feet and fled down the passage. Anthony did not pursue him, but went back into his own room.

'So much for the Comrades of the Red Hand,' he remarked. 'Picturesque appearance, but easily routed by direct action. How the hell did that fellow get in, I wonder? There's one thing that stands out pretty clearly – this isn't going to be quite such a soft job as I thought. I've already fallen foul of both the Loyalist and the Revolutionary parties. Soon, I suppose, the Nationalists and the Independent Liberals will be sending up a delegation. One thing's fixed. I start on that manuscript tonight.'

Looking at his watch, Anthony discovered that it was nearly nine o'clock, and he decided to dine where he was. He did not anticipate any more surprise visits, but he felt that it was up to him to be on his guard. He had no intention of allowing his suitcase to be rifled whilst he was downstairs in the Grill Room. He rang the bell and asked for the menu, selected a couple of dishes and ordered a bottle of Chambertin. The waiter took the order and withdrew.

Whilst he was waiting for the meal to arrive, he got out the package of manuscript and put it on the table with the letters.

There was a knock at the door, and the waiter entered with a small table and the accessories of the meal. Anthony had strolled over to the mantelpiece. Standing there with his back to the room, he was directly facing the mirror, and idly glancing in it he noticed a curious thing.

The waiter's eyes were glued on the parcel of manuscript. Shooting little glances sideways at Anthony's immovable back, he moved softly round the table. His hands were twitching and he kept passing his tongue over his dry lips. Anthony observed him more closely. He was a tall man, supple like all waiters, with a clean-shaven, mobile face. An Italian, Anthony thought, not a Frenchman.

At the critical moment Anthony wheeled round abruptly. The waiter started slightly, but pretended to be doing something with the salt-cellar.

'What's your name?' asked Anthony abruptly.

'Giuseppe, monsieur.'

'Italian, eh?'

'Yes, monsieur.'

Anthony spoke to him in that language, and the man answered fluently enough. Finally Anthony dismissed him with a nod, but all the while he was eating the excellent meal which Giuseppe served to him, he was thinking rapidly.

Had he been mistaken? Was Giuseppe's interest in the parcel just ordinary curiosity? It might be so, but remembering the feverish intensity of the man's excitement, Anthony decided against that theory. All the same, he was puzzled.

'Dash it all,' said Anthony to himself, 'everyone can't be after the blasted manuscript. Perhaps I'm fancying things.'

Dinner concluded and cleared away, he applied himself to the perusal of the memoirs. Owing to the illegibility of the late Count's handwriting, the business was a slow one. Anthony's yawns succeeded one another with suspicious rapidity. At the end of the fourth chapter, he gave it up.

So far, he had found the memoirs insufferably dull, with no hint of scandal of any kind.

He gathered up the letters and the wrapping of the manu-

script which were lying in a heap together on the table and
locked them up in the suitcase. Then he locked the door, and
as an additional precaution put a chair against it. On the chair
he placed the water-bottle from the bathroom.

Surveying these preparations with some pride, he undressed
and got into bed. He had one more shot at the Count's
memoirs, but felt his eyelids drooping, and stuffing the manuscript under his pillow, he switched out the light and fell asleep
almost immediately.

It must have been some four hours later that he awoke with
a start. What had awakened him he did not know – perhaps
a sound, perhaps only the consciousness of danger which in
men who have led an adventurous life is very fully developed.

For a moment he lay quite still, trying to focus his impres-
sions. He could hear a very stealthy rustle, and then he became
aware of a denser blackness somewhere between him and the
window – on the floor by the suitcase.

With a sudden spring, Anthony jumped out of bed, switching the light on as he did so. A figure sprang up from where
it had been kneeling by the suitcase.

It was the waiter, Giuseppe. In his right hand gleamed a
long thin knife. He hurled himself straight upon Anthony, who
was by now fully conscious of his own danger. He was
unarmed and Giuseppe was evidently thoroughly at home with
his own weapon.

Anthony sprang to one side, and Giuseppe missed him with
the knife. The next minute the two men were rolling on the
floor together, locked in a close embrace. The whole of
Anthony's faculties were centred on keeping a close grip of
Giuseppe's right arm so that he would be unable to use the
knife. He bent it slowly back. At the same time he felt
the Italian's other hand clutching at his windpipe, stifling him,
choking. And still, desperately, he bent the right arm back.

There was a sharp tinkle as the knife fell on the floor. At
the same time, the Italian extricated himself with a swift twist
from Anthony's grasp. Anthony sprang up too, but made the
mistake of moving towards the door to cut off the other's

retreat. He saw, too late, that the chair and the water-bottle were just as he had arranged them.

Giuseppe had entered by the window, and it was the window he made for now. In the instant's respite given him by Anthony's move towards the door, he had sprung out on the balcony, leaped over to the adjoining balcony and had disappeared through the adjoining window.

Anthony knew well enough that it was of no use to pursue him. His way of retreat was doubtless fully assured. Anthony would merely get himself into trouble.

He walked over to the bed, thrusting his hand beneath the pillow and drawing out the memoirs. Lucky that they had been there and not in the suitcase. He crossed over to the suitcase and looked inside, meaning to take out the letters.

Then he swore softly under his breath.

The letters were gone.

CHAPTER VI

The Gentle Art of Blackmail

It was exactly five minutes to four when Virginia Revel, rendered punctual by a healthy curiosity, returned to the house in Pont Street. She opened the door with her latchkey, and stepped into the hall to be immediately confronted by the impassive Chilvers.

'I beg pardon, ma'am, but a – a person has called to see you –'

For the moment, Virginia did not pay attention to the subtle phraseology whereby Chilvers cloaked his meaning.

'Mr Lomax? Where is he? In the drawing-room?'

'Oh, no, ma'am, not Mr Lomax.' Chilvers' tone was faintly reproachful. 'A person – I was reluctant to let him in, but he said his business was most important – connected with the late Captain, I understood him to say. Thinking therefore that you might wish to see him, I put him – er – in the study.'

Virginia stood thinking for a minute. She had been a widow now for some years, and the fact that she rarely spoke of her husband was taken by some to indicate that below her careless demeanour was a still-aching wound. By others it was taken to mean the exact opposite, that Virginia had never really cared for Tim Revel, and that she found it insincere to profess a grief she did not feel.

'I should have mentioned, ma'am,' continued Chilvers, 'that the man appears to be some kind of foreigner.'

Virginia's interest heightened a little. Her husband had been in the Diplomatic Service, and they had been together in Herzoslovakia just before the sensational murder of the King and Queen. This man might probably be a Herzoslovakian, some old servant who had fallen on evil days.

'You did quite right, Chilvers,' she said with a quick, approving nod. 'Where did you say you put him? In the study?'

She crossed the hall with her light buoyant step, and opened the door of the small room that flanked the dining-room.

The visitor was sitting in a chair by the fireplace. He rose on her entrance and stood looking at her. Virginia had an excellent memory for faces, and she was at once quite sure that she had never seen the man before. He was tall and dark, supple in figure, and quite unmistakably a foreigner; but she did not think he was of Slavonic origin. She put him down as Italian or possibly Spanish.

'You wish to see me?' she asked. 'I am Mrs Revel.'

The man did not answer for a minute or two. He was looking her slowly over, as though appraising her narrowly. There was a veiled insolence in his manner which she was quick to feel.

'Will you please state your business?' she said, with a touch of impatience.

'You are Mrs Revel? Mrs Timothy Revel?'

'Yes. I told you so just now.'

'Quite so. It is a good thing that you consented to see me, Mrs Revel. Otherwise, as I told your butler, I should have been compelled to do business with your husband.'

Virginia looked at him in astonishment, but some impulse quelled the retort that sprang to her lips. She contented herself by remarking dryly:

'You might have found some difficulty in doing that.'

'I think not. I am very persistent. But I will come to the point. Perhaps you recognize this?'

He flourished something in his hand. Virginia looked at it without much interest.

'Can you tell me what it is, madame?'

'It appears to be a letter,' replied Virginia, who was by now convinced that she had to do with a man who was mentally unhinged.

'And perhaps you note to whom it is addressed,' said the man significantly, holding it out to her.

'I can read,' Virginia informed him pleasantly. 'It is addressed to a Captain O'Neill at Rue de Quenelles No 15 Paris.'

The man seemed to be searching her face hungrily for something he did not find.

'Will you read it, please?'

Virginia took the envelope from him, drew out the enclosure and glanced at it, but almost immediately she stiffened and held it out to him again.

'This is a private letter – certainly not meant for my eyes.'

The man laughed sardonically.

'I congratulate you, Mrs Revel, on your admirable acting. You play your part to perfection. Nevertheless, I think that you will hardly be able to deny the signature!'

'The signature?'

Virginia turned the letter over – and was struck dumb with astonishment. The signature, written in a delicate slanting hand, was Virginia Revel. Checking the exclamation of astonishment that rose to her lips, she turned again to the beginning of the letter and deliberately read the whole thing through. Then she stood a minute lost in thought. The nature of the letter made it clear enough what was in prospect.

'Well, madame?' said the man. 'That is your name, is it not?'

'Oh, yes,' said Virginia. 'It's my name.'

'But not my handwriting,' she might have added.

Instead she turned a dazzling smile upon her visitor.

'Supposing,' she said sweetly, 'we sit down and talk it over?'

He was puzzled. Not so had he expected her to behave. His instinct told him that she was not afraid of him.

'First of all, I should like to know how you found me out?'

'That was easy.'

He took from his pocket a page torn from an illustrated paper, and handed it to her. Anthony Cade would have recognized it.

She gave it back to him with a thoughtful little frown.

'I see,' she said. 'It was very easy.'

'Of course you understand, Mrs Revel, that that is not the only letter. There are others.'

'Dear me,' said Virginia, 'I seem to have been frightfully indiscreet.'

Again she could see that her light tone puzzled him. She was by now thoroughly enjoying herself.

'At any rate,' she said, smiling sweetly at him, 'it's very kind of you to call and give them back to me.'

There was a pause as he cleared his throat.

'I am a poor man, Mrs Revel,' he said at last, with a good deal of significance in his manner.

'As such you will doubtless find it easier to enter the Kingdom of Heaven, or so I have always heard.'

'I cannot afford to let you have these letters for nothing.'

'I think you are under a misapprehension. Those letters are the property of the person who wrote them.'

'That may be the law, madame, but in this country you have a saying "Possession is nine points of the law." And, in any case, are you prepared to invoke the aid of the law?'

'The law is a severe one for blackmailers,' Virginia reminded him.

'Come, Mrs Revel, I am not quite a fool. I have read these letters – the letters of a woman to her lover, one and all breathing dread of discovery by her husband. Do you want me to take them to your husband?'

'You have overlooked one possibility. Those letters were written some years ago. Supposing that since then – I have become a widow.'

He shook his head with confidence.

'In that case – if you had nothing to fear – you would not be sitting here making terms with me.'

Virginia smiled.

'What is your price?' she asked in a businesslike manner.

'For one thousand pounds I will hand the whole packet over to you. It is very little that I am asking there; but, you see, I do not like the business.'

'I shouldn't dream of paying you a thousand pounds,' said Virginia with decision.

'Madame, I never bargain. A thousand pounds, and I will place the letters in your hands.'

Virginia reflected.

'You must give me a little time to think it over. It will not be easy for me to get such a sum together.'

'A few pounds on account perhaps – say fifty – and I will call again.'

Virginia looked up at the clock. It was five minutes past four, and she fancied that she had heard the bell.

'Very well,' she said hurriedly. 'Come back tomorrow, but later than this. About six.'

She crossed over to a desk that stood against the wall, unlocked one of the drawers, and took out an untidy handful of notes.

'There is about forty pounds here. That will have to do for you.'

He snatched at it eagerly.

'And now go at once, please,' said Virginia.

He left the room obediently enough. Through the open door, Virginia caught a glimpse of George Lomax in the hall, just being ushered upstairs by Chilvers. As the front door closed, Virginia called to him.

'Come in here, George. Chilvers, bring us tea in here, will you please?'

She flung open both windows, and George Lomax came into the room to find her standing erect with dancing eyes and wind-blown hair.

'I'll shut them in a minute, George, but I felt the room ought to be aired. Did you fall over the blackmailer in the hall?'

'The what?'

'Blackmailer, George. B-L-A-C-K-M-A-I-L-E-R: blackmailer. One who blackmails.'

'My dear Virginia you can't be serious!'

'Oh, but I am, George.'

'But who did he come here to blackmail?'

'Me, George.'

'But, my dear Virginia, what have you been doing?'

'Well, just for once, as it happens, I hadn't been doing anything. The good gentleman mistook me for someone else.'

'You rang up the police, I suppose?'

'No, I didn't. I suppose you think I ought to have done so.'

'Well –' George considered weightily. 'No, no, perhaps not – perhaps you acted wisely. You might be mixed up in some unpleasant publicity in connexion with the case. You might even have had to give evidence –'

'I should have liked that,' said Virginia. 'I would love to be summoned, and I should like to see if judges really do make all the rotten jokes you read about. It would be most exciting. I was at Vine Street the other day to see about a diamond brooch I had lost, and there was the most perfectly lovely inspector – the nicest man I ever met.'

George, as was his custom, let all irrelevancies pass.

'But what did you do about this scoundrel?'

'Well, George, I'm afraid I let him do it.'

'Do what?'

'Blackmail me.'

George's face of horror was so poignant that Virginia had to bite her under-lip.

'You mean – do I understand you to mean – that you did not correct the misapprehension under which he was labouring?'

Virginia shook her head, shooting a sideways glance at him.

'Good heavens, Virginia, you must be mad.'

'I suppose it would seem that way to you.'

'But why? In God's name, why?'

'Several reasons. To begin with, he was doing it so beautifully – blackmailing me, I mean – I hate to interrupt an artist when he's doing his job really well. And then, you see, I'd never been blackmailed –'

'I should hope not, indeed.'

'And I wanted to see what it felt like.'

'I am quite at a loss to comprehend you, Virginia.'

'I knew you wouldn't understand.'

'You did not give him money, I hope?'

'Just a trifle,' said Virginia apologetically.

'How much?'

'Forty pounds.'

'Virginia!'

'My dear George, it's only what I pay for an evening dress. It's just as exciting to buy a new experience as it is to buy a new dress – more so, in fact.'

George Lomax merely shook his head, and Chilvers appearing at that moment with the tea urn, he was saved from having to express his outraged feelings. When tea had been brought in, and Virginia's deft fingers were manipulating the heavy silver teapot, she spoke again on the subject.

'I had another motive too, George – a brighter and better one. We women are usually supposed to be cats, but at any rate I'd done another woman a good turn this afternoon. This man isn't likely to go off looking for another Virginia Revel. He thinks he's found his bird all right. Poor little devil, she was in a blue funk when she wrote that letter. Mr Blackmailer would have had the easiest job in his life there. Now, though he doesn't know it, he's up against a tough proposition. Starting with the great advantage of having led a blameless life, I shall toy with him to his undoing – as they say in books. Guile, George, lots of guile.'

George still shook his head.

'I don't like it,' he persisted. 'I don't like it.'

'Well, never mind, George dear. You didn't come here to talk about blackmailers. What did you come here for, by the way? Correct answer: "To see *you*!" Accent on the you, and press her hand with significance unless you happen to have been eating heavily buttered muffin, in which case it must all be done with the eyes.'

'I did come to see you,' replied George seriously. 'And I am glad to find you alone.'

'"Oh, George, this is so sudden." Says she, swallowing a currant.'

'I wanted to ask a favour of you. I have always considered you, Virginia, as a woman of considerable charm.'

'Oh, George!'

'And also as a woman of intelligence!'

'Not really? How well the man knows me.'

'My dear Virginia, there is a young fellow arriving in England tomorrow whom I should like you to meet.'

'All right, George, but it's your party – let that be clearly understood.'

'You could, I feel sure, if you chose, exercise your considerable charm.'

Virginia cocked her head a little on one side.

'George dear, I don't "charm" as a profession, you know. Often I like people – and then, well, they like me. But I don't think I could set out in cold blood to fascinate a helpless stranger. That sort of thing isn't done, George, it really isn't. There are professional sirens who would do it much better than I should.'

'That is out of the question, Virginia. This young man, he is a Canadian, by the way, of the name of McGrath –'

'"A Canadian of Scottish descent." Says she, deducing brilliantly.'

'Is probably quite unused to the higher walks of English society. I should like him to appreciate the charm and distinction of a real English gentlewoman.'

'Meaning me?'

'Exactly.'

'Why?'

'I beg your pardon?'

'I said why? You don't boom the real English gentlewoman with every stray Canadian who sets foot upon our shores. What is the deep idea, George? To put it vulgarly, what do *you* get out of it?'

'I cannot see that that concerns you, Virginia.'

'I couldn't possibly go out for an evening and fascinate unless I knew all the whys and wherefores.'

'You have a most extraordinary way of putting things, Virginia. Anyone would think –'

'Wouldn't they? Come on, George, part with a little more information.'

'My dear Virginia, matters are likely to be a little strained shortly in a certain Central European nation. It is important, for reasons which are immaterial, that this – Mr – er – McGrath should be brought to realize that the restoring of the monarchy in Herzoslovakia is imperative to the peace of Europe.'

'The part about the peace of Europe is all bosh,' said Virginia calmly, 'but I'm all for monarchies every time, especially for a picturesque people like the Herzoslovakians. So you're running a king in the Herzoslovakian Stakes, are you? Who is he?'

George was reluctant to answer, but did not see his way to avoid the question. The interview was not going at all as he had planned. He had foreseen Virginia as a willing, docile tool, receiving his hints gratefully, and asking no awkward questions. This was far from being the case. She seemed determined to know all about it and this George, ever doubtful of female discretion, was determined at all costs to avoid. He had made a mistake. Virginia was not the woman for the part. She might, indeed, cause serious trouble. Her account of her interview with the blackmailer had caused him grave apprehension. A most undependable creature, with no idea of treating serious matters seriously.

'Prince Michael Obolovitch,' he replied, as Virginia was obviously waiting for an answer to her question. 'But please let that go no further.'

'Don't be absurd, George. There are all sorts of hints in the papers already, and articles cracking up the Obolovitch dynasty and talking about the murdered Nicholas IV as though he were a cross between a saint and a hero instead of a stupid little man besotted by a third-rate actress.'

George winced. He was more than ever convinced that he had made a mistake in enlisting Virginia's aid. He must stave her off quickly.

'You are right, my dear Virginia,' he said hastily, as he rose to his feet to bid her farewell. 'I should not have made the suggestion I did to you. But we are anxious for the Dominions to see eye to eye with us on this Herzoslovakian crisis, and McGrath has, I believe, influence in journalistic circles. As an ardent monarchist, and with your knowledge of the country, I thought it a good plan for you to meet him.'

'So that's the explanation, is it?'

'Yes, but I dare say you wouldn't have cared for him.'

Virginia looked at him for a second and then she laughed.

'George,' she said, 'you're a rotten liar.'

'Virginia!'

'Rotten, absolutely rotten! If I had had your training, I could have managed a better one than that – one that had a chance of being believed. But I shall find out all about it, my poor George. Rest assured of that. The Mystery of Mr McGrath. I shouldn't wonder if I got a hint or two at Chimneys this weekend.'

'At Chimneys? You are going to Chimneys?'

George could not conceal his perturbation. He had hoped to reach Lord Caterham in time for the invitation to remain un-issued.

'Bundle rang up and asked me this morning.'

George made a last effort.

'Rather a dull party, I believe,' he said. 'Hardly in your line, Virginia.'

'My poor George, why didn't you tell me the truth and trust me? It's still not too late.'

George took her hand and dropped it again limply.

'I have told you the truth,' he said coldly, and he said it without a blush.

'That's a better one,' said Virginia approvingly. 'But it's still not good enough. Cheer up, George, I shall be at Chimneys all right, exerting my considerable charm – as you put it. Life has become suddenly very much more amusing. First a blackmailer, and then George in diplomatic difficulties. Will he tell all to the beautiful woman who asks for his confidence so

pathetically? No, he will reveal nothing until the last chapter.
Goodbye, George. One last fond look before you go? No? Oh,
George, dear, don't be sulky about it!'

Virginia ran to the telephone as soon as George had
departed with a heavy gait through the front door.

She obtained the number she required and asked to speak
to Lady Eileen Brent.

'Is that you, Bundle? I'm coming to Chimneys all right
tomorrow. What? Bore me? No, it won't. Bundle, wild horses
wouldn't keep me away! So there!'

CHAPTER VII

Mr McGrath Refuses an Invitation

The letters were gone!

Having once made up his mind to the fact of their disappearance, there was nothing to do but accept it. Anthony realized very well that he could not pursue Giuseppe through the corridors of the Blitz Hotel. To do so was to court undesired publicity, and in all probability to fail in his object all the same.

He came to the conclusion that Giuseppe had mistaken the packets of letters, enclosed as they were in the other wrappings, for the memoirs themselves. It was likely therefore that when he discovered his mistake he would make another attempt to get hold of the memoirs. For this attempt Anthony intended to be fully prepared.

Another plan that occurred to him was to advertise discreetly for the return of the package of letters. Supposing Giuseppe to be an emissary of the Comrades of the Red Hand, or, which seemed to Anthony more probable, to be employed by the Loyalist party, the letters could have no possible interest for either employer and he would probably jump at the chance of obtaining a small sum of money for their return.

Having thought out all this, Anthony returned to bed and slept peacefully until morning. He did not fancy that Giuseppe would be anxious for a second encounter that night.

Anthony got up with his plan of campaign fully thought out. He had a good breakfast, glanced at the papers which were full of the new discoveries of oil in Herzoslovakia, and then demanded an interview with the manager and being Anthony Cade, with a gift for getting his own way by means of quiet determination he obtained what he asked for.

The manager, a Frenchman with an exquisitely suave manner, received him in his private office.

'You wished to see me, I understand, Mr – er – McGrath?'

'I did. I arrived at your hotel yesterday afternoon and I had dinner served to me in my own rooms by a waiter whose name was Giuseppe.'

He paused.

'I dare say we have a waiter of that name,' agreed the manager indifferently.

'I was struck by something unusual in the man's manner, but thought nothing more of it at the time. Later, in the night, I was awakened by the sound of someone moving softly about the room. I switched on the light, and found this same Giuseppe in the act of rifling my leather suitcase.'

The manager's indifference had completely disappeared now.

'But I have heard nothing of this,' he exclaimed. 'Why was I not informed sooner?'

'The man and I had a brief struggle – he was armed with a knife, by the way. In the end he succeeded in making off by way of the window.'

'What did you do then, Mr McGrath?'

'I examined the contents of my suitcase.'

'Had anything been taken?'

'Nothing of – importance,' said Anthony slowly.

The manager leaned back with a sigh.

'I am glad of that,' he remarked. 'But you will allow me to say, Mr McGrath, that I do not quite understand your attitude in the matter. You made no attempt to arouse the hotel? To pursue the thief?'

Anthony shrugged his shoulders.

'Nothing of value had been taken, as I tell you. I am aware, of course, that strictly speaking it is a case for the police –'

He paused, and the manager murmured without any particular enthusiasm:

'For the police – of course –'

'In any case, I was fairly certain that the man would manage to make good his escape, and since nothing was taken, why bother with the police?'

The manager smiled a little.

'I see that you realize, Mr McGrath, that I am not at all anxious to have the police called in. From my point of view it is always disastrous. If the newspapers can get hold of anything connected with a big fashionable hotel such as this, they always run it for all it is worth, no matter how insignificant the real subject may be.'

'Quite so,' agreed Anthony. 'Now I told you that nothing of value had been taken, and that was perfectly true in a sense. Nothing of any value to the thief was taken, but he got hold of something which is of considerable value to me.'

'Ah?'

'Letters, you understand.'

An expression of superhuman discretion, only to be achieved by a Frenchman, settled down upon the manager's face.

'I comprehend,' he murmured. 'But perfectly. Naturally, it is not a matter for the police.'

'We are quite agreed upon that point. But you will understand that I have every intention of recovering these letters. In the part of the world where I come from, people are used to doing things for themselves. What I require from you therefore is the fullest possible information you can give me about this waiter, Giuseppe.'

'I see no objection to that,' said the manager after a moment or two's pause. 'I cannot give you the information offhand, of course, but if you will return in half an hour's time I will have everything ready to lay before you.'

'Thank you very much. That will suit me admirably.'

In half an hour's time, Anthony returned to the office again to find that the manager had been as good as his word. Jotted down on a piece of paper were all the relevant facts known about Giuseppe Manelli.

'He came to us, you see, about three months ago. A skilled and experienced waiter. Has given complete satisfaction. He has been in England about five years.'

Together the two men ran over a list of the hotels and restaurants where the Italian had worked. One fact struck Anthony as being possibly of significance. At two of the hotels in question there had been serious robberies during the time that Giuseppe was employed there, though no suspicion of any kind had attached to him in either case. Still, the fact was significant.

Was Giuseppe merely a clever hotel thief? Had his search of Anthony's suitcase been only part of his habitual professional tactics? He might just possibly have had the packet of letters in his hand at the moment when Anthony switched on the light, and have shoved it into his pocket mechanically so as to have his hands free. In that case, the thing was mere plain or garden robbery.

Against that, there was to be put the man's excitement of the evening before when he had caught sight of the papers lying on the table. There had been no money or object of value there such as would excite the cupidity of an ordinary thief.

No, Anthony felt convinced that Giuseppe had been acting as a tool for some outside agency. With the information supplied to him by the manager, it might be possible to learn something about Giuseppe's private life and so finally track him down. He gathered up the sheet of paper and rose.

'Thank you very much indeed. It's quite unnecessary to ask, I suppose, whether Giuseppe is still in the hotel?'

The manager smiled.

'His bed was not slept in, and all his things have been left behind. He must have rushed straight out after his attack upon you. I don't think there is much chance of our seeing him again.'

'I imagine not. Well, thank you very much indeed. I shall be staying on here for the present.'

'I hope you will be successful in your task, but I confess that I am rather doubtful.'

'I always hope for the best.'

One of Anthony's first proceedings was to question some of

the other waiters who had been friendly with Giuseppe, but he obtained very little to go upon. He wrote out an advertisement on the lines he had planned, and had it sent to five of the most widely read newspapers. He was just about to go out and visit the restaurant at which Giuseppe had been previously employed when the telephone rang. Anthony took up the receiver.

'Hullo, what is it?'

A toneless voice replied.

'Am I speaking to Mr McGrath?'

'You are. Who are you?'

'This is Messrs Balderson and Hodgkins. Just a minute, please. I will put you through to Mr Balderson.'

'Our worthy publishers,' thought Anthony. 'So they are getting worried too, are they? They needn't. There's a week to run still.'

A hearty voice struck suddenly upon his ear.

'Hullo! That Mr McGrath?'

'Speaking.'

'I'm Mr Balderson of Balderson and Hodgkins. What about that manuscript, Mr McGrath?'

'Well,' said Anthony, 'what about it?'

'Everything about it. I understand, Mr McGrath, that you have just arrived in this country from South Africa. That being so, you can't possibly understand the position. There's going to be trouble about that manuscript, Mr McGrath, big trouble. Sometimes I wish we'd never said we'd handle it.'

'Indeed?'

'I assure you it's so. At present I'm anxious to get it into my possession as quickly as possible, so as to have a couple of copies made. Then, if the original is destroyed – well, no harm will be done.'

'Dear me,' said Anthony.

'Yes, I expect it sounds absurd to you, Mr McGrath. But, I assure you, you don't appreciate the situation. There's a determined effort being made to prevent its ever reaching this office. I say to you quite frankly and without humbug that if you attempt to bring it yourself it's ten to one that you'll never get here.'

'I doubt that,' said Anthony. 'When I want to get anywhere, I usually do.'

'You're up against a very dangerous lot of people. I wouldn't have believed it myself a month ago. I tell you, Mr McGrath, we've been bribed and threatened and cajoled by one lot and another until we don't know whether we're on our heads or our heels. My suggestion is that you do not attempt to bring the manuscript here. One of our people will call upon you at the hotel and take possession of it.'

'And supposing the gang does him in?' asked Anthony.

'The responsibility would then be ours – not yours. You would have delivered it to our representative and obtained a written discharge. The cheque for – er – a thousand pounds which we are instructed to hand to you will not be available until Wednesday next by the terms of our agreement with the executors of the late – er – author – you know whom I mean, but if you insist I will send my own cheque for that amount by the messenger.'

Anthony reflected for a minute or two. He had intended to keep the memoirs until the last day of grace, because he was anxious to see for himself what all the fuss was about. Nevertheless, he realized the force of the publisher's arguments.

'All right,' he said, with a little sigh. 'Have it your own way. Send your man along. And if you don't mind sending that cheque as well I'd rather have it now, as I may be going out of England before next Wednesday.'

'Certainly, Mr McGrath. Our representative will call upon you first thing tomorrow morning. It will be wiser not to send anyone direct from the office. Our Mr Holmes lives in South London. He will call in on his way to us, and will give you a receipt for the package. I suggest that tonight you should place a dummy packet in the manager's safe. Your enemies will get to hear of this, and it will prevent any attack being made upon your apartments tonight.'

'Very well, I will do as you direct.'

Anthony hung up the receiver with a thoughtful face.

Then he went on with his interrupted plan of seeking news of the slippery Giuseppe. He drew a complete blank, however. Giuseppe had worked at the restaurant in question, but nobody seemed to know anything of his private life or associates.

'But I'll get you, my lad,' murmured Anthony, between his teeth. 'I'll get you yet. It's only a matter of time.'

His second night in London was entirely peaceful.

At nine o'clock the following morning, the card of Mr Holmes from Messrs Balderson and Hodgkins was sent up, and Mr Holmes followed it. A small, fair man with a quiet manner. Anthony handed over the manuscript, and received in exchange a cheque for a thousand pounds. Mr Holmes packed up the manuscript in the small brown bag he carried, wished Anthony good morning, and departed. The whole thing seemed very tame.

'But perhaps he'll be murdered on the way there,' Anthony murmured aloud, as he stared idly out of the window. 'I wonder now – I very much wonder.'

He put the cheque in an envelope, enclosed a few lines of writing with it, and sealed it up carefully. Jimmy, who had been more or less in funds at the time of his encounter with Anthony at Bulawayo, had advanced him a substantial sum of money which was, as yet, practically untouched.

'If one job's done with, the other isn't,' said Anthony to himself. 'Up to now, I've bungled it. But never say die. I think that, suitably disguised, I shall go and have a look at 487 Pont Street.'

He packed his belongings, went down and paid his bill, and ordered his luggage to be put on a taxi. Suitably rewarding those who stood in his path, most of whom had done nothing whatever materially to add to his comfort, he was on the point of being driven off, when a small boy rushed down the steps with a letter.

'Just come for you, this very minute, sir.'

With a sigh, Anthony produced yet another shilling. The

taxi groaned heavily and jumped forward with a hideous crashing of gears, and Anthony opened the letter.

It was rather a curious document. He had to read it four times before he could be sure of what it was all about. Put in plain English (the letter was not in plain English, but in the peculiar involved style common to missives issued by government officials) it presumed that Mr McGrath was arriving in England from South Africa today – Thursday, it referred obliquely to the memoirs of Count Stylptitch, and begged Mr McGrath to do nothing in the matter until he had had a confidential conversation with Mr George Lomax, and certain other parties whose magnificence was vaguely hinted at. It also contained a definite invitation to go down to Chimneys as the guest of Lord Caterham, on the following day, Friday.

A mysterious and thoroughly obscure communication. Anthony enjoyed it very much.

'Dear old England,' he murmured affectionately. 'Two days behind the times, as usual. Rather a pity. Still, I can't go down to Chimneys under false pretences. I wonder, though, if there's an inn handy? Mr Anthony Cade might stay at the inn without anyone being the wiser.'

He leaned out of the window, and gave new directions to the taxi driver, who acknowledged them with a snort of contempt.

The taxi drew up before one of London's more obscure hostelries. The fare, however, was paid on a scale befitting its point of departure.

Having booked a room in the name of Anthony Cade, Anthony passed into a dingy writing-room took out a sheet of notepaper stamped with the legend Hotel Blitz, and wrote rapidly.

He explained that he had arrived on the preceding Tuesday, that he had handed over the manuscript in question to Messrs Balderson and Hodgkins, and he regretfully declined the kind invitation of Lord Caterham as he was leaving England almost immediately. He signed the letter 'Yours faithfully, James McGrath.'

And now,' said Anthony, as he affixed the stamp to the envelope. 'To business. Exit James McGrath, and Enter Anthony Cade.'

CHAPTER VIII

A Dead Man

On that same Thursday afternoon Virginia Revel had been playing tennis at Ranelagh. All the way back to Pont Street, as she lay back in the long, luxurious limousine, a little smile played upon her lips as she rehearsed her part in the forthcoming interview. Of course it was within the bounds of possibility that the blackmailer might not reappear, but she felt pretty certain that he would. She had shown herself an easy prey. Well, perhaps this time there would be a little surprise for him!

When the car drew up at the house, she turned to speak to the chauffeur before going up the steps.

'How's your wife, Walton? I forgot to ask.'

'Better I think, ma'am. The doctor said he'd look in and see her about half past six. Will you be wanting the car again?'

Virginia reflected for a minute.

'I shall be away for the weekend. I'm going by the 6.40 from Paddington, but I shan't need you again – a taxi will do for that. I'd rather you saw the doctor. If he thinks it would do your wife good to go away for the weekend, take her somewhere, Walton. I'll stand the expense.'

Cutting short the man's thanks with an impatient nod of the head, Virginia ran up the steps, delved into her bag in search of her latch-key, remembered she hadn't got it with her, and hastily rang the bell.

It was not answered at once, but as she waited there a young man came up the steps. He was shabbily dressed, and carried in his hand a sheaf of leaflets. He held one out to Virginia with the legend on it plainly visible: 'Why Did I Serve My Country?' In his left hand he held a collecting box.

'I can't buy two of those awful poems in one day,' said Virginia pleadingly. 'I bought one this morning. I did, indeed, honour bright.'

The young man threw back his head and laughed. Virginia laughed with him. Running her eyes carelessly over him, she thought him a more pleasing specimen than usual of London's unemployed. She liked his brown face, and the lean hardness of him. She went so far as to wish she had a job for him.

But at that moment the door opened, and immediately Virginia forgot all about the problem of the unemployed, for to her astonishment the door was opened by her own maid, Elise.

'Where's Chilvers?' she demanded sharply, as she stepped into the hall.

'But he is gone, madame, with the others.'

'What others? Gone where?'

'But to Datchet, madame – to the cottage, as your telegram said.'

'My telegram?' said Virginia, utterly at sea.

'Did not madame send a telegram? Surely there can be no mistake. It came but an hour ago.'

'I never sent any telegram. What did it say?'

'I believe it is still on the table *là-bas*.'

Elise retired, pouncing upon it, and brought it to her mistress in triumph.

'*Voilà*, madame!'

The telegram was addressed to Chilvers and ran as follows:

'Please take household down to cottage at once, and make preparations for weekend party there. Catch 5.49 train.'

There was nothing unusual about it, it was just the sort of message she herself had frequently sent before, when she had arranged a party at her riverside bungalow on the spur of the moment. She always took the whole household down, leaving an old woman as caretaker. Chilvers would not have seen anything wrong with the message, and like a good servant had carried out his orders faithfully enough.

'Me, I remained,' explained Elise, 'knowing that madame would wish me to pack for her.'

'It's a silly hoax,' cried Virginia, flinging down the telegram angrily. 'You know perfectly well, Elise, that I am going to Chimneys. I told you so this morning.'

'I thought madame had changed her mind. Sometimes that does happen, does it not, madame?'

Virginia admitted the truth of the accusation with a half-smile. She was busy trying to find a reason for this extraordinary practical joke. Elise put forward a suggestion.

'*Mon Dieu!*' she cried, clasping her hands. 'If it should be the malefactors, the thieves! They send the bogus telegram and get the *domestiques* all out of the house, and then they rob it.'

'I suppose that might be it,' said Virginia doubtfully.

'Yes, yes madame, that is without a doubt. Every day you read in the papers of such things. Madame will ring up the police at once – at once – before they arrive and cut our throats.'

'Don't get so excited, Elise. They won't come and cut our throats at six o'clock in the afternoon.'

'Madame, I implore you, let me run out and fetch a policeman now, at once.'

'What on earth for? Don't be silly, Elise. Go up and pack my things for Chimneys, if you haven't already done it. The new Cailleaux evening dress, and the white crêpe marocain, and – yes, the black velvet – black velvet is so political, is it not?'

'Madame looks ravishing in the eau de nil satin,' suggested Elise, her professional instincts reasserting themselves.

'No, I won't take that. Hurry up, Elise, there's a good girl. We've got very little time. I'll send a wire to Chilvers at Datchet, and I'll speak to the policeman on the beat as we go out and tell him to keep an eye on the place. Don't start rolling your eyes again, Elise – if you get so frightened before anything has happened, what would you do if a man jumped out from some dark corner and stuck a knife into you?'

Elise gave vent to a shrill squeak, and beat a speedy retreat up the stairs, darting nervous glances over her shoulder as she went.

Virginia made a face at her retreating back, and crossed the hall to the little study where the telephone was. Elise's suggestion of ringing up the police station seemed to her a good one, and she intended to act upon it without any further delay.

She opened the study door and crossed to the telephone. Then, with her hand on the receiver, she stopped. A man was sitting in the big armchair, sitting in a curious huddled position. In the stress of the moment, she had forgotten all about her expected visitor. Apparently he had fallen asleep whilst waiting for her.

She came right up to the chair, a slightly mischievous smile upon her face. And then suddenly the smile faded.

The man was not asleep. *He was dead.*

She knew it at once, knew it instinctively even before her eyes had seen and noted the small shining pistol lying on the floor, the little-singed hole just above the heart with the dark stain round it, and the horrible dropped jaw.

She stood quite still, her hands pressed to her sides. In the silence she heard Elise running down the stairs.

'Madame! Madame!'

'Well, what is it?'

She moved quickly to the door. Her whole instinct was to conceal what had happened – for the moment anyway – from Elise. Elise would promptly go into hysterics, she knew that well enough, and she felt a great need for calm and quiet in which to think things out.

'Madame, would it not be better if I should draw the chain across the door? These malefactors, at any minute they may arrive.'

'Yes, if you like. Anything you like.'

She heard the rattle of the chain, and then Elise running upstairs again, and drew a long breath of relief.

She looked at the man in the chair and then at the telephone.

Her course was quite clear, she must ring up the police at once.

But still she did not do so. She stood quite still, paralysed with horror and with a host of conflicting ideas rushing through her brain. The bogus telegram! Had it something to do with this? Supposing Elise had not stayed behind? She would have let herself in – that is, presuming she had had her latch-key with her as usual to find herself alone in the house with a murdered man – a man whom she had permitted to blackmail her on a former occasion. Of course she had an explanation of that; but thinking of that explanation she was not quite easy in her mind. She remembered how frankly incredible George had found it. Would other people think the same? Those letters now – of course, she hadn't written them, but would it be so easy to prove that?

She put her hands on her forehead, squeezing them tight together.

'I must think,' said Virginia. 'I simply must think.'

Who had let the man in? Surely not Elise. If she had done so, she would have been sure to have mentioned the fact at once. The whole thing seemed more and more mysterious as she thought about it. There was really only one thing to be done – ring up the police.

She stretched out her hand to the telephone, and suddenly she thought of George. A man – that was what she wanted – an ordinary level-headed, unemotional man who would see things in their proper proportion and point out to her the best course to take.

Then she shook her head. Not George. The first thing George would think of would be his own position. He would hate being mixed up in this kind of business. George wouldn't do at all.

Then her face softened. Bill, of course! Without more ado, she rang up Bill.

She was informed that he had left half an hour ago for Chimneys.

'Oh, damn!' cried Virginia, jamming down the receiver. It

was horrible to be shut up with a dead body and to have no one to speak to.

And at that minute the front-door bell rang.

Virginia jumped. In a few minutes it rang again. Elise, she knew, was upstairs packing and wouldn't hear it.

Virginia went out in the hall, drew back the chain, and undid all the bolts that Elise had fastened in her zeal. Then, with a long breath, she threw open the door. On the steps was the unemployed young man.

Virginia plunged headlong with a relief born of overstrung nerves.

'Come in,' she said. 'I think perhaps I've got a job for you.'

She took him into the dining-room, pulled forward a chair for him, sat herself facing him, and stared at him very attentively.

'Excuse me,' she said, 'but are you – I mean –'

'Eton and Oxford,' said the young man. 'That's what you wanted to ask me, wasn't it?'

'Something of the kind,' admitted Virginia.

'Come down in the world entirely through my own incapacity to stick to regular work. This isn't regular work you're offering me, I hope?'

A smile hovered for a moment on her lips.

'It's very irregular.'

'Good,' said the young man in a tone of satisfaction.

Virginia noted his bronzed face and long lean body with approval.

'You see,' she explained. 'I'm in rather a hole, and most of my friends are – well, rather high up. They've all got something to lose.'

'I've nothing whatever to lose. So go ahead. What's the trouble?'

'There's a dead man in the next room,' said Virginia. 'He's been murdered, and I don't know what to do about it.'

She blurted out the words as simply as a child might have done. The young man went up enormously in her estimation by the way he accepted her statement. He might have been

used to hearing a similar announcement made every day of
his life.

'Excellent,' he said, with a trace of enthusiasm. 'I've always
wanted to do a bit of amateur detective work. Shall we go and
view the body, or will you give me the facts first?'

'I think I'd better give you the facts.' She paused for a
moment to consider how best to condense her story, and then
began speaking quietly and concisely:

'This man came to the house for the first time yesterday
and asked to see me. He had certain letters with him – love
letters, signed with my name –'

'But which weren't written by you,' put in the young man
quietly.

Virginia looked at him in some astonishment.

'How did you know that?'

'Oh, I deduced it. But go on.'

'He wanted to blackmail me – and I – well, I don't know
if you'll understand, but I – let him.'

She looked at him appealingly, and he nodded his head
reassuringly.

'Of course I understand. You wanted to see what it felt
like.'

'How frightfully clever of you! That's just what I did feel.'

'I *am* clever,' said the young man modestly. 'But, mind you,
very few people would understand that point of view. Most
people, you see, haven't got any imagination.'

'I suppose that's so. I told this man to come back today –
at six o'clock. I arrived home from Ranelagh to find that a
bogus telegram had got all the servants except my maid out
of the house. Then I walked into the study and found the man
shot.'

'Who let him in?'

'I don't know. I think if my maid had done so she would
have told me.'

'Does she know what has happened?'

'I have told her nothing.'

The young man nodded, and rose to his feet.

'And now to view the body,' he said briskly. 'But I'll tell you this – on the whole it's always best to tell the truth. One lie involves you in such a lot of lies – and continuous lying is so monotonous.'

'Then you advise me to ring up the police?'

'Probably. But we'll just have a look at the fellow first.'

Virginia led the way out of the room. On the threshold she paused, looking back at him.

'By the way,' she said, 'you haven't told me your name yet?'

'My name? My name's Anthony Cade.'

CHAPTER IX

Anthony Disposes of a Body

Anthony followed Virginia out of the room, smiling a little to himself. Events had taken quite an unexpected turn. But as he bent over the figure in the chair he grew grave again.

'He's still warm,' he said sharply. 'He was killed less than half an hour ago.'

'Just before I came in?'

'Exactly.'

He stood upright, drawing his brows together in a frown. Then he asked a question of which Virginia did not at once see the drift:

'Your maid's not been in this room, of course?'

'No.'

'Does she know that you've been into it?'

'Why – yes. I came to the door to speak to her.'

'After you'd found the body?'

'Yes.'

'And you said nothing?'

'Would it have been better if I had? I thought she would go into hysterics – she's French, you know, and easily upset – I wanted to think over the best thing to do.'

Anthony nodded, but did not speak.

'You think it a pity, I can see?'

'Well, it was rather unfortunate, Mrs Revel. If you and the maid had discovered the body together, immediately on your return, it would have simplified matters very much. The man would then definitely have been shot *before* your return to the house.'

'Whilst now they might say he was shot *after* – I see –'

He watched her taking in the idea, and was confirmed in his first impression of her formed when she had spoken to him on the steps outside. Besides beauty, she possessed courage and brains.

Virginia was so engrossed in the puzzle presented to her that it did not occur to her to wonder at this strange man's ready use of her name.

'Why didn't Elise hear the shot, I wonder?' she murmured.

Anthony pointed to the open window, as a loud backfire came from a passing car.

'There you are. London's not the place to notice a pistol shot.'

Virginia turned with a little shudder to the body in the chair.

'He looks like an Italian,' she remarked curiously.

'He is an Italian,' said Anthony. 'I should say that his regular profession was that of a waiter. He only did black-mailing in his spare time. His name might very possibly be Giuseppe.'

'Good heavens!' cried Virginia. 'Is this Sherlock Holmes?'

'No,' said Anthony regretfully. 'I'm afraid it's just plain or garden cheating. I'll tell you all about it presently. Now you say this man showed you some letters and asked you for money. Did you give him any?'

'Yes, I did.'

'How much?'

'Forty pounds.'

'That's bad,' said Anthony, but without manifesting any undue surprise. 'Now let's have a look at the telegram.'

Virginia picked it up from the table and gave it to him. She saw his face grow grave as he looked at it.

'What's the matter?'

He held it out, pointing silently to the place of origin.

'Barnes,' he said. 'And you were at Ranelagh this afternoon. What's to prevent you having sent it off yourself?'

Virginia felt fascinated by his words. It was as though a net was closing tighter and tighter round her. He was forcing her to see all the things which she had felt dimly at the back of her mind.

Anthony took out his handkerchief and wound it round his hand, then he picked up the pistol.

'We criminals have to be so careful,' he said apologetically. 'Fingerprints, you know.'

Suddenly she saw his whole figure stiffen. His voice, when he spoke, had altered. It was terse and curt.

'Mrs Revel,' he said, 'have you ever seen this pistol before?'

'No,' said Virginia wonderingly.

'Are you sure of that?'

'Quite sure.'

'Have you a pistol of your own?'

'No.'

'Have you ever had one?'

'No, never.'

'You are sure of that?'

'Quite sure.'

He stared at her steadily for a minute, and Virginia stared back in complete surprise at his tone.

Then, with a sigh, he relaxed.

'That's odd,' he said. 'How do you account for this?'

He held out the pistol. It was a small, dainty article, almost a toy – though capable of doing deadly work. Engraved on it was the name Virginia.

'Oh, it's impossible!' cried Virginia.

Her astonishment was so genuine that Anthony could but believe in it.

'Sit down,' he said quietly. 'There's more in this than there seemed to be first go off. To begin with, what's our hypothesis? There are only two possible ones. There is, of course, the real Virginia of the letters. She may have somehow or other tracked him down, shot him, dropped the pistol, stolen the letters, and taken herself off. That's quite possible, isn't it?'

'I suppose so,' said Virginia unwillingly.

'The other hypothesis is a good deal more interesting. Whoever wished to kill Giuseppe, wished also to incriminate you

– in fact, that may have been their main object. They could get *him* easily enough anywhere, but they took extraordinary pains and trouble to get him *here*, and whoever they were they knew all about you, your cottage at Datchet, your usual household arrangements, and the fact that you were at Ranelagh this afternoon. It seems an absurd question, but have you any enemies, Mrs Revel?'

'Of course I haven't – not that kind, anyway.'

'The question is,' said Anthony, 'what are we going to do now? There are two courses open to us. A: ring up the police, tell the whole story, and trust to your unassailable position in the world and your hitherto blameless life. B: an attempt on my part to dispose successfully of the body. Naturally my private inclinations urge me to B. I've always wanted to see if I couldn't conceal a crime with the necessary cunning, but have had a squeamish objection to shedding blood. On the whole, I expect A's the soundest. Then here's a sort of bowdlerized A. Ring up the police, etc, but suppress the pistol and the blackmailing letters – that is, if they are on him still.'

Anthony ran rapidly through the dead man's pockets.

'He's been stripped clean,' he announced. 'There's not a thing on him. There'll be dirty work at the crossroads over those letters yet. Hullo, what's this? Hole in the lining – something got caught there, torn roughly out, and a scrap of paper left behind.'

He drew out the scrap of paper as he spoke, and brought it over to the light. Virginia joined him.

'Pity we haven't got the rest of it,' he muttered. 'Chimneys 11.45 Thursday – Sounds like an appointment.'

'Chimneys?' cried Virginia. 'How extraordinary!'

'Why extraordinary? Rather high-toned for such a low fellow?'

'I'm going to Chimneys this evening. At least I was.'

Anthony wheeled round on her.

'What's that? Say that again.'

'I was going to Chimneys this evening,' repeated Virginia. Anthony stared at her.

'I begin to see. At least, I may be wrong – but it's an idea. Suppose someone wanted badly to prevent your going to Chimneys?'

'My cousin George Lomax does,' said Virginia with a smile. 'But I can't seriously suspect George of murder.'

Anthony did not smile. He was lost in thought.

'If you ring up the police, it's goodbye to any idea of getting to Chimneys today – or even tomorrow. And I should like you to go to Chimneys. I fancy it will disconcert our unknown friends. Mrs Revel, will you put yourself in my hands?'

'It's to be Plan B, then?'

'It's to be Plan B. The first thing is to get that maid of yours out of the house. Can you manage that?'

'Easily.'

Virginia went out in the hall and called up the stairs.

'Elise. Elise.'

'Madame?'

Anthony heard a rapid colloquy, and then the front door opened and shut. Virginia came back into the room.

'She's gone. I sent her for some special scent – told her the shop in question was open until eight. It won't be, of course. She's to follow after me by the next train without coming back here.'

'Good,' said Anthony approvingly. 'We can now proceed to the disposal of the body. It's a timeworn method, but I'm afraid I shall have to ask you if there's such a thing in the house as a trunk?'

'Of course there is. Come down to the basement and take your choice.'

There was a variety of trunks in the basement. Anthony selected a solid affair of suitable size.

'I'll attend to this part of it,' he said tactfully. 'You go upstairs and get ready to start.'

Virginia obeyed. She slipped out of her tennis kit, put on a soft brown travelling dress and a delightful little orange hat, and came down to find Anthony waiting in the hall with a neatly strapped trunk beside him.

'I should like to tell you the story of my life,' he remarked, 'but it's going to be rather a busy evening. Now this is what you've got to do. Call a taxi, have your luggage put on it, including the trunk. Drive to Paddington. There have the trunk put in the Left Luggage Office. I shall be on the platform. As you pass me, drop the cloakroom ticket. I will pick it up and return it to you, but in reality I shall keep it. Go on to Chimneys, and leave the rest to me.'

'It's awfully good of you,' said Virginia. 'It's really dreadful of me saddling a perfect stranger with a dead body like this.'

'I like it,' returned Anthony nonchalantly. 'If one of my friends, Jimmy McGrath, were here, he'd tell you that anything of this kind suits me down to the ground.'

Virginia was staring at him.

'What name did you say? Jimmy McGrath?'

Anthony returned her glance keenly.

'Yes. Why? Have you heard of him?'

'Yes – and quite lately.' She paused irresolutely, and then went on. 'Mr Cade, I must talk to you. Can't you come down to Chimneys?'

'You'll see me before very long, Mrs Revel – I'll tell you that. Now, exit Conspirator A by back door slinkingly. Exit Conspirator B in blaze of glory by front door to taxi.'

The plan went through without a hitch. Anthony, having picked up a second taxi, was on the platform and duly retrieved the fallen ticket. He then departed in search of a somewhat battered second-hand Morris Cowley which he had acquired earlier in the day in case it should be necessary to his plans.

Returning to Paddington in this, he handed the ticket to the porter, who got the trunk out of the cloakroom and wedged it securely at the back of the car. Anthony drove off.

His objective now was out of London. Through Notting Hill, Shepherd's Bush, down Goldhawk Road, through Brentford and Hounslow till he came to the long stretch of road midway between Hounslow and Staines. It was a well-frequented road, with motors passing continuously. No footmarks or tyremarks were likely to show. Anthony stopped the car at a certain spot. Getting down, he first obscured the number-plate with mud. Then, waiting until he heard no car coming in either direction, he opened the trunk, heaved out Giuseppe's body, and laid it neatly down by the side of the road, on the inside of a curve, so that the headlights of passing motors would not strike on it.

Then he entered the car again and drove away. The whole business had occupied exactly one minute and a half. He made a detour to the right, returning to London by way of Burnham Beeches. There again he halted the car, and choosing a giant of the forest he deliberately climbed the huge tree. It was something of a feat, even for Anthony. To one of the topmost branches he affixed a small brown-paper parcel, concealing it in a little niche close to the bole.

'A very clever way of disposing of the pistol,' said Anthony to himself with some approval. 'Everybody hunts about on the ground, and drags ponds. But there are very few people in England who could climb that tree.'

Next, back to London and Paddington Station. Here he left the trunk – at the other cloakroom this time, the one on the Arrival side. He thought longingly of such things as good rump steaks, juicy chops, and large masses of fried potatoes. But he shook his head ruefully, glancing at his wristwatch. He fed the Morris with a fresh supply of petrol, and then took the road once more. North this time.

It was just after half past eleven that he brought the car to rest in the road adjoining the park of Chimneys. Jumping out he scaled the wall easily enough, and set out towards the house. It took him longer than he thought, and presently he broke into a run. A great grey mass loomed up out of the darkness – the venerable pile of Chimneys. In the distance a stable clock chimed the three-quarters.

11.45 – the time mentioned on the scrap of paper. Anthony was on the terrace now, looking up at the house. Everything seemed dark and quiet.

'They go to bed early, these politicians,' he murmured to himself.

And suddenly a sound smote upon his ears – the sound of a shot. Anthony spun round quickly. The sound had come from within the house – he was sure of that. He waited a minute, but everything was still as death. Finally he went up to one of the long french windows from where he judged the sound that had startled him had come. He tried the handle. It was locked. He tried some of the other windows, listening intently all the while. But the silence remained unbroken.

In the end he told himself that he must have imagined the sound, or perhaps mistaken a stray shot coming from a poacher in the woods. He turned and retraced his steps across the park, vaguely dissatisfied and uneasy.

He looked back at the house, and whilst he looked a light sprang up in one of the windows on the first floor. In another minute it went out again, and the whole place was in darkness once more.

CHAPTER X

Chimneys

Inspector Badgworthy in his office. Time, 8.30 A.M. A tall portly man, Inspector Badgworthy, with a heavy regulation tread. Inclined to breathe hard in moments of professional strain. In attendance Constable Johnson, very new to the Force, with a downy unfledged look about him, like a human chicken.

The telephone on the table rang sharply, and the inspector took it up with his usual portentous gravity of action.

'Yes. Police station Market Basing. Inspector Badgworthy speaking. What?'

Slight alteration in the inspector's manner. As he is greater than Johnson, so others are greater than Inspector Badgworthy.

'Speaking, my lord. I beg your pardon, my lord? I didn't quite hear what you said?'

Long pause, during which the inspector listens, quite a variety of expressions passing over his usually impassive countenance. Finally he lays down the receiver, after a brief 'At once, my lord.'

He turned to Johnson, seeming visibly swelled with importance.

'From his lordship – at Chimneys – murder.'

'Murder,' echoed Johnson, suitably impressed.

'Murder it is,' said the inspector, with great satisfaction.

'Why, there's never been a murder here – not that I've ever heard of – except the time that Tom Pearse shot his sweetheart.'

'And that, in a manner of speaking, wasn't murder at all, but drink,' said the inspector, deprecatingly.

'He weren't hanged for it,' agreed Johnson gloomily. 'But this is the real thing, is it, sir?'

'It is, Johnson. One of his lordship's guests, a foreign gentleman, discovered shot. Open window, and footprints outside.'

'I'm sorry it were a foreigner,' said Johnson, with some regret.

It made the murder seem less real. Foreigners, Johnson felt, were liable to be shot.

'His lordship's in a rare taking,' continued the inspector. 'We'll get hold of Dr Cartwright and take him up with us right away. I hope to goodness no one will get messing with those footprints.'

Badgworthy was in a seventh heaven. A murder! At Chimneys! Inspector Badgworthy in charge of the case. The police have a clue. Sensational arrest. Promotion and kudos for the aforementioned inspector.

'That is,' said Inspector Badgworthy to himself, 'if Scotland Yard doesn't come butting in.'

The thought damped him momentarily. It seemed so extremely likely to happen under the circumstances.

They stopped at Dr Cartwright's, and the doctor, who was a comparatively young man, displayed a keen interest. His attitude was almost exactly that of Johnson.

'Why, bless my soul,' he exclaimed. 'We haven't had a murder here since the time of Tom Pearse.'

All three of them got into the doctor's little car, and started off briskly for Chimneys. As they passed the local inn, the Jolly Cricketers, the doctor noticed a man standing in the doorway.

'Stranger,' he remarked. 'Rather a nice-looking fellow. Wonder how long he's been here, and what he's doing staying at the Cricketers? I haven't seen him about at all. He must have arrived last night.'

'He didn't come by train,' said Johnson.

Johnson's brother was the local railway porter, and Johnson was therefore always well up in arrivals and departures.

'Who was here for Chimneys yesterday?' asked the inspector.

'Lady Eileen, she come down by the 3.40, and two gentlemen with her, an American gent and a young Army chap – neither of them with valets. His lordship come down with a foreign gentleman, the one that's been shot as likely as not, by the 5.40, and the foreign gentleman's valet. Mr Eversleigh come by the same train. Mrs Revel came by the 7.25, and another foreign-looking gentleman came by it too, one with a bald head and a hook nose. Mrs Revel's maid came by the 8.56.'

Johnson paused, out of breath.

'And there was no one for the Cricketers?'

Johnson shook his head.

'He must have come by car then,' said the inspector. 'Johnson, make a note to institute inquiries at the Cricketers on your way back. We want to know all about any strangers. He was very sunburnt, that gentleman. Likely as not, he's come from foreign parts too.'

The inspector nodded his head with great sagacity, as though to imply that that was the sort of wide-awake man he was – not to be caught napping under any consideration.

The car passed in through the park gates of Chimneys. Descriptions of that historic place can be found in any guidebook. It is also No 3 in *Historic Homes of England*, price 21s. On Thursday, coaches come over from Middlingham and view those portions of it which are open to the public. In view of all these facilities, to describe Chimneys would be superfluous.

They were received at the door by a white-headed butler whose demeanour was perfect.

'We are not accustomed,' it seemed to say, 'to having murder committed within these walls. But these are evil days. Let us meet disaster with perfect calm, and pretend with our dying breath that nothing out of the usual has occurred.'

'His lordship,' said the butler, 'is expecting you. This way, if you please.'

He led them to a small cosy room which was Lord Caterham's refuge from the magnificence elsewhere, and announced them.

'The police, my lord, and Dr Cartwright.'

Lord Caterham was pacing up and down in a visibly agitated state.

'Ha! Inspector, you've turned up at last. I'm thankful for that. How are you, Cartwright? This is the very devil of a business, you know. The very devil of a business.'

And Lord Caterham, running his hands through his hair in a frenzied fashion until it stood upright in little tufts, looked even less like a peer of the realm than usual.

'Where's the body?' asked the doctor, in curt business-like fashion.

Lord Caterham turned to him as though relieved at being asked a direct question.

'In the Council Chamber – just where it was found – I wouldn't have it touched. I believed – er – that that was the correct thing to do.'

'Quite right, my lord,' said the inspector approvingly.

He produced a notebook and pencil.

'And who discovered the body? Did you?'

'Good Lord, no,' said Lord Caterham. 'You don't think I usually get up at this unearthly hour in the morning, do you? No, a housemaid found it. She screamed a good deal, I believe. I didn't hear her myself. Then they came to me about it, and of course I got up and came down – and there it was, you know.'

'You recognized the body as that of one of your guests?'

'That's right, Inspector.'

'By name?'

This perfectly simple question seemed to upset Lord Caterham. He opened his mouth once or twice, and then shut it again. Finally he asked feebly:

'Do you mean – do you mean – what was his name?'

'Yes, my lord.'

'Well,' said Lord Caterham, looking slowly round the room,

as though hoping to gain inspiration. 'His name was – I should say it was – yes, decidedly so – Count Stanislaus.'

There was something so odd about Lord Caterham's manner, that the inspector ceased using his pencil and stared at him instead. But at that moment a diversion occurred which seemed highly welcome to the embarrassed peer.

The door opened and a girl came into the room. She was tall, slim and dark, with an attractive boyish face, and a very determined manner. This was Lady Eileen Brent, commonly known as Bundle, Lord Caterham's eldest daughter. She nodded to the others, and addressed her father directly.

'I've got him,' she announced.

For a moment the inspector was on the point of starting forward under the impression that the young lady had captured the murderer red-handed, but almost immediately he realized that her meaning was quite different.

Lord Caterham uttered a sigh of relief.

'That's a good job. What did he say?'

'He's coming over at once. We are to "use the utmost discretion".'

Her father made a sound of annoyance.

'That's just the sort of idiotic thing George Lomax would say. However, once he comes, I shall wash my hands of the whole affair.'

He appeared to cheer up a little at the prospect.

'And the name of the murdered man was Count Stanislaus?' queried the doctor.

A lightning glance passed between father and daughter, and then the former said with some dignity:

'Certainly. I said so just now.'

'I asked because you didn't seem quite sure about it before,' explained Cartwright.

There was a faint twinkle in his eye, and Lord Caterham looked at him reproachfully.

'I'll take you to the Council Chamber,' he said more briskly.

They followed him, the inspector bringing up the rear, and darting sharp glances all around him as he went, much as though he expected to find a clue in a picture frame, or behind a door.

Lord Caterham took a key from his pocket and unlocked a door, flinging it open. They all passed into a big room panelled in oak, with three french windows giving on the terrace. There was a long refectory table and a good many oak chests, and some beautiful old chairs. On the walls were various paintings of dead and gone Caterhams and others.

Near the left-hand wall, about halfway between the door and the window, a man was lying on his back, his arms flung wide.

Dr Cartwright went over and knelt down by the body. The inspector strode across to the windows, and examined them in turn. The centre one was closed, but not fastened. On the steps outside were footprints leading up to the window, and a second set going away again.

'Clear enough,' said the inspector, with a nod. 'But there ought to be footprints on the inside as well. They'd show up plain on this parquet floor.'

'I think I can explain that,' interposed Bundle. 'The housemaid had polished half the floor this morning before she saw the body. You see, it was dark when she came in here. She went straight across to the windows, drew the curtains, and began on the floor, and naturally didn't see the body which is hidden from that side of the room by the table. She didn't see it until she came right on top of it.'

The inspector nodded.

'Well,' said Lord Caterham, eager to escape. 'I'll leave you here, Inspector. You'll be able to find me if you – er – want me. But Mr George Lomax is coming over from Wyvern Abbey shortly, and he'll be able to tell you far more than I could. It's his business really. I can't explain, but he will when he comes.'

Lord Caterham beat a precipitate retreat without waiting for a reply.

'Too bad of Lomax,' he complained. 'Letting me in for this. What's the matter, Tredwell?'

The white-haired butler was hovering deferentially at his elbow.

'I have taken the liberty, my lord, of advancing the breakfast hour as far as you are concerned. Everything is ready in the dining-room.'

'I don't suppose for a minute I can eat anything,' said Lord Caterham gloomily, turning his footsteps in that direction. 'Not for a moment.'

Bundle slipped her hand through his arm, and they entered the dining-room together. On the sideboard were half a score of heavy silver dishes, ingeniously kept hot by patent arrangements.

'Omelette,' said Lord Caterham, lifting each lid in turn. 'Eggs and bacon, kidneys, devilled bird, haddock, cold ham, cold pheasant. I don't like any of these things, Tredwell. Ask the cook to poach me an egg, will you?'

'Very good, my lord.'

Tredwell withdrew. Lord Caterham, in an absent-minded fashion, helped himself plentifully to kidneys and bacon, poured himself out a cup of coffee, and sat down at the long table. Bundle was already busy with a plateful of eggs and bacon.

'I'm damned hungry,' said Bundle with her mouth full. 'It must be the excitement.'

'It's all very well for you,' complained her father. 'You young people like excitement. But I'm in a very delicate state of health. Avoid all worry, that's what Sir Abner Willis said – avoid all worry. So easy for a man sitting in his consulting-room in Harley Street to say that. How can I avoid worry when that ass Lomax lands me with a thing like this? I ought to have been firm at the time. I ought to have put my foot down.'

With a sad shake of the head, Lord Caterham rose and carved himself a plate of ham.

'Codders has certainly done it this time,' observed Bundle cheerfully. 'He was almost incoherent over the telephone. He'll be here in a minute or two, spluttering nineteen to the dozen about discretion and hushing it up.'

Lord Caterham groaned at the prospect.

'Was he up?' he asked.

'He told me,' replied Bundle, 'that he had been up and dictating letters and memoranda ever since seven o'clock.'

'Proud of it, too,' remarked her father. 'Extraordinarily selfish, these public men. They make their wretched secretaries get up at the most unearthly hours in order to dictate rubbish to them. If a law was passed compelling them to stop in bed until eleven, what a benefit it would be to the nation! I wouldn't mind so much if they didn't talk such balderdash. Lomax is always talking to me of my "position". As if I had any. Who wants to be a peer nowadays?'

'Nobody,' said Bundle. 'They'd much rather keep a prosperous public-house.'

Tredwell reappeared silently with two poached eggs in a little silver dish which he placed on the table in front of Lord Caterham.

'What's that, Tredwell?' said the latter, looking at them with faint distaste.

'Poached eggs, my lord.'

'I hate poached eggs,' said Lord Caterham peevishly. 'They're so insipid. I don't like to look at them even. Take them away, will you, Tredwell?'

'Very good, my lord.'

Tredwell and the poached eggs withdrew as silently as they came.

'Thank God no one gets up early in this house,' remarked Lord Caterham devoutly. 'We shall have to break this to them when they do, I suppose.'

He sighed.

'I wonder who murdered him,' said Bundle. 'And why?'

'That's not our business, thank goodness,' said Lord Caterham. 'That's for the police to find out. Not that Badgworthy will ever find anything. On the whole I rather hope it was Nosystein.'

'Meaning –'

'The all-British syndicate.'

'Why should Mr Isaacstein murder him when he'd come down here on purpose to meet him?'

'High finance,' said Lord Caterham vaguely. 'And that reminds me, I shouldn't be at all surprised if Isaacstein wasn't an early riser. He may blow in upon us at any minute. It's a habit in the city. I believe that, however rich you are, you always catch the 9.17.'

The sound of a motor being driven at great speed was heard through the open window.

'Codders,' cried Bundle.

Father and daughter leaned out of the window and hailed the occupant of the car as it drew up before the entrance.

'In here, my dear fellow, in here,' cried Lord Caterham, hastily swallowing his mouthful of ham.

George had no intention of climbing in through the window. He disappeared through the front door, and reappeared ushered in by Tredwell, who withdrew at once.

'Have some breakfast,' said Lord Caterham, shaking him by the hand. 'What about a kidney?'

George waved the kidney aside impatiently.

'This is a terrible calamity, terrible, terrible.'

'It is indeed. Some haddock?'

'No, no. It must be hushed up – at all costs it must be hushed up.'

As Bundle had prophesied, George began to splutter.

'I understand your feelings,' said Lord Caterham sympathetically. 'Try an egg and bacon, or some haddock.'

'A totally unforeseen contingency – national calamity – concessions jeopardized –'

'Take time,' said Lord Caterham. 'And take some food. What you need is some food, to pull you together. Poached eggs now? There were some poached eggs here a minute or two ago.'

'I don't want any food,' said George. 'I've had breakfast, and even if I hadn't had any I shouldn't want it. We must think what is to be done. You have told no one as yet?'

'Well, there's Bundle and myself. And the local police. And Cartwright. And all the servants of course.'

George groaned.

'Pull yourself together, my dear fellow,' said Lord Caterham kindly. '(I wish you'd have some breakfast.) You don't seem to realize that you can't hush up a dead body. It's got to be buried and all that sort of thing. Very unfortunate, but there it is.'

George became suddenly calm.

'You are right, Caterham. You have called in the local police, you say? That will not do. We must have Battle.'

'Battle, murder and sudden death,' inquired Lord Caterham, with a puzzled face.

'No, no, you misunderstand me. I referred to Superintendent Battle of Scotland Yard. A man of the utmost discretion. He worked with us in that deplorable business of the Party funds.'

'What was that?' asked Lord Caterham, with some interest.

But George's eye had fallen upon Bundle, as she sat half in and half out of the window, and he remembered discretion just in time. He rose.

'We must waste no time. I must send off some wires at once.'

'If you write them out, Bundle will send them through the telephone.'

George pulled out a fountain pen and began to write with incredible rapidity. He handed the first one to Bundle, who read it with a great deal of interest.

'God! what a name,' she remarked. 'Baron How Much?'

'Baron Lolopretjzyl.'

Bundle blinked.

'I've got it, but it will take some conveying to the post office.'

George continued to write. Then he handed his labours to Bundle and addressed the master of the house:

'The best thing that you can do, Caterham –'

'Yes,' said Lord Caterham apprehensively.

'Is to leave everything in my hands.'

'Certainly,' said Lord Caterham, with alacrity. 'Just what I was thinking myself. You'll find the police and Dr Cartwright in the Council Chamber. With the – er – with the body, you know. My dear Lomax, I place Chimneys unreservedly at your disposal. Do anything you like.'

'Thank you,' said George. 'If I should want to consult you –'

But Lord Caterham had faded unobtrusively through the farther door. Bundle had observed his retreat with a grim smile.

'I'll send off those telegrams at once,' she said. 'You know your way to the Council Chamber?'

'Thank you, Lady Eileen.'

George hurried from the room.

CHAPTER XI

Superintendent Battle Arrives

So apprehensive was Lord Caterham of being consulted by George that he spent the whole morning making a tour of his estate. Only the pangs of hunger drew him homeward. He also reflected that by now the worst would surely be over.

He sneaked into the house quietly by a small side door. From there he slipped neatly into his sanctum. He flattered himself that his entrance had not been observed, but there he was mistaken. The watchful Tredwell let nothing escape him. He presented himself at the door.

'You'll excuse me, my lord –'

'What is it, Tredwell?'

'Mr Lomax, my lord, is anxious to see you in the library as soon as you return.'

By this delicate method Tredwell conveyed that Lord Caterham had not yet returned unless he chose to say so.

Lord Caterham sighed, and then rose.

'I suppose it will have to be done sooner or later. In the library, you say?'

'Yes, my lord.'

Sighing again, Lord Caterham crossed the wide spaces of his ancestral home, and reached the library door. The door was locked. As he rattled the handle, it was unlocked from inside, opened a little way, and the face of George Lomax appeared, peering out suspiciously.

His face changed when he saw who it was.

'Ah, Caterham, come in. We were just wondering what had become of you.'

Murmuring something vague about duties on the estate, repairs for tenants, Lord Caterham sidled in apologetically.

There were two other men in the room. One was Colonel Melrose, the chief constable. The other was a squarely built middle-aged man with a face so singularly devoid of expression as to be quite remarkable.

'Superintendent Battle arrived half an hour ago,' explained George. 'He has been round with Inspector Badgworthy, and seen Dr Cartwright. He now wants a few facts from us.'

They all sat down, after Lord Caterham had greeted Melrose and acknowledged his introduction to Superintendent Battle.

'I need hardly tell you, Battle,' said George, 'that this is a case in which we must use the utmost discretion.'

The superintendent nodded in an offhand manner that rather took Lord Caterham's fancy.

'That will be all right, Mr Lomax. But no concealments from us. I understand that the dead gentleman was called Count Stanislaus – at least, that that is the name by which the household knew him. Now was that his real name?'

'It was not.'

'What was his real name?'

'Prince Michael of Herzoslovakia.'

Battle's eyes opened just a trifle, otherwise he gave no sign.

'And what, if I may ask the question, was the purpose of his visit here? Just pleasure?'

'There was a further object, Battle. All this in the strictest confidence, of course.'

'Yes, yes, Mr Lomax.'

'Colonel Melrose?'

'Of course.'

'Well, then, Prince Michael was here for the express purpose of meeting Mr Herman Isaacstein. A loan was to be arranged on certain terms.'

'Which were?'

'I do not know the exact details. Indeed, they had not yet been arranged. But in the event of coming to the throne, Prince Michael pledged himself to grant certain oil concessions to those companies in which Mr Isaacstein is interested. The

British Government was prepared to support the claim of Prince Michael to the throne in view of his pronounced British sympathies.'

'Well,' said Superintendent Battle, 'I don't suppose I need go further into it than that. Prince Michael wanted the money, Mr Isaacstein wanted oil, and the British Government was ready to do the heavy father. Just one question. Was anyone else after those concessions?'

'I believe an American group of financiers had made overtures to His Highness.'

'And been turned down, eh?'

But George refused to be drawn.

'Prince Michael's sympathies were entirely pro-British,' he repeated.

Superintendent Battle did not press the point.

'Lord Caterham, I understand that this is what occurred yesterday. You met Prince Michael in town and journeyed down here in company with him. The Prince was accompanied by his valet, a Herzoslovakian named Boris Anchoukoff, but his equerry, Captain Andrassy, remained in town. The Prince, on arriving, declared himself greatly fatigued, and retired to the apartments set aside for him. Dinner was served to him there, and he did not meet the other members of the house party. Is that correct?'

'Quite correct.'

'This morning a housemaid discovered the body at approximately 7.45 A.M. Dr Cartwright examined the dead man and found that death was the result of a bullet fired from a revolver. No revolver was found, and no one in the house seems to have heard the shot. On the other hand the dead man's wristwatch was smashed by the fall, and marks the crime as having been committed at exactly a quarter to twelve. Now what time did you retire to bed last night?'

'We went early. Somehow or other the party didn't seem to "go", if you know what I mean, Superintendent. We went up about half past ten, I should say.'

'Thank you. Now I will ask you, Lord Caterham, to give

me a description of all the people staying in the house.'

'But, excuse me, I thought the fellow who did it came from outside?'

Superintendent Battle smiled.

'I dare say he did. I dare say he did. But all the same I've got to know who was in the house. Matter of routine, you know.'

'Well, there was Prince Michael and his valet and Mr Herman Isaacstein. You know all about them. Then there was Mr Eversleigh –'

'Who works in my department,' put in George condescendingly.

'And who was acquainted with the real reason of Prince Michael's being here?'

'No, I should not say that,' replied George weightily. 'Doubtless he realized that something was in the wind, but I did not think it necessary to take him fully into my confidence.'

'I see. Will you go on, Lord Caterham?'

'Let me see, there was Mr Hiram Fish.'

'Who is Mr Hiram Fish?'

'Mr Fish is an American. He brought over a letter of introduction from Mr Lucius Gott – you've heard of Lucius Gott?'

Superintendent Battle smiled acknowledgement. Who had not heard of Lucius C. Gott, the multi-millionaire?

'He was specially anxious to see my first editions. Mr Gott's collection is, of course, unequalled, but I've got several treasures myself. This Mr Fish was an enthusiast. Mr Lomax had suggested that I ask one or two extra people down here this weekend to make things seem more natural, so I took the opportunity of asking Mr Fish. That finishes the men. As for the ladies, there is only Mrs Revel – and I expect she brought a maid or something like that. Then there was my daughter, and of course the children and their nurses and governesses and all the servants.'

Lord Caterham paused and took a breath.

'Thank you,' said the detective. 'A mere matter of routine, but necessary as such.'

'There is no doubt, I suppose,' asked George ponderously, 'that the murderer entered by the window?'

Battle paused for a minute before replying slowly.

'There were footsteps leading up to the window, and footsteps leading away from it. A car stopped outside the park at 11.40 last night. At twelve o'clock a young man arrived at the Jolly Cricketers in a car, and engaged a room. He put his boots outside to be cleaned – they were very wet and muddy, as though he had been walking through the long grass in the park.'

George leant forward eagerly.

'Could not the boots be compared with the footprints?'

'They were.'

'Well?'

'They exactly correspond.'

'That settles it,' cried George. 'We have the murderer. This young man – what is his name, by the way?'

'At the inn he gave the name of Anthony Cade.'

'This Anthony Cade must be pursued at once, and arrested.'

'You won't need to pursue him,' said Superintendent Battle.

'Why?'

'Because he's still there.'

'What?'

'Curious, isn't it?'

Colonel Melrose eyed him keenly.

'What's in your mind, Battle? Out with it.'

'I just say it's curious, that's all. Here's a young man who ought to cut and run, but he doesn't cut and run. He stays here, and gives us every facility for comparing footmarks.'

'What do you think, then?'

'I don't know what to think. And that's a very disturbing state of mind.'

'Do you imagine –' began Colonel Melrose, but broke off as a discreet knock came at the door.

George rose and went to it. Tredwell, inwardly suffering from having to knock at doors in this low fashion, stood dignified upon the threshold, and addressed his master.

'Excuse me, my lord, but a gentleman wishes to see you on urgent and important business, connected, I understand, with this morning's tragedy.'

'What's his name?' asked Battle suddenly.

'His name, sir, is Mr Anthony Cade, but he said it wouldn't convey anything to anybody.'

It seemed to convey something to the four men present. They all sat up in varying degrees of astonishment.

Lord Caterham began to chuckle.

'I'm really beginning to enjoy myself. Show him in, Tredwell. Show him in at once.'

CHAPTER XII

Anthony Tells his Story

'Mr Anthony Cade,' announced Tredwell. 'Enter suspicious stranger from village inn,' said Anthony.

He made his way towards Lord Caterham with a kind of instinct rare in strangers. At the same time he summed up the other three men in his own mind thus: '1, Scotland Yard. 2, local dignitary – probably chief constable. 3, harassed gentleman on the verge of apoplexy – possibly connected with the Government.'

'I must apologize,' continued Anthony, still addressing Lord Caterham. 'For forcing my way in like this, I mean. But it was rumoured round the Jolly Dog, or whatever the name of your local pub may be, that you had had a murder up here, and as I thought I might be able to throw some light upon it I came along.'

For a moment or two, no one spoke. Superintendent Battle because he was a man of ripe experience who knew how infinitely better it was to let everyone else speak if they could be persuaded upon to do so, Colonel Melrose because he was habitually taciturn, George because he was in the habit of having notice given to him of the question, Lord Caterham because he had not the least idea of what to say. The silence of the other three, however, and the fact that he had been directly addressed, finally forced speech upon the last-named.

'Er – quite so – quite so,' he said nervously. 'Won't – you – er – sit down?'

'Thank you,' said Anthony.

George cleared his throat portentously.

'Er – when you say you can throw light upon this matter, you mean? – '

'I mean,' said Anthony, 'that I was trespassing upon Lord Caterham's property (for which I hope he will forgive me) last night at about 11.45, and that I actually heard the shot fired. I can at any rate fix the time of the crime for you.'

He looked round at the three in turn, his eyes resting longest on Superintendent Battle, the impassivity of whose face he seemed to appreciate.

'But I hardly think that that's news to you,' he added gently.

'Meaning by that, Mr Cade?' asked Battle.

'Just this. I put on shoes when I got up this morning. Later, when I asked for my boots, I couldn't have them. Some nice young constable had called round for them. So I naturally put two and two together, and hurried up here to clear my character if possible.'

'A very sensible move,' said Battle noncommittally.

Anthony's eyes twinkled a little.

'I appreciate your reticence, Inspector. It is Inspector, isn't it?'

Lord Caterham interposed. He was beginning to take a fancy to Anthony.

'Superintendent Battle of Scotland Yard. This is Colonel Melrose, our chief constable, and Mr Lomax.'

Anthony looked sharply at George.

'Mr George Lomax?'

'Yes.'

'I think, Mr Lomax,' said Anthony, 'that I had the pleasure of receiving a letter from you yesterday.'

George stared at him.

'I think not,' he said coldly.

But he wished that Miss Oscar were here. Miss Oscar wrote all his letters for him, and remembered who they were to and what they were about. A great man like George could not possibly remember all these annoying details.

'I think, Mr Cade,' he hinted, 'that you were about to give us some – er – explanation of what you were doing in the grounds last night at 11.45?'

His tone said plainly: 'And whatever it may be, we are not likely to believe it.'

'Yes, Mr Cade, what *were* you doing?' said Lord Caterham with lively interest.

'Well,' said Anthony regretfully, 'I'm afraid it's rather a long story.'

He drew out his cigarette case.

'May I?'

Lord Caterham nodded, and Anthony lit a cigarette, and braced himself for the ordeal.

He was aware, none better, of the peril in which he stood. In the short space of twenty-four hours, he had become embroiled in two separate crimes. His actions in connexion with the first would not bear looking into for a second. After deliberately disposing of one body and so defeating the aims of justice, he had arrived upon the scene of the second crime at the exact moment when it was being committed. For a young man looking for trouble, he could hardly have done better.

'South America,' thought Anthony to himself, 'simply isn't in it with this!'

He had already decided upon his course of action. He was going to tell the truth – with one trifling alteration, and one grave suppression.

'The story begins,' said Anthony, 'about three weeks ago – in Bulawayo. Mr Lomax, of course, knows where that is – outpost of the Empire – "What do we know of England who only England know?" all that sort of thing. I was conversing with a friend of mine, a Mr James McGrath –'

He brought out the name slowly, with a thoughtful eye on George. George bounded in his seat and repressed an exclamation with difficulty.

'The upshot of our conversation was that I came to England to carry out a little commission for Mr McGrath, who was unable to go himself. Since the passage was booked in his name, I travelled as James McGrath. I don't know what particular kind of offence that was – the superintendent can tell me, I dare say, and run me in for so many months' hard if necessary.'

'We'll get on with the story, if you please, sir,' said Battle, but his eyes twinkled a little.

'On arrival in London I went to the Blitz Hotel, still as James McGrath. My business in London was to deliver a certain manuscript to a firm of publishers, but almost immediately I received deputations from the representatives of two political parties of a foreign kingdom. The methods of one were strictly constitutional, the methods of the other were not. I dealt with them both accordingly. But my troubles were not over. That night my room was broken into, and an attempt at burglary was made by one of the waiters at the hotel.'

'That was not reported to the police, I think?' said Superintendent Battle.

'You are right. It was not. Nothing was taken, you see. But I did report the occurrence to the manager of the hotel, and he will confirm my story, and tell you that the waiter in question decamped rather abruptly in the middle of the night. The next day, the publishers rang me up, and suggested that one of their representatives would call upon me and receive the manuscript. I agreed to this, and the arrangement was duly carried out on the following morning. Since I have heard nothing further, I presume the manuscript reached them safely. Yesterday, still as James McGrath, I received a letter from Mr Lomax –'

Anthony paused. He was by now beginning to enjoy himself. George shifted uneasily.

'I remember,' he murmured. 'Such a large correspondence. The name, of course, being different, I could not be expected to know. And I may say,' George's voice rose a little, firm in assurance of moral stability, 'that I consider this – this – masquerading as another man in the highest degree improper. I have no doubt, no doubt whatever that you have incurred a severe legal penalty.'

'In this letter,' continued Anthony, unmoved, 'Mr Lomax made various suggestions concerning the manuscript in my charge. He also extended an invitation to me from Lord Caterham to join the house party here.'

'Delighted to see you, my dear fellow,' said the nobleman. 'Better late than never – eh?'

George frowned at him.

Superintendent Battle bent an unmoved eye upon Anthony.

'And is that your explanation of your presence here last night, sir?' he asked.

'Certainly not,' said Anthony warmly. 'When I am asked to stay at a country house, I don't scale the wall late at night, tramp across the park, and try the downstairs windows. I drive up to the front door, ring the bell and wipe my feet on the mat. I will proceed. I replied to Mr Lomax's letter, explaining that the manuscript had passed out of my keeping, and therefore regretfully declining Lord Caterham's kind invitation. But after I had done so, I remembered something which had up till then escaped my memory.' He paused. The moment had come for skating over thin ice. 'I must tell you that in my struggle with the waiter Giuseppe, I had wrested from him a small bit of paper with some words scribbled on it. They had conveyed nothing to me at the time, but I still had them, and the mention of Chimneys recalled them to me. I got the torn scrap out and looked at it. It was as I had thought. Here is the piece of paper, gentlemen, you can see for yourselves. The words on it are "*Chimneys 11.45 Thursday*".'

Battle examined the paper attentively.

'Of course,' continued Anthony, 'the word Chimneys might have nothing whatever to do with this house. On the other hand, it might. And undoubtedly this Giuseppe was a thieving rascal. I made up my mind to motor down here last night, satisfy myself that all was as it should be, put up at the inn, and call upon Lord Caterham in the morning and put him on his guard in case some mischief should be intended during the weekend.'

'Quite so,' said Lord Caterham encouragingly. 'Quite so.'

'I was late getting here – had not allowed enough time.

Consequently I stopped the car, climbed over the wall and ran across the park. When I arrived on the terrace, the whole house was dark and silent. I was just turning away when I heard a shot. I fancied that it came from inside the house, and I ran back, crossed the terrace, and tried the windows. But they were fastened, and there was no sound of any kind from inside the house. I waited a while, but the whole place was as still as the grave, so I made up my mind that I had made a mistake, and that what I had heard was a stray poacher – quite natural conclusion to come to under the circumstances, I think.'

'Quite natural,' said Superintendent Battle expressionlessly.

'I went on to the inn, put up as I said – and heard the news this morning. I realized, of course, that I was a suspicious character – bound to be under the circumstances, and came up here to tell my story, hoping it wasn't going to be handcuffs for one.'

There was a pause. Colonel Melrose looked sideways at Superintendent Battle.

'I think the story seems clear enough,' he remarked.

'Yes,' said Battle. 'I don't think we'll be handing out any handcuffs this morning.'

'Any questions, Battle?'

'There's one thing I'd like to know. What was this manuscript?'

He looked across at George, and the latter replied with a trace of unwillingness:

'The memoirs of the late Count Stylptitch. You see –'

'You needn't say anything more,' said Battle. 'I see perfectly.'

He turned to Anthony.

'Do you know who it was that was shot, Mr Cade?'

'At the Jolly Dog it was understood to be a Count Stanislaus or some such name.'

'Tell him,' said Battle laconically to George Lomax.

George was clearly reluctant, but he was forced to speak:

'The gentleman who was staying here incognito as Count

Stanislaus was His Highness Prince Michael of Herzoslovakia.'

Anthony whistled.

'That must be deuced awkward,' he remarked.

Superintendent Battle, who had been watching Anthony closely, gave a short grunt as though satisfied of something, and rose abruptly to his feet.

'There are one or two questions I'd like to ask Mr Cade,' he announced. 'I'll take him into the Council Chamber with me if I may.'

'Certainly, certainly,' said Lord Caterham. 'Take him anywhere you like.'

Anthony and the detective went out together.

The body had been moved from the scene of the tragedy. There was a dark stain on the floor where it had lain, but otherwise there was nothing to suggest that a tragedy had ever occurred. The sun poured in through the three windows, flooding the room with light, and bringing out the mellow tone of the old panelling. Anthony looked around him with approval.

'Very nice,' he commented. 'Nothing much to beat old England, is there?'

'Did it seem to you at first that it was in this room the shot was fired?' asked the superintendent, not replying to Anthony's eulogium.

'Let me see.'

Anthony opened the window and went out on the terrace, looking up at the house.

'Yes, that's the room all right,' he said. 'It's built out, and occupies all the corner. If the shot had been fired anywhere else, it would have sounded from the *left*, but this was from behind me or to the right if anything. That's why I thought of poachers. It's at the extremity of the wing, you see.'

He stepped back across the threshold, and asked suddenly, as though the idea had just struck him:

'But why do you ask? You know he was shot here, don't you?'

'Ah!' said the superintendent. 'We never know as much as we'd like to know. But, yes, he was shot here all right. Now you said something about trying the windows, didn't you?'

'Yes. They were fastened from the inside.'

'How many of them did you try?'

'All three of them.'

'Sure of that, sir?'

'I'm in the habit of being sure. Why do you ask?'

'That's a funny thing,' said the superintendent.

'What's a funny thing?'

'When the crime was discovered this morning, the middle one was open – not latched, that is to say.'

'Whew!' said Anthony, sinking down on the window-seat, and taking out his cigarette case. 'That's rather a blow. That opens up quite a different aspect of the case. It leaves us two alternatives. Either he was killed by someone in the house, and that someone unlatched the window after I had gone to make it look like an outside job – incidentally with me as Little Willie – or else, not to mince matters, I'm lying. I dare say you incline to the second possibility, but, upon my honour, you're wrong.'

'Nobody's going to leave this house until I'm through with them, I can tell you that,' said Superintendent Battle grimly.

Anthony looked at him keenly.

'How long have you had the idea that it might be an inside job?' he asked.

Battle smiled.

'I've had a notion that way all along. Your trail was a bit too – flaring, if I may put it that way. As soon as your boots fitted the footmarks, I began to have my doubts.'

'I congratulate Scotland Yard,' said Anthony lightly.

But at that moment, the moment when Battle apparently admitted Anthony's complete absence of complicity in the crime, Anthony felt more than ever the need of being upon his guard. Superintendent Battle was a very astute officer. It would not do to make any slip with Superintendent Battle about.

'That's where it happened, I suppose?' said Anthony, nodding towards the dark patch upon the floor.

'Yes.'

'What was he shot with – a revolver?'

'Yes, but we shan't know what make until they get the bullet out at the autopsy.'

'It wasn't found then?'

'No, it wasn't found.'

'No clues of any kind?'

'Well, we've got this.'

Rather after the manner of a conjurer, Superintendent Battle produced a half-sheet of notepaper. And, as he did so, he again watched Anthony closely without seeming to do so.

But Anthony recognized the design upon it without any sign of consternation.

'Aha! Comrades of the Red Hand again. If they're going to scatter this sort of thing about, they ought to have it lithographed. It must be a frightful nuisance doing every one separately. Where was this found?'

'Underneath the body. You've seen it before, sir?'

Anthony recounted to him in detail his short encounter with that public-spirited association.

'The idea is, I suppose, that the Comrades did him in.'

'Do you think it likely, sir?'

'Well, it would be in keeping with their propaganda. But I've always found that those who talk most about blood have never actually seen it run. I shouldn't have said the Comrades had the guts myself. And they're such picturesque people too. I don't see one of them disguising himself as a suitable guest for a country house. Still, one never knows.'

'Quite right, Mr Cade. One never knows.'

Anthony looked suddenly amused.

'I see the big idea now. Open window, trail of footprints, suspicious stranger at the village inn. But I can assure you, my dear Superintendent, that whatever I am, I am not the local agent of the Red Hand.'

Superintendent Battle smiled a little. Then he played his last card.

'Would you have any objection to seeing the body?' he shot out suddenly.

'None whatever,' rejoined Anthony.

Battle took a key from his pocket, and preceding Anthony down the corridor, paused at a door and unlocked it. It was one of the smaller drawing-rooms. The body lay on a table covered with a sheet.

Superintendent Battle waited until Anthony was beside him, and then whisked away the sheet suddenly.

An eager light sprang into his eyes at the half-uttered exclamation and the start of surprise which the other gave.

'So you *do* recognize him, Mr Cade?' he said, in a voice that he strove to render devoid of triumph.

'I've seen him before, yes,' said Anthony, recovering himself. 'But not as Prince Michael Obolovitch. He purported to come from Messrs Balderson and Hodgkins, and he called himself Mr Holmes.'

CHAPTER XIII

The American Visitor

Superintendent Battle replaced the sheet with the slightly crestfallen air of a man whose best point has fallen flat. Anthony stood with his hands in his pockets lost in thought.

'So that's what old Lollipop meant when he talked about "other means",' he murmured at last.

'I beg your pardon, Mr Cade?'

'Nothing, Superintendent. Forgive my abstraction. You see I – or rather my friend, Jimmy McGrath, has been very neatly done out of a thousand pounds.'

'A thousand pounds is a nice sum of money,' said Battle.

'It isn't the thousand pounds so much,' said Anthony, 'though I agree with you that it's a nice sum of money. It's being done that maddens me. I handed over that manuscript like a little woolly lamb. It hurts, Superintendent, indeed it hurts.'

The detective said nothing.

'Well, well,' said Anthony. 'Regrets are vain, and all may not yet be lost. I've only got to get hold of dear old Stylptitch's reminiscences between now and next Wednesday and all will be gas and gaiters.'

'Would you mind coming back to the Council Chamber, Mr Cade? There's one little thing I want to point out to you.'

Back in the Council Chamber, the detective strode over at once to the middle window.

'I've been thinking, Mr Cade. This particular window is very stiff; very stiff indeed. You might have been mistaken in thinking that it was fastened. It might just have stuck. I'm sure – yes, I'm almost sure, that you *were* mistaken.'

Anthony eyed him keenly.

'And supposing I say that I'm quite sure I was not?'

'Don't you think you could have been?' said Battle, looking at him very steadily.

'Well, to oblige you, Superintendent, yes.'

Battle smiled in a satisfied fashion.

'You're quick in the uptake, sir. And you'll have no objection to saying so, careless like, at a suitable moment?'

'None whatever. I –'

He paused, as Battle gripped his arm. The superintendent was bent forward, listening.

Enjoining silence on Anthony with a gesture, he tiptoed noiselessly to the door, and flung it suddenly open.

On the threshold stood a tall man with black hair neatly parted in the middle, china-blue eyes with a particularly innocent expression, and a large placid face.

'Your pardon, gentlemen,' he said in a slow drawling voice with a pronounced transatlantic accent. 'But is it permitted to inspect the scene of the crime? I take it that you are both gentlemen from Scotland Yard?'

'I have not that honour,' said Anthony. 'But this gentleman is Superintendent Battle of Scotland Yard.'

'Is that so?' said the American gentleman, with a great appearance of interest. 'Pleased to meet you, sir. My name is Hiram P. Fish, of New York City.'

'What was it you wanted to see, Mr Fish?' asked the detective.

The American walked gently into the room, and looked with much interest at the dark patch on the floor.

'I am interested in crime, Mr Battle. It is one of my hobbies. I have contributed a monograph to one of our weekly periodicals on the subject "Degeneracy and the Criminal".'

As he spoke, his eyes went gently round the room, seeming to note everything in it. They rested just a shade longer on the window.

'The body,' said Superintendant Battle, stating a self-evident fact, 'has been removed.'

'Surely,' said Mr Fish. His eyes went on to the panelled

walls. 'Some remarkable pictures in this room, gentlemen. A Holbein, two Van Dycks, and, if I am not mistaken, a Velazquez. I am interested in pictures – and likewise in first editions. It was to see his first editions that Lord Caterham was so kind as to invite me down here.'

He sighed gently.

'I guess that's all off now. It would show a proper feeling, I suppose, for the guests to return to town immediately?'

'I'm afraid that can't be done, sir,' said Superintendent Battle. 'Nobody must leave the house until after the inquest.'

'Is that so? And when is the inquest?'

'May be tomorrow, may not be until Monday.' We've got to arrange for the autopsy and see the coroner.

'I get you,' said Mr Fish. 'Under the circumstances, though it will be a melancholy party.'

Battle led the way to the door.

'We'd best get out of here,' he said. 'We're keeping it locked still.'

He waited for the other two to pass through, and then turned the key and removed it.

'I opine,' said Mr Fish, 'that you are seeking for fingerprints?'

'Maybe,' said the superintendent laconically.

'I should say too, that, on a night such as last night, an intruder would have left footprints on the hardwood floor.'

'None inside, plenty outside.'

'Mine,' explained Anthony cheerfully.

The innocent eyes of Mr Fish swept over him.

'Young man,' he said, 'you surprise me.'

They turned a corner, and came out into the big wide hall, panelled like the Council Chamber in old oak, and with a wide gallery above it. Two other figures came into sight at the far end.

'Aha!' said Mr Fish. 'Our genial host.'

This was such a ludicrous description of Lord Caterham that Anthony had to turn his head away to conceal a smile.

'And with him,' continued the American, 'is a lady whose

name I did not catch last night. But she is bright – she is very bright.'

With Lord Caterham was Virginia Revel.

Anthony had been anticipating this meeting all along. He had no idea how to act. He must leave it to Virginia. Although he had full confidence in her presence of mind, he had not the slightest idea what line she would take. He was not long left in doubt.

'Why, it's Mr Cade,' said Virginia. She held out both hands to him. 'So you found you could come down after all?'

'My dear Mrs Revel, I had no idea Mr Cade was a friend of yours,' said Lord Caterham.

'He's a very old friend,' said Virginia, smiling at Anthony, with a mischievous glint in her eye. 'I ran across him in London unexpectedly yesterday, and told him I was coming down here.'

Anthony was quick to give her her pointer.

'I explained to Mrs Revel,' he said, 'that I had been forced to refuse your kind invitation – since it had really been extended to quite a different man. And I couldn't very well foist a perfect stranger on you under false pretences.'

'Well, well, my dear fellow,' said Lord Caterham, 'that's all over and done with now. I'll send down to the Cricketers for your bag.'

'It's very kind of you, Lord Caterham, but –'

'Nonsense, of course you must come to Chimneys. Horrible place, the Cricketers – to stay in, I mean.'

'Of course, you must come, Mr Cade,' said Virginia softly.

Anthony realized the altered tone of his surroundings. Already Virginia had done much for him. He was no longer an ambiguous stranger. Her position was so assured and unassailable that anyone for whom she vouched was accepted as a matter of course. He thought of the pistol in the tree at Burnham Beeches, and smiled inwardly.

'I'll send for your traps,' said Lord Caterham to Anthony. 'I suppose, in the circumstances, we can't have any shooting.

A pity. But there it is. And I don't know what the devil to do with Isaacstein. It's all very unfortunate.'

The depressed peer sighed heavily.

'That's settled, then,' said Virginia. 'You can begin to be useful right away, Mr Cade, and take me out on the lake. It's very peaceful there and far from crime and all that sort of thing. Isn't it awful for poor Lord Caterham having a murder done in his house? But it's George's fault really. This is George's party, you know.'

'Ah!' said Lord Caterham. 'But I should never have listened to him!'

He assumed the air of a strong man betrayed by a single weakness.

'One can't help listening to George,' said Virginia. 'He always holds you so that you can't get away. I'm thinking of patenting a detachable lapel.'

'I wish you would,' chuckled her host. 'I'm glad you're coming to us, Cade. I need support.'

'I appreciate your kindness very much, Lord Caterham,' said Anthony. 'Especially,' he added, 'when I'm such a suspicious character. But my staying here makes it easier for Battle.'

'In what way, sir?' asked the superintendent.

'It won't be so difficult to keep an eye on me,' explained Anthony gently.

And by the momentary flicker of the superintendent's eyelids he knew that his shot had gone home.

CHAPTER XIV

Mainly Political and Financial

Except for that involuntary twitch of the eyelids, Superintendent Battle's impassivity was unimpaired. If he had been surprised at Virginia's recognition of Anthony, he did not show
it. He and Lord Caterham stood together and watched those
two go out through the garden door. Mr Fish also watched
them.

'Nice young fellow, that,' said Lord Caterham.

'Vurry nice for Mrs Revel to meet an old friend,' murmured
the American. 'They have been acquainted some time, pre-
soomably?'

'Seems so,' said Lord Caterham. 'But I've never heard her
mention him before. Oh, by the way, Battle, Mr Lomax has
been asking for you. He's in the Blue Morning-room.'

'Very good, Lord Caterham. I'll go there at once.'

Battle found his way to the Blue Morning-room without
difficulty. He was already familiar with the geography of the
house.

'Ah, there you are, Battle,' said Lomax.

He was striding impatiently up and down the carpet. There
was one other person in the room, a big man sitting in a
chair by the fireplace. He was dressed in very correct English
shooting clothes which nevertheless sat strangely upon him.
He had a fat yellow face, and black eyes, as impenetrable as
those of a cobra. There was a generous curve to the big nose
and power in the square lines of the vast jaw.

'Come in, Battle,' said Lomax irritably. 'And shut the door
behind you. This is Mr Herman Isaacstein.'

Battle inclined his head respectfully.

He knew all about Mr Herman Isaacstein, and though the great financier sat there silent, whilst Lomax strode up and down and talked, he knew who was the real power in the room.

'We can speak more freely now,' said Lomax. 'Before Lord Caterham and Colonel Melrose, I was anxious not to say too much. You understand, Battle? These things mustn't get about.'

'Ah!' said Battle. 'But they always do, more's the pity.'

Just for a second he saw a trace of a smile on the fat yellow face. It disappeared as suddenly as it had come.

'Now, what do you really think of this young fellow – this Anthony Cade?' continued George. 'Do you still assume him to be innocent?'

Battle shrugged his shoulders very slightly.

'He tells a straight story. Part of it we shall be able to verify. On the face of it, it accounts for his presence here last night. I shall cable to South Africa, of course, for information about his antecedents.'

'Then you regard him as cleared of all complicity?'

Battle raised a large square hand.

'Not so fast, sir. I never said that.'

'What is your idea about the crime, Superintendent Battle?' asked Isaacstein, speaking for the first time.

His voice was deep and rich, and had a certain compelling quality about it. It had stood him in good stead at board meetings in his younger days.

'It's rather too soon to have ideas, Mr Isaacstein. I've not got beyond asking myself the first question.'

'What is that?'

'Oh, it's always the same. Motive. Who benefits by the death of Prince Michael? We've got to answer that before we can get anywhere.'

'The Revolutionary party of Herzoslovakia –' began George.

Superintendent Battle waved him aside with something less than his usual respect.

'It wasn't the Comrades of the Red Hand, sir, if you're thinking of them.'

'But the paper – with the scarlet hand on it?'

'Put there to suggest the obvious solution.'

George's dignity was a little ruffled.

'Really, Battle, I don't see how you can be so sure of that.'

'Bless you, Mr Lomax, we know all about the Comrades of the Red Hand. We've had our eye on them ever since Prince Michael landed in England. That sort of thing is the elementary work of the department. They'd never be allowed to get within a mile of him.'

'I agree with Superintendent Battle,' said Isaacstein. 'We must look elsewhere.'

'You see, sir,' said Battle, encouraged by this support, 'we do know a little about the case. If we don't know who gains by his death, we do know who loses by it.'

'Meaning?' said Isaacstein.

His black eyes were bent upon the detective. More than ever, he reminded Battle of a hooded cobra.

'You and Mr Lomax, not to mention the Loyalist party of Herzoslovakia. If you'll pardon the expression, sir, you're in the soup.'

'Really, Battle,' interposed George, shocked to the core.

'Go on, Battle,' said Isaacstein. 'In the soup describes the situation very accurately. You're an intelligent man.'

'You've got to have a king. You've lost your king – like that!' He snapped his large fingers. 'You've got to find another in a hurry, and that's not an easy job. No, I don't want to know the details of your scheme, the bare outline is enough for me, but, I take it, it's a big deal?'

Isaacstein bent his head slowly.

'It's a very big deal.'

'That brings me to my second question. Who is the next heir to the throne of Herzoslovakia?'

Isaacstein looked across at Lomax. The latter answered the question, with a certain reluctance, and a good deal of hesitation:

'That would be – I should say – yes, in all probability Prince Nicholas would be the next heir.'

'Ah!' said Battle. 'And who is Prince Nicholas?'

'A first cousin of Prince Michael's.'

'Ah!' said Battle. 'I should like to hear all about Prince Nicholas, especially where he is at present.'

'Nothing much is known of him,' said Lomax. 'As a young man, he was most peculiar in his ideas, consorted with Socialists and Republicans, and acted in a way highly unbecoming to his position. He was sent down from Oxford, I believe, for some wild escapade. There was a rumour of his death two years later in the Congo, but it was only a rumour. He turned up a few months ago when news of the royalist reaction got about.'

'Indeed?' said Battle. 'Where did he turn up?'

'In America.'

'America!'

Battle turned to Isaacstein with one laconic word:

'Oil?'

The financier nodded.

'He represented that if the Herzoslovakians chose a king, they would prefer him to Prince Michael as being more in sympathy with modern enlightened ideas, and he drew attention to his early democratic views and his sympathy with Republican ideals. In return for financial support, he was prepared to grant concessions to a certain group of American financiers.'

Superintendent Battle so far forgot his habitual impassivity as to give vent to a prolonged whistle.

'So that is it,' he muttered. 'In the meantime, the Loyalist party supported Prince Michael, and you felt sure you'd come out on top. And then this happens!'

'You surely don't think –' began George.

'It was a big deal,' said Battle. 'Mr Isaacstein says so. And I should say that what he calls a big deal *is* a big deal.'

'There are always unscrupulous tools to be got hold of,' said Isaacstein quietly. 'For the moment, Wall Street wins. But they've not done with me yet. Find out who killed Prince Michael, Superintendent Battle, if you want to do your country a service.'

'One thing strikes me as highly suspicious,' put in George. 'Why did the equerry, Captain Andrassy, not come down with the Prince yesterday?'

'I've inquired into that,' said Battle. 'It's perfectly simple. He stayed in town to make arrangements with a certain lady, on behalf of Prince Michael, for next weekend. The Baron rather frowned on such things, thinking them injudicious at the present stage of affairs, so His Highness had to go about them in a hole-and-corner manner. He was, if I may say so, inclined to be a rather – er – dissipated young man.'

'I'm afraid so,' said George ponderously. 'Yes, I'm afraid so.'

'There's one other point we ought to take into account, I think,' said Battle, speaking with a certain amount of hesitation. 'King Victor's supposed to be in England.'

'King Victor?'

Lomax frowned in an effort at recollection.

'Notorious French crook, sir. We've had a warning from the Sûreté in Paris.'

'Of course,' said George. 'I remember now. Jewel thief, isn't he? Why, that's the man –'

He broke off abruptly. Isaacstein, who had been frowning abstractedly at the fireplace, looked up just too late to catch the warning glance telegraphed from Superintendent Battle to the other. But being a man sensitive to vibrations in the atmosphere, he was conscious of a sense of strain.

'You don't want me any longer, do you, Lomax?' he inquired.

'No, thank you, my dear fellow.'

'Would it upset your plans if I returned to London, Superintendent Battle?'

'I'm afraid so, sir,' said the superintendent civilly. 'You see, if you go, there will be others who'll want to go also. And that would never do.'

'Quite so.'

The great financier left the room, closing the door behind him.

'Splendid fellow, Isaacstein,' murmured George Lomax perfunctorily.

'Very powerful personality,' agreed Superintendent Battle.

George began to pace up and down again.

'What you say disturbs me greatly,' he began. 'King Victor! I thought he was in prison?'

'Came out a few months ago. French police meant to keep on his heels, but he managed to give them the slip straight away. He would too. One of the coolest customers that ever lived. For some reason or other, they believe he's in England, and have notified us to that effect.'

'But what should he be doing in England?'

'That's for you to say, sir,' said Battle significantly.

'You mean? – You think? – You know the story, of course – ah, yes, I can see you do. I was not in office, of course, at the time, but I heard the whole story from the late Lord Caterham. An unparalleled catastrophe.'

'The Koh-i-noor,' said Battle reflectively.

'Hush, Battle!' George glanced suspiciously round him. 'I beg of you, mention no names. Much better not. If you must speak of it, call it the K.'

The superintendent looked wooden again.

'You don't connect King Victor with this crime, do you, Battle?'

'It's just a possibility, that's all. If you cast your mind back, sir, you'll remember that there were four places where a – er – certain royal visitor might have concealed the jewel. Chimneys was one of them. King Victor was arrested in Paris three days after the – disappearance, if I may call it that, of the K. It was always hoped that he would some day lead us to the jewel.'

'But Chimneys has been ransacked and overhauled a dozen times.'

'Yes,' said Battle sapiently. 'But it's never much good looking when you don't know where to look. Only suppose now, that this King Victor came here to look for the thing, was surprised by Prince Michael, and shot him.'

'It's possible,' said George. 'A most likely solution of the crime.'

'I wouldn't go as far as that. It's possible, but not much more.'

'Why is that?'

'Because King Victor has never been known to take a life,' said Battle seriously.

'Oh, but a man like that – a dangerous criminal –'

But Battle shook his head in a dissatisfied manner.

'Criminals always act true to type, Mr Lomax. It's surprising. All the same –'

'Yes?'

'I'd rather like to question the Prince's servant. I've left him purposely to the last. We'll have him in here, sir, if you don't mind.'

George signified his assent. The superintendent rang the bell. Tredwell answered it, and departed with his instructions.

He returned shortly accompanied by a tall fair man with high cheekbones, and very deep-set blue eyes, and an impassivity of countenance, which almost rivalled Battle's.

'Boris Anchoukoff?'

'Yes.'

'You were valet to Prince Michael?'

'I was His Highness' valet, yes.'

The man spoke good English, though with a markedly harsh foreign accent.

'You know that your master was murdered last night?'

A deep snarl, like the snarl of a wild beast, was the man's only answer. It alarmed George, who withdrew prudently towards the window.

'When did you see your master last?'

'His Highness retired to bed at half past ten. I slept, as always, in the anteroom next to him. He must have gone down to the room downstairs by the other door, the door that gave on the corridor. I did not hear him go. It may be that I was drugged. I have been an unfaithful servant, I slept while my master woke. I am accursed.'

George gazed at him, fascinated.

'You loved your master, eh?' said Battle, watching the man closely.

Boris' features contracted painfully. He swallowed twice. Then his voice came, harsh with emotion.

'I say this to you, English policeman, I would have died for him! And since he is dead, and I still live, my eyes shall not know sleep, or my heart rest, until I have avenged him. Like a dog will I nose out his murderer and when I have discovered him – Ah!' His eyes lit up. Suddenly he drew an immense knife from beneath his coat and brandished it aloft. 'Not all at once will I kill him – oh no! – first I will slit his nose, and cut off his ears and put out his eyes, and then – then, into his black heart, I will thrust this knife.'

Swiftly he replaced the knife, and turning, left the room. George Lomax, his eyes always protuberant, but now goggling almost out of his head, stared at the closed door.

'Pure-bred Herzoslovakian, of course,' he muttered. 'Most uncivilized people. A race of brigands.'

Superindentent Battle rose alertly to his feet.

'Either that man's sincere,' he remarked, 'or he's the best bluffer I've ever seen. And if it's the former, God help Prince Michael's murderer when that human bloodhound gets hold of him.'

CHAPTER XV

The French Stranger

Virginia and Anthony walked side by side down the path which led to the lake. For some minutes after leaving the house they were silent. It was Virginia who broke the silence at last with a little laugh.

'Oh, dear,' she said, 'isn't it dreadful? Here I am so bursting with the things I want to tell you, and the things I want to know, that I simply don't know where to begin. First of all' – she lowered her voice – '*What have you done with the body?* How awful it sounds, doesn't it! I never dreamt that I should be so steeped in crime.'

'I suppose it's quite a novel sensation for you,' agreed Anthony.

'But not for you?'

'Well, I've never disposed of a corpse before, certainly.'

'Tell me about it.'

Briefly and succinctly, Anthony ran over the steps he had taken on the previous night. Virginia listened attentively.

'I think you were very clever,' she said approvingly when he had finished. 'I can pick up the trunk again when I go back to Paddington. The only difficulty that might arise is if you had to give an account of where you were yesterday evening.'

'I can't see that can arise. The body can't have been found until late last night – or possibly this morning. Otherwise there would have been something about it in this morning's papers. And whatever you may imagine from reading detective stories, doctors aren't such magicians that they can tell you exactly how many hours a man has been dead. The exact time of his death will be pretty vague. An alibi for last night would be far more to the point.'

'I know. Lord Caterham was telling me all about it. But the Scotland Yard man is quite convinced of your innocence now, isn't he?'

Anthony did not reply at once.

'He doesn't look particularly astute,' continued Virginia.

'I don't know about that,' said Anthony slowly. 'I've an impression that there are no flies on Superintendent Battle. He appears to be convinced of my innocence – but I'm not sure. He's stumped at present by my apparent lack of motive.'

'Apparent?' cried Virginia. 'But what possible reason could you have for murdering an unknown foreign count?'

Anthony darted a sharp glance at her.

'You were at one time or other in Herzoslovakia, weren't you?' he asked.

'Yes. I was there with my husband, for two years, at the Embassy.'

'That was just before the assassination of the King and Queen. Did you ever run across Prince Michael Obolovitch?'

'Michael? Of course I did. Horrid little wretch! He suggested, I remember, that I should marry him morganatically.'

'Did he really? And what did he suggest you should do about your existing husband?'

'Oh, he had a sort of David and Uriah scheme all made out.'

'And how did you respond to this amiable offer?'

'Well,' said Virginia, 'unfortunately one had to be diplomatic. So poor little Michael didn't get it as straight from the shoulder as he might have done. But he retired hurt all the same. Why all this interest about Michael?'

'Something I'm getting at in my own blundering fashion. I take it that you didn't meet the murdered man?'

'No. To put it like a book he "retired to his own apartments immediately on arrival".'

'And of course you haven't seen the body?'

Virginia, eyeing him with a good deal of interest, shook her head.

'Could you get to see it, do you think?'

'By means of influence in high places – meaning Lord Caterham – I dare say I could. Why? Is it an order?'

'Good Lord, no,' said Anthony, horrified. 'Have I been as dictatorial as all that? No, it's simply this. Count Stanislaus was the incognito of Prince Michael of Herzoslovakia.'

Virginia's eyes opened very wide.

'I see.' Suddenly her face broke into its fascinating one-sided smile. 'I hope you don't suggest that Michael went to his rooms simply to avoid seeing me?'

'Something of the kind,' admitted Anthony. 'You see, if I'm right in my mind that someone wanted to prevent your coming to Chimneys, the reason seems to lie in your knowing Herzoslovakia. Do you realize that you're the only person here who knew Prince Michael by sight?'

'Do you mean that this man who was murdered was an imposter?' asked Virginia abruptly.

'That is the possibility that crossed my mind. If you can get Lord Caterham to show you the body, we can clear up that point at once.'

'He was shot at 11.45,' said Virginia thoughtfully. 'The time mentioned on that scrap of paper. The whole thing's horribly mysterious.'

'That reminds me. Is that your window up there? The second from the end over the Council Chamber?'

'No, my room is in the Elizabethan wing, the other side. Why?'

'Simply because as I walked away last night, after thinking I heard a shot, the light went up in that room.'

'How curious! I don't know who has that room, but I can find out by asking Bundle. Perhaps they heard the shot?'

'If so, they haven't come forward to say so. I understood from Battle that nobody in the house heard the shot fired. It's the only clue of any kind that I've got, and I dare say it's a pretty rotten one, but I mean to follow it up for what it's worth.'

'It's curious, certainly,' said Virginia thoughtfully.

They had arrived at the boathouse by the lake, and had been leaning against it as they talked.

'And now for the whole story,' said Anthony. 'We'll paddle gently about on the lake, secure from the prying ears of Scotland Yard, American visitors, and curious housemaids.'

'I've heard something from Lord Caterham,' said Virginia. 'But not nearly enough. To begin with, which are you really, Anthony Cade or Jimmy McGrath?'

For the second time that morning, Anthony unfolded the history of the last six weeks of his life – with this difference that the account given to Virginia needed no editing. He finished up with his own astonished recognition of 'Mr Holmes'.

'By the way, Mrs Revel,' he ended, 'I've never thanked you for imperilling your mortal soul by saying that I was an old friend of yours.'

'Of course you're an old friend,' cried Virginia. 'You don't suppose I'd lumber you with a corpse, and then pretend you were a mere acquaintance next time I met you? No, indeed!'

She paused.

'Do you know one thing that strikes me about all this?' she went on. 'That there's some extra mystery about those memoirs that we haven't fathomed yet.'

'I think you're right,' agreed Anthony. 'There's one thing I'd like you to tell me,' he continued.

'What's that?'

'Why did you seem so surprised when I mentioned the name of Jimmy McGrath to you yesterday at Pont Street? Had you heard it before?'

'I had, Sherlock Holmes. George – my cousin, George Lomax, you know – came to see me the other day, and suggested a lot of frightfully silly things. His idea was that I should come down here and make myself agreeable to this man, McGrath, and Delilah the memoirs out of him somehow.

He didn't put it like that, of course. He talked a lot of nonsense about English gentlewomen, and things like that, but his real meaning was never obscure for a moment. It was just the sort of rotten thing poor old George would think of. And then I wanted to know too much, and he tried to put me off with lies that wouldn't have deceived a child of two.'

'Well, his plan seems to have succeeded, anyhow,' observed Anthony. 'Here am I, the James McGrath he had in mind, and here are you being agreeable to me.'

'But alas, for poor old George, no memoirs! Now I've got a question for you. When I said I hadn't written those letters, you said you knew I hadn't – you couldn't know any such thing?'

'Oh, yes, I could,' said Anthony, smiling. 'I've got a good working knowledge of psychology.'

'You mean your belief in the sterling worth of my moral character was such that –'

But Anthony was shaking his head vigorously.

'Not at all. I don't know anything about your moral character. You might have a lover, and you might write to him. But you'd never lie down to be blackmailed. The Virginia Revel of those letters was scared stiff. You'd have fought.'

'I wonder who the real Virginia Revel is – where she is, I mean. It makes me feel as though I had a double somewhere.'

Anthony lit a cigarette.

'You know that one of the letters was written from Chimneys?' he asked at last.

'What?' Virginia was clearly startled. 'When was it written?'

'It wasn't dated. But it's odd, isn't it?'

'I'm perfectly certain no other Virginia Revel has ever stayed at Chimneys. Bundle or Lord Caterham would have said something about the coincidence of the name if she had.'

'Yes. It's rather queer. Do you know, Mrs Revel, I am beginning to disbelieve profoundly in this other Virginia Revel.'

'She's very elusive,' agreed Virginia.

'Extraordinarily elusive. I am beginning to think that the

person who wrote those letters deliberately used your name.'

'But why?' cried Virginia. 'Why should they do such a thing?'

'Ah, that's just the question. There's the devil of a lot to find out about everything.'

'Who do you really think killed Michael?' asked Virginia suddenly. 'The Comrades of the Red Hand?'

'I suppose they might have done so,' said Anthony in a dissatisfied voice. 'Pointless killing would be rather characteristic of them.'

'Let's get to work,' said Virginia. 'I see Lord Caterham and Bundle strolling together. The first thing to do is to find out definitely whether the dead man is Michael or not.'

Anthony paddled to shore and a few moments later they had joined Lord Caterham and his daughter.

'Lunch is late,' said his lordship in a depressed voice. 'Battle has insulted the cook, I expect.'

'This is a friend of mine, Bundle,' said Virginia. 'Be nice to him.'

Bundle looked earnestly at Anthony for some minutes, and then addressed a remark to Virginia as though he had not been there.

'Where do you pick up these nice-looking men, Virginia? "How do you do it?" says she enviously.'

'You can have him,' said Virginia generously. 'I want Lord Caterham.'

She smiled upon the flattered peer, slipped her hand through his arm and they moved off together.

'Do you talk?' asked Bundle. 'Or are you just strong and silent?'

'Talk?' said Anthony. 'I babble. I murmur. I burble – like the running brook, you know. Sometimes I even ask questions.'

'As, for instance?'

'Who occupies the second room on the left from the end?'

He pointed to it as he spoke.

'What an extraordinary question!' said Bundle. 'You

intrigue me greatly. Let me see – yes – that's Mademoiselle Brun's room. The French governess. She endeavours to keep my young sisters in order. Dulcie and Daisy – like the song, you know. I dare say they'd have called the next one Dorothy May. But mother got tired of having nothing but girls and died. Thought someone else could take on the job of providing an heir.'

'Mademoiselle Brun,' said Anthony thoughtfully. 'How long has she been with you?'

'Two months. She came to us when we were in Scotland.'

'Ha!' said Anthony. 'I smell a rat.'

'I wish I could smell some lunch,' said Bundle. 'Do I ask the Scotland Yard man to have lunch with us, Mr Cade? You're a man of the world, you know about the etiquette of such things. We've never had a murder in the house before. Exciting, isn't it. I'm sorry your character was so completely cleared this morning. I've always wanted to meet a murderer and see for myself if they're as genial and charming as the Sunday papers always say they are. God! what's that?'

'That' seemed to be a taxi approaching the house. Its two occupants were a tall man with a bald head and a black beard, and a smaller and younger man with a black moustache. Anthony recognized the former, and guessed that it was he – rather than the vehicle which contained him – that had rung the exclamation of astonishment from his companion's lips.

'Unless I much mistake,' he remarked, 'that is my old friend, Baron Lollipop.'

'Baron what?'

'I call him Lollipop for convenience. The pronouncing of his own name tends to harden the arteries.'

'It nearly wrecked the telephone this morning,' remarked Bundle. 'So that's the Baron, is it? I foresee he'll be turned on to me this afternoon – and I've had Isaacstein all the morning. Let George do his own dirty work, say I, and to hell with politics. Excuse me leaving you, Mr Cade, but I must stand by poor old Father.'

Bundle retreated rapidly to the house.

Anthony stood looking after her for a minute or two and thoughtfully lighted a cigarette. As he did so, his ear was caught by a stealthy sound quite near him. He was standing by the boathouse, and the sound seemed to come from just round the corner. The mental picture conveyed to him was that of a man vainly trying to stifle a sudden sneeze.

'Now I wonder – I very much wonder who's behind the boathouse,' said Anthony to himself. 'We'd better see, I think.'

Suiting the action to the word, he threw away the match he had just blown out, and ran lightly and noiselessly round the corner of the boathouse.

He came upon a man who had evidently been kneeling on the ground and was just struggling to rise to his feet. He was tall, wore a light-coloured overcoat and glasses, and for the rest, had a short pointed black beard and slightly foppish manner. He was between thirty and forty years of age, and altogether of a most respectable appearance.

'What are you doing here?' asked Anthony.

He was pretty certain that the man was not one of Lord Caterham's guests.

'I ask your pardon,' said the stranger, with a marked foreign accent and what was meant to be an engaging smile. 'It is that I wish to return to the Jolly Cricketers and I have lost my way. Would Monsieur be so good as to direct me?'

'Certainly,' said Anthony. 'But you don't go there by water, you know.'

'Eh?' said the stranger, with the air of one at a loss.

'I said,' repeated Anthony, with a meaning glance at the boathouse, 'that you won't get there by water. There's a right of way across the park – some distance away, but all this is the private part. You're trespassing.'

'I am most sorry,' said the stranger. 'I lost my direction entirely. I thought I would come up here and inquire.'

Anthony refrained from pointing out that kneeling behind a boathouse was a somewhat peculiar manner of prosecuting inquiries. He took the stranger kindly by the arm.

'You go this way,' he said. 'Right round the lake and straight on – you can't miss the path. When you get on it, turn to the left, and it will lead you to the village. You're staying at the Cricketers, I suppose?'

'I am, Monsieur. Since this morning. Many thanks for your kindness in directing me.'

'Don't mention it,' said Anthony. 'I hope you haven't caught cold.'

'Eh?' said the stranger.

'From kneeling on the damp ground, I mean,' explained Anthony. 'I fancied I heard you sneezing.'

'I may have sneezed,' admitted the other.

'Quite so,' said Anthony. 'But you shouldn't suppress a sneeze, you know. One of the most eminent doctors said so only the other day. It's frightfully dangerous. I don't remember exactly what it does to you – whether it's an inhibition or whether it hardens your arteries, but you must never do it. Good morning.'

'Good morning, and thank you, monsieur, for setting me on the right road.'

'Second suspicious stranger from village inn,' murmured Anthony to himself, as he watched the other's retreating form. 'And one that I can't place, either. Appearance that of a French commercial traveller. I don't quite see him as a Comrade of the Red Hand. Does he represent yet a third party in the harassed state of Herzoslovakia? The French governess has the second window from the end. A mysterious Frenchman is found slinking round the grounds, listening to conversations that are not meant for his ears. I'll bet my hat there's something in it.'

Musing thus, Anthony retraced his steps to the house. On the terrace, he encountered Lord Caterham, looking suitably depressed, and two new arrivals. He brightened a little at the sight of Anthony.

'Ah, there you are,' he remarked. 'Let me introduce you to Baron – er – er – and Captain Andrassy. Mr Anthony Cade.'

The Baron stared at Anthony with growing suspicion.

'Mr Cade?' he said stiffly. 'I think not.'

'A word alone with you, Baron,' said Anthony. 'I can explain everything.'

The Baron bowed, and the two men walked down the terrace together.

'Baron,' said Anthony. 'I must throw myself upon your mercy. I have so far strained the honour of an English gentleman as to travel to this country under an assumed name. I represented myself to you as Mr James McGrath – but you must see for yourself that the deception involved was infinitesimal. You are doubtless acquainted with the works of Shakespeare, and his remarks about the unimportance of the nomenclature of roses? This case is the same. The man you wanted to see was the man in possession of the memoirs. I was that man. As you know only too well, I am no longer in possession of them. A neat trick, Baron, a very neat trick. Who thought of it, you or your principal?'

'His Highness' own idea it was. And for anyone but him to carry it out he would not permit.'

'He did it jolly well,' said Anthony, with approval. 'I never took him for anything but an Englishman.'

'The education of an English gentleman did the Prince receive,' explained the Baron. 'The custom of Herzoslovakia it is.'

'No professional could have pinched those papers better,' said Anthony. 'May I ask, without indiscretion, what has become of them?'

'Between gentlemen,' began the Baron.

'You are too kind, Baron,' murmured Anthony. 'I've never been called a gentleman so often as I have in the last forty-eight hours.'

'I to you say this – I believe them to be burnt.'

'You believe, but you don't know, eh? Is that it?'

'His Highness in his own keeping retained them. His purpose it was to read them and then by the fire destroy them.'

'I see,' said Anthony. 'All the same, they are not the kind of light literature you'd skim through in half an hour.'

'Among the effects of my martyred master they have not discovered been. It is clear, therefore, that burnt they are.'

'Hm!' said Anthony. 'I wonder?'

He was silent for a minute or two and then went on.

'I have asked you these questions, Baron, because, as you may have heard, I myself have been implicated in the crime. I must clear myself absolutely, so that no suspicion attaches to me.'

'Undoubtedly,' said the Baron. 'Your honour demands it.'

'Exactly,' said Anthony. 'You put these things so well. I haven't got the knack of it. To continue, I can only clear myself by discovering the real murderer, and to do that I must have all the facts. This question of the memoirs is very important. It seems to me possible that to gain possession of them might be the motive of the crime. Tell me, Baron, is that a very far-fetched idea?'

The Baron hesitated for a moment or two.

'You yourself the memoirs have read?' he asked cautiously at length.

'I think I am answered,' said Anthony, smiling. 'Now, Baron, there's just one thing more. I should like to give you fair warning that it is still my intention to deliver that manuscript to the publishers on Wednesday next, the 13th of October.'

The Baron stared at him.

'But you have no longer got it?'

'On Wednesday next, I said. Today is Friday. That gives me five days to get hold of it again.'

'But if it is burnt?'

'I don't think it is burnt. I have good reasons for not believing so.'

As he spoke they turned the corner of the terrace. A massive figure was advancing towards them. Anthony, who had not yet seen the great Mr Herman Isaacstein, looked at him with considerable interest.

'Ah, Baron,' said Isaacstein, waving a big black cigar he was smoking, 'this is a bad business – a very bad business.'

'My good friend, Mr Isaacstein, it is indeed,' cried the Baron. 'All our noble edifice in ruins is.'

Anthony tactfully left the two gentlemen to their lamentations, and retraced his steps along the terrace.

Suddenly he came to a halt. A thin spiral of smoke was rising into the air apparently from the very centre of the yew hedge.

'It must be hollow in the middle,' reflected Anthony 'I've heard of such things before.'

He looked swiftly to right and left of him. Lord Caterham was at the farther end of the terrace with Captain Andrassy. Their backs were towards him. Anthony bent down and wriggled his way through the massive yew.

He had been quite right in his supposition. The yew hedge was really not one, but two, a narrow passage divided them. The entrance to this was about halfway up, on the side of the house. There was no mystery about it, but no one seeing the yew hedge from the front would have guessed at the probability.

Anthony looked down the narrow vista. About halfway down, a man was reclining in a basket chair. A half-smoked cigar rested on the arm of the chair, and the gentleman himself appeared to be asleep.

'Hm!' said Anthony to himself. 'Evidently Mr Hiram Fish prefers sitting in the shade.'

CHAPTER XVI

Tea in the Schoolroom

Anthony regained the terrace with the feeling uppermost in his mind that the only safe place for private conversations was the middle of the lake.

The resonant boom of a gong sounded from the house, and Tredwell appeared in a stately fashion from a side door.

'Luncheon is served, my lord.'

'Ah!' said Lord Caterham, brisking up a little. 'Lunch!'

At that moment two children burst out of the house. They were high-spirited young women of twelve and ten, and though their names might be Dulcie and Daisy, as Bundle had affirmed, they appeared to be more generally known as Guggle and Winkle. They executed a kind of war dance, interspersed with shrill whoops till Bundle emerged and quelled them.

'Where's Mademoiselle?' she demanded.

'She's got the migraine, the migraine, the migraine!' chanted Winkle.

'Hurrah!' said Guggle, joining in.

Lord Caterham had succeeded in shepherding most of his guests into the house. Now he laid a restraining hand on Anthony's arm.

'Come to my study,' he breathed. 'I've got something rather special there.'

Slinking down the hall, far more like a thief than like the master of the house, Lord Caterham gained the shelter of his sanctum. Here he unlocked a cupboard and produced various bottles.

'Talking to foreigners always makes me so thirsty,' he explained apologetically. 'I don't know why it is.'

There was a knock on the door, and Virginia popped her head round the corner of it.

'Got a special cocktail for me?' she demanded.

'Of course,' said Lord Caterham hospitably. 'Come in.'

The next few minutes were taken up with serious rites.

'I needed that,' said Lord Caterham with a sigh, as he replaced his glass on the table. 'As I said just now, I find talking to foreigners particularly fatiguing. I think it's because they're so polite. Come along. Let's have some lunch.'

He led the way to the dining-room. Virginia put her hand on Anthony's arm, and drew him back a little.

'I've done my good deed for the day,' she whispered. 'I got Lord Caterham to take me to see the body.'

'Well?' demanded Anthony eagerly.

One theory of his was to be proved or disproved.

Virginia was shaking her head.

'You were wrong,' she whispered. 'It's Prince Michael all right.'

'Oh!' Anthony was deeply chagrined.

'And Mademoiselle had the migraine,' he added aloud, in a dissatisfied tone.

'What has that got to do with it?'

'Probably nothing, but I wanted to see her. You see, I've found out that Mademoiselle has the second room from the end – the one where I saw the light go up last night.'

'That's interesting.'

'Probably there's nothing in it. All the same, I mean to see Mademoiselle before the day is out.'

Lunch was somewhat of an ordeal. Even the cheerful impartiality of Bundle failed to reconcile the heterogeneous assembly. The Baron and Andrassy were correct, formal, full of etiquette, and had the air of attending a meal in a mausoleum. Lord Caterham was lethargic and depressed. Bill Eversleigh stared longingly at Virginia. George, very mindful of the trying position in which he found himself, conversed weightily with the Baron and Mr Isaacstein. Guggle and Winkle, completely beside themselves with joy at having a murder in the house, had to be continually checked and kept under, whilst Mr Hiram Fish slowly masticated his food, and drawled out dry remarks in his own peculiar idiom. Superintendent Battle had considerately vanished, and nobody knew what had become of him.

'Thank God that's over,' murmured Bundle to Anthony, as they left the table. 'And George is taking the foreign contingent over to the Abbey this afternoon to discuss State secrets.'

'That will possibly relieve the atmosphere,' agreed Anthony.

'I don't mind the American so much,' continued Bundle. 'He and Father can talk first editions together quite happily in some secluded spot. Mr Fish' – as the object of their conversation drew near – 'I'm planning a peaceful afternoon for you.'

The American bowed.

'That's too kind of you, Lady Eileen.'

'Mr Fish,' said Anthony, 'had quite a peaceful morning.'

Mr Fish shot a quick glance at him.

'Ah, you observed me, then, in my secluded retreat? There are moments, sir, when far from the madding crowd is the only motto for a man of quiet tastes.'

Bundle had drifted on, and the American and Anthony were left together. The former dropped his voice a little.

'I opine,' he said, 'that there is considerable mystery about this little dust-up?'

'Any amount of it,' said Anthony.

'That guy with the bald head was perhaps a family connexion?'

'Something of the kind.'

'These Central European nations beat the band,' declared Mr Fish. 'It's kind of being rumoured around that the deceased gentleman was a Royal Highness. Is that so, do you know?'

'He was staying here as Count Stanislaus,' replied Anthony evasively.

To this Mr Fish offered no further rejoinder than the somewhat cryptic:

'Oh, boy!'

After which he relapsed into silence for some moments.

'This police captain of yours,' he observed at last. 'Battle, or whatever his name is, is he the goods all right?'

'Scotland Yard think so,' replied Anthony dryly.

'He seems kind of hidebound to me,' remarked Mr Fish. 'No hustle to him. This big idea of his, letting no one leave the house, what is there to it?'

He darted a very sharp look at Anthony as he spoke.

'Everyone's got to attend the inquest tomorrow morning, you see.'

'That's the idea is it? No more to it than that? No question of Lord Caterham's guests being suspected?'

'My dear Mr Fish!'

'I was getting a mite uneasy – being a stranger in this country. But of course it was an outside job – I remember now. Window found unfastened, wasn't it?'

'It was,' said Anthony, looking straight in front of him.

Mr Fish sighed. After a minute or two he said in a plaintive tone:

'Young man, do you know how they get the water out of a mine?'

'How?'

'By pumping – but it's almighty hard work! I observe the figure of my genial host detaching itself from the group over yonder. I must join him.'

Mr Fish walked gently away, and Bundle drifted back again.

'Funny Fish, isn't he?' she remarked.

'He is.'

'It's no good looking for Virginia,' said Bundle sharply.

'I wasn't.'

'You were. I don't know how she does it. It isn't what she says, I don't even believe it's what she looks. But, oh, boy! she gets there every time. Anyway, she's on duty elsewhere for the time. She told me to be nice to you, and I'm going to be nice to you – by force if necessary.'

'No force required,' Anthony assured her. 'But, if it's all the same to you, I'd rather you were nice to me on the water, in a boat.'

'It's not a bad idea,' said Bundle meditatively.

They strolled down to the lake together.

'There's just one question I'd like to ask you,' said Anthony as he paddled gently out from the shore, 'before we turn to really interesting topics. Business before pleasure.'

'Whose bedroom do you want to know about now?' asked Bundle with weary patience.

'Nobody's bedroom for the moment. But I would like to know where you got your French governess from.'

'The man's bewitched,' said Bundle. 'I got her from an agency, and I pay her a hundred pounds a year, and her Christian name is Geneviève. Anything more you want to know?'

'We'll assume the agency,' said Anthony. 'What about her references?'

'Oh, glowing! She lived for ten years with the Countess of What Not.'

'What Not being? –'

'The Comtesse de Breteuil, Château de Breteuil, Dinard.'

'You didn't actually see the Comtesse yourself? It was all done by letter?'

'Exactly.'

'Hm!' said Anthony.

'You intrigue me,' said Bundle. 'You intrigue me enormously. Is it love or crime?'

'Probably sheer idiocy on my part. Let's forget it.'

'"Let's forget it," says he negligently, having extracted all the information he wants. Mr Cade, who do you suspect? I rather suspect Virginia as being the most unlikely person. Or possibly Bill.'

'What about you?'

'Member of the aristocracy joins in secret the Comrades of the Red Hand. It would create a sensation all right.'

Anthony laughed. He liked Bundle, though he was a little afraid of the shrewd penetration of her sharp grey eyes.

'You must be proud of all this,' he said suddenly, waving his hand towards the great house in the distance.

Bundle screwed up her eyes and tilted her head on one side.

'Yes – it means something, I suppose. But one's too used to it. Anyway, we're not here very much – too deadly dull. We've been at Cowes and Deauville all the summer after town, and then up to Scotland. Chimneys has been swathed in dust-sheets for about five months. Once a week they take the dust-sheets off and coaches full of tourists come and gape and listen to Tredwell. "On your right is the portrait of the fourth Marchioness of Caterham, painted by Sir Joshua Reynolds," etc, and Ed or Bert, the humorist of the party, nudges his girl and says, "Eh! Gladys, they've got two pennyworth of pictures here, right enough." And then they go and look at more pictures and yawn and shuffle their feet and wish it was time to go home.'

'Yet history has been made here once or twice, by all accounts.'

'You've been listening to George,' said Bundle sharply. 'That's the kind of thing he's always saying.'

But Anthony had raised himself on his elbow, and was staring at the shore.

'Is that a third suspicious stranger I see standing disconsolately by the boathouse? Or is it one of the house party?'

Bundle lifted her head from the scarlet cushion.

'It's Bill,' she said.

'He seems to be looking for something.'

'He's probably looking for me,' said Bundle, without enthusiasm.

'Shall we row quickly in the opposite direction?'

'That's quite the right answer, but it should be delivered with more enthusiasm.'

'I shall row with double vigour after that rebuke.'

'Not at all,' said Bundle. 'I have my pride. Row me to where that young ass is waiting. Somebody's got to look after him, I suppose. Virginia must have given him the slip. One of these days, inconceivable as it seems, I might want to marry George, so I might as well practise being "one of our well-known political hostesses".'

Anthony pulled obediently towards the shore.

'And what's to become of me, I should like to know?' he complained. 'I refuse to be the unwanted third. Is that the children I see in the distance?'

'Yes. Be careful, or they'll rope you in.'

'I'm rather fond of children,' said Anthony. 'I might teach them some nice quiet intellectual game.'

'Well, don't say I didn't warn you.'

Having relinquished Bundle to the care of the disconsolate Bill, Anthony strolled off to where various shrill cries disturbed the peace of the afternoon. He was received with acclamation.

'Are you any good at playing Red Indians?' asked Guggle sternly.

'Rather,' said Anthony. 'You should hear the noise I make when I'm being scalped. Like this.' He illustrated.

'Not so bad,' said Winkle grudgingly. 'Now do the scalper's yell.'

Anthony obliged with a blood-curdling noise. In another minute the game of Red Indians was in full swing.

About an hour later, Anthony wiped his forehead, and ventured to inquire after Mademoiselle's migraine. He was pleased to hear that that lady had entirely recovered. So popular had he become that he was urgently invited to come and have tea in the schoolroom.

'And then you can tell us about the man you saw hung,' urged Guggle.

'Did you say you'd got a bit of the rope with you?' asked Winkle.

'It's in my suitcase,' said Anthony solemnly. 'You shall each have a piece of it.'

Winkle immediately let out a wild Indian yell of satisfaction.

'We'll have to go and get washed, I suppose,' said Guggle gloomily. 'You will come to tea, won't you? You won't forget?'

Anthony swore solemnly that nothing should prevent him keeping the engagement. Satisfied, the youthful pair beat a retreat towards the house. Anthony stood for a minute looking after them, and, as he did so, he became aware of a man leaving the other side of a little copse of trees and hurrying away across the park. He felt almost sure that it was the same black-bearded stranger he had encountered that morning. Whilst he was hesitating whether to go after him or not the trees just ahead of him were parted and Mr Hiram Fish stepped out into the open. He started slightly when he saw Anthony.

'A peaceful afternoon, Mr Fish?' inquired the latter.

'I thank you, yes.'

Mr Fish did not look as peaceful as usual however. His face was flushed, and he was breathing hard as though he had been running. He drew out his watch and consulted it.

'I guess,' he said softly, 'it's just about time for your British institution of afternoon tea.'

Closing his watch with a snap, Mr Fish ambled gently away in the direction of the house.

Anthony stood in a brown study and awoke with a start to the fact that Superintendent Battle was standing beside him. Not the faintest sound had heralded his approach, and he seemed literally to have materialized from space.

'Where did you spring from?' asked Anthony irritably.

With a slight jerk of his head, Battle indicated the little copse of trees behind them.

'It seems a popular spot this afternoon,' remarked Anthony.

'You were very lost in thought, Mr Cade.'

'I was indeed. Do you know what I was doing, Battle? I was trying to put two and one and five and three together so as to make four. And it can't be done, Battle, it simply can't be done.'

'There's difficulties that way,' agreed the detective.

'But you're just the man I wanted to see. Battle, I want to go away. Can it be done?'

True to his creed, Superintendent Battle showed neither emotion nor surprise. His reply was easy and matter of fact.

'That depends, sir, as to where you want to go.'

'I'll tell you exactly, Battle. I'll lay my cards upon the table. I want to go Dinard, to the château of Madame la Comtesse de Breteuil. Can it be done?'

'When do you want to go, Mr Cade?'

'Say tomorrow after the inquest. I could be back here by Sunday evening.'

'I see,' said the superintendent, with peculiar solidity.

'Well, what about it?'

'I've no objection, provided you go where you say you're going, and come straight back here.'

'You're a man in a thousand, Battle. Either you have taken an extraordinary fancy to me or else you're extraordinarily deep. Which is it?'

Superintendent Battle smiled a little, but did not answer.

'Well, well,' said Anthony, 'I expect you'll take your precautions. Discreet minions of the law will follow my suspicious footsteps. So be it. But I do wish I knew what it was all about.'

'I don't get you, Mr Cade.'

'The memoirs – what all the fuss is about. Were they only memoirs? Or have you got something up your sleeve?'

Battle smiled again.

'Take it like this. I'm doing you a favour because you've made a favourable impression on me, Mr Cade. I'd like you to work in with me over this case. The amateur and the professional, they go well together. The one has the intimacy, so to speak, and the other the experience.'

'Well,' said Anthony slowly, 'I don't mind admitting that I've always wanted to try my hand at unravelling a murder mystery.'

'Any ideas about the case at all, Mr Cade?'

'Plenty of them,' said Anthony. 'But they're mostly questions.'

'As, for instance?'

'Who steps into the murdered Michael's shoes? It seems to me that that is important?'

A rather wry smile came over Superintendent Battle's face. 'I wondered if you'd think of that, sir. Prince Nicholas

Obolovitch is the next heir – first cousin of this gentleman.'

'And where is he at the present moment?' asked Anthony, turning away to light a cigarette. 'Don't tell me you don't know, Battle, because I shan't believe you.'

'We've reason to believe that he's in the United States. He was until quite lately, at all events. Raising money on his expectations.'

Anthony gave vent to a surprised whistle.

'I get you,' said Anthony. 'Michael was backed by England, Nicholas by America. In both countries a group of financiers are anxious to obtain the oil concessions. The Loyalist party adopted Michael as their candidate – now they'll have to look elsewhere. Gnashing of teeth on the part of Isaacstein and Co and Mr George Lomax. Rejoicings in Wall Street. Am I right?'

'You're not far off,' said Superintendent Battle.

'Hm!' said Anthony. 'I almost dare swear that I know what you were doing in that copse.'

The detective smiled, but made no reply.

'International politics are very fascinating,' said Anthony, 'but I fear I must leave you. I have an appointment in the schoolroom.'

He strode briskly away towards the house. Inquiries of the dignified Tredwell showed him the way to the schoolroom. He tapped on the door and entered, to be greeted by squeals of joy.

Guggle and Winkle immediately rushed at him and bore him in triumph to be introduced to Mademoiselle.

For the first time, Anthony felt a qualm. Mademoiselle Brun was a small, middle-aged woman with a sallow face, pepper-and-salt hair, and a budding moustache!

As the notorious foreign adventuress she did not fit into the picture at all.

'I believe,' said Anthony to himself, 'I'm making the most utter fool of myself. Never mind, I must go through with it now.'

He was extremely pleasant to Mademoiselle, and she, on her part, was evidently delighted to have a good-looking young man invade her schoolroom. The meal was a great success.

But that evening, alone in the charming bedchamber that had been allotted to him, Anthony shook his head several times.

'I'm wrong,' he said to himself. 'For the second time, I'm wrong. Somehow or other, I can't get the hang of this thing.'

He stopped in his pacing of the floor.

'What the devil –' began Anthony.

The door was being softly opened. In another minute a man had slipped into the room, and stood deferentially by the door.

He was a big fair man, squarely built, with high Slavonic cheekbones, and dreamy fanatic eyes.

'Who the devil are you?' asked Anthony, staring at him.

The man replied in perfect English.

'I am Boris Anchoukoff.'

'Prince Michael's servant, eh?'

'That is so. I served my master. He is dead. Now I serve you.'

'It's very kind of you,' said Anthony. 'But I don't happen to want a valet.'

'You are my master now. I will serve you faithfully.'

'Yes – but – look – here – I don't need a valet. I can't afford one.'

Boris Anchoukoff looked at him with a touch of scorn.

'I do not ask for money. I served my master. So will I serve you – to the death!'

Stepping quickly forward, he dropped on one knee, caught Anthony's hand and placed it on his forehead. Then he rose swiftly and left the room as suddenly as he had come.

Anthony stared after him, his face a picture of astonishment.

'That's damned odd,' he said to himself. 'A faithful sort of dog. Curious the instincts these fellows have.'

He rose and paced up and down.

'All the same,' he muttered, 'it's awkward – damned awkward – just at present.'

CHAPTER XVII

A Midnight Adventure

The inquest took place on the following morning. It was extraordinarily unlike the inquests as pictured in sensational fiction. It satisfied even George Lomax in its rigid suppression of all interesting details. Superintendent Battle and the coroner working together with the support of the chief constable, had reduced the proceedings to the lowest level of boredom.

Immediately after the inquest, Anthony took an unostentatious departure.

His departure was the one bright spot in the day for Bill Eversleigh. George Lomax, obsessed with the fear that something damaging to his department might leak out, had been exceedingly trying. Miss Oscar and Bill had been in constant attendance. Everything useful and interesting had been done by Miss Oscar. Bill's part had been to run to and fro with countless messages, to decode telegrams, and to listen by the hour to George's repeating himself.

It was a completely exhausted young man who retired to bed on Saturday night. He had had practically no chance to talk to Virginia all day, owing to George's exactions, and he felt injured and ill-used. Thank goodness, that Colonial fellow had taken himself off. He had monopolized far too much of Virginia's society, anyway. And of course if George Lomax went on making an ass of himself like this – his mind seething with resentment, Bill fell asleep. And, in dreams, came consolation. For he dreamt of Virginia.

It was an heroic dream, a dream of burning timbers in which he played the part of the gallant rescuer. He brought down Virginia from the topmost storey in his arms. She was unconscious. He laid her on the grass. Then he went off to find a packet of sandwiches. It was most important that he should find that packet of sandwiches. George had it but instead of giving it up to Bill, he began to dictate telegrams. They were now in the vestry of a church, and any minute Virginia might arrive to be married to him. Horror! He was wearing pyjamas. He must get home at once and find his proper clothes. He rushed out to the car. The car would not start. No petrol in the tank! He was getting desperate. And then a big General bus drew up and Virginia got out of it on the arm of the bald-headed Baron. She was deliciously cool, and exquisitely dressed in grey. She came over to him and shook him by the shoulders playfully. 'Bill,' she said. 'Oh, Bill.' She shook him harder. 'Bill,' she said. 'Wake up. Oh, do wake up!'

Very dazed, Bill woke up. He was in his bedroom at Chimneys. But part of the dream was with him still. Virginia was leaning over him, and was repeating the same words with variations.

'Wake up, Bill. Oh, do wake up! Bill.'

'Hullo!' said Bill, sitting up in bed. 'What's the matter?'

Virginia gave a sigh of relief.

'Thank goodness. I thought you'd never wake up. I've been shaking you and shaking you. Are you properly awake now?'

'I think so,' said Bill doubtfully.

'You great lump,' said Virginia. 'The trouble I've had! My arms are aching.'

'These insults are uncalled for,' said Bill, with dignity. 'Let me say, Virginia, that I consider your conduct most unbecoming. Not at all that of a pure young widow.'

'Don't be an idiot, Bill. Things are happening.'

'What kind of things?'

'Queer things. In the Council Chamber. I thought I heard a door bang somewhere, and I came down to see. And then I saw a light in the Council Chamber. I crept along the passage, and peeped through the crack of the door. I couldn't see much, but what I could see was so extraordinary that I felt I must see more. And then, all of a sudden, I felt that I should like a nice, big strong man with me. And you were the nicest and biggest and strongest man I could think of, so I came in and tried to wake you up quietly. But I've been ages doing it.'

'I see,' said Bill. 'And what do you want me to do now? Get up and tackle the burglars?'

Virginia wrinkled her brows.

'I'm not sure that they are burglars. Bill, it's very queer – But don't let's waste time talking. Get up.'

Bill slipped obediently out of bed.

'Wait while I don a pair of boots – the big ones with nails in them. However big and strong I am. I'm not going to tackle hardened criminals with bare feet.'

'I like your pyjamas, Bill,' said Virginia dreamily. 'Brightness without vulgarity.'

'While we're on the subject,' remarked Bill, reaching for his second boot, 'I like that thingummybob of yours. It's a pretty shade of green. What do you call it? It's not just a dressing-gown, is it?'

'It's a negligé,' said Virginia. 'I'm glad you've led such a pure life, Bill.'

'I haven't,' said Bill indignantly.

'You've just betrayed the fact. You're very nice, Bill, and I like you. I dare say that tomorrow morning – say about ten o'clock, a good safe hour for not unduly exciting the emotions – I might even kiss you.'

'I always think these things are best carried out on the spur of the moment,' suggested Bill.

'We've other fish to fry,' said Virginia. 'If you don't want to put on a gasmask and a shirt of chain-mail, shall we start?'

'I'm ready,' said Bill.

He wriggled into a lurid silk dressing-gown, and picked up a poker.

'The orthodox weapon,' he observed.

'Come on,' said Virginia, 'and don't make a noise.'

They crept out of the room and along the corridor, and

then down the wide double staircase. Virginia frowned as they reached the bottom of it.

'Those boots of yours aren't exactly domes of silence, are they, Bill?'

'Nails will be nails,' said Bill. 'I'm doing my best.'

'You'll have to take them off,' said Virginia firmly.

Bill groaned.

'You can carry them in your hand. I want to see if you can make out what's going on in the Council Chamber. Bill, it's awfully mysterious. Why should burglars take a man in armour to pieces?'

'Well, I suppose they can't take him away whole very well. They disarticulate him, and pack him neatly.'

Virginia shook her head, dissatisfied.

'What should they want to steal a mouldy old suit of armour for? Why, Chimneys is full of treasures that are much easier to take away.'

Bill shook his head.

'How many of them are there?' he asked, taking a firmer grip of his poker.

'I couldn't see properly. You know what a keyhole is. And they only had a flashlight.'

'I expect they've gone by now,' said Bill hopefully.

He sat on the bottom stair and drew off his boots. Then, holding them in his hand, he crept along the passage that led to the Council Chamber, Virginia close behind him. They halted outside the massive oak door. All was silent within, but suddenly Virginia pressed his arm, and he nodded. A bright light had shown for a minute through the keyhole.

Bill went down on his knees, and applied his eye to the orifice. What he saw was confusing in the extreme. The scene of the drama that was being enacted inside was evidently just to the left, out of his line of vision. A subdued chink every now and then seemed to point to the fact that the invaders were still dealing with the figure in armour. There were two of these, Bill remembered. They stood together by the wall just under the Holbein portrait. The light of the electric torch was evidently being directed upon the operations in progress. It left the rest of the room nearly in darkness. Once a figure flitted across Bill's line of vision, but there was not sufficient light to distinguish anything about it. It might have been that of a man or a woman. In a minute or two it flitted back again and then the subdued chinking sounded again. Presently there came a new sound, a faint tap-tap as of knuckles on wood.

Bill sat back on his heels suddenly.

'What is it?' whispered Virginia.

'Nothing. It's no good going on like this. We can't see anything, and we can't guess what they're up to. I must go in and tackle them.'

He drew on his boots and stood up.

'Now, Virginia, listen to me. We'll open the door as softly as possible. You know where the switch of the electric light is?'

'Yes, just by the door.'

'I don't think there are more than two of them. There may be only one. I want to get well into the room. Then, when I say "Go" I want you to switch on the lights. Do you understand?'

'Perfectly.'

'And don't scream or faint or anything. I won't let anyone hurt you.'

'My hero!' murmured Virginia.

Bill peered at her suspiciously through the darkness. He heard a faint sound which might have been either a sob or a laugh. Then he grasped the poker firmly and rose to his feet. He felt that he was fully alive to the situation.

Very softly, he turned the handle of the door. It yielded and swung gently inwards. Bill felt Virginia close beside him. Together they moved noiselessly into the room.

At the farther end of the room, the torch was playing upon the Holbein picture. Silhouetted against it was the figure of a man, standing on a chair and gently tapping on the panelling. His back, of course, was to them, and he merely loomed up as a monstrous shadow.

What more they might have seen cannot be told, for at that

moment Bill's nails squeaked upon the parquet floor. The man swung round, directing the powerful torch full upon them and almost dazzling them with the sudden glare.

Bill did not hesitate.

'Go,' he roared to Virginia, and sprang for his man, as she obediently pressed down the switch of the electric lights.

The big chandelier should have been flooded with light; but instead, all that happened was the click of the switch. The room remained in darkness.

Virginia heard Bill curse freely. The next minute the air was filled with panting, scuffling sounds. The torch had fallen to the ground and extinguished itself in the fall. There was the sound of a desperate struggle going on in the darkness, but as to who was getting the better of it, and indeed as to who was taking part in it, Virginia had no idea. Had there been anyone else in the room besides the man who was tapping the panelling? There might have been. Their glimpse had been only a momentary one.

Virginia felt paralysed. She hardly knew what to do. She dared not try to join in the struggle. To do so might hamper and not aid Bill. Her one idea was to stay in the doorway, so that anyone trying to escape should not leave the room that way. At the same time, she disobeyed Bill's express instructions and screamed loudly and repeatedly for help.

She heard doors opening upstairs, and a sudden gleam of light from the hall and the big staircase. If only Bill could hold his man until help came.

But at that minute there was a final terrific upheaval. They must have crashed into one of the figures in armour, for it fell to the ground with a deafening noise. Virginia saw dimly a figure springing for the window, and at the same time heard Bill cursing and disengaging himself from fragments of armour.

For the first time, she left her post, and rushed wildly for the figure at the window. But the window was already unlatched. The intruder had no need to stop and fumble for it. He sprang out and raced away down the terrace and round the corner of the house. Virginia raced after him. She was young and athletic, and she turned the corner of the terrace not many seconds after her quarry.

But there she ran headlong into the arms of a man who was emerging from a small side door. It was Mr Hiram P. Fish.

'Gee! It's a lady,' he exclaimed. 'Why, I beg your pardon, Mrs Revel. I took you for one of the thugs fleeing from justice.'

'He's just passed this way,' cried Virginia breathlessly. 'Can't we catch him?'

But even as she spoke, she knew it was too late. The man must have gained the park by now, and it was a dark night with no moon. She retraced her steps to the Council Chamber, Mr Fish by her side, discoursing in a soothing monotone upon the habits of burglars in general, of which he seemed to have a wide experience.

Lord Caterham, Bundle and various frightened servants were standing in the doorway of the Council Chamber.

'What the devil's the matter?' asked Bundle. 'Is it burglars? What are you and Mr Fish doing, Virginia? Taking a midnight stroll?'

Virginia explained the events of the evening.

'How frightfully exciting,' commented Bundle. 'You don't usually get a murder and a burglary crowded into one weekend. What's the matter with the lights in here? They're all right everywhere else.'

That mystery was soon explained. The bulbs had simply been removed and laid in a row against the wall. Mounted on a pair of steps, the dignified Tredwell, dignified even in undress, restored illumination to the stricken apartment.

'If I am not mistaken,' said Lord Caterham in his sad voice as he looked around him, 'this room has recently been the centre of somewhat violent activity.'

There was some justice in the remark. Everything that could have been knocked over had been knocked over. The floor was littered with splintered chairs, broken china, and fragments of armour.

'How many of them were there?' asked Bundle. 'It seems to have been a desperate fight.'

'Only one, I think,' said Virginia. But, even as she spoke she hesitated a little. Certainly only one person – a man – had passed out through the window. But as she had rushed after him, she had a vague impression of a rustle somewhere close at hand. If so, the second occupant of the room could have escaped through the door. Perhaps, though, the rustle had been an effect of her own imagination.

Bill appeared suddenly at the window. He was out of breath and panting hard.

'Damn the fellow!' he exclaimed wrathfully. 'He's escaped. I've been hunting all over the place. Not a sign of him.'

'Cheer up, Bill,' said Virginia, 'better luck next time.'

'Well,' said Lord Caterham, 'what do you think we'd better do now? Go back to bed? I can't get hold of Badgworthy at this time of night. Tredwell, you know the sort of thing that's necessary. Just see to it, will you?'

'Very good, my lord.'

With a sigh of relief, Lord Caterham prepared to retreat.

'That beggar, Isaacstein, sleeps soundly,' he remarked, with a touch of envy. 'You'd have thought all this row would have brought him down.' He looked across at Mr Fish. 'You found time to dress, I see,' he added.

'I flung on a few articles of clothing, yes,' admitted the American.

'Very sensible of you,' said Lord Caterham. 'Damned chilly things, pyjamas.'

He yawned. In a rather depressed mood, the house party retired to bed.

CHAPTER XVIII

Second Midnight Adventure

The first person that Anthony saw as he alighted from his train on the following afternoon was Superintendent Battle. His face broke into a smile.

'I've returned according to contract,' he remarked. 'Did you come down here to assure yourself of the fact?'

Battle shook his head.

'I wasn't worrying about that, Mr Cade. I happen to be going to London, that's all.'

'You have such a trustful nature, Battle.'

'Do you think so, sir?'

'No. I think you're deep – very deep. Still waters, you know, and all that sort of thing. So you're going to London?'

'I am, Mr Cade.'

'I wonder why.'

The detective did not reply.

'You're so chatty,' remarked Anthony. 'That's what I like about you.'

A far off twinkle showed in Battle's eyes.

'What about your own little job, Mr Cade?' he inquired. 'How did that go off?'

'I've drawn blank, Battle. For the second time I've been proved hopelessly wrong. Galling, isn't it?'

'What was the idea, sir, if I may ask?'

'I suspected the French governess, Battle. A: upon the grounds of her being the most unlikely person, according to the canons of the best fiction. B: because there was a light in her room on the night of the tragedy.'

'That wasn't much to go upon.'

'You are quite right. It was not. But I discovered that she

had only been here a short time, and I also found a suspicious Frenchman spying round the place. You know all about him, I suppose?'

'You mean the man who calls himself M. Chelles? Staying at the Cricketers? A traveller in silk.'

'That's it, is it? What about him? What does Scotland Yard think?'

'His actions have been suspicious,' said Superintendent Battle expressionlessly.

'Very suspicious, I should say. Well, I put two and two together. French governess in the house, French stranger outside. I decided that they were in league together, and I hurried off to interview the lady with whom Mademoiselle Brun had lived for the last ten years. I was fully prepared to find that she had never heard of any such person as Mademoiselle Brun, but I was wrong, Battle. Mademoiselle is the genuine article.'

Battle nodded.

'I must admit,' said Anthony, 'that as soon as I spoke to her I had an uneasy conviction that I was barking up the wrong tree. She seemed so absolutely the governess.'

Again Battle nodded.

'All the same, Mr Cade, you can't always go by that. Women especially can do a lot with make-up. I've seen quite a pretty girl with the colour of her hair altered, a sallow complexion stain, slightly reddened eyelids and, most efficacious of all, dowdy clothes, who would fail to be identified by nine people out of ten who had seen her in her former character. Men haven't got quite the same pull. You can do something with the eyebrows, and of course different sets of false teeth alter the whole expression. But there are always the ears – there's an extraordinary lot of character in ears, Mr Cade.'

'Don't look so hard at mine, Battle,' complained Anthony. 'You make me quite nervous.'

'I'm not talking of false beards and grease-paint,' continued the superintendent. 'That's only for books. No, there are very few men who can escape identification and put it over on you.

In fact there's only one man I know who has a positive genius for impersonation. King Victor. Ever heard of King Victor, Mr Cade?'

There was something so sharp and sudden about the way the detective put the question that Anthony checked the words that were rising to his lips.

'King Victor?' he said reflectively instead. 'Somehow, I seem to have heard the name.'

'One of the most celebrated jewel thieves in the world. Irish father, French mother. Can speak five languages at least. He's been serving a sentence, but his time was up a few months ago.'

'Really? And where is he supposed to be now?'

'Well, Mr Cade, that's what we'd rather like to know.'

'The plot thickens,' said Anthony lightly. 'No chance of his turning up here, is there? But I suppose he wouldn't be interested in political memoirs – only in jewels.'

'There's no saying,' said Superintendent Battle. 'For all we know, he may be here already.'

'Disguised as the second footman? Splendid. You'll recognize him by his ears and cover yourself with glory.'

'Quite fond of your little joke, aren't you, Mr Cade? By the way, what do you think of that curious business at Staines?'

'Staines?' said Anthony. 'What's been happening at Staines?'

'It was in Saturday's papers. I thought you might have seen about it. Man found by the roadside shot. A foreigner. It was in the papers again today, of course.'

'I did see something about it,' said Anthony carelessly. 'Not suicide, apparently.'

'No. There was no weapon. As yet the man hasn't been identified.'

'You seem very interested,' said Anthony, smiling. 'No connexion with Prince Michael's death, is there?'

His hand was quite steady. So were his eyes. Was it his fancy that Superintendent Battle was looking at him with peculiar intentness?

'Seems to be quite an epidemic of that sort of thing,' said Battle. 'But, well, I dare say there's nothing in it.'

He turned away, beckoning to a porter as the London train came thundering in. Anthony drew a faint sigh of relief.

He strolled across the park in an unusually thoughtful mood. He purposely chose to approach the house from the same direction as that from which he had come on the fateful Thursday night, and as he drew near to it he looked up at the windows cudgelling his brains to make sure of the one where he had seen the light. Was he quite sure that it was the second from the end?

And, doing so, he made a discovery. There was an angle at the corner of the house in which was a window set farther back. Standing on one spot, you counted this window as the first, and the first one built out over the Council Chamber as the second, but move a few yards to the right and the part built out over the Council Chamber appeared to be the end of the house. The first window was invisible, and the two windows of the rooms over the Council Chamber would have appeared the first and second from the end. Where exactly had he been standing when he had seen the light flash up?

Anthony found the question very hard to determine. A matter of a yard or so made all the difference. But one point was made abundantly clear. It was quite possible that he had been mistaken in describing the light as ocurring in the second room from the end. It might equally well have been the *third*.

Now who occupied the third room? Anthony was determined to find that out as soon as possible. Fortune favoured him. In the hall Tredwell had just set the massive silver urn in its place on the tea-tray. Nobody else was there.

'Hullo, Tredwell,' said Anthony. 'I wanted to ask you something. Who has the third room from the end on the west side? Over the Council Chamber, I mean.'

Tredwell reflected for a minute or two.

'That would be the American gentleman's room, sir. Mr Fish.'

'Oh, is it? Thank you.'

'Not at all, sir.'

Tredwell prepared to depart, then paused. The desire to be the first to impart news makes even pontifical butlers human.

'Perhaps you have heard, sir, of what occurred last night?'

'Not a word,' said Anthony. 'What did occur last night?'

'An attempt at robbery, sir!'

'Not really? Was anything taken?'

'No sir. The thieves were dismantling the suits of armour in the Council Chamber when they were surprised and forced to flee. Unfortunately they got clear away.'

'That's very extraordinary,' said Anthony. 'The Council Chamber again. Did they break in that way?'

'It is supposed, sir, that they forced the window.'

Satisfied with the interest his information had aroused, Tredwell resumed his retreat, but brought up short with a dignified apology.

'I beg your pardon, sir. I didn't hear you come in, and didn't know you were standing just behind me.'

Mr Isaacstein, who had been the victim of the impact, waved his hand in a friendly fashion.

'No harm done, my good fellow. I assure you no harm done.'

Tredwell retired looking contemptuous, and Isaacstein came forward and dropped into an easy-chair.

'Hullo, Cade, so you're back again. Been hearing all about last night's little show?'

'Yes,' said Anthony. 'Rather an exciting weekend, isn't it?'

'I should imagine that last night was the work of local men,' said Isaacstein. 'It seems a clumsy, amateurish affair.'

'Is there anyone about here who collects armour?' asked Anthony. 'It seems a curious thing to select.'

'Very curious,' agreed Mr Isaacstein. He paused a minute, and then said slowly: 'The whole position here is very unfortunate.'

There was something almost menacing in his tone.

'I don't quite understand,' said Anthony.

'Why are we all being kept here in this way? The inquest was over yesterday. The Prince's body will be removed to

London, where it is being given out that he died of heart failure. And still nobody is allowed to leave the house. Mr Lomax knows no more than I do. He refers me to Superintendent Battle.'

'Superintendent Battle has something up his sleeve,' said Anthony thoughtfully. 'And it seems the essence of his plan that nobody should leave.'

'But, excuse me, Mr Cade, you have been away.'

'With a string tied to my leg. I've no doubt that I was shadowed the whole time. I shouldn't have been given a chance of disposing of the revolver or anything of that kind.'

'Ah, the revolver,' said Isaacstein thoughtfully. 'That has not yet been found, I think?'

'Not yet.'

'Possibly thrown into the lake in passing.'

'Very possibly.'

'Where is Superintendent Battle? I have not seen him this afternoon.'

'He's gone to London. I met him at the station.'

'Gone to London? Really? Did he say when he would be back?'

'Early tomorrow, so I understand.'

Virginia came in with Lord Caterham and Mr Fish. She smiled a welcome at Anthony.

'So you're back, Mr Cade. Have you heard all about our adventures last night?'

'Why, trooly, Mr Cade,' said Hiram Fish. 'It was a night of strenuous excitement. Did you hear that I mistook Mrs Revel for one of the thugs?'

'And in the meantime,' said Anthony, 'the thug? –'

'Got clear away,' said Mr Fish mournfully.

'Do pour out,' said Lord Caterham to Virginia. 'I don't know where Bundle is.'

Virginia officiated. Then she came and sat down near Anthony.

'Come to the boathouse after tea,' she said in a low voice. 'Bill and I have got a lot to tell you.'

Then she joined lightly in the general conversation.

The meeting at the boathouse was duly held.

Virginia and Bill were bubbling over with their news. They agreed that a boat in the middle of the lake was the only safe place for confidential conversation. Having paddled out a sufficient distance, the full story of last night's adventure was related to Anthony. Bill looked a little sulky. He wished Virginia would not insist on bringing this Colonial fellow into it.

'It's very odd,' said Anthony, when the story was finished. 'What do you make of it?' he asked Virginia.

'I think they were looking for something,' she returned promptly. 'The burglar idea is absurd.'

'They thought the something, whatever it was, might be concealed in the suits of armour, that's clear enough. But why tap the panelling? That looks more as though they were looking for a secret staircase, or something of that kind.'

'There's a priest's hole at Chimneys, I know,' said Virginia. 'And I believe there's a secret staircase as well. Lord Caterham would tell us all about it. What I want to know is, what can they have been looking for?'

'It can't be the memoirs,' said Anthony. 'They're a great bulky package. It must have been something small.'

'George knows, I expect,' said Virginia. 'I wonder whether I could get it out of him. All along I've felt there was something behind all this.'

'You say there was only one man,' pursued Anthony, 'but that there might possibly be another, as you thought you heard someone going towards the door as you sprang to the window.'

'The sound was very slight,' said Virginia. 'It might have been just my imagination.'

'That's quite possible, but in case it wasn't your imagination the second person must have been an inmate of the house. I wonder now –'

'What are you wondering at?' asked Virginia.

'The thoroughness of Mr Hiram Fish, who dresses himself completely when he hears screams for help downstairs.'

'There's something in that,' agreed Virginia. 'And then there's Isaacstein, who sleeps through it all. That's suspicious too. Surely he couldn't?'

'There's that fellow Boris,' suggested Bill. 'He looks an unmitigated ruffian. Michael's servant, I mean.'

'Chimneys is full of suspicious characters,' said Virginia. 'I dare say the others are just as suspicious of us. I wish Superintendent Battle hadn't gone to London. I think it's rather stupid of him. By the way, Mr Cade, I've seen that peculiar-looking Frenchman about once or twice, spying round the park.'

'It's a mix-up,' confessed Anthony. 'I've been away on a wild-goose chase. Made a thorough ass of myself. Look here, to me the whole question seems to resolve itself into this: did the men find what they were looking for last night?'

'Supposing they didn't?' said Virginia. 'I'm pretty sure they didn't, as a matter of fact.'

'Just this, I believe they'll come again. They know, or they soon will know, that Battle's in London. They'll take the risk and come again tonight.'

'Do you really think so?'

'It's a chance. Now we three will form a little syndicate. Eversleigh and I will conceal ourselves with due precautions in the Council Chamber –'

'What about me?' interrupted Virginia. 'Don't think you're going to leave me out of it.'

'Listen to me, Virginia,' said Bill. 'This is men's work –'

'Don't be an idiot, Bill. I'm in on this. Don't you make any mistake about it. The syndicate will keep watch tonight.'

It was settled thus, and the details of the plan were laid. After the party had retired to bed, first one and then another of the syndicate crept down. They were all armed with powerful electric torches, and in the pocket of Anthony's coat lay a revolver.

Anthony had said that he believed another attempt to resume the search would be made. Nevertheless, he did not expect that the attempt would be made from outside. He

believed that Virginia had been correct in her guess that someone had passed her in the dark the night before, and as he
stood in the shadow of an old oak dresser it was towards the
door and not the window that his eyes were directed. Virginia
was crouching behind a figure in armour on the opposite wall,
and Bill was by the window.

The minutes passed, at interminable length. One o'clock
chimed, then the half-hour, then two, then half-hour. Anthony
felt stiff and cramped. He was coming slowly to the conclusion
that he had been wrong. No attempt would be made tonight.

And then he stiffened suddenly, all his senses on the alert.
He had heard a footstep on the terrace outside. Silence again,
and then a low scratching noise at the window. Suddenly it
ceased, and the window swung open. A man stepped across
the sill into the room. He stood quite still for a moment, peering round as though listening. After a minute or two, seem-
ingly satisfied, he switched on a torch he carried, and turned
it rapidly round the room. Apparently he saw nothing unusual.
The three watchers held their breath.

He went over to the same bit of panelled wall he had been
examining the night before.

And then a terrible knowledge smote Bill. He was going to
sneeze! The wild race through the dew-laden park the night
before had given him a chill. All day he had sneezed intermit-
tently. A sneeze was due now, and nothing on earth would
stop it.

He adopted all the remedies he could think of. He pressed
his upper lip, swallowed hard, threw back his head and looked
at the ceiling. As a last resort he held his nose and pinched it
violently. It was of no avail. He sneezed.

A stifled, checked, emasculated sneeze, but a startling sound
in the deadly quiet of the room.

The stranger sprang round, and in the same minute,
Anthony acted. He flashed on his torch, and jumped full for
the stranger. In another minute they were down on the floor
together.

'Lights,' shouted Anthony.

Virginia was ready at the switch. The lights came on true and full tonight. Anthony was on top of his man. Bill leant down to give him a hand.

'And now,' said Anthony, 'let's see who you are, my fine fellow.'

He rolled his victim over. It was the neat, dark-bearded stranger from the Cricketers.

'Very nice indeed,' said an approving voice.

They all looked up startled. The bulky form of Superintendent Battle was standing in the open doorway.

'I thought you were in London, Superintendent Battle,' said Anthony.

Battle's eyes twinkled.

'Did you sir?' he said. 'Well, I thought it would be a good thing if I was thought to be going.'

'And it has been,' agreed Anthony, looking down at his prostrate foe.

To his surprise there was a slight smile on the stranger's face.

'May I get up, gentlemen?' he inquired. 'You are three to one.'

Anthony kindly hauled him on to his legs. The stranger settled his coat, pulled up his collar, and directed a keen look at Battle.

'I demand pardon,' he said, 'but do I understand that you are a representative from Scotland Yard?'

'That's right,' said Battle.

'Then I will present to you my credentials.' He smiled rather ruefully. 'I would have been wise to do so before.'

He took some papers from his pocket and handed them to the Scotland Yard detective. At the same time, he turned back the lapel of his coat and showed something pinned there.

Battle gave an exclamation of astonishment. He looked through the papers and handed them back with a little bow.

'I'm sorry you've been man-handled, monsieur,' he said, 'but you brought it on yourself, you know.'

He smiled, noting the astonished expression on the faces of the others.

'This is a colleague we have been expecting for some time,' he said. 'M. Lemoine, of the Sûreté in Paris.'

CHAPTER XIX

Secret History

They all stared at the French detective, who smiled back at them.

'But yes,' he said, 'it is true.'

There was a pause for a general readjusting of ideas. Then Virginia turned to Battle.

'Do you know what I think, Superintendent Battle?'

'What do you think, Mrs Revel?'

'I think the time has come to enlighten us a little.'

'To enlighten you? I don't quite understand, Mrs Revel.'

'Superintendent Battle, you understand perfectly. I dare say Mr Lomax has hedged you about with recommendations of secrecy – George would, but surely it's better to tell us than have us stumbling on the secret all by ourselves, and perhaps doing untold harm. M. Lemoine, don't you agree with me?'

'Madame, I agree with you entirely.'

'You can't go on keeping things dark for ever,' said Battle, 'I've told Mr Lomax so. Mr Eversleigh is Mr Lomax's secretary, there's no objection to his knowing what there is to know. As for Mr Cade, he's been brought into the thing willy-nilly, and I consider he's a right to know where he stands. But –'

Battle paused.

'I know,' said Virginia. 'Women are so indiscreet! I've often heard George say so.'

Lemoine had been studying Virginia attentively. Now he turned to the Scotland Yard man.

'Did I hear you just now address Madame by the name of Revel?'

'That is my name,' said Virginia.

'Your husband was in the Diplomatic Service, was he not?

And you were with him in Herzoslovakia just before the assassination of the late King and Queen.'

'Yes.'

Lemoine turned again.

'I think Madame has a right to hear the story. She is indirectly concerned. Moreover' – his eyes twinkled a little – 'Madame's reputation for discretion stands very high in diplomatic circles.'

'I'm glad they give me a good character,' said Virginia, laughing. 'And I'm glad I'm not going to be left out of it.'

'What about refreshments?' said Anthony. 'Where does the conference take place? Here?'

'If you please, sir,' said Battle, 'I've a fancy for not leaving this room until morning. You'll see why when you've heard the story.'

'Then I'll go and forage,' said Anthony.

Bill went with him and they returned with a tray of glasses, siphons and other necessaries of life.

The augmented syndicate established itself comfortably in the corner by the window, being grouped round a long oak table.

'It's understood, of course,' said Battle, 'that anything that's said here is said in strict confidence. There must be no leakage. I've always felt it would come out one of these days. Gentlemen like Mr Lomax who want everything hushed up take bigger risks than they think. The start of this business was just over seven years ago. There was a lot of what they call reconstruction going on – especially in the Near East. There was a good deal going on in England, strictly on the QT with that old gentleman, Count Stylptitch, pulling the strings. All the Balkan States were interested parties, and there were a lot of royal personages in England just then. I'm not going into details but Something disappeared – disappeared in a way that seemed incredible unless you admitted two things – that the thief was a royal personage and that at the same time it was the work of a high-class professional. M. Lemoine here will tell you how that well might be.'

The Frenchman bowed courteously and took up the tale.

'It is possible that you in England may not even have heard of our famous and fantastic King Victor. What his real name is, no one knows, but he is a man of singular courage and daring, one who speaks five languages and is unequalled in the art of disguise. Though his father is known to have been either English or Irish, he himself has worked chiefly in Paris. It was there, nearly eight years ago, that he was carrying out a daring series of robberies and living under the name of Captain O'Neill.'

A faint exclamation escaped Virginia. M. Lemoine darted a keen glance at her.

'I think I understand what agitates Madame. You will see in a minute. Now we of the Sûreté had our suspicions that this Captain O'Neill was none other than "King Victor", but we could not obtain the necessary proof. There was also in Paris at the time a clever young actress, Angèle Mory, of the Folies Bergères. For some time we had suspected that she was associated with the operations of King Victor. But again no proof was forthcoming.

'About that time, Paris was preparing for the visit of the young King Nicholas IV of Herzoslovakia. At the Sûreté we were given special instructions as to the course to be adopted to ensure the safety of His Majesty. In particular we were warned to superintend the activities of a certain Revolutionary organization which called itself the Comrades of the Red Hand. It is fairly certain now that the Comrades approached Angèle Mory and offered her a huge sum if she would aid them in their plans. Her part was to infatuate the young King, and decoy him to some spot agreed upon with them. Angèle Mory accepted the bribe and promised to perform her part.

'But the young lady was cleverer and more ambitious than her employers suspected. She succeeded in captivating the King who fell desperately in love with her and loaded her with jewels. It was then that she conceived the idea of being – not a king's mistress, but a queen! As everyone knows, she realized her ambition. She was introduced into Herzoslovakia as the

Countess Varaga Popoleffsky, an offshoot of the Romanoffs, and became eventually Queen Veraga of Herzoslovakia. Not bad for a little Parisian actress! I have always heard that she played the part extremely well. But her triumph was not to be long-lived. The Comrades of the Red Hand, furious at her betrayal, twice attempted her life. Finally they worked up the country to such a pitch that a revolution broke out in which both the King and Queen perished. Their bodies, horribly mutilated and hardly recognizable, were recovered, attesting to the fury of the populace against the low-born foreign Queen.

'Now, in all this, it seems certain that Queen Varaga still kept in with her confederate, King Victor. It is possible that the bold plan was his all along. What is known is that she continued to correspond with him, in a secret code, from the Court of Herzoslovakia. For safety the letters were written in English, and signed with the name of an English lady then at the Embassy. If any inquiry had been made, and the lady in question had denied her signature, it is possible that she would not have been believed, for the letters were those of a guilty woman to her lover. It was your name she used, Mrs Revel.'

'I know,' said Virginia. Her colour was coming and going unevenly. 'So that is the truth of the letters! I have wondered and wondered.'

'What a blackguardly trick,' cried Bill indignantly.

'The letters were addressed to Captain O'Neill at his rooms in Paris, and their principal purpose may have light shed upon it by a curious fact which came to light later. After the assassination of the King and Queen, many of the crown jewels which had fallen, of course, into the hands of the mob, found their way to Paris, and it was discovered that in nine cases out of ten the principal stones had been replaced by paste – and mind you, there were some very famous stones among the jewels of Herzoslovakia. So as a queen, Angèle Mory still practised her former activities.

'You see now where we have arrived. Nicholas IV and Queen Varaga came to England and were the guests of the late Marquis of Caterham, then Secretary of State for Foreign Affairs. Herzoslovakia is a small country, but it could not be left out. Queen Varaga was necessarily received. And there we have a royal personage and at the same time an expert thief. There is also no doubt that the – er – substitute which was so wonderful as to deceive anyone but an expert could only have been fashioned by King Victor, and indeed the whole plan, in its daring and audacity, pointed to him as the author.'

'What happened?' asked Virginia.

'Hushed up,' said Superintendent Battle laconically. 'Not a mention of it's ever been made public to this day. We did all that could be done on the quiet – and that was a good deal more than you'd ever imagine, by the way. We've got methods of our own that would surprise. That jewel didn't leave England with the Queen of Herzoslovakia – I can tell you that much. No, Her Majesty hid it somewhere – but where we've never been able to discover. But I shouldn't wonder' – Superintendent Battle let his eyes wander gently round – 'if it wasn't somewhere in this room.'

Anthony leapt to his feet.

'What? After all these years?' he cried incredulously. 'Impossible.'

'You do not know the peculiar circumstances, monsieur,' said the Frenchman quickly. 'Only a fortnight later, the revolution in Herzoslovakia broke out, and the King and Queen were murdered. Also, Captain O'Neill was arrested in Paris and sentenced on a minor charge. We hoped to find the packet of code letters in his house, but it appears that this had been stolen by some Herzoslovakian go-between. The man turned up in Herzoslovakia just before the revolution, and then disappeared completely.'

'He probably went abroad,' said Anthony thoughtfully. 'To Africa as likely as not. And you bet he hung on to that packet. It was as good as a gold mine to him. It's odd how things come about. They probably called him Dutch Pedro or something like that out there.'

He caught Superintendent Battle's expressionless glance bent upon him, and smiled.

'It's not really clairvoyance, Battle,' he said, 'though it sounds like it. I'll tell you presently.'

'There is one thing that you have not explained,' said Virginia. 'Where does this link up with the memoirs? There must be a link, surely?'

'Madame is very quick,' said Lemoine approvingly. 'Yes, there is a link. Count Stylptitch was also staying at Chimneys at the time.'

'So that he might have known about it?'

'*Parfaitement.*'

'And, of course,' said Battle, 'if he's blurted it out in his precious memoirs, the fat will be in the fire. Especially after the way the whole thing was hushed up.'

Anthony lit a cigarette.

'There's no possibility of there being a clue in the memoirs as to where the stone was hidden?' he asked.

'Very unlikely,' said Battle decisively. 'He was never in with the Queen – opposed the marriage tooth and nail. She's not likely to have taken him into her confidence.'

'I wasn't suggesting such a thing for a minute,' said Anthony. 'But by all accounts he was a cunning old boy. Unknown to her, he may have discovered where she hid the jewel. In that case, what would he have done, do you think?'

'Sat tight,' said Battle, after a moment's reflection.

'I agree,' said the Frenchman. 'It was a ticklish moment, you see. To return the stone anonymously would have presented great difficulties. Also, the knowledge of its whereabouts would give him great power – and he liked power, that strange old man. Not only did he hold the Queen in the hollow of his hand, but he had a powerful weapon to negotiate with at any time. It was not the only secret he possessed – oh, no! – he collected secrets like some men collect rare pieces of china. It is said that, once or twice before his death, he boasted to people of the things he could make public if the fancy took him. And once at least he declared that he intended to make some startling revelations in his memoirs. Hence' – the Frenchman smiled rather dryly – 'the general anxiety to get hold of them. Our own secret police intended to seize them, but the Count took the precaution to have them conveyed away before his death.'

'Still, there's no real reason to believe that he knew this particular secret,' said Battle.

'I beg your pardon,' said Anthony quietly. 'There are his own words.'

'What?'

Both detectives stared at him as though unable to believe their ears.

'When Mr McGrath gave me that manuscript to bring to England, he told me the circumstances of his one meeting with Count Stylptitch. It was in Paris. At some considerable risk to himself, Mr McGrath rescued the Count from a band of Apaches. He was, I understand – shall we say a trifle – exhilarated? Being in that condition, he made two rather interesting remarks. One of them was to the effect that he knew where the Koh-i-noor was – a statement to which my friend paid very little attention. He also said that the gang in question were King Victor's men. Taken together, those two remarks are very significant.'

'Good lord,' ejaculated Superintendent Battle. 'I should say they were. Even the murder of Prince Michael wears a different aspect.'

'King Victor has never taken a life,' the Frenchman reminded him.

'Supposing he were surprised when he was searching for the jewel?'

'Is he in England, then?' asked Anthony sharply. 'You say that he was released a few months ago. Didn't you keep track of him?'

A rather rueful smile overspread the French detective's face.

'We tried to, monsieur. But he is a devil, that man. He gave us the slip at once – at once. We thought, of course, that he would make straight for England. But no. He went – where do you think?'

'Where?' said Anthony.

He was staring intently at the Frenchman, and absent-mindedly fingers played with a box of matches.

'To America. To the United States.'

'What?'

There was sheer amazement in Anthony's tone.

'Yes, and what do you think he called himself? What part do you think he played over there? The part of Prince Nicholas of Herzoslovakia.'

The matchbox fell from Anthony's hand, but his amazement was fully equalled by that of Battle.

'Impossible.'

'Not so, my friend. You, too, will get the news in the morning. It has been the most colossal bluff. As you know, Prince Nicholas was rumoured to have died in the Congo years ago. Our friend, King Victor, seizes on that – difficult to prove a death of that kind. He resurrects Prince Nicholas, and plays him to such purpose that he gets away with a tremendous haul of American dollars – all on account of the supposed oil concessions. But by a mere accident, he was unmasked, and had to leave the country hurriedly. This time he did come to England. And that is why I am here. Sooner or later he will come to Chimneys. That is, if he is not already here!'

'You think – that?'

'I think he was here the night Prince Michael died, and again last night.'

'It was another attempt, eh?' said Battle.

'It was another attempt.'

'What has bothered me,' continued Battle, 'was wondering what had become of M. Lemoine here. I'd had word from Paris that he was on his way over to work with me, and couldn't make out why he hadn't turned up.'

'I must indeed apologize,' said Lemoine. 'You see, I arrived on the morning after the murder. It occurred to me at once that it would be as well for me to study things from an unofficial standpoint without appearing officially as your colleague. I thought that great possibilities lay that way. I was, of course, aware that I was bound to be an object of suspicion, but that in a way furthered my plan since it would not put the people I was after on their guard. I can assure you that I have seen a good deal that is interesting on the last two days.'

'But look here,' said Bill, 'what really did happen last night?'

'I am afraid,' said M. Lemoine, 'that I gave you rather violent exercise.'

'It was you I chased, then?'

'Yes. I will recount things to you. I came up here to watch, convinced that the secret had to do with this room since the Prince had been killed here. I stood outside on the terrace. Presently I became aware that someone was moving about in this room. I could see the flash of a torch now and again. I tried the middle window and found it unlatched. Whether the man had entered that way earlier, or whether he had left it so as a blind in case he was disturbed, I do not know. Very gently, I pushed it back and slipped inside the room. Step by step I felt my way until I was in a spot where I could watch operations without likelihood of being discovered myself. The man himself I could not see clearly. His back was to me, of course, and he was silhouetted against the light of the torch so that his outline only could be seen. But his actions filled me with surprise. He took to pieces first one and then the other of those two suits of armour, examining each one piece by piece. When he had convinced himself that what he sought was not there, he began tapping the panelling of the wall under that picture. What he would have done next, I do not know. The interruption came. *You* burst in –' He looked at Bill.

'Our well-meant interference was really rather a pity,' said Virginia thoughtfully.

'In a sense, madame, it was. The man switched out his torch, and I, who had no wish as yet to be forced to reveal my identity, sprang for the window. I collided with the other two in the dark, and fell headlong. I sprang up and out through the window. Mr Eversleigh, taking me for his assailant, followed.'

'I followed you first,' said Virginia. 'Bill was only second in the race.'

'And the other fellow had the sense to stay still and sneak out through the door. I wonder he didn't meet the rescuing crowd.'

'That would present no difficulties,' said Lemoine. 'He would be a rescuer in advance of the rest, that was all.'

'Do you really think this Arsène Lupin fellow is actually among the household now?' asked Bill, his eyes sparkling.

'Why not?' said Lemoine. 'He could pass perfectly as a servant. For all we may know, he may be Boris Anchoukoff, the trusted servant of the late Prince Michael.'

'He is an odd-looking bloke,' agreed Bill.

But Anthony was smiling.

'That's hardly worthy of you, M. Lemoine,' he said gently.

The Frenchman smiled too.

'You've taken him on as your valet now, haven't you, Mr Cade?' asked Superintendent Battle.

'Battle, I take off my hat to you. You know everything. But just as a matter of detail, he's taken me on, not I him.'

'Why was that, I wonder, Mr Cade?'

'I don't know,' said Anthony lightly. 'It's a curious taste, but perhaps he may have liked my face. Or he may think I murdered his master and wish to establish himself in a handy position for executing revenge upon me.'

He rose and went over to the windows, pulling the curtains.

'Daylight,' he said, with a slight yawn. 'There won't be any more excitements now.'

Lemoine rose also.

'I will leave you,' he said. 'We shall perhaps meet again later in the day.'

With a graceful bow to Virginia, he stepped out of the window.

'Bed,' said Virginia, yawning. 'It's all been very exciting.

Come on, Bill, go to bed like a good little boy. The breakfast-table will see us not, I fear.'

Anthony stayed at the window looking after the retreating form of M. Lemoine.

'You wouldn't think it,' said Battle behind him, 'but that's supposed to be the cleverest detective in France.'

'I don't know that I wouldn't,' said Anthony thoughtfully. 'I rather think I would.'

'Well,' said Battle, 'he was right about the excitements of this night being over. By the way, do you remember my telling you about that man they'd found shot near Staines?'

'Yes. Why?'

'Nothing. They've identified him, that's all. It seems he was called Giuseppe Manuelli. He was a waiter at the Blitz in London. Curious, isn't it?'

CHAPTER XX

Battle and Anthony Confer

Anthony said nothing. He continued to stare out of the window. Superintendent Battle looked for some time at his motionless back.

'Well, goodnight, sir,' he said at last, and moved to the door.

Anthony stirred.

'Wait a minute, Battle.'

The superintendent halted obediently. Anthony left the window. He drew out a cigarette from his case and lighted it. Then, between two puffs of smoke, he said:

'You seem very interested in this business at Staines?'

'I wouldn't go as far as that, sir. It's unusual, that's all.'

'Do you think the man was shot where he was found, or do you think he was killed elsewhere and the body brought to that particular spot afterwards?'

'I think he was shot somewhere else, and the body brought there in a car.'

'I think so too,' said Anthony.

Something in the emphasis of his tone made the dectective look up sharply.

'Any ideas of your own, sir? Do you know who brought him there?'

'Yes,' said Anthony. 'I did.'

He was a little annoyed at the absolutely unruffled calm preserved by the other.

'I must say you take these shocks very well, Battle,' he remarked.

'"Never display emotion". That was a rule that was given to me once, and I've found it very useful.'

'You live up to it, certainly,' said Anthony. 'I can't say I've ever seen you ruffled. Well, do you want to hear the whole story?'

'If you please, Mr Cade.'

Anthony pulled up two of the chairs, both men sat down, and Anthony recounted the events of the preceding Thursday night.

Battle listened immovably. There was a far-off twinkle in his eyes as Anthony finished.

'You know, sir,' he said, 'you'll get into trouble one of these days.'

'Then, for the second time, I'm not to be taken into custody?'

'We always like to give a man plenty of rope,' said Superintendent Battle.

'Very delicately put,' said Anthony. 'Without unduly stressing the end of the proverb.'

'What I can't make out, sir,' said Battle, 'is why you decided to come across with this now?'

'It's rather difficult to explain,' said Anthony. 'You see, Battle, I've come to have really a very high opinion of your abilities. When the moment comes, you're always there. Look at tonight. And it occurred to me that, in withholding this knowledge of mine, I was seriously cramping your style. You deserve to have access to all the facts. I've done what I could, and up to now I've made a mess of things. Until tonight, I couldn't speak for Mrs Revel's sake. But now that those letters have been definitely proved to have nothing whatever to do with her, any idea of her complicity becomes absurd. Perhaps I advised her badly in the first place, but it struck me that her statement of having paid this man money to suppress the letters, simply as a whim, might take a bit of believing.'

'It might, by a jury,' agreed Battle. 'Juries never have any imagination.'

'But you accept it quite easily?' said Anthony, looking curiously at him.

'Well, you see, Mr Cade, most of my work has lain amongst

these people. What they call the upper classes, I mean. You see, the majority of people are always wondering what the neighbours will think. But tramps and aristocrats don't – they just do the first thing that comes into their heads, and they don't bother to think what anyone thinks of them. I'm not meaning just the idle rich, the people who give big parties, and so on. I mean those that have had it born and bred in them for generations that nobody else's opinion counts but their own. I've always found the upper classes the same – fearless, truthful, and sometimes extraordinarily foolish.'

'This is a very interesting lecture, Battle. I suppose you'll be writing your reminiscences one of these days. They ought to be worth reading too.'

The detective acknowledged the suggestion with a smile, but said nothing.

'I'd like rather to ask you one question,' continued Anthony. 'Did you connect me at all with the Staines affair? I fancied, from your manner, that you did.'

'Quite right. I had a hunch that way. But nothing definite to go upon. Your manner was very good, if I may say so, Mr Cade. You never overdid the carelessness.'

'I'm glad of that,' said Anthony. 'I've a feeling that ever since I met you you've been laying little traps for me. On the whole I've managed to avoid falling into them, but the strain has been acute.'

Battle smiled grimly.

'That's how you get a crook in the end, sir. Keep him on the run, to and fro, turning and twisting. Sooner or later, his nerve goes, and you've got him.'

'You're a cheerful fellow, Battle. When will you get me, I wonder?'

'Plenty of rope, sir,' quoted the superintendent, 'plenty of rope.'

'In the meantime,' said Anthony, 'I am still the amateur assistant?'

'That's it, Mr Cade.'

'Watson to your Sherlock, in fact?'

'Detective stories are mostly bunkum,' said Battle unemotionally. 'But they amuse people,' he added, as an afterthought. 'And they're useful sometimes.'

'In what way?' asked Anthony curiously.

'They encourage the universal idea that the police are stupid. When we get an amateur crime, such as a murder, that's very useful indeed.'

Anthony looked at him for some minutes in silence. Battle sat quite still, blinking now and then, with no expression whatsoever on his square placid face. Presently he rose.

'Not much good going to bed now,' he observed. 'As soon as he's up, I want to have a few words with his lordship. Anyone who wants to leave the house can do so now. At the same time I should be much obliged to his lordship if he'll extend an informal invitation to his guests to stay on. You'll accept it, sir, if you please, and Mrs Revel also.'

'Have you ever found the revolver?' asked Anthony suddenly.

'You mean the one Prince Michael was shot with? No, I haven't. Yet it must be in the house or grounds. I'll take a hint from you, Mr Cade, and send some boys up bird's-nesting. If I could get hold of the revolver, we might get forward a bit. That, and the bundle of letters. You say that a letter with the heading "Chimneys" was amongst them? Depend upon it that was the last one written. The instructions for finding the diamond are written in code in that letter.'

'What's your theory of the killing of Giuseppe?' asked Anthony.

'I should say he was a regular thief, and that he was got hold of, either by King Victor or by the Comrades of the Red Hand, and employed by them. I shouldn't wonder at all if the Comrades and King Victor aren't working together. The organization has plenty of money and power, but it isn't very strong in brain. Giuseppe's task was to steal the memoirs – they couldn't have known that you had the letters – it's a very odd coincidence that you should have, by the way.'

'I know,' said Anthony. 'It's amazing when you come to think of it.'

'Giuseppe gets hold of the letters instead. Is at first vastly chagrined. Then sees the cutting from the paper and has the brilliant idea of turning them to account on his own by blackmailing the lady. He has, of course, no idea of their real significance. The Comrades find out what he is doing, believe that he is deliberately double-crossing them, and decree his death. They're very fond of executing traitors. It has a picturesque element which seems to appeal to them. What I can't quite make out is the revolver with "Virginia" engraved upon it. There's too much finesse about that for the Comrades. As a rule, they enjoy plastering their Red Hand sign about – in order to strike terror into other would-be-traitors. No, it looks to me as though King Victor had stepped in there. But what his motive was, I don't know. It looks like a very deliberate attempt to saddle Mrs Revel with the murder, and, on the surface, there doesn't seem any particular point in that.'

'I had a theory,' said Anthony. 'But it didn't work out according to plan.'

He told Battle of Virginia's recognition of Michael. Battle nodded his head.

'Oh, yes, no doubt as to his identity. By the way, that old Baron has a very high opinion of you. He speaks of you in most enthusiastic terms.'

'That's very kind of him,' said Anthony. 'Especially as I've given him full warning that I mean to do my utmost to get hold of the missing memoirs before Wednesday next.'

'You'll have a job to do that,' said Battle.

'Y-es. You think so? I suppose King Victor and Co have got the letters.'

Battle nodded.

'Pinched them off Giuseppe that day in Pont Street. Prettily planned piece of work, that. Yes, they've got 'em all right, and they've decoded them, and they know where to look.'

Both men were on the point of passing out of the room.

'In here?' said Anthony, jerking his head back.

'Exactly, in here. But they haven't found the prize yet, and they're going to run a pretty risk trying to get it.'

'I suppose,' said Anthony, 'that you've got a plan in that subtle head of yours?'

Battle returned no answer. He looked particularly stolid and unintelligent. Then, very slowly, he winked.

'Want my help?' asked Anthony.

'I do. And I shall want someone else's.'

'Who is that?'

'Mrs Revel's. You may have noticed it, Mr Cade, but she's a lady who has a particularly beguiling way with her.'

'I've noticed it all right,' said Anthony.

He glanced at his watch.

'I'm inclined to agree with you about bed, Battle. A dip in the lake and a hearty breakfast will be far more to the point.'

He ran lightly upstairs to his bedroom. Whistling to himself, he discarded his evening clothes, and picked up a dressing-gown and a bath towel.

Then suddenly he stopped dead in front of the dressing-table, staring at the object that reposed demurely in front of the looking-glass.

For a moment he could not believe his eyes. He took it up, examined it closely. Yes, there was no mistake.

It was the bundle of letters signed Virginia Revel. They were intact. Not one missing.

Anthony dropped into a chair, the letters in his hand.

'My brain must be cracking,' he murmured. 'I can't understand a quarter of what is going on in this house. Why should the letters reappear like a damned conjuring trick? Who put them on my dressing-table? Why?'

And to all these very pertinent questions he could find no satisfactory reply.

CHAPTER XXI

Mr Isaacstein's Suitcase

At ten o'clock that morning, Lord Caterham and his daughter
were breakfasting. Bundle was looking very thoughtful.

'Father,' she said at last.

Lord Caterham, absorbed in *The Times*, did not reply.

'Father,' said Bundle again, more sharply.

Lord Caterham, torn from his interested perusal of forthcoming sales of rare books, looked up absent-mindedly.

'Eh?' he said. 'Did you speak?'

'Yes. Who is it who's had breakfast?'

She nodded towards a place that had evidently been occupied. The rest were all expectant.

'Oh, what's-his-name.'

'Fat Iky?'

Bundle and her father had enough sympathy between them
to comprehend each other's somewhat misleading observations.

'That's it.'

'Did I see you talking to the detective this morning before
breakfast?'

Lord Caterham sighed.

'Yes, he buttonholed me in the hall. I do think the hours
before breakfast should be sacred. I shall have to go abroad.
The strain on my nerves – '

Bundle interrupted unceremoniously.

'What did he say?'

'Said everyone who wanted to could clear out.'

'Well,' said Bundle, 'that's all right. That's what you've
been wanting.'

'I know. But he didn't leave it at that. He went on to say

that nevertheless he wanted me to ask everyone to stay on.'

'I don't understand,' said Bundle, wrinkling her nose.

'So confusing and contradictory,' complained Lord Caterham. 'And before breakfast too.'

'What did you say?'

'Oh, I agreed, of course. It's never any good arguing with these people. Especially before breakfast,' continued Lord Caterham, reverting to his principal grievance.

'Who have you asked so far?'

'Cade. He was up very early this morning. He's going to stop on. I don't mind that. I can't quite make the fellow out; but I like him – I like him very much.'

'So does Virginia,' said Bundle, drawing a pattern on the table with her fork.

'Eh?'

'And so do I. But that doesn't seem to matter.'

'And I asked Isaacstein,' continued Lord Caterham.

'Well?'

'But fortunately he's got to go back to town. Don't forget to order the car for the 10.50, by the way.'

'All right.'

'Now if I can only get rid of Fish too,' continued Lord Caterham, his spirits rising.

'I thought you liked talking to him about your mouldy old books.'

'So I do, so I do. So I did, rather. But it gets monotonous when one finds that one is always doing all the talking. Fish is very interested, but he never volunteers any statements of his own.'

'It's better than doing all the listening,' said Bundle. 'Like one does with George Lomax.'

Lord Caterham shuddered at the remembrance.

'George is all very well on platforms,' said Bundle. 'I've clapped him myself, though of course I know all the time that he's talking balderdash. And anyway, I'm a Socialist –'

'I know, my dear, I know,' said Lord Caterham hastily.

'It's all right,' said Bundle. 'I'm not going to bring politics into the home. That's what George does – public speaking in private life. It ought to be abolished by Act of Parliament.'

'Quite so,' said Lord Caterham.

'What about Virginia?' asked Bundle. 'Is she to be asked to stop on?'

'Battle said everybody.'

'Says he firmly! Have you asked her to be my stepma yet?'

'I don't think it would be any good,' said Lord Caterham mournfully. 'Although she did call me a darling last night. But that's the worst of these attractive young women with affectionate dispositions. They'll say anything, and they mean absolutely nothing by it.'

'No,' agreed Bundle. 'It would have been much more hopeful if she'd thrown a boot at you or tried to bite you.'

'You modern young people seem to have such unpleasant ideas about love-making,' said Lord Caterham plaintively.

'It comes from reading *The Sheik*,' said Bundle. 'Desert love. Throw her about, etc.'

'What is *The Sheik*?' asked Lord Caterham simply. 'Is it a poem?'

Bundle looked at him with commiserating pity. Then she rose and kissed the top of his head.

'Dear old Daddy,' she remarked, and sprang lightly out of the window.

Lord Caterham went back to the salerooms.

He jumped when addressed suddenly by Mr Hiram Fish, who had made his usual noiseless entry.

'Good morning, Lord Caterham.'

'Oh, good morning,' said Lord Caterham. 'Good morning. Nice day.'

'The weather is delightful,' said Mr Fish.

He helped himself to coffee. By way of food, he took a piece of dry toast.

'Do I hear correctly that the embargo is removed?' he asked after a minute or two. 'That we are all free to depart?'

'Yes – er – yes,' said Lord Caterham 'As a matter of fact, I hoped, I mean, that I shall be delighted' – his conscience

drove him on – 'only too delighted if you will stay on for a
little.'

'Why, Lord Caterham –'

'It's been a beastly visit, I know,' Lord Caterham hurried
on. 'Too bad. Shan't blame you for wanting to run away.'

'You misjudge me, Lord Caterham. The associations have
been painful, no one could deny that point. But the English
country life, as lived in the mansions of the great, has a powerful attraction for me. I am interested in the study of those
conditions. It is a thing we lack completely in America. I shall
be only too delighted to accept your vurry kind invitation and
stay on.'

'Oh, well,' said Lord Caterham, 'that's that. Absolutely
delighted, my dear fellow, absolutely delighted.'

Spurring himself on to a false geniality of manner, Lord
Caterham murmured something about having to see his bailiff
and escaped from the room.

In the hall, he saw Virginia just descending the staircase.

'Shall I take you in to breakfast?' asked Lord Caterham
tenderly.

'I've had it in bed, thank you, I was frightfully sleepy this
morning.'

She yawned.

'Had a bad night, perhaps?'

'Not exactly a bad night. From one point of view decidedly
a good night. Oh, Lord Caterham' – she slipped her hand
inside his arm and gave it a squeeze – '*I am* enjoying myself.
You were a darling to ask me down.'

'You'll stop on for a bit then, won't you? Battle is lifting
the – the embargo, but I want you to stay particularly. So
does Bundle.'

'Of course I'll stay. It's sweet of you to ask me.'

'Ah!' said Lord Caterham.

He sighed.

'What is your secret sorrow?' asked Virginia. 'Has anyone
bitten you?'

'That's just it,' said Lord Caterham mournfully.

Virginia looked puzzled.

'You don't feel, by any chance, that you want to throw a boot at me? No, I can see you don't. Oh, well, it's of no consequence.'

Lord Caterham drifted sadly away, and Virginia passed out through a side door into the garden.

She stood there for a moment, breathing in the crisp October air which was infinitely refreshing to one in her slightly jaded state.

She started a little to find Superintendent Battle at her elbow. The man seemed to have an extraordinary knack of appearing out of space without the least warning.

'Good morning, Mrs Revel. Not too tired, I hope?'

Virginia shook her head.

'It was a most exciting night,' she said. 'Well worth the loss of a little sleep. The only thing is, today seems a trifle dull after it.'

'There's a nice shady place down under that cedar tree,' remarked the superintendent. 'Shall I take a chair down to it for you?'

'If you think it's the best thing for me to do,' said Virginia solemnly.

'You're very quick, Mrs Revel. Yes, it's quite true, I do want a word with you.'

He picked up a long wicker chair and carried it down the lawn. Virginia followed him with a cushion under her arm.

'Very dangerous place, that terrace,' remarked the detective. 'That is, if you want to have a private conversation.'

'I'm getting excited again, Superintendent Battle.'

'Oh, it's nothing important.' He took out a big watch and glanced at it. 'Half past ten. I'm starting for Wyvern Abbey in ten minutes to report to Mr Lomax. Plenty of time. I only wanted to know if you could tell me a little more about Mr Cade.'

'About Mr Cade?'

Virginia was startled.

'Yes, where you first met him, and how long you've known him and so forth.'

Battle's manner was easy and pleasant enough. He even refrained from looking at her and the fact that he did so made her vaguely uneasy.

'It's more difficult than you think,' she said at last. 'He did me a great service once –'

Battle interrupted her.

'Before you go any further, Mrs Revel, I'd just like to say something. Last night, after you and Mr Eversleigh had gone to bed, Mr Cade told me all about the letters and the man who was killed in your house.'

'He did?' gasped Virginia.

'Yes, and very wisely too. It clears up a lot of misunderstanding. There's only one thing he didn't tell me – how long he had known you. Now I've a little idea of my own about that. You shall tell me if I'm right or wrong. I think that the day he came to your house in Pont Street was the first time you had ever seen him. Ah! I see I'm right. It was so.'

Virginia said nothing. For the first time she felt afraid of this stolid man with the expressionless face. She understood what Anthony had meant when he said there were no flies on Superintendent Battle.

'Has he ever told you anything about his life.' the detective continued. 'Before he was in South Africa, I mean. Canada? Or before that, the Sudan? Or about his boyhood?'

Virginia merely shook her head.

'And yet I'd bet he's got something worth telling. You can't mistake the face of a man who's led a life of daring and adventure. He could tell you some interesting tales if he cared to.'

'If you want to know about his past life, why don't you cable to that friend of his, Mr McGrath?' Virginia asked.

'Oh, we have. But it seems he's up-country somewhere. Still, there's no doubt Mr Cade was in Bulawayo when he said he was. But I wondered what he'd been doing before he came to South Africa. He'd only had that job with Castle's about a month.' He took out his watch again. 'I must be off. The car will be waiting.'

Virginia watched him retreat to the house. But she did not move from her chair. She hoped that Anthony might appear and join her. Instead came Bill Eversleigh, with a prodigious yawn.

'Thank God, I've got a chance to speak to you at last, Virginia,' he complained.

'Well, speak to me very gently, Bill darling, or I shall burst into tears.'

'Has someone been bullying you?'

'Not exactly bullying me. Getting inside my mind and turning it inside out. I feel as though I'd been jumped on by an elephant.'

'Not Battle?'

'Yes, Battle. He's a terrible man really.'

'Well, never mind Battle. I say, Virginia, I do love you so awfully –'

'Not this morning, Bill. I'm not strong enough. Anyway, I've always told you the best people don't propose before lunch.'

'Good Lord,' said Bill. 'I could propose to you before breakfast.'

Virginia shuddered.

'Bill, be sensible and intelligent for a minute. I want to ask your advice.'

'If you'd once make up your mind to it, and say you'd marry me, you'd feel miles better, I'm sure. Happier, you know, and more settled down.'

'Listen to me, Bill. Proposing to me is your *idée fixe*. All men propose when they're bored and can't think of anything to say. Remember my age and my widowed state, and go and make love to a pure young girl.'

'My darling Virginia – Oh, Blast! here's that French idiot bearing down on us.'

It was indeed M. Lemoine, black-bearded and correct of demeanour as ever.

'Good morning, madame. You are not fatigued, I trust?'

'Not in the least.'

'That is excellent. Good morning, Mr Eversleigh.'

'How would it be if we promenaded ourselves a little, the three of us?' suggested the Frenchman.

'How about it, Bill?' said Virginia.

'Oh, all right,' said the unwilling young gentleman by her side.

He heaved himself up from the grass, and the three of them walked slowly along, Virginia between the two men. She was sensible at once of a strange undercurrent of excitement in the Frenchman, though she had no clue as to what caused it.

Soon, with her usual skill, she was putting him at his ease, asking him questions, listening to his answers, and gradually drawing him out. Presently he was telling them anecdotes of the famous King Victor. He talked well, albeit with a certain bitterness as he described the various ways in which the detective bureau had been outwitted.

But all the time, despite the real absorption of Lemoine in his own narrative Virginia had a feeling that he had some other object in view. Moreover, she judged that Lemoine, under cover of his story, was deliberately striking out his own course across the park. They were not just strolling idly. He was deliberately guiding them in a certain direction.

Suddenly, he broke off his story and looked round. They were standing just where the drive intersected the park before turning an abrupt corner by a clump of trees. Lemoine was staring at a vehicle approaching them from the direction of the house.

Virginia's eyes followed his.

It's the luggage cart,' she said, 'taking Isaacstein's luggage and his valet to the station.'

Is that so?' said Lemoine. He glanced down at his own watch and started. 'A thousand pardons. I have been longer here than I meant – such charming company. Is it possible, do you think, that I might have a lift to the village?'

He stepped out on to the drive and signalled with his arm.

The luggage cart stopped, and after a word or two of explanation Lemoine climbed in behind. He raised his hat politely to Virginia, and drove off.

The other two stood and watched the cart disappearing with puzzled expressions. Just as the cart swung round the bend, a suitcase fell off into the drive. The cart went on.

'Come on,' said Virginia to Bill. 'We're going to see something interesting. That suitcase was thrown out.'

'Nobody's noticed it,' said Bill.

They ran down the drive towards the fallen piece of luggage. Just as they reached it, Lemoine came round the corner of the bend on foot. He was hot from walking fast.

'I was obliged to descend,' he said pleasantly. 'I found that I had left something behind.'

'This?' said Bill, indicating the suitcase.

It was a handsome case of heavy pigskin, with the initials H. I. on it.

'What a pity!' said Lemoine gently. 'It must have fallen out. Shall we lift it from the road?'

Without waiting for a reply, he picked up the suitcase, and carried it over to the belt of trees. He stooped over it, something flashed in his hand, and the lock slipped back.

He spoke, and his voice was totally different, quick and commanding.

'The car will be here in a minute,' he said. 'Is it in sight?'

Virginia looked back towards the house.

'No.'

'Good.'

With deft fingers he tossed the things out of the suitcase. Gold-topped bottle, silk pyjamas, a variety of socks. Suddenly his whole figure stiffened. He caught up what appeared to be a bundle of silk underwear, and unrolled it rapidly.

A slight exclamation broke from Bill. In the centre of the bundle was a heavy revolver.

'I hear the horn,' said Virginia.

Like lightning, Lemoine repacked the suitcase. The revolver he wrapped in a silk handkerchief of his own, and slipped into his pocket. He snapped the locks of the suitcase, and turned quickly to Bill.

'Take it. Madame will be with you. Stop the car, and explain that it fell off the luggage cart. Do not mention me.'

Bill stepped quickly down to the drive just as the big Lanchester limousine with Isaacstein inside it came round the corner. The chauffeur slowed down, and Bill swung the suitcase up to him.

'Fell off the luggage cart,' he explained. 'We happened to see it.'

He caught a momentary glimpse of a startled yellow face as the financier stared at him, and then the car swept on again.

They went back to Lemoine. He was standing with the revolver in his hand, and a look of gloating satisfaction in his face.

'A long shot,' he said. 'A very long shot. But it came off.'

CHAPTER XXII

The Red Signal

Superintendent Battle was standing in the library at Wyvern Abbey.

George Lomax, seated before a desk overflowing with papers, was frowning portentously.

Superintendent Battle had opened proceedings by making a brief and business-like report. Since then, the conversation had lain almost entirely with George, and Battle had contented himself with making brief and usually monosyllabic replies to the other's questions.

On the desk, in front of George, was the packet of letters Anthony had found on his dressing-table.

'I can't understand it at all,' said George irritably, as he picked up the packet. 'They're in code, you say?'

'Just so, Mr Lomax.'

'And where does he say he found them – on his dressing-table?'

Battle repeated, word for word, Anthony Cade's account of how he had come to regain possession of the letters.

'And he brought them at once to you? That was quite proper – quite proper. But who could have placed them in his room?'

Battle shook his head.

'That's the sort of thing you ought to know,' complained George. 'It sounds to me very fishy – very fishy indeed. What do we know about this man Cade, anyway? He appears in a most mysterious manner – under highly suspicious circumstances – and we know nothing whatever about him. I may say that I, personally, don't care for his manner at all. You've made inquiries about him, I suppose?'

Superintendent Battle permitted himself a patient smile.

'We wired at once to South Africa, and his story has been confirmed on all points. He was in Bulawayo with Mr McGrath at the time he stated. Previous to their meeting, he was employed by Messrs Castle, the tourist agents.'

'Just what I should have expected,' said George. 'He has the kind of cheap assurance that succeeds in a certain type of employment. But about these letters – steps must be taken at once – at once –'

The great man puffed himself out and swelled importantly. Superintendent Battle opened his mouth, but George forestalled him.

'There must be no delay. These letters must be decoded without any loss of time. Let me see, who is the man? There is a man – connected with the British Museum. Knows all there is to know about ciphers. Ran the department for us during the war. Where is Miss Oscar? She will know. Name something like Win – Win –'

'Professor Wynwood,' said Battle.

'Exactly. I remember perfectly now. He must be wired to immediately.'

'I have done so, Mr Lomax, an hour ago. He will arrive by the 12.10.'

'Oh, very good, very good. Thank heaven, something is off my mind. I shall have to be in town today. You can get along without me, I suppose?'

'I think so, sir.'

'Well, do your best, Battle, do your best. I am terribly rushed just at present.'

'Just so, sir.'

'By the way, why did not Mr Eversleigh come over with you?'

'He was still asleep, sir. We've been up all night, as I told you.'

'Oh, quite so. I am frequently up nearly the whole night myself. To do the work of thirty-six hours in twenty-four, that is my constant task! Send Mr Eversleigh over at once when you get back, will you, Battle?'

'I will give him your message, sir.'

'Thank you, Battle. I realize perfectly that you had to repose a certain amount of confidence in him. But do you think it was strictly necessary to take my cousin, Mrs Revel, into your confidence also?'

'In view of the name signed to those letters, I do, Mr Lomax.'

'An amazing piece of effrontery,' murmured George, his brow darkened as he looked at the bundle of letters. 'I remember the late King of Herzoslovakia. A charming fellow, but weak – deplorably weak. A tool in the hands of an unscrupulous woman. Have you any theory as to how these letters came to be restored to Mr Cade?'

'It's my opinion,' said Battle, 'that if people can't get a thing one way – they try another.'

'I don't quite follow you,' said George.

'This crook, this King Victor, he's well aware by now that the Council Chamber is watched. So he'll let us have the letters, and let us do the decoding, and let us find the hiding-place. And then – trouble! But Lemoine and I between us will attend to that.'

'You've got a plan, eh?'

'I wouldn't go so far as to say I've got a plan. But I've got an idea. It's a very useful thing sometimes, an idea.'

Thereupon Superintendent Battle took his departure.

He had no intention of taking George any further into his confidence.

On the way back, he passed Anthony on the road and stopped. 'Going to give me a lift back to the house?' asked Anthony. 'That's good.'

'Where have you been, Mr Cade?'

'Down to the station to inquire about trains.'

Battle raised his eyebrows.

'Thinking of leaving us again?' he inquired.

'Not just at present,' laughed Anthony. 'By the way, what's upset Isaacstein? He arrived in the car just as I left, and he looked as though something had given him a nasty jolt.'

'Mr Isaacstein?'

'Yes.'

'I can't say, I'm sure. I fancy it would take a good deal to jolt him.'

'So do I,' agreed Anthony. 'He's quite one of the strong silent yellow men of finance.'

Suddenly Battle leant forward and touched the chauffeur on the shoulder.

'Stop, will you? And wait for me here.'

He jumped out of the car, much to Anthony's surprise. But in a minute or two, the latter perceived M Lemoine advancing to meet the English detective, and gathered that it was a signal from him which had attracted Battle's attention.

There was a rapid colloquy between them, and then the superintendent returned to the car and jumped in again, bidding the chauffeur drive on.

His expression had completely changed.

'They've found the revolver,' he said suddenly and curtly.

'What?'

Anthony gazed at him in great surprise.

'Where?'

'In Isaacstein's suitcase.'

'Oh, impossible!'

'Nothing's impossible,' said Battle. 'I ought to have remembered that.'

He sat perfectly still, tapping his knee with his hand.

'Who found it?'

Battle jerked his head over his shoulder.

'Lemoine. Clever chap. They think no end of him at the Sûreté.'

'But doesn't this upset all your ideas?'

'No,' said Superintendent Battle very slowly. 'I can't say it does. It was a bit of a surprise, I admit, at first. But it fits in very well with one idea of mine.'

'Which is?'

But the superintendent branched off on to a totally different subject.

'I wonder if you'd mind finding Mr Eversleigh for me, sir? There's a message for him from Mr Lomax. He's to go over to the Abbey at once.'

'All right,' said Anthony. The car had just drawn up at the great door. 'He's probably in bed still.'

'I think not,' said the detective. 'If you'll look, you'll see him walking under the trees there with Mrs Revel.'

'Wonderful eyes you have, haven't you, Battle?' said Anthony as he departed on his errand.

He delivered the message to Bill, who was duly disgusted.

'Damn it all,' grumbled Bill to himself, as he strode off to the house, 'why can't Codders sometimes leave me alone? And why can't these blasted Colonials stay in their Colonies? What do they want to come over here for, and pick out all the best girls? I'm fed up to the teeth with everything.'

'Have you heard about the revolver?' asked Virginia breathlessly, as Bill left them.

'Battle told me. Rather staggering, isn't it? Isaacstein was in a frightful state yesterday to get away, but I thought it was just nerves. He's about the one person I'd have pitched upon as being above suspicion. Can you see any motive for his wanting Prince Michael out of the way?'

'It certainly doesn't fit in,' agreed Virginia thoughtfully.

'Nothing fits in anywhere,' said Anthony discontentedly. 'I rather fancied myself as an amateur detective to begin with, and so far all I've done is to clear the character of the French governess at vast trouble and some little expense.'

'Is that what you went to France for?' inquired Virginia.

'Yes, I went to Dinard and had an interview with the Comtesse de Breteuil, awfully pleased with my own cleverness, and fully expecting to be told that no such person as Mademoiselle Brun had ever been heard of. Instead of which I was given to understand that the lady in question had been the mainstay of the household for the last seven years. So, unless the Comtesse is also a crook, that ingenious theory of mine falls to the ground.'

Virginia shook her head.

'Madame de Breteuil is quite above suspicion. I know her quite well, and I fancy I must have come across Mademoiselle at the château. I certainly knew her face quite well – in that vague way one does know governesses and companions and people one sits opposite to in trains. It's awful, but I never really look at them properly. Do you?'

'Only if they're exceptionally beautiful,' admitted Anthony.

'Well, in this case –' she broke off. 'What's the matter?'

Anthony was staring at a figure which detached itself from the clump of trees and stood there rigidly at attention. It was the Herzoslovakian, Boris.

'Excuse me,' said Anthony to Virginia, 'I must just speak to my dog a minute.'

He went across to where Boris was standing.

'What's the matter? What do you want?'

'Master,' said Boris, bowing.

'Yes, that's all very well, but you mustn't keep following me about like this. It looks odd.'

Without a word, Boris produced a soiled scrap of paper, evidently torn from a letter, and handed it to Anthony.

'What's this?' said Anthony.

There was an address scrawled on the paper, nothing else.

'He dropped it,' said Boris. 'I bring it to the master.'

'Who dropped it?'

'The foreign gentleman.'

'But why bring it to me?'

Boris looked at him reproachfully.

'Well, anyway, go away now,' said Anthony. 'I'm busy.'

Boris saluted, turning sharply on his heel, and marched away. Anthony rejoined Virginia, thrusting the piece of paper into his pocket.

'What did he want?' she asked curiously. 'And why do you call him your dog?'

'Because he acts like one,' said Anthony, answering the last question first. 'He must have been a retriever in his last incarnation, I think. He's just brought me a piece of a letter which he says the foreign gentleman dropped. I suppose he means Lemoine.'

'I suppose so,' acquiesced Virginia.

'He's always following me round,' continued Anthony. 'Just like a dog. Says next to nothing. Just looks at me with his big round eyes. I can't make him out.'

'Perhaps he meant Isaacstein,' suggested Virginia. 'Isaacstein looks foreign enough, heaven knows.'

'Isaacstein,' muttered Anthony impatiently. 'Where the devil does he come in?'

'Are you ever sorry that you've mixed yourself up in all this?' asked Virginia suddenly.

'Sorry? Good Lord, no. I love it. I've spent most of my life looking for trouble, you know. Perhaps, this time, I've got a little more than I bargained for.'

'But you're well out of the wood now,' said Virginia, a little surprised by the unusual gravity of his tone.

'Not quite.'

They strolled on for a minute or two in silence.

'There are some people,' said Anthony, breaking the silence, 'who don't conform to the signals. An ordinary well-regulated locomotive slows down or pulls up when it sees the red light hoisted against it. Perhaps I was born colour-blind. When I see the red signal – I can't help forging ahead. And in the end, you know, that spells disaster. Bound to. And quite right really. That sort of thing is bad for traffic generally.'

He still spoke very seriously.

'I suppose,' said Virginia, 'that you have taken a good many risks in your life?'

'Pretty nearly every one there is – except marriage.'

'That's rather cynical.'

'It wasn't meant to be. Marriage, the kind of marriage I mean, would be the biggest adventure of the lot.'

'I like that,' said Virginia, flushing eagerly.

'There's only one kind of woman I'd want to marry – the kind who is worlds removed from my type of life. What would we do about it? Is she to lead my life, or am I to lead hers?'

'If she loved you –'

'Sentimentality, Mrs Revel. You know it is. Love isn't a drug that you take to blind you to your surroundings – you can make it that, yes, but it's a pity – love can be a lot more than that. What do you think the King and his beggarmaid thought of married life after they'd been married a year or two? Didn't she regret her rags and her bare feet and her carefree life? You bet she did. Would it have been any good his renouncing his crown for her sake? Not a bit of good, either. He'd have made a damned bad beggar, I'm sure. And no woman respects a man when he's doing a thing thoroughly badly.'

'Have you fallen in love with a beggarmaid, Mr Cade?' inquired Virginia softly.

'It's the other way about with me, but the principle's the same.'

'And there's no way out?' asked Virginia.

'There's always a way out,' said Anthony gloomily. 'I've got a theory that one can always get anything one wants if one will pay the price. And do you know what the price is, nine times out of ten? Compromise. A beastly thing, compromise, but it steals upon you as you near middle age. It's stealing upon me now. To get the woman I want I'd – I'd even take up regular work.'

Virginia laughed.

'I was brought up to a trade, you know,' continued Anthony.

'And you abandoned it?'

'Yes.'

'Why?'

'A matter of principle.'

'Oh!'

'You're a very unusual woman,' said Anthony suddenly, turning and looking at her.

'Why?'

'You can refrain from asking questions.'

'You mean that I haven't asked you what your trade was?'

'Just that.'

Again they walked on in silence. They were nearing the house now, passing close by the scented sweetness of the rose garden.

'You understand well enough, I dare say,' said Anthony, breaking the silence. 'You know when a man's in love with you. I don't suppose you care a hang for me – or for anyone else – but, by God, I'd like to make you care.'

'Do you think you could?' asked Virginia, in a low voice.

'Probably not, but I'd have a damned good try.'

'Are you sorry you ever met me?' she said suddenly.

'Lord, no. It's the red signal again. When I first saw you – that day in Pont Street, I knew I was up against something that was going to hurt like fun. Your face did that to me – just your face. There's magic in you from head to foot – some women are like that, but I've never known a woman who had so much of it as you have. You'll marry someone respectable and prosperous, I suppose, and I shall return to my disreputable life, but I'll kiss you once before I go – I swear I will.'

'You can't do it now,' said Virginia softly. 'Superintendent Battle is watching us out of the library window.'

Anthony looked at her.

'You're rather a devil, Virginia,' he said dispassionately. 'But rather a dear too.'

Then he waved his hand airily to Superintendent Battle.

'Caught any criminals this morning, Battle?'

'Not as yet, Mr Cade.'

'That sounds hopeful.'

Battle with an agility surprising in so stolid a man, vaulted out of the library window and joined them on the terrace.

'I've got Professor Wynwood down here,' he announced in a whisper. 'Just this minute arrived. He's decoding the letters now. Would you like to see him at work?'

His tone suggested that of the showman speaking of some pet exhibit. Receiving a reply in the affirmative, he led them up to the window and invited them to peep inside.

Seated at a table, the letters spread out in front of him and writing busily on a big sheet of paper, was a small red-haired man of middle age. He grunted irritably to himself as he wrote and every now and then rubbed his nose violently until its hue almost rivalled that of his hair.

Presently he looked up.

'That you, Battle? What do you want me down here to unravel this tomfoolery for? A child in arms could do it. A baby of two could do it on his head. Call this thing a cipher? It leaps to the eye, man.'

'I'm glad of that, Professor,' said Battle mildly. 'But we're not all so clever as you are, you know.'

'It doesn't need cleverness,' snapped the professor. 'It's routine work. Do you want the whole bundle done? It's a long business, you know – requires diligent application and close attention and absolutely no intelligence. I've done the one dated "Chimneys" which you said was important. I might as well take the rest back to London and hand 'em over to one of my assistants. I really can't afford the time myself. I've come away now from a real teaser, and I want to get back to it.'

His eyes glistened a little.

'Very well, Professor,' assented Battle. 'I'm sorry we're such small fry. I'll explain to Mr Lomax. It's just this one letter that all the hurry is about. Lord Caterham is expecting you to stay for lunch, I believe.'

'Never have lunch,' said the professor. 'Bad habit, lunch. A banana and a water biscuit is all any sane and healthy man should need in the middle of the day.'

He seized his overcoat, which lay across the back of a chair. Battle went round to the front of the house, and a few minutes later Anthony and Virginia heard the sound of a car driving away.

Battle rejoined them, carrying in his hand the half-sheet of paper which the Professor had given him.

'He's always like that,' said Battle, referring to the departed professor. 'In the very deuce of a hurry. Clever man, though. Well, here's the kernel of Her Majesty's letter. Care to have a look at it?'

Virginia stretched out a hand, and Anthony read it over her shoulder. It had been, he remembered, a long epistle, breathing mingled passion and despair. The genius of Professor Wynwood had transformed it into an essentially business-like communication

Operations carried out successfully, but S double-crossed us. Has removed stone from hiding-place. Not in his room. I have searched. Found following memorandum which I think refers to it: RICHMOND SEVEN STRAIGHT EIGHT LEFT THREE RIGHT.

'S?' said Anthony. 'Stylptitch, of course. Cunning old dog. He changed the hiding-place.'

'Richmond,' said Virginia thoughtfully. 'Is the diamond concealed somewhere at Richmond, I wonder?'

'It's a favourite spot for royalties,' agreed Anthony.

Battle shook his head.

'I still think it's a reference to something in this house.'

'I know,' cried Virginia suddenly.

Both men turned to look at her.

'The Holbein portrait in the Council Chamber. They were tapping on the wall just below it. And it's a portrait of the Earl of Richmond!'

'You've got it,' said Battle, and slapped his leg.

He spoke with an animation quite unwonted.

'That's the starting-point, the picture, and the crooks know no more than we do what the figures refer to. Those two men in armour stand directly underneath the picture, and their first idea was that the diamond was hidden in one of them. The measurements might have been inches. That failed, and their next idea was a secret passage or stairway, or a sliding panel. Do you know of any such thing, Mrs Revel?'

Virginia shook her head.

'There's a priest's hole, and at least one secret passage, I know,' she said. 'I believe I've been shown them once, but I can't remember much about them now. Here's Bundle, she'll know.'

Bundle was coming quickly along the terrace towards them.

'I'm taking the Panhard up to town after lunch,' she remarked. 'Anyone want a lift? Wouldn't you like to come, Mr Cade? We'll be back by dinnertime.'

'No, thanks,' said Anthony. 'I'm quite happy and busy down here.'

'The man fears me,' said Bundle. 'Either my driving or my fatal fascination! Which is it?'

'The latter,' said Anthony. 'Every time.'

'Bundle, dear,' said Virginia, 'is there any secret passage leading out of the Council Chamber?'

'Rather. But it's only a mouldy one. Supposed to lead from Chimneys to Wyvern Abbey. So it did in the old, old days, but it's all blocked up now. You can only get along it for about a hundred yards from this end. The one upstairs in the White Gallery is ever so much more amusing, and the priest's hole isn't half bad.'

'We're not regarding them from an artistic standpoint,' explained Virginia. 'It's business. How do you get into the Council Chamber one?'

'Hinged panel. I'll show it you after lunch if you like.'

'Thank you,' said Superintendent Battle. 'Shall we say at 2.30?'

Bundle looked at him with lifted eyebrows.

'Crook stuff?' she inquired.

Tredwell appeared on the terrace.

'Luncheon is served, my lady,' he announced.

CHAPTER XXIII

Encounter in the Rose Garden

At 2.30 a little party met together in the Council Chamber: Bundle, Virginia, Superintendent Battle, M. Lemoine and Anthony Cade.

'No good waiting until we can get hold of Mr Lomax,' said Battle. 'This is the kind of business one wants to get on with quickly.'

'If you've got any idea that Prince Michael was murdered by someone who got in this way, you're wrong,' said Bundle. 'It can't be done. The other end's blocked completely.'

'There is no question of that, milady,' said Lemoine quickly. 'It is quite a different search that we make.'

'Looking for something, are you?' asked Bundle quickly. 'Not the historic what-not, by any chance?'

Lemoine looked puzzled.

'Explain yourself, Bundle,' said Virginia encouragingly. 'You can when you try.'

'The thingummybob,' said Bundle. 'The historic diamond of purple princes that was pinched in the dark ages before I grew to years of discretion.'

'Who told you this, Lady Eileen?' asked Battle.

'I've always known. One of the footmen told me when I was twelve years old.'

'A footman,' said Battle. 'Lord! I'd like Mr Lomax to have heard that!'

'Is it one of George's closely guarded secrets?' asked Bundle. 'How perfectly screaming! I never really thought it was true. George always was an ass – he must know that servants know everything.'

She went across to the Holbein portrait, touched a spring

concealed somewhere at the side of it, and immediately, with a creaking noise, a section of the panelling swung inwards, revealing a dark opening.

'*Entrez, messieurs et mesdames,*' said Bundle dramatically. 'Walk up, walk up, walk up, dearies. Best show of the season, and only a tanner.'

Both Lemoine and Battle were provided with torches. They entered the dark aperture first, the others close on their heels.

'Air's nice and fresh,' remarked Battle. 'Must be ventilated somehow.'

He walked on ahead. The floor was rough uneven stone, but the walls were bricked. As Bundle had said, the passage extended for a bare hundred yards. Then it came to an abrupt end with a fallen heap of masonry. Battle satisfied himself that there was no way of egress beyond, and then spoke over his shoulder.

'We'll go back, if you please. I wanted just to spy out the land, so to speak.'

In a few minutes they were back again at the panelled entrance.

'We'll start from here,' said Battle. 'Seven straight, eight left, three right. Take the first as paces.'

He paced seven steps carefully, and bending down examined the ground.

'About right, I should fancy. At one time or another, there's been a chalk mark made here. Now then, eight left. That's not paces, the passage is only wide enough to go Indian file, anyway.'

'Say it in bricks,' suggested Anthony.

'Quite right, Mr Cade. Eight bricks from the bottom or the top on the left-hand side. Try from the bottom first – it's easier.'

He counted up eight bricks.

'Now three to the right of that. One, two, three – Hullo – Hullo, what's this?'

'I shall scream in a minute,' said Bundle, 'I know I shall. *What* is it?'

Superintendent Battle was working at the brick with the point of his knife. His practised eye had quickly seen that this particular brick was different from the rest. A minute or two's work, and he was able to pull it right out. Behind was a small dark cavity. Battle thrust in his hand.

Everyone waited in breathless expectancy.

Battle drew out his hand again.

He uttered an exclamation of surprise and anger.

The others crowded round and stared uncomprehendingly at the three articles he held. For a moment it seemed as though their eyes must have deceived them.

A card of small pearl buttons, a square of coarse knitting, and a piece of paper on which were inscribed a row of capital E's!

'Well,' said Battle. 'I'm – I'm danged. What's the meaning of this?'

'*Mon Dieu*,' muttered the Frenchman. '*Ça, c'est un peu trop fort!*'

'But what does it mean?' cried Virginia, bewildered.

'Mean?' said Anthony. 'There's only one thing it can mean. The late Count Stylptitch must have had a sense of humour! This is an example of that humour. I may say that I don't consider it particularly funny myself.'

'Do you mind explaining your meaning a little more clearly, sir?' said the Superintendent Battle.

'Certainly. This was the Count's little joke. He must have suspected that his memorandum had been read. When the crooks came to recover the jewel, they were to find instead this extremely clever conundrum. It's the sort of thing you pin on to yourself at Book Teas, when people have to guess what you are.'

'It has a meaning, then?'

'I should say, undoubtedly. If the Count had meant to be merely offensive, he would have put a placard with "Sold" on it, or a picture of a donkey or something crude like that.'

'A bit of knitting, some capital E's, and a lot of buttons,' muttered Battle discontentedly.

'*C'est inouï,*' said Lemoine angrily.

'Cipher No 2,' said Anthony. 'I wonder whether Professor Wynwood would be any good at this one?'

'When was this passage last used, milady?' asked the Frenchman of Bundle.

Bundle reflected.

'I don't believe anyone's been into it for over two years. The priest's hole is the show exhibit for Americans and tourists generally.'

'Curious,' murmured the Frenchman.

'Why curious?'

Lemoine stooped and picked up a small object from the floor.

'Because of this,' he said. 'This match has not lain here for two years – not even two days.'

'Any of you ladies or gentlemen drop this, by any chance?' he asked.

He received a negative all round.

'Well, then,' said Superintendent Battle, 'we've seen all there is to see. We might as well get out of here.'

The proposal was assented to by all. The panel had swung to, but Bundle showed them how it was fastened from the inside. She unlatched it, swung it noiselessly open, and sprang through the opening, alighting in the Council Chamber with a resounding thud.

'Damn!' said Lord Caterham, springing up from an armchair in which he appeared to have been taking forty winks.

'Poor old Father,' said Bundle. 'Did I startle you?'

'I can't think,' said Lord Caterham, 'why nobody nowadays ever sits still after a meal. It's a lost art. God knows Chimneys is big enough but even here there doesn't seem to be a single room where I can be sure of a little peace. Good Lord, how many of you are there? Reminds me of the pantomimes I used to go to as a boy when hordes of demons used to pop up out of trapdoors.'

'Demon No 7,' said Virginia, approaching him, and patting

him on the head. 'Don't be cross. We're just exploring secret passages, that's all.'

'There seems to be a positive boom in secret passages today,' grumbled Lord Caterham, not yet completely mollified. 'I've had to show that fellow Fish round them all this morning.'

'When was that?' asked Battle quickly.

'Just before lunch. It seems he'd heard of the one in here. I showed him that, and then took him up to the White Gallery, and we finished up with the priest's hole. But his enthusiasm was waning by that time. He looked bored to death. But I made him go through with it.' Lord Caterham chuckled at the remembrance.

Anthony put a hand on Lemoine's arm.

'Come outside,' he said softly. 'I want to speak to you.'

The two men went out together through the window. When they had gone a sufficient distance from the house, Anthony drew from his pocket the scrap of paper that Boris had given him that morning.

'Look here,' he said. 'Did you drop this?'

Lemoine took it and examined it with some interest.

'No,' he said. 'I have never seen it before. Why?'

'Quite sure?'

'Absolutely sure, monsieur.'

'That's very odd.'

He repeated to Lemoine what Boris had said. The other listened with close attention.

'No, I did not drop it. You say he found it in that clump of trees?'

'Well, I assumed so, but he did not actually say so.'

'It is just possible that it might have fluttered out of M Isaacstein's suitcase. Question Boris again.' He handed the paper back to Anthony. After a minute or two he said: 'What exactly do you know of this man Boris?'

Anthony shrugged his shoulders.

'I understood he was the late Prince Michael's trusted servant.'

'It may be so, but make it your business to find out. Ask

someone who knows, such as the Baron Lolopretjzyl. Perhaps this man was engaged but a few weeks ago. For myself, I have believed him honest. But who knows? King Victor is quite capable of making himself into a trusted servant at a moment's notice.'

'Do you really think –'

Lemoine interrupted him.

'I will be quite frank. With me, King Victor is an obsession. I see him everywhere. At this moment even I ask myself – this man who is talking to me, this M Cade, is he, perhaps, King Victor?'

'Good Lord,' said Anthony, 'you have got it badly.'

'What do I care for the diamond? For the discovery of the murderer of Prince Michael? I leave those affairs to my colleague of Scotland Yard whose business it is. Me, I am in England for one purpose, and one purpose only, to capture King Victor and capture him red-handed. Nothing else matters.'

'Think you'll do it?' asked Anthony, lighting a cigarette.

'How should I know?' said Lemoine, with sudden despondency.

'Hm!' said Anthony.

They had regained the terrace. Superintendent Battle was standing near the french window in a wooden attitude.

'Look at poor old Battle,' said Anthony. 'Let's go and cheer him up.' He paused a minute, and said, 'You know, you're an odd fish in some ways, M Lemoine.'

'In what ways, M Cade?'

'Well,' said Anthony, 'in your place, I should have been inclined to note down that address that I showed you. It may be of no importance – quite conceivably. On the other hand, it might be very important indeed.'

Lemoine looked at him for a minute or two steadily. Then, with a slight smile, he drew back the cuff of his left coat-sleeve. Pencilled on the white shirt-cuff beneath were the words 'Hurstmere, Langly Road, Dover.'

'I apologize,' said Anthony. 'And I retire worsted.'

He joined Superintendent Battle.

'You look very pensive, Battle,' he remarked.

'I've got a lot to think about, Mr Cade.'

'Yes, I expect you have.'

'Things aren't dovetailing. They're not dovetailing at all.'

'Very trying,' sympathized Anthony. 'Never mind, Battle, if the worst comes to the worst, you can always arrest me. You've got my guilty footprints to fall back upon, remember.'

But the superintendent did not smile.

'Got any enemies here that you know of, Mr Cade?' he asked.

'I've an idea that the third footman doesn't like me,' replied Anthony lightly. 'He does his best to forget to hand me the choicest vegetables. Why?'

'I've been getting anonymous letters,' said Superintendent Battle. 'Or rather an anonymous letter, I should say.'

'About me?'

Without answer Battle took a folded sheet of cheap notepaper from his pocket, and handed it to Anthony. Scrawled on it in an illiterate handwriting were the words:

Look out for Mr Cade. He isn't wot he seems.

Anthony handed it back with a light laugh.

'That all? Cheer up, Battle. I'm really a king in disguise, you know.'

He went into the house, whistling lightly as he walked along. But as he entered his bedroom and shut the door behind him, his face changed. It grew set and stern. He sat down on the edge of the bed and stared moodily at the floor.

'Things are getting serious,' said Anthony to himself. 'Something must be done about it. It's all damned awkward . . .'

He sat there for a minute or two, then strolled to the window. For a moment or two he stood looking out aimlessly and then his eyes became suddenly focused on a certain spot, and his face lightened.

'Of course,' he said. 'The rose garden! That's it! The rose garden.'

He hurried downstairs again and out into the garden by a

side door. He approached the rose garden by a circuitous route. It had a little gate at either end. He entered by the far one, and walked up to the sundial which was on a raised hillock in the exact centre of the garden.

Just as Anthony reached it, he stopped dead and stared at another occupant of the rose garden who seemed equally surprised to see him.

'I didn't know that you were interested in roses, Mr Fish,' said Anthony gently.

'Sir,' said Mr Fish, 'I am considerably interested in roses.'

They looked at each other warily, as antagonists seek to measure their opponents' strength.

'So am I,' said Anthony.

'Is that so?'

'In fact, I dote upon roses,' said Anthony airily.

A very slight smile hovered upon Mr Fish's lips, and at the same time Anthony also smiled. The tension seemed to relax.

'Look at this beauty now,' said Mr Fish, stooping to point out a particularly fine bloom. 'Madame Abel Chatenay, I pressoom it to be. Yes, I am right. This white rose, before the war, was known as Frau Carl Drusky. They have, I believe, renamed it. Over-sensitive, perhaps, but truly patriotic. The La France is always popular. Do you care for red roses at all, Mr Cade? A bright scarlet rose now –'

Mr Fish's slow, drawling voice, was interrupted. Bundle was leaning out of a first-floor window.

'Care for a spin to town, Mr Fish? I'm just off.'

'Thank you, Lady Eileen, but I am vurry happy here.'

'Sure you won't change your mind, Mr Cade?'

Anthony laughed and shook his head. Bundle disappeared.

'Sleep is more in my line,' said Anthony, with a wide yawn. 'A good after-luncheon nap!' He took out a cigarette. 'You haven't got a match, have you?'

Mr Fish handed him a matchbox. Anthony helped himself, and handed back the box with a word of thanks.

'Roses,' said Anthony, 'are all very well. But I don't feel particularly horticultural this afternoon.'

With a disarming smile, he nodded cheerfully.

A thundering noise sounded from just outside the house.

'Pretty powerful engine she's got in that car of hers,' remarked Anthony. 'There, off she goes.'

They had a view of the car speeding down the long drive.

Anthony yawned again, and strolled towards the house.

He passed in through the door. Once inside, he seemed as though changed to quicksilver. He raced across the hall, out through one of the windows on the farther side, and across the park. Bundle, he knew, had to make a big detour by the lodge gates, and through the village.

He ran desperately. It was a race against time. He reached the park wall just as he heard the car outside. He swung himself up and dropped into the road.

'Hi!' cried Anthony.

In her astonishment, Bundle swerved half across the road. She managed to pull up without accident. Anthony ran after the car, opened the door, and jumped in beside Bundle.

'I'm coming to London with you,' he said. 'I meant to all along.'

'Extraordinary person,' said Bundle. 'What's that you've got in your hand?'

'Only a match,' said Anthony.'

He regarded it thoughtfully. It was pink, with a yellow head. He threw away his unlighted cigarette, and put the match carefully into his pocket.

CHAPTER XXIV

The House at Dover

'You don't mind, I suppose,' said Bundle after a minute or two, 'if I drive rather fast? I started later than I meant to do.'

It had seemed to Anthony that they were proceeding at a terrific speed already, but he soon saw that that was nothing compared to what Bundle could get out of the Panhard if she tried.

'Some people,' said Bundle, as she slowed down momentarily to pass through a village, 'are terrified of my driving. Poor old Father, for instance. Nothing would induce him to come up with me in this old bus.'

Privately, Anthony thought Lord Caterham was entirely justified. Driving with Bundle was not a sport to be indulged in by nervous, middle-aged gentlemen.

'But you don't seem nervous a bit,' continued Bundle approvingly, as she swept round a corner on two wheels.

'I'm in pretty good training, you see,' explained Anthony gravely. 'Also,' he added, as an afterthought, 'I'm rather in a hurry myself.'

'Shall I speed her up a bit more?' asked Bundle kindly.

'Good Lord, no,' said Anthony hastily. 'We're averaging about fifty as it is.'

'I'm burning with curiosity to know the reason for this sudden departure,' said Bundle, after executing a fanfare upon the klaxon which must temporarily have deafened the neighbourhood. 'But I suppose I mustn't ask? You're not escaping from justice, are you?'

'I'm not quite sure,' said Anthony. 'I shall know soon.'

'That Scotland Yard man isn't as much of a rabbit as I thought,' said Bundle thoughtfully.

'Battle's a good man,' agreed Anthony.

'You ought to have been in diplomacy,' remarked Bundle. 'You don't part with much information, do you?'

'I was under the impression that I babbled.'

'Oh! Boy! You're not eloping with Mademoiselle Brun, by any chance?'

'Not guilty!' said Anthony with fervour.

There was a pause of some minutes during which Bundle caught up and passed three other cars. Then she asked suddenly:

'How long have you known Virginia?'

'That's a difficult question to answer,' said Anthony, with perfect truth. 'I haven't actually met her very often, and yet I seem to have known her a long time.'

Bundle nodded.

'Virginia's got brains,' she remarked abruptly. 'She's always talking nonsense, but she's got brains all right. She was frightfully good out in Herzoslovakia, I believe. If Tim Revel had lived he'd have had a fine career – and mostly owing to Virginia. She worked for him tooth and nail. She did everything in the world she could for him – and I know why, too.'

'Because she cared for him?' Anthony sat looking very straight ahead of him.

'No, because she didn't. Don't you see? She didn't love him – she never loved him, and so she did everything on earth she could to make up. That's Virginia all over. But don't you make any mistake about it. Virginia was never in love with Tim Revel.'

'You seem very positive,' said Anthony, turning to look at her.

Bundle's little hands were clenched on the steering wheel, and her chin was stuck out in a determined manner.

'I know a thing or two. I was only a kid at the time of her marriage, but I heard one or two things, and knowing Virginia I can put them together easily enough. Tim Revel was bowled over by Virginia – he was Irish, you know, and most attractive, with a genius for expressing himself well. Virginia was quite young – eighteen. She couldn't go anywhere without seeing Tim in a state of picturesque misery, vowing he'd shoot himself or take to drink if she didn't marry him. Girls believe these things – or used to – we've advanced a lot in the last eight years. Virginia was carried away by the feeling she thought she'd inspired. She married him – and she was an angel to him always. She wouldn't have been half as much of an angel if she'd loved him. There's a lot of the devil in Virginia. But I can tell you one thing – she enjoys her freedom. And anyone will have a hard time persuading her to give it up.'

'I wonder why you tell me all this?' said Anthony slowly.

'It's interesting to know about people, isn't it? Some people, that is.'

'I've wanted to know,' he acknowledged.

'And you'd never have heard from Virginia. But you can trust me for an inside tip from the stables. Virginia's a darling. Even women like her because she isn't a bit of a cat. And anyway,' Bundle ended, somewhat obscurely, 'one must be a sport, mustn't one?'

'Oh, certainly,' Anthony agreed. But he was still puzzled. He had no idea what had prompted Bundle to give him so much information unasked. That he was glad of it, he did not deny.

'Here are the trams,' said Bundle, with a sigh. 'Now, I suppose, I shall have to drive carefully.'

'It might be as well,' agreed Anthony.

His ideas and Bundle's on the subject of careful driving hardly coincided. Leaving indignant suburbs behind them they finally emerged into Oxford Street.

'Not bad going, eh?' said Bundle, glancing at her wrist-watch.

Anthony assented fervently.

'Where do you want to be dropped?'

'Anywhere. Which way are you going?'

'Knightsbridge way.'

'All right, drop me at Hyde Park Corner.'

'Goodbye,' said Bundle, as she drew up at the place indicated. 'What about the return journey?'

'I'll find my own way back, thanks very much.'

'I *have* scared him,' remarked Bundle.

'I shouldn't recommend driving with you as a tonic for nervous old ladies, but personally I've enjoyed it. The last time I was in equal danger was when I was charged by a herd of wild elephants.'

'I think you're extremely rude,' remarked Bundle. 'We've not even had one bump today.'

'I'm sorry if you've been holding yourself in on my account,' retorted Anthony.

'I don't think men are really very brave,' said Bundle.

'That's a nasty one,' said Anthony. 'I retire, humiliated.' Bundle nodded and drove on. Anthony hailed a passing taxi. 'Victoria Station,' he said to the driver as he got in.

When he got to Victoria he paid off the taxi and inquired for the next train to Dover. Unfortunately he had just missed one.

Resigning himself to a wait of something over an hour, Anthony paced up and down, his brows knit. Once or twice he shook his head impatiently.

The journey to Dover was uneventful. Arrived there, Anthony passed quickly out of the station and then, as though suddenly remembering, he turned back again. There was a slight smile on his lips as he asked to be directed to Hurstmere, Langly Road.

The road in question was a long one, leading right out of the town. According to the porter's instructions, Hurstmere was the last house. Anthony trudged along steadily. The little pucker had reappeared between his eyes. Nevertheless there was a new elation in his manner, as always when danger was near at hand.

Hurstmere was, as the porter had said, the last house in Langly Road. It stood well back, enclosed in its own grounds, which were ragged and overgrown. The place, Anthony judged, must have been empty for many years. A large iron gate swung rustily on its hinges, and the name on the gate-post was half obliterated.

'A lonely spot,' muttered Anthony to himself, 'and a good one to choose.'

He hesitated a minute or two, glanced quickly up and down the road – which was quite deserted – and then slipped quietly past the creaking gate into the overgrown drive. He walked up it a little way, and then stood listening. He was still some distance from the house. Not a sound could be heard any-where. Some fast-yellowing leaves detached themselves from one of the trees overhead and fell with a soft rustling sound that was almost sinister in the stillness. Anthony started; then smiled.

'Nerves,' he murmured to himself. 'Never knew I had such things before.'

He went on up the drive. Presently, as the drive curved, he slipped into the shrubbery and so continued his way unseen from the house. Suddenly he stood still, peering out through the leaves. Some distance away a dog was barking, but it was a sound nearer at hand that had attracted Anthony's attention.

His keen hearing had not been mistaken. A man came rapidly round the corner of the house, a short square, thick-set man, foreign in appearance. He did not pause but walked steadily on, circling the house and disappearing again.

Anthony nodded to himself.

'Sentry,' he murmured. 'They do the thing quite well.'

As soon as he had passed, Anthony went on, diverging to the left, and so following in the footsteps of the sentry.

His own footsteps were quite noiseless.

The wall of the house was on his right, and presently he came to where a broad blur of light fell on the gravelled walk. The sound of several men talking together was clearly audible.

'My God! what double-dyed idiots,' murmured Anthony to himself. 'It would serve them right to be given a fright.'

He stole up to the window, stooping a little so that he should not be seen. Presently he lifted his head very carefully to the level of the sill and looked in.

Half a dozen men were sprawling round a table. Four of them were big thick-set men, with high cheekbones, and eyes set in Magyar slanting fashion. The other two were rat-like little men with quick gestures. The language that was being spoken was French, but the four big men spoke it with uncertainty and a hoarse guttural intonation.

'The boss?' growled one of these. 'When will he be here?'

One of the smaller men shrugged his shoulders.

'Any time now.'

'About time, too,' growled the first man. 'I have never seen him, this boss of yours, but, oh, what great and glorious work might we not have accomplished in these days of idle waiting!'

'Fool,' said the other little man bitingly. 'Getting nabbed by the police is all the great and glorious work you and your precious lot would have been likely to accomplish. A lot of blundering gorillas!'

'Aha!' roared another big thick-set fellow. 'You insult the Comrades? I will soon set the sign of the Red Hand round your throat.'

He half rose, glaring ferociously at the Frenchman, but one of his companions pulled him back again.

'No quarrelling,' he grunted. 'We're to work together. From all I heard, this King Victor doesn't stand for being disobeyed.'

In the darkness, Anthony heard the footsteps of the sentry coming on his round again, and he drew back behind a bush.

'Who's that?' said one of the men inside.

'Carlo – going his rounds.'

'Oh! What about the prisoner?'

'He's all right – coming round pretty fast now. He's recovered well from the crack on the head we gave him.'

Anthony moved gently away.

'God! What a lot,' he muttered. 'They discuss their affairs with an open window, and that fool Carlo goes his round with the tread of an elephant – and the eyes of a bat. And to crown all, the Herzoslovakians and the French are on the point of coming to blows. King Victor's headquarters seem to be in a parlous condition. It would amuse me, it would amuse me very much, to teach them a lesson.'

He stood irresolute for a minute, smiling to himself.

From somewhere above his head came a stifled groan.

Anthony looked up. The groan came again.

Anthony glanced quickly from left to right. Carlo was not due round again just yet. He grasped the heavy virginia creeper and climbed nimbly till he reached the sill of a window. The window was shut, but with a tool from his pocket he soon succeeded in forcing up the catch.

He paused a minute to listen, then sprang lightly inside the room. There was a bed in the far corner and on that bed a man was lying, his figure barely discernible in the gloom.

Anthony went over to the bed, and flashed his pocket torch on the man's face. It was a foreign face, pale and emaciated, and the head was swathed in heavy bandages.

The man was bound hand and foot. He stared up at Anthony like one dazed.

Anthony bent over him, and as he did so he heard a sound behind him and swung round, his hand travelling to his coat pocket.

But a sharp command arrested him.

'Hands up, sonny. You didn't expect to see me here, but I happened to catch the same train as you at Victoria.'

It was Mr Hiram Fish who was standing in the doorway. He was smiling and in his hand was a big blue automatic.

CHAPTER XXV

Tuesday Night at Chimneys

Lord Caterham, Virginia and Bundle were sitting in the library after dinner. It was Tuesday evening. Some thirty hours had elapsed since Anthony's rather dramatic departure.

For at least the seventh time Bundle repeated Anthony's parting words, as spoken at Hyde Park Corner.

'I'll find my own way back,' echoed Virginia thoughtfully. 'That doesn't look as though he expected to be away as long as this. And he's left all his things here.'

'He didn't tell you where he was going?'

'No,' said Virginia, looking straight in front of her. 'He told me nothing.'

After this, there was a silence for a minute or two. Lord Caterham was the first to break it.

'On the whole,' he said, 'keeping an hotel has some advantages over keeping a country house.'

'Meaning –'

'That little notice they always hang up in your room. Visitors intending departure must give notice before twelve o'clock.'

Virginia smiled.

'I dare say,' he continued, 'that I am old-fashioned and unreasonable. It's the fashion, I know, to pop in and out of a house. Same idea as an hotel – perfect freedom of action, and no bill at the end!'

'You are an old grouser,' said Bundle. 'You've had Virginia and me. What more do you want?'

'Nothing more, nothing more,' Lord Caterham assured them hastily. 'That's not it at all. It's the principle of the thing. It gives one such a restless feeling. I'm quite willing to admit that it's been an almost ideal twenty-four hours. Peace – perfect peace. No burglaries or other crimes of violence, no detectives, no Americans. What I complain of is that I should have enjoyed it all so much more if I'd felt really secure. As it is, all the time, I've been saying to myself, "One or the other of them is bound to turn up in a minute." And that spoilt the whole thing.'

'Well, nobody has turned up,' said Bundle. 'We've been left severely alone – neglected, in fact. It's odd the way Fish disappeared. Didn't he say anything?'

'Not a word. Last time I saw him he was pacing up and down the rose garden yesterday afternoon, smoking one of those unpleasant cigars of his. After that he seems to have just melted into the landscape.'

'Somebody must have kidnapped him,' said Bundle hopefully.

'In another day or two, I expect we shall have Scotland Yard dragging the lake to find his dead body,' said her father gloomily. 'It serves me right. At my time of life, I ought to have gone quietly abroad and taken care of my health, and not allowed myself to be drawn into George Lomax's wild-cat schemes. I –'

He was interrupted by Tredwell.

'Well,' said Lord Caterham, irritably, 'what is it?'

'The French detective is here, my lord, and would be glad if you could spare him a few minutes.'

'What did I tell you?' said Lord Caterham. 'I knew it was too good to last. Depend upon it, they've found Fish's dead body doubled up in the goldfish pond.'

Tredwell, in a strictly respectful manner, steered him back to the point at issue.

'Am I to say that you will see him, my lord?'

'Yes, yes. Bring him in here.'

Tredwell departed. He returned a minute or two later announcing in a lugubrious voice:

'Monsieur Lemoine.'

The Frenchman came in with a quick, light step. His walk,

more than his face, betrayed the fact that he was excited about something.

'Good evening, Lemoine,' said Lord Caterham. 'Have a drink, won't you?'

'I thank you, no.' He bowed punctiliously to the ladies. 'At last I make progress. As things are, I felt that you should be acquainted with the discoveries – the very grave discoveries that I have made in the course of the last twenty-four hours.'

'I thought there must be something important going on somewhere,' said Lord Caterham.

'My lord, yesterday afternoon one of your guests left this house in a curious manner. From the beginning, I must tell you, I have had my suspicions. Here is a man who comes from the wilds. Two months ago he was in South Africa. Before that – where?'

Virginia drew a sharp breath. For a moment the Frenchman's eyes rested on her doubtfully. Then he went on:

'Before that – where? None can say. And he is just such a one as the man I am looking for – gay, audacious, reckless, one who would dare anything. I send cable after cable, but I can get no word as to his past life. Ten years ago he was in Canada, yes, but since then – silence. My suspicions grow stronger. Then I pick up one day a scrap of paper where he has lately passed along. It bears an address – the address of a house in Dover. Later, as though by chance, I drop that same piece of paper. Out of the tail of my eye, I see this Boris, the Herzoslovakian, pick it up and take it to his master. All along I have been sure that this Boris is an emissary of the Comrades of the Red Hand. We know that the Comrades are working in with King Victor over this affair. If Boris recognized his chief in Mr Anthony Cade, would he not do just what he has done – transferred his allegiance? Why should he attach himself otherwise to an insignificant stranger? It was suspicious, I tell you, very suspicious.

'But almost I am disarmed, for Anthony Cade brings this same paper to me at once and asks me if I have dropped it. As I say, almost I am disarmed – but not quite! For it may mean that he is innocent, or it may mean that he is very, very clever. I deny, of course, that it is mine or that I dropped it. But in the meantime I have set inquiries on foot. Only today I have news. The house at Dover has been precipitately abandoned, but up till yesterday afternoon it was occupied by a body of foreigners. Not a doubt but that it was King Victor's headquarters. Now see the significance of these points. Yesterday afternoon, Mr Cade clears out from here precipitately. Ever since he dropped that paper, he must know that the game is up. He reaches Dover and immediately the gang is disbanded. What the next move will be, I do not know. What is quite certain is that Mr Anthony Cade will not return here. But knowing King Victor as I do, I am certain that he will not abandon the game without having one more try for the jewel. And that is when I shall get him!'

Virginia stood up suddenly. She walked across to the mantelpiece and spoke in a voice that rang cold like steel.

'You are leaving one thing out of account, I think, M Lemoine,' she said. 'Mr Cade is not the only guest who disappeared yesterday in a suspicious manner.'

'You mean, madame? –'

'That all you have said applies equally well to another person. What about Mr Hiram Fish?'

'Oh Mr Fish!'

'Yes, Mr Fish. Did you not tell us that first night that King Victor had lately come to England from America? So has Mr Fish come to England from America. It is true that he brought a letter of introduction from a very well-known man, but surely that would be a simple thing for a man like King Victor to manage. He is certainly not what he pretends to be. Lord Caterham has commented on the fact that when it is a question of the first editions he is supposed to have come here to see he is always the listener, never the talker. And there are several suspicious facts against him. There was a light in his window the night of the murder. Then take that evening in the Council Chamber. When I met him on the terrace he was fully dressed. *He* could have dropped the paper. You didn't actually *see* Mr

Cade do so. Mr Cade may have gone to Dover. If he did it was simply to investigate. He may have been kidnapped there. I say that there is far more suspicion attaching to Mr Fish's actions than to Mr Cade's.'

The Frenchman's voice rang out sharply:

'From your point of view, that well may be, madame. I do not dispute it. And I agree that Mr Fish is not what he seems.'

'Well, then?'

'But that makes no difference. *You see, madame, Mr Fish is a Pinkerton's man.*'

'What?' cried Lord Caterham.

'Yes, Lord Caterham. He came over here to trail King Victor. Superintendent Battle and I have known this for some time.'

Virginia said nothing. Very slowly she sat down again. With those few words the structure that she had built up so carefully was scattered in ruins about her feet.

'You see,' Lemoine was continuing, 'we have all known that eventually King Victor would come to Chimneys. It was the one place we were sure of catching him.'

Virginia looked up with an odd light in her eyes, and suddenly she laughed.

'You've not caught him yet,' she said.

Lemoine looked at her curiously.

'No, madame. But I shall.'

'He's supposed to be rather famous for outwitting people, isn't he?'

The Frenchman's face darkened with anger.

'This time, it will be different,' he said between his teeth.

'He's a very attractive fellow,' said Lord Caterham. 'Very attractive. But surely – why, you said he was an old friend of yours, Virginia?'

'That is why,' said Virginia composedly, 'I think M Lemoine must be making a mistake.'

And her eyes met the detective's steadily, but he appeared in no wise discomfited.

'Time will show, madame,' he said.

'Do you pretend that it was he who shot Prince Michael?' she asked presently.

'Certainly.'

But Virginia shook her head.

'Oh no!' she said. 'Oh, no! That is one thing I am quite sure of. Anthony Cade never killed Prince Michael.'

Lemoine was watching her intently.

'There is a possibility that you are right, madame,' he said slowly. 'A possibility, that is all. It may have been the Herzo-slovakian, Boris, who exceeded his orders and fired that shot. Who knows, Prince Michael may have done him some great wrong, and the man sought revenge.'

'He looks a murderous sort of fellow,' agreed Lord Cater-ham. 'The housemaids, I believe, scream when he passes them in the passages.'

'Well,' said Lemoine. 'I must be going now. I felt it was due to you, my lord, to know exactly how things stand.'

'Very kind of you, I'm sure,' said Lord Caterham. 'Quite certain you won't have a drink? All right, then. Goodnight.'

'I hate that man with his prim little black beard and his eyeglasses,' said Bundle, as soon as the door had shut behind him. 'I hope Anthony *does* snoo him. I'd love to see him dancing with rage. What do you think about it all, Virginia?'

'I don't know,' said Virginia. 'I'm tired. I shall go up to bed.'

'Not a bad idea,' said Lord Caterham. 'It's half past eleven.'

As Virginia was crossing the wide hall, she caught sight of a broad back that seemed familiar to her discreetly vanishing through a side door.

'Superintendent Battle,' she called imperiously.

The superintendent, for it was indeed he, retraced his steps with a shade of unwillingness.

'Yes, Mrs Revel?'

'M Lemoine has been here. He says – Tell me, is it true, really true, that Mr Fish is an American detective?'

Superintendent Battle nodded.

'That's right.'

'You have known it all along?'

Again Superintendent Battle nodded.

Virginia turned away towards the staircase.

'I see,' she said. 'Thank you.'

Until that minute she had refused to believe.

And now? –

Sitting down before her dressing-table in her own room, she faced the question squarely. Every word that Anthony had said came back to her fraught with a new significance.

Was this the 'trade' that he had spoken of?

The trade that he had given up. But then –

An unusual sound disturbed the even tenor of her meditations. She lifted her head with a start. Her little gold clock showed the hour to be after one. Nearly two hours she had sat here thinking.

Again the sound was repeated. A sharp tap on the window-pane. Virginia went to the window and opened it. Below on the pathway was a tall figure which even as she looked stooped for another handful of gravel.

For a moment Virginia's heart beat faster – then she recognized the massive strength and square-cut outline of the Herzoslovakian, Boris.

'Yes,' she said in a low voice. 'What is it?'

At the moment it did not strike her as strange that Boris should be throwing gravel at her window at this hour of the night.

'What is it?' she repeated impatiently.

'I come from the master,' said Boris in a low tone which nevertheless carried perfectly. 'He has sent for you.'

He made the statement in a perfectly matter-of-fact tone.

'Sent for me?'

'Yes, I am to bring you to him. There is a note. I will throw it up to you.'

Virginia stood back a little, and a slip of paper, weighted with a stone, fell accurately at her feet. She unfolded it and read:

My dear (Anthony had written) – *I'm in a tight place, but I mean to win through. Will you trust me and come to me?*

For quite two minutes Virginia stood there, immovable, reading those few words over and over again.

She raised her head, looking round the well-appointed luxury of the bedroom as though she saw it with new eyes.

Then she leaned out of the window again.

'What am I to do?' she asked.

'The detectives are the other side of the house, outside the Council Chamber. Come down and out through the side door. I will be there. I have a car waiting outside in the road.'

Virginia nodded. Quickly she changed her dress for one of fawn tricot, and pulled on a little fawn leather hat.

Then, smiling a little, she wrote a short note, addressed it to Bundle and pinned it to the pin-cushion.

She stole quietly downstairs and undid the bolts of the side door. Just a moment she paused, then, with a little gallant toss of the head, the same toss of the head with which her ancestors had gone into action in the Crusades, she passed through.

CHAPTER XXVI

The 13th of October

At ten o'clock on the morning of Wednesday, the 13th of October, Anthony Cade walked into Harridge's Hotel and asked for Baron Lolopretjzyl who was occupying a suite there.

After suitable and imposing delay, Anthony was taken to the suite in question. The Baron was standing on the hearthrug in a correct and stiff fashion. Little Captain Andrassy, equally correct as to demeanour, but with a slightly hostile attitude, was also present.

The usual bows, clicking of heels, and other formal greetings of etiquette took place. Anthony was, by now, thoroughly conversant with the routine.

'You will forgive this early call I trust, Baron,' he said cheerfully, laying down his hat and stick on the table. 'As a matter of fact, I have a little business proposition to make to you.'

'Ha! Is that so?' said the Baron.

Captain Andrassy, who had never overcome his initial distrust of Anthony, looked suspicious.

'Business,' said Anthony, 'is based on the well-known principle of supply and demand. You want something, the other man has it. The only thing left to settle is the price.'

The Baron looked at him attentively, but said nothing.

'Between a Herzoslovakian nobleman and an English gentleman the terms should be easily arranged,' said Anthony rapidly.

He blushed a little as he said it. Such words do not rise easily to an Englishman's lips, but he had observed on previous occasions the enormous effect of such phraseology upon the Baron's mentality. True enough, the charm worked.

'That is so,' said the Baron approvingly, nodding his head. 'That is entirely so.'

Even Captain Andrassy appeared to unbend a little, and nodded his head also.

'Very good,' said Anthony. 'I won't beat about the bush any more –'

'What is that, you say?' interrupted the Baron. 'To beat about the bush? I do not comprehend?'

'A mere figure of speech, Baron. To speak in plain English, *you* want the goods, *we* have them! The ship is all very well, but it lacks a figurehead. By the ship, I mean the Loyalist party of Herzoslovakia. At the present minute you lack the principal plank of your political programme. You are minus a prince! Now supposing – only supposing, that I could supply you with a prince?'

The Baron stared.

'I do not comprehend you in the least,' he declared.

'Sir,' said Captain Andrassy, twirling his moustache fiercely, 'you are insulting!'

'Not at all,' said Anthony. 'I'm trying to be helpful. Supply and demand, you understand. It's all perfectly fair and square. No princes supplied unless genuine – see trademark. If we come to terms, you'll find it's quite all right. I'm offering you the real genuine article – out of the bottom drawer.'

'Not in the least,' the Baron declared again, 'do I comprehend you.'

'It doesn't really matter,' said Anthony kindly. 'I just want you to get used to the idea. To put it vulgarly, I've got something up my sleeve. Just get hold of this. You want a prince. Under certain conditions, I will undertake to supply you with one.'

The Baron and Andrassy stared at him. Anthony took up his hat and stick again and prepared to depart.

'Just think it over. Now, Baron, there is one thing further. You must come down to Chimneys this evening – Captain Andrassy also. Several very curious things are likely to happen there. Shall we make an appointment? Say in the Council

Chamber at nine o'clock? Thank you, gentlemen, I may rely upon you to be there?'

The Baron took a step forward and looked searchingly in Anthony's face.

'Mr Cade,' he said, not without dignity, 'it is not, I hope, that you wish to make fun of me?'

Anthony returned his gaze steadily.

'Baron,' he said, and there was a curious note in his voice, 'when this evening is over, I think you will be the first to admit that there is more earnest than jest about this business.'

Bowing to both men, he left the room.

His next call was in the City where he sent in his card to Mr Herman Isaacstein.

After some delay, Anthony was received by a pale and exquisitely dressed underling with an engaging manner, and a military title.

'You wanted to see Mr Isaacstein, didn't you?' said the young man. 'I'm afraid he's most awfully busy this morning – board meetings and all that sort of thing, you know. Is it anything that I can do?'

'I must see him personally,' said Anthony, and added carelessly, 'I've just come up from Chimneys.'

The young man was slightly staggered by the mention of Chimneys.

'Oh!' he said doubtfully. 'Well, I'll see.'

'Tell him it's important,' said Anthony.

'Message from Lord Caterham?' suggested the young man.

'Something of the kind,' said Anthony, 'but it's imperative that I should see Mr Isaacstein at once.'

Two minutes later Anthony was conducted into a sumptuous inner sanctum where he was principally impressed by the immense size and roomy depths of the leather-covered armchairs.

Mr Isaacstein rose to greet him.

'You must forgive my looking you up like this,' said Anthony. 'I know that you're a busy man, and I'm not going to waste more of your time than I can help. It's just a little matter of business that I want to put before you.'

Isaacstein looked at him attentively for a minute or two out of his beady black eyes.

'Have a cigar,' he said unexpectedly, holding out an open box.

'Thank you,' said Anthony. 'I don't mind if I do.'

He helped himself.

'It's about this Herzoslovakian business,' continued Anthony as he accepted a match. He noted the momentary flickering of the other's steady gaze. 'The murder of Prince Michael must have rather upset the applecart.'

Mr Isaacstein raised one eyebrow, murmured 'Ah?' interrogatively and transferred his gaze to the ceiling.

'Oil,' said Anthony, thoughtfully surveying the polished surface of the desk. 'Wonderful thing, oil.'

He felt the slight start the financier gave.

'Do you mind coming to the point, Mr Cade?'

'Not at all. I imagine, Mr Isaacstein, that if those oil concessions are granted to another company you won't be exactly pleased about it?'

'What's the proposition?' asked the other, looking straight at him.

'A suitable claimant to the throne, full of pro-British sympathies.'

'Where have you got him?'

'That's my business.'

Isaacstein acknowledged the retort by a slight smile, his glance had grown hard and keen.

'The genuine article? I can't stand for any funny business?'

'The absolute genuine article.'

'Straight?'

'Straight.'

'I'll take your word for it.'

'You don't seem to take much convincing?' said Anthony, looking curiously at him.

Herman Isaacstein smiled.

'I shouldn't be where I am now if I hadn't learnt to know whether a man is speaking the truth or not,' he replied simply. 'What terms do you want?'

'The same loan, on the same conditions, that you offered to Prince Michael.'

'What about yourself?'

'For the moment, nothing, except that I want you to come down to Chimneys tonight.'

'No,' said Isaacstein, with some decision. 'I can't do that.'

'Why?'

'Dining out – rather an important dinner.'

'All the same, I'm afraid you'll have to cut it out – for your own sake.'

'What do you mean?'

Anthony looked at him for a full minute before he said slowly:

'Do you know that they've found the revolver, the one Michael was shot with? Do you know where they found it? In your suitcase.'

'What?'

Isaacstein almost leapt from his chair. His face was frenzied.

'What are you saying? What do you mean?'

'I'll tell you.'

Very obligingly, Anthony narrated the occurrences in connexion with the finding of the revolver. As he spoke the other's face assumed a greyish tinge of absolute terror.

'But it's false,' he screamed out as Anthony finished. 'I never put it there. I know nothing about it. It is a plot.'

'Don't excite yourself,' said Anthony soothingly. 'If that's the case you'll easily be able to prove it.'

'Prove it? How can I prove it?'

'If I were you,' said Anthony gently, 'I'd come to Chimneys tonight.'

Isaacstein looked at him doubtfully.

'You advise it?'

Anthony leant forward and whispered to him. The financier fell back in amazement, staring at him.

'You actually mean –'

'Come and see,' said Anthony.

CHAPTER XXVII

The 13th of October (*contd*)

The clock in the Council Chamber struck nine.

'Well,' said Lord Caterham, with a deep sigh. 'Here they all are, just like little Bo-Peep's flock, back again and wagging their tails behind them.'

He looked sadly round the room.

'Organ grinder complete with monkey,' he murmured, fixing the Baron with his eye. 'Nosy Parker of Throgmorton Street –'

'I think you're rather unkind to the Baron,' protested Bundle, to whom these confidences were being poured out. 'He told me that he considered you the perfect example of English hospitality among the *haute noblesse*.'

'I dare say,' said Lord Caterham. 'He's always saying things like that. It makes him most fatiguing to talk to. But I can tell you I'm not nearly as much of the hospitable English gentleman as I was. As soon as I can I shall let Chimneys to an enterprising American, and go and live in an hotel. There, if anyone worries you, you can just ask for your bill and go.'

'Cheer up,' said Bundle. 'We seem to have lost Mr Fish for good.'

'I always found him rather amusing,' said Lord Caterham, who was in a contradictory temper. 'It's that precious young man of yours who has let me in for this. Why should I have this board meeting called in my house? Why doesn't he rent The Larches or Elmhurst, or some nice villa residence like that at Streatham, and hold his company meetings there?'

'Wrong atmosphere,' said Bundle.

'No one is going to play any tricks on us, I hope?' said her father nervously. 'I don't trust that French fellow, Lemoine.

The French police are up to all sorts of dodges. Put india-rubber bands round your arm, and then reconstruct the crime and make you jump, and it's registered on a thermometer. I know that when they call out "Who killed Prince Michael?" I shall register a hundred and twenty-two or something perfectly frightful, and they'll haul me off to jail at once.'

The door opened and Tredwell announced:

'Mr George Lomax. Mr Eversleigh.'

'Enter Codders, followed by faithful dog,' murmured Bundle.

Bill made a beeline for her, whilst George greeted Lord Caterham in the genial manner he assumed for public occasions.

'My dear Caterham,' said George, shaking him by the hand, 'I got your message and came over, of course.'

'Very good of you, my dear fellow, very good of you. Delighted to see you.' Lord Caterham's conscience always drove him on to an excess of geniality when he was conscious of feeling none. 'Not that it was my message, but that doesn't matter at all.'

In the meantime Bill was attacking Bundle in an undertone.

'I say. What's it all about? What's this I hear about Virginia bolting off in the middle of the night? She's not been kidnapped has she?'

'Oh, no,' said Bundle. 'She left a note pinned to the pincushion in the orthodox fashion.'

'She's not gone off with anyone, has she? Not with that Colonial Johnny? I never liked the fellow, and, from all I hear, there seems to be an idea floating around that he himself is the super-crook. But I don't quite see how that can be?'

'Why not?'

'Well, this King Victor was a French fellow, and Cade's English enough.'

'You don't happen to have heard that King Victor was an accomplished linguist, and, moreover, was half Irish?'

'Oh, Lord! Then that's why he's made himself scarce, is it?'

'I don't know about his making himself scarce. He disappeared the day before yesterday, as you know. But this morning we got a wire from him saying he would be down here at 9 PM tonight, and suggesting that Codders should be asked over. All these other people have turned up as well – asked by Mr Cade.'

'It is a gathering,' said Bill, looking round. 'One French detective by window, one English ditto by fireplace. Strong foreign element. The Stars and Stripes don't seem to be represented?'

Bundle shook her head.

'Mr Fish has disappeared into the blue. Virginia's not here either. But everyone else is assembled, and I have a feeling in my bones, Bill, that we are drawing very near to the moment when somebody says "James, the footman", and everything is revealed. We're only waiting now for Anthony Cade to arrive.'

'He'll never show up,' said Bill.

'Then why call this company meeting, as Father calls it?'

'Ah, there's some deep idea behind that. Depend upon it. Wants us all here while he's somewhere else – you know the sort of thing.'

'You don't think he'll come, then?'

'No fear. Run his head into the lion's mouth? Why, the room's bristling with detectives and high officials.'

'You don't know much about King Victor, if you think that would deter him. By all accounts, it's the kind of situation he loves above all, and he always manages to come out on top.'

Mr Eversleigh shook his head doubtfully.

'That would take some doing – with the dice loaded against him. He'll never –'

The door opened again and Tredwell announced:

'Mr Cade.'

Anthony came straight across to his host.

'Lord Caterham,' he said, 'I'm giving you a frightful lot of trouble, and I'm awfully sorry about it. But I really do think that tonight will see the clearing up of the mystery.'

Lord Caterham looked mollified. He had always had a secret liking for Anthony.

'No trouble at all,' he said heartily.

'It's very kind of you,' said Anthony. 'We're all here, I see. Then I can get on with the good work.'

'I don't understand,' said George Lomax weightily. 'I don't understand in the least. This is all very irregular. Mr Cade has no standing – no standing whatever. The position is a very difficult and delicate one. I am strongly of the opinion –'

George's flood of eloquence was arrested. Moving unobtrusively to the great man's side, Superintendent Battle whispered a few words in his ear. George looked perplexed and baffled.

'Very well, if you say so,' he remarked grudgingly. Then added in a louder tone, 'I'm sure we are all willing to listen to what Mr Cade has to say.'

Anthony ignored the palpable condescension of the other's tone.

'It's just a little idea of mine, that's all,' he said cheerfully. 'Probably all of you know that we got hold of a certain message in cipher the other day. There was a reference to Richmond, and some numbers.' He paused. 'Well, we had a shot at solving it – and we failed. Now in the late Count Stylptitch's memoirs (which I happen to have read) there is a reference to a certain dinner – a "flower" dinner which everyone attended wearing a badge representing a flower. The Count himself wore the exact duplicate of that curious device we found in the cavity in the secret passage. It represented a rose. If you remember, it was all *rows* of things – buttons, letter Es, and finally rows of knitting. Now, gentlemen, what is there in this house that is arranged in rows? Books, isn't that so? Add to that, that in the catalogue of Lord Caterham's library there is a book called *The Life of the Earl of Richmond*, and I think you will get a very fair idea of the hiding-place. Starting at the volume in question, and using the numbers to denote shelves and books, I think you will find that the – er – object of our search is concealed in a dummy book, or in a cavity behind a particular book.'

Anthony looked round modestly, obviously waiting for applause.

'Upon my word, that's very ingenious,' said Lord Caterham.

'Quite ingenious,' admitted George condescendingly. 'But it remains to be seen –'

Anthony laughed.

'The proof of the pudding's in the eating – eh? Well, I'll soon settle that for you.' He sprang to his feet. 'I'll go to the library –'

He got no farther. M Lemoine moved forward from the window.

'Just one moment, Mr Cade. You permit, Lord Caterham?'

He went to the writing-table, and hurriedly scribbled a few lines. He sealed them up in an envelope, and then rang the bell. Tredwell appeared in answer to it. Lemoine handed him the note.

'See that that is delivered at once, if you please.'

'Very good, sir,' said Tredwell.

With his usual dignified tread he withdrew.

Anthony, who had been standing, irresolute, sat down again.

'What's the big idea, Lemoine?' he asked gently.

There was a sudden sense of strain in the atmosphere.

'If the jewel is where you say it is – well, it has been there for over seven years – a quarter of an hour more does not matter.'

'Go on,' said Anthony. 'That wasn't all you wanted to say?'

'No, it was not. At this juncture it is – unwise to permit any one person to leave the room. Especially if that person has rather questionable antecedents.'

Anthony raised his eyebrows and lighted a cigarette.

'I suppose a vagabond life is not very respectable,' he mused.

'Two months ago, Mr Cade, you were in South Africa. That is admitted. Where were you before that?'

Anthony leaned back in his chair, idly blowing smoke rings.

'Canada. Wild North-west.'

'Are you sure you were not in prison? A French prison?'

Automatically, Superintendent Battle moved a step nearer the door, as if to cut off a retreat that way, but Anthony showed no signs of doing anything dramatic.

Instead, he stared at the French detective, and then burst out laughing.

'My poor Lemoine. It is a monomania with you! You do indeed see King Victor everywhere. So you fancy that I am that interesting gentleman?'

'Do you deny it?'

Anthony brushed a fleck of ash from his coat-sleeve.

'I never deny anything that amuses me,' he said lightly. 'But the accusation is really too ridiculous.'

'Ah! you think so?' The Frenchman leant forward. His face was twitching painfully, and yet he seemed perplexed and baffled – as though something in Anthony's manner puzzled him. 'What if I tell you, monsieur, that this time – this time – I am out to get King Victor, and nothing shall stop me!'

'Very laudable,' was Anthony's comment. 'You've been out to get him before, though, haven't you, Lemoine? And he's got the better of you. Aren't you afraid that that may happen again? He's a slippery fellow, by all accounts.'

The conversation had developed into a duel between the detective and Anthony. Everyone else in the room was conscious of the tension. It was a fight to a finish between the Frenchman, painfully in earnest, and the man who smoked so calmly and whose words seemed to show that he had not a care in the world.

'If I were you, Lemoine,' continued Anthony, 'I should be very, very careful. Watch your step, and all that sort of thing.'

'This time,' said Lemoine grimly, 'there will be no mistake.'

'You seem very sure about it all,' said Anthony. 'But there's such a thing as evidence, you know.'

Lemoine smiled, and something in his smile seemed to attract Anthony's attention. He sat up and stubbed out his cigarette.

'You saw that note I wrote just now?' said the French detective. 'It was to my people at the inn. Yesterday I received from France the fingerprints and the Bertillon measurements of King Victor – the so-called Captain O'Neill. I have asked for them to be sent up to me here. In a few minutes we shall *know* whether you are the man!'

Anthony stared steadily at him. Then a little smile crept over his face.

'You're really rather clever, Lemoine. I never thought of that. The documents will arrive, you will induce me to dip my fingers in the ink, or something equally unpleasant, and you will measure my ears and look for my distinguishing marks. And if they agree –'

'Well,' said Lemoine, 'if they agree – eh?'

Anthony leaned forward in his chair.

'Well, if they do agree,' he said very gently, 'what then?'

'What then?' The detective seemed taken aback. 'But – I shall have proved then that you are King Victor!'

But for the first time, a shade of uncertainty crept into his manner.

'That will doubtless be a great satisfaction to you,' said Anthony. 'But I don't quite see where it's going to hurt me. I'm not admitting anything, but supposing, just for the sake of argument, that I was King Victor – I might be trying to repent, you know.'

'Repent?'

'That's the idea. Put yourself in King Victor's place, Lemoine. Use your imagination. You've just come out of prison. You're getting on in life. You've lost the first fine rapture of the adventurous life. Say, even that you meet a beautiful girl. You think of marrying and settling down somewhere in the country where you can grow vegetable marrows. You decide from henceforth to lead a blameless life. Put yourself in King Victor's place. Can't you imagine feeling like that?'

'I do not think that I should feel like that,' said Lemoine with a sardonic smile.

'Perhaps you wouldn't,' admitted Anthony. 'But then you're not King Victor, are you? You can't possibly know what he feels like.'

'But it is nonsense, what you are saying there,' spluttered the Frenchman.

'Oh, no, it isn't. Come now, Lemoine, if I'm King Victor, what have you against me after all? You could never get the necessary evidence in the old, old days, remember. I've served my sentence, and that's all there is to it. I suppose you could arrest me for the French equivalent of "Loitering with intent to commit a felony", but that would be poor satisfaction, wouldn't it?'

'You forget,' said Lemoine. 'America! How about this business of obtaining money under false pretences, and passing yourself off as Prince Nicholas Obolovitch?'

'No good, Lemoine,' said Anthony, 'I was nowhere near America at the time. And I can prove that easily enough. If King Victor impersonated Prince Nicholas in America, then I'm not King Victor. You're sure he *was* impersonated? That it wasn't the man himself?'

Superintendent Battle suddenly interposed.

'The man was an imposter all right, Mr Cade.'

'I wouldn't contradict you, Battle,' said Anthony. 'You have such a habit of being always right. Are you equally sure that Prince Nicholas died in the Congo?'

Battle looked at him curiously.

'I wouldn't swear to that, sir. But it's generally believed.'

'Careful man. What's your motto? Plenty of rope, eh? I've taken a leaf out of your book. I've given M Lemoine plenty of rope. I've not denied his accusations. But, all the same, I'm afraid he's going to be disappointed. You see I always believe in having something up one's sleeve. Anticipating that some little unpleasantness might arise here, I took the precaution to bring a trump card along with me. It – or rather he – is upstairs.'

'Upstairs?' said Lord Caterham, very interested.

'Yes, he's been having rather a trying time of it lately, poor fellow. Got a nasty bump on the head from someone. I've been looking after him.'

Suddenly the deep voice of Mr Isaacstein broke in: 'Can we guess who he is?'

'If you like,' said Anthony, 'but –'

Lemoine interrupted with sudden ferocity:

'All this is foolery. You think to outwit me yet again. It may be true what you say – that you were not in America. You are too clever to say it if it were not true. But there is something else. Murder! Yes, murder. The murder of Prince Michael. He interfered with you that night as you were looking for the jewel.'

'Lemoine, have you ever known King Victor do murder?' Anthony's voice rang out sharply. 'You know as well – better than I do, that he has never shed blood.'

'Who else but you could have murdered him?' cried Lemoine. 'Tell me that!'

The last word died on his lips, as a shrill whistle sounded from the terrace outside. Anthony sprang up, all his assumed nonchalance laid aside.

'You ask me who murdered Prince Michael?' he cried. 'I won't tell you – I'll *show* you. That whistle was the signal I've been waiting for. The murderer of Prince Michael is in the library now.'

He sprang out through the window, and the others followed him as he led the way round the terrace, until they came to the library window. He pushed the window, and it yielded to his touch.

Very softly he held aside the thick curtain, so that they could look into the room.

Standing by the bookcase was a dark figure, hurriedly pulling out and replacing volumes, so absorbed in the task that no outside sound was heeded.

And then, as they stood watching, trying to recognize the figure that was vaguely silhouetted against the light of the electric torch it carried, someone sprang past them with a sound like the roar of a wild beast.

The torch fell to the ground, was extinguished, and the sounds of a terrific struggle filled the room. Lord Caterham groped his way to the lights and switched them on.

Two figures were swaying together. And as they looked the

end came. The short sharp crack of a pistol shot, and the small figure crumbled up and fell. The other figure turned and faced them – it was Boris, his eyes alight with rage.

'She killed my master,' he growled. 'Now she tries to shoot me. I would have taken the pistol from her and shot her, but it went off in the struggle. St Michael directed it. The evil woman is dead.'

'A woman?' cried George Lomax.

They drew nearer. On the floor, the pistol still clasped in her hand, and an expression of deadly malignity on her face, lay – Mademoiselle Brun.

CHAPTER XXVIII

King Victor

'I suspected her from the first,' explained Anthony. 'There was a light in her room on the night of the murder. Afterwards, I wavered. I made inquiries about her in Brittany, and came back satisfied that she was what she represented herself to be. I was a fool. Because the Comtesse de Breteuil had employed a Mademoiselle Brun and spoke highly of her, it never occurred to me that the real Mademoiselle Brun might have been kidnapped on her way to her new post, and that it might be a substitute taking her place. Instead I shifted my suspicions to Mr Fish. It was not until he had followed me to Dover, and we had had a mutual explanation, that I began to see clearly. Once I knew that he was a Pinkerton's man, trailing King Victor, my suspicions swung back again to their original object.

'The thing that worried me most was that Mrs Revel had definitely recognized the woman. Then I remembered that it was only *after* I had mentioned her being Madame de Breteuil's governess. And all she had said was that that accounted for the fact that the woman's face was familiar to her. Superintendent Battle will tell you that a deliberate plot was formed to keep Mrs Revel from coming to Chimneys. Nothing more nor less than a dead body, in fact. And though the murder was the work of the Comrades of the Red Hand, punishing supposed treachery on the part of the victim, the staging of it, and the absence of the Comrade's sign-manual, pointed to some abler intelligence directing operations. From the first, I suspected some connexion with Herzoslovakia. Mrs Revel was the only member of the house party who had been to the country. I suspected at first that someone was impersonating

Prince Michael, but that proved to be a totally erroneous idea. When I realized the possibility of Mademoiselle Brun's being an imposter, and added to that the fact that her face was familiar to Mrs Revel, I began to see daylight. It was evidently very important that she should not be recognized, and Mrs Revel was the only person likely to do so.'

'But who was she?' said Lord Caterham. 'Someone Mrs Revel had known in Herzoslovakia?'

'I think the Baron might be able to tell us,' said Anthony.

'I?' The Baron stared at him, then down at the motionless figure.

'Look well,' said Anthony. 'Don't be put off by the make-up. She was an actress once, remember.'

The Baron stared again. Suddenly he started.

'God in heaven,' he breathed, 'it is not possible.'

'What is not possible?' asked George. 'Who is the lady? You recognize her, Baron?'

'No, no, it is not possible.' The Baron continued to mutter. 'She was killed. They were both killed. On the steps of the palace. Her body was recovered.'

'Mutilated and unrecognizable,' Anthony reminded him. 'She managed to put up a bluff. I think she escaped to America, and has spent a good many years lying low in deadly terror of the Comrades of the Red Hand. They promoted the revolution, remember, and, to use an expressive phrase, they always had it in for her. Then King Victor was released, and they planned to recover the diamond together. She was searching for it that night when she came suddenly upon Prince Michael, and he recognized her. There was never much fear of her meeting him in the ordinary way of things. Royal guests don't come in contact with governesses, and she could always retire with a convenient migraine, as she did the day the Baron was here.

'However, she met Prince Michael face to face when she least expected it. Exposure and disgrace stared her in the face. She shot him. It was she who placed the revolver in Isaacstein's suitcase, so as to confuse the trail, and she who returned the letters.'

Lemoine moved forward.

'She was coming down to search for the jewel that night, you say,' he said. 'Might she not have been going to meet her accomplice, King Victor, who was coming from outside? Eh? What do you say to that?'

Anthony sighed.

'Still at it, my dear Lemoine? How persistent you are! You won't take my hint that I've got a trump card up my sleeve?'

But George, whose mind worked slowly, now broke in.

'I am still completely at sea. Who was this lady, Baron? You recognize her, it seems?'

But the Baron drew himself up and stood very straight and stiff.

'You are in error, Mr Lomax. To my knowledge I have not this lady seen before. A complete stranger she is to me.'

'But –'

George stared at him – bewildered.

The Baron took him into a corner of the room, and murmured something into his ear. Anthony watched with a good deal of enjoyment, George's face turning slowly purple, his eyes bulging, and all the incipient symptoms of apoplexy. A murmur of George's throaty voice came to him.

'Certainly . . . certainly . . . by all means . . . no need at all . . . complicate situation . . . utmost discretion.'

'Ah!' Lemoine hit the table sharply with his hand. 'I do not care about all this! The murder of Prince Michael – that was not my affair. I want King Victor.'

Anthony shook his head gently.

'I'm sorry for you, Lemoine. You're really a very able fellow. But, all the same, you're going to lose the trick. I'm about to play my trump card.'

He stepped across the room and rang the bell. Tredwell answered it.

'A gentlemen arrived with me this evening, Tredwell.'

'Yes, sir, a foreign gentleman.'

'Quite so. Will you kindly ask him to join us here as soon as possible?'

'Yes, sir.'

Tredwell withdrew.

'Entry of the trump card, the mysterious Monsieur X,' remarked Anthony. '*Who is he?* Can anyone guess?'

'Putting two and two together,' said Herman Isaacstein, 'what with your mysterious hints this morning, and your attitude this afternoon, I should say there was no doubt about it. Somehow or other you've managed to get hold of Prince Nicholas of Herzoslovakia.'

'You think the same, Baron?'

'I do. Unless yet another imposter you have put forward. But that I will not believe. With me, your dealings most honourable have been.'

'Thank you, Baron. I shan't forget those words. So you are all agreed?'

His eyes swept round the circle of waiting faces. Only Lemoine did not respond, but kept his eyes fixed sullenly on the table.

Anthony's quick ears had caught the sound of footsteps outside in the hall.

'And yet, you know,' he said with a queer smile, 'you're all wrong!'

He crossed swiftly to the door and flung it open.

A man stood on the threshold – a man with a neat black beard, eyeglasses, and a foppish appearance slightly marred by a bandage round the head.

'Allow me to present to you the real Monsieur Lemoine of the Sûreté.'

There was a rush and a scuffle, and then the nasal tones of Mr Hiram Fish rose bland and reassuring from the window:

'No, you don't, sonny – not this way. I have been stationed here this whole evening for the particular purpose of preventing your escape. You will observe that I have you covered well and good with this gun of mine. I came over to get you, and I've got you – but you sure are some lad!'

CHAPTER XXIX

Further Explanations

'You owe us an explanation, I think, Mr Cade,' said Herman Isaacstein, somewhat later in the evening.

'There's nothing much to explain,' said Anthony modestly. 'I went to Dover and Fish followed me under the impression that I was King Victor. We found a mysterious stranger imprisoned there, and as soon as we heard his story we knew where we were. The same idea again, you see. The real man kidnapped, and the false one – in this case King Victor himself – takes his place. But it seems that Battle here always thought there was something fishy about his French colleague, and wired to Paris for his fingerprints and other means of identification.'

'Ah!' cried the Baron. 'The fingerprints. The Bertillon measurements that that scoundrel talked about?'

'It was a clever idea,' said Anthony. 'I admired it so much that I felt forced to play it up. Besides, my doing so puzzled the false Lemoine enormously. You see, as soon as I had given the tip about the "rows" and where the jewel really was, he was keen to pass on the news to his accomplice, and at the same time to keep us all in that room. The note was really to Mademoiselle Brun. He told Tredwell to deliver it at once, and Tredwell did so by taking it upstairs to the schoolroom. Lemoine accused me of being King Victor, by that means creating a diversion and preventing anyone from leaving the room. By the time all that had been cleared up and we adjourned to the library to look for the stone, he flattered himself that the stone would be no longer there to find!'

George cleared his throat.

'I must say, Mr Cade,' he said pompously, 'that I consider

your action in that matter highly reprehensible. If the slightest hitch had occurred in your plans, one of our national possessions might have disappeared beyond the hope of recovery. It was foolhardy, Mr Cade, reprehensibly foolhardy.'

'I guess you haven't tumbled to the little idea, Mr Lomax,' said the drawling voice of Mr Fish. 'That historic diamond was never behind the books in the library.'

'Never?'

'Not on your life.'

'You see,' explained Anthony, 'that little device of Count Stylptitch's stood for what it had originally stood for – a rose. When that dawned upon me on Monday afternoon, I went straight to the rose garden. Mr Fish had already trumbled to the same idea. If, standing with your back to the sundial, you take seven paces straight forward, then eight to the left and three to the right, you come to some bushes of a bright red rose called Richmond. The house has been ransacked to find the hiding-place, but nobody has thought of digging in the garden. I suggest a little digging party tomorrow morning.'

'Then the story about the books in the library –'

'An invention of mine to trap the lady. Mr Fish kept watch on the terrace, and whistled when the psychological moment had arrived. I may say that Mr Fish and I established martial law at the Dover house, and prevented the Comrades from communicating with the false Lemoine. He sent them an order to clear out, and word was conveyed to him that this had been done. So he went happily ahead with his plans for denouncing me.'

'Well, well,' said Lord Caterham cheerfully, 'everything seems to have been cleared up most satisfactorily.'

'Everything but one thing,' said Mr Isaacstein.

'What is that?'

The great financier looked steadily at Anthony.

'What did you get me down here for? Just to assist at a dramatic scene as an interested onlooker?'

Anthony shook his head.

'No, Mr Isaacstein. You are a busy man whose time is money. Why did you come down here originally?'

'To negotiate a loan.'

'With whom?'

'Prince Michael of Herzoslovakia.'

'Exactly. Prince Michael is dead. Are your prepared to offer the same loan on the same terms to his cousin Nicholas?'

'Can you produce him? I thought he was killed in the Congo?'

'He was killed all right. I killed him. Oh, no, I'm not a murderer. When I say I killed him, I mean that I spread the report of his death. I promise you a prince, Mr Isaacstein. Will *I* do?'

'You?'

'Yes, I'm the man. Nicholas Sergius Alexander Ferdinand Obolovitch. Rather long for the kind of life I proposed to live, so I emerged from the Congo as plain Anthony Cade.'

Little Captain Andrassy sprang up.

'But this is incredible – incredible,' he spluttered. 'Have a care, sir, what you say.'

'I can give you plenty of proofs,' said Anthony quietly. 'I think I shall be able to convince the Baron here.'

The Baron lifted his hand.

'Your proofs I will examine, yes. But of them for me there is no need. Your word alone sufficient for me is. Besides, your English mother you much resemble. All along have I said: "This young man on one side or the other most highly born is."'

'You have always trusted my word, Baron,' said Anthony. 'I can assure you that in the days to come I shall not forget.'

Then he looked over at Superintendent Battle, whose face had remained perfectly expressionless.

'You can understand,' said Anthony with a smile, 'that my position has been extremely precarious. Of all of those in the house I might be supposed to have the best reason for wishing Michael Obolovitch out of the way, since I was the next heir to the throne. I've been extraordinarily afraid of Battle all along. I always felt that he suspected me, but that he was held up by lack of motive.'

'I never believed for a minute that you'd shot him, sir,' said Superintendent Battle. 'We've got a feeling in such matters. But I knew that you were afraid of something, and you puzzled me. If I'd known sooner who you really were I dare say I'd have yielded to the evidence, and arrested you.'

'I'm glad I managed to keep one guilty secret from you. You wormed everything else out of me all right. You're a damned good man at your job Battle. I shall always think of Scotland Yard with respect.'

'Most amazing,' muttered George. 'Most amazing story I ever heard. I – I can really hardly believe it. You are quite sure, Baron, that –'

'My dear Mr Lomax,' said Anthony, with a slight hardness in his tone, 'I have no intention of asking the British Foreign Office to support my claim without bringing forward the most convincing documentary evidence. I suggest that we adjourn now, and that you, the Baron, Mr Isaacstein and myself discuss the terms of the proposed loan.'

The Baron rose to his feet, and clicked his heels together.

'It will be the proudest moment of my life, sir,' he said solemnly, 'when I see you King of Herzoslovakia.'

'Oh, by the way, Baron,' said Anthony carelessly, slipping his hand through the other's arm, 'I forgot to tell you. There's a string tied to this. I'm married, you know.'

The Baron retreated a step or two. Dismay overspread his countenance.

'Something wrong I knew there would be,' he boomed. 'Merciful God in heaven! He has married a black woman in Africa!'

'Come, come, it's not so bad as all that,' said Anthony laughing. 'She's white enough – white all through, bless her.'

'Good. A respectable morganatic affair it can be, then.'

'Not a bit of it. She's to play Queen to my King. It's no use shaking your head. She's fully qualified for the post. She's the daughter of an English peer who dates back to the time of the Conqueror. It's very fashionable just now for royalties to marry into the aristocracy – and she knows something of Herzoslovakia.'

'My God!' cried George Lomax, startled out of his usual careful speech. 'Not – not – Virginia Revel?'

'Yes,' said Anthony. 'Virginia Revel.'

'My dear fellow,' cried Lord Caterham, 'I mean – sir, I congratulate you. I do indeed. A delightful creature.'

'Thank you, Lord Caterham,' said Anthony. 'She's all you say and more.'

But Mr Isaacstein was regarding him curiously.

'You'll excuse my asking your Highness, but when did this marriage take place?'

Anthony smiled back at him.

'As a matter of fact,' he said, 'I married her this morning.'

CHAPTER XXX

Anthony Signs on for a New Job

'If you will go on, gentlemen, I will follow you in a minute,' said Anthony.

He waited while the others filed out, and then turned to where Superintendent Battle was standing apparently absorbed in examining the panelling.

'Well, Battle? Want to ask me something, don't you?'

'Well, I do, sir, though I don't know how you knew I did. But I always marked you out as being specially quick in the uptake. I take it that the lady who is dead was the late Queen Varaga?'

'Quite right, Battle. It'll be hushed up, I hope. You can understand what I feel about family skeletons.'

'Trust Mr Lomax for that, sir. No one will ever know. That is, a lot of people will know, but it won't get about.'

'Was that what you wanted to ask me about?'

'No, sir – that was only in passing. I was curious to know just what made you drop your own name – if I'm not taking too much of a liberty?'

'Not a bit of it. I'll tell you. I killed myself for the purest motives, Battle. My mother was English, I'd been educated in England, and I was far more interested in England than in Herzoslovakia. And I felt an absolute fool knocking about the world with a comic-opera title tacked on to me. You see, when I was very young, I had democratic ideas. Believed in the purity of ideals, and the equality of all men. I especially disbelieved in kings and princes.'

'And since then?' asked Battle shrewdly.

'Oh, since then, I've travelled and seen the world. There's damned little equality going about. Mind you, I still believe in democracy. But you've got to force it on people with a strong hand – ram it down their throats. Men don't want to be brothers – they may some day, but they don't now. My belief in the brotherhood of man died the day I arrived in London last week, when I observed people standing in a Tube train resolutely refuse to move up and make room for those who entered. You won't turn people into angels by appealing to their better natures just yet awhile – but by judicious force you can coerce them into behaving more or less decently to one another to go on with. I still believe in the brotherhood of man, but it's not coming yet awhile. Say another ten thousand years or so. It's no good being impatient. Evolution is a slow process.'

'I'm very interested in these views of yours, sir,' said Battle with a twinkle. 'And if you'll allow me to say so, I'm sure you'll make a very fine king out there.'

'Thank you, Battle,' said Anthony with a sigh.

'You don't seem very happy about it, sir?'

'Oh, I don't know. I dare say it will be rather fun. But it's tying oneself down to regular work. I've always avoided that before.'

'But you consider it your duty, I suppose, sir?'

'Good Lord, no! What an idea. It's a woman – it's always a woman, Battle. I'd do more than be a king for her sake.'

'Quite so, sir.'

'I've arranged it so that the Baron and Isaacstein can't kick. The one wants a king, and the other wants oil. They'll both get what they want, and I've got – oh, Lord, Battle, have you ever been in love?'

'I am much attached to Mrs Battle, sir.'

'Much attached to Mrs – oh, you don't know what I'm talking about! It's entirely different!'

'Excuse me, sir, that man of yours is waiting outside the window.'

'Boris? So he is. He's a wonderful fellow. It's a mercy that pistol went off in the struggle and killed the lady. Otherwise Boris would have wrung her neck as sure as Fate, and then you would have wanted to hang him. His attachment to the Obolovitch dynasty is remarkable. The queer thing was that as soon as Michael was dead he attached himself to me – and yet he couldn't possibly have known who I really was.'

'Instinct,' said Battle. 'Like a dog.'

'Very awkward instinct I thought it at the time. I was afraid it might give the show away to you. I suppose I'd better see what he wants.'

He went out through the window. Superintendent Battle, left alone, looked after him for a minute, then apparently addressed the panelling.

'He'll do,' said Superintendent Battle.

Outside Boris explained himself.

'Master,' he said, and led the way along the terrace.

Anthony followed him, wondering what was forward.

Presently Boris stopped and pointed with his forefinger. It was moonlight, and in front of them was a stone seat on which sat two figures.

'He *is* a dog,' said Anthony to himself. 'And what's more a pointer!'

He strode forward. Boris melted into the shadows.

The two figures rose to meet him. One of them was Virginia – the other –

'Hullo, Joe,' said a well-remembered voice. 'This is a great girl of yours.'

'Jimmy McGrath, by all that's wonderful,' cried Anthony. 'How in the name of fortune did you get here?'

'That trip of mine into the interior went phut. Then some dagos came monkeying around. Wanted to buy that manuscript off me. Next thing I as near as nothing got a knife in the back one night. That made me think that I'd handed you out a bigger job than I knew. I thought you might need help, and I came along after you by the very next boat.'

'Wasn't it splendid of him?' said Virginia. She squeezed Jimmy's arm. 'Why didn't you ever tell me how frightfully nice he was? You are, Jimmy, you're a perfect dear.'

'You two seem to be getting along all right,' said Anthony.

'Sure thing,' said Jimmy. 'I was snooping round for news of you, when I connected with this dame. She wasn't at all what I thought she'd be – some swell haughty society lady that'd scare the life out of me.'

'He told me all about the letters,' said Virginia. 'And I feel almost ashamed not to have been in real trouble over them when he was such a knight-errant.'

'If I'd known what you were like,' said Jimmy gallantly, 'I'd not have given him the letters. I'd have brought them to you myself. Say, young man, is the fun really over? Is there nothing for me to do?'

'By Jove,' said Anthony, 'there is! Wait a minute.'

He disappeared into the house. In a minute or two he returned with a paper package which he cast into Jimmy's arms.

'Go round to the garage and help yourself to a likely looking car. Beat it to London and deliver that parcel at 17 Everdean Square. That's Mr Balderson's private address. In exchange he'll hand you a thousand pounds.'

'What? It's not the memoirs? I understood that they'd been burnt.'

'What do you take me for?' demanded Anthony. 'You don't think I'd fall for a story like that, do you? I rang up the publishers at once, found out that the other was a fake call, and arranged accordingly. I made up a dummy package as I'd been directed to do. But I put the real package in the manager's safe and handed over the dummy. The memoirs have never been out of my possession.'

'Bully for you, my son,' said Jimmy.

'Oh, Anthony,' cried Virginia. 'You're not going to let them be published?'

'I can't help myself. I can't let a pal like Jimmy down. But you needn't worry. I've had time to wade through them, and I see now why people always hint that bigwigs don't write their own reminiscences but hire someone to do it for them. As a writer, Stylptitch is an insufferable bore. He proses on about statecraft, and doesn't go in for any racy and indiscreet anecdotes. His ruling passion of secrecy held strong to the end. There's not a word in the memoirs from beginning to end to flutter the susceptibilities of the most difficult politician. I rang up Balderson today, and arranged with him that I'd deliver the manuscript tonight before midnight. But Jimmy can do his own dirty work now that he's here.'

'I'm off,' said Jimmy. 'I like the idea of that thousand pounds – especially when I'd made up my mind it was down and out.'

'Half a second,' said Anthony. 'I've got a confession to make to you, Virginia. Something that everyone else knows, but that I haven't yet told you.'

'I don't mind how many strange women you've loved so long as you don't tell me about them.'

'Women!' said Anthony, with a virtuous air. 'Women indeed? You ask James here what kind of women I was going about with the last time he saw me.'

'Frumps,' said Jimmy solemnly. 'Utter frumps. Not one a day under forty-five.'

'Thank you, Jimmy,' said Anthony, 'you're a true friend. No, it's much worse than that. I've deceived you as to my real name.'

'Is it very dreadful?' said Virginia, with interest. 'It isn't something silly like Pobbles, is it? Fancy being called Mrs Pobbles.'

'You are always thinking the worst of me.'

'I admit that I did once think you were King Victor, but only for about a minute and a half.'

'By the way, Jimmy, I've got a job for you – gold prospecting in the rocky fastnesses of Herzoslovakia?'

'Is there gold there?' asked Jimmy eagerly.

'Sure to be,' said Anthony. 'It's a wonderful country.'

'So you're taking my advice and going there?'

'Yes,' said Anthony. 'Your advice was worth more than you knew. Now for the confession. I wasn't changed at nurse, or anything romantic like that, but nevertheless I am really Prince Nicholas Obolovitch of Herzoslovakia.'

'Oh, Anthony,' cried Virginia. 'How perfectly screaming! And I have married you! What are we going to do about it?'

'We'll go to Herzoslovakia and pretend to be kings and queens. Jimmy McGrath once said that the average life of a king or queen out there is under four years. I hope you don't mind?'

'Mind?' cried Virginia. 'I shall love it!'

'Isn't she great?' murmured Jimmy.

Then, discreetly, he faded into the night. A few minutes later the sound of a car was heard.

'Nothing like letting a man do his own dirty work,' said Anthony with satisfaction. 'Besides, I didn't know how else to get rid of him. Since we were married I've not had one minute alone with you.'

'We'll have a lot of fun,' said Virginia. 'Teaching the brigands not to be brigands, and the assassins not to assassinate, and generally improving the moral tone of the country.'

'I like to hear these pure ideals,' said Anthony. 'It makes me feel my sacrifice has not been in vain.'

'Rot,' said Virginia calmly, 'you'll enjoy being a king. It's in your blood, you know. You were brought up to the trade of royalty, and you've got a natural aptitude for it, just like plumbers have a natural bent for plumbing.'

'I never think they have,' said Anthony. 'But, damn it all, don't let's waste time talking about plumbers. Do you know that at this very minute I'm supposed to be deep in conference with Isaacstein and old Lollipop? They want to talk about oil. Oil, my God! They can just await my kingly pleasure. Virginia, do you remember my telling you once that I'd have a damned good try to make you care for me?'

'I remember,' said Virginia softly. 'But Superintendent Battle was looking out of the window.'

'Well, he isn't now,' said Anthony.

He caught her suddenly to him, kissing her eyelids, her lips, the green gold of her hair . . .

'I do love you so, Virginia,' he whispered. 'I do love you so. Do you love me?'

He looked down at her – sure of the answer.

Her head rested against his shoulder, and very low, in a sweet shaken voice, she answered:

'Not a bit!'

'You little devil,' cried Anthony, kissing her again. 'Now I know for certain that I shall love you until I die . . .'

CHAPTER XXXI

Sundry Details

Scene – Chimneys, 11 A.M. Thursday morning.

Johnson, the police constable, with his coat off, digging.

Something in the nature of a funeral feeling seems to be in the air. The friends and relations stand round the grave that Johnson is digging.

George Lomax has the air of the principal beneficiary under the will of the deceased. Superintendent Battle, with his immovable face, seems pleased that the funeral arrangements have gone so nicely. As the undertaker, it reflects credit upon him. Lord Caterham has that solemn and shocked look which Englishmen assume when a religious ceremony is in progress.

Mr Fish does not fit into the picture so well. He is not sufficiently grave.

Johnson bends to his task. Suddenly he straightens up. A little stir of excitement passes round.

'That'll do, sonny,' said Mr Fish. 'We shall do nicely now.'

One perceives at once that he is really the family physician.

Johnson retires. Mr Fish, with due solemnity, stoops over the excavation. The surgeon is about to operate.

He brings out a small canvas package. With much ceremony he hands it to Superintendent Battle. The latter, in his turn, hands it to George Lomax. The etiquette of the situation has now been carefully complied with.

George Lomax unwraps the package, slits up the oilsilk inside it, burrows into further wrapping. For a moment he holds something on the palm of his hand – then quickly shrouds it once more in cottonwool.

He clears his throat.

'At this auspicious moment,' he begins, with the clear delivery of the practised speaker.

Lord Caterham beats a precipitate retreat. On the terrace he finds his daughter.

'Bundle, is that car of yours in order?'

'Yes. Why?'

'Then take me up to town in it immediately. I'm going abroad at once – today.'

'But, Father –'

'Don't argue with me, Bundle. George Lomax told me when he arrived this morning that he was anxious to have a few words with me privately on a matter of the utmost delicacy. He added that the King of Timbuctoo was arriving in London shortly. I won't go through it again, Bundle, do you hear? Not for fifty George Lomaxes! If Chimneys is so valuable to the nation, let the nation buy it. Otherwise I shall sell it to a syndicate and they can turn it into an hotel.'

'Where is Codders now?'

Bundle is rising to the situation.

'At the present minute,' replied Lord Caterham, looking at his watch, 'he is good for at least fifteen minutes about the Empire.'

Another picture.

Mr Bill Eversleigh, not invited to be present at the graveside ceremony, at the telephone.

'No, really, I mean it . . . I say, don't be huffy . . . Well, you will have supper tonight, anyway? . . . No, I haven't. I've been kept to it with my nose at the grindstone. You've no idea what Codders is like . . . I say, Dolly, you know jolly well what I think about you . . . You know I've never cared for anyone but you . . . Yes, I'll come to the show first. How does the old wheeze go? "And the little girl tries, Hooks and Eyes" . . .'

Unearthly sounds. Mr Eversleigh trying to hum the refrain in question.

And now George's peroration draws to a close.

'. . . the lasting peace and prosperity of the British Empire!'

'I guess,' said Mr Hiram Fish *sotto voce* to himself and the world at large, 'that this has been a great little old week.'

Postscript

After the success of The Man in the Brown Suit, *The Bodley Head offered Agatha Christie a much more favourable contract. Still feeling cheated by the way in which they had treated her, she refused.*

Her existing contract, however, still tied her to The Bodley Head. Christie sent them a novel based on a long short story written a few years before, dealing with various supernatural happenings. She patched it up and added additional characters. Eventually, this work would be completed as The Hound of Death and Other Stories, *published elsewhere in 1933. The Bodley Head refused to publish the book on the grounds of it not being a straightforward detective novel. This allowed Agatha Christie to move on faster and, on Hugh Massie's advice, she chose a new Publisher. Now having only one book to finish before breaking free from her old publishers, she wrote* The Secret of Chimneys.

'The next book I wrote was a completely light-hearted one, rather in the style of The Secret Adversary. *This was more fun and quicker to write, and my work reflected the lightheartedness that I felt at this particular period, when everything was going so well.'*

Christie's family had just moved from London to Sunningdale, in the countryside, where she rented a flat in a large Victorian house situated within the magnificent gardens of Scotswood. Archie enjoyed the proximity to the Golf Course, Rosalind cycled round the garden on her fairy cycle and Agatha was beginning to realise that she might have become a professional writer.

The joyful and carefree life during the months at Scotswood is reflected in the free and casual construction of The Secret of Chimneys, *which combines two plots: a European, political intrigue, reminiscent of* The Prisoner of Zenda; *and the adventures of an international jewellery thief named 'King Victor'.*

Dedicated to her nephew, James Watts Jr – the son of her sister

Madge – The Secret of Chimneys *marks the end of Agatha Christie's apprenticeship. The novel also introduces a new character, – Superintendent Battle, of Scotland Yard, – who reappears several times in Christie's oeuvre. We find him again in* The Seven Dials Mystery *(1929),* Cards on the Table *(1936),* Murder is Easy *(1939) and* Towards Zero *(1944).*

Appreciated by the authorities for his discretion and his remarkable skills, Battle's role in The Secret of Chimneys *is not yet fully developed. In later novels, he will become a much more important character.*

All Agatha Christie titles are available from HarperCollins:

❏	1920s Agatha Christie Volume One	0 00 649630 X	£7.99
❏	1920s Agatha Christie Volume Two	0 00 649656 3	£7.99
❏	1920s Agatha Christie Volume Three	0 00 649897 3	£7.99
❏	1920s Agatha Christie Volume Four	0 00 649898 1	£7.99
❏	The Mary Westmacott Collection Volume One	0 00 647987 1	£5.99
❏	The Mary Westmacott Collection Volume Two	0 00 649329 7	£6.99
❏	The Mousetrap	0 00 649618 0	£5.99
❏	Witness for the Prosecution	0 00 649045 X	£4.99

All these books are available from your local bookseller or can be ordered direct from the publishers.

To order direct just tick the titles you want and fill in the form below:

Name: _____

Address: _____

Postcode: _____

Send to HarperCollins Paperbacks Mail Order, Dept 8, HarperCollins *Publishers*, Westerhill Road, Bishopbriggs, Glasgow G64 2QT.

Please enclose a cheque or postal order or your authority to debit your Visa/Mastercard account –

Credit card no: _____

Expiry date: _____

Signature: _____

to the value of the cover price plus:

UK & BFPO: Add £1.00 for the first book and 25p for each additional book ordered.

Overseas orders including Eire: Please add £2.95 service charge.

Books will be sent by surface mail but quotes for airmail despatches will be given on request.

24 HOUR TELEPHONE ORDERING SERVICE FOR ACCESS/MASTERCARD CARDHOLDERS –

TEL: GLASGOW 0141 772 2281 or LONDON 0181 307 4052

Due to the many and varied queries from the loyal fans of Agatha Christie it was decided to form an *Agatha Christie Society* to open the channels of communication between those fans and the various media who strive to bring her works, in their various forms, to the public

If you wish to apply for membership of the Society, please write to:
Agatha Christie Society, PO Box 985, London SW1X 9XA